THE JACK EMERY SERIES

BOOKS 1-3

STEVE P. VINCENT

First published by Steve P. Vincent in 2017

This edition published in 2018 by Steve P. Vincent

Copyright © Steve P. Vincent 2017

The moral right of the author has been asserted.

The Jack Emery Series

Cover by Amanda Pillar

Edited by Kylie Mason

❀ Created with Vellum

For Vanessa Pratt

FIREPLAY

JACK EMERY 0.5

PROLOGUE

A flash of lightning illuminated the cell with pale light for only a split second, long enough for Hewad Ghilzai to see his friend on the floor. Positioned unnaturally, he hadn't moved since the American soldiers had left several hours ago. Hewad hadn't moved either. He was too scared. He'd been hurt too many times.

Hewad held his knees to his chest and kept his back against the wall. His mind was empty and his tear ducts were dry. Only his grief and the smell of human feces kept his attention in this world at all. He awaited the next. He'd taken the fight to the infidel and ended up in a place worse than hell.

He'd done everything right. Had Allah abandoned him? On most nights the stars provided enough light to see the outline of his bed, the latrine pail, and the grilled steel that penned him in, but tonight he couldn't see an inch in front of his hand. The world was as dark as the heart of his captors, except when lightning lashed at the mountains.

Footsteps approached and a faint light lit the corridor outside his cell. He instinctively hugged his knees tighter and his eyes shot towards the door. As he waited the footsteps grew louder and the light brighter. He whimpered as the heavy door unlocked with a clunk and opened with a squeal.

"Evening, haji." The soldier's drawl was unmistakable, even as the cell door slammed shut. "I thought you could use some company, what with the storm and all."

Hewad said nothing. He hadn't always been so passive and afraid. The blows from combat boots and rifle butts had started a conversion that mutilations and degradation had completed. He was a broken man, a spent soul trapped in a body that had nearly expired.

"Nothing to say?" The soldier sighed as he held the flashlight up to Hewad's face. "You had some spunk, haji, but now you're as lively as your friend over there."

Hewad lifted his hands to shield his eyes as the soldier laughed at his own joke. The light felt like another assault after so much darkness, though it was nothing compared to whatever struck him across the side of the head. It staggered him. He fell onto his side, curled into a ball, and tried to protect himself as best he could.

Blows rained on him and he felt himself starting to black out when he heard an earsplitting boom and felt an enormous shockwave. He rolled onto his back and opened his eyes, confused. The flashlight was on the ground, illuminating the chaos. The soldier lay still and half of the wall was missing.

Hewad blinked several times and his senses slowly returned. His pain was intense, but in the depths of his mind excitement sparked. He looked at the soldier for several minutes, waiting for him to move. Finally, he inched closer, paused, and then scurried over and felt for a pulse. None. Allah had delivered him.

He shoved the man. When the body didn't move Hewad's eyes widened and he clawed for the man's canteen, unscrewed the lid, and drank deeply. Some of the water spilled to the sand as he sucked at it, gulping and coughing as he fought to overcome the most incredible thirst.

When the water ran out he glanced at the soldier's sidearm. To take it would be to re-enter the fight, to forget the next life for the moment and take up arms again in this world. He stared at the weapon for several long moments and then looked at the hole that had been blown in the wall. He knew the will of Allah.

Hewad took the soldier's weapon and boots and then staggered to his feet. He walked toward the hole in the wall, where the lightning had struck the steel window grill and fractured much of the poor-quality wall. He hesitated briefly. To step through would mean death if he was captured, but to stay would be to spit in the face of Allah's mercy. He spat on the soldier instead.

Hewad stepped outside.

CHAPTER 1

J ack Emery smiled wryly and looked up from his laptop. He'd never faced such an odd juxtaposition before: Aussie rock blaring inside an American armored vehicle driving through the Afghan desert. It left him barely able to think or work as the squealing guitars threatened to pierce the sound barrier. In his experience, it was just how the marines liked it.

"Sound like home?" Lieutenant Daniel Ortiz laughed as he shouted over the music. "I told you bringing that thing along was a waste of time!"

Jack set the laptop aside and had to raise his own voice to be heard. "I thought I'd try to get some work done!"

"Sorry about that, buddy! You want to hang with marines you have to party with marines!" Ortiz grinned and then turned his head to look out the window.

Jack winced at the thought of all the work he had to do. He'd been embedded with the 8th Marines for three months, sending three reports a week to EMCorp and its affiliates. It wasn't a huge workload, but after so long it was getting hard to find interesting things to write about, given the war was now a simmering insurgency. In the last week he'd filed two stories about US troops building schools.

He looked out the front windshield and could see nothing but the desert and the dust kicked up from the Humvee at the head of the column. He shuffled back into the seat and struggled to get comfortable as the music switched to the next track. As a roaring drum solo kicked off the wailing electric guitars, there was a massive explosion and the lead Humvee burst into a fireball.

"Fuck!" Jack gripped his laptop.

"IED!" Ortiz had to shout over the music.

As the Humvee ahead of them started to slow, ablaze and bleeding smoke, Jack reached for the overhead rail and the driver braked hard. The vehicle skidded and slid sideways, the road not giving the tires any purchase. The sound of the locked wheels skidding across the dirt and gravel was one of the worst Jack had ever heard. He wasn't a religious man, but he closed his eyes and prayed.

The vehicle stopped as Jack opened his eyes and reached for his video camera. He glanced right. The music had stopped and Ortiz had started to bark commands to his unit over the radio. Jack looked left, over his shoulder, where flames licked at the blackened husk of the unmoving Humvee. Nobody could have survived that explosion.

"Talk to me! Any movement?" Ortiz's voice was tense as he spoke into the radio.

Jack's mind started to speed up again as the other vehicles in the convoy reported no contacts. It was quite common for the insurgents to hit a convoy with one roadside bomb, but there had also been instances where a single blast had been the prologue to a greater assault. Jack followed as the marines climbed out of their vehicles and formed a perimeter.

Jack felt instinctively for the 'PRESS' lettering that covered his Kevlar vest as he followed Ortiz to the flamed-out Humvee. He kept filming as he drew closer. Even though he probably wouldn't use the video, he'd be able to get some stills to go with his report. It was hard to believe that four marines had probably been talking shit inside the vehicle just a minute ago.

"Fucking hell." Ortiz spat in disgust. "How can you fight these guys?"

Jack kept silent. He doubted Ortiz was addressing him. He'd just lost friends.

Jack heard a shout. "Hey! LT! We've got a solo contact about a mile out."

Ortiz snapped instantly from mourner to commander and started to jog toward the marines, who were taking cover behind the bulk of a

Humvee. Jack followed, arriving a few seconds after Ortiz. He took a few deep breaths, trying to stay calm. He'd been in combat plenty, but had never been on the end of an IED attack. There was a particular type of fear reserved for an enemy that you couldn't see.

"Report." Ortiz's voice had an edge that Jack hadn't heard before. He'd just lost a quarter of his convoy in the blink of an eye.

The marine who'd reported the contact lowered his binoculars, handed them to Ortiz and pointed out into the desert.

Jack squinted. Though he thought he could see an individual drawing closer, he knew the desert played tricks on the eye. His heart pounded. He wanted desperately for it to be a lone individual and not a Taliban or Al Qaeda attack. He didn't fancy being in the middle of a firefight this far from friendly backup. He kept filming as the unidentified man drew closer.

"One guy, hands in the air and with no visible weaponry." Ortiz exhaled loudly through his nose. "What's his game, I wonder? The bomber?"

"Or a suicide bomber?" Jack spoke before he'd realized it.

Ortiz shook his head. "Nah, we shoot long before they get close enough."

Jack nodded. As several of the marines kept their rifles trained on the approaching man, Jack stood back a few yards and watched. Ortiz stood still until the Afghani closed to within fifty yards. At that point he used the interpreter to order the man to stop, take off his outer garments, keep his hands in the air, and drop to his knees. The man did it all without hesitation or protest.

"Something isn't right here, LT." One of the marines protested.

"Shut the fuck up and move in, Hills," Ortiz snarled. "If I want you to check your grandmother's Ouija board to make sure things are safe, I'll be sure to ask."

Jack followed Ortiz and five other marines as they approached the man, leaving the others behind to guard the vehicles. Despite having so many weapons trained on him, the man said nothing and stayed still. His body was covered in sores, scars, and bruises. Once the man had stripped the only thing he wore was underwear and a pair of tan-colored boots.

"What's your name?" Ortiz waited for the translator to finish. "Did you plant the bomb that blew up my vehicle?"

"My name is Hewad." The man's voice was calm, even spiritual, as he spoke in his native tongue and the translator gave it meaning. "Yes. I did."

"Hewad what?" Ortiz took a step closer. "I need your surname."

"Hewad Ghilzai."

Before Ortiz could reply, the marine who'd been pawing through Ghilzai's pile of clothing spoke. "There's a marine sidearm here, LT, and those are marine boots."

Ortiz's gaze flicked back to Ghilzai. "Where did you get the boots and weapon?"

"Camp Navitas." Ghilzai smiled. "God delivered them to me. Now I must go."

Jack kept filming as Ghilzai tried to stand with a smile on his face. Gunfire roared all around as the marines took no chances. Ghilzai's body slumped to the hot sand, his blood completing a horrible scene. Jack filmed closely until Ortiz came close and put a hand on his shoulder. Jack took the cue and flicked off the camera. He had what he needed and these men had been through enough.

"What now?" Jack's gaze flicked back and forth between the body, Ortiz, and the other marines.

"We go pay a visit." The fury in Ortiz's eyes was matched by the edginess of his voice.

Suddenly, Jack felt he might have something to write about.

∿

"As you can see, Mr Emery, the facility we're running is top notch." Major Brad Brinson waved a hand out over the yard where, on the other side of the chain link fence, inmates were playing soccer or chatting in small groups. "I trust your story will say as much?"

Jack ignored the threat in Brinson's words. Any journalist worth their salt was subject to threats, bribes, intimidations, and warnings on a weekly basis. He couldn't help but think that Brinson was feeding him horse shit. He shrugged. "The Press Corps will have right of refusal, as always."

Brinson frowned but said nothing. He turned away and resumed the walk along the path, where marines armed with rifles kept watch over matters. On the surface, Jack had to admit that the facility looked fine: well run, adequately staffed, and with inmates cared for in basic but suitable conditions. But deep in his gut he felt like it didn't stack up.

After Ortiz had radioed the attack in, they'd waited for a few hours for a relief convoy to arrive to take care of the cleanup. The delay had given Ortiz and the other marines some time to grieve and to think through the shooting of Hewad Ghilzai. That time hadn't provided clarity, however. Jack was still confused about those chaotic five minutes. He couldn't understand it, but knew there was a story.

While Jack had never heard of Camp Navitas, Ortiz had told him it was a small marine outpost in Helmand Province that doubled as a small prison. While they waited for the cleanup crew, Ortiz had made a request on Jack's behalf and approval had been granted. They'd arrived and been greeted by Brinson. After a quick tour, the major clearly expected them to leave.

"Just one more question, if you'll indulge me?" Jack pushed his luck. He'd only get once chance. "Tell me about Hewad Ghilzai."

Major Brinson stiffened. "Not much to tell. The little shit got lucky. Lightning struck the bars of his cell a few weeks back. The shockwave took out one of my men and weakened the wall. He grabbed a weapon and made a run for it. Given how many of our boys he's responsible for killing, I'm glad he's dead."

Jack wasn't satisfied with the explanation or the tour. He wanted to know more and to see more. He looked at his watch. "Gee, it's getting late."

Brinson smiled like a mouse that'd triggered the trap but made off with the cheese. "You guys better be off. Don't worry, there's not much else to see."

Jack hesitated. He looked over to Ortiz, who stood off to the side with his hands in his pockets and his eyes hidden behind sunglasses. A slight raise of the eyebrow was the only sign Jack gave to Ortiz that he was after some support. He turned back to Brinson and was about to speak when Ortiz spat on the ground and stepped forward to join them.

"Too late to move out now." Ortiz looked up at the sky and rubbed his chin. "It's too far back to Leatherneck. We'll need to billet here until dawn, Major."

The smile vanished from Brinson's face. He glared at Jack, Ortiz, and the other two marines as if they were annoyances. "Impossible, we don't have room."

"I hear a space has just opened up, Major." Jack smiled. "One of your prisoners was shot dead a few hours from here."

Brinson glared. "I don't appreciate – "

Ortiz sighed. "Do I need to get the colonel on the line? It's 104 degrees, major, and the orders were clear: every possible courtesy and all that."

"You're out of line, Lieutenant." Brinson's voice had menace.

Jack tapped his tape recorder, which was still going. "It would let me start on the story and I could give you a look before we head off tomorrow."

Brinson's eyes narrowed. He was clearly weighing up something and Jack wondered again what he had to hide. To have the chance to find out, Jack had to hope the potential to shape his story and the threat of escalation to Colonel Williams would overcome Brinson's displeasure at the idea of them staying. Jack needed time to snoop around.

"Okay." Brinson nodded. "But I hope you like bunk beds, Mr Emery. One of my guys will sort you out."

Ortiz saluted and waited as Brinson returned it lazily and then stalked off. As they waited to be told where to go, Jack and Ortiz leaned against the chain link fence and watched the inmates play. Jack looped his hands through the fence, and then winced as he cut himself on a rough strip. He looked down and saw blood and then glanced up at the inmates. It struck him then how many had scars and bruises.

"I hope you know what you're doing, Jack." Ortiz spoke softly. "I'm going to be in a shit ton of trouble with the colonel."

Jack grinned. "This is what I do."

❧

JACK PRESSED AGAINST THE WALL, hoping that the cold stone might somehow hide him from the beam of light that snaked towards him, left and right, ever closer as a marine approached with a flashlight. After all of his effort to stay at Camp Navitas overnight, he'd barely made it out of his room and now it looked like the gig was up. Ortiz wouldn't be impressed if Jack was busted, nor would Jack's editor. He took a deep breath.

"Hey, Mike!" a voice shouted. "Major Brinson wants you posted outside the journalist's door."

Jack closed his eyes. He hoped the new voice was calling out to the guy holding the torch.

"I'm rostered on to B wing." Another man, closer to Jack, called back and then let out a long sigh. "I wish he'd make up his mind. Who's taking over from me?"

"Nobody. Now get moving."

Jack's eyes shot open and locked onto the beam of light. It had stopped moving towards him. He heard another sigh and then watched as the light shifted direction. The marine's boots gave dull thuds as he walked away, the sound growing fainter with each footstep. Finally, after going so close to being exposed by the guards, Jack was alone in the darkness.

He took a couple of deep breaths and then pushed himself off the wall. He stuck his head around the corner and then moved down the hallway as quietly as he could. At the end of the corridor he turned left and made his way toward one of the three detention blocks he'd been walked past but not allowed to enter when Brinson had given them the tour. Brinson had told him that each block housed twelve detainees.

He reached the heavy steel door that barred the way into the cell block. Luckily, it was more focused on keeping inmates in than snooping reporters out, meaning he could open it with the turn of a handle. He walked inside and closed the door behind him. No guards were posted inside, but there was always a chance one would happen along. Whatever he was hoping to find, he had to find it quickly.

The light on his cell phone was all Jack could use to search. It was hard to get used to walking around in the dark, but many American firebases and camps on the fringe of insurgent territory went dark at night. Navitas was no different. As he walked deeper into the cell block, the smell was the first thing he noticed, followed by the cries and whimpers of broken men from behind simple but effective grilled steel cell doors.

He hesitated and then decided that if he was going to trespass he may as well go the whole hog. "Hello? Does anyone speak English?"

He was met with silence, though the whimpering stopped. He tried again. "I'm an Australian reporter. I'd like to talk about Hewad."

He stood still as some of the inmates chatted amongst themselves in Pashto or Dari – Jack wasn't sure which. It was a long shot that any of them would be able to understand him, know Ghilzai, and be willing to speak with him, but he had to try. The alternative was to search aimlessly through the camp and risk getting caught with no guarantee of a story.

The chattering increased and, finally, one of the Afghans approached the door to his cell. He gripped the bars with his hands and spoke. "You know Hewad?"

Jack flashed the light towards the man. "I met him. He's dead now. He blew up an American vehicle and they shot him."

"Trust him to do something like that." The detainee's English was patchy, but good enough to understand. "We thought he was crazy."

Jack's mind started to fire, but he kept calm. The surest way to scare off a source was to jump too excitedly at a lead. "You knew him well?"

The other man laughed and then suppressed it, as if he'd momentarily forgotten where he was. The few teeth he had left were rotten. "I should. He married my sister."

Jack smiled. He shouldn't take a liking to the man, but it was hard not to. "Hewad had American boots and a weapon. He told me if I came here I'd find answers."

The prisoner laughed. He took a step back, pulled his tattered shirt over his head, and turned around. Even in the pale light offered by the phone, Jack could see fresh wounds alongside scars. He could see welts and burns, angry and red, and bruises as dark as the night. The man's whole body was broken and wounded. Jack had seen combat injuries before, and these weren't that. This was something else.

"How long have you been here?" Jack kept his voice low, feeling as if the man's revelations made his snooping even riskier.

The prisoner shrugged. "Many months. Nearly a year. Who knows? I've been here the longest though."

So the wounds could only have been caused by one thing. "And they mistreat you?"

Another shrug. "They do what they do. To me and everyone else until we die. Except Hewad. He was the most devout. God freed him and he struck back."

"Do you mind if I take some photographs? I'll report this to the world."

"Do what you want. I'm a dead man anyway."

Jack spent a few moments photographing the man's injuries with his phone. The shots weren't great, but they'd suffice. Jack was surprised when the prisoner called out to other detainees to show him their wounds. He gathered dozens of photographs of the nine men before deciding he'd pushed his luck – and that of the prisoners – far enough. He noted down the names of each prisoner and then moved to leave the cell block.

On a whim he paused and turned back to the prisoner who spoke English, still standing at the bars of his cell. "Which cell belonged to Hewad?"

The man pointed. Jack walked over and flashed his light inside the cell. Not surprisingly, it was empty, though there was an enormous bloodstain on the sandy floor of the cell. He looked up and saw clearly how Hewad had escaped, through the giant hole in the wall. He took some more snaps and started to piece it together in his head. Camp Navitas was a giant torture chamber.

He'd risked enough and had enough for a story. There was nothing else to be gained, but plenty to be lost by sticking around. With one final glance at the prisoners he cut the light on his phone, left the cellblock, and then snuck back toward his room. No marines interrupted his journey, though Jack did pause around the corner from his room.

He pulled the phone out of his pocket and undid the button on his brown chinos. Within a few seconds, he had the phone in between his ass cheeks. It wasn't the nicest part of his job, but if Brinson was worried enough about what was hidden in his facility to put a guard on Jack's door, then there was a chance they'd search him. He turned the corner and approached the door.

The marine on the door nearly had a kitten when he saw Jack walking toward him. His flashlight switched on and pointed at Jack. "I hope you can explain this, sir."

Jack smiled and raised his hands in the air, trying to lighten the mood. "Just ducked out for a walk. Sorry."

"I've been here for thirty minutes, sir." The marine didn't sound convinced. "I believe the major was clear about the rules of you staying here overnight."

"I'm Australian, mate. Rules are optional for us." Jack laughed and patted the marine on the shoulder. "What he doesn't know won't hurt him, will it?"

The marine sighed. "I'll need to search you quickly."

Jack clenched his cheeks. He doubted the guard would look too closely.

CHAPTER 2

The departure from Navitas hadn't gone as Jack had expected. Major Brinson hadn't even been there when, early in the morning, Jack had climbed into the Humvee with Ortiz and the other marines and set off for Camp Leatherneck. He'd expected bluster from Brinson – threats about his story and chastisement for wandering from his room. Instead, he'd been given a sandwich.

"So did you get anything worthwhile?" Ortiz shook his head as they raced along the road. "Those were some cranky motherfuckers."

Jack looked up from his laptop. Tellingly, the other two marines in the vehicle were nodding at Ortiz's words. They knew something was up. "Well, I…"

Ortiz interrupted and pointed to the driver and front seat passenger. "If you're worried about these two, don't be. They've been through hell with me."

Jack still hesitated. The story he was writing to go with the pictures he'd taken would rock America and the Marine Corps. Though allegations of torture had surrounded the CIA for years following September 11, the military had mostly kept its hands clean with the exception of Abu Ghraib. From what Jack had seen, this was as bad – systematic and at scale. It angered him.

He knew that the minute he spoke about the story it would take on a life of its own. Though he'd spent the last few months embedded with

Ortiz and his troops, and he was confident that most men and women in uniform would be as appalled as he was by the torture, there was no guarantee. Jack closed his eyes, reached up, and scratched his forehead. He opened his eyes and Ortiz was staring at him.

"Look, Jack." Ortiz's gaze didn't waver. "Whatever happened at that camp contributed to the death of four of my men. Shit happens in war, but if someone screwed up I want to know before you put it on the front page of the *Standard*."

"Okay." Jack sighed. Suddenly, he felt bad for questioning these men. They'd welcomed him, protected him, and shown him around the country for months. He handed the laptop to Ortiz. "Check it out."

Jack watched as Ortiz took the computer and worked his way through the story. The marine's facial expression shifted from curious to concerned to angry. By the time he reached the end of the story he'd seen Jack's claims and the photos that backed them up – the beatings, the burnings, the electrocution, the rectal abuse. The detainees hadn't held back and neither had Jack.

"Fuck." Ortiz handed the laptop to the marine in the front seat. "I thought we'd learned from Iraq."

"It's an important story." Jack shrugged. "But it's going to cause a firestorm. I'll keep your names out of it."

Ortiz grunted. He seemed satisfied by Jack's concession, given nobody in the Humvee was guilty of anything. It was only by sheer chance that they'd been the patrol to trigger Ghilzai's bomb and then been able to question the man enough to get a lead before he'd been shot. What shocked Jack most of all was the scale of the abuse at Navitas – at least thirty detainees and a dozen marines were involved.

The driver interrupted Jack's thoughts. "Hey, LT? We've got company. A couple of ANA hummers and a truck."

Jack was confused about why an Afghan National Army convoy would be tailing them. Ortiz and the driver shared a look in the rear vision mirror, after which the Humvee started to speed up. Clearly the marines were nervous too. Whatever beef the Afghans had could be sorted once they reached Leatherneck and were safely under the watchful eye of a few hundred US guns.

Ortiz picked up the radio receiver. "Lizard Four calling Leatherneck Actual."

As he listened in and waited for a reply, Jack turned around in his seat and peered out the back window. Their pursuers were definitely gunning their engines to catch up, leaving a cloud of dust in their wake. He turned back around in his seat. The other marines were tense, readying their rifles as they waited for the response over the radio.

The radio crackled. "Lizard Four, this is Leatherneck Actual, report."

"We're en route from Camp Navitas to Camp Leatherneck and we've got ANA vehicles riding our six pretty hard." Ortiz paused. "Was it scheduled?"

"Standby, Lizard Four."

Jack grabbed his laptop from the marine in the front seat. He had a feeling that things were about to go south as he plugged in the satellite internet dongle. As he waited for it to connect, he looked behind them again. The convoy was closing even though the driver of the Humvee had stepped on the gas. He turned to the front and saw a speck in the distance.

"What's that?" Jack pointed. It looked like a tank.

Ortiz looked up from his weapon. His eyes widened. "It's an old T-62."

The driver laughed. "It's a museum piece, LT."

Ortiz wasn't amused. "It's still got enough to split us open like a melon."

Jack inched forward in his seat. "They want us to stop. They want my photographs."

The radio crackled again. "Lizard Four, ANA liaison reports no vehicle convoys within fifty miles of you at this time. Act at your discretion. Over."

Ortiz's eyes narrowed and he cussed. It was the first time Jack had felt scared in his marrow since being in Afghanistan. Through all the firefights, incidents and even the explosion of the IED he'd been in friendly hands. Being surrounded by a whole lot of marines was like a condom for an embedded reporter. It felt good to know you're covered. This situation felt a bit more precarious though.

"They're getting closer!" The driver looked back in the mirror. "What do you want to do, LT?"

"Pull us over. Whatever is about to happen, I'd rather do it away from that tank." Ortiz turned to Jack. "Whatever you're doing, you've got thirty seconds."

Jack nodded and looked back at his machine. He tried not to think about the approaching convoy and focused on uploading some of the more significant photos to his Dropbox account. He also uploaded the story he'd been writing. As the Humvee slowed and then stopped and the convoy pulled to a stop behind them, the upload finished.

"Done!" Jack cleared his browser cache, deleted the photos and documents from his hard drive and then yanked out the satellite dongle. He threw the camera SD card and the dongle underneath the seat. "What now?"

Ortiz climbed out under the watchful guns of the ANA troops who'd surrounded the vehicle. Jack couldn't hear what was being said, but there was lots of pointing and gesturing. The leader of the Afghan group also seemed fond of waving a piece of paper in Ortiz's face. The whole situation was an open powder keg with a match held over it.

Eventually, Ortiz opened the door with a look of fury etched onto his face. "These gentlemen are taking you into custody. They also need your computer."

Jack nodded and unbuckled his seatbelt. "What's the charge?"

"All sorts of stuff. It's just to scare you." Ortiz smiled. "We're going to tail the convoy and we'll be with you all the way to Lashkar Gah. You'll be fine."

"Okay." Jack opened the door and climbed out of the vehicle. He let himself be handcuffed. He was scared, but had no choice. "Lead the way, fellas."

∼

THERE WASN'T a lot to be said about the room that Jack found himself in. He'd sat for hours at a small table, swinging on his chair and thinking about the defense he'd have to mount against the charges. Once that got boring, he'd simply stared at the wall. He'd been told through a translator that he'd have to wait a short while, but Rome had been built quicker than this.

He was happy that the images and the start of his story were safely stowed in his Dropbox account. Whatever was to come, they'd be waiting for him whenever he was freed. He was also confident that he'd covered his tracks with the computer and the SD card to a basic level. His efforts wouldn't hold up to detailed forensic examination of his computer, but it would satisfy a passing glance.

The story was a bombshell and he was certain that neither Brinson nor the ANA had any idea what he'd managed to learn. Short of such an examination of his computer, or them torturing the information and the

Dropbox login out of him, it was hidden like a dormant virus ready for him to trigger. He was excited by the potential and was sure that his editor would be as well.

Eventually, the steel door creaked open on its hinges. Jack turned his head in time for the door to hit the wall with a loud bang as two Afghani men in military uniforms walked into the room. A third man – a Westerner – followed them in, wearing civilian clothes and half-framed glasses. He was too small to be military, which meant he was either a diplomat or an intelligence officer.

Without a word, the two officers sat in the chairs directly opposite Jack, while the Westerner sat to Jack's left. The two military men started to lay some papers out on the table. Jack leaned forward in his chair, ready for his eyes to feast on what was in front of him. He wanted to learn what they had and what they intended to hit him with. He was disappointed that he couldn't read any of it.

"Mr Emery." The officer on the left was all business. "I'm Major Gholem-Ali Jafari, Afghan National Army. My colleague is Lieutenant Doost Mohammad. We're here to dissuade you from reporting on classified material."

Jack said nothing. He wanted to figure out who was the good cop and who was the bad cop. The major spoke excellent English with an Oxford accent, probably the brother of a local warlord parachuted into a position of authority. The lieutenant kept his face expressionless. The Westerner was the real mystery. He had his arms crossed and his eyes locked on Jack. He was the threat.

Jafari continued. "You have no right to silence here. You're facing serious charges and if you find yourself before a judge you'll spend the rest of this decade in prison. I suggest you start talking, Mr Emery."

They didn't beat around the bush – accusations and the threat of long-term incarceration. Jack turned to the Westerner. "Who're you?"

"My name is Sonny Vacaro." The Westerner spoke with a southern drawl as he tapped his thumbs on the table. "I just – "

"Where are you from, Sonny Vacaro?" Jack wasn't sure interrupting was the best idea, but he had to get something of a handle on the situation.

"Alabama."

Jack persisted. "And your professional home?"

"Classified." Vacaro smiled like a shark.

"Right." Jack sighed. 'Your name isn't Sonny Vacaro, either.'

"Classified."

Jack snorted. "Right."

"Look, Jack." Vacaro uncrossed his arms and leaned forward. "We're the only thing keeping you from an Afghan prison cell with a dirt floor and pit latrine."

"Okay." Jack swallowed hard, trying to resist the urge to press Vacaro's buttons further. "I've done nothing wrong. Ask what you want."

"Now we're getting somewhere." Vacaro waved a hand lazily towards the documents on the table. "A number of Taliban and Al Qaeda prisoners have confessed that you recorded their lies and took photos of some of the injuries they suffered prior to capture. I'm concerned you have the wrong picture, Jack."

Jack scoffed. The ANA officers and Vacaro were throwing around threats like candy and there were some documents he couldn't read on the table. He'd had tougher shits than this and he'd heard more compelling narrative out of *New York Standard* interns. It was time to test what they knew, what they suspected, and what they had no idea about.

"Look, this feels a bit like amateur hour at the Comedy Club." Jack reached up and ran a hand through his hair. "I don't *have* a story, so you'll need to piece it together for me."

Vacaro bit his lip as if lost in thought. After a moment he nodded and spoke again. "Did you record a conversation with Hewad Ghilzai when he was under guard by members of the 8th Marines?"

"Sure, the recording is on my computer, which you have."

Vacaro nodded, shared a look with the ANA officers, and then continued. "Good. Now, did that conversation lead you to Camp Navitas where, after a tour from Major Bradley Brinson, you arranged to stay the night on a thin pretext?"

"I'd dispute that – "

Jafari cut in. "You then snuck around the camp and spoke to nine dangerous criminals and terrorists. They fed you lies and you also took photographs."

Vacaro didn't seem thrilled with the interruption. He glared at Jafari and then turned to Jack. "I think what my colleague here is trying to say is that, in a vacuum, whatever you heard there may sound damning. But you need to be careful here, Jack."

Jack smiled. "I'd dispute that too. The only thing you'll find in my possession is a recording of my discussion with Ghilzai. I have no testimony from any prisoners and I have no photos."

Vacaro sighed. "You're not an American, Jack. If you were you'd have more protection in this room. I don't care if you trespassed. I don't care if you spoke to some Afghans. I do care if you're going to parlay those facts into damaging lies."

Jack inched forward in his seat and placed his hands, palms down, on the table. He glanced in the direction of each man for a few seconds, using the time to collect his thoughts. This was the crossroads: he could deny everything or come clean and promise to keep quiet. Both options had risks, but despite his unease there was only one choice for him to make. He was a news man.

He smiled. "No comment."

"Are you sure you want to walk down this path?"

Jack shrugged, despite the tinge of doubt he felt. "I'm a pretty well-known reporter who works for the largest media conglomerate on the planet. Are you sure?"

"Very well. We'll see if a few days in that prison I mentioned changes your mind. I don't care about you, Jack, but I can't have you reporting falsehoods."

Jack sat back as Vacaro nodded at the lieutenant, who appeared to be little more than a prop. The junior officer stood, walked towards the door, and bashed on it twice with his fist. The heavy sound rang out like the death knell on Jack's freedom. He was fearful of what was to come, but he couldn't abandon this story so easily, especially after the interest Vacaro had shown in burying it.

The door swung open and two uniformed ANA soldiers stepped in, joined by a pair of marines. Jack's eyes widened. It was a surprise to see the two militaries working so closely together to bust this story out of him. As they walked closer, stood him up, and cuffed him, he felt like he was floating above his body. His mind started to recalibrate. This was more than Brinson and some dodgy marines.

This was big.

~

JACK'S THROAT felt as if it was tearing open as he screamed out in agony. He tried to pull his hand back, to protect it, but the restraints kept it where it was – flat on the table and palm up, an easy target for the rod that had just come down on it hard and sent fire burning up his arm. He bucked against the chair, trying to free himself and screaming insults at his captors.

His nostrils flared and his eyes blinked quickly as the pain receded. His hair was soaked with sweat and stuck to his forehead. Rivulets of sweat rolled down his face, stung his eyes, and filled his mouth with salty moisture that seemed to mock his thirst. He wanted to see them, but a hood covered his head. They waited for the answer. Sure as death they'd ask it again in a minute, he wouldn't answer, they'd hit him and ask again.

Best he could tell, he'd been in their custody for nearly two days, and the attention they'd given him was a painful exclamation point on the interview with Vacaro and the ANA officers. Their treatment had been harsh and had left him in no doubt that they wanted him to give them everything he knew. He was determined not to tell them about the Dropbox dump.

It had been easy to handle at first – no food and little sleep. Every time he'd started to doze off, they'd beam the lights down on him. That had graduated to not being able to use the bathroom and, when that had failed to garner answers from him, they'd started to hurt him. Fists and boots, followed by the rod. He'd had enough already and it had barely started. He wondered how any of the Afghan prisoners took much more than this.

An American voice punctuated his thoughts and his pain. "Tell us how to access the photographs you took and this all ends, Jack."

His head slumped. He didn't want to tell them about the photos, but he couldn't endure this. He hadn't filed the story and he didn't have any sources to protect. The only thing he had to lose was a good story, but it wasn't worth his freedom or his life. He wanted to hold out but they'd break him eventually. From what he'd seen in the cells at Navitas, there was a lot worse to come.

"I feel like you want to tell me something, Jack." The voice persisted.

Jack raised his head. "I – "

Jack was interrupted by pounding against the interrogation room door. He jerked his head toward it, even though he couldn't see anything from underneath the hood. He heard a deep sigh from one of his interrogators and then the clicking sound of boots on the concrete floor. Jack didn't think much of it until he heard several low, angry voices speaking.

He couldn't hear what was being said, though the anger of his interrogator was clear. He shook his head and clamped his teeth together, determined now to hold out after his moment of weakness and his near betrayal of the photos and the story. After a few moments of back and forth conversation near the door, the voices grew louder and several new footsteps could be heard.

The light burned Jack's eyes and he squeezed them shut as the hood was pulled off his head. His mind screamed with confusion. He could hear voices but couldn't process what they were saying, until slowly everything returned to normal and he started to regain his senses. He opened his eyes and looked around, confused by the five men who surrounded him.

The only man not wearing a military uniform spoke. "Mr Emery, my name is Keith Baird, I'm a staffer at the Australian Embassy in Kabul."

Jack blinked a couple of times and tried to lift his hands, but they were still bound on the table. "What do you want?"

"I want you, actually." Baird smiled sadly. "I'm just sorry it took me so long to hear about your… predicament. Sorrier still it took me so long to get here."

Baird waved a piece of paper at the soldiers. "This is an order from the Afghan Justice Minister ordering you to release this man into my custody."

Just like that, Jack nearly cried as the four military men – three American and one Afghani – worked to free him from his restraints. He didn't get his hopes up until his hands were free. He felt his wrists and rubbed his raw, abused palms against his legs. He stood, resisting the urge to take a swing at one of the soldiers and then walked to stand behind Baird.

In less than five minutes he was out of the compound and riding in a black SUV with Baird towards Kabul. They sat in silence in the back seat, as if Baird was waiting for him to speak. The soldiers had watched them leave, their expressions blank. Jack had wanted some sign that his departure meant something to them, but he received none.

Finally, once they'd been driving for a bit, Baird spoke. "Tell me where you want to head from here, Jack? Once we're back in Kabul, I mean."

Jack continued to stare out of the window. "I need to spend some time getting to the bottom of a story."

"Anything you need. You'll have a room at the Embassy for a few days to tidy up loose ends and then we'll see you safety to the airport." Baird patted him on the shoulder. "I hope it's a good story. You've caused a huge stir. The Australian Foreign Minister had to shout a bit to get you out of there."

Jack turned to face Baird. "It concerns the torture and abuse of Afghan prisoners by United States Marine Corps troops. It's organized and I have proof."

Baird whistled. "I guess I better get ready for the flurry of diplomatic protests. But that's no matter. If there's a story you need to tell it."

"Thanks." Jack nodded and turned back to look out of the window.

CHAPTER 3

J ack exhaled deeply as he swung back on the office chair and stared up at the ceiling. He reached up and rubbed his eyes, wishing again that the Embassy had some real coffee. He'd been burning the candle at both ends to get to the bottom of the story for three days and this, combined with the lack of sleep he'd had while in prison, had him slow on his feet. He knew he should stop and rest, but the story was too important.

He sighed, leaned forward, and resumed tapping away on his laptop. He'd spent his time at the Australian Embassy in Kabul digging as deeply as he could into Brinson, Navitas, and the role of the US Marine Corps in torture and prisoner abuse. Though Baird and the other staff had stayed out of his way, he hadn't found much online and the few sources he'd reached out to hadn't been much help.

The only thing of use had been some media coverage about pressure on the CIA to wind-down the extraordinary rendition program – the extrajudicial transfer of prisoners to other countries that had become a means of torture by proxy by the United States. It seemed that the high point of pressure on the Agency had coincided with the opening of Navitas, which Jack assumed had been torturing Afghans from the day it opened.

Though it could just be a coincidence, he didn't feel like it was. The attention he'd received – the detention, the beating, and the diplomatic pressure that Baird said was being placed on Australia to hand him over – all spoke to something important that influential people felt it vital to cover up. It was more than some rogue Marines kicking some Taliban and Al Qaeda fighters around.

He'd called Josefa Takaloka, his editor at the *Standard*, who'd pressured Jack to just write the story as it stood. Jo had thought the story good enough to run and didn't want to risk Jack's safety by digging deeper. Jack had stalled and asked for a few more days to uncover something that proved his hunch – that this was a far deeper cancer than a single camp.

His phone started to buzz on the table, breaking his reverie. He looked down and was surprised by the name flashing on the screen. He answered. "Jack Emery."

"Jack, it's Dan Ortiz." There was a pause. "Where are you? I've got some information to share with you but I can't talk over the phone."

"I'm at the Australian Embassy. It's the only place I'm safely able to work at the moment." Jack hated saying it aloud. "I'm sorry, Dan. I can't risk it."

Ortiz laughed. "And what do you think I'm risking even by calling you? You're going to want to hear this."

Jack thought about it. While Ortiz had given Jack no reason to be suspicious of him, he did work for the same branch of the armed forces that Jack was investigating. On the other hand, he knew he had barely any time left to close up his story, with the patience of his editor, the Australian Embassy, and the Afghan Justice Minister growing thin. Everyone wanted him out of the country. Each extra day was a risk.

Besides, the business of a reporter was out in the field, not hiding inside a government compound. He lifted the phone to his mouth. "Okay."

"Great." Ortiz seemed relieved. "Where should we meet?"

Jack didn't hesitate. "Faisal Market. North entrance. One hour."

He terminated the call and gathered his things. He walked out of the small office and asked a staffer to organize a car, ignoring the protests that he stay inside the compound. The location of the Embassy was classified and he was a guest, but he was still a free man. It was made clear to him as the car pulled up that once he left the building he was on his own until he returned. If he returned.

Fifty minutes and some traffic later he was at Faisal Market. He grabbed a kabob from a street vendor and waited slightly away from where he'd told Ortiz to meet him. He wanted to be sure what he was getting into before he committed. As he ate, he kept his eyes peeled for any sign of trouble, but as the minutes ticked by he felt more comfortable. He trusted Ortiz.

Finally, Ortiz came into view. He was disguised in chinos, a white cotton shirt, and dark sunglasses. Importantly, from what Jack could tell, Ortiz was alone. He watched as Ortiz stopped in place, raised his glasses, and looked around. After a few minutes Jack threw the remains of his food in a bin and walked over to Ortiz.

He walked up behind Ortiz. "Hi, Dan."

Ortiz turned around and flashed a smile. "Your field craft is good, Jack."

Jack grinned and shrugged. "You spend a few years in the White House Press Corps and you learn a thing or two about stalking prominent Americans."

Ortiz gave a small laugh and then his expression darkened. "I need your phone, Jack."

"What?"

"Your phone. I need it. I can't talk to you without it."

Jack hesitated, then reached into his pocket and handed over his phone. "Please don't break it."

Ortiz took the phone, opened the back, and removed the battery and the SIM card. He then handed them back to Jack. "Now you can't be listened to, but they still know you're here. We only have a couple of minutes."

Jack nodded. "I'm in danger every second I'm in this country, Dan. It's clear to me that I've kicked over an ant hill, but I'm not sure how deep below the ground it goes. Or how nasty the ants inside are."

"It goes real deep and they're nasty fuckers, Jack." Ortiz turned and gestured for Jack to follow. "Walk with me."

Jack followed. They walked inside the Faisal Market, immediately overwhelmed by smells and hawkers competing for their attention. "So?"

"So." Ortiz twisted his head to face Jack, even as he walked. "You know about the CIA rendition program?"

"Yep."

"Well, turns out all that public attention on the Agency has forced them to shut down some of their more ambitious programs." Ortiz paused to look at a wallet. "It's expanded to include the Marine Corps, among other agencies. Smaller scale. Less visible."

Jack's eyes widened. He'd thought the timing was strange, and now Ortiz was confirming it. "Can you substantiate this?"

Ortiz's brow furrowed and he nodded. "Sure can. I made some inquiries after our run-in with Brinson. A friend I went to Officer Candidate School with figured out what I was looking into and had a word in my ear. He disagrees with what's going on and can provide the proof, but the kicker is that you need to be out of the country before he releases it."

"But – "

Ortiz patted Jack on the back. "No plane, no proof. It's that simple, Jack."

Jack nodded. He could deal with this. Once he was out of the country he'd contact Ortiz and get what he needed. If it fell through for whatever reason, he had enough in his pictures and the testimony of the tortured to run a story anyway. At worst, it was a bombshell. At best, it was nuclear. He had to get back to the Embassy for long enough to collect his things and book a flight before he could leave this desert.

Ortiz reached into his pocket and pulled out a pager. "You'll get a message on this when I know you're out of the country and my man is ready with the information."

"Okay." Jack took the pager and pocketed it, struggling not to laugh at the low-tech approach. "I'll keep it close."

Ortiz walked away and Jack watched him leave as the bustle of the market continued to move around him like a rising tide against a small island. Once Ortiz was out of sight, he took one final look around and exhaled deeply. He took his cell phone out of his pocket, reassembled it and started to dial his Embassy contact. He stopped dead when he felt something press into his back.

"Hello, Jack."

~

JACK'S EYES were squeezed shut as he tried to move his head away from the cold steel barrel pressed into his temple, but Brinson simply pushed the pistol against him harder. He was afraid of the lengths Brinson would go to in order to protect his secrets, even as his mind cursed his stupidity. He'd walked right into Brinson's grasp.

He was bundled into the back of a car with Brinson in the back and two men in front. As the black sedan roared forward and Jack was pushed back in his seat, his eyes flicked between Brinson and the world outside. They were leaving Kabul and the relative safety he'd enjoyed. US and Afghani authorities alike would do nothing to help him, and he was in the hands of a man who had every interest in silencing him.

"Please, just let me go." Jack's voice wavered slightly and the barrel pressed ever harder. "I won't report the story. I won't report *anything*."

Brinson laughed. "You had your chance. You didn't have to snoop around Navitas. You could have given up your story. You could have gone home."

"But – "

Brinson pressed on. "Instead, you kept digging and asking questions. I'm not going to hurt you, but you can't be allowed to live. Goodbye, Jack."

Jack cowered away. He clenched his muscles and gritted his teeth as the pistol clicked and gave a slight kick. A second after Brinson pulled the trigger, however, he still seemed to be alive. His nostrils flared and he inhaled deeply. He swung his hands around and clubbed Brinson, despite the handcuffs, over and over again. The other man just laughed as he weathered the blows. His laughter only grew louder.

"You're a bastard." Jack fumed, as he took a deep breath and placed his hands back on his legs. It wasn't smart to antagonize a guy with a gun. "A fucking bastard."

Brinson lowered the pistol and laughed. "That's what I like about you, Jack. You've got fire. I wish my men could have some fun with you. Unfortunately, your fate is sealed."

"Why?"

Brinson shrugged. "We were just a small outpost amongst the sand until you did your best Lois fucking Lane impression and stumbled into danger. I'm not a bad guy. We tried to get you to back off, Jack. But you just wouldn't fucking listen."

"My wife accuses me of that all the time."

Brinson grunted and sat back in his seat. The conversation had clearly finished for now. Jack had no idea where they were taking him but he assumed it was back to Navitas, where they'd kill him and quietly make his body disappear. He figured he had about eight hours to live. What irked him most was that he'd told nobody about the Dropbox account. Josefa knew there was a story, but not how to unlock any of it.

He closed his eyes and settled into the drive, racking his brain for any possible way to escape. It was useless. Brinson had frisked him and taken all of his gear. His hands were cuffed and he had three marines sitting within six feet of him. While he hoped that Ortiz or the Embassy would help, Brinson was right. He was screwed.

He must have fallen asleep, because when he woke there was no sign of the city, just desert on either side of the road. Jack looked to his left, where Brinson was staring out the window with the pistol still in hand. Somewhere along the way they'd picked up an escort: a pair of ANA Humvees in front of them and another behind. He sighed. Any chance of escape had fallen from minimal to zero.

Jack turned to Brinson. "I need to use the bathroom."

Major Brinson sighed. "Really? You'll be dead in two hours, Jack."

Jack nodded. Brinson sighed again, told his men to pull over, and then dug around in the bag at his feet for some toilet paper. He tossed it to Jack as the car moved onto the gravel shoulder of the road and ground to a halt. The Marine riding in the front passenger seat climbed out, opened Jack's door, and jerked him roughly out of the car. Jack marched a hundred feet away and squatted.

As he shat, Jack looked back to the convoy. Only the man who'd pulled him out of the sedan was watching Jack. The marine leaned against the vehicle with apparent impatience. He had a sidearm with him, but no rifle. The other marines had stayed in the vehicle and the ANA Humvees showed no sign of activity as they idled with their troops inside.

Jack exaggerated the time it was taking him to finish as his mind raced. This was likely his one chance to escape, even though the possibility of any attempt succeeding was nearly zero. There were a dozen or so armed men less than a football field away, he had no weapons or supplies, and there was nothing but desert ahead.

He closed his eyes and breathed deeply. He thought of his wife, Erin, waiting back in New York, oblivious to the danger he was in. She'd be the most upset by his death or, more likely, his unexplained disappearance. He doubted the marines would be in a hurry to release details about his fate. He'd be another anonymous body claimed by the sand.

He opened his eyes again. He'd decided. This was his only chance. He kept low as he wiped his ass and pulled up his pants, keeping his eye on the convoy. Nobody was paying him more than the loosest attention. As best as he could tell, he might get another fifty yards away from them before they noticed what he was doing and the bullets started to fly. But he had to try.

He stood at his full height, turned, and sprinted off into the desert.

~

JACK GRUNTED as he hit the ground hard. His face burned as it skidded across the gravelly sand, as if a hundred little needles full of molten lava had been injected into his face all at once. His hands and feet flailed as he struggled to get to his feet again. His mind was screaming at him. He had to keep running. Keep moving. Keep trying to escape. He'd gained more distance on them than he'd hoped, but they'd be closing.

He climbed onto his hands and knees and shook his head, trying to clear some of the fog. He did a quick stocktake of his limbs and everything appeared intact. He struggled to his feet and resumed his run, not knowing where he was going but needing to escape. He focused on turning his legs over, clearing his mind, ignoring the pain and the threat behind him.

He made it another hundred yards and then he turned around to look. He could see a few men running three hundred yards back. One of the ANA Humvees was also pursuing and would be on him in a few moments. He turned and kept running, confused by the low hum he could hear in the distance. The hum turned into a buzz, then into a roar. He didn't dare look around. He didn't have the time.

The amount of sand the pair of helicopters kicked up as they roared overhead was impressive, and they did little to help Jack's attempts to remain upright. His heart sank with the knowledge that Brinson must have called in air support. His run slowed to a jog, despite his pursuers. With helicopters in the air there was no point running.

As he slowed to a walk he realized, deep in the recesses of his mind, that there was no way helicopters could have arrived in the short time he'd been running. He heard the chattering of machinegun fire. He turned around and watched as tracer rounds spewed from the side of one of the helicopters toward the convoy. The other helicopter added rocket fire to the carnage.

He turned around and ran again as the choppers rained death upon the convoy. They had US Marine Corps markings, which confused him further. He didn't know what to think any more, but he figured he couldn't go wrong with getting away from all of it. He started to run again. Ahead of him, another chopper had appeared and started to descend. In the door, Ortiz waved.

Jack didn't know if anyone was left on his tail as the choppers behind him did their work, but he didn't look back. He just ran as hard as he could towards the door and hoped like hell that he didn't take one in the back before he got there. The distance closed as the chopper touched down and kept its rotors spinning. Forty yards, then thirty. His lungs burned hot as he pushed himself on.

He staggered forward another few inches. He wanted to live, but he couldn't run anymore. He was spent, he could barely think straight, and it was difficult to keep putting one foot in front of another. After another few steps toward the now-grounded helicopter, he fell to his knees and then onto his hands. He sucked at the hot desert air, struggling to breathe.

He stared at the sand, his lungs heaving for air. He wanted to slump into it but he wasn't sure how long the rescue chopper would wait. He took one more deep breath and then steeled himself for one more try. He wanted to live. As he was about to try to climb to his feet, he felt a hand grip his arm. He looked up and saw Ortiz smiling down at him.

"Come on, Jack." Ortiz yanked his arm and helped Jack to his feet. "We've got thirty seconds before people start to notice that the birds have stopped."

Jack staggered to his feet and let himself be guided towards the open door of the chopper. Once he was seated safely inside, Ortiz slid the door shut and they were airborne in seconds. Jack slowly caught his breath and started to breathe normally. Only then did he start to sob. It was uncontrollable. The stress of the last few days had finally overwhelmed him.

"No shame in it, Jack."

He looked up at Ortiz. "What?"

Ortiz smiled. "No shame."

Jack nodded. He wasn't sure if Ortiz was saying what he really believed or was just trying to make him feel better, but he appreciated the effort. He felt a bond with the man like few he'd had in his life. He slowly calmed down and settled back in his seat. He watched as Ortiz reached into his combat vest, pulled out a packet of smokes, and started to hand them around.

"Give me one of those." Jack reached out and plucked a cigarette from the packet.

"Knew we'd make a deviant out of you." Ortiz grinned as reached out to light Jack's cigarette.

Jack took a drag and coughed. "How did you find me, Dan?"

"The pager had a tracker. Turns out some Corps brass weren't thrilled about being sucked into the rendition program and we thought it likely that Brinson would make a move on you. As far as anyone will know, Brinson's convoy was hit by Taliban and the helos were on patrol."

Jack's eyes widened. He had no idea that politics within the Marine Corps ran so deep. "What about my story?"

Ortiz smiled. "Once you get back to the States you'll have your information, Jack. Unfortunately Major Brinson, the brainchild of the program, was killed on a patrol."

Jack nodded. He understood. He was being given his life and his story in return for keeping his mouth shut about the Marine Corps cleaning up their mess. He didn't know what politics were playing out between the Marine Corps and the CIA, or even what else would occur in future, but all he knew was that he wanted out of Afghanistan. He'd had enough of the country's hospitality.

Jack closed his eyes. The sound of the helicopter's rotors slicing through the air was rhythmic, and no further words were needed between the two of them. He took another deep drag of the cigarette, exhaled, and coughed only lightly. He'd never smoked before and had no intention of starting, but it seemed a fitting way to end the week from hell.

As soon as he was home he was going to have a whisky, sleep next to his wife, and wake up only for bacon. The story could wait a day or two.

EPILOGUE

Pulitzer Prize winner.

Jack was still getting used to it. He smiled as he killed the ignition, put the car into park, and lifted the handbrake. The light in the main bedroom was on, spilling through the small cracks at either end of the curtain. He hadn't expected Erin to wait up for him, given how sick she'd been earlier in the day. That she had was a pleasant surprise, the final flourish on a night of celebration and recognition. He hefted the Pulitzer – still surprised by its weight – and climbed out of the car. He couldn't wait to show Erin and to go into work on Monday.

Things were on the up.

THE FOUNDATION

JACK EMERY 1

For anyone that likes to daydream, imagine and ask "what if…?"

Keep it up.

PROLOGUE

Chen Shubian cursed under his breath at the old Hewlett Packard as it whirred to life. He was seated at the rear of a little internet café on the outskirts of Taipei, watching the light in the middle of the case occasionally flash with activity. He was losing patience and about to force a restart when the Microsoft logo appeared.

Chen shook his head. "Vista."

He dug a small envelope from his pocket and tore it open. Inside was a piece of paper with an alphanumeric code, meaningless to most people. It was Chen's key to the private server set up by his employers. They'd found him on the Darknet, a refugee searching for his vengeance, and brought him to their community. Now, the private server allowed them to conduct business outside the view of the authorities.

The code wasn't all that was required to access the server. He plugged his Hello Kitty USB into the front slot of the computer and tapped his fingers on the desk as the ancient machine whirred some more. He typed the code into the black command box that appeared on the screen and hit enter. The black box was replaced by an ordinary-looking web browser.

Chen clicked the only bookmark on the browser, which took him to a message board where likeminded people connected to chat about politics, sport and blowing up international infrastructure. A message at the top of the screen reminded users to ensure the security of the network, lest they end up in residence at Guantanamo Bay.

Chen searched his pockets again and found a small photo. He put it below the computer screen and stared at it for a few moments. His mother and father stared back at him, standing on either side of a slender fifteen-year-old boy with straight, shiny, black hair. The photo had been taken the last time Chen and his parents were all together.

Chen's life had changed forever when his father—an employee of a large American investment bank—had been arrested on a routine business trip from Taiwan to China. He had been charged with espionage and executed after a show trial. In grief, Chen's mother had taken her own life soon after the death of her husband.

Chen blamed China, but he also blamed the American bank that had left his father to rot. They'd obviously determined that their business interests in China were more important and had done nothing to help his father. The thirst for vengeance against China had guided Chen's life ever since: from school, to university, to the Taiwanese Army and then its Special Operations Command. It had honed his anger and his skills.

Though the attack he planned would rock China, his employers assured him that the act would also cause great heartache for the United States. It was a happy coincidence.

He smiled with pride as he browsed the thread, which connected him with others slighted by China and united them all under one cause. He left a message for those who would help him undertake the attack, confirming the final details. He typed another to his employers in the endeavor, noting that their funding had been received and confirming the details of their meeting in a few days' time.

When he was finished, he ejected the USB and all signs of the message board vanished from the screen. Chen left the internet café as anonymously as he'd entered, satisfied that everything was in place for the attack. He had no expectation that he'd bring down the Chinese Government, though he did believe that a heavy enough blow could cause a fracture in the monolith. He felt a small degree of guilt for the innocents who'd die, but their lives were the price of vengeance.

Men of decisive action changed the world, and if it had been good enough for Mao, who'd driven Chen's ancestors from mainland China to Taiwan, then it was certainly good enough for him.

ACT I

CHAPTER 1

In London today, Ernest McDowell, Managing Director of EMCorp, fronted the British Parliamentary inquiry into the phone hacking of UK politicians, sports stars and celebrities. During his testimony, Mr McDowell denied all prior knowledge of the crimes, but also noted that the company's head of UK operations had been fired and the London Telegraph had been closed. Despite these moves, and Mr McDowell's assurances that he'd stamp out any remaining rogue behavior in his company, the inquiry chairman seemed unimpressed. Mr McDowell will not enjoy any breathing room when he arrives home in the US, with a similar investigation about to get underway in the United States Senate and mounting pressure from his board to step down.

Jarvis Green, BBC World News, *August 31*

J ack Emery woke with a groan, face down in a pool of vomit. The sickly soup had matted his hair and dried on his face. He dry retched, one more protest from a body familiar with this type of abuse. He had the worst hangover of all time, or at least this side of the crucifixion. He rolled out of the puddle and onto his back. As he moved, his head felt like it was a tumble dryer. Once he was still, he took a minute to do a physical stocktake. He moved his fingers and toes, then his limbs, pleased that everything seemed to be in working order— more or less.

"That's a start." His voice was raspy, and he considered calling for a crime scene unit to stencil some chalk around him, haul him off and call it even.

He opened his eyes and looked around, glad that he'd found his way back to his hotel. He stood, walked unsteadily to the window and opened the curtains. Despite the frost on the window and his aching body, the sight of New York City made him smile. The skyscrapers and the bustle. It was chaotic, but somehow it all worked. He turned to the bed, mad at himself for lacking the sense to pass out onto it rather than the floor. At least he didn't have to make it every day. It was the only advantage of being forced to stay at the Wellington Hotel for the past month.

He sighed and decided to bury that particular set of thoughts for the time being. None of it was going away in a hurry, so there was no sense adding mental anguish to his physical trauma. He needed a shower, a shave and breakfast. He staggered to the bathroom and started the shower.

As Jack waited for the stream of water to become warm, then scalding, he stole a look at himself in the mirror. It wasn't pretty. His hair was greasy, his skin dry; he was showing every second of his thirty-five years. He stepped into the shower and successfully washed away the stink of stale beer and vomit.

Once out, he toweled off and then tore at his stubble using the terrible complimentary razor. He felt a bit fresher, and left the bathroom to do his best to find some clean clothes among the piles of dirty laundry that littered the room. He dressed and slipped on the same shoes from the night before, complete with speckles of vomit. He gathered his keys, office security pass, cell phone and wallet, then made his way to the first-floor diner. He pushed open the double doors and took in the scene with distaste. No matter how many times he ate here, it never looked welcoming. He sat.

It didn't take long for a waitress to shuffle over. "What can I get you?"

Then his phone beeped. He fumbled around for it and looked at the message. He absentmindedly waved the waitress away. As he stared at the text, bile rose in his throat

Not attending this morning? I didn't think you'd sabotage your career to avoid me.

Erin. Tall, blond, beautiful. Good colleague and great shag. Unfaithful wife.

Jack looked at his watch and realized he should have been at the morning *New York Standard* staff meeting, being handed the assignment of a lifetime. Instead, he was in a diner. His life was a mess.

"Bitch."

Thoughts of breakfast forgotten, he went outside and hailed a cab. He jumped in and gave the driver the address. As the cab drove downtown, Jack's head never left his hands. He'd wanted the job for months, but had probably lost it because of his self-annihilation.

The cab pulled to a stop and the driver turned his head. "Eight seventy, pal."

"Thanks, mate." Jack gave a ten-dollar note to the driver. "Keep the change."

"Thanks, pal. You Australian?" The driver gave a toothless smile. "See you 'round."

Jack rushed into the *New York Standard* building, through the security gates and into the elevator. He tapped his foot impatiently as the elevator climbed to the eightieth floor, and as soon as the doors opened he burst into a run past the reception desk. Every additional second he was late reduced the chance of him getting the China gig.

He slowed as he reached the large wooden door and placed his hand on the knob. He took a second to compose himself, but knew he looked like shit: out of breath and sweaty. He sighed, opened the door and stepped inside. Two dozen pairs of eyes bored into him like lasers.

The booming voice he didn't want to hear came from the head of the table. "Nice of you to join us, Jack."

"Thought I'd let the rest of you get some work done." Jack kept his eyes down.

Nobody spoke while Jack found his way to his usual seat. Coffee cups and all manner of food covered much of the table. At its head in a high-backed leather chair sat the paper's managing editor, Josefa Tokaloka, a Pacific Islander turned American citizen who'd been with EMCorp for decades. Everyone else sat on far more modest chairs.

Jack found his seat and looked up to see Tokaloka's eyes on him. They held the stare for an awkward few seconds. Eventually, Tokaloka nodded so slightly that Jack thought he might be the only one who noticed, and that was it. He knew there would be no chewing out, the point had been made.

Tokaloka looked back down at his papers. "As I was saying, this stuff from Britain is killing us. We've done nothing wrong, but we're one of the few brands in the company that can say that. Keep yourselves clean. If you're in doubt, don't do it. I don't want anyone deciding they don't have to play by the rules."

Jack looked around and saw plenty of nods. The troubles at the *London Telegraph* office—the hacking, the denials—had led to a decision by Ernest McDowell to close the whole paper. A century-and-a-half-old institution gone overnight, with hundreds of colleagues out the door. There had been issues elsewhere, as well, including the US.

"Anyway, only one more thing to cover. China." Tokaloka paused. "Erin, it's yours."

Jack's head moved so fast he risked whiplash. The World Trade Organization Conference in Shanghai was supposed to be his gig, the career boost he needed to get over his current malaise. Tokaloka had obviously decided otherwise and abandoned him. He'd had a hunch he would lose the gig when he was late, but not to her.

Jack slammed his hands on the table and stood. "Hold on one bloody minute, Jo. That job was mine!"

Tokaloka stared at him. "You're too flaky at the moment. You walk in here late and looking like shit. It's not good enough. You're benched until you get it together."

Jack was about to argue, but decided against it. Making a scene would just dig him into a deeper hole with the boss. He bit his tongue and sat.

Tokaloka turned to Erin. "I want you on the ground in two days. You're going to be as busy as hell, but you'll have Celeste along to help."

Erin flashed the smile Jack had fallen in love with. "Happy to help, Jo. Thanks for the opportunity."

Tokaloka nodded. "Right, we're done."

Jack stayed where he was as the room exploded with conversation and staff rose to go to their desks. He was still in shock. He'd spent weeks doing the prep work on the WTO conference. While he knew his mind had been off-track for a few months, he could still do the job. Tokaloka taking it away wounded him. They were friends, after all.

Jack waited for the bustle to clear and for the sting of losing the China assignment to ease. When he looked up, he was confronted by Erin, Celeste Adams alongside her. He was trapped, and couldn't escape without looking like a fool. He hated to admit it, but Erin looked great. He knew that if she offered, he'd take her to the nearest secluded place, undress her and mess up that blond hair. That would never happen, though, because she'd continued to shine while he'd spiraled down into a dark mire.

"Got a minute, Jack?" Her voice was soft.

"Fuck off, Erin."

"Suit yourself, just remember it's me trying to heal this, at least a little." She shook her head as she turned and strode away.

"Heal yourself! We might've had a chance if you had." Jack's words were wasted, because Erin was already out of earshot.

Celeste smiled. "That had nothing to do with me. I'm just shadowing whatever she does, which apparently includes relationship destruction." She was younger and different to his wife in every way: average height, where Erin was tall; preferred dresses to the hard, boxy pant suits that Erin wore; and had a mane of fiery red hair that flowed across her shoulders.

Jack snorted and changed the topic. "You're one of the refugees from London, right? Your accent is as strong as mine used to be."

"Yeah." She laughed. "I started at the *Telegraph* a few weeks before they shut up shop. I hadn't done anything wrong, so I managed to get a job here. I'm trying to adjust."

"Listen to Erin. She'll be your ticket to bigger things."

"Got it. I'll see you around."

As Celeste left him, Jack's cell phone beeped. It was a message from Jo.

You're letting me down, Jack. I need more of the Pulitzer Prize winner and less of the current version. It's time to bite the bullet on your divorce, my friend. I want you to meet me for a beer later in the week.

Jack sighed and started to type his reply.

No hard feelings, but did it have to be her? Meeting the lawyer tomorrow.

ERNEST MCDOWELL—MOGUL, *visionary, ruthless bastard.*

Ernest stared at the magazine for a long while. His deeply lined face stared back at him from under gray hair. He sighed, picked up the magazine and threw it at the small table. It fluttered the short distance and landed cover up alongside a few papers and other weekly news magazines, though none of the others had his face on them.

"Never should have rejected that buyout, right Peter?"

His assistant didn't take the bait, even though Ernest was sure that, deep down, Peter Weston was feeling vindicated. A few years ago, Ernest had declined an opportunity to buy the same magazine that now plagued him, despite Peter's advice to the contrary. Ernest had rarely gone against his advice since then.

Peter smiled from the seat opposite. "Don't worry about it."

"Easy for you to say." Ernest sighed. "It's not every day you get subjected to a dozen-page hatchet job in the largest weekly news magazine in the United States."

"It's poorly researched and full of errors. It won't do any damage." Peter waved his hand. "There are bigger things to worry about."

Ernest laughed. "You mean the British Parliament going for my jugular or the US Senate going for my balls?"

Peter laughed. "Quite a dilemma, I suppose."

Ernest massaged his temples with the tips of his forefingers, trying to see off his headache. He wasn't sure if it was caused by the sound of the aircraft engines, which droned in his ears like a fleet of mosquitoes, or the million or so conflicting ideas ricocheting around inside his head.

He sank deeper into the brown leather seats of the Gulfstream IV. He hated these trans-Atlantic flights, even if he did get to ride on a private jet. He was looking forward to getting home after a few days in London, which had cost Ernest his head of UK operations and the *Telegraph*.

"Want a drink?" Peter held up his hand to get the attention of the flight attendant. "I think you need one."

Ernest looked up as the woman swayed down the aisle with a bottle of Laphroaig and a pair of glasses. She knew their poison.

"I'll take it neat, thanks, Clara." Peter flashed her a grin.

She nodded at him and smiled at Ernest. "One for you, Mr McDowell?"

"Not now."

Peter laughed. "Normally you'd be all for a little recreational drinking on such a long flight."

Ernest frowned. "Not now."

He watched absentmindedly as Clara poured Peter's drink. Ernest knew that he was being difficult, mad at himself because he hadn't yet found a way to control the situation. He'd work it out eventually, but for now he was content to feel sorry for himself. Once Clara had finished, she left them.

"I want to know how I managed to build this company, see off three wives, raise a daughter, stare down takeover attempts and get us through the global economic meltdown, only to be undone by an ambitious jerk hacking the phone of a former British prime minister!"

Peter was silent for a few moments as he sipped his drink. Ernest didn't mind. He'd learned to appreciate Peter's careful, considered advice. "It was more than just one cowboy, Ernest. It was a systematic regime of criminal activity. We were right to shut it down, but despite that, we'll take our hits."

Ernest took a deep breath and exhaled slowly. "We already have. They want more."

"The UK issues will dissipate. We're through your testimony and you've cut away most of the cancer. The problems we have there were an appetizer."

Peter was right. The evidence of EMCorp wrongdoing had first emerged in the UK and it was limited to the activity of one overly ambitious newspaper. It had burned hot for a few months, and led to the Parliamentary inquiry, but Ernest's contrition and swift action had cooled things down a bit. A much larger fight was looming at home.

He closed his eyes. "The British are used to this sort of thing from Fleet Street. But trying to get the Senate and Patrick Mahoney to back off is a larger challenge."

Peter said nothing as he took another sip of his drink and leaned back in his seat.

"I really do hate the fat bastard, Peter."

Peter laughed. "Well, given the fat bastard chairs the Senate Judiciary Subcommittee on Privacy, Technology and the Law, which is on you like a fly on shit, he's a problem."

Ernest snorted. "Usually it'd be easy, but we can't even threaten to disrupt his re-election in a few months' time. He's retiring."

"Wouldn't be easy even if he wasn't." Peter shrugged. "We've got nothing. He's clean."

"Hate it when that happens."

They sat in silence for several minutes. Ernest stared into space while Peter occasionally sipped his whisky. He wondered how it had come to this, after all this time. He'd built EMCorp—the largest media company in the world—from the ground up. He'd thought it was impregnable, but now it was beset on all sides. He felt old.

Ernest's reverie was broken by the buzz of the plane intercom. The sound pierced to the very heart of his bad mood and made him want to strangle the pilot with the phone cord. Peter placed his drink on the table and rose to answer the phone.

Peter spoke in a series of pauses. "What is it? Sandra? What's wrong?"

Ernest's interest was immediately piqued when his wife's name was mentioned.

"Ohio?" Peter frowned. "Why was she there? An attack? Be sure that she is."

Ernest's heart pounded as Peter hung up. "What is it?"

"It's your wife." Peter paused. "She's been admitted to hospital in Ohio."

"Which one?"

"Sandra."

Ernest glared. "Not which wife, Peter. Don't be an idiot. Which hospital?"

"It's in Columbus. She's alright, but she's had another severe panic attack. She's insisting on seeing you."

"We should go." Ernest sighed. "Why the hell was she in Ohio?"

"Charity gig. We can't for a few days, Ernest. We're meeting Mahoney in Washington tomorrow. Once that's done, we'll go and see her."

Ernest stood and his back staged a protest in the form of sharp pain. He paced as he processed this new information. He'd hated these last few weeks most of all because, just when he had things figured out, the game would change again. Sandra would have to wait.

"Doesn't she fucking understand what we're dealing with here? The last thing I need is her going off the deep end again."

"The tabloids will get a hold of it and have a field day. But at the least we can keep it quiet in Ohio and give Sandra some peace."

"Owning the only major paper there helps." Ernest scratched his chin. "Okay, let her cool her heels. But I want to be out of Washington as soon as possible."

"I'll make sure we're fueled and ready to leave Dulles tomorrow night, as soon as we're done with the senator."

∽

MICHELLE DOMINIQUE'S guilty pleasure was the ten-minute casual snooze she took after silencing her wailing alarm clock. She liked that the simple press of a button granted time to reflect on the day ahead, safe in the cocoon of self-denial that although the day was close, it hadn't quite arrived.

Today was different. She'd slept in and the day was well and truly here. Michelle watched the clock with one eye open, the rest of her body coiled under the covers. She dared it to grind the last painful minute to 11am, and when the alarm started she pounded the snooze button several times. Ten more minutes. On most mornings she'd wake much earlier, but she'd had a very interesting night.

She sighed as the bed's other occupant started to stir and she felt a hardness press against her back. For him, seemingly, the ten-minute snooze was an excuse for mischief. She searched her memory for his name, but it abandoned her, probably in response to the tequila the night before. He pressed in closer.

"Good morning, gorgeous." His hand cupped her breast, too hard. "Was hoping you wouldn't be working today and we could get to know each other."

She closed her eyes. This was the part Michelle hated. While she was happy to indulge in what her grandmother called the physical trappings of Satan, she hated the next morning. She just wished the split could be as free and easy as their efforts the night before. She had work to do.

"Why? I've got to get moving."

His hand started moving south. "Come on, babe, there's always time for a quickie."

"I thought that's what last night was supposed to be." Her voice had all the innocence of a former St Augustine's choir girl's.

His hand froze and he gave little more than a grunt in response.

"You can call a cab, or there's a bus stop out the front."

Not wanting to entertain his advances any longer, Michelle stretched her legs out and committed the crime of rising before the second alarm. She stood and walked to the shower, earning a sigh of acceptance from the man. Yet again, she promised herself that, one day, she'd pick a man based on him being something more than an attractive Neanderthal. One day.

It was just easier this way, she'd decided long ago. Michelle Dominique. Single. Hates cats and children. Her job was demanding and she had planned a future that was more demanding still. She was in no hurry to settle down and have it all end in the horrible drudgery of suburbia.

She closed the bathroom door and untied the mess that was her post-sex hairstyle. Her reflection worried her. Too thin. She'd been working too much lately and had probably lost a bit too much weight. Her face looked hollow with stress and lack of sleep. She vowed to look after herself better.

"Just a few more months."

She showered and completed her morning routine. Once out of the bathroom, she was pleased to discover that her companion had gracefully exited. Careful not to dislodge the towel holding her wet hair in place, she dressed in a black dress and blood-red pumps, then looked in the mirror again and nodded. Good enough.

Michelle walked to the kitchen and opened her fridge. Though she had a nice enough apartment, the food situation was bleak. Some beer, a bottle of milk and a jar of pickles. She was just not home enough to make stocking it worthwhile. She sighed, grabbed the milk and some muesli from the pantry and combined them to make a dismal breakfast.

As she ate, she checked the news on her iPad. It was the usual leftist rubbish and propaganda, though the stories from the right of politics depressed her as well. She flicked through it all very quickly, getting across the major items. She was about to close the browser window when a small item caught her attention.

"Oh Ernest, Ernest, Ernest." A small dribble of milk escaped her mouth and ran down her chin. She swiped at it. "You're in a bad spot."

She knew that Ernest McDowell was in trouble in the UK, but the scandals engulfing him at home in the United States were about to get much worse. She closed the browser and opened up Skype. She dialed the first name in the contact list: Anton. It took a while to connect, and she smiled at the thought she might have woken him.

Her smile grew when he answered the call wearing nothing but a towel. "Hello, Anton, sorry to disturb you."

He frowned, and the light above him reflected off his shaved head. "An email wouldn't have sufficed? And wipe that smile, or I'm going to think you planned this."

"Seen the news?" She lifted another spoonful of muesli into her mouth.

He raised an eyebrow. "What in particular?"

She swallowed and gave a wide smile. "McDowell will be fronting the US Senate next month. Told you so. Democrats want a piece. Republicans aren't any better, either."

He seemed to consider the news for a second or two. While they were in broad agreement about most things to do with the Foundation for a New America, the topic of Ernest McDowell had divided them in recent months. She wanted him on the hook, Anton didn't see the point. Maybe this would convince him.

"So?" Anton was clearly unimpressed. "He'll just take his lumps."

"He could be an asset if we handle him correctly."

"I remember the last time you said that. Cost us four lives." He shook his head. "No. You need to focus on China and your Congressional campaign."

Michelle grimaced internally, but did her best to keep the expression on her face even. He was right to point out that she'd compromised an entire cell in Houston on what, in hindsight, had been a hunch. But that was the risk in the high-stakes game they played. The fallout had been contained and the organization had moved on. But she conceded the point—for now.

"China is under control. My flight is booked and the assets are in place. Don't worry about that. My Congressional campaign is going fine, as well."

Anton smiled. "Now you're talking. Relax, though, while your campaign is on track, we need to think about the others who are running. McDowell is a distraction."

She wasn't going to win this, but tried one more time. "He'd make it easier. Having the influence of his company under our belt would all but ensure success. Every candidate we put up would stroll across the line."

He started to say something, but seemed to reconsider. He frowned, and enough lines formed on his forehead to tell her she'd broken through and he was considering her point. "I'm not convinced, but let's talk about it more in Shanghai. He could be handy, but he's also the sort who'd out us and take the flak, just for fun."

"Okay, fair enough." Michelle was happy enough that McDowell was back on the agenda. "I've got to get ready for my flight. I'll see you in Shanghai."

CHAPTER 2

Celeb Weekly can report exclusively that Sandra Cheng, socialite wife of Ernest McDowell, has been admitted to hospital in Ohio after a breakdown at a charity function. The latest admission is her third in as many months. A source close to the McDowell family has expressed doubts about her mental health and revealed that Ms Cheng is distressed about events involving her husband's company. Ms Cheng, a high-profile lawyer prior to her marriage, gave up her private practice upon marrying Mr McDowell. It appears that despite impressive public achievements in her own right, Ms Cheng is struggling to cope with the increased scrutiny of recent months.

Cherry Adams, Celeb Weekly, *September 1*

"I can have my assistant work up the forms and courier them to your office. You'll have them by the end of the day, and then it's up to you to sign them." Winston Clay raised an eyebrow. "As long as you're sure, Jack?"

Jack wasn't, but he nodded anyway. He'd decided at some point during the meeting that he really didn't like Clay, who was one of the better divorce lawyers in New York. Though he needed him, he was tempted to tip over the coffee table and storm out of the room. Instead he continued to sit and listen to advice he didn't want to hear, which also cost him a fortune.

Clay stood and extended his hand across the coffee table. Jack stayed put, sinking further into the leather armchair that probably cost more than he—a minted Pulitzer Prize winner—earned in a month. After a few seconds, Clay dropped his hand and retook his seat. Jack reached up, scratched his nose and stared out the window behind the lawyer.

Clay sighed. "If you still have doubts, Jack, there are options that fall well short of divorce. Not that I'm trying to put myself out of business, you understand, but could counseling work? Time apart?"

Jack leaned forward and took hold of the glass of scotch on the coffee table. He threw back the remains with a flick of his wrist, then put the glass back. Morning drinking was for losers, but he didn't care much right now. He'd replayed the events of that terrible night a million times in his head, and it made less sense with each pass.

He'd thought Erin would be fast asleep by the time he got home. Instead, he'd found her upright in bed, surrounded by a hundred tissues and an empty bottle of red. Blind drunk on wine and antidepressants, she'd told him everything. How she'd slept with the neighbor, many times, but was now laden with guilt.

The next day, with sunlight flooding their room and a clearer head, she'd recanted. Jack had tried to speak to her about it, but after her denials he'd given up and left the house a shattered man. While he'd first spoken to Clay a while ago, having to stay for so long at the Wellington Hotel and losing the China gig had convinced him to proceed.

Jack shifted his gaze down slightly, and looked straight at Clay. "I'm sure, Winston. She slept with my neighbor, got drunk, admitted to it, got sober and then denied it all again. She hasn't given me any reason to think there's any hope, or that she even gives a damn."

Clay shrugged. "Your call. I just want you to be across your range of options before you pull the trigger. You need to think about your finances, handling the fallout…"

"Give her half. I just want it over with. It's done." To say those words broke Jack's heart again."

"That's quite unusual, Jack." Clay's eyes narrowed. "You need to protect your interests and—"

"I understand." Jack sighed. "You've done your job, now do what I ask."

He'd built a life with Erin. They'd pursued careers, supported each other, consoled each other and loved each other. Now he simply wanted to be done with it. With her. He wanted to retreat into a dark hole with a bottle of nice scotch, and wake up only after the decade or so it would take to stop hurting.

Clay nodded and stood for the second time, hand outstretched. "Okay, Jack."

Jack stood and shook his hand. "Thanks."

"And Jack, on a personal note, some advice free of charge. Clean yourself up, get a massage. You look like shit."

Jack gave a thumbs up to Clay and walked to the door. He deliberately didn't look around at the oak bookshelves or the six-figure artwork in the office. He'd made that mistake last time and felt enraged when the bill had come. It was all paid for by sad men and women who'd had their lives together guillotined, with Clay the executioner.

ERNEST WONDERED how many of his tax dollars were paying for the office of Senator Patrick Mahoney, Democrat for Massachusetts. The office looked as if it had been painted by a drunk spinning around on a chair and then furnished by a child. It hurt Ernest's sense of good taste. He and Peter sat opposite the senator, a bullfrog of a man who spilled over the sides of his chair. Between them was a hardwood desk, which had apparently belonged to a Kennedy. Or so Mahoney said.

Ernest took a deep breath and leaned forward. "So what you're telling me, Senator, is that the US Senate is ready to destroy my company?"

Mahoney smiled. "That's about the sum of it. Your enterprise has become a little too big, a little too powerful, and now you've trampled on the civil rights of Americans."

Ernest bit his lip, but couldn't resist. "Unlike drone attacks, indefinite detention without charge or all-pervasive electronic signals interception and intelligence?"

"All perfectly legal, Ernest." Mahoney smiled like a shark. "The conduct of your company, on the other hand, was not. That necessitates a reaction."

The allegations against EMCorp in the US were as serious as those in the United Kingdom, if Ernest was being honest. Though, to the best of his knowledge, the company had dealt with and disclosed all misconduct, it was an almighty assumption. It was also a gamble, given the looming inquiry. If more illegal activity emerged, he'd be scuttled.

Ernest wondered if the company had just become too big for him to control, even as he did his best to fight Mahoney and his ilk.

Ernest felt his face flush. "I'll concede that we're in a bit of trouble, Senator. But I didn't think you and your colleagues were quite so stupid."

Mahoney frowned. "I don't follow."

"I suspect you don't. You're probably daft enough to think that it's policy and good governance that gets representatives re-elected, Senator."

Mahoney leaned back in his chair and Ernest felt his anger grow. He hoped that the other man would tip back just far enough to fall over and maybe snap his neck on the way down. No such luck—Mahoney continued to stare straight at him and started to tap his finger on the armrest.

"I know the public like their bread and circuses, Ernest. Who manufactures them is largely irrelevant. Though it's currently your company, you're not indispensable."

"You're wrong. Who manufactures the content, and with it the message, is very important. While I respect the right of our duly elected representatives to destroy one of the greatest bastions of freedom that the American people have, they should know that I have an almighty bark, Senator, and quite a substantial bite."

Mahoney smiled. "I'm retiring from public life at the coming election. Given it's only a few months away, I'm not sure which is more underwhelming, your sense of self-importance or your threats. Both are at odds with reality."

"I don't agree, Senator. It's entirely plausible that you're done with public life, but I'm yet to meet a thirty-year veteran of the hill who doesn't care about his legacy."

Mahoney raised an eyebrow. "I'm listening."

"The key to securing your achievements is sitting in front of you, and you're doing a pretty good job of pissing him off. I'm also doing all I can to fix the issues that EMCorp has had and I can assure you there won't be a repeat." Ernest knew this was his chance. He let his words sink in before he continued. "Back off, remove the noose from around my neck, and you'll have friendly smoke blown up your ass for the next century."

Mahoney seemed to consider his offer for a moment, then shook his head. "Not good enough, Ernest. I get more out of destroying you than working with you. I'll be a hero."

Ernest looked to Peter for support.

Peter sat forward. "Need we remind you, Senator, of the generous donations that came your way following the *Boston Chronicle* endorsement at the last election?"

"The support surely was appreciated, son, but I've got the public baying for blood."

Ernest sighed. It was time to cut to the chase. "What're you proposing?"

"An understanding. If you dig your heels in, it will end in sanctions against your company, including its dismantling, and destruction of your own wealth and influence. But all I really want is a scalp to hang on my wall."

Ernest said nothing; he knew where this was going.

"Instead, I propose that you come before the committee and announce you're stepping down as head of the company. Whoever takes over—I don't care who it is—promises to fix the problems. You lose the power, but your company is intact and I get my scalp."

Ernest was in awe of Mahoney's gall. He'd tried reason, he'd tried bribery; he had one option left. He looked at Peter and gave him a slight nod. He watched as Peter searched for a single piece of paper from among his notes and day planner. Once he found it, he calmly placed it face down on the desk.

"I'm afraid I can't accept your proposal. I didn't really want to bring this up, Senator. But we've uncovered some...anomalies in your past." He knew exactly what was on the sheet of paper: nothing. Despite months of looking for something, anything, to bury Mahoney, he was clean. Ernest had nothing he could use against the senator except a blank sheet of paper and his reputation for smear.

Mahoney sat in silence and his face drained of color. Ernest was surprised, and wondered what it was that he and Peter hadn't managed to uncover.

He pushed home his advantage. "I've got the largest army of dirt diggers on the planet. They're very good at it. The ball is in your court, Senator."

Mahoney shook his head. "You can't prove anything. Besides, I can't just halt a committee hearing, son. There are other members you'd have to ride roughshod over."

Mahoney was right, but Ernest had planted a seed of doubt. He laughed. "Oh, I don't want to stop it. I want to make a mockery of it and destroy its conveners."

Ernest only wished he was as confident as his bluster suggested.

~

MICHELLE SIPPED her coffee and grimaced as it assaulted her taste buds. She wondered why she kept faith with the company when she was disappointed every time. She'd walk in, order a grande from the overly cheery staff, and sit down in one of the comfortable chairs. Lulled into a false sense of hope, she'd take a sip, then curse.

Anton laughed. "I know how much you love Starbucks."

She sneered at him. "Yeah, like cancer."

Anton made a face, the small benign tumor he'd had cut out a few months ago apparently still a sore spot. "No need to get personal."

Michelle snorted and looked up at the entrance again, irritated. She was jet lagged from the eighteen-hour flight from New York to Shanghai, via Chicago, and was in no mood to wait. Once the meeting was done, she was going straight to her hotel room to get some sleep.

"Where is he?" She knew it was a pointless question, given they were situated in the back corner. If he had arrived they'd have seen it.

"How should I know? He's your man."

"No, Anton. He's not mine, or yours, or ours. That's the point."

He rolled his eyes. "Relax, I didn't mean it literally."

She was about to take further issue when the door chime sounded. She looked up and saw an Asian man in full business attire. He stood in the doorway and as he scanned the tables he looked ordinary in every way. Most importantly, he wore a red and black striped tie. Michelle raised her hand and gave him a small wave.

"He's here."

The Chinese man saw her, gave a small nod and moved to the counter to order. Michelle and Anton waited in silence. Michelle used the time to gather her thoughts and Anton wore a poker face. The meeting was mainly to reassure Anton about the man she'd selected to complete the operation. The next few minutes needed to go well.

Michelle stood and held out her hand as the man joined them with a cup of tea in hand. "I appreciate you joining us, Chen. This is my colleague, Anton."

Chen shook her hand. "Good afternoon, Michelle and Anton. It's a pleasure to finally meet the enablers of my vengeance."

Michelle smiled again, and after the two men shook hands she gestured Chen toward the vacant chair and sat in her own. She glanced at Anton, who now sat with his elbows resting on his knees and his chin cupped in his hand. She knew this look. She'd seen it dozens of times. He was going to pounce.

"Are you prepared to die?" Anton's tone was casual, as if he was asking how the tea tasted or what the weather was going to be like.

Chen showed no expression. "I am trained to do the job, and I will live up to my commitments. That's all you need to know."

"I beg to differ. Great piles of my organization's money and effort have been poured into this mission, which is key to our broader agenda. I'll ask whatever I please."

Michelle didn't speak, but watched Chen lift his tea and sip it. A lot of her influence within the Foundation had been staked on the selection of Chen Shubian for the operation. She'd found him on the Darknet, carefully cultivated his fury, then connected him to the Foundation's server. Since then, she'd worked painstakingly with Chen to plan the operation, including the selection of others to assist him.

While her position as number two to Anton gave her a lot of power within the Foundation, he didn't suffer fools or mistakes. Since she'd joined a decade prior, she'd seen how ruthless he could be to friends as well as foes. If, at the end of the meeting, Anton had any doubts about Chen's commitment, a Foundation for a New America wet squad would make the Taiwanese man disappear. Better that than a messy operation.

Anton continued. "You were chosen by my associate because you have the skills and commitment to achieve our objectives. I don't care about your motivation and you shouldn't care about ours. We're a happy alliance of convenience that will result in thousands dead, vengeance done and a world changed. But I still insist on excellence."

Chen laughed softly, and the sound chilled Michelle. "I have planned wisely. My equipment is excellent, my companions sound and my preparations meticulous."

"I'm glad to hear it, but I still have some concerns about your willingness to see this through."

"Sitting here together is proof that we've already won." Chen looked around. "If the secret police had any clue that I was a threat, we'd be rotting in prison."

Anton smiled. "Glad you're on board. You have my blessings and the green light. I wish you well."

Michelle waited impassively as Anton stood, and had started to stand when he gestured for them to remain seated. "You two finish your drinks. I want to get some shopping in before we unleash your handiwork, Chen."

Chen smiled, but said nothing.

Michelle waited until Anton was out of earshot. "Nicely done, he can be quite difficult. You handled it well."

He shrugged. "The last matter I need confirmed is that my identity will remain anonymous. I have a family that needs to be protected."

Michelle nodded. "The only way a soul will know is if you fuck it up, and that's entirely up to you."

"That won't happen."

"Well, here's to you, then." She raised her coffee in salute and took a long sip, then grimaced again, having forgotten how poor it was.

Chen smiled slightly as he stood to leave. "Make sure you have a good view, I will make the night as bright as day."

CHAPTER 3

"The first day of the WTO Conference is in the books, Garth, and traffic disruption to date has been horrendous. But I'm sure what is most concerning the Chinese Government are the large protests taking place across Shanghai. While the authorities have kept things in order for the most part, the audacity of the protests must frustrate them, given China's reputation for strong-arm tactics. The few protesters I spoke to this morning linked the protests to separatist campaigns in Tibet and Xinjiang, rather than opposition to the WTO. In particular, the Tibetan and Uyghur protestors said the conference offered a unique opportunity to air their concerns while the eyes of the world are on Shanghai."

Erin Emery, News Tonight, *September 3*

Chen had eagerly anticipated another ride on the Shanghai Maglev. When he'd arrived three days ago, he'd ridden the wondrous train from the airport to the city. Man's ability to create something so remarkable—a transit system where the train rode above the track, without needing to touch the rail—amazed him. He didn't understand the science, but was amazed nonetheless.

With his business in Shanghai nearly concluded, he arrived at the Longyang Road metro station for the Maglev that would take him to Pudong International Airport. The station was amazing, wrapped in a large curved roof that made Chen feel like he was in a spaceship. He waited on the platform with a mix of tired-looking businessmen and tourists.

After a few minutes, the train pulled into the station. The doors on the other side of the carriage opened and the passengers disembarked. Once the carriage was empty, the doors on Chen's side opened and he stepped onto the train, took a seat near the door and put his backpack on the seat beside him. The train wasn't scheduled to depart for a few minutes, so he clasped his hands and waited.

An old woman stepped onto the carriage just as the intercom beeped, warning that the doors were about to close. She was hunched over heavily on her cane. Chen moved his bag off the seat beside him and gestured for her to sit. The old woman smiled at him warmly and sat with an audible sigh of relief. The doors of the carriage closed and the wondrous machine began to move.

As the train gathered speed and he settled in for the seven-minute journey, Chen pulled his cell phone from his pocket and sent a quick message. It would set in motion the synchronized attacks he'd planned for Shanghai—several large bombs, a few targeted killings and a wave of cyberterrorist strikes. Half the incidents targeted the arteries that made Shanghai move, the other half aimed to disrupt the World Trade Organization conference. All were designed to inflict the maximum amount of damage.

He smiled at the perfection of his timing, knowing he'd be out of the country before the Shanghai authorities knew the full extent of what had hit them. He'd leave a horrible, destructive wake that would have ramifications for the entire region and rock China to its very foundations. His vengeance would be complete.

His thoughts were interrupted by an announcement that the Maglev was arriving at the airport. He checked his watch, pleased that he had a bit of time to get a snack and a drink before his flight. He moved closer to the doors and looked outside as the train slowed and the platform came up alongside. The train stopped and the doors opened.

He was about to step off when the old woman waved at him, before coughing several times. "Your bag! Young man! Your bag!"

Chen felt a degree of panic as he waved at the woman. "The bag isn't mine. I'll inform the stationmaster that somebody has left it unattended."

The woman smiled and placed the bag back down on the seat. Chen moved out of the way as passengers bustled past him, including the kind old woman. As he waited, he made sure that nobody removed the bag. At the last possible moment he stepped off the carriage, relieved that the bag was still in place and the train was ready to go.

He raised his cell phone, entered a number and then waited. As the train pulled out of the station and built up speed, he marveled again at the science that made it work. Once it was out of sight he hit the green call button. He waited ten seconds to be sure and then hung up.

He couldn't help smiling when he heard the explosion in the distance, a muffled boom that shook the glass windows of the station. Within seconds, a plume of dark, greasy, brown smoke rose into the sky, confirmation that his strike had been successful. Without further delay, he turned around and walked to the platform exit. He opened the back of the cheap phone and took out the SIM card. He threw the phone into one trash bin and snapped the SIM card in half before dropping it into another.

His next decision was what to eat in the terminal once he'd passed through security. He really felt like pizza.

~

"A TOAST to my soon to be ex-wife!" Jack raised his glass.

The patrons closest to him joined his salute to Erin as Jack laughed and drained half of the double whisky in one motion. The news break had shown the replay of a report by Erin from Shanghai. It was bad enough that she'd received the gig for the *Standard*, but she was also apparently a darling with the TV guys. Thankfully, the news break was over and the network had crossed back to the baseball.

He was just glad he hadn't been able to hear her voice over the noise in the bar. While Clay's staff had delivered the papers to Erin's lawyers the day before, the news had apparently not reached her, or else she was unconcerned. She looked as fresh, happy and gorgeous as ever. He hated that, but most of all, he hated the fact that he still cared. It was another kick in the balls.

For his part, Jack had made a formidable effort to forget the whole thing, enlisting the help of Josefa and Shane Solomon. He'd worked with Josefa for a decade, and known Shane for just as long. Jack followed the whisky with a long pull from his beer. He slumped back into his seat and looked around the table. The others stared back at him, concern evident on their faces.

"I knew you were struggling, Jack, but this is something else." Josefa reached out and pulled Jack's beer away from him. "Maybe this wasn't my best idea."

Shane laughed. "I bet Jack thinks it was."

Jack flared. "Fuck off, Shane. You left your wife to marry your secretary. I left mine because she was fucking the neighbor."

With his beer now out of reach, he considered ordering another from the big-breasted waitress. She was the one highlight of the bar, which was the lowest of low. The tables were scuffed by the love and care of thousands of drinkers and the carpet was stained in some places, sticky in others. He ignored the rest of the conversation at the table and turned his attention to the game. Though he wasn't much of a baseball fan and had never watched it at home in Australia, it would do.

He was just about to find that waitress when jeers sounded out across the bar as the game feed was cut. Jack snorted as one fan threw a beer bottle at the screen, but missed. A razor sharp news anchor appeared, doing his best to get the public up to speed on some momentous event. He looked anxious, though Jack couldn't hear what he was saying. It was the news ticker across the bottom of the screen that told him everything: thousands dead, a city attacked and a country in chaos.

It spoke of Shanghai.

"Hey, shut up, fellas." Josefa stood and pointed to the screen. "Turn the sound up!"

As Jack stood and swayed, nearly losing his feet, the barman turned up the volume and the sound of the broadcast flooded the bar. "*...it appears as if the attacks, which began just minutes ago, have struck at the heart of the Shanghai summit. The hotel housing the world's media has been severely damaged, and it appears that other parts of Shanghai are also under attack, including the Bund.*"

"Erin's there." Jack tried to clear the cobwebs from his head as he looked between Josefa and Shane. "That's where she's staying."

"Stay calm, Jack." Josefa placed a hand on his shoulder. "I'm sure she's fine. Shanghai is a big place."

"No!" Jack cried out in distress. "Her report was from outside of that hotel, Jo!"

Josefa nodded as Jack continued to watch, unable to peel his eyes away from the screen. The bar was silent. The vision shifted to shaky footage of a large building, racked with fire. Whoever was filming ran toward the building. The shot panned down to a woman, huddled in the fetal position, bloody and frantic.

"That's Celeste." Josefa pulled his cell phone from his pocket. "I need to make a call. Shane, keep an eye on Jack."

Jack watched as closely as he could for any sign of Erin, but the vision cut back to the presenter in the studio.

"That was footage from what appears to be the focal point of the attacks, the Grand Hyatt Shanghai, where international media are staying during the WTO conference."

Jack slammed his fist on the table, knocking two drinks over in the process. He remained standing, frozen in place, not knowing what to do or where to go but needing to do something. The thought of Erin, wounded and alone in Shanghai, felt too much for him to process.

He also knew how this sort of disaster was reported—drip-fed information, half-truths and speculation by reporters. Added to that would be interviews with subject experts usually starved for relevance, who took the opportunity to pitch sensational theories. Good for the viewer, but not necessarily for someone with a missing loved one.

He strode toward the exit, though he had to push past patrons who were chatting loudly about the attacks. Once outside, he tripped and landed roughly on the sidewalk. He was breathing heavily and felt like vomiting. Nothing came except sobs. He felt two people move closer, and turned to see Josefa and Shane standing over him.

Shane crouched down. "I think she'll be alright. Jo's on it, I'm sure she'll be fine."

Jack nodded and tried to regain his feet, but failed spectacularly. He landed on his right wrist and a shot of pain lanced up his arm. He cried out, and Shane placed a hand on his shoulder, no doubt to reassure him but also probably to prevent him from doing further injury.

Josefa was in the middle of another call, obviously having tried Erin with no luck. "We've got people over there, Ernest, we need to help them."

While it reassured Jack that Erin was about to have the resources of the company looking out for her, it wasn't enough. Despite how much she'd hurt him, he still felt a connection to her that went as deep as his marrow. He needed to act. He pulled out his cell phone and held it out to Shane.

"I need to get over there, Shane." He paused. "I need to find her."

Shane nodded. "I'll get you on the next flight."

~

MICHELLE FELT like a god as she surveyed Shanghai from one of the top-floor rooms of the Marriott Courtyard Shanghai. She'd chosen the room carefully to ensure a view of the Shanghai New International Expo Centre, the site of the WTO conference. She was relieved that the attacks had gone well, at least if judged by the amount of smoke that billowed from a dozen different places across the city. In front of her was the evidence that she had the ability to achieve anything. Yet it was more than that: it felt like the final cremation of her past, a signal that her rebirth was complete.

Though she'd had a rough family life, which explained her slightly obsessive interest in guns, she'd made it to Yale and studied law and political science. While her grades had been outstanding for two years, that had changed after an internship with a senator during spring break. They'd slept together and she'd thought it was a relationship, but later found out that she'd been the latest in a long line of wide-eyed interns. Her grades had plummeted and all thoughts of her future had changed. From that moment onwards she'd hated the Washington establishment to her core.

But years later, as a graduate, Anton had spotted her potential and recruited her, then spent the next few years slowly introducing her to the truth behind the Foundation for a New America. Her career since had been fighting for the American rebirth and for the Foundation's power. Now they were on the verge of success.

She shook her head and focused on the scene in front of her. There would be time to reflect once she was back in the States, but until then she needed to be alert and careful. Martial law had been declared since the attacks and the airport and other major facilities were closed. Hungry for updates, she'd been forced to rely on state television and what she could see from her hotel window. She'd smiled at the grainy picture on TV of the burnt-out remains of the Shanghai Maglev, derailed and embedded in the side of a building. She couldn't have asked for a better visual from a Hollywood studio.

Chen had done well. Michelle knew that no matter how quickly the fires were put out, and how swiftly the wounded healed, it would take China years to get over this. They could fix the Maglev and rebuild the other targets, but it would take far longer to soothe the anger. She was counting on it. The Foundation was counting on it.

She turned away from the window and smiled when she saw Anton asleep, naked, on top of the bed covers. Once the attacks were underway, she'd taken him to bed. The sex had been furious and energetic—an outlet for the pent-up stress and emotion of the previous few days. It seemed a fitting climax to this part of their plan. She crossed the room and sat on the edge of the bed, next to where Anton was asleep. She put a hand on his shoulder and gave it a squeeze. He was awake in seconds, staring up at her. He looked satiated, but she still saw the deep intelligence and cunning in his eyes.

He lifted himself up onto one elbow. "What is it?"

"It's time to go. We've done what we needed. I don't want to push our luck."

He smiled. Michelle didn't feel it was friendly. "Not quite everything."

"What do you mean?" She stared at him. "What've you done?"

He stared straight into her eyes. "Leaving Chen alive is too risky. I've sent a team."

Michelle was dumbstruck. This was the first time she'd felt disconnected from him. The attacks had been designed to help preserve the correct world order—and America's place in it—by pointing the Chinese at Taiwan. They'd painstakingly linked the evidence trail back to the island and its government, leaving little doubt who was responsible and what the Chinese reaction would be.

More importantly, with China focused on the island rather than its greater strategic interests, America would have the opportunity to flex its muscle and pull itself off the mat after the financial crisis. It would also signal the beginning of the next part of their plan: for the Foundation—and Michelle—to get a significant presence in the US Congress. Enough of a presence to exert more control.

A minute ago, she'd felt closer to him than ever. Now, Anton was playing a new game. There had been no talk of outing Chen. She'd been his handler. She'd helped him to plan the attacks. Most importantly, she'd given him access to their secure network. He'd repaid her efforts beyond her wildest imagination. The thought of terminating him such success was an anathema to her.

"Are you insane? We gave our word. The man has a family."

"They'll be taken care of as well." Anton laughed. "Bit late for sanctimony. We just killed thousands of innocent people from thousands of families."

"This is different. He's our man."

"He's a loose end that needs tying up. Once he's dead, nothing can be linked back to the Foundation." He sighed. "Look, Michelle, you've still got a lot to learn. I'll get us some room service and we'll talk about it some more, okay?"

She ground her teeth. "I don't want room service. I agreed with the plan, Anton, and I still agree with our purpose. But I don't like being in the dark one bit, and I don't like selling out our people either. There's nothing to be gained by killing Chen."

But he'd made up his mind, and she knew he wouldn't change it. In making this decision, Anton was revealing a part of himself she hadn't seen before. He'd always been ruthless, but until now she'd never considered that he'd so ruthlessly deal with someone who'd done a good job. She had to wonder if she'd suffer the same fate one day.

She lay down next to Anton, who was now on his back with his head resting in his hands. She didn't say anything, but rolled over and feigned sleep to consider her options. It felt like everything had changed. She was a woman of her word. She'd promised Chen that his family would be safe.

A few hours passed. When she was sure Anton was asleep again, she climbed carefully out of bed, grabbed her cell phone and walked to the bathroom. She locked the door and dialed a number from the address book. It rang for what seemed like an eternity until the call was picked up.

"This is Rodriguez."

She exhaled with relief. "This is Dominique. Are you still in Taipei?"

"Sure am. At the embassy."

"Okay. A Taiwanese family need to be looked after. I'll text you their details. I want them taken to the States. Set them up with a house and some cash. This is urgent."

"Okay, shouldn't be a problem, but I'll need Anton's green light. This will blow my cover at the embassy."

She paused. She'd anticipated this. "Anton is indisposed. You can consider this from the top, though."

"Your call." Rodriguez sounded unconvinced. "I'll take care of it."

CHAPTER 4

China's Foreign Minister has expressed outrage at the attacks on Shanghai and blamed Taiwan, describing it as the single most destructive act against the Chinese mainland since the Japanese atrocities of the Second World War. It's hard to argue, with a death toll in excess of ten thousand, French colonial buildings along the Bund damaged, the Maglev train derailed and dozens of other buildings damaged or destroyed. In response to the attacks, China has announced that military readiness has been stepped up and military assets and missiles in the south-east of the country prepared to strike Taiwan if necessary.

   Garth Angell, Foreign Correspondent, *September 4*

"I just need to get to Shanghai!" Jack leaned in closer to the small Japanese woman behind the Air China ticket counter. "My wife is missing and I need to reach her!"

The woman nodded sadly. Though he was enraged, Jack could see that she was unsure about how to proceed with the shouting *gaijin* in front of her.

"*Sumimasen*, sir. I am sorry. I'm unable to get you on a flight to Shanghai. Many airlines have stopped flying, and the remainder are full. There are no available seats aboard Air China or any of our partner airlines. Have you tried Japan Airlines?"

Jack stared at her for a long few moments, then took a deep breath and ran a hand through his hair. "Yeah, and everyone else. Look, money is no object. I'll buy you a Ferrari. I just need a seat." Technically it was true, with Ernest McDowell footing the bill.

Despite this, the woman shook her head and looked behind him. Jack turned to see two Japanese police officers standing rigidly, batons in one hand and radios in the other. They nodded at him, and gestured with their white-gloved hands for him to step away from the counter and over to the side.

Jack exhaled deeply. "Sorry, guys. I know it's not her fault. I just need to get over there. This is important, you know?"

The policemen looked at each other. They clearly didn't know, but just wanted Jack to stop harassing the desk staff. His shoulders sagged. They'd probably seen the same thing a hundred times in recent days, and stood with him while he calmed down. After a few minutes one of them patted him on the shoulder and they moved on.

Jack didn't push his luck. While he was glad he hadn't been arrested, he was clearly no longer welcome at the Air China counter. It had been his last port of call for the day—he'd tried every other airline that was still flying from Tokyo to Shanghai. He'd have to renew his attempts to beg, bully or bribe a ticket tomorrow.

He sighed and walked away from the ticketing area, resigned to the fact that he was probably not going to reach Erin any time soon. He made his way to the bar that had become his second home since arriving at Narita, in between irregular sleep on plastic chairs and abuse of airline staff. The bar was empty, apart from a few people killing time. It frustrated him that even though he couldn't get where he wanted to go, others could. In one corner sat a Japanese man with a briefcase at his side, laptop out. In one of the booths, a couple faced each other and talked with passionate eyes and expressive faces, their relationship not yet weighed down by the baggage of time.

He nodded at the bartender and pointed at the nearest beer tap. "Kirin, please."

The bartender smiled and Jack watched as he slowly filled the glass. He found himself hypnotized by the slow swirl of froth through the amber liquid. He longed for the numbness that the beer would induce, once he'd had enough of it. He craved it. He needed it.

The bartender placed the beer in front of him. "Four-hundred and twenty yen."

"Airport prices." Jack fished around in his pocket for a 500-yen coin, which he handed to the bartender. "Thanks. Keep the change."

As the bartender walked away, Jack's cell phone rang. He fumbled around in his pocket and dug it out. He didn't recognize the number. "Hello?"

"Jack? Oh, Jack, thank God. It's Celeste." The relief in her voice was clear.

The beer shook in Jack's hands, so much that he placed it on the bar. Celeste was calling. Erin might be alive. Or might not be. Celeste was calling. Not Erin. It was too soon to know for sure, or so the US Embassy had told him. Celeste seemed relieved, so it might be good news. Or might not be. He wanted answers. But didn't.

He felt empty. "Hi, Celeste."

"Jack? The line isn't great. I'm calling from Beijing Airport. They evacuated me out of Shanghai for some minor medical treatment, but I'm fine. It took me a while to find a phone and get sorted, but I spoke to Jo. I'm flying to Tokyo."

"Why?"

"I'm sorry, Jack." Her voice started to break and he heard a sob. "Erin is gone. She was standing near me when the bomb went off."

Jack sagged. "How? I saw you on the TV…"

Another pause. "It was a large piece of shrapnel. I'm so sorry. I waited with her as long as I could. She was gone by the time they forced me into an ambulance."

Jack felt dizzy. He leaned toward the bar to catch himself, but failed. He slipped off the stool and hit his head on the bar on the way down. The phone clattered down next to him. He reached up and touched his head, then looked at his hand. Blood. He'd split his head open. He closed his eyes and tried to compose himself.

Celeste's words had kicked in the doors of his preparation, and he felt the grief rushing in. He'd thought himself mentally fortified for Erin's death, though he'd hoped she was still alive. The reality of it was unbearable. The woman he'd loved, despite their recent issues, was gone. He picked up the phone.

"Jack?" Celeste's voice dripped with concern. "Jack? Jack, are you okay?"

He just wanted to be alone. "Thanks for telling me."

He hung up and stood. He righted the stool, sat again and a single tear streaked down his cheek. It was all over. His wife was dead. Deep down, ever since he'd left the bar in New York, he'd known it was likely Erin was dead. The life they'd built together was in ruins. The events of the last few months seemed trivial now.

He took a mouthful of his beer and considered what he'd see if he was outside of his body. He'd see a wreck of a man, mourning the death of his wife and the wasteland of his life. He'd see a man with a beer and little else. He'd pity him. For a while he thought of nothing, just tried to clear his head of the noise, the mess and the despair.

Soon, the sobs came, long and drawn out. Each one felt like it penetrated him to his core. He was as alone in the airport as he was in the world.

~

ERNEST CONCEDED that the hospital was quite nice, with a sloped driveway and an impressive garden that gave way to a four-story white building at the center of it all. It was far better than the rest of Ohio, at least. He was frustrated that it had taken him nearly a week to visit his wife after the meeting with Mahoney, because of issues with the US and UK governments, crazies blowing up half of Shanghai and leaving several of his journalists dead or missing.

"You know, Peter, this place is a pain in my ass to get to. Are you sure there's no way we can get her moved to another facility? In New York, perhaps?"

Peter shook his head. "I'm afraid the doctors were insistent. She's to stay at this facility in this fine state. They say that to move her will be detrimental to her wellbeing."

Ernest sighed as the car came to a halt. He opened the door and climbed out of the black sedan with a groan; his back was giving him hell. At least the driver had parked in the spot closest to the hospital front door, ignoring the "CEO" sign. They entered a cavernous lobby so white it hurt his eyes through the double automatic doors.

A large security guard was seated behind a desk with his feet up and his stomach protruding, the buttons on his blue shirt threatening to burst from the strain. Ernest could barely mask his contempt for Sandra's gatekeeper. He approached the desk and the guard pointed at the guest book on the counter. Ernest stared for several seconds, before scrawling his name and the time on the page without a word. Peter did likewise.

The guard took his feet off the desk, rummaged around in a drawer on the reception desk and held out a meaty hand clenching two identity tags. "You'll need to put these on your jackets, gentlemen."

Ernest looked at the tags, then down at his suit jacket, appalled at the idea of a pinhole in his five-thousand-dollar suit. He raised an eyebrow at the guard, who didn't seem to recognize that he was talking to Forbes' fifteenth richest man.

"No tag, no entry, sir." The guard shrugged. "I don't make the rules."

"Fucking hell. Peter, give me your jacket."

Peter frowned.

Ernest slid off his jacket. "I saw that look, stop whining, I'll buy you a new one."

In most circles Peter would be considered well dressed, but their suits couldn't be compared and Ernest was in no mood to haggle. After a short pause, Peter undid the button on his jacket and gave it to Ernest. Ernest slid the jacket over his shoulders and clipped on the security pass. The jacket fit well enough and he handed his own to Peter.

"Wait here."

The guard waved Ernest through and after a short walk down the hall, he found Sandra's room. He peered in through the small circular window on the door before he entered. She was seated near the room's largest window, which gave a good view into the garden. He opened the door as quietly as he could to avoid disturbing her, but as usual it didn't work.

"Good morning, Ernest." Her voice was cool. "Nice of you to fit me into your schedule. I haven't seen this little of you since our honeymoon."

He leaned down to kiss her on the cheek, but backed off when she pulled away. "Sorry, it's been a frantic week."

She shrugged. "It doesn't matter. Though when you didn't visit right away the staff were a bit worried I might get sad and end myself. I couldn't stop laughing."

The couple of days in hospital had clearly ticked her off. She still looked beautiful though, even in her pajamas. Peter had done some digging about her incident. Sandra had harassed a couple at a charity function, but the couple had laughed it off as stress. Though no harm was done, it was a concern. Ernest felt guilty that it had taken so long to get here, but he had other responsibilities. She knew that.

He gestured for her to move over on the sofa and sat next to her. He placed a hand on her leg and she placed her hand on top of his. They sat in silence for a few minutes. Ernest exhaled deeply and tried to relax. It felt like the first moment he'd been off the clock in weeks. He closed his eyes, and she cuddled in to him. It was as close to perfect as he could remember.

He thought about their marriage. He'd courted her, briefly, but in reality Ernest was sure that Sandra had targeted him. He didn't mind, he loved her and she was an impressive woman in her own right. When Sandra had arrived on the scene, she'd been an enigma. An intelligent Chinese beauty who was completely opposite to his previous wives. This fact hadn't stopped the two of them being regulars in the trash magazine society pages, and Sandra had found herself compelled to quit her legal career because of the publicity. He'd considered trying to have a child with her, to add to the adult daughter he already had, but at his age he'd decided against it.

"I'm glad you're here." She lay down in his lap. He struggled to think of a more serene moment they'd spent together in the past few months.

"Sandra? What can I do to help?"

"Short of staying here with me?" She laughed sadly. "I want all of it to go away. The hacking, the inquiries, the attacks in Shanghai. I can't handle it all."

He smiled down at her, though she couldn't see his face. "I'm working on the first two. The hacking has stopped and I'm doing my best with the inquiries. It's bleak."

"Okay."

"As for the terrorist attacks, I can't do much about them, Sandra. I lost some people over there, and a few more are injured."

He felt her tense up. "I'm worried, Ernest. Please be fair in reporting it. We don't need your usual henchmen stoking the flames of war."

Ernest frowned. She knew his business and what made it profitable as much as he did. "What happens next is up to the Chinese, Sandra."

MICHELLE SIGHED as the car sped along the quiet road. She was seated in the passenger seat next to her driver, Mr Liu, on the way to a small private airport in the middle of nowhere. They'd left Shanghai in the afternoon. Now, hours into the drive, Michelle just wanted to get on the plane and close her eyes. That was still a few hours away though.

She was mad at Anton for his betrayal of Chen, but madder yet at his ability to get out of the country from a normal airport—he'd managed to get a commercial flight, but it was Foundation procedure not to have two leaders on the one plane. By the time her flight had come around, it had been canceled. Now she had to fly out of a dustbowl airport. The only consolation was that Chen's family should have been extracted by now, though it would anger Anton and probably cause her problems down the track.

Mr Liu, who'd been silent for the whole drive, suddenly cursed under his breath in Mandarin. She knew enough of the language to recognize he'd said something about sons of whores. The car headlights picked out a drab sedan parked across the road and blocking it. She feared that this surprise was not a good one. As their car drew closer, she could see two men in Chinese military uniforms leaning against the sedan. While they seemed casual, talking and smoking, she felt threatened.

"Want me to turn around?" Liu spoke calmly in English.

Michelle swallowed hard. "I don't think that'd be the stealthy way to handle this."

He shrugged and kept driving. Spotting the car, one of the soldiers stood up straight and sauntered into the middle of the road. He held up his hand with the palm facing outward and blew a small whistle. Liu stopped the car a few yards away from the impromptu checkpoint. He killed the engine but left the headlights on. Liu was experienced in dealing with Chinese authorities, including in less than official ways, so she could do little except hope that he was worth what the Foundation was paying him.

The man who'd stopped their car seemed fresh-faced. He was probably newly minted from the recruit factory. She felt her heart beat faster as the young soldier approached the car on the driver's side. Behind him, the older soldier unbuckled the holster on the belt under his paunch. She regretted not having a weapon of her own, but it was too much of a risk to carry a firearm in the circumstances. Her cover wouldn't hold up under too much scrutiny.

The younger soldier tapped on the window and Liu wound it down. Michelle sat, powerless as they exchanged pleasantries in Mandarin. She knew it would take a few moments of skirting the issue before the two Chinese men reached the point. She followed along with parts of the conversation. The soldier eventually said something about the regional airport being closed, and having to search the car. Liu scoffed and threatened to involve the Party if the soldier didn't move immediately.

Without warning, the man pushed his head inside the car and started shouting. Michelle had been the beneficiary of enough combat and survival training to know the signs of danger. She unbuckled her belt as carefully as she could as the soldier started pointing at her, to which Liu shouted back and slapped his hand away. Michelle lost the thread of the exchange as the two men shouted too quickly for her to follow.

With no gun and no other weapon, flight was looking like her only option. She reached for the door handle as the soldier shouted at Liu to freeze. As the first gunshot cannoned in her ear, she pulled on the handle and leaped from the car. She ran as fast as she could toward the darkness. She had no idea where she was, or where she was going, but she had to get away from the car and the soldiers.

Liu was probably dead and she had no way to protect herself. She had to keep moving. She ran into the scrub on the side of the road, but there was nowhere obvious to hide. Distance and darkness were her only friends, but after another few steps she stumbled and fell, hitting her head on the ground. Before she could rise, a fierce blow to her midsection drove the air out of her.

"Don't move." A voice said in broken English. It was different to the young soldier's. It had to be the older one. "This does not need to be painful."

Michelle closed her eyes as a pistol barrel was pressed against the back of her head. This was it. After all that she had achieved, it was going to end on the roadside in the dark in the middle of the Chinese countryside. Nobody would know about her death, or mourn her. She didn't know what to do, but she wouldn't beg. There was no point. This was an orchestrated hit—Liu was already dead, and she was about to be.

She did not look at him. "Get it over with, you fuck!"

He laughed, then the world exploded with a bang as loud as two asteroids colliding.

She lifted her hands to her ringing ears and felt something wet on her left cheek. Blood. And something that felt like marshmallow—a small piece of the soldier's brain.

She opened her eyes and turned around, confused. Liu was standing over her and the body of the old Chinese soldier, a flashlight in one hand and a pistol in the other. He crouched down and wrapped one arm awkwardly around her.

"How?" Her voice wavered only slightly. "How did you survive?"

Liu shrugged, barely visible in the torchlight. He lifted his shirt and she saw Kevlar.

"Well, thanks. Are you okay?"

"A few ribs will be broken, but nothing too bad."

Michelle shivered and huddled into him. "Why would they attack us?"

"Money. The young one said he'd let us live if we gave him more than he had been given to kill us. I gave him a bullet."

Michelle's eyes widened. "It was a hit? Ordered by who?"

Liu said nothing. His silence was damning. He knew as well as she did that there was only one other person in China who knew who she was and the significance of the Foundation. Only one who'd known where she would be. Liu had foiled that plan, because of his paranoia and a Kevlar vest. She stumbled to her feet and they walked back to the car in silence.

She didn't say anything as he started the car and resumed their drive to the airport. Only then did Michelle dare to breathe evenly, despite both of them being covered in blood and the car smelling like gun smoke. She'd survived. It made her more determined to get back to the States. Anton had betrayed Chen and now he'd betrayed her. He was tying up all loose ends.

There was only one thing that could be done.

She had to kill Anton.

CHAPTER 5

Taiwan has rejected allegations by China that it is responsible for the terrorist attacks on Shanghai, despite evidence produced by China that suggests Taiwan is linked to the attacks. The crisis appears no closer to cooling down, with reports of dangerous maneuvers of military aircraft by both nations. As China continues its forceful rhetoric, Taiwan has called for international condemnation to pressure China to stop any further aggressive military posturing. As tensions in the region grow, the US Secretary of State has called for calm, a plea mirrored by Japan, South Korea and other regional powers.

    Kelly Vacaro, Al Jazeera, *September 5*

As the Narita Express pulled into Tokyo Central Station, Jack's head hurt so badly from the hangover that he could barely remember the code to the luggage lock. He entered the combination and was relieved when it opened with a small click. He wrestled with his case—a small Samsonite that contained his hastily packed clothes and personal items—and got ready to disembark.

Since Celeste's phone call informing him of Erin's death, he'd given up on his attempts to get a flight to China. He'd made some calls, and the Chinese weren't going to release her body until the investigations concerning the attack were completed. He'd also spent some time getting to the bottom of a few bottles of liquor, which he was now paying the price for.

He'd faced a choice: return to the States right away, or home to Australia, but he liked the idea of a few days' rest in Tokyo. The train came to a stop and the doors opened, and he stepped off the train, inhaling deeply. Given the hour, he was surprised at the large number of people milling about, getting on and off. If this was Tokyo before dawn, he didn't look forward to the peak-hour rush.

He stood on the platform. He knew the name of his hotel and where it was on a map, but that was no help. The walls were covered in arrows and Japanese characters. Helpfully, these were accompanied by English translations underneath, though they may as well have been written in Latin—none of the locations sounded right. With no help in sight, Jack picked a direction and walked. Eventually he found a booth with a big blue I and went inside. Behind the desk sat a friendly looking Japan Rail staff member.

Jack tried his patchy Japanese on for size. "*Konichi wa.*"

The Japan Rail employee smiled. "*Konichi wa*, sir, good morning."

"Ah. You speak English?" Jack wrestled his case alongside him and placed his satchel on the counter.

"A little, sir. Can I help?"

Jack smoothed the crumpled map out onto the counter. "I'm looking for the Mercure Hotel in Ginza, but I can't find the right exit."

"First time in Japan, sir?" The man looked down at Jack's map.

"Sure is."

After a few seconds he looked up and pointed in the direction Jack had just come. "That way. Head outside and find *Chuo-dori*. Then it's straight ahead."

Jack was dubious, but felt too embarrassed to ask for more assistance. He expressed his thanks, gathered his things and left the little booth. Once he'd emerged from the station, he looked up and saw the street sign he needed. Smiling with relief, he started walking. He'd traveled less than a block when his cell phone rang. Jack stopped and fumbled around his pockets to find it. He looked down at the display and saw it was Josefa Tokaloka calling. He hurried to answer before Jo hung up.

"Hi, Jo."

"Hi, Jack." Jo paused. "I'm sorry again about Erin."

Jack sighed. "Thanks."

"No luck getting to Shanghai?"

"No. And there's no point now anyway, if they're not releasing her body until the investigations are complete. I've decided to rest a few days in Tokyo then head home."

"I'm here for you, Jack. Whatever you need."

Jack knew that Jo was genuine. He was one of the few people who'd stuck by him, more or less, in the last few months, when most had obviously considered it too hard. Erin's death just made it all the worse. For some reason, he found himself thinking of Afghanistan. Things had been simpler then. Embedded with a unit in the Green Zone for two years, he'd met some great people and seen plenty. Hell, the worst thing he'd seen had won him a Pulitzer, though he'd agonized for weeks about filing that story.

"I want to get back to work, Jo." Jack was surprised that he'd blurted it out before he'd had a chance to think about it. "Is there anything I can do? It's either that or drink."

"No, Jack." Jo's voice was firm. "You only found out about Erin yesterday, work is the last thing you need. You need time to heal."

"That's not what I want. I've had too much time to myself in the last few months. It's part of the reason things are so shitty at the moment. I want to work. Give me anything."

Jo paused again and then sighed. "Well, you being in Japan is opportune."

"Name it."

"It's against my better judgment, but if you're determined to get back to work, the Navy is deploying the USS *George Washington* battle group out of Yokosuka late tomorrow. They want a few embeds and you're my most experienced option. It's yours if you want it, but I'd prefer you didn't."

Jack smiled. It sounded perfect. Onboard the carrier, he'd travel where he was told, sleep where he was told, eat when and what he was told, and focus on work. Better, given the ship was sailing into a potential conflict zone, there was half a chance it could be a dry environment. He'd have a much easier time staying off the booze.

"They're sending a carrier to China? That's a real bright idea."

Josefa laughed. "Just flying the flag, I guess. Warn China off being stupid."

"That sounds pretty stupid to me, but I'm on it."

"Okay. I should let you know, though, Celeste is in Japan and she'll be joining you."

Jack paused for a second, unsure what to say. His recent history with

Celeste hadn't exactly been great. "I'd rather do it alone. I'm surprised she's even up to it."

"You can talk." Jo paused. "She's okay. The doctors have cleared her and she's refusing to come back to the States. She wants to keep busy. There are worse places she could be than next to you. Honestly, I think she feels a bit guilty about Erin, so tread carefully."

"You're not going to let me work if I don't agree?"

"Nope."

Jack sighed. "I'll call you from the train."

He ended the call. While he was glad he didn't have to navigate his way to the hotel, he now had to find his way back in to the station, find the ticket counter and get to Yokosuka. Still, the job gave him something to keep him occupied, which was the main thing.

And if it got him a little bit closer to Shanghai, so much the better.

As usual, Ernest had arrived for the meeting of the EMCorp board earlier than necessary; he liked to have time to get into his groove, sip his coffee and wait. As others entered the room, he'd size them up from a position of strength, considering any advantages or disadvantages. He would plot.

Not today.

Today the room closed in around him, suffocating. He felt exhausted and vulnerable, tired and beaten. This was usually his arena, where he fought his greatest foes. More often than not he'd subjugate them and emerge victorious. Today though, he felt like a Roman slave, given a sword and told to go fight a lion.

He turned to face Peter, who was sitting in the usual position to his left, ready to take the minutes. "They're going to get me this time, Peter."

Peter looked up from his paperwork. "Don't count on it. They're all bluff and bluster. They've had you on the ropes before and never managed to bring you down."

"This might be the day. Too much baggage. Too much politics. Too many ex-wives diluting my stock holding, waiting for their turn to help stick the knife in one last time."

Peter sighed. "You might be okay. Hit them hard from the outset, draw your line in the sand and force them to cross it. It's the only chance."

Ernest nodded and turned back to the table. He arranged his papers as the boardroom door opened and the rest of the board filed in, escorted by Ernest's secretary. He kept his face blank and didn't say anything. His few allies on the board would know how dire things were and he saw no need to give his enemies an advantage.

"Thanks, everyone." Peter paused as the others settled. "I confirm that we have a quorum and that the board meeting is open."

Ernest looked around the room absentmindedly as Peter recalled the minutes from the previous meeting. He knew that a challenge would come today. He could feel it. But he didn't know who'd have the balls to do it. This situation was as fluid as it was professionally deadly. He had a list of suspects, but only time would tell.

The two most senior and most obvious candidates were Steve Wilson, who'd sat on the board for a decade, and Dan Grattan, the Chief Operating Officer. Neither liked him much, but they didn't feel right. Ernest was certain that the challenge would come from one of the lesser lights, preordained by the others. He readied himself.

"So, if there are no objections to the minutes, we'll endorse them and move on."

"Okay, thanks, Peter. I just want to note that we've got some people missing or deceased." Ernest cleared his throat. "Now, the first order of business is—"

"Sorry for interrupting, Ernest." Al Preston leaned forward. "I've got an extraordinary motion burning a hole in my pocket."

Ernest waved a hand. "Let's hear it then."

Preston seemed slightly taken aback. "Well, thing is, a few of us believe the time might have come for you to stand aside, Ernest. Voluntarily, if possible."

Ernest laughed boisterously for several long seconds. "A half-assed appeal to my better judgment, Al? Fuck your beliefs, you'll need to do better than that."

Preston looked shocked, and momentarily lost his composure. "Ernest, please, it doesn't need to be like—"

"Sure, it does. I gave your father his place on this board, rest his soul, and I did the same for you. I'll drop dead before I step down for you. Now shut up."

Ernest sat back and grinned as murmurs and sideways glances were shared by the other eighteen board members. They obviously hadn't expected him to be so belligerent, and he thought for a second that Preston's plea might be it. Peter's advice to hit them hard and early might have worked.

He noticed movement to his left. He looked and felt his confidence and bluster vanish in a second as Duncan McColl, the EMCorp Chief Financial Officer—and one of Ernest's closest friends—stood. He had a somber expression on his face and wouldn't look at Ernest.

"Of all people, Duncan, I thought you'd be solid."

"I'm sorry, Ernest." McColl started to pace. "I've been here nearly as long as you. And I've always been silent on the issues you've walked us into, but it's time."

Ernest said nothing as McColl walked behind each board member. It was a tactic Ernest liked to employ himself from time to time, because it put people off guard, and now McColl was copying it. He'd have laughed at the absurdity of it all if the situation wasn't so dire.

"We can't have it, Ernest. The newspaper arm of the company is dying, the United Kingdom is a mess, there are new scandals by the day and our share price is bleeding. We could handle all that, we really could, but now there's to be a US Senate inquiry as well? You've put the United States operations at risk. It's over. We ask again—"

"Judas!" Ernest shouted.

"I'm sorry?"

"I was ready for an attack by any of these other plebeians, Duncan, and just about ready to turn my back and let them sink the knife in. But you?"

"I don't do this lightly, Ernest. But given the troubles we're sailing into, it's with the greatest respect and sincerity that—"

"Oh, fuck your sincerity!" Ernest slammed the table with both fists, causing his coffee to spill over his papers. He turned to Peter. "What's my total shareholding?"

Peter was matter of fact. "Between your personal holdings and the trust for your daughter, about thirty-seven percent. Add in your wife and it jumps to forty."

"Well, there you have it. In short, gentlemen, I've got you all by the short and curly hairs." He looked to the only female board member. "Sorry, Janice."

McColl was unrepentant, but seemed slightly crestfallen. "Ernest, be reasonable. Think of what's best for the company."

"I've been doing that for the past thirty-five years, Duncan, and I've survived longer than many of the doomsayers who've sat in these very chairs, telling me how wrong I was. If you're so fucking confident, then call a spill, and let's see who the shareholders back. Here's the rub, though: I've got a fair head start."

McColl shook his head. "Are you so confident that you're right again? That you're not going to annihilate this company with your little tantrum?"

Ernest laughed. "Not in the slightest, but I've earned the right to find out. We're going to stay the course, stare down these inquiries, and emerge on the other side."

McColl looked up and down the table, clearly seeking the support of his co-conspirators to carry the argument further. When none materialized, he sat down. Ernest could tell his CFO was crushed. Despite his anger, he felt regret at what was to come.

"I thank you all for the faith placed in me." His voice was cold. "I'd like to adjourn for five minutes, given the drama. But before we do, Duncan, your services as CFO will no longer be required, and I'd ask that you step down from the board as well."

McColl's head shot up and he looked around the table. When nobody defended him, his nostrils flared. "This is an outrage! I only prosecuted the case you wanted me to. Now you're too gutless to speak in my favor."

"That'll be all, Duncan."

McColl spat into the middle of the table. "I resign."

As McColl stormed from the room, Ernest turned to Peter and spoke softly. "Thank you, Peter. I can't believe I nearly let myself be done in by these puffed-up cowards."

"It's fine. Besides, don't thank me until you've seen the cost of that suit you promised to replace. It's beautiful."

Ernest laughed. "Better sell the Bentley."

❧

CHEN SIGHED with exhaustion as he searched his pockets for his keys. He'd left Shanghai without incident following the attacks, and after a stopover in Osaka, he'd arrived home in Taipei. The indirect route had been a precaution, but now he wanted to kiss his wife, hug his children and reacquaint himself with his pillow. He was sure he'd sleep for days.

When he opened the door of his apartment he was surprised by the darkness and silence that welcomed him. The house should have been abuzz with the sounds of his children playing and the smells of his wife's cooking. He flicked on the light switch.

"Hello?"

There was no response. He stepped further inside and looked around. There was no hint of anyone, but also no sign of a struggle or disturbance. It took him a few minutes to check the other rooms— bedroom, bathroom, living room. His family had either gone out for the night or disappeared into thin air.

Their abscene wasn't right. His wife was a homebody. She liked spending time in the house with their two children. The situation was so unusual that Chen nearly considered calling his mother-in-law. He climbed the stairs to the living room and sank into the sofa with a deep sigh.

It was then that he saw an envelope on the coffee table. He reached over and picked it up. He considered it, checked it front and back, but there was nothing to indicate who it was from. He hesitated for just a second, then shrugged and opened it. Inside was a slip of paper with two words written on it.

Call M.D.

He stared at it, and struggled to link the disappearance of his family with the message. He needed to get to the bottom of it, so he pulled out his burner cell phone and dialed the emergency number he'd memorized. The phone rang for a long time, and Chen thought it would ring out. Finally, she answered.

"About fucking time." Michelle Dominique's voice was terse.

Chen was taken aback by her tone. "My plane was delayed in Osaka."

She seemed unrepentant. "Whatever. You're lucky you're not dead or stranded."

"Stranded where?"

"Taiwan. China. East fucking Asia. Who cares?"

"Why?"

"You've been compromised." He could hear the doubt in her voice. "There's probably a team on their way to you."

The phrase struck at Chen's confidence like a hammer. He'd been sure that he'd carried out his operation flawlessly. "How? I was assured that wouldn't happen."

"Doesn't matter. We've already extracted your family."

Chen was shocked. "They went willingly?"

"Not exactly. Your wife has a nice bruise, I hear. Couldn't be avoided."

His anger flashed. "If you've hurt them—"

"Relax. I sent a team to get you and your family out safely. You weren't there. I could have abandoned them, and you, and you'd all be dead. I got them out. Remember that."

"I want to see them."

"Look, you're not getting it. Anton sold you out. He sold me out too. I'm risking my life for yours. Now get with the fucking program and go to the airport."

Chen took a deep breath. "I understand, and thank you. I will repay your service to my family, and I'll express my displeasure with Mr Clark in person."

"Worry about that later. Now go."

He ended the call, opened the back of the phone and removed the SIM card. He put the phone in his pocket and snapped the SIM card in half. Standard procedure, as automatic to him as breathing. He thought about the ramifications of the call. He'd been compromised by Anton. His family was gone, but probably safe.

He exhaled. Things were okay, but he had to move. Chen knew it was only a matter of time before they were knocking on his door. He needed to get to the airport.

He rushed to the bedroom and went to the bedside table. He opened the bottom drawer, lifted it from its runner and pulled it out completely. He looked into the gap where he'd hidden his kit. There were enough false identity papers, money and contacts contained within that small hiding space to last a great many years. He stacked the cash in one pile on the bed. Next to it he stacked the IDs and a few other things he needed.

He left the handgun and first aid supplies behind, because neither could be easily loaded onto a commercial flight. Satisfied he had all that was helpful, he reached under the bed and found his small carry-on case. He stuffed the money and the documents inside, covered them with clothes and zipped the lid closed. He replaced the drawer, then hefted the small case and walked to the front door.

He knew this was the last time he'd see this place, where his children were conceived and raised. He knew he'd never hug his wife inside these walls again.

He had a heavy heart, but no choice. It was time to go.

CHAPTER 6

Taipei has descended into panic following the launch of a Chinese rocket over the island of Taiwan. The rocket, launched from the Chinese mainland, was captured on film by dozens of citizens before it landed in the ocean south of the island. Locals are taking it as a sign of China's rage at the Shanghai attacks, and their claims of Taiwanese involvement. The Taiwanese Government, meanwhile, has denied all links to the attacks, and has appealed for the diplomatic support of the international community to avert war.

Sanjay Pahani, The Times of India, *September 6*

Jack walked along the main pier of the American naval base at Yokosuka, escorted by a burly Marine sergeant. The man had said nothing for the five-minute walk, which Jack was thankful for—it was about all he wanted to hear right now. The port was alive with activity as many of the berthed naval vessels were readied for sea. Jack had stopped several times to gawk at the aircraft carrier USS *George Washington* and its accompanying ships, and each time the sergeant had waited with his hands folded behind his back.

As they reached the gangplank of the carrier, the sergeant led him to a large man in an officer's uniform, who was looking up at the ship. "I have Mr Emery, Admiral."

The officer turned to them and returned the sergeant's salute with a lazy wave. The sergeant turned on his heel and walked away.

"Mr Emery? I'm so sorry to hear about your wife." Jack was taken aback by the Admiral's thick southern accent. He was old, but had a certain bearing and a lot of decorations on his chest. "I'm Carl McCulloch, commander of this here procession."

Jack shook the other man's hand. "Thanks for the kind words and pleasure to meet you, sir. I appreciate you meeting me, but I could have found my way. I'm sure you've got more important work to do."

"Oh, you'd be surprised." McCulloch jerked a thumb over his shoulder, toward the ocean. "I earn my living out there. In port, I've got staff to do everything as long as I bark loud enough. Besides, half the point of this expedition is to give the folks back home a look-see in the region. I can only do that through you, so you're my new best friend."

Jack was surprised that McCulloch was being so candid. Usually embeds were spoon-fed content by the Pentagon press corps, but the admiral's admission showed how worried the United States was about the situation unfolding between China and Taiwan. It seemed that his coverage from aboard the carrier was as important to the flag-waving mission as the ships and crew themselves. It gave him leverage. Jack liked that.

Jack nodded toward the aircraft carrier. "Quite an impressive display, Admiral."

"Sure is. Worth more zeroes than you can count and can do whatever we need doing."

Jack raised an eyebrow. "You don't think it'll inflame the situation?"

McCulloch shrugged and turned, gesturing for Jack to follow him aboard the ship. "Tough question. Off the record? If China make a proper job of attacking the Taiwanese, we're in the game anyway. We're not trying to provoke the Chinese. Hell, this sort of thing has often worked in the past to help keep the peace."

Jack laughed as he walked alongside McCulloch. "Keep the peace? By sailing a fleet past their front door?"

"Sounds crazy, and I understand the skepticism, but the balance of power in this region is fragile." McCulloch turned down a hallway. "China, Taiwan, South Korea and Japan all have legitimate fears and grievances at the best of times."

"Nothing so bad as half of Shanghai being blown up, I'd think."

"You'd be surprised, son. The folk in this region don't forget easily. They still hold grudges from centuries ago. It's our job to mediate and be the counterweight to too much ambition on any one side. The policy has worked for half a century."

"Surely the Chinese understand it's not Taiwan's fault. Despite the bit of evidence that has trickled out, it seems capital-S stupid."

"Speculation isn't my business." McCulloch shrugged. "Who knows? But the State Department thinks that things are different now. China and Taiwan have been cautiously friendly for the last few years, but that's gone—Shanghai changed everything. China blames the island, and they're going to keep flexing some muscle. That's why we just need to cool everyone down."

Jack wasn't sure he believed the premise that more guns equaled less likelihood of conflict. "Guess we'll have to see."

"Damn right."

They walked in silence through the maze of long corridors, Jack doubted he'd be able to find his way back to the deck. As they went deeper into the ship, junior sailors stood to the side and saluted.

Eventually they reached a door and McCulloch paused in front of it. "Here we are, Mr Emery. If you'll excuse me, I've got a fleet to get moving."

"Of course, Admiral, appreciate the chat."

"Welcome aboard the *George Washington*. We'll catch up once we're underway and you're settled in a bit." McCulloch turned and walked away.

Jack opened the heavy steel door and stepped inside his quarters. He was immediately taken aback by the sight of Celeste Adams seated on the bed. While he'd known that she'd be here, he was shocked at how she looked. Her face was covered in grazes and scratches, and her left arm was in a sling. She smiled at him.

He put his bag down in the doorway and approached her. "Looks like you've seen better days."

"Hi, Jack." She stood and held her one good arm out. He was surprised when she put the arm around him. "Thought you could use a friendly face once you got aboard."

He recoiled instinctively from the contact, but she persisted. He gave in and put his arms around her as well. He held her loosely, awkwardly, not sure what was expected. In truth, he wished it was Erin he was holding, despite their issues. He wondered for the first time if agreeing to work on board the carrier was a mistake.

Eventually, after she pulled away and looked at him, he fumbled for words before the moment became awkward. "I'm glad you're alive."

"You're glad I'm alive?" Celeste's laughter broke the tension. "Erin told me you were strange at times, Jack, but come on."

"You know what I mean." Jack smiled at the memory of Erin, who'd used to say that a lot. "Too many good people died over there."

"Yeah." Her voice trailed off. "You've got a nice room. Bigger than mine, anyway."

Jack looked around. The cabin was not spacious, but he was certain it was better than most of the men and women on board enjoyed. A single bed ran the length of one wall, and there was a small table with two chairs against the opposite wall. There was also a small door that probably led to the bathroom.

She sat back down on the bed and punched the pillow. "Feels okay."

"Yeah, it'll do."

They sat in silence, before Jack turned to her and blurted out what he'd been thinking for several minutes. "How did it happen, Celeste? How did she die?"

She continued to stare straight ahead and didn't look at him as she spoke. "We were both outside the hotel. Erin had just filed and we were going to get a drink when it went off. I felt the shockwave. It knocked me over and stunned me. But once my head cleared, I realized what had happened. The front of the hotel was just gone. The rest was on fire."

Jack felt empty. He wanted more. "That's it? She didn't say anything? Do anything?"

"Most of the rest is a blur. Erin was still alive, barely. I did some first aid, but there was a lot of blood and she didn't last long. Then they bundled me into an ambulance."

Jack exhaled heavily. "I saw you on the news and hoped she might be okay. But when you called me in Tokyo..."

"I'm so sorry, Jack. I don't know what to say." She smiled sadly. "I was just lucky."

He felt his head cloud over, and he suddenly felt sick. He continued to stare at her, and finally she looked at him. They locked eyes, and Jack could see the strain etched on her face. "There's something else, Celeste. Something you're not telling me."

She smiled sadly, and a tear splashed down her cheek. "The last thing she said before she died was to tell you that she loved you and was sorry."

∼

MICHELLE HELD her breath as she eased the door to her apartment open. The light from inside the apartment peeked out like a small, curious child as she crouched and probed her finger slowly inside the crack. When her finger grazed a thin steel wire, she exhaled with relief, reached inside and unhooked it.

She stood up, pushed the door open and hauled her case through, careful not to trip over the limp wire. It would be ironic to be blown up by her own trap, when she'd just organized to have a chunk of Shanghai destroyed, and she enjoyed a small chuckle as she closed the door behind her and locked it. She turned on the lights.

Evidently, nobody had disturbed her apartment. On the other hand, she also knew that while her defensive tripwires and a few other surprises would keep casual interest away, it wouldn't deter a pro. She'd half expected to return from China to a room full of gunmen, but things seemed safe, though it was ironic that the training she'd been provided by the Foundation was now being used to defend against its leader.

She shook her head as she wound up the wire and separated it from the grenade, but stopped short of putting the trap away. There was a fairly good chance she'd need to set it again soon. While Anton had clearly decided to end her, she'd escaped that situation and Chen and his family were safe. There was a chance Anton wouldn't try anything too ambitious on home soil, given she had her own support network within the Foundation.

But if he did decide to make a move, the clock was ticking. With the Congressional midterm elections drawing closer, if Anton had decided to remove her from play, he'd have a much harder time of it once she was elected. That put him on a timetable that was dangerous to her ongoing health.

She made her way to the kitchen, threw her keys on the kitchen counter and took a beer from the fridge. In the living room she found her pistol in a drawer and felt safer for it. After the close call in China, she'd vowed to never be so helpless again. She found her way to the couch, put the gun on the cushion beside her and took a long pull of the beer.

Anton wanted her out of the picture, but that knowledge meant nothing without proof. Her supporters would only move on him with proof or provocation. For now, she had no mechanism to bring the matter to a head. She opened her eyes and placed her beer on the coffee table. It was time to test a theory. She picked up her cell phone and dialed.

The call was answered in less than a second. "Foundation for a New America, you're speaking with Grace, how may I help you?"

"Hi Grace, it's Michelle." She paused for a moment and took a deep breath. "I'm back in the country and I need to speak to Anton."

There was a delay, which did not surprise Michelle one bit. "Just hold on for a moment, can you, Ms Dominique?"

Michelle tapped her foot as the hold music played. She knew exactly what was happening, but needed to be sure. Grace was asking her manager, who sat alongside her. The manager would buzz Anton on the intercom. Anton would refuse to take her call. The manager would tell Grace, who'd give her apologies to Michelle and suggest she try another time, or try his direct line.

The music stopped. "Ms Dominique? I'm afraid he's unable to take your call. He's also unavailable for the rest of the day. I suggest you call tomorrow or try his private line."

Michelle terminated the call. It was the first time that Anton had ever refused to speak to her. Thankfully, with Shanghai now sorted, she had more opportunity to focus on other matters. She was surer than ever that the way to shift momentum in her favor was through control of Ernest McDowell and EMCorp. She picked up the phone and dialed again.

"What?" Senator Patrick Mahoney had a level of aggression that surprised her.

Michelle laughed softly. "Senator, I trust you're well?"

"As usual, Ms Dominique, much better when I'm speaking to you."

Michelle didn't blame him for the sarcasm. Though the Foundation had their friends in the Capitol Building, most duly elected representatives were suspicious of her and the organization. Most of the conversations she had with them were a mixture of carrot and stick, and more than one congressman or senator had been whacked.

"I want a meeting. At your convenience, of course."

Mahoney snorted. "Of course. When and where, Ms Dominique?"

"Your office. I'll come tomorrow at noon. We need to discuss the EMCorp inquiry."

"Why? It's open and shut, really. Especially since he threatened me."

That was news to Michelle. "Don't be too cocky, Senator."

She hung up the phone. If all went to plan, the result of the inquiry would soon be a foregone conclusion. She hoped it would be clear to McDowell that he needed to take drastic action to save his company. He would be backed up against a cliff, with the ocean below. She intended to be the one to save him, or push him over.

It all depended on his attitude.

She picked up the beer again and finished it. While she thought about the situation further, she peeled the label and tore the damp paper into several smaller pieces. She thought of Ernest McDowell, of Anton, of the Foundation and its plan for an American rebirth and controlling the agenda from Congress. It was coming together.

Her goals weren't modest, but neither were her successes so far.

Shanghai was just the beginning.

ERNEST WALKED BRISKLY through the crowd of the charity function. He skirted around clusters of guests and dodged waiters with trays of drinks and canapés, protecting their precious cargo from potential disaster with practiced hands. A few looked his way in anger, then relented when they realized who'd nearly bowled them over.

He'd almost reached the safety of the bar when he felt a tap on his shoulder. He turned and feigned surprise. "Oh, hello, Catherine, how nice to see you."

She smiled coldly and handed him a glass of champagne. "Found you."

Ernest looked down at the champagne flute. The liquid inside bubbled away, and for a brief moment he considered how a slight flick of his wrist would fling the contents all over his ex-wife, enabling his escape. He thought better of it.

He waved toward the bar. "I was just enjoying a drink. What can I help you with?"

"What can you do for me?" A nasty snarl grew on her face. "You can give me what's mine. You can answer the fucking phone when I call."

Ernest sighed. While it had cost several million dollars to cut away the cancer that Catherine Salerno had been, the outcome had been positive. A watertight prenuptial agreement and a sympathetic judge who'd been considerate of her narcotics issues had seen him escape relatively unscathed. Daddy Salerno, a Supreme Court Justice, was still a danger, but if things stayed civil, he left Ernest alone.

"I owe you nothing, Catherine. Our relationship ended with the court ruling. You've got every dime you'll ever see out of me."

He stepped back as two large men approached from behind her. The larger of the two tapped Catherine on the shoulder and whispered something in her ear. A dark look came over her face. He knew it well: shock, mixed with anger and just a touch of indignation. Only Catherine's father could paint that particular picture. One of the suited men put a hand on her waist and led her away. The other came closer to Ernest, discretely apologized and said he'd find her a cab.

Ernest sighed with relief. "Thanks. She's unwell."

"We know. Justice Salerno sends his regards." The man turned and walked briskly after his colleague.

Ernest leaned on the bar. He put down his champagne and ordered a whisky, the barman pouring him a double without any hesitation. Ernest downed half of the drink in one gulp. While the burn of the whisky as it followed the path to his stomach satisfied him, he'd pay for it tomorrow. He was tired. In Washington for the Senate hearing, he'd been roped into a charity function at Sandra's behest. She was fresh out of hospital, despite his protests. The evening had been organized months ago, and he'd agreed to attend and do his best to drum up some money for the cause.

Fortunately, he hadn't had to do much. Sandra was a natural, and he just needed to keep out of her way and let her do her thing: raise large amounts of money with a smile and a few minutes of conversation. He searched for his wife and spotted her across the room, resplendent in a navy blue ball gown, complete with a scandalous split up the left side. She still took his breath away. She moved from group to group, not letting herself get bogged down but leaving each guest she spoke to with a smile on their face and fresh concern for cancer-stricken children.

Ernest downed the rest of his whisky and plucked another champagne flute from the tray of a passing waitress. He gave her a pained smile and received a wink for his troubles. He pushed himself away from the bar and stepped into the crowd, determined to at least stay through the speeches. He was quickly engaged in conversation with a rotund investment banker and his trophy wife. He took the path of least resistance, nodding at everything the man said while he considered what was bigger, the banker's account balance or his wife's cleavage. It would be a close call.

Ernest held up a hand as the banker continued to prattle on. "Hey, President is on, better listen up."

As the applause lifted the mood of the room, Ernest smiled at the sight of the President of the United States, Philip Kurzon, his friend since college.

Kurzon waited for the applause to die down. "Ladies and gentlemen, thank you all for coming tonight to support such a great cause. Ms Cheng and her fellow directors do a great job at events such as this one, helping the families of childhood cancer victims stay together while they're in treatment. Let's give them a round of applause."

Ernest joined the rest of the crowd in polite applause.

Kurzon frowned and glanced at the glass prompter, positioned slightly to his left. "I'd ask that you give generously to the fine cause we're here to support tonight. I was planning on saying more on that, but certain fast-moving international events have forced my hand and made this speech a little less intimate than I'd intended."

Kurzon gripped the lectern and leaned forward. "In recent days, the People's Republic of China has suffered great trauma at the hands of a well-organized group of terrorists. This is a pain the United States of America is familiar with, and we stand united in fury with China that this could happen again."

He paused briefly. "However, it appears that the PRC is using this attack as justification for aggression against its neighbors. Though some evidence appears to link Taiwan to these attacks, the United States does not consider it compelling. Nor do we consider it a legitimate basis for Chinese saber rattling.

"Yet earlier today, a missile was fired from the south of China over Taiwan. Though it splashed down in the ocean south of the island, it represents an escalation that's both worrying and unacceptable. It is quite disgusting that China would respond to acts of terror by terrorizing the civilians of Taiwan."

Kurzon lifted his hands, palms facing upward, the model of reassurance and calm. "I speak now to the government of the People's Republic of China. Stand your forces down. Work with the United States and the international community to secure justice for your dead."

Ernest's eyes widened. It was not often you saw the leader of the free world plead with the leaders of the oppressed world to stay in their own backyard. Not so bluntly, at any rate. He had a feeling that the speech would push his looming Senate testimony from the front pages, especially in the papers he didn't own.

Kurzon continued. "For our part, we will not be idle. To ensure ongoing peace in the region, I've ordered the USS *George Washington* carrier group to deploy from Yokosuka, Japan, to the South China Sea. There, the carrier and its aircraft will provide the world with eyes and ears into what's happening in that region.

"I've requested that members of our media travel with the carrier, to document this mission and ensure the world can see the truth. It's my hope that the nations of the region step back from the precipice of war, and recognize the prosperity and security we all gain from continued peace.

"But let me be clear. The United States is bound by an Act of Congress to defend Taiwan. With force, if it becomes necessary."

Ernest wasn't surprised by anything in the speech, having caught wind of it earlier in the day. Kurzon left the stage and Ernest decided to leave the party as conversation started to buzz with the ramifications of the announcement. He was certain that Sandra would understand his early departure. She knew he had a lot on his mind.

He nodded at the doormen when they opened the oak doors of the convention center. As he started his walk down the marble stairs that led to the car park, a tall, black-haired woman pushed herself off one of the decorative pillars to intercept him. He was also aware of the two large, suited men standing nearby.

"Mr McDowell, can I have a minute of your time?"

He kept walking. "I'm sorry, miss. I've got a very busy day tomorrow. If you need to make an appointment, my assistant would be more than happy to take your enquiry."

"I'd really like you to hear me out!"

He didn't look back as she called after him.

CHAPTER 7

"Carl, the President has given the strongest possible warning to the Chinese about where America stands. He expressed the sympathy of the American people and offered cooperation on an investigation, but on the other hand made it clear that China better not step an inch further towards a military confrontation with Taiwan."

"So what options are on the table here, Admiral?"

"Without a doubt, the decision to move a carrier group into the South China Sea is an escalation in the US response. It gives the Joint Chiefs the option to aggressively defend Taiwan by air and sea, to monitor developments and, if they choose, to strike at China."

Interview with retired Admiral Jay Calloway, Counterpoint, *September 7*

Michelle stood outside the door to one of the better suites at the Jefferson Hotel. She took a deep breath, then nodded at Andrei and Erik Shadd. The two hulking Czechs counted down from three in their native tongue and at zero, Erik gave the door a heavy kick. It gave little resistance to the strength of the six and a half foot–tall behemoth.

"What the fuck?" Michelle heard from inside.

She followed Andrei and Erik into the cavernous space, lit by the torch app on one of their phones. They moved through the sitting area and into the bedroom at the same time as the bedside lamp flicked on.

She sat in an armchair near the window and made sure to keep the bulk of one of the Shadd brothers between her and the bed.

She watched from the comfort of the chair as Ernest McDowell, bleary-eyed and confused, looked from her to the two men and back again. She noticed his eyes drift down to the suit jackets the brothers wore. He must have spent enough time with bodyguards to spot the tell-tale bulge of a concealed handgun.

*Tap…tap…tap…*Michelle said nothing, simply tapping her pen on the side table.

"Will you be tapping that damn pen all day?" McDowell exploded eventually. "Or are you going to tell me what the hell you want?"

She laid the pen on the table, then leaned forward, rested her elbows on her knees and steepled her fingers. "Ernest McDowell. Eighty-two. Married to Sandra Cheng, prominent lawyer turned socialite. Fourth marriage. One child to a previous wife. Masters in journalism and…theology?"

McDowell shrugged. "Easy subject. Left me more time to chase skirts. I'd like to congratulate you for managing to find your way to my Wikipedia profile. Who're you?"

Michelle laughed. "Quite forward. I like it. Explains the four wives. My name is Michelle Dominique."

McDowell frowned. "Whatever you want, was it entirely necessary to break into my hotel room to achieve it?"

"I gave you the chance to talk last night. Your refusal forced more drastic action, including my friends here." Technically it was true. In more normal circumstances, Michelle would have spent additional time working her way into McDowell's life. As it was, with Anton gunning for her, events in China proceeding at breakneck pace and the election just a few months away, she needed to get a move on with EMCorp. Having the brothers with her—a protection against Anton's adventures —was just a happy coincidence on occasions such as this.

He looked to Andrei and Erik again. "Fine. So what do you want?"

She stood up and walked over to the drinks cabinet. She browsed the labels before settling on the Bombay Sapphire. She turned over two glasses and poured. "Are you aware of the danger America faces today, Ernest?"

He didn't reply.

She dropped a couple of ice cubes into each glass. "Of course you are. Your papers got good mileage out of hundreds of our boys coming home from Afghanistan in pieces last year."

She poured the tonic, then carried both glasses over and handed him one, which he put on his bedside table. "I'm here to help ensure the elimination of the greatest threat to America since the terrorists we've battled for the last decade: weakness and complacency. Congress is deadlocked by the two parties fighting to be the most petty. Our financial might is in ruins. Our military is weary. Our freedoms are curbed more each year. This complacency, this weakness will lead to our destruction."

McDowell snorted, his skepticism plain on his face. "Forgive me, but this is all sounding a little Tom Clancy to me. I just run newspapers."

"Don't be a fool, Ernest. The media in this country is the hinge that great change turns on. It decides whether a president is free to act in America's interests. It shapes opinions. It changes governments and fortunes. Companies like yours remodel the world."

"They sure do." McDowell yawned. "You should get one of your own."

Michelle smiled, but didn't rise to his bait. "Today the front lines are newspapers and blogs, Twitter feeds and Facebook posts, television stations and talk-back radio. And this space is populated by sheep, but led by only a few, including you. My organization seeks to harness these assets for a greater good: making America great again."

McDowell raised an eyebrow. "Nice theory. And who exactly do you work for?"

"The Foundation for a New America." Michelle left it at that. McDowell didn't need to know about her difficulties with Anton.

"Okay. And what're you trying to achieve with this little monologue?"

"Rebirth."

He snorted. "You could just get a good man, a good bottle of red, wait nine months and you'd have your birth, miss."

"Smart. Rebirth for America. Whenever it has grown stale, America has always rejuvenated itself through war: the War of Independence, and the birth of modern America; the Civil War, and the forging of an American social identity; the Spanish–American War, and the arrival of the United States on the world stage; World Wars One and Two, and America becoming a global power; the Cold War, and America becoming the Superpower."

McDowell seemed to consider her statement carefully. "Your thesis has problems. What about Nicaragua, Lebanon, Vietnam, Iraq, Afghanistan? Wars that the US has fought, and lost. Or at least not won."

He was done with batting away her statements with bluster and derision, and was now engaging in the contest of ideas. She knew she had his interest. "Tactical missteps. America has thrived from big conflict, from the contest of big nations and big ideas."

"So what exactly are you suggesting, Ms Dominique? What's your end game?"

This was her chance. If Michelle was going to enlist McDowell and his company to her cause, she had to hit him between the eyes. It was the key to shifting the balance against Anton and ultimately prying power from him, while still keeping the Foundation intact enough to make its—*her*— run for Congressional control.

"War between the United States and the People's Republic of China." She smiled sweetly. "Then, the rejuvenation of America through dozens of my colleagues and me in Congress, able to fix the problems."

"Ah." He laughed. "Republicans? Can't beat the Democrats fairly the last few times around, so you look for the wacky way to do it? Usually I sympathize with your side of politics, miss, but I am increasingly daunted by their level of crazy."

"No, we're not Republicans, though we do hide ourselves among them for now. They loathe our message, and are equally responsible for this mess. No, Congress requires a new force."

"You're nuts." He shook his head. "Isn't there a chance that America will lose this theoretical war of yours?"

Michelle shrugged. "Empires on the wrong side of great conflicts have fallen, but America has yet to fail. What's worse? To try and fail, or to never try and be overtaken?"

"Well, whatever. But keep me out of it."

"History is on my side, Ernest. Unfortunately, technology is on yours. While the reality of America's need for war hasn't changed, the means for fighting those wars has. I've already explained how the media fits in. I'm interested in how far you're willing to go to help stamp out these problems."

"Not an inch."

Michelle sighed and signaled to Erik, who drew an envelope out of his jacket pocket and walked over to hand it to McDowell. He looked at it in confusion. "What's this?"

"This is the means for you to destroy the good Senator Mahoney. The whole nasty business of the Senate committee will just go away. If you make the right choice, it's also the way to create a greater future for your family and all Americans. The right future. The future I decide."

"And the cost?"

She rolled the dice. "Print what we tell you to, just every now and then. It will help us to stoke the right flames, and to get my colleagues and me the public support we need. Things will be fine. It won't be difficult, given what the public expects of news. Surely that's a better option than letting them ruin you and dismantle your company."

She waited and continued to sip her drink as McDowell weighed up his options. The bait in front of him must be impossibly tempting— exactly as she'd designed. She knew that with McDowell and his organization on her side, the war was nearly guaranteed, her power base against Anton would expand and the Congressional run of Michelle and the other Foundation-aligned candidates was much more likely to succeed.

"I don't see the link?"

"We create an incident, you stoke the flames, war erupts, public dissatisfied with response of President Kurzon and both major parties and clamor for change." She sighed. "You're our ticket to the party, Ernest, and I'm your ticket to destroying your enemies and keeping your company. It really is the perfect scenario."

McDowell stared at her, then placed the unopened envelope on the bed. "I'm sorry to have wasted your time breaking into my suite. I don't like being at the mercy of anyone, but given the choice, I'll try my hand with the government. At least I can see them coming. Unlike you and your friends here."

Michelle shook her head and put her empty glass on the table. She'd known that this was a strong possibility, but had hoped he'd take the easy route. "How unfortunate. I hope you don't come to regret this decision, Ernest."

∾

ERNEST WAS SEATED at a table in the Senate inquiry hearing room. In front of him was the bench from where the eleven senators would judge his fate, while behind him, the public gallery was full to bursting. He'd been offended by their stares and glared back until the EMCorp Director of Legal Affairs, Saul Alweiss, had discreetly told him that stink-eyeing the public wouldn't look great on CSPAN.

As he tapped his foot and worked his way through the day's third coffee, Ernest hated to admit that Saul was right. The wrong look and his testimony would get wall-to-wall coverage on television and in print. He didn't relish the thought. Since Saul's quiet word he'd simply stared straight ahead, sipped his coffee and showed no emotion. He couldn't help the leg shake that he'd inherited from his father.

He thought back to the invasion of his hotel room earlier that morning. While he'd initially written Michelle Dominique off as a nut, he'd done some digging. There was more to her than met the eye, including a Congressional tilt in the coming midterm elections. She clearly had some crackpot theories, so even if she could get him out of his current mire, it wouldn't be worth the cost.

"Will they get on with it any time soon?"

Alweiss smiled and leaned forward. "Usually takes them a while to get going."

"It's ten am. Don't these bastards do any work?" Ernest kept his voice down. "I'm usually well into my day by now."

While Saul had handed the first part of the hearing, Ernest was glad his time to speak had arrived. The Senate Judiciary Subcommittee on Privacy, Technology and the Law had oversight of laws and policies governing collection of information by the private sector and enforcement of privacy laws. Because of the activities of EMCorp, Ernest was squarely in their sights. Part of him was terrified about what the hearings would bring.

Alweiss placed a hand on his knee. "Keep your cool, Ernest. Everything hinges on that."

Ernest laid his palms down flat on the wooden table as the senators walked in to the room. Last to enter was Senator Mahoney, Chairman of the Subcommittee, who took his seat on the middle of the bench. As the senators settled in, Mahoney stared straight at Ernest with a large, shit-eating grin on his face. Ernest was sad that he was too old to leap the table and stab the bastard with a pen.

After a few moments of quiet chatter between the senators, Mahoney cleared his throat. His microphone carried the sound across the room well enough that most people seemed to get the point. Chatter stopped and people readied themselves for the showdown. Ernest stopped shaking his foot, put down his coffee and sat up straight in his chair. He stared at Mahoney, who started to speak.

"Good morning, everybody. I call to order the third day of the inquiry into the conduct of EMCorp within the borders of the United States." Mahoney paused, apparently for dramatic effect. "Mr McDowell, thanks for joining us this morning."

"And a good afternoon to you, too." Ernest managed to draw a few short laughs from the gallery. "Glad to be of service to the duly elected representatives of our fine democracy."

Mahoney bristled, but continued. "As you know, EMCorp, the company you chair and have a large holding in, has been embroiled in significant controversy overseas, most notably the United Kingdom. The opening two days of this inquiry heard a catalog of allegations. Our role is to determine the extent of misconduct in the US."

Ernest waited until Mahoney was done, then lifted his coffee cup and drained the contents. He looked to each of the eleven members of the committee in turn then spoke. "Nice editorial, Senator. Give me a call once you're out of politics."

Mahoney laughed. "I'll take the first question, Mr McDowell. Quite simply, can you guarantee EMCorp hasn't engaged in illegal behavior of the kind that we've seen overseas inside the United States, beyond what has already been declared?"

Ernest looked to Alweiss, who took the question. "No corporate leader could offer such a guarantee, Senator. But we're confident that, beyond what we've already disclosed to the authorities and to the markets, no further activity along those lines has occurred in the United States. The company has performed a full audit."

Mahoney tapped his pen on the bench, seemingly annoyed that Alweiss had answered the question. "While I thank your lawyer for his response, Mr McDowell, it's apparent to many people, myself included, that the level of control that your company has over the political and economic direction of this nation is far too high—"

Ernest tried to interrupt. "Sorry, Senator."

Mahoney persisted. "I was speaking, Mr McDowell. I'd actually liken it to a man, even a large one, being crushed to death by a snake. The man is this country, your company is the snake. Though the man might be strong, he has nothing to compete with the constricting strength of the snake, ever tighter."

Ernest knew he was in trouble. This was about more than potential illegal activities—it was a power play. Mahoney was playing for keeps, and despite his looming retirement, he had the power base in Washington to have a chance in the game. This was going to be the biggest fight of his professional life.

With Mahoney finished, another senator leaned in to her microphone. "Mr McDowell, do you have anything to say from the outset?"

"Yes, I do, actually, miss." Ernest paused and looked at the senator's name plate. "Sorry, Senator Woodyatt. Yes, I do."

When the senator nodded for him to proceed, Ernest looked at Alweiss, who shook his head only a fraction. Ernest ignored it. "I find substantial levels of media ownership to be wholly compatible with the entrepreneurial spirit of this country. I started this company and it's now a global enterprise employing thousands of Americans.

"Regardless of troubles elsewhere, I'd hoped that at home, at least, EMCorp would be welcome, yet here I sit. It's a sad day indeed when such a committee can begin a witch hunt in such a manner. So let's get on with it."

Ernest sat back in his chair. Alweiss had a blank look on his face and was probably considering the weaseling he'd have to do to reverse the damage of the statement. Mahoney had an even bigger grin on his face, but the other senators seemed unconcerned. The CSPAN cameras were on Ernest and several cameras flashed.

He knew that this was going to end badly and that the committee had the power to orchestrate sweeping changes to his company. He'd seen off the EMCorp board only to run headlong into this mess. He wondered again about Michelle Dominique and her offer, before shaking his head and readying himself for the next question.

MICHELLE'S BOOTS clicked on the red bricks as she walked to the dining hall at a brisk pace. She'd spent the afternoon doing one of her occasional lectures at Georgetown University, but a flurry of student questions had made her late for a coffee date. She hated being late. The lectures were just part of the façade of legitimacy that all of the senior staff at the Foundation had to have, but they also helped with her campaign.

She looked back over her shoulder and smiled at the sight of Andrei Shadd. Though he kept a respectable distance, she had no doubt that she was well protected. Given the likelihood of a second attempt on her life by Anton, she'd made a habit of having one of the Czech brothers in tow whenever she was out. The brothers were part of the dark work that the Foundation did. There was a cell in each major US state and some foreign countries, each responsible for agitation, low-level terrorism and whatever else needed doing. Beyond that, there was an investment branch that sponsored overseas subversives, and a wet squad of ex-special forces guys. The light side was a think tank, well funded and politically hyperactive. It was involved in everything from presidential campaigns to policy advocacy and research. It looked and acted every bit the legitimate organization. It also carried a lot of punch in Washington.

As she neared the door of the Leo J. O'Donovan Dining Hall, she rubbed her hands together, trying to coax some warmth back into them. She took out her cell phone, and fired off a quick text to Andrei. *I'll need some privacy, Andrei. No interruptions unless someone hits the big red button.* A glance was all it took to see he understood. She entered the hall.

The room was abuzz with the evening undergrad rush, each seeking a slice of pizza or equally dismal fare. The tables were full with groups of students eating or doing work on their laptops. There was very little spare space, and Michelle was worried that she'd missed her appointment. She paused and looked around, then nearly jumped into the air when someone placed a hand on her shoulder.

"Sorry." Sarah McDowell flashed her white teeth and held out a cup. The dimples on her cheeks were pronounced and she was pleased with herself. "Couldn't resist."

Michelle took the coffee from Sarah with a smile and leaned in to kiss her on the cheek. "Hey, Sarah, how's it going?"

Sarah turned and nodded back toward the door. "Alright. Thought I'd get us some takeaways. It's crazy in here."

Michelle nodded. "Hey, tough break for your dad today."

The younger woman frowned, and Michelle realized she'd need to be careful. Even though Sarah McDowell seemingly took very little interest in the professional affairs of her father and his business empire, she was still a loving and loyal daughter. Michelle risked poisoning the well of opportunity with misplaced words.

"They didn't give him a chance." Sarah pushed the door open and Michelle followed her outside. "He's going to get crucified."

Michelle glanced toward Andrei, who'd had the foresight to sit well away from the dining hall. "How many days of questioning does he have?"

Sarah brushed her blond hair behind her head. "At least a couple, his assistant tells me. Peter isn't usually wrong."

They walked together in silence for a few moments, past the law building and toward the center of the Georgetown campus. While parts of her plan were ticking along nicely, her efforts to recruit McDowell to her cause had been a massive failure. For now, at least. The inquiry had been hotter than she'd expected, so she retained some hope.

Sarah broke the silence. "How was your lecture?"

"It was alright. First time I've spoken on terrorism since my PhD, so I think I was a bit rusty. But they had an appetite for it, given everything that's happening in China."

Sarah nodded and frowned. "What was the gist of it?"

"Outrage about the attacks in China on one hand, the need for us to stand beside Taiwan and renew our focus on the threat of terrorism on the other. My political advisors thought it would be a good idea to get some talking points on the record."

"Dad lost some staff over there. You must have heard."

Michelle feigned surprise. Since meeting Sarah at a gallery opening, she'd gone to huge effort to avoid expressing much knowledge of EMCorp. Sarah knew only that she was a conservative, and involved in politics. Sarah was studying art, and they'd become decent enough friends.

"How's that guy you've been seeing?"

"No good." Sarah seemed content to leave it at that.

Michelle nodded and took a sip of her coffee. The effort to divest Sarah of her infatuation with a transfer student from the Wharton Business School had been worth it. He'd had too much husband potential for Michelle to allow the relationship to flourish. It was a shame he'd refused to take a hint, and she'd had to destroy his reputation. His promising career was now in ruins. He'd also never marry Sarah and be in the box seat for control of EMCorp. Michelle didn't like surprises, and the boyfriend had been one of those. Her relationship with Sarah was insurance against McDowell making the wrong choices.

CHAPTER 8

In scenes nearly as vocal as those playing out in the South China Sea, the United States Senate Judiciary Subcommittee on Privacy, Technology and the Law spent a seventh day grilling Ernest McDowell, Chief Executive Officer of EMCorp. Sources from inside the company told Business Daily that many company executives expect it to be broken up, or other significant measures to be taken, to reduce its dominance in the US and global media market. Mr McDowell, looking more distressed by the day, was angered when the Committee chairman, Senator Patrick Mahoney, asked what should be done with his company, replying, "Nothing."

Francis McKay, Business Daily, *September 14*

Ernest had waited for hours in the most modern office he'd ever seen. It had angular chairs, an odd lamp, a coffee table shaped like a lightning bolt and all manner of other visual dross. It was lucky for the manufacturers that people paid a fortune for such crap, because he figured that once the business community came to its senses, a whole lot of furniture makers would be out of a living.

He lifted his coffee, took a mouthful then placed the cup down carefully on the lightning bolt. He was tired and knew that she was deliberately making him wait, to get him off guard and angry. But he had no control, so there was no sense in a tantrum. All the delay did was give him time to reflect on the disaster the last week had been. Although the Committee clearly had an agenda and a giant axe to grind, the previous night he'd been dealt the killer blow: a call from a despondent Saul Alweiss. He hadn't beaten around the bush—Saul had found proof within EMCorp of fresh phone hacking in the United States; it was only a matter of time before the evidence was discovered by the Senate inquiry; and if he was a religious man, he should start praying for deliverance. It made Ernest's testimony and denials at the inquiry worthless.

Eventually the door to the office opened with a mechanical whir. Michelle Dominique walked through the door and feigned surprise. "Ernest, nice of you to visit."

He snorted and doubted very much she'd been oblivious to his presence, but he kept the thought to himself. He had to admit that she was dressed to kill. Her black hair flowed over her shoulders in a way that made him think of Medusa and her snakes. Her white blouse and black skirt took none of the attention away from her legs, which were bound by knee-high black leather boots.

He shook her outstretched hand. "If I didn't know any better, I'd think you spent the last hour dressing to distract me."

"Hardly, you're a married man. And I have no desire to be wife number, what is it—five?" She smirked and nodded her head in the direction of her office. "Let's go in here."

He said nothing as they crossed the waiting area and entered her office. Clearly she had different tastes in furniture to whoever was responsible for the waiting area, with hardwood the order of the day. He couldn't deny that her view of the Washington Mall was spectacular as well, as she sat in a brown leather lounge chair and he sat opposite.

Her eyes were locked on to his. "I must admit I don't have any idea why you're here. I thought we left things fairly concrete in your hotel."

"I've changed my mind about your proposal. I'm in. Limited editorial control as long as you can make my little problem go away, as you inferred."

She laughed at him and his heart sank. "Do you make a habit of trying to revive the dead, Ernest? Strange fetish, and to each their own, I suppose. But I'm afraid our business is concluded. Events and my plans have moved on without you."

Ernest had expected this. He'd declined her attempts to control him and his company prior to the Senate hearing, and things had only become worse since. He was now at her mercy, and would have to fight hard to secure whatever terms she deemed to give. In terms of the balance of power, he was the Japan to her United States, circa 1945, and a couple of his cities had just been nuked.

"There must be something I could do that would change your mind. I'm desperate."

She winked. "Oh Ernest! You flatter! I'm sure that plenty of bright, beautiful young things have asked similar of you in the past, and you've been all too happy to take them up on it. But I'm afraid I'm not interested in old men in that way, no matter how rich."

He ignored her jibe. "I'm prepared to offer more than you previously asked for in return for your support."

Michelle leaned back in her seat and looked up to the ceiling. "Well, that's a different story."

She didn't immediately decline, as he'd expected. Instead, she seemed to consider her next move carefully. He was anxious. The next few minutes and the direction of the conversation would change much in Ernest's life, one way or another.

She looked back at him. "I'm still going to decline. You rejected me, put all your chips on black, and the big green zero has come up. I've moved on, I suggest you do the same."

He looked at her in desperation. "The committee is going to split up my company, Ms Dominique. They'll ruin me and tear it apart."

She shrugged and stood. "As I said they would. Not my problem, Ernest. You had your chance, blew it, and there's no hard feelings. But you can't really expect me to backtrack now things have become worse for you."

Ernest felt it all start to slip away. Decades of working to acquire, spread, fine tune and protect his media empire. Countless birthdays and anniversaries missed. Friends and relationships sacrificed. Billions of dollars of profit and loss. His empire, his life. Within days, it would be broken up and all but destroyed.

"I don't believe for a second you've given up on your efforts to control my company, Ms Dominique. Not after such a fine speech in my hotel room."

She laughed. "I was head of the debating team in college, Ernest, I say a lot of persuasive things. Having you on side would have helped, but we've moved past this."

"I want the deal."

He looked up at her and she stared back, a look of pity in her eyes.

"Oh, very well. I'm prepared to offer you the same deal on my part. I will, in essence, save your behind."

"You won't regret it." He exhaled loudly. "You've lifted a weight off my shoulders."

"I'm not finished." She leaned forward. "My part of the bargain hasn't changed. Yours, however, will be very different—my price for your delay in accepting."

He'd expected something like this, but was glad she'd listened to his pleas. "Okay. Name it and it's yours."

He felt some of his confidence disappear when she grinned at him.

~

MICHELLE KNEW SHE HAD HIM. Sitting in front of her was a man at his most desperate. He was facing the crushing reality of the Senate inquiry going against him, and he'd do just about anything to save his company.

She needed to get him under control, but also reduce his ability to go against the agreement they were about to make. She could have asked for the beating heart of his daughter—his heir—and he might have given it up. Thankfully for Sarah McDowell, Ernest's daughter was already under control. Michelle had other targets in mind to further reduce his options. At the same time, she had to keep up the façade of negotiation. She leaned back in her seat. He was still in the same position, as if he feared that by moving, even an inch, he'd break the tenuous chance of a deal between them and be cast adrift into the maelstrom of uncertainty.

"The deal has changed, Ernest."

"What're your terms, then?"

Michelle readied herself. There was a small chance that he'd be so outraged that he'd simply walk out. She doubted it though. It was a bet on his love for his company over his love for his family. With Sarah McDowell in her camp, she now needed to deal with the stock holding of Sandra Cheng. It was time to test his resolve and tighten the screws.

"You divorce your wife."

His head shot up and his eyes flared in protest. "Divorce my wife? She's nothing to you, a non-practicing lawyer who's spent more time in hospital than by my side in recent months. That's ridiculous."

Michelle shrugged. "Those are my terms."

She watched as he processed her words. No doubt he felt her

reasons were petty, designed merely to inflict pain for his initial recalcitrance. But that couldn't be further from the truth. Michelle never relied on others, not entirely, and as soon as she'd locked her sights on EMCorp, she'd developed plans to control it, with or without Ernest McDowell. That meant befriending Sarah McDowell, removing Sandra Cheng and the Foundation buying stock of its own at the right time.

"There must be something else." He leaned forward, desperation in his eyes. "You can't force me to destroy my family to save my company. I don't understand what you gain."

Michelle was enjoying his rambling, but she had had enough. She decided it was time to push. "There are no other conditions that I'm interested in considering, Ernest. You asked for this meeting, not me, and you're welcome to use the door over there. If you do, be sure to pass on my best to the senator and his colleagues. But if you are interested in the deal, you need to decide right now. My patience is at an end."

His bluster disappeared and he cradled his head in his hands. "Is that really what it's going to take?"

"Afraid so."

He seemed to consider her terms for a long few moments, then sighed. "You've got a deal. Get rid of the Senate inquiry. Once they're off my back, I'll do what you ask."

Michelle smiled. "I don't like the precedent of you dictating terms, but in this case they're fair enough. I'll get things in motion tonight, and the inquiry should be history in a day or two. But you best hold up your end when the time comes. I think you understand the extremes to which I'm able to project my displeasure."

"Indeed."

"You can start with having a front page editorial in the *Standard* tomorrow, calling for America to protect Taiwan, deploy assets, recognition—all that jazz. A sign of goodwill."

He grunted, stood and exited without another word. Now that she had him, Michelle would have to act swiftly to hold up her end of the bargain. It would have been much easier to make the Senate inquiry go away before it had convened, but now things were underway, far more drastic action was needed.

She knew that the conspiracy theorists would look back in decades to come and point at the events as an example of the power of corporate America. As usual, she mused darkly, they'd miss the point entirely. The deaths, the professional ruin, all would be orchestrated behind the scenes, with no possible link back to the Foundation.

Things were moving, and it was time for her to make her final push. Shanghai had been a success, EMCorp was in her pocket, war was looking likely and the election was soon.

There were only a few things left to do.

≈

JACK STOOD on the observation platform high above the flight deck of the USS *George Washington*. This was one of several times in the past few days that he'd watched in awe as men and women in brightly colored vests moved without apparent pattern around the deck. Yet the more he watched, the more he saw the routine—the choreography of jets taking off and landing under careful instruction. It mesmerized him.

Jack was only now starting to appreciate the sheer force that the carrier, with all its planes and attendant ships, allowed the United States Navy to project. He felt as if this ship would be enough to stop one nation, injured and angry, from striking at another, frightened but defiant. It really was proof that weapons built for war could help to enforce peace between nations.

The clear night sky provided the perfect backdrop for his thoughts, complete with full moon and millions of stars. The observation platform had become his second home on board the ship whenever he wasn't working, a place where he could be alone and think. It was one of the few places on the ship where that was possible, home as it was to thousands of men and women.

Tonight, as he stared out into the night, he was grateful that nobody else was nearby. Between the roar of the jets taking off or landing every few minutes, he thought of many things. He thought of Erin, of Shanghai, of work and of life. He was proud that he'd so far managed to avoid the bottle, but didn't like the introspection that sobriety forced. He wasn't quite ready for the decisions that came next in many parts of his life.

He leaned on the rail for a few more minutes while his mind wandered. Then he heard the screech of the bulkhead door behind him as someone pushed it open. He involuntarily tensed at the intrusion.

"Hi, Jack. You've been out here for hours. I think the admiral is going to send out a search party if you don't surface soon."

Jack continued to stare straight ahead. He sensed her move closer, nearly close enough to touch him. Celeste stopped and settled in a spot just behind him, slightly to his left. He was glad that the roar of another plane taking off conveniently overwhelmed the awkward silence.

"Impressive, isn't it?"

He shrugged. "Probably enough to conquer some countries."

"Mightn't be enough though. The Chinese seem pretty pissed."

Another pause. "Sorry, but is there something you wanted, Celeste?"

Her voice quivered slightly. "I'm sorry. I shouldn't have told you what she said."

Jack turned to face her. She was looking up at the sky. He exhaled loudly. "You've done nothing to be sorry for. I've been a dick."

"No, you haven't, Jack. You're allowed to feel and act any way you want right now. Your whole world has been thrown upside down."

He reached out and grabbed hold of her shoulders. When she didn't look at him, he squeezed her shoulders slightly. Finally, she turned. "Celeste, I'm sorry."

She smiled weakly and pulled away a little. "I was just checking my emails. I had one from Jo. He's telling us to change slant on this one and ramp up the focus on Taiwanese nationalism and how important it is for the US to support it—to a ridiculous extent."

Jack laughed. "Welcome to the company. Not often we get told which way the wind blows, but Ernest can be pretty bloody convincing."

She frowned. "I don't believe Ernest is *that* explicit about his agenda. I mean, I've heard stories, but—"

"They're true." Jack shrugged. "He's a ruthless bastard and we write what he tells us to write whenever he's interested enough to tell us. It's worse than that, in this case. I spoke to Jo an hour ago on the sat phone."

"Oh?"

"He gave me the same message that you got in the email. They're running with a pretty explosive editorial tomorrow—a demand for preemptive US strikes to keep Chinese brinksmanship in check. He also told me it's straight from the top."

Celeste walked over to the rail of the observation deck. "Are they trying to start a war?"

Jack shrugged. "Don't worry too much. Even though there's a war brewing, it's being held in check by this very ship. I'll take the lead on the reports, you just help me with the background. I won't make you write the piece that sparks the powder keg."

"Thanks." She looked relieved.

Jack turned to go inside the carrier just as everything around him went bright and a shockwave hit him. As he stumbled and fell, he heard the explosion and Celeste cry out. He managed to brace, but he still landed hard on the deck. His ears started to ring with a high-pitched whine.

He felt the cold steel of the walkway on his cheek. He tried to move, but couldn't. He was not sure how long he lay there, stunned, but it was long enough for the whine in his ears to subside. Through the gap in the safety rail, he could see several fires burning on the far side of the flight deck. The flames combined with the dozens of flashing red LEDs to light the night sky in a hellish scene. Men and women screamed.

Jack lifted his head and looked at Celeste. She hadn't moved. He was about to try to get to his feet when everything went black.

ACT II

CHAPTER 9

While it's unclear exactly what's taken place aboard the USS George Washington, to have a US carrier stranded in such a hot zone is a difficult situation. We've already seen the Chinese scramble aircraft, claiming that the carrier is in its territorial waters and demanding it leave or be towed to a Chinese port—two outcomes the US would fight hard to avoid. The situation with the carrier adds more kindling to an already heated situation with China and Taiwan.

Hiroshi Kawahara, Asashi Shinbun, *September 15*

Jack's shoes clanked on the steel floor of the long, straight corridor. It was as if with each step the carrier was groaning again at the punishment it had taken. His nostrils were filled with the heady mix of burning rubber, insulation and electrical wire. Though most of the fires were out, the stink remained.

He was taking things slowly. Although he'd been let out of the infirmary with a few stitches and some aspirin, his head still ached. He couldn't blame the doctors for being more concerned about the real casualties—those with burns and shrapnel—than with his cut lip and sore head. Celeste had likewise been released.

"Step aside!"

Jack moved to the wall and sank into it as much as the cold, hard steel would allow. He waited as a small team of men and women rushed past him without a glance in his direction. In the hours since the attack on the *Washington*, the same crew he'd watched maneuver jet planes had worked to put out fires or clean up debris.

Once the path was clear, he walked through a final bulkhead and up a small flight of stairs. He paused at the top and looked around at the banks of computers. Harried-looking men and women were crowded around several of the terminals. Above it all, on a raised platform, sat Admiral McCulloch. He looked like a man in control.

"Permission to come aboard, Admiral?" Jack spoke loudly enough that the man in the chair looked his way.

"Ah, Mr Emery." McCulloch smiled. "Granted."

He stepped into the Combat Information Center, which felt strangely untouched by the attack. He walked to where McCulloch sat and wondered when the man had last slept. Nonetheless, McCulloch's aura of authority amazed Jack. He'd half expected chaos. Instead, all was calm, though the ship was listless and pathetic.

"Bad time, Admiral?"

McCulloch gestured for Jack to sit next to him in the executive officer's vacant seat. "As good a time as any. Glad you're okay, though. You had a fall?"

Jack shrugged. "Not too bad. Any idea what happened?"

McCulloch sighed. "Off the record? Chinese sub. A new one. Got right inside our guard, kicked us in the balls and got away again."

Jack's eyes widened. He knew a scoop when he heard one. "Anything for me on the record?"

McCulloch laughed. "You crazy? I'm not giving you your next Pulitzer. If I say a word, and you print it, the nukes might start flying. I'm no coward, but I don't want to be stranded here if that happens. The Pentagon isn't saying shit. I think they might still be in shock. And if they're not talking, neither am I."

"Fair enough, Admiral. You should know, though, that the word from my superiors is to talk up Taiwanese independence, the outrageous actions of China, and so on."

McCulloch snorted. "That's going to do wonders for our health and wellbeing."

"Hopefully we won't be here to find out."

"I wouldn't count on it. We're sitting ducks. We've lost all propulsion and we're trying to patch a great big hole in the side of the ship. We're afloat but going nowhere soon."

Jack was staggered to think about the amount of damage required to bring such a large ship to a halt. If the explosion had been caused by a Chinese submarine attack, as McCulloch had suggested, it represented a massive increase in the stakes. It wouldn't take much more to trigger a war. Jack was surprised it hadn't already happened.

"Why are you telling me this, Admiral?"

"Posterity, son. I've seen too many of my contemporaries hang from the rafters after the fact. I want this documented, and I want history to remember we tried to avoid a war."

Jack smiled. "I can do that."

"Good. The Joint Chiefs have ordered the USS *John C Stennis* to make a beeline from the Persian Gulf, but it will take a while to get here. The USS *Nimitz* is halfway to Norfolk for its refit but has turned around. Nothing is close enough right now."

"So there's no help coming?"

"Oh, we've always got stuff in town. Some air power out of Japan and Guam. Some subs and surface boats. We've got enough to deny the Chinese sea control, if it comes to that, but we can't project power or do a lot of the things we usually take for granted."

"Who knew it would be this easy?"

"That's the problem with steaming full speed ahead into somebody else's war." McCulloch sighed. "Sometimes they don't like it when you appear on the horizon."

"At least we've got a mini-Air Force on board."

McCulloch stared at him blankly. "You haven't noticed the silence? The torpedo took out some pretty important widgets. My engineers are working on it, but all those jets are shiny paperweights unless we can get this tub fixed."

Jack's mouth went dry as he realized the implications—the carrier was static and had no air power umbrella. It didn't seem like a winning proposition. "Will the Chinese attack again?"

"I can't see why they would. They've proven their new nuke subs can get inside our defenses. There's no need to show off and spike the ball in the end zone."

One of the radio operators cut in. "Incoming transmission, sir. Chairman of the Joint Chiefs."

"Patch it through to my phone, Mr Jones." McCulloch turned to Jack. "You'll need to excuse me, son."

Jack nodded and stood. Clearly McCulloch was not going to start speaking to his boss until Jack had left the CIC, so he made his way out of the room as quickly as he could. McCulloch and his crew had been more than welcoming, and he didn't want to push his luck at a sensitive time.

He snaked his way back through the ship to his cabin. On the way, he saw more evidence of damage and the crews trying hard to fix it. Jack did his best to stay out of their way and at a respectful distance. He reached his cabin, kicked off his shoes and sprawled out on his narrow bed. He closed his eyes.

Jack's eyes shot open and he sat up in confusion when there was a knock on the door. He'd obviously fallen asleep. "Come in."

He rose to his feet as McCulloch entered and gestured for Jack to remain seated. "No need to get up."

"Admiral? What can I do for you?"

McCulloch sighed. "I need to get a few things on the record, for use if and when this little party gets kicking."

Jack frowned. "What do you mean?"

"My call was from the Chairman of the Joint Chiefs. The Chinese are insisting that we've drifted into their waters following the 'accident' and demanding we either abandon ship, allow them to rescue us or leave their waters."

Jack saw where this was heading. "I'm guessing there's a few problems with most of those options."

"You could say that. We're not moving without a tow truck, we're not letting them on board and we're certainly not abandoning a few billion dollars' worth of carrier that easily."

"So what can I do for you, Admiral?"

"I want it recorded that the Joint Chiefs have told us there's nothing close enough to defend us, but that our orders are to hold the airspace if at all possible. They've also expressly forbidden us from entertaining any options of surrender or compromise. I'm just starting to feel like we're the tripwire here. I'll need you to capture a few things."

Jack nodded. "I'll get my gear."

～

"GOOD MORNING, *New York, this is Dan Cuperino with your news on the hour.*"

Ernest opened his eyes with a groan. He resisted all temptation to throw the alarm clock across the room, or even to whack it a few times with his fist. Sandra stirred next to him and hugged in close, her head resting on his chest as he wrapped his arms around her. She was asleep again in a second despite the noise of the radio, an ability he never failed to marvel at.

"*First this morning, there is shock around the capital as news of the arrest of Democratic Senator Patrick Mahoney on fraud and perjury charges surfaces. Early reports indicate that the arrest stems from testimony the senator gave to the Supreme Court nearly a decade ago, which DC police are now saying they can prove was false. We'll have more on this as details come to hand.*"

Ernest closed his eyes as his head spun. While he'd known that something like this was coming, he hadn't expected it to come so quickly. He was surprised that Dominique had held up her end of the bargain quite so boldly. Whatever her means, it was impossible to doubt her efficiency. Less than twenty-four hours after he'd agreed to her terms, she'd delivered.

Ernest turned the radio off and rolled onto his side. He scooped his wife closer into a hug, having not yet quite come to terms with the cost of saving his company. Mahoney was now the least of his concerns. He held Sandra tight, and she mumbled a little and stirred in his arms, but not enough to indicate any discomfort. He held her for several minutes, thoughts and options racing around his brain.

He knew Dominique would get everything she wanted: editorial control of his company whenever she desired and effective control over him. She'd have the means to influence, if not outright control, public opinion all over the world. It was a power Ernest had used at times, but soon it would be in her hands, not his.

The loss of his wife was a cost nearly too great to pay. But he knew, deep down, that it was no choice for him. His wives had come and gone, but the one constant in his life had been EMCorp. He had spent half a century building his empire, and it would be impossible for him to enter the last years of his life without it. It was his legacy. If given the choice, it was no choice at all.

She'd been a fine wife, the best of them all, by far. Intelligent, beautiful, resourceful and discreet, she'd been by his side during some of the more difficult years of his professional life. He wanted to hold her for days, weeks even, before delivering the news. She'd be shattered. Her whole life had been put on hold for their marriage. He'd compensate Sandra well.

He leaned over to check the time, and was surprised that a full hour had passed since the news. He hugged Sandra a little tighter and she snuggled in closer. He knew that this would be the last time he'd ever hold his wife, and possibly the last time he'd ever hold a woman, given his age. He'd never been the sort to procure sexual comfort through financial means, and he'd vowed years ago to never marry again.

He slid his feet into the slippers that waited on the floor like obedient pets. His back ached and his head hurt as he shuffled off to the shower. Sandra didn't even stir. She was used to his early starts and wouldn't rise for a few more hours yet, snoozing in blissful ignorance about the bomb he would be dropping on their relationship later in the day. He could have told her now, but whether from cowardice or altruism, he decided it would wait. When he closed the door to the ensuite, he felt like he was closing the door on part of his life. Whatever her motivation, Michelle Dominique had achieved what she wanted. Ernest had grave fears for the future of his company and the United States of America. The woman was now in charge of the greatest media company in the world, about to start a war and might even get a bunch of her people into Congress.

He ran the shower. When it was hot he stripped off his pajamas, stepped inside and closed the door. The hot water did nothing to wipe away the disgust he felt at himself, but he was resigned to his decision. Later in the day, he'd phone Sandra and tell her, then let Dominique know. In coming days, he'd organize a settlement, Sandra would move out with a lot of cash and he'd be free to get on with his life, minus his heart.

He was a man in control of his company again, or at least partially. Yet he felt nothing but dread.

~

MICHELLE WONDERED what it felt like to live in the White House and to work in the Oval Office—to sleep, eat and work within the four walls of one building, albeit an impressive one, leaving only under heavy guard for stage-managed occasions and the rare, discreet, family holiday.

While she knew that it was refurnished in line with each new president's tastes, there were also leftovers from past administrations, such as the original *Resolute* desk, a gift from Queen Victoria and made from the timbers of a nineteenth-century British frigate. The sense of duty and the burden of history must feel overwhelming to anyone who sat at that desk. From there, wars had been started, waged and finished. Economies had been changed at the stroke of a pen. Rights given or taken away. Great social achievements in education, health, taxation and social welfare made.

She didn't think that President Philip Kurzon was a garish man, or overly comfortable with the trappings of his wealth or power. She'd visited him in this office a few times during his first five years in office. Initially, he'd made minimal changes—a new rug, some curtains. But now into his second term, he'd redecorated.

Instead of opting for the less informal couches, she was surprised the President had elected to sit at his desk, with Michelle opposite. She was sure it was a bad precedent for him to lean back in his chair, feet resting on the century old desk, but he didn't seem to care.

"Ms Dominique, if I'm going to lead my country into its biggest war in eighty years—with a disgraced senator on my plate to boot—I'd ask you not to judge my posture."

It certainly looked like events were taking a toll on him. While the news about the USS *George Washington* had had half a day to sink in, it would still be a shock to the United States' political establishment for weeks to come.

"Of all the men in all of the offices in the world, you're the most entitled to have your feet on the desk, or anywhere you damn please, if you'll excuse me." It was late in the evening, and she was probably not his last appointment. When she'd called to ask to see him, she'd taken what she could get. Despite the power of the Foundation, and its tendrils that spread through all aspects of life in the capital, she was still sitting opposite the most powerful man in the world.

"I'm too used to snapping at my doctor and my wife." Kurzon smiled. "Now what is it I can do for you, Ms Dominique? I was surprised to see you in my diary."

Michelle had no doubt about that. Though she'd met him a few times on Foundation business, it had always been alongside Anton. That was precisely why she was here. Anton had refused to meet with her, and every other effort she'd made to get him out of his compound had been unsuccessful. Despite that setback, she had received some good news earlier—confirmation that McDowell had told his wife about the divorce.

"I wanted to meet with you personally, Mr President, to say the Foundation and all of its resources will be supporting the war effort."

He laughed. "All of your resources, Ms Dominique? I understand that Anton Clark is still the head honcho of your group of hatchet men."

Michelle didn't rise to the bait. "I'm working on that."

He exhaled deeply. "Besides, I'm not sure I need placards and megaphones right now, or an out-of-date sense of American exceptionalism."

She bristled. "You may not share our views, Mr President, but there's a lot of candidates in the upcoming midterms who do. You know that."

"Yourself included, if you win your seat?" He waved his hand, as though to shoo her retort away. "I don't listen to wingnuts like you. You're so far to the extreme right of the Republican Party that you aren't even really welcome on your side of the aisle. If they think you're nuts, Ms Dominique, why should I listen?"

"With respect, sir, all matters of ideology, policy and priorities must be put aside at times like this. You should know that you have the full support of the entire nation in what's to come. The attack on the *Washington* strikes to the core of America's place in Asia and the world."

"Noble sentiments, but not overly realistic, I'm afraid. We still don't know the motive for the attack on the carrier. I hope to avoid war."

"Now you're being fooli—"

"No. War isn't guaranteed. I wish everyone would stop acting like it is. The best result would be for the Chinese to back down and let a proper investigation take place. The evidence linking Taiwan to the attacks is tenuous, but there may even be a case for us just surrendering the field and letting them have Taiwan."

"War is guaranteed, Mr President. That is, if you want your country ascendant, your economy strong and your legacy secure."

He waved his hand. "At any rate, I've ordered other assets to the region, and the Air Force has deployed aircraft to Taiwan itself. I hope they won't be needed."

Michelle pursed her lips in thought. If Kurzon had forward deployed a significant number of troops onto the island, war was inevitable. China wouldn't take a backward step while US troops were in town, nor would the US concede, especially after the incident with the *Washington*.

She leaned forward in her seat. "They will be, Mr President. You simply cannot allow an attack on a United States Navy aircraft carrier to go unanswered."

As soon as he nodded, Michelle knew the tinderbox that would set the world on fire was waiting to be lit.

CHAPTER 10

There's been significant fallout in Washington following the arrest of Senator Patrick Mahoney, chairman of the Senate Judiciary Subcommittee on Privacy, Technology and the Law inquiry into the activities of EMCorp. The newly appointed chairwoman of the inquiry, Senator Lyn Eddings, raised eyebrows this morning when she hinted that it may be abandoned outright.

"After our initial hearings, which included a substantial interview with Mr McDowell, we must consider whether there's sufficient evidence of misconduct to continue with an inquiry," Senator Eddings said. "Senator Mahoney had certain views on the viability of the inquiry, and it's true to say that some of my colleagues and I have a somewhat divergent view."

Frank Parzinkas, Your News Today, *September 16*

Jack continued to stare straight down the barrel of the small camcorder, which Celeste wielded with some difficulty, given her injured arm. "For all the latest from aboard the USS *George Washington*, join us on the *New York Standard* live video blog at twelve noon eastern for a Q&A session."

Celeste laughed as she lowered the camera. "One take. You'd think you'd done this before!"

"A few times. Blame the fusion of media." Jack scratched his nose, which had been itchy for the entire three-minute spot. "Used to be a newspaper was a newspaper."

"Delivered by horse and cart?" Celeste smirked.

Jack punched her arm gently. "Cute. Now we're a newspaper, with video, blogs, chatrooms and forums. And that doesn't even include the social media guys."

He started to walk back toward the heavy steel door that would lead them back inside the confines of the *Washington*. Celeste followed alongside, fiddling with the playback on the camera and watching his clip over again.

"Want to get a bite?" Celeste didn't look up from the camera. "Fish fingers tonight."

Jack smiled. "Sounds tempting, but no. I want to get some sleep."

The short video was just part of his day's work, the cherry on top of a two thousand-word feature he'd written for Josefa. Since the word had come down to push the Taiwan independence angle, Jack had been working up the piece, which would be on the front page of the *Standard*.

Jack was disturbed by the silence as they walked to the door. Though activity on the flight deck had slowly increased, the ship wasn't fully fighting fit, with bilge pumps working to clear away the water the carrier had taken on. The sight of the escorts on the horizon made him feel any better. The fleet was still well protected.

As Jack reached out to the door handle, klaxons started to wail and red LED lights flashed up and down the deck. "Bandits inbound! All hands to station."

Celeste cursed as she dropped the camera and grabbed his arm. "What the fuck now? Can't they just leave us alone?"

"We need to move!" Jack wrapped his arm around her and hurried her away from the door. "We need to get to the chopper."

In his mind, Jack rehearsed the scenario that one of the carrier's junior officers had taken them through the previous day. McCulloch hadn't wanted to risk the two of them being aboard the carrier in the event of another attack, so Jack had been briefed about exactly what to do if the fireworks started again. He'd been told in no uncertain terms that flashing lights and alarms meant it was time to go.

They sprinted to the helipad as quickly as they could, careful to stay out of the path of the aircraft that were beginning to ramp up their engines. If the Chinese were inbound, McCulloch would want everything in the air, including the MH-60R Seahawk that would ferry the few non-essentials aboard the ship to safety.

"Just stick together and we'll be okay." Jack looked at Celeste, who nodded. "The group is designed to swat away any attack."

When they reached the squat gray Seahawk, it already had its rotors firing. The helicopter was surrounded with seamen loading the few passengers it was assigned to carry. As Jack and Celeste drew closer, the junior officer who'd briefed him on the process the day earlier waved him in. Jack pointed Celeste to the door of the helicopter and ran over to the lieutenant.

The lieutenant had to raise his voice to be heard. "We've got a whole load of Chinese bombers inbound, under heavy escort. We're sending you to the USS *Shiloh*. It's smaller than the carrier, so less likely to get painted by an anti-ship missile. It's also got more fireworks than a Chinese New Year to keep you safe. You'll be fine over there, sir."

"Thanks! Stay safe." He had to shout.

The other man smiled. "Been about seventy years since one of these tubs was sunk."

Jack nodded and ran for the helicopter. He reached the door and was pulled aboard by a crew member, who slid the door shut. Jack took a seat next to Celeste and looked over at her, but she didn't move and continued to stare straight ahead. He placed a hand on her knee and gave it a slight squeeze.

The crew member who'd helped Jack aboard walked over to them with a practiced ease, his hand held out. "Here, take these."

Jack took the two sets of large headphones. "What're they for?"

"Knowledge. You guys are reporters, right? So report. If shit goes bad here, the world is going to need to know. Just don't tell anyone I gave those to you."

Jack nodded as the wheels lifted off the deck. He placed the headset over his ears as the crew member returned to his seat. He held out the other headset for Celeste. She took it, but left them on her lap for the time being. The helicopter banked, and his ears were assaulted with radio reports from what could only be the fleet combat information center, its various ships and aircraft squadrons.

After a few minutes, he started to understand the gist of what was happening. It frightened him. He eased back into his seat and listened as the reports rolled in.

"One hundred and ninety-seven bandits at extreme range, and more every second."

"Squadrons, check in."

"Royal Maces, en route and on point."

"Diamondbacks, ready to engage."

"Eagles launching."

"Dambusters, awaiting takeoff."

Jack did the arithmetic in his head and felt trapped. No matter how mighty the carrier and its battle group, if they could only get a squadron or two in place before the Chinese started firing their missiles, he knew that bad things were going to follow. He looked out the window of the Seahawk and saw nothing but blue ocean. There was nowhere to run.

"All assets, this is Admiral McCulloch. You're about to get a little taste of how General Custer felt at Little Big Horn. Let's swat as many of these bastards as we can. Good luck."

Jack wondered how anyone could stay so calm in such a situation, with the safety of thousands resting on his shoulders. But the admiral's southern twang was somehow reassuring. In the minutes that followed, the radio chatter was mostly concerned with ships and aircraft getting into position for what was to come. As the number of Chinese aircraft inbound continued to rise, it was clear that the US forces were outgunned.

Jack turned to Celeste. "It's beginning." She looked over at him and nodded, placing her headset on as the helicopter banked again.

"Mr President." Jack recognized the call sign for the *Washington*. "This is Mace Prime, we've got what you could call a target-rich environment, over. Permission to engage?"

McCulloch's voice boomed in his headset. "Denied. Do not fire until fired upon or until they enter our threat box. Our rules of engagement are ironclad."

Jack wasn't sure about holding fire until you had a couple of hundred missiles coming your way, but nor was he a three-star admiral. He also understood McCulloch's reluctance to start World War Three unless absolutely necessary. Historians would be discussing McCulloch's actions for decades to come.

The minutes ticked away. Then McCulloch cut into the radio feed. "Right, they're in the threat box, put them down."

Jack heard acceptance of the order from both flight leaders and the fleet gunnery officers. Soon after, the radio was awash with confirmation of missiles being fired by both sides. Reports of aircraft running empty of missiles started to roll in, and other voices reported the fleet escorts were filling the air with defensive missiles. Still the Chinese missiles kept coming.

McCulloch spoke a second later. "All assets shift focus to the missiles. Disengage from the Chinese birds and protect the group."

Celeste grabbed Jack's hand as he closed his eyes and listened to the radio. He hadn't felt this helpless since Afghanistan, when he'd been in a convoy that had been attacked by insurgents. Surrounded, he'd had to wait in a Humvee while the Marines he was embedded with drove off the threat.

He opened his eyes and saw the deck of the cruiser USS *Shiloh* come into sight out of the window of the Seahawk. It seemed serene, stationary in the water as its two vertical missile launchers fired for the final time, then radioed that they were as dry at the rest of the fleet.

"Fire all close in defense!" McCulloch shouted over the radio, in a tone that made events sound pretty bleak. "Everything you've got, people."

There was a muffled boom in the distance. Nobody on the helicopter said a word, but many screamed or gritted their teeth. There was a second boom, closer, as the helicopter started to descend onto the deck of the *Shiloh*. Others followed. It was impossible to tell whether it was Chinese missiles being shot down, or US ships being hit.

"Attention all assets, this is Admiral McCulloch. The *Washington* has been hit twice and breached. We're abandoning ship. USS *Shiloh* has the command."

Jack began to wonder if he was living the last few moments of his life. He was reassured as the deck of the *Shiloh* came into view, a hundred feet below.

He turned to Celeste and smiled. "We'll be okay."

She smiled back.

The window outside the Seahawk lit up as the *Shiloh* exploded, and a huge ball of flame climbed into the air toward the Seahawk. Jack was driven back into his seat as the pilot banked and climbed again. He smelled smoke. He turned his head to find the Seahawk was aflame, a massive hole in the rear of the aircraft.

The helicopter lost altitude in seconds. Jack could do nothing but squeeze Celeste's knee as the Seahawk ploughed into the South China Sea.

~

ERNEST'S private office in the penthouse of the *New York Standard* building was unique. From this office, decisions had been made that had changed the world. He'd helped governments to rise and to fall, influenced public opinion, and moderated the trends and fashions of whole generations. While Ernest's tastes in furniture and decor were modest, the office had been redecorated several times, most recently at the behest of Sandra. She'd protested that since he spent eighteen hours a day here, or so it seemed, it should have some nice things in it. After he'd agreed, it had taken mere days for the room to transform, from new chairs and paintings, to small touches like the books on display. At first, he was glad his wife had persisted, since the office felt more welcoming. Now he hated it. It was a stark reminder of what he'd lost in order to save the company.

He shook his head and returned to the present. He chewed on a bagel and savored the cream cheese, listening while Peter gave a rundown of the day's news. It was a key part of his day, their morning ritual, and one that required Peter to be up earlier than Ernest—no small feat.

"Plenty about the Senate inquiry. Looks like the consensus is that Mahoney was the inquisitor and without him it will blow over."

Ernest pursed his lips. He hadn't told Peter about his deal with Dominique and saw no reason to now. "I'm certainly glad that's gone away, but I'm annoyed that we never managed to find the dirt on him. We'll need to do better next time."

Peter laughed. "Don't be so dark. It will be fine. The senator has been dealt with and the committee will go away."

Ernest wasn't so sure. He resented having to be a patsy to that woman and her organization. Already she'd started to call to make small demands. They'd been subtle: massages of the truth here or an omitted fact there; mostly harmless. But Ernest knew that with each passing day she'd try to extract more from their relationship.

On the other hand, he had to admit that Dominique had proven ruthlessly effective in the prosecution of their agreement. Within days, Mahoney had been disgraced, the Senate inquiry was a memory and the political mire that had dragged down his company for months was starting to relent.

"What sort of coverage is the divorce announcement getting? Am I the worst husband and father on the planet?"

"Close enough. Let me show you." Peter put a separate folder on the desk and opened it. It was piled high with articles.

"Fan mail?"

Peter nodded. "Basically all along the lines of: what's he thinking; how could he be so cruel; she has a mental illness; it must be some slut breaking them up; is anyone surprised, given it's wife number four; so on, so forth."

"Could be worse, then?"

"Probably not. Are you sure your divorce is absolutely necessary?"

Ernest closed his eyes. It probably wasn't. He could have weathered the storm, faced the Senate head on and likely seen a dismantling of his lifetime's work. But he had made a decision and followed through. After Sandra's initial pleading, she hadn't said a word to him. All of their contact since had been through lawyers and the paperwork was nearly complete. The pre-nuptial agreement would leave her a rich woman.

While the loss cut him deeply, he kept his feelings and his reasons to himself. "It was necessary and there's no point revisiting it. Leave it at that."

Peter looked a bit confused, but nodded his acceptance. There was a knock on the door and it was flung open before Ernest had a chance to summon whoever was on the other side. One of his junior assistants looked flustered as he rushed across the room and placed a piece of paper in Peter's hand. The man nodded at them and left the room without a word.

Peter read the document and went white. "Shit, looks like China has gone and made the rest of the day's news irrelevant."

"What do you mean?"

"That stranded carrier, they've sunk it."

"When?"

"A few hours ago. We've got people aboard."

Ernest's head spun with the political and economic ramifications of the news, even before Peter had stopped talking. He was not prepared for his phone to ring, and even less prepared for who it was. He stared at the caller ID and willed the phone to stop ringing. He gestured for Peter to leave, and waited until he was alone before he finally answered.

"Took you long enough." Michelle Dominique spoke before he'd had a chance to say hello. "The point of giving me your direct line was not making me wait."

"Sorry, but I've just seen the news—with the world about to go to hell and all, what do a few extra seconds matter?"

"Whatever. I want it spun. Pro-Taiwanese independence. Moral outrage that our good boys and girls would get blown up like this. China evil. Taiwan good."

Ernest sighed. Since their agreement, he'd ordered his editors to start slanting things in that direction. The *New York Standard* had a strong front-page feature about it, and other EMCorp papers and television affiliates had run it to death. He'd done all he could, within reason, short of an outright declaration of support for a preemptive US strike.

He resisted the urge to fight her on this. "So you want us to further stoke the flames of war. Are you sure that's the best move at this point?"

"I don't want your advice, Ernest. I want results." There was a pause. "I also want criticism of the Kurzon administration's handling of the crisis. You need to stoke public dissatisfaction and pave the way for my people to be elected in November."

He heard a click and the phone went dead. He sighed and closed his eyes. He knew he'd better get used to it—getting calls from her like his editors were used to getting from him—but he still didn't like it. For someone who'd run his own operation with an iron fist for decades, it was a culture shock he'd continued to struggle with.

For now, he had work to do. Ernest kept the phone in his hand and dialed the number of one of his best friends in the world. When the secretary of the President of the United States answered, he explained that he needed to speak with the President urgently and was put right through.

"How's the wife, Ernest?" President Phillip Kurzon offered in greeting.

'Which one?"

It was their standard opening banter, but when friends got as old as the two of them, routine jokes could still bring a degree of comfort and amusement, even with a war breaking out. They'd been college roommates. Philip Kurzon had gone on to marry his sweetheart and lived happily with her since. Ernest had quite a different story.

"Ernest, that's a nasty business with Sandra. Are you sure it can't be salvaged?"

"I'm sure. The divorce will be finalized soon. As for the others, I haven't heard from Elle or Edith and Catherine is as unpredictable as ever. That's all of them. How's yours?"

"The usual. Incredible woman, my wife. I think she has a harder job than I do. Grandson made quarterback, you know?"

"Pass on my congratulations." Ernest paused. "Anyway, I do have some business to discuss with you, and I'm sure you're busy."

'Thanks, I know why you're calling. What've you got?"

"Not very much, just wanted to let you know we're running hard for Taiwan on this one. I know that puts you in a bind, but I really don't have a choice."

While Ernest, a Republican supporter, and Kurzon, a Democratic president, disagreed on politics, it had never affected their friendship. No president reached the Oval Office without a patron in the media, and Ernest had thrown all of the support he could behind his first campaign. In return, he'd gained a powerful friend.

"I'm not surprised, but the last thing I need is more fuel on this particular fire."

"They sunk a carrier, Phil."

"And besides nuke them, what exactly would you have me do? The Joint Chiefs tell me I've got few conventional options with the *Washington* gone. I've got a meeting with Frank Maas in an hour, that'll tell me if the Agency has any ideas."

Ernest massaged his temples with his fingers. "Is the military situation that bad?"

"Normally, no. But they sank one carrier, the next nearest are in the Gulf and somewhere near San Francisco, and anything I send from the East Coast will take far too long to get there. We're going to war, but it's with one hand tied behind our back."

"Recognition for Taiwan?" Ernest pushed his luck.

The phone was silent for a few long moments. "It's really a formality after they hit the carrier. State is already working it through. The Euros aren't getting involved for now, but the Japanese, Koreans and Australians are howling. This is all off the record."

"Of course."

"Anyway, Ern, thanks for letting me know. Nice to know you'll be calling on me to beat the drums of war as hard as I can. I've got work to do. Call my office next week and we'll organize a round next time you're in DC, it's been too long since we caught up."

"You got it. Thanks, Phil. Bye."

Ernest sighed. While the President knew war was now inevitable, he clearly hoped to keep the engagement limited. Yet Dominique was using

EMCorp and its public influence to corner the President of the United States with public opinion.

Ernest, and his company, had become a strategic asset.

~

JACK FELT VERY ALONE as he looked around the deck of the Chinese rescue boat, which he shared with a dozen or so armed soldiers and a large number of survivors. The sailors who'd been saved from drowning stared into the darkness or at the deck, and didn't engage each other in conversation or protest their captivity.

Their captors, on the other hand, barked orders through translators and weren't averse to using the butt of a rifle to make their point. They shared around bottled water and some meager food rations happily enough, but any dissent—real or imagined—was quickly dealt with.

Jack shivered. Though he had no injuries, he'd been unable to get warm since his plunge into the South China Sea, despite having three blankets draped over him. The dampness combined with the seasonal chill to make warmth impossible. He didn't mind so much. At least he knew he was alive.

The Seahawk had plunged into the ocean seconds after the USS *Shiloh* had exploded. He'd had no time to react before the helicopter was upside down and completely submerged. It had been hard enough to get out of his seatbelt, let alone outside the chopper. If not for the gaping hole in the fuselage, he'd have drowned. Several others had.

Celeste had been alive when he'd lost her. He'd helped her to unbuckle and they'd both reached the surface, but in the confusion of fire and terror that followed, they'd lost each other. He thought she was alive, but it was equally possible that she'd drowned before the arrival of the Chinese rescue boats, a mix of naval and civilian ships that made for a strange flotilla. He'd been lucky to get aboard one of the first few.

Best he could tell, most or all of the carrier group's warships were gone.

Besides the *Shiloh*, he'd been able to see one of the escorting destroyers crippled and continue to burn long after being abandoned. Beyond that, Jack had no idea what had happened to the rest of fleet, its escort submarine or the *Washington* air wing that had been aloft when their carrier started to go under. He hoped they'd had enough fuel to get to Taiwan or somewhere else.

He had been witness to the end of American naval dominance in the Pacific Ocean. Though the Chinese had no doubt taken significant losses as well, the result of their attack had been the loss of a ship thought impregnable and the death of sailors who'd paid the price for that hubris. No doubt the attack would have other ramifications as well.

Jack's face suddenly stung, his reverie broken by the cold hand of a Chinese naval officer. The slap was firm but not brutal. The officer spoke to Jack in Mandarin, his tone professional. Jack relied on the English translator next to the officer to make sense of what was being said.

"My comrade said you should pay attention." The translator's tone was entirely civil. "You aren't a navy man, so he wishes to know your name, occupation and role."

Jack rubbed his cheek, trying to will away the pain of the slap. He shook his head. "I'm Jack Emery. I had no role aboard the ship. I'm a journalist for the *New York Standard*."

He watched as the two men exchanged words. As they spoke, Jack looked around the small boat. This vessel had only a few dozen of the rescued, compared to the hundreds picked up by some of the larger ships. He looked back to the pair discussing his fate. As the translator spoke, the officer's expression grew darker. Jack was fairly sure that the officer didn't relish having foreign media on his vessel. Then, as if a dark cloud had lifted, the officer smiled at the translator and then at Jack. It didn't feel like a happy one.

The translator spoke. "Are you sure that's your answer?"

Jack stared at him. "Yes, of course. I need to get to Japan or the US. I also had a colleague on the helicopter that was shot down. She might be among the rescued."

"That will take some time, I'm afraid. We believe you may be a spy. You'll be under the guard of the People's Liberation Army Navy until we can confirm or disprove this."

Jack's mind raced. While China didn't have the most sterling human rights record, they were generally hands off with members of the foreign press. "That's crazy."

"That's fact."

"And suppose I jump overboard?"

The translator stiffened. "The troops on this vessel have orders to shoot if necessary."

Jack's shoulders slumped and he sighed. "So what next, then?"

The translator smiled. "There are procedures in place. I'm sure you understand."

Jack didn't, but he didn't get any further chance to contest the point as the translator nodded, turned and walked away.

He ground his teeth, resigned to the fact that he was in the custody of the Chinese for however long they pleased. Whatever happened on the trip between the rescue site and the mainland, Jack knew that nothing good was waiting for him. He simply hoped that Celeste had survived.

CHAPTER 11

Following the sinking of the USS George Washington, the United States has delivered a declaration of war to the Chinese Ambassador to the United States. As the US continues to deploy additional assets to the area, the Air Force has launched wide-ranging air and cruise missile strikes against the Chinese mainland. While details are sketchy, it appears the US strikes were aimed at major Chinese airfields and port facilities. We'll bring you more information as it comes to hand. Meanwhile, the United States has formally recognized Taiwan as an independent state. Though there's been no reaction by the Chinese, it's unlikely that this move will do anything to calm tensions in the region, already white hot following the attack on the carrier and the retaliation by the US Air Force.

    Kate Winston, Reuters, *September 18*

I n an attempt to get his mind off the pain that throbbed around his body with every beat of his heart, Jack thought of happier times with Erin. He'd expected his treatment at the hands of the Chinese to be rudimentary, but had never considered the possibility of the brutality he'd been subjected to. The darkness bothered him nearly as much as the odor that seemed to permeate every inch of the prison, a combination of sweat, human filth and the putrid, slightly sweet smell of charred flesh. The smell added to the continual, dull moan of human misery—a cacophony of wails, high and low. Occasionally, he heard a sharp cry of pain or terror.

It was all testimony to the work being done around the clock to extract information, real or imagined, from those unlucky enough to be here. He'd had a taste of such treatment on his first night, when a pair of uniformed men had visited and kicked him around. One of them had welcomed him in patchy English, before laughing at his attempt to cower away from the pain. They'd left Jack in darkness, and he'd been on the floor since. His only comfort was a metal pail for his bodily functions, which he suspected was more for the convenience of his jailers than their prisoner. Blood, piss and spittle could be hosed away, Jack figured, but shit would probably block the drains.

He dozed off. Some time later, he woke and gave an involuntary whimper as the lock on the steel cell door gave a loud click. The heavy door swung open on poorly oiled hinges. He looked up, and there was enough light in the passageway for him to see a small, bespectacled Chinese man with a toolbox in his hand.

Jack wasn't sure what to expect. The man said something in Mandarin, and Jack was instantly blinded by harsh overhead lighting. He shielded his eyes against the pain of the first real light he'd seen in days, listening to the footsteps of the man as he entered the room and the screech of the door closing behind him. He was not sure how much time had passed between the first beating and now, but as Jack regained his sight, he saw it had been long enough for some of the blood he'd lost to dry in irregular streaks on the cell floor. The gruesome display wouldn't be out of place in a gallery of modern art.

The new arrival dropped to his knees beside Jack and put his toolbox on the ground. He opened it and removed his tools. They were terrible instruments: some sharp, some blunt, some Jack had no idea about. But one message was loud and clear: this man could inflict pain. Jack backed into the corner, away from him.

The man spoke softly. "I'm here to hear your confession."

Jack closed his eyes as he felt a tear streak down his cheek. "I have nothing for you."

"Start with your name."

"Jack Emery."

"You're a spy, posing as a journalist. You were on board the US Navy aircraft carrier that was inside Chinese territorial waters."

Jack was slightly taken aback. He'd spent lots of time since his capture puzzled by his treatment. While China wasn't usually averse to impinging on the rights of the international media, they usually kept the heat to a low simmer. He wasn't sure why he was getting the special treatment, but suspected it was the pro-Taiwanese coverage.

He opened his eyes and stared at the man. "A spy? I'm a reporter. A pretty bloody famous one, too. Google me and you'll work out that I'm no spy."

The man laughed. "That's one of the more fanciful stories I've heard."

Jack felt his heartbeat quicken, and his mouth went dry. He had no doubts about what was in store should he remain here much longer. His heart pleaded with him to say something to the man, to convince him of the futility of what was to come, but his head knew it was pointless.

"Mr Emery, if you give me what I need, you'll remained imprisoned here but otherwise unharmed for however long the conflict lasts. Once it's over, you'll be free to join your lady friend back in the United States."

"Celeste? You have Celeste?"

"Of course. She's another valued guest. Now, if you don't give me what I need, things become more complicated. You'll be deprived of sleep, comfort, food and any relief. You'll also experience pain unimagined, until your very nerves are screaming at you."

Jack closed his eyes. The beating he'd already taken would be nothing compared with any of that. He also felt a deeper fear, knowing they had Celeste. He'd thought she might be dead, which in many ways would be preferable to the Chinese hospitality. The man had clearly told him she was alive because she could be used against Jack.

"Close your eyes, Mr Emery, but don't think that the darkness behind your eyelids protects you. You do have a real choice, but only one is correct."

Jack felt hopeless. "Why are you doing this? All of this?"

The man laughed. "I'll indulge you. My leaders have decided the time has come to reckon with Taiwan. Given that the American bulldog stands in the way, it was necessary to smack it on the nose with a newspaper."

"You sank a carrier to send a message?" Jack shook his head. "Look, I don't even care. You know I'm no spy. There's no point in torturing me. I just want to go home."

"I do know that the company you work for has become a strategic element in this war. If my government can't control it, we can render it inert." He shrugged "Just business."

Jack's heart sank. If he'd had hopes of being released, or at least having an easier time of it, they'd now vanished. Suddenly Josefa's instructions to cover the conflict in favor of Taiwan made sense. For whatever reason, Ernest McDowell had cast his lot in the war. It meant Jack was in for a nasty time.

The other man slapped him lightly. "Now, I expect the same candor from you, Mr Emery. Concede that your coverage on board the American carrier was flawed. Admit that the ship was in Chinese territorial waters, and I will inform my superiors that they are mistaken about your espionage. It's inevitable, so we may as well get it over with."

Jack said nothing for several moments. He cowered in the corner as the other man waited for him to offer something to stay the threat of torture. Then, clearly tired of waiting, the man cocked a fist back. Jack tried to lift his arm to defend against the blow, but was too slow.

The fist slammed into his face. He wailed in pain as his nose gave a sickening crunch and the back of his head slammed into the blood-smeared concrete. He groaned but remained conscious, his head on fire. He continued to groan as the other man moved his head close enough that Jack could smell the cigarettes on his breath.

"I've seen some of the Falun Gong fanatics hold out until death, as well as some enemy spies, trained for such interrogation. But you're a journalist. Why do you fight?"

Jack coughed several times, and spat blood onto the floor. "Because I don't know what you want me to tell you."

"Aren't you afraid of me, Mr Emery?"

"I've been in the White House press corps." Jack coughed again. "This is little league in comparison, and you're the cheerleader that the entire offensive line is banging."

The other man chuckled and then moved back on the floor slightly. Jack was pretty sure he'd caught the drift. Despite his bravado, Jack suddenly wished that he hadn't insulted his captor. It would just mean more pain. As if on cue, he heard the scrape of metal against a whetstone.

"It is men like you who make my job a pleasure, Mr Emery. The ones who break immediately are no fun, they make my job feel like sweeping the floor. But every now and then, someone like you comes along, who gives me joy in my profession. You'll break, though. Everyone does. Some just break quicker than others."

ERNEST MOUTHED his thanks as the waiter laid a napkin across his lap. He considered the wine list for only a moment before settling on a bottle of the 1997 Penfolds Grange. The waiter nodded, thanked the two of them and backed away, leaving Ernest and Peter alone. Ernest sighed.

"While we're here there's a thousand or so corpses floating in the South China Sea, boys in Chinese custody, and pilots risking their lives over hostile territory."

Peter nodded. "Not to mention a country coming to terms with the destruction of American exceptionalism."

"You don't say." They'd spent the morning digesting the blanket coverage of the war and putting a particular slant on things. Ernest didn't tell him it was Dominique's slant.

He reached for a bread roll from the basket in the middle of the table. He tore it open, taking out some of his pent-up anger on the unfortunate sourdough. In addition to all the other carnage, he had reporters missing. Ernest had lost people before—like any proprietor who'd been in the game long enough—but never this many.

"Any word from our people?"

Peter buttered his own roll. "It's coming in slowly, but Fran O'Rourke from the *Independent* is still with what's left of the fleet on their way back to Yokosuka. Christian Malley has been picked up by the Chinese, but there has been no word on Jack Emery, or the other *Standard* reporter, Celeste Adams. They were on board the *Washington*."

"So they're dead or captured." Ernest assaulted the bread with a thick layer of butter.

"Yeah." Peter's voice trailed off. "Watch your cholesterol."

"Not now, Peter."

They sat in silence as the waiter returned with the wine and poured a glass for both of them. Ernest half expected a comment from Peter about watching his liver, but none came. In truth, Ernest was sure Peter felt as bad as he did about having so many people—EMCorp people—missing or dead.

Ernest picked up his glass and took a mouthful of the wine. It was as good as he remembered. He was about to have another when an Asian man approached the table from the side and came to a stop a respectful few feet away. Ernest sighed. This was the last thing he wanted to deal with right now.

"Ambassador." Ernest turned to look at him.

The Chinese Ambassador to the United States, Du Xiaoming, gave a small cough. "Excuse me, gentlemen, I noticed you were dining and wanted to pay my respects."

Peter stood and Ernest was glad that he took the cue.

"Just off to the gents. Please excuse me, Ambassador."

Du nodded at Peter and took the newly occupied seat. Ernest said nothing as Peter walked away, but signaled the waiter to bring another glass. It gave him time to think. He'd had some minor dealings with the ambassador in the past, mainly about EMCorp expansion into China, and knew that this was a business meeting. Ernest just didn't know the type of business they'd be discussing.

"What can I do for you, Ambassador?"

Du smiled again. "This is just a neighborly visit, as you Americans like to call it. A courtesy, since your dogs have strayed into our yard."

Ernest felt his face flush, but any potential outburst was stayed when the waiter placed a glass in front of the ambassador and filled it.

"May I take your order, gentlemen?"

"Steak, James, just the usual." Ernest gestured toward the ambassador. "And…"

Du kept his face even. "Two please."

"Certainly." The waiter took their menus then left them.

Ernest leaned forward to avoid any chance of prying ears. "You're talking about the three embeds? You know they're a part of the business."

Du shrugged. "Your people, your risk. I'm afraid my government is seeing things quite a bit differently, though. All three are in custody and facing espionage charges."

Ernest sat back in his chair, lifted his glass and took a sip of wine. He never took his eyes off Du, who sat impassively. Ernest knew he was now neck deep in negotiation for the lives and welfare of his staff.

He put the glass down and inched forward again. "They're reporters, Ambassador. They were reporting events as they unfolded. They're not spies. I want them released."

Du held his gaze for a few moments, then nodded slightly. "Your company's reporting of the developing situation concerns my government. Now they've trespassed, their return will require adjustments in their owner's priorities."

It took all of Ernest's self-control not to scream in frustration. The deal with Dominique was to blame for this meeting, and for the fact that his people were probably being roughed up. He'd dug himself out of one hole only to land right in another. He had no doubt that the Chinese would release Emery, Adams and Malley tomorrow, for the right price. But it would be steep.

"Their reporting was fair and balanced. I don't know what more you want."

Du took a sip of wine. "That's the thing about neighborly disputes, isn't it? One side has a view, the other side has a view, but who knows who's right?"

"Maybe. But sooner or later it must be resolved."

"Yes, but unfortunately for you, we have your dogs. And their condition worsens with each passing day because of the grief they feel at not being at home with their owner."

Ernest flared. "If you've hurt them, it will be on your head."

Du held up a hand. "I haven't harmed anyone. But dogs must be trained."

There was a long pause. Neither of them spoke as they stared at each other across the table. Unfortunately for Ernest, the ambassador was right. It was EMCorp staff in danger, primarily because of his deal with Michelle Dominique. He had nothing to bargain with that he hadn't already promised to her. He forced his temper to subside.

Ernest sighed. "Where to from here, Ambassador?"

"We agree to disagree, and we part ways as friends, I'd suggest."

"Alright." Ernest wasn't satisfied, but there was nothing to be gained by more pushing.

"But one last friendly observation." Du spoke softly. "The world is changing and the great tectonic plates are shifting. The time has come for everyone to pick sides. As the plates grind against each other, only a stupid man would place himself or his company in between. Please, heed my words if you value the health and wellbeing of your dogs."

~

MICHELLE KEPT her gaze locked on Anton as he continued to shout, his spittle washing over her like rain. He'd been at it for a good ten seconds. She didn't break eye contact with him as she removed her glasses, wiped them clean on her cardigan and placed them back on.

"Are you done?" She stared at him from across the desk. "This is quite annoying."

"You cut off my funds, corner me, kill my security detail. And all for nothing." He pounded the table with his fist. "Don't you have anything to say for yourself?"

"I'm probably going to need a shower, whenever you decide you're done."

He huffed and sat down, giving her a small victory. Anton had been holed up in his compound, running the Foundation remotely since his return from China. They'd had an uneasy peace while Michelle put things in place for her takeover, until this morning. She'd cut off his funds and sent an email to the organization informing everyone that she was stepping up to take charge, while Anton was indisposed. It was a total lie, but combined with her recent efforts to ensnare McDowell and meet with the President, he'd had no choice but to react. He'd agreed to meet at a neutral office building. Things had probably seemed like they were going well for him, until the Shadd brothers had killed his security detail and left the two of them alone in the small office.

She was certain that he could recognize the balance of power shifting. She had control of the Foundation in her hand.

"I'm going to need more than that from you, Michelle. I'm currently weighing up the merits of continuing to allow you to breathe."

She laughed. "You don't frighten me, Anton. Nor do you recognize that you've lost all control. It's all slipping away."

He apparently didn't hear what she'd said. "This is the most shocking betrayal of me and our cause I could imagine."

Michelle made no attempt to hide her anger. "Is that so? I'd consider you trying to kill me to be worse."

He froze, unsure for the first time. "What're you talking about?"

"China."

"You're being ridiculous, Michelle. If I wanted you dead, you'd be dead."

She knew it was time to strike. She grabbed a metal paperweight off the desk and, before he could react, threw it at him as hard as she could. The paperweight hit his skull and gave a satisfying crack. She vaulted the desk in one bound as he screeched in agony, reaching up toward his head. She advanced on him with a bloody, single-minded focus as he staggered backward. He looked up and seemed to recognize her intent. As she closed in, she ducked under his hastily thrown roundhouse. She threw a quick jab at his stomach, which caused him to double over.

"I didn't mind when you kept me in the dark, because we were both motivated to make America great again."

She lifted her knee and connected with his nose, which caused his head to jerk back. He slumped to the floor.

"I didn't mind when you changed the plan, took credit and denied me mine, even though I did most of the heavy lifting."

She reached down to the floor and picked up a pen that had been knocked over in the scuffle, as he rose back to his full height with his hands over his nose.

"I didn't even mind when you arranged the death of Chen and his family, despite your promises, because I managed to save them."

She was surprised when he threw another punch. This one connected square with her jaw. Her vision exploded with color and she staggered to one knee. She winced as Anton followed up with a brutal kick to her midriff. She tasted blood in her mouth, but knew that if she didn't get up quickly, he was a more than capable foe.

She pushed herself off the floor, rushed toward him and tackled him around the waist. They fell in a sprawling heap. She climbed on top of him and swung several punches at his head, which he defended as best he could. She growled in frustration and punched him one last time. He held his hands up in surrender.

"I did mind when you tried to have me killed, and didn't have the good grace to do it properly or fuck off when you failed."

His eyes widened in apparent fear, then horror, as she raised the pen. "What're you doing?"

She brought the pen down, hard. The tip penetrated his eye socket and she pushed until the shaft would go no deeper. After a second or two he stopped flailing. She screamed as loudly as she could and felt the fury rush out of her. She leaned back on his stomach, and could smell the putrid scent of his bowels as they evacuated.

"What needs to be done." She climbed up off the lifeless body.

She'd been prepared to achieve the Foundation's goals together, but Anton had been too paranoid for that. That paranoia had cost him his life. She was now the nominal leader of the Foundation. She had people counting on her, plans that depended on her. She also knew that there were others, trusted lieutenants of Anton, who'd attempt to unseat her if they found out the method of his death. She'd need help tying up loose ends. The Shadd brothers would make his body disappear.

Once she had total control of the Foundation, America was next.

CHAPTER 12

As the United States and China continue to trade blows, there appears to be little hope of halting the escalation of the conflict. This has potentially grave ramifications for the families of captured US servicemen and women, many of whom have shared with the New York Standard their fears about possible mistreatment or torture of their loved ones. In response to questions from this publication, the Chinese Ambassador to the United States stated that all detained personnel were being treated in line with China's international obligations. This publication—like the rest of the EMCorp family—continues to advocate peace and calls for China to halt its campaign of aggression and allow Taiwan to peacefully join the community of nations.

Editorial, New York Standard, *September 21*

"Turn it off, Peter." Ernest placed his head in his hands. "For heaven's sake, turn it off."

Peter reached over to the laptop and pressed a button to stop the audio recording of Jack Emery and Christian Malley being tortured. The screams of Ernest's staff were visceral and spoke of a deep pain. He'd heard them curse their torturer and cry out for their mothers, for God and for anyone else to help them. To Ernest, it felt as if they called out to him.

They sat in silence, but the recordings he'd heard burned Ernest to his core. Worse still, he knew it was decisions that he'd made that had placed his people in danger. Usually Ernest liked to distance himself from the people under his direction, and he had made decisions before that had ended livelihoods and changed life trajectories. This was different.

He looked up at Peter, who appeared as stunned as Ernest felt. "We have to get them out of there. They're not soldiers or spies. They'll be dead in a couple of weeks under this sort of treatment."

Peter looked down at the floor. "I put in a call to Dan Whelan at Princeton. In his opinion, under such stress, if the Chinese don't relent a little they'll be suffering immense psychological stress. They might not last that long."

Ernest's head was aching. How was he to navigate the release of his people while having to honor agreement he'd made to Dominique and the Foundation? He regretted not telling Peter about the deal, but it was too late to share now. The Chinese, via the ambassador, had made it clear that the way to ensure his people stayed alive was to alter the tone of EMCorp's reporting of the war. He was trapped in a pincer. The only option he liked was the idea of making it somebody else's problem.

"We need to take it to the authorities. Give them the files and whatever support they need. It's the only way to get them out of there."

Peter shrugged. "Who's going to care, with everything else that's going on?"

"We need to do something to help them! I'll call the President."

"You're being irrational. The US Government has more on its mind at the moment."

"We could try the Pentagon? Surely some of their people are being held at the same prison. Get them out, and our people. Two birds with one stone and all that."

"Tried that. Yes, they have people there, but no, they're not going in. With thousands of their own dead, wounded or captured, a few journos don't top their list."

Ernest exhaled loudly. "So we're on our own."

"Everyone is frightened. The hawks want the nukes to come out."

Ernest had considered the chances of government intervention to be slim. His next consideration had been a private operation—mercenaries, who'd blast in, extract his people and get out. But he'd been told that nobody would run a private op in the PRC. He'd even privately asked Dominique to help, to no avail except her howling with laughter.

He sighed and leaned back in his chair. He had to comply with the

Chinese request if he wanted his people back. But maybe there was one other way. He knew that every second he delayed meant more pain for his people, so if he danced the right dance, he could secure their return to the United States. Once that was achieved, he could deal with the consequences of what he was about to do.

He looked at Peter. "Okay, thanks. You've given me a bit to think about."

Peter took the cue to leave the room and started to gather his papers. As he departed, Ernest flicked through his business card holder, picked up his phone and dialed. When the phone was answered, he asked for the ambassador and waited for a couple of minutes with the sound of a local radio station his only company.

Eventually, the music stopped. "This is Ambassador Du."

"It's Ernest McDowell."

"Ah." Ernest could nearly feel Du's grin. "I've been expecting your call, Mr McDowell."

"I'll bet. You sent me the files, after all. I need to speak with your premier."

"I don't know what files you're talking about, but you may speak to me. In this matter, I speak with all the authority you'll need." Du paused. "Off the record, of course."

"If necessary to free my reporters, absolutely."

"I'll keep it short, since time is of the essence. As I mentioned at lunch the other day, your company has become a strategic asset in this conflict. This is of grave concern, made worse by the sheer scale of anti-China coverage in recent days."

Ernest was taken aback by the ambassador's blunt accusation. While his agreement with Dominique had indeed made him pick a side, he hadn't intended for it to manifest itself in quite this way. The coverage of the conflict by EMCorp's stable of media assets had all slanted in a particular direction, in line with Dominique's wishes, but she'd ordered it ramped up hugely. The Chinese had clearly noticed.

"I'll simply say that there were matters beyond my control that amended my attitude on this conflict. I won't apologize, but I'm willing to compromise."

"It was Mao who said, as communists, we gain control with the power of the gun, and maintain control with the power of the pen."

"How can I help with that?"

"We require immediate cessation of your pro-Taiwanese coverage, and a complete reversal of your editorial direction."

"I've been told that a lot in the last few weeks." Ernest laughed. "Do I have any choice?"

"No, not particularly."

"Then your terms are acceptable. Release my people."

"It will be done within twenty-four hours. I've been permitted to authorize travel of your private jet to China pick them up. I'll be in touch."

Du hung up and Ernest exhaled deeply. He'd promised the impossible. But he didn't have a choice, he'd done what was necessary to get his people back, and kicked the problem further down the road. He'd bought time, but his only chance, long term, was to try rework the deal with Dominique. He'd placed the noose tighter around his own neck.

~

A SINGLE SHAFT of light from underneath the door penetrated the darkness of the cell.

For several days now, Jack had mentally clung to it as if it was the final lifeboat on the *Titanic*. The abuse of his body had been nothing compared with the desolation of his mind. He was just glad he could recognize what was happening. But he knew that with each passing second his old life slipped a little farther away. With each beating, each threat to his life, each breakdown, he became more desperate. More despondent.

The door screeched open, and he flinched involuntarily; while he loved the small sliver of light, he feared its growth into a bright inferno. When it did, more abuse was imminent. He pushed himself weakly along the floor of his cell, hoping he might be able to hide.

The guards spoke in Mandarin as they entered the cell. He was surprised when they didn't immediately kick him or hurl insults. Instead, they picked him up off the floor. Each grabbed one of his arms and dragged him from the cell. They handled him firmly, but not too roughly. The possibilities assaulted his brain. More torture? Freedom? Or some other vile option he hadn't considered? Whatever was in store, for at least a minute or two, he'd been spared. What replaced it really didn't matter. While Jack might hope for his freedom, he'd be content with a little sunlight or a day free of pain.

He clearly wasn't to be kept waiting. They reached a steel door and the guard on his left side opened it. Sunlight flared in, stinging his eyes but warming his spirit. He was marched outside and before his eyes could adjust he felt the sharp pain of gravel underneath his bare feet. It crunched under the boots of the guards as they walked, but cut into his skin. Jack kept silent, knowing that any dissent or complaint would be met with brutality. His concerns about small, loose stones were chased away a moment later by the booming sounds of gunshots followed by shouts in Mandarin.

Jack's heart raced. As his eyes adjusted, he could see his fate. A rank of uniformed soldiers stood at attention and in a straight line across the gravel courtyard. Opposite them, a man was heaped, dead, in front of a stone wall. The wall was pockmarked with bullet holes and streaked with blood.

Another man was marched to the wall by a pair of guards. The doomed man didn't fight back, despite being tall and stout enough to try. He stood against the wall. It looked like he'd been beaten half to death, and his face was bloodied and bruised purple. Jack watched in silent horror, determined to cry out in defense of the man but kept in check by his fear. Jack's bladder released as the Chinese officer in charge of the firing squad ordered his men to the ready. His shame, fear and embarrassment trickled down his leg as the order was given. Shots barked out and the man slumped to the ground, a small spray of his blood adding to the grotesque mix on the wall behind.

Jack's shoulders slumped and the guards took up the slack to support his weight. They carried him toward the wall, slowly but with purpose. He did his best to resist, but their grip was strong and his body was weak. The grim procession stopped briefly when a third guard stood in front of Jack and handcuffed his hands to an iron ring in the wall. The guards moved away, chatting to one another.

Despite his best efforts, there was no beating them. He closed his eyes and steeled himself. Many seconds passed, and Jack wondered if he'd passed into blackness already. He was pretty sure he hadn't, however, when a radio crackled and a voice blared out. When the guards nearby laughed with each other, his hunch was confirmed. He heard the footsteps of a guard.

"Not for you today, my friend."

Jack started to sob as they grabbed him again and marched him back inside, relieved that he had been spared, but fearing what was going to replace it. He walked for several minutes, toward whatever fresh abuse was in store for him. He turned or stopped whenever they demanded, and eventually he was facing a steel door. It was not his normal cell. He was kicked inside.

"Jack?" He heard her voice over the slam of the door. "What have they done to you?"

He said nothing as Celeste approached him. He didn't resist as she took his head in her hands and inspected his face like a mother might a recalcitrant, dirty-faced child. He looked at her without word and as she completed her inspection, he did one of his own. She had bruises and injuries too, and looking down, he saw that her clothing was largely torn into useless rags. She was barely covered, and her body had other wounds.

"Eyes up here, mister." She smiled sadly. "I'm glad you're alive, Jack. Though it looks like you've seen better days."

Jack returned his eyes to her, ashamed that his gaze had lingered a little too long on her body. "I thought they'd done the same to you."

"Not quite." She wrapped her arms around him gently, so his wounds wouldn't scream. "They raped me, Jack."

Jack was speechless. He should have expected that, but it didn't make the news any easier to grasp. If they were single-minded in their efforts to break the reporters so that Ernest would agree to their terms, then physical brutality was just one of the available weapons. He pulled back from her embrace and saw she was crying.

He hugged her back. "I'm sorry, Celeste." He didn't know what else to say.

"What was all this for? What does it all mean? We're reporters, for fuck's sake!" She exhaled loudly. "What stopped them?"

"Orders. The torturer made it clear that this was all about getting to Ernest. I think it might have worked."

"Well, whatever the reason, I'm glad to have the company."

They said nothing for a while. He felt human for the first time in days, as safe in her arms as a newborn in its mother's embrace. He felt a mix of relief at being spared Malley's fate and fear of what was still to come, but whatever the next move was going to be, at least he wasn't alone. He hugged her and laughed.

She drew back from him slightly. "What's so funny?"

"I'm in here with you. I could just as easily be slumped outside with a bullet in me."

She nodded and sat on the concrete floor, gesturing for him to sit too. He didn't resist when she gently moved his head to her lap; it felt like a pillow after so many days without sleep. He enjoyed her strokes on his cheeks, and realized it was the first time he'd lay down in days without water, or light, or pain to break up his attempts to sleep.

She leaned in close and whispered in his ear. "Let's just stay sane until we're out."

He closed his eyes. "We might never be out."

$\sim$

CHEN SIGHED as he looked through the night-vision binoculars. He'd spent several hours on his stomach and now the front of his clothing was cold and damp. It was a less than glamorous way to spend an evening, but it was vital to getting in and out with his head still on his shoulders and with the information he needed.

The men guarding Anton Clark's house were in sight. The amount of security made Chen's job harder. More warm bodies moving about always did. The guards were all part of a small security detail that kept Anton's family and property free from threat, though it had done nothing to protect him from Michelle Dominique sticking a pen in his eye. He knew they could outgun anything he had access to at such short notice. He couldn't worry too much about that, but he could stay hidden and hope his superior training would win out if he was seen. He was just glad that Dominique had managed to craft a story about Anton being overseas on business. The cover seemed to have held up.

He put the binoculars down and pulled himself up to his knees. He brushed his gloved hands over the front of him, removing the leaves and other natural detritus from his clothes. Within a few seconds he'd placed the binoculars in one of the many pockets on his combat vest and zipped it closed. Taking mental stock of his equipment, Chen made sure nothing was loose and he hadn't dropped anything on the ground. His Heckler and Koch USP Tactical pistol was loaded in its holster on his right hip. On his other hip, he had a small combat knife. Most importantly, among all sorts of utility equipment that he might need in the vest pockets, he had a pair of USB drives.

Chen took a deep breath and started off. He drew his pistol and walked as quickly as he could through the scrub. It took ten minutes to reach the first difficult part—the road. He took another breath, looked both ways, crouched as low as he could and walked rapidly across. When he was just near the base of the wall, he heard a small scrape to his left. He turned with alarm at the sound, raised his handgun toward the noise and pressed his finger slightly on the trigger.

He released the trigger immediately when he saw a boy, probably about thirteen, in the very dim light, staring at him with wide eyes. Chen cursed that he hadn't seen the boy during his reconnaissance, but it didn't matter now. He lowered his pistol slightly and quickly approached the boy. He was frozen, so Chen reached out and put a gloved hand over his mouth. The boy tensed and no doubt feared the worst as Chen crouched down towards him.

He put his mouth close to the boy's ear. "You look old enough to realize what's at stake."

The boy nodded vigorously and gave a barely audible moan.

"I need you to keep calm. You'll be fine and home with your mother tonight if you do. But I need you to be quiet. Understand?"

The boy nodded again.

Chen slowly removed his hand from the boy's mouth, and to his relief the boy said nothing and didn't move an inch. He could use him. Chen dug in his pocket, pulled out a few hundred dollars and held the money up in front of the boy. Eyes wide with recognition, the boy's eyes flicked back and forth between the cash and Chen's face.

"You can have all of this if you listen very carefully. In a few minutes I want you to throw some coins I'll give you over the fence, right there." He pointed to the compound.

"Okay." The boy's voice was barely a whisper. He seemed to relax a little now that his life was not in immediate danger and there was the promise of a large amount of cash. Americans—always about the profit. He handed the boy the wad of cash and a few coins. He squeezed the boy's hand shut around the coins, lest he drop them.

"Count to one hundred and eighty, then throw the coins."

"Okay." The boy smiled. "Easy."

Chen hadn't planned on this, but he could use it to his advantage. Anton's guards had a timed routine that took them around the property every thirteen minutes. Chen needed them to be as far from the house as possible and the coins would help delay them when they were.

"Once it's done you need to run straight home. Don't stay near here and don't tell anyone about me. You found the money."

The boy nodded and started to move to where Chen had pointed. Chen wasted no time, leaving the boy and creeping along the wall. He stopped just short of one of the gates. He hugged the wall and waited. He hoped that Dominique's hacker had taken out the cameras. He was alert to any sound, hopeful that the coins would land on the ground inside and distract the guards for an extra few seconds. The coast would be clear.

He looked at the watch on his wrist, which he'd synced with the watch given to the boy. Once the clock hit three minutes, he sprang into action. Chen hoped the boy had done his job and was long gone, but he didn't spare him another thought. He tried the gate latch with one hand. It was locked, but it took only a second for him to pick. He pushed the gate open.

He followed a preplanned route across the garden and to the house that should get him to the target of the entire expedition: the computer in Anton's study. He thought he might make it without incident until he rounded a corner and found two very surprised security guards.

As Chen's gun came up, the guards froze in place and started to draw their pistols. He knew it was the automatic response of most American law enforcement and security personnel, when they should have sought cover. It was their deadly mistake. His own pistol was on them before either hand reached a holster.

He fired two shots at the first guard; a sound akin to compressed air being released and the pattering of two spent bullet cases dancing across the hardwood were the only evidence. The guard didn't get the chance to make much more than a muffled gurgle as a bullet penetrated his throat, severing the carotid. The second bullet hit him in the chest.

The other guard continued to draw his weapon as Chen brought his own pistol onto target. The man's fate was sealed by his instinctive look to his left, where his colleague had just been. The man looked back to Chen, his eyes wide, before Chen put a bullet between them. The guard dropped limp, and his gun fell from his hands.

Chen moved quickly to the two men. One was clearly dead, while the other writhed on the expensive hardwood floor as his lifeblood escaped from his throat, forming a crimson pool next to him. Chen put a bullet in his head. He took both their weapons and threw them into the pot of a houseplant.

After a few more corners he reached the home office and pushed the door open. The room was empty. Chen closed the door behind him, moved to the computer and sat at the horribly modern glass desk. The laptop blinked on when he opened the lid. He clicked on Anton's username and entered the password. An hourglass appeared for a second and then a chime sounded. He was glad Dominique had been right about the password. He grabbed the two USB sticks from his pocket.

He inserted his own USB first and copied the documents folder from Anton's computer onto it. Chen turned and trained his pistol on the door, but nobody interrupted him for the minute or so it took the job to complete. Once the dump was complete, he pulled out the first USB and inserted the second. Automatically, an algorithm was activated and started the attack, just as Dominique had promised. When it had finished its work, he pulled it out of its slot and the computer went to sleep. Nobody would ever know he'd touched it.

He smiled at the wizardry of it all as he put the sticks in his pocket, then moved to the study door. Anton's computer had been savaged. Dominique would now have all the files she'd need to run the Foundation, along with any of Anton's secrets. A few pesky files that she'd wanted destroyed were gone, too, while others had been planted.

Chen had paid her back for extracting his family from Taiwan and now had all of Anton's documents as insurance.

Within five minutes he'd be back in the trees. He'd be home in Wisconsin in a day.

CHAPTER 13

CHINA LAUNCHES ALL OUT MISSILE AND AIR ATTACK ON TAIWAN!
After a week of high tension and tactical strikes, the island of Taiwan woke this morning to the sound of jet engines and the heat of explosions, as China launched the heaviest attacks yet in the conflict. The United States Air Force and ground-based missile defense units failed to halt the onslaught, leaving Taipei heavily damaged. China has reportedly delivered a letter to the United States Ambassador in Beijing. Reuters has learned that this letter was a guarantee that China will not use nuclear weapons. Despite this, it may only be a matter of time before China launches a full-scale invasion.
Correspondents, Reuters, September 28

Jack couldn't hear the explosion, but he could feel the heat of it. He was unable to escape, surrounded by fire. He looked around. Celeste was next to him, mouth open in mute terror, no words able to escape. Others were flailing their arms. One man, Jack didn't know him, had a shard of steel through his stomach that he gripped and tried to pull out, just as they plunged into the icy water of the South China Sea.

Jack's eyes shot open and he sat up on the air mattress. He winced in pain and rubbed his eyes, confused. A second ago he'd been on the Seahawk as it plunged into the ocean, but now he was in his hotel room. He exhaled deeply and lay down. Never before had the cobweb on the plain white ceiling that housekeeping never got around to cleaning been such a welcome sight. He was home.

"You awake?" Celeste stirred on the bed. "You okay?"

"Sorry."

She smiled. "It's alright. Anyone ever tell you you snore really loudly?"

"Every friend, roommate and girlfriend since puberty." He laughed. "Erin, too."

He felt a small measure of regret as her smile disappeared, replaced by a frown. "Which one this time? The Chinese cell?"

"Nope, the chopper just as the destroyer blew up. We hit the ocean and I wake up." Jack snorted. "I guess I don't like the cold even in my dreams."

Celeste laughed softly. "At least your mind gives you a bit of variety in the nightmares."

Jack was more glad than ever that Celeste had offered to stay at his hotel room once they'd arrived back in the States. Ostensibly it had been to look after him, but he did not doubt that she welcomed the company and support as well. Neither of them had family in America, and Celeste had sold him on the idea of sticking together. He'd agreed, on the condition that she took the better bed.

He turned his head to look up at her. "What were you treated with last night?"

"The rape." She didn't open her eyes. "Again."

"I'm sorry, Celeste."

"Wasn't you doing it."

That much was true. While Jack's nightmares ranged from the helicopter going down, the variety of torture he'd received and others that didn't make much sense, Celeste had only one. The rape. He struggled up, his body screaming in pain the whole time, and sat on the edge of her bed. He placed a hand on her shoulder and she finally looked at him.

"I'm here if you want to talk about it."

She smiled weakly. "I don't want to add to your smorgasbord of head-fuckery."

He squeezed her shoulder. "Try me."

She stared at him for a long moment, seeming to size him up, then nodded slightly. "On the first night, three men entered and stripped me naked."

Jack immediately felt uncomfortable. "You don't have to talk about this if it's too hard."

She stared at the wall, not even acknowledging that she'd heard him. "They laughed at me and took my clothes. The next day, they returned and did it."

"Did what?"

"They held me down. They watched one another." Her bottom lip quivered slightly, and Jack placed his arm around her. "The third day was the worst. Objects..."

Jack closed his eyes. "I'm sorry, Celeste."

"Like I said, not your fault." Her voice trailed off. "They returned my clothes just before they threw you in with me. I knew then that something must have happened."

"Yeah. Ernest gave them whatever they were after."

She nodded, and closed her eyes again.

Jack still hadn't managed to speak with Ernest McDowell, despite his best efforts. From the prison, they'd been taken along with Christian Malley to a private airfield, placed aboard an EMCorp jet and flown home. They'd eaten, been looked over by a whole team of medical personnel and slept for hours on end. Once they'd landed, the two of them had been chauffeured to the hotel. But his calls to McDowell had been for naught.

He laid down on the bed beside Celeste, who was already asleep. He reached over to the side table and found his phone and earphones. He listened to the news, and felt a sense of hurt that the radio announcer who prattled away in his ear didn't interrupt the broadcast to curse the world on his behalf. Jack had learned that no matter how long you spent in bed, it took a great deal of time to heal when you had been abused.

At least this morning there was some fresh news—as depressing as it was—about the attacks on Taiwan. For the past week the US and Chinese airforces had danced with each other, but been unable to deliver a killing blow. That had apparently changed this morning—half of Taipei had been hit.

At some point he must have dozed off, because he woke up with a new program in his ears and a mouth as dry as the Sahara. He sighed, removed the earphones and did his best to sit upright. He reached for a glass of water, took a mouthful and placed it back. He let his head collapse onto the pillow and cursed under his breath at the spike of pain.

In the week spent at the hotel, he'd been able to gather his thoughts.

It felt like he'd taken only a few breaths in the last month, given the incredible speed at which events had spiraled out of control. The divorce. The bombings. Erin's death. The sinking of the USS *George Washington*. His torture. The war between China and Taiwan. He felt like he was at the center of it all.

His phone rang. He picked it up off the side table. "Hello?"

"Hi, Jack? Peter Weston calling."

Jack frowned, unsure why Ernest McDowell's assistant was calling him. He switched the call to speaker. "Hi, Peter."

"How're you feeling?"

Jack laughed. "It's a regular party town over here. Come over if you like, but don't forget the scotch."

Peter laughed. "Maybe another time? Ernest wanted me to invite you and a guest to the company box at the Yankees playoff game. If you're feeling up to it by then."

Jack didn't even consider it for a moment. "Baseball tickets? Not for me. Stupid sport. But thanks anyway."

"You sure? They're expensive tickets." There was a note of incredulity in Peter's voice. "Ernest would appreciate it if you could make it."

Jack was about to decline for the second time when Celeste shoved him lightly. He looked at her and she gave him a thumbs up. He'd have hell to pay if he didn't accept. He reasoned that it would probably be worth it if it took her mind off her experiences, even for an afternoon.

"Alright, I'll be there. I'll be bringing along Celeste Adams." Jack looked at Celeste. Her eyes had grown wide and she nodded vigorously. He smiled at her.

"Great. Someone will email you the details. I'll give Celeste a call and invite her if you like."

Jack paused. "She accepts."

"I'm sure she will." Peter sounded confused. "But I'll still have to call."

"Celeste is here, she accepts."

Celeste leaned into the phone. "Hi, Peter."

Weston was silent for just a second too long. "Oh, well, you two have fun."

"Plan to. Speak later, Peter, thanks." Jack hung up.

"Plan to what?"

"Nothing. But he thinks we're fucking."

Celeste went beet red, then punched him in the arm again, lightly, before lying down with a sigh. "Thanks a lot. You've really done wonders for my career there, Jack."

"You'll just have to impress him at the game."

Jack rolled onto his back and closed his eyes. He was content to be warm and safe for the time being. He'd recuperate, mourn for Erin and then work out what came next. Hopefully it would include getting his life back on track. It wasn't much of a plan, but it was enough for now.

"I love baseball." Celeste rolled over. "It's going to be wonderful."

"It's going to be horrible."

~

ERNEST CLOSED the lid of his laptop with too much force. It slammed shut, causing the ice in the glass next to the computer to jingle a little. He let out a long sigh as he swung back in the leather chair, closed his eyes and massaged his temples. He'd been at his desk for fourteen hours, trying to catch up on work that had piled up in the past few weeks. The days spent dealing with the Senate committee and the EMCorp board, the negotiations with Michelle Dominique and China—and freeing his people—had put him behind with everything else.

But what had finally broken him for the day was a pair of emails he'd only reached a minute ago. One, from Dominique, suggested a particular line on the next day's coverage, while another, from the Chinese, suggested a different approach. While the emails were couched in polite terms and carefully manicured to appear appropriate if they fell into the wrong hands, he knew they weren't suggestions at all. For Ernest, there could be no clearer illustration of the prison he'd engineered for himself.

He didn't regret the choices he'd made at various points to save himself, his company and his staff. He consoled himself with the fact that, in a time of great stress, he'd done what he'd had to do. Not everyone in his position would have. But the deal with the Chinese, on the back of the one with Dominique, had placed him in an impossible bind. He felt the agreements strangling the life out of him.

He'd hoped the arrangement would last a little longer, but it wouldn't. He felt old, and knew that if there was to be a reckoning for the decisions he'd made, it may as well be now. With another sigh, he opened his eyes and reached for the phone on the desk. He dialed in a number he'd committed to memory and switched the call to loudspeaker. The phone rang and Ernest used this time to steel himself for the coming conversation.

"Hello, Ernest." Dominique's tone was impatient. "I hope this is important."

"It is. I need to renegotiate our deal."

She gave a small laugh. "Why would you need to do that?"

He rubbed his head. "I'm in a hopeless situation, but I want to honor both our agreement and another I've made. I can only do that if you're flexible."

There was a pause. "Being flexible wouldn't really be in my interests, Ernest, nor would it lead to you honoring our agreement in any way. My terms were clear. I delivered. The Senate inquiry has gone away and your company is off the hook in the United States. I expect you to continue to live up to your end of the bargain."

Any hope he'd had for a reasonable negotiation was out the window. "I had all good intentions of honoring my agreement with you, but things have changed."

She laughed again. "The Chinese? Yes, Ernest."

He was genuinely shocked. "You know? How?"

"I know you made a deal with the Chinese, that's clear. I don't know why, nor do I care."

He changed the topic. "I don't like being backed into corners and forced into impossible decisions I don't want to make."

"I know." She sounded chirpy again. "And it's precisely why I used the Senate inquiry to bait you. And now you're mine, to be blunt."

"What I'm proposing will help you retain some day-to-day control over editorial direction. It's the best I can offer."

"Not interested."

"I suggest you think again. You've got me, but I do have the means to slip your net. If I step down from the board entirely, then you're left with nothing."

She laughed. "Oh, I love the fishing analogies. Let's keep those going. Think of me as a fisherman, which I'm not, by the way. I've just caught a whale—that's you—and now it's struggling on the hook, fighting to get free. At the same time, the whale—that's you, remember —got your tail caught on *another* hook—the Chinese."

Ernest was growing tired of her, but hid his annoyance. "I don't quite understand the point."

"The point is: I've caught the big daddy, the trophy. I don't care what else happens, there's no way I'm letting go, no matter how much it wriggles. The Chinese can rip your fucking tail off, but your head and your company are mine. I'll rip your head off if I have to, but you're not getting away."

He swung back in his chair again while he thought. He ran through as many scenarios as possible, but he saw no other option than to break faith with one side. Having decided that, it became an exercise in risk assessment: while crossing Dominique would cause him pain, crossing the Chinese government in the current climate was unthinkable. He'd take the angry wolf pack over an angry dragon.

"Ernest?" She sounded annoyed. "Is that all?"

He gave a long sigh. "Yes. We're done unless you're willing to negotiate. Contact me."

"You've got little time to change your mind, Ernest. Don't throw everything away."

He was about to reply when the call cut out.

～

MICHELLE SWIRLED the amber liquid around in the tumbler then brought it up to her nose. She inhaled the scent of the whisky before lifting it to her lips and taking a small sip, then another. When her glass was empty, she leaned forward and placed it on the table. She smiled and leaned back, looking down the length of the table at the assembled men and women, each the leader of a Foundation cell. For all intents and purposes, this was the entire leadership of the Foundation now that Anton was gone.

"Anton is dead."

She kept a passive face as the cell leaders digested the news. A few gasped, another swore under his breath and the others just stared at her or looked around the table. She waited as the news sank in and for the most animated of them to regain their composure.

The leader of the Foundation's West Coast cell, Vanessa Dunstan, leaned forward. "How? Why weren't we told right away?"

Michelle considered her response. She knew that if there was going to be civil war among the Foundation in the aftermath of her actions, it would be led from California. Dunstan and her cell were the furthest from the Foundation's power centers of Washington and New York, both geographically and ideologically. She'd opposed some of the more extreme methods employed in recent years, and made no secret of it.

"I didn't want anything captured electronically." Michelle shrugged. "I also decided it was better to bring everyone together to sort out succession quickly and cleanly."

Dunstan rolled her eyes. "I bet you did. You still haven't answered the how."

Michelle knew that Dunstan had been close to Anton, and that intimacy had kept her adventures at least partially in check over the years. While it was unlikely that Michelle would get the same level of cooperation, she also knew that there was no sense hiding from the truth. Some of it, anyway. They could never know the real reason she'd killed him: that he'd tried to take her out, and she'd taken control as a result.

"I killed him." She looked Dunstan straight in the eye. Her tone was even, completely matter of fact. "I discovered evidence that he was acting unilaterally to explode a nuclear device in Cleveland, and paint Islamic fundamentalists as responsible."

The room erupted. Michelle had wondered if any of them would assault her, though she had a fully armed Andrei Shadd a shout away. The usually reserved head of the Midwest cell, Mike Douglas, tapped his finger on the table, increasingly loudly, to get the attention of the room.

Once the room was silent, he spoke. "And why would he do that?"

"I don't know, but if he'd succeeded, it would have diverted the attention of the President and his administration from the war with China, and placed America's sight on the wrong target. It also would have made a mess of our efforts to get a large number of us into Congress."

Douglas nodded. "It sure fucking would have."

"We've wasted a decade and trillions fighting in meaningless deserts, more of that needs to be avoided."

A look of grave doubt appeared on Dunstan's face, her forehead creasing with stress lines. "Very well, if it's as you say, it needed to be done. I trust you have proof?"

Michelle shrugged. "Plenty—I'll make it available to you all after the meeting. I regret it, but my actions were necessary. We set it up to look like a street assault."

Dunstan nodded. None of the others spoke up. She'd won.

"Very well, if there's nothing else on that matter, we need to elect a director. There are too many balls in the air to not have someone in charge of the juggling."

There were nods up and down the table. The people gathered were used to quick-moving situations. Anton's death was forgotten.

The head of the New England cell, Bruno Cagliari, cleared his throat. "I'd like to nominate Michelle. She has the experience, contacts and the most in-depth knowledge of our current operations. Our cause will thrive or die on the success of a plan she and Anton developed. I throw New England's lot in with her."

Michelle gave Cagliari a barely perceptible nod. He'd be rewarded later. "Thanks, Bruno. I accept the nomination, but I'd also invite others to put their hand up."

She looked down the length of the table and the representatives remained silent. She had them. Apparently the weight of her claim, along with the lack of support from the others, had aborted any power play by Dunstan. She felt the rewards were finally coming her way, after so long and so much planning. When no other nomination came forward, others began to swear their cells over to her.

"The Mid-Atlantic cell is yours."

"The South East is on board with the new administration."

Michelle had a nervous moment when the leaders of the South and Midwest cells, Duke Callister and Mike Douglas, shared a wordless exchange. They were traditionalists and the staunchest conservatives, even in a room full of them, and she was not sure they'd go for a woman who'd just murdered the boss. Finally, Callister leaned in and whispered something in Douglas' ear. Michelle exhaled deeply when Douglas nodded.

Duke Callister spoke for the two of them. "If this evidence is as compelling as you say it is, Michelle, we're on side. But you'd better hope it is."

She nodded and smiled at him. "It is. I appreciate your support, Duke."

Michelle knew she was close, all she needed was the Mountain cell and Dunstan's West Coast. With the others on board—and the South in particular—she knew they didn't have the strength to resist her control. She looked at Dunstan and then at Mark Harrison, head of the Mountain cell.

Harrison looked at Dunstan, then shrugged. "Okay, but I don't like it. You've got an inch of wriggle room, Michelle."

That left Dunstan. Michelle stared at her, right down the other end of the table. "Vanessa?"

Dunstan sighed. "Okay."

Michelle was elated, but didn't show her emotion. "Okay. Next order of business is an update from the director. In short, everything is on track and we're about to see the rewards. We're unblemished by Shanghai and the war has started nicely. The next part of our plan is more of us in Congress. I'd ask that you all focus your efforts on that."

Dunstan scoffed. "I never understood this part of the plan, and how you expect the media to warm to our agenda, given their lack of enthusiasm in the past."

"Easy. Through control of EMCorp. Which I've had for the last few weeks."

She smiled, and enjoyed their reaction. They were more shocked by this news than they'd been about Anton's death. She omitted the fact that the head of EMCorp was being a particularly large pain in her behind and might slip loose. This was no time to dilute her authority or have them doubt her achievements.

She stood and held her hands out. "We've got our endgame within reach and now we've got the means to broadcast exactly what we want."

Douglas nodded and crossed his arms. Cagliari smiled. Even Vanessa Dunstan looked content as she spoke. "Well done, Michelle."

"Right, now that's covered, I think it's a good time to take a five-minute break. We'll discuss regular business after that."

She didn't wait for agreement. She left the room, aware that nobody else had moved. As soon as she was outside, they'd be gossiping about the changed environment, but she had control. Once out of earshot, she pulled her phone from her purse and dialed.

Through her friendship with Sarah McDowell, Michelle had put contingencies in place for controlling EMCorp if Ernest got out of control. Now she was ascendant in the Foundation, she couldn't risk him following through on his threats from earlier in the day. Losing EMCorp after announcing it was in hand would be a loss of prestige with her colleagues. It would also make achieving her agenda all the more difficult. Better to cut her losses. If she couldn't have him, nobody could.

"Chen? It's me. I need you on a flight to New York. I've got another job for you."

She hung up. Just as the Foundation meeting was about to reconvene, she wrote a quick text. *Sarah, let's catch up, I've got some wonderful news for you.*

CHAPTER 14

As the war continues to escalate between the armed forces of the United States and China, Americans pause for a few hours today for the beginning of the Major League Baseball playoffs. The build-up has been subdued this year, but that's done nothing to dull the excitement of the New York Yankees fans, who are out in force to cheer on their home-town team against the visiting Red Sox. This year's coverage will include crosses to US troops serving in Taiwan, in Japan and on ships in the South China Sea, and the broadcast will include a special tribute to their service.

Michael Pompei, Chicago Tribune, *October 5*

J ack was impressed. While he'd only agreed to attend the first game of the American League Division Series out of a sense of obligation to Ernest, since he'd arrived at Yankee Stadium with Celeste they'd each had a smile on their faces. It seemed like the perfect way to finish their recovery. While the nightmares of their torture remained, some of the physical damage had healed. Jack felt almost human again.

Once a stadium staff member had spotted the lanyards they were wearing, they'd been escorted to the cavernous EMCorp corporate suite. Jack felt like some sort of king as they walked through the double doors, even though he knew the service being heaped upon him was only because of the color of his pass.

He turned to Celeste. "Pretty impressive, isn't it?"

The suite was deep and rectangular, with floor-to-ceiling glass on one side showing off the field. On the far wall was a full-service bar. Guests had a choice of sitting at one of the dozen or so dining tables or in the leather recliners along the window with a view of the field. The room was already full, though it was over an hour until the opening pitch.

"Sure is." Celeste beamed as she eyed the bar. "It's going to be great. Want a drink?"

Jack hesitated. "You go ahead."

She smiled and left him. A few months earlier, he'd have been up for the free booze. Now, he just wanted to sit in a corner, out of the way, until the game started. He avoided the large huddles of people making small talk and ignored the glances from the other guests as he crossed the room. Those who knew him were probably curious about his wellbeing, but he didn't want to talk to anyone at the moment.

He nearly managed to find his way to a table and sit down when he was intercepted by a tall man with a broad smile and newsreader good looks, who stretched out his hand. "Warwick Jenkins. I work at the *Boston Herald*. You're Jack Emery, right? Hell of a story, you making it off that carrier."

Jack was surprised that Jenkins knew so much, given the details of their release had been tightly guarded. Jack watched the man's eyes drift to the cuts and bruises on his face. For the first time, he knew how an attractive woman felt. Jenkins' roaming eyes felt like an assault that he was powerless to stop without being rude. He didn't know Jenkins, but if he was here then he was important to Ernest.

Jack gave his best attempt at a smile and shook Jenkins' hand. "Just lucky, I guess. Lots of guys didn't make it."

"You're just modest, son."

Jack tried to change the topic. "Surprised you're not in the office, if not for the injuries, I'm sure I'd be missing the game."

"The war? We've got that covered. I don't miss a Red Sox playoff game for anything short of nuclear winter. You watch, tonight the war will be number two on the news." Jenkins laughed. "Say, I'd love you to meet my wife. We're suckers for an Australian accent. Spent some time in Sydney a few years ago."

Jack's mind was scrambling to find an excuse when Ernest appeared alongside them. It was the first time Jack had seen him since his return from China. He nearly blurted out his thanks. Though he knew the price for his release must have been high, he didn't know exactly what Ernest had had to agree to. He intended to find out and somehow repay him, but for now he needed to stay professional.

Ernest patted him on the back. "Hi, Warwick, good to see you. Jack, I'd like you to meet someone, he'll be here in a minute."

Jenkins clearly knew how to take a hint. "Mr McDowell, good to see you, and Jack, good to meet you. Let's talk soon."

Jack exhaled and smiled at Ernest as Jenkins backed away from the conversation. "Thanks for the intervention."

Ernest patted him on the shoulder. "Don't mention it. I didn't invite you here to be a social piñata. How are you, Jack?"

Jack hesitated, unsure how to answer. "I'm out of there, thanks to you, that's what counts. I wanted to say thanks."

"Don't mention it."

Jack leaned in closer. "I have a fair idea why I was tortured. What did they extract out of you to secure my release?"

Ernest's eyes narrowed and he started to say something, but hesitated. "That's not your concern, Jack. Relax and enjoy yourself. I need to find my daughter."

～

CHEN CEASED his climb up the ladder and opened the access hatch as quietly as possible. He pulled himself through, closed the hatch carefully and locked it behind him. He had plenty of time to prepare. The day had gone to plan and he was slightly ahead of schedule with the game about to start.

He walked to the far side of the space. The walls were covered in dust and grime, as well as an amusing cartoon some tradesman had made years ago, presumably of his employer. He was glad to see the case he needed was on the concrete floor. He next looked to the small ventilation hatch on one wall and saw the key to the whole plan—the height and breadth of view the steel grate provided. It was as perfect as Michelle Dominique's representative has promised.

Following the job at Anton Clark's house, he'd agreed to her request for one more piece of wet work. In his head, he'd owed her one job for saving his family and another for saving him after the Shanghai attacks. If she'd wanted to, she could have hung them out to dry. Chen was an honorable man. He paid his debts. After this, they'd be square.

The space allowed one of the most breathtaking views in the entire stadium, from a location few knew about and even fewer visited. Importantly, it also gave a clear view to some of the corporate suites. He knew all of this thanks to the briefing pack that had been provided, along with his rifle and uniform. He thought again about his disguise. An amazing beast, the cleaner, often maligned, never considered. Invisible. He'd moved his way through the stadium and to his perch without being questioned.

He moved to the case and opened it. He took in the beauty of one of the tools of his trade. It was pristine, cold and deadly, even disassembled into a half-dozen pieces. The long-barreled sniper rifle was as clean and beautiful as the day it had been manufactured. South African by design, it was light and portable, its sight able to zoom many times the magnification of the human eye. Most importantly, Chen had used it before and considered it suitable to cover the mission.

He assembled the weapon in silence and worked through all possible scenarios in his head. He mentally rehearsed the shot and how he'd escape from the scene. He could count on a few seconds of paralyzed fear that would grip the crowd and the authorities alike. If all went to plan, it should be a relatively easy job. In and out quickly.

If not, then all bets were off.

As he slid the gun onto its tripod, he didn't think for a second about the life of the man about to be snuffed out. He'd done something to irritate the wrong people, and that was it. To Chen, it was a business transaction, as normal as ordering dinner. He owed Michele Dominique one more job, and this was her chosen payment.

With the gun in place he stripped off his janitor's uniform and changed into some New York Yankees gear. All was now in place for the job to proceed. He slid up alongside the weapon, looked down the sight and touched his finger lightly on the trigger. He slowed his breathing and waited with well-practiced patience for the right time.

∼

ERNEST SHOOK hands with Claire Paine and left the conversation. Paine was a political reporter he'd been trying to poach for a while, but since she'd won a Pulitzer the price had gone up. She'd declined Ernest's latest offer, so Ernest saw no point in continuing to talk to her.

He walked to the bar and asked for a whisky. As it was poured, he mused darkly about the last phone call he'd shared with Michelle Dominique. She hadn't been happy at his request to revise their deal, and it had been several days since he'd heard from her. His attempts to contact her had been fruitless.

He needed to think about something else. He scanned the room and smiled as he watched his daughter fend off the advances of the latest young suitor. Since Sarah had abruptly lost interest in the Wharton grad she'd been dating, word had reached every young, eligible bachelor on the East Coast. Even here, among friends, she was targeted.

While it would have been easy for him to march over and rain fire and brimstone down on the young, overly drunk EMCorp sales executive, he waited. He'd learned long ago that she could take care of herself, and there was no point in ruining a promising career unless it was absolutely necessary.

As her suitor leaned in to whisper something into her ear, he also placed his hand on the small of Sarah's back. The hand then began to trend downward. Ernest recognized a grope when he saw one and felt a flash of anger. Sarah was wearing a conservative gray tunic dress, but that clearly wasn't enough to dissuade those intending ill. As soon as the hand reached ground zero, Sarah took a step back and swung her small purse right into the exec's face. He didn't get his free hand up in time to defend the shot, but he did remove his other hand from her backside without delay. Sarah glowered at him and he backed away, mumbling some sort of apology.

Ernest chuckled and picked his whisky up from the bar. As he walked over to his daughter, he reflected on her fire and her focus— traits they shared. Despite this, he hadn't managed to focus her in the same direction as he had taken. While he'd been driven to succeed in business, Sarah was interested in art and theater.

"You okay?" He leaned in to kiss her on the cheek. "I hope you're not getting into too much mischief."

Her eyebrows furrowed in mock contempt. "It's your staff trying to get me into mischief. It's like they see a big dollar sign above my head or something."

He laughed. "Not quite. More likely they see a dollar sign above my head and a big green arrow pointing at me above yours. I'm an old man, after all. Won't last forever."

"Don't be stupid." She punched him softly on the arm. "Besides, you better last a few more years yet, because I sure as hell don't want your company."

He thought about saying something, but decided against it. They'd had that particular argument a few too many times. "Enjoying yourself?"

She shrugged and smiled. "Prefer Broadway."

He laughed. Truth be told, he hadn't really enjoyed the pre-game reception and the meal. His mind was on other things and he couldn't escape the crushing knowledge that a reckoning was coming. He was playing with fire, and it was only a matter of time before he got burned.

His gloom was penetrated by the mighty roar in the stadium, which seeped through the glass windows of the suite. A few of his guests shushed others as the stadium announcer gave some cheesy tribute to the American troops currently battling the Chinese in the skies above Taiwan. Once the announcer was finished, the national anthem was sung.

A short while later the game started. Ernest watched the first Yankees hitter put one into the stands. The reaction on the field seemed subdued compared to the scenes in the crowd, as grown men jumped up and spilled their eight-dollar beers and cold burgers. A few of the guests in the EMCorp skybox cheered and one Red Sox fan groaned, but most gave it little thought, continuing to chat and enjoy the hospitality.

"Wow, that was awesome." Sarah laughed.

He had a momentary pang of regret, and thought for a moment that he should have just taken his daughter to the game and jettisoned the freeloaders. The thought passed quickly. As much as he loved his daughter, it was commercial necessity that he use the box widely for events like this.

He turned to Sarah and smiled. "Plenty of time left for some more fireworks."

CHEN THOUGHT it would have been all too easy to pull the trigger the moment Ernest McDowell entered the crosshairs. The amateur—or immature—killer might have taken the shot, which was both simple and inviting. Even some professionals would have been hard pressed to turn down one of the easiest kills of their careers.

But those weren't the instructions.

At the crux of it, he knew that despite the veneer of legitimacy and professional standards of the special forces, retired or not, he was paid to kill people and break stuff. The same colleagues who would have taken the shot, though, were thugs; they had no restraint, no appreciation for detail or the art of their trade.

He was different. He followed specifications exactly. It was the reason he'd kept vigil on Ernest McDowell for forty minutes, not taking the first shot, but waiting for the best one. A perfect shot that not only produced the desired result, but gave the best chance for escape from the scene with minimum fuss.

He'd watched McDowell enjoy the highs and suffer the lows of the game so far alongside his daughter. McDowell seemed to pay no attention to the hangers-on who were also in the box. One innings had passed, and then another, until finally the time to strike had come.

With little emotion, Chen made sure his breathing was slow and waited. He had a perfect understanding of his weapon and his finger pressed on the trigger as much as possible without firing. He applied slow pressure until the precise moment. He was a hair's breadth away from his final squeeze when he aborted the shot.

McDowell's daughter had wrapped her arms around him for a hug. He eased off on the trigger and readjusted his aim slightly. He inhaled deeply, and then exhaled. He took the new target profile into account, inhaled again, and as he exhaled he squeezed the trigger slowly. This time it was enough to fire the weapon.

He nearly screamed. The girl had fucked it up. He could see the small spray of fine red mist through his sight and knew the shot had hit. But even as the man fell limp a moment after the round struck home, and chaos and confusion erupted in the box, he knew the shot was off: the girl had punched McDowell on the arm just as Chen had fired.

The movement had been enough to put the shot through McDowell's neck, instead of the center of his head. He knew it would probably still be enough to do the job, but it was not the perfection he sought.

～

JACK FROZE. His mind was screaming in protest at the scene in front of him, only vaguely aware of his glass of Coke falling to the ground. Each second felt like an eternity, and all he could seem to recognize was the clunking of the ice on the floor and the slosh of the liquid on the carpet.

His immediate instinct in that first second or two was to run, but as the others in the suite began to scream and run away from the source of the violence, he stood still. His feet felt like they were set in cement, refusing to move forward, as much as his mind refused to let him run away.

A woman's voice called out in distress: "Somebody fucking help my dad!"

Jack's feet started to move, his vision widening and life speeding up again. Past the panicked guests who were rushing right at him, he saw several people huddled around a figure on the floor. He had a sinking feeling he knew who it was and what had happened. He had to help.

He turned to Celeste. "Get out of here!"

He didn't wait for an answer as he broke into a run. His legs moved faster with each step as he ran the length of the function room. A few times he had to push his way forcefully through the crowd, and the closer he got the more chaos there was. Jack's mind had not had so much to process since China.

Ernest McDowell was on his back, writhing in pain and surrounded by blood. His daughter Sarah and a few others were crowded over him, while Peter Weston was shouting for help. When Jack reached Ernest's side he fell to his knees. Ernest was gulping for air, but when he saw Jack his eyes bulged wider than Jack thought possible.

Jack grimaced. "Ernest, just take it easy, help is nearly here."

Ernest tried to speak, but the gurgling sound that emerged from his throat sounded as if he were trying to suck all the air from the room.

"Where's the fucking help, Peter? He's going to bleed to death." Jack looked up to Sarah. "And someone get her out of here, she doesn't need to see this."

Ernest coughed and tried to speak again, but all that came out was a gargling sound. Jack didn't know much about medicine, but the very dark blood running down Ernest's neck and mouth was not a good sign. Jack's eyes widened in surprise as Celeste slid down beside him and put her hand over the wound to stem the bleeding.

"I told you to get out of here!" He stared at her. "It's not safe!"

Celeste gave him a dark look. "He saved me too, Jack."

"They're here!" Peter's voice sounded relieved. "The paramedics are here."

Jack looked up. A pair of paramedics were rushing to Ernest's side.

One of them kneeled and took over from Celeste, placing a gloved hand over the wound. The other waved them all away.

"We'll take it from here, everyone. You all need to step back."

Jack started to climb to his feet and back away, but felt someone squeeze his hand. He looked down. Ernest was pressing his cell phone firmly into Jack's hand. He grabbed it and looked around. Celeste had noticed and raised an eyebrow, but nobody else seemed to see as he slipped the bloodied phone into his pocket.

~

LESS THAN THREE minutes after his shot had struck home, Chen had finished disassembling his rifle. He walked back to the access hatch and paused only to press a button on his cell phone. He put his hand on the hatch as he heard the small charges he'd placed at four locations around the stadium detonate. The explosions weren't very large, merely designed to make a lot of noise and blow out smoke. They'd add to the gunshot and together be enough to send the crowd rushing for the exits faster than the police and venue security could handle. The confusion was his ticket out.

With one last check of his surroundings, making sure no trace was left of his presence, he opened the hatch. He looked down the ladder and saw that despite the mayhem of the past few minutes, the passage was deserted. He closed the hatch on the way down and grunted as he dropped the last few feet to the concrete below.

He put on a crumpled Yankees cap that had been in the case. He looked the part, complete with an old jersey. He walked quickly along the maze of passages that led him back to the main concourse, where he quietly joined the tidal wave of people rushing to the exits.

He saw a few police officers and security staff. They were trying hard to wrest back control of the situation, but they had no chance. They were too late to catch him. He was no longer vulnerable to detection. He'd packed up and left the scene flawlessly, now just another scared fan.

Within five minutes, one suspect suddenly became thousands. There would be an unparalleled manhunt, but with no DNA, footage or fingerprints, the job was complete. A few might remember the Asian Yankees fan with the briefcase, but for all that they may as well have seen Elvis.

Chen allowed himself a small, barely discernible smirk. For all the money spent on security, it was still easy. The art of killing was not complex once emotion was removed, it simply required thought and planning like any other worthwhile human endeavor. The engineer doesn't build a bridge without a plan, nor should a killer pull the trigger. There had been no messy bomb killing hundreds, just a single round and a clean getaway. To Chen, it was another face filed away among many. While he was mad his shot hadn't been perfect, he hoped the result was the right one.

Even the best got it wrong sometimes.

CHAPTER 15

There has been significant fallout from the attack on Ernest McDowell, billionaire owner of EMCorp. The Department of Homeland Security has stated it has credible evidence linking the attacks to terrorists and, as the investigation continues, the attack has caused chaos in the markets this morning. The Dow and the NASDAQ, which have both been hammered by the war with China, experienced further falls at the opening bell. EMCorp's board attempted to soothe the market by announcing caretaker arrangements, though EMCorp shares were off 14.2%.

Maree Silaski, Wall Street Journal, *October 6*

Jack was fascinated by the complex series of machines keeping Ernest alive. He'd watched them for hours, the monitors that bleeped, the screens with colored lines and an array of constantly changing numbers. Another machine—the respirator —inflated and deflated with its own rhythm, ensuring that Ernest continued to breathe.

Jack had been there from the moment Ernest exited surgery. The only others allowed into the suite were Peter Weston, Josefa Tokaloka and Ernest's daughter, Sarah. They'd kept a constant vigil for the last day, sharing some dark jokes about the suite being big enough for all of them to move into permanently.

Nothing had changed with Ernest's condition in those hours, all Jack had noticed was the increase in the number of well-wishers sending flowers, presents and other trinkets. It had been a constant stream. While the hospital had flexed their muscles and restricted the number of visitors, they seemed powerless to stop the avalanche of gifts.

He had spent hours searching through the cell phone Ernest had handed him. He knew that the phone must have some answers, given the energy Ernest had expended handing it to him. At first, he'd tried to unlock the phone using any date or number of significance he could find on Ernest's Wikipedia page. None had worked, until he'd tried Sarah McDowell's birthday. The problem was that there was so much on the phone it would take days or weeks to dig through everything and find what Ernest wanted found. Jack wouldn't give up.

He sighed and looked away from the machines. He knew that his presence here would make no difference to Ernest's recovery, but he didn't leave. He was not a religious man, so there was no point in praying. So he waited and watched the machines keep Ernest alive. He owed it to the man who'd secured his release from China. Was this the price that had been paid? Was he the reason Ernest was lying there?

Jack heard the electric door behind him whir open. He turned to see Peter Weston entering the room with an armful of flowers and cards. Jack patted his pocket, making sure the phone was still there, then smiled sadly at Peter as he placed the gifts on a coffee table. Peter collapsed into the armchair next to Jack.

Peter looked up at him and rubbed his temples. "Still here?"

"Yeah, there's been no change."

"You can go home for a while. Nobody will think less of you."

Jack shrugged. "I would. I owe him. Sitting here is hardly a big deal."

Peter nodded and sank back into his seat. They sat in silence for several minutes. Jack considered telling Peter about the phone, but held off for now. Ernest had handed the phone to him, not to Peter, and he wondered if there was a reason. Maybe Ernest had distrusted Peter, in which case telling him about the phone would be a mistake.

Peter sighed, breaking Jack's reverie. "Cops came by the office earlier."

Jack nodded. "They came here again too. Just confirmed a few facts. I still don't really understand it though. It was the sort of attack normally aimed at a president, except Ernest didn't have the Secret Service by his side."

"Homeland Security is saying terrorists, but I'm not buying it." Peter shook his head. "He's a prominent man, with a lot of enemies. The cops won't find anything."

Jack was silent as he watched Peter closely. He had a pained look on his face, especially when he spoke of the enemies Ernest had made. Jack considered that Peter had probably been at Ernest's side when he'd made some of them. He made his decision, rummaged around in his pocket and pulled out the phone.

"It was a pro—had to have been. We do have one thing the cops don't, though." Jack held up the cell phone.

Peter's eyes widened. "Where did you get that?"

"Ernest handed it to me as the ambulance crews rushed toward him. He was so intent on me having it, I'm convinced there's something important on it."

Peter inhaled sharply. "And is there?"

Jack shrugged. "No way to tell. There's so much on it that it would take a dozen journalists a month to sift through it all."

"Well, whatever information he wanted you to have, I hope you get to the bottom of it. Let me know if you want some help."

"I'm sure you've got other things to worry about."

Peter looked over at the still form of his boss, lying on the hospital bed. "Ernest being in a coma has caused some problems."

"What do you mean?"

"There's a few rumblings on the board. Nothing I can't handle. Just certain individuals taking the opportunity to make waves while Ernest is incapacitated."

Jack sighed. "Sounds like we've both got plenty to be getting on with. I just wonder if we'll get anywhere."

"What choice is there?"

"None. I owe Ernest too much to give up. I'll keep searching through this phone until my thumbs bleed. We'll get to the bottom of this."

Jack sighed and closed his eyes. He was tired. He hadn't slept properly since the shooting, and it was starting to catch up with him.

He woke a few hours later, looked around, and saw Peter asleep in the second armchair. After a few seconds' thought, he decided to try his luck on the voicemails. He plugged his headphones into the phone and dialed.

"*You have no new messages.*" The voice was polite and feminine. "*To hear all saved messages, please press 3.*"

Jack pressed the button.

The first message played: *"Hi Dad, just wanted to make sure..."*

Time passed slowly as the voicemail messages he listened to—or truthfully, half listened to—blended into one. He found it hard to believe that one man had so much contact with so many people. He dozed off again at one point, because he woke having dreamt of Erin. With a sigh, he pressed a button for the next message.

"Ernest, we had a deal. Stop being a fool. You don't have a lot of time left to make the right decision."

"Bingo!"

❧

MICHELLE SAT on a plastic chair in the middle of the hardwood floor of the Georgetown University basketball stadium, home of the Hoyas. She kept a pleasant smile on her face as students, faculty and some members of the public filtered into the bleachers. The usual butterflies that fluttered in her stomach before a major speech were there again, made worse by the uncertainty of the situation. She'd be fine once she was underway.

When the crowd was settled, the dean of the Graduate School of Arts and Sciences introduced her and gave a brief biography of her career to date. Michelle kept the smile throughout, but her mind was focused on the events of the last few days. She'd planned this speech carefully around her run for Congress, Ernest McDowell's death, and the fate of EMCorp. McDowell's ongoing ability to breathe was a significant problem.

She'd decided that McDowell's recalcitrance about their deal was too great a risk. With Anton dead, the Foundation cells under control, the war kicking along and the rest of her agenda ready to fly, the last thing she needed was problems from a geriatric business magnate. She'd put insurance in place for the control of EMCorp in the event of McDowell's death, so she'd ordered Chen to do the job.

Unfortunately, he'd failed.

The audience broke into enthusiastic applause. She smiled broadly, stood to approach the lectern then thanked the dean. It was all a blur until she laid her speech notes on the lectern, brushed some imaginary dirt from her dress and looked up. Then there was clarity. She gave a small wave and waited for the applause to subside, then cleared her throat.

"Good evening. As you know, if not for a fatal street assault, my late colleague Anton Clark would have been addressing you tonight. So first off I'd like to acknowledge his contribution to American public life, and the enormous void that his passing has left. He was a fountain from which torrents of intellect flowed."

There was more applause, subdued this time. If only they knew that every significant political event to strike the United States in the last few months was her responsibility—they'd storm the court and probably toss her severed head through the ring. It was a burden she carried gladly. There was nobody else who could put the country on the right path in such a manner.

"His death is one in a series of dire events that's afflicted our country, and the world, in recent months. The death of so many Americans in Shanghai, the underhanded sinking of the USS *George Washington* without a declaration of war, and—in recent days—the mysterious shooting of Ernest McDowell. Worst of all, of course, is the war."

She gazed into the crowd and was happy to see Sarah McDowell smile sadly in the front row, wiping a tear from her eye. Michelle knew that the next few lines would be the ones picked up by the television cameras. She glanced over carefully rehearsed words. It was the coming together of the remaining strands of her plan—with a few amendments, after Chen's failure.

"These events have led me to ask some important questions of myself. I've reflected on what I can do to aid our country in the most desperate crisis we've faced since we had our finger over the button, ready to deal with a nuclear force hosted by Castro. All Americans should ask the same."

She smiled straight at Sarah. While McDowell's daughter had been the central plank of Michelle's insurance policy, even with her father alive she was important. With Ernest McDowell in a coma, Sarah— beautiful and educated—became a massive lightning rod for public opinion. The public, and the EMCorp board, would fall in behind her.

"I've come up with two things. Firstly, I've ordered that much of the financial assets of the Foundation for a New America be spent purchasing a significant shareholding in EMCorp in the coming weeks. Despite the attack on Mr McDowell sending the share price tumbling, I want EMCorp to continue being a strong voice for America."

Michelle took a deep breath.

"Secondly, as I seek a mandate from the people to join Congress, I promise that if elected, I will not be joining the legislative sewer that has passed for our democracy in the last decade, for which both major parties are responsible. Instead, and with the support of as many likeminded Congressional colleagues as I can find, I will be a strong and unyielding voice for bringing strength and leadership back to America. It is time to fix the problems and bring America back to greatness."

This time the applause was thunderous. She made sure to give each of the cameras a good two-second look straight down the barrel. She held her hands up and waved the applause away, grinning from ear to ear. She waved again, then stepped away from the lectern and approached Sarah. The younger woman was beaming as they embraced. Michelle held the hug, to be sure that the cameras picked it up.

"Well done, Michelle, that was inspirational." Sarah's voice was soft enough only she could hear. "Thanks for the kind words about Dad."

Michelle pulled away slightly and nodded. "I just hope he pulls through. His absence is the last thing the country needs right now."

Michelle's timetable had been pushed forward by Ernest McDowell's double dealings, and complicated by Chen's failure. With the looming purchase of a huge shareholding by the Foundation, and Sarah's help, she was well placed to take control of the company when McDowell finally kicked the bucket. When he did, Sarah would become the star at the center of the story.

Sarah nodded. "I'm glad you're investing in the company. Though the family business isn't really my thing, it's nice to have a friend until he pulls through."

CHAPTER 16

"Thanks, Stan. As you mentioned, things are getting bleak on the island. Despite the best efforts of the US Navy, the Chinese naval and submarine blockade has stopped most shipments of food and medical supplies to Taiwan. While the US has managed to airlift enough food onto the island to prevent mass starvation and people are able to eat at crisis shelters, there's a growing sense of desperation. This comes as the capital was rocked by another day of non-stop missile attacks, and as reports filter in of Chinese special forces troops active in the hills south of Taipei."

Royce Miller, Asia Today, *October 11*

Michelle sat back in her seat and watched as Chen's wife refilled the three delicate bone china tea cups with practiced grace. Not a single drop was spilled, and the whole process seemed effortless. When she was done, she placed the teapot back on the heat mat, stood and picked up her own cup.

"I'll leave you two to discuss your business." She smiled at Michelle. "But I want to thank you again for saving my family."

Michelle smiled as she leaned forward to pick up the tea. "No thanks are necessary."

The other woman nodded, then left the room. Michelle didn't speak until the door had closed and she was certain nobody would overhear the conversation, using the time to plan her approach.

She looked to Chen, who seemed relaxed. "Your wife moves like a ninja, or a ballet dancer, I can't decide which."

Chen gave a small laugh. "It's hell on the children. They don't ever hear her coming."

Michelle lifted the cup of tea to her mouth and took a small sip. It was a stupid move, and her tongue screamed in pain at the intrusion of the boiling liquid, far too hot for her taste. She did her best to mask any discomfort, but when she looked up at Chen, he had the slightest smile on his face. Scalded, she placed the cup carefully back on the table.

"Ernest McDowell is alive." Her voice was matter of fact. "That is unacceptable."

"So I saw on the news." He lifted his own tea and took a small sip, apparently with no discomfort. "Good for his family, but not for your organization."

"Indeed. I needed him dead."

Chen looked her straight in the eye. "It's through no fault of mine that he lives. The operation was a success. I inserted, took the shot, and got out."

Michelle couldn't believe what she was hearing. "He's alive, Chen."

"Because he shifted as I pulled the trigger. It was bad luck, and when he fell to the ground he was out of my gun sights. He's alive by the grace of his God."

Michelle sighed. She hadn't expected this to be easy. Chen had told her explicitly when she'd asked him to kill McDowell that this was the last job he'd do for her. But nor had she expected that he'd fight her so hard. She needed to convince him to finish the job, to march into McDowell's hospital room and yank a cord or two. Sarah McDowell's positive reaction to her Georgetown speech the day before had convinced Michelle that she'd have the support of McDowell's daughter once the old man was dead. Sarah would inherit his shares the moment his heart stopped beating, which for Michelle was good enough. Sarah McDowell was malleable.

She leaned forward. "I need the job finished. His continued ability to breathe will have unacceptable consequences, to say the least."

Her ideal situation had been to control EMCorp through manipulation of McDowell, but failing that, the best option was his death. In recent days she'd instructed the Foundation to prepare to buy up a great deal of EMCorp stock. She'd also put in motion efforts to blackmail, bribe or outright bully other board members onto her side.

But with McDowell still conceivably in the picture, every contingency had gone to shit. Michelle had little to show for her efforts a week after she'd told the Foundation cell leaders that she was in the driver's seat.

"Ernest McDowell needs to die. I want you to finish the job. Say what you want about deities and bad luck, but you owe a debt to me, and I expect it to be made good."

She looked into Chen's eyes, and his black irises suddenly seemed like unforgiving vortexes that sucked her in and nearly extinguished the flame of her confidence. He leaned forward slightly and placed his tea cup on the table. He lifted his hand to his chin to scratch it. For the first time with this man, she felt like she was not in control.

His face was completely expressionless. "I don't see it that way. I told you I owed you two jobs: one for extracting me and one for extracting my family. You asked me to take care of Anton Clark's computer and I did. Then you asked me to shoot Ernest McDowell, and I did. I've repaid the debts."

Michelle gave a small laugh. "If I gave everyone I owed favors to the same spiel, I'd be dead in a week. I wanted you to kill him. There's a pretty big fucking difference."

Chen shrugged. "You told me to shoot him. I shot him. Death was not guaranteed. Your instructions should have been clearer. I will not be moved on this."

Michelle struggled to contain her anger. "You know as well as I do, Chen, that when you play in the big leagues, sometimes you need to work a bit harder."

"I understand, and that's why I took care of your deceased boss." His tone was calm.

"I killed him, in case you forget."

"But I removed the knife from your throat."

She hated to admit that he had a point. She'd been hoping to convince him to take one last action on her behalf, but his efforts to plant the evidence on Anton's computer and help her take over the Foundation had been invaluable. Deep down, she'd prefer to leave him and his family alone, but she didn't have that luxury.

Michelle knew there was no point pushing the issue further. He didn't seem like the sort who would change his mind once it was made up. She smiled and lifted her tea. She took another cautious sip and was glad that she wasn't scalded for her efforts. She swallowed, placed the cup carefully back on the table and stood.

"Patronage can be revoked, Chen. I hope you'll reconsider your decision. Please thank your wife for the tea."

~

JACK HAD one clue to unlock the mystery of Ernest's shooting—an unidentified female voice. He'd tried to call the number back, but it was disconnected. A burner phone. It seemed hopeless, but he'd made stories and a career out of less. Like a police detective, he knew he needed an overlooked fact, a new angle or a chance encounter. If he pulled the right thread, the whole mess would untangle before his eyes.

Since finding the voicemail on Ernest's phone, he'd spent most of the last few days in his office at the *New York Standard* trying to find that thread. He could do pretty much whatever the hell he liked without reproach at the moment, because his experiences in the last few months had made others treat him with a light touch. They seemed surprised that he was at work at all.

He'd decided he could do nothing with the mystery woman's voice for now, and the hours spent trawling through Ernest's phone had otherwise proven fruitless, so he'd focused on finding some other blemish in Ernest's life that might explain the attack. He typed the date of the shooting into Wikipedia, but found nothing.

With a frustrated sigh, he swung back on his chair. He needed a break. He looked away from the computer and up at the television in the corner of his office. It was a good enough distraction as any and better than the scotch he'd sworn off. He lifted the remote from his desk and turned on the TV.

The screen flashed to life and showed a news replay of a speech given at Georgetown a few nights prior. He knew no easier way to get his mind back on the job than a few minutes of watching this sort of thing, though he had to admit the attractive speaker would keep his attention for longer than usual.

"Firstly, I've ordered that much of the financial assets of the Foundation for a New America be spent purchasing a significant shareholding in EMCorp in the coming weeks."

Jack's eyes narrowed, then widened. He continued to listen as he leaned forward in his chair and dug through his pocket until he found Ernest's phone. As quickly as he could, and while the speech was still going, he pulled up the mystery woman's voicemail and played it on loudspeaker.

"Ernest, we had a deal. Stop being a fool. You don't have a lot of time left to make the right decision."

He played it again, to be sure. After the second playback, he was convinced that it was the woman on the screen, announcing that her organization was buying shares in EMCorp and that she was ready to shake Congress up. A broad smile crossed his face, and he had to stop himself from cheering aloud when a box appeared on the screen.

Michelle Dominique
Director, Foundation for a New America

He typed her name into Google as he continued to look at the woman on the screen. She was beautiful, black haired, well dressed. The page delivered instantly: a profile, a website for her foundation—a treasure chest that would take him no time to unlock. He wasn't sure if she was the one who'd ordered Ernest shot, and even if she had, he had no idea why, but deep down he knew this was the thread he'd been looking for.

A coffee cup slammed—a little too loudly—on his desk. He hadn't heard anyone enter his office, but the shock was soon replaced with a smile when he spun around in his chair to see Celeste with her own coffee in hand.

"How long have you been sitting here for?" Her voice was terse as she put a hand on one hip. "You've got to sleep at some point."

"A while." He laughed. "Think I just figured it out."

"Oh?"

"Yeah, these guys." He pointed to the laptop, then up at the television. "Her. She left a nasty message on Ernest's voicemail, and she's buying a chunk of the company."

Celeste leaned over his shoulder and read what was on the screen. "Foundation for a New America. Looks like your average, run-of-the-mill conservative think tank."

"I've heard of them, vaguely. Extreme right-wingers. They hang out with the Republicans but aren't really welcome."

"All sounds promising." Celeste patted him on the shoulder. "Come on, time for lunch. Let's game plan this."

CHAPTER 17

What this war has shown, more than any other in history, is the difference of warfare in the modern age. Smart weaponry has reduced the number of men needed to prosecute a war, but increased the drain of material and financial resources. The Chinese sank the George Washington, the US retaliated and struck at a number of Chinese air and naval bases, and now both sides are in stalemate over Taiwan. Billions of dollars' worth of military equipment is wrecked daily, and while both states have the power to deny the other the air, sea and land, neither has the strength to exert much control. The concern expressed by United Nations Secretary General Hans Voeckler is that as the frustration continues, both sides will be tempted to use nuclear weapons to end the deadlock.

Jim Teague, Jane's Defence Weekly, *October 15*

J ack held up his phone and took a few more photos of the woman. It hadn't been hard to find her, given how much of a public figure she was, and since then he'd watched her from a distance for almost a week. Michelle Dominique, Director of the Foundation for a New America and Congressional nominee. He pushed himself off the wall he'd been leaning on and walked in an easy stride to intercept her.

After hearing her voice on the news, and matching it to the voicemail, he'd hopped a short flight from New York to Washington. He'd spent his days trailing her, and his nights digging deeper into her character. She was his sole focus. He was intent on learning more about this woman, who was somehow entwined in Ernest's shooting. Unfortunately, she was surprisingly private and he'd struggled to find much dirt.

Now he walked twenty yards behind her, careful not to get too close. Not that it mattered all that much, since she didn't seem overly aware of her surroundings. Whatever her part in all of this, he doubted she was some kind of super spy. After another block, she slowed near a bar and entered.

He had a choice to make. He could go in now and try to engineer some sort of contact, or he could wait and see what happened. He deferred to his professional judgment. There was no point in waiting any longer. An idea formed in his head, which he spent the next few minutes turning into a plan.

He crossed the road and entered the bar. It was more upmarket than he was used to. A bar ran the length of the small room and soft lighting accentuated curves and forgave blemishes. There were leather booths, which afforded privacy to those who wanted it. He had no doubt that the step up in class would be reflected in the drink prices.

Jack felt at home, or close enough. As he closed the door behind him and approached the bar, heads turned—he knew he was being sized up. In this sort of place, that analysis consisted of two things: how much he earned and how attractive he was. Lucky he was wearing the most expensive suit he owned.

He stepped closer to the bar with all the confidence he could muster and looked around. He recognized his target standing at the bar. Dominique was one of the few who hadn't turned to look at him when he'd entered. Her jet black hair flowed down the back of her dress and confidence seemed to radiate off her.

As he stood next to her, he was terrified that she'd recognize him, but he had to take the chance. He left just the right distance between them to ensure he didn't arouse her suspicions, but not enough for someone else to slip in between them. Jack rested his elbows on the bar and when the barman looked his way, he slid a fifty onto the counter.

The barman looked at the note, then up at him with a smile. "What can I get you?"

"Whisky on the rocks." Jack had no intention of drinking, but the act was necessary.

The barman frowned. "Any in particular, sir? We've got quite a few."

"Surprise me." Jack turned to Dominique. "And I'll get the lady's drink too."

Jack turned his head back to the barman and kept calm. He sensed slight movement to his left as the ice hit the bottom of the glass with a clink. He felt her gaze upon him as the top-shelf Irish whisky was poured over ice with the measured practice of a professional. He heard Dominique clear her throat as the barman put the scotch and a small bowl of nuts on the bar with a smile, then placed another whisky in front of her.

Dominique took the drink but left the nuts. "Thanks."

As she walked away, Jack exhaled heavily, glad that she hadn't recognized him. Though he wasn't exactly a household name, a lot of Washington insiders knew who he was. Newsprint clearly still gave him a fair bit of anonymity. His name was known by most, but his face wasn't. He remained perched on the bar as the barman returned with his change, but Jack waved at him to keep it.

The barman smiled and gestured his head in Dominique's direction. "Hey, thanks, buddy. Looks like you're in with a good shot."

Jack grinned. "I've got no idea what you mean."

Jack rapped his knuckles on the bar and walked to the only vacant booth, right at the back of the bar. Dominique was nowhere in sight, and his heart was threatening to leap out of his chest with its rhythmic thumping. He sat and took a few deep breaths to calm himself as he waited. Though tempted to take a sip of whisky to calm his nerves, his recent addiction was still too raw, and he left it alone.

A minute or so after he'd sat down, Dominique passed. He caught her scent: it was something floral but not overpowering, made all the more intoxicating by knowing he was close to getting her answers. Before he knew it, she'd placed her own drink on the table and was sliding up closer to him in the booth.

"Thanks for the drink." Her voice was soft but thick with suggestion.

Jack kept his voice even, despite his nerves and excitement. "No problem."

She smiled slightly. "What's your name?"

Jack knew he had her attention, but it was potentially fleeting. There were a dozen other guys in the bar who'd give her exactly what he could, probably better. He pressed his leg into hers and she responded in kind. He dug into his pocket and placed a fake business card on the table.

She picked up the card and considered it. "So, James Ewing. Farzo? What's that?"

"Social media, video conferencing, that sort of thing. It's a start-up I'm working on."

"Sounds dull." She placed the card back on the table. "I'm Michelle."

He grinned. "It is, until it outgrows Facebook. What do you do for a living, Michelle?"

"Lobbyist." She clearly didn't want to say any more. She lifted her drink to her mouth, drained it then placed the glass back on the table so firmly that the ice clinked.

"Get you another drink?" While Jack knew things might be easier with Dominique if she had booze in her, he couldn't shake the feeling that he was acting predatorily.

"Yours will do." She grabbed his drink and downed it in one go. She obviously knew how to have a good time. "Let's get out of here?"

Jack tried his best not to look stunned. He hadn't expected her to be so forward. "Um, my hotel is miles away."

This was his gambit. Getting Dominique interested, getting her into bed and escaping the next day with his story intact would be the easy part. But the entire effort hinged on whether he could get to her place, search through her things, and get a feel for who she was. Finding something useful would be a bonus. She started to stand and he hoped.

"My place is close." She shrugged. "Come on."

Jack stood and followed her to the exit. He was aware of every pair of eyes in the bar tracking him, scoring him much higher than when he'd walked in. Even though he had a purpose to all this, he had to admit he enjoyed the attention. He reconsidered his feelings from a moment ago.

Predatory or not, he had no qualms about his actions. He knew that he was about to start down the very slippery slope that had made his colleagues in Britain think that hacking phones was logical. But he didn't care. He was in control again. He felt like a lion stalking a gazelle.

He was going to enjoy this.

~

JACK STOPPED and winced as Dominique stirred next to him. He'd been about to get up and start searching, but wanted to be sure that she was sound asleep. The minutes passed and he waited, eyes wide open. He looked at the clock on the bedside table. Midnight. Plenty of time.

Besides, she'd warned him the night before that she was intending to sleep in, so he could leave if he wanted to be up and off early. He wondered if she was as blunt with all the men she bedded, and decided it was a safe bet. She hadn't been what he'd expected. She'd been harsh, demanding, physical. He'd had to work harder to satiate her than any woman he'd been with, and they'd tried things Jack never had before. Not even with Erin.

It gave him all the more motivation to do the next part right. He needed information, and this was the last place he could think of to get it. He listened and waited. She stirred again slightly, one more time, before she started to snore softly. When he was sure she was asleep, he pulled back the covers and moved quietly into the ensuite. Once inside, he took his time and sat on the toilet far longer than needed to conduct his business. He wanted to be sure she stayed asleep.

When he left the bathroom she hadn't stirred. He dug around in the pocket of his jeans, which were on the floor next to the bed. He grabbed his keys as quietly as he could and moved toward the door. Once through it he closed it softly. He turned on the flashlight on his key ring and moved the small, bright beam of light around the apartment.

He didn't really know where to start, so he went straight to the iPad on the coffee table. He sat on the couch with it and put the flashlight between his teeth as he rolled back the lime green cover. The screen lit up, nearly as bright as the flashlight. A box asking for a code popped up. He cursed. It would have been all too easy for her to have no security on the iPad, but she wasn't that stupid. He probably had three tries to get the password right before he was locked out. He tried one random, four-digit code. The iPad buzzed, and "Wrong Passcode—Try Again" flashed in red at the top of the password box. He tried another. It buzzed again. He knew he could have one more try, but there'd be no surer way to inform her that he'd been rifling through her stuff than a locked iPad.

He sighed. While the iPad was the obvious place to find incriminating documents and information, it was closed to him. He shut the cover and put the iPad back down on the table where he'd found it. He took the flashlight out of his mouth and waved the beam around the room again.

He spent the next twenty minutes fruitlessly searching the apartment. He searched the kitchen, living area and main bathroom, but found nothing of worth. He knew there was one room most likely to contain some information, and he'd deliberately left it to last. He opened the door to the study, which seemed to pull double duty as a study, second bedroom, clothes storage room and general junk depot. There was no computer, but there was a desk littered with documents and a safe.

He left the safe alone, having no illusions that he was MacGyver, able to open it with a paperclip. Instead, he went straight for the notepad. He grabbed a lead pencil from the stationary caddy and tried the oldest trick in the book. He scribbled the lead pencil all over the yellow paper, and writing appeared.

Chen–608-558-2015.

A phone number. An Asian name. It might be nothing, or it could be a lead. He tore off the sheet of paper, crushed it into a ball and placed the pencil back in the caddy. He'd be able to look up the number easily enough later. He searched through the pile of documents on the desk but found nothing of use, though there was a boarding pass stub for Shanghai.

He left the study and made his way back to the bedroom. On his way through he looked longingly at the iPad, sorely tempted to try again, but he left it. He returned to the bedroom and put the keys and the screwed-up piece of paper into his jeans. He climbed back into the bed. Leaving now would just make her suspicious. Next to him, Dominique stirred, rolled over and placed an arm over his midsection.

"Thanks for last night." Her voice was heavy with sleep. "I really enjoyed it."

"No problem."

His mind buzzed with the possibilities of what he'd found. He knew it could end up being nothing, or it could be the key to unlocking the whole puzzle. He had a number, and knew she'd been in Shanghai. He'd have to call in a favor to get the number traced to an address, but that wouldn't be hugely difficult. He'd leave first thing in the morning and start down the path that had just opened for him. He hoped it led somewhere.

He felt energized. It was enough for now.

CHAPTER 18

There has been a major development in the war between the United States and China today, as Japan announced it would be committing air and naval assets to the conflict. The Japanese Government has justified the move by stating the forces would be used in self-defense only. Japanese Prime Minister Hiroshi Matsui stressed that the Japanese forces were tasked solely to protect Japanese shipping lanes through the South China Sea. Japan has lost three merchant ships in the conflict so far and the deployment of the highly capable Japanese military will free up US assets currently spent defending convoys.

Kris Brady, New York Standard, *October 16*

Michelle woke for the second time. She'd enjoyed the sleep in, and was particularly glad that Ewing had left without much fuss. It made for a nice change, as did the quality of the sex. She stretched like a cat, relishing the fact that she had the bed to herself. She had loose plans to sleep for a bit longer, followed by coffee and then a jog. Her plans were interrupted in their infancy by her cell phone, which buzzed on the nightstand.

She considered leaving it, but then sighed and hit the answer button. "What?"

"It's Andrei Shadd."

"What the fuck, Andrei? It's my day off, and it's too early."

There was a pause on the other end. "Sorry, Michelle, but I think your iPad has been stolen, and I thought you'd want to know."

She frowned. "No, it hasn't. I used it yesterday."

"I can't explain it then. The security guys recorded someone trying to unlock it. Whoever it was got nothing, but the guys have remotely wiped it."

"It's in my apartment. Unless Spiderman broke in while I was sleeping, there was no need to wipe it. Not fucking impressed, Andrei."

The phone line was quiet.

She stretched her legs out again under the covers. Her body ached—a good ache. "I want whatever you wiped restored by the time I'm out of the shower."

"Doesn't work like that. It's all gone, and the last backup was over a month ago. You should really plug it in more often, Michelle. The manufacturer recommends once—"

"Fuck off, Andrei. Send me the details of whoever broke into it, I need to know who to hate on for a couple of days."

She hung up and threw the phone on top of the covers. She stretched out again and winced as a sharp pain stabbed her in the back, and wondered again what some of those positions had been last night. She'd have to remember them. She was just dozing off again when her mind screamed and her eyes shot open.

She'd been half asleep during the phone call, so had failed to connect the dots. It hit her like a brick. She rushed out of bed, tripped in the covers and fell to the floor. With a curse, she got up and ran to the living room. Her iPad was where she'd left it, on the coffee table, undisturbed. Her fears had been unfounded.

"Fucking idiots."

Ewing had probably just wanted to check his Facebook account. He hadn't seemed like the brightest spark, so she severely doubted that he was an international super spy, as Andrei seemed to think. She was about to call him back and abuse him some more, just so she'd feel better, when her phone beeped.

The message was from Andrei, and contained the information she'd wanted—a log of activity that confirmed someone had tried to unlock the iPad at a ridiculously early hour. She'd thought he might have done it once the sun had come up, or just before he'd left, but the odd timing aroused her suspicions.

"Fuck."

She did a quick scan of the room, but couldn't see anything obvious missing. If she'd been robbed, the diamond earrings she'd left on the kitchen bench as they'd undressed would be gone. So would the iPad, for that matter. She rushed to the only place in the apartment she cared about, because it contained information that could ruin her.

Her safe was in plain sight in the study, but she'd been assured it was the hardest to crack in the world, short of those found in banks. It was intact and seemingly undisturbed, though some of the papers on her desk had been rifled through. But none of those mattered.

She knew she was being stupid, but she put in the code to the safe, waited until it beeped then entered the second code. It beeped again and she opened it quickly. Her body flooded with relief when she saw that the single manila folder was still there, along with a decent amount of cash, a handgun, some USB sticks and her duplicate ID.

She closed the safe and sank to the floor. She exhaled heavily and spent a few moments trying to regain her composure. Whatever he'd been looking for, the things that could destroy her life and her work were safe. She cursed at her carelessness. She'd underestimated the possibility that one of her casual pickups could mean her harm.

She called Andrei back. "You were right."

She had a hunch he was smiling on the other end. "Oh?"

"I had a guy here last night. My iPad and my safe look like they're okay, and I doubt he got much else, but I can't be sure. I want you to find out what you can."

"Got a name?"

"James Ewing. Probably fake though." She ground her teeth. "I think I got played."

"Leave it with me." He paused. "That all?"

She thought for a few seconds. Michelle didn't think she'd been compromised, but that didn't remove the horrible feeling in her stomach. She had enough to worry about without free agents ruining her plans. She'd considered another, different problem for days, but this seemed to be the perfect time to make a decision.

"Andrei?" Her voice was laced with anger. "I want Chen Shubian taken care of. Family too. Clean and final."

"I'll get the local cell onto it."

She lowered the phone from her ear and ended the call. Chen had failed her, and then declined her request to finish the job. She'd wanted to give him the benefit of the doubt, given his previous service, but he was someone who knew too much and offered her too little. The decision was made.

She sighed and shook her head. "I've become Anton."

～

CHEN'S EYES shot open and his mind was immediately alert to the high-pitched squeal from just outside his bedroom. He held his breath and listened again for the sound—a loose floorboard that his wife had implored him to fix half-a-dozen times. Chen had been reluctant, though, as the sound of the floorboard being stepped on, even by the lightest person, had inadvertently become a good alarm against sneaky children out of bed in the night.

There was no further sound.

Chen smiled, despite his annoyance at being woken up. Ongoing silence meant that the children were frozen in place, aware that Dad was about to come and march them off to bed with a swift spank for their troubles. He swung his feet out of the bed and sat up. The full moon had cast a shadowy hue over the whole room, and he envied his wife still sleeping soundly beside him.

He was about to stand when he heard the creak again.

"Shhh!"

Chen's plans changed in an instant. That wasn't his children outside the door, imploring someone to silence. He swung back into bed and rolled over to his wife. Resting on his side, he put one hand over her mouth and shook her head gently but with intent. In the light of the moon he could see her eyes open, as alert as Chen had been upon waking. She had learned long ago to sleep very lightly.

When he knew she was not going to speak, he removed his hand from her mouth and tapped her on the chin: once, twice, three times. She knew the signal. Her eyes widened a little, but she nodded and immediately started to rise. They could do this in the complete darkness, but the moonlight made it easier. As she slid out of bed and onto the floor, Chen knew that she'd do what needed to be done.

He knew he was almost out of time. As quickly as he could, he rolled back to his side of the bed and opened the drawer on his side table. He pulled out his favorite pistol—the Heckler and Koch USP Tactical. In complete silence, he checked the gun was loaded, pressed the safety off and lay back in bed. He pointed the gun at the door and waited as he heard his wife slide under the bed. It was the safest place she could be.

He aimed, and was surprised that whoever was invading his household chose to open his door slowly and quietly, rather than burst in to get the jump on him. Chen didn't move as the door opened fully and a large, balaclava-clad man entered the room cautiously. It was nearly too easy. Chen squeezed the trigger once, then again, then one final time.

One of the rounds hit the man in the head, and he fell to the ground with a thud. Chen was already moving. He slid out of bed and aimed the gun at the wall. Whoever was on the other side had obviously seen the first man fall. He had partly contained the threat, now he needed to seize the initiative.

Chen felt sorry for them. He knew their playbook better than they did. Chen knelt, using his bed as some degree of cover, and fired four rounds into the wall, low enough to hit anyone standing outside but high enough that the bullets would whiz over the head of any children in the vicinity. His children.

The drywall gave way to the bullets like a bar of soap to a razor blade. Chen heard a cry of shock, and knew he'd hit something. One neutralized, another wounded. If they were following standard doctrine, there would be a team of four spread among his house, chasing their objectives. Two more. His children were still in grave danger.

He left his wife to hold the room, knowing that she'd give anybody who entered a dose of buckshot from the Remington 12-gauge she was cradling. He moved swiftly to the door of the bedroom and stepped around the corner. The wounded man he'd shot through the wall was whimpering, with several bullet wounds. Though he was no longer a threat, Chen put a round into his skull to be sure.

He reloaded and moved further into the hallway, which was lit by a single bulb. Chen turned the corner, low, and ducked lower still when he heard the impact of a bullet in the wall behind him. At least his attackers were using silenced weapons, so the police and the neighbors would stay away. Less fortunate was the sight of the third balaclava-clad man holding his daughter hostage. He saw confusion and fear in her eyes.

"Let her go." Chen raised his pistol. "Let her go, now."

"We're here for you, not the k—."

Chen didn't let him finish. He fired, glad there was enough light for perfect aim. The attacker's head jerked back slightly as Chen put a round through the man's open mouth. A fine mist of blood and brain matter evacuated from the back of his head and Chen was already moving up the hallway toward his daughter.

She started to cry as he reached her, and squealed as Chen put another round in her attacker's head. He put his arm around her, lifted her and carried her to the master bedroom, where he called out to his wife before entering, lest she fill him with shot. Once inside the bedroom, he let his daughter run to his wife and turned around again.

His senses burned, trying to locate the fourth attacker. There were always four.

Chen heard the back door slam. The fourth attacker must have lost his nerve and started to run. He threw the pistol onto the floor. Having to shoot inside had been bad enough, but he knew he couldn't fire off a few shots in the backyard of a quiet Wisconsin street without drawing police attention. Even with a silenced pistol, it was too risky.

He ran for the back door, thankful that the house was small. He burst through the door and it swung back hard on its frame with a loud bang. As he ran across the yard, Chen saw his prey was at the fence but struggling to climb over. He closed the distance quickly and pulled the man back.

The attacker cried out in surprise and landed heavily on top of Chen's wife's favorite flower pots. Chen picked up a large, pointed piece of broken ceramic pot. He pulled the man by the collar, just as his pistol was rising in Chen's direction. Chen drove the point of the shard into the man's face with all the force his adrenalin and training allowed.

It was enough. The man went limp as the clay pierced his skull and slid into his brain. Just to be sure, Chen rammed the piece into the man's face again, then once more, creating a series of bloody craters. Done, he dragged the man's dead weight back into the house, leaving a bloody smear.

Once he was inside and the door was shut, he shouted up the hall: "We need to go!"

When he reached the master bedroom, he watched the scene with a combination of awe and admiration. His wife had already gathered the children. They were frantic but as disciplined as always. She'd also gathered the single getaway bag they kept for emergencies and had car keys in her hand.

"Go to the car, it's safe now."

As they left the room, he went to the other side of the bedroom. In less than a minute he'd gathered the second getaway bag he kept for himself. It had a fresh pistol, cash, fake documents and everything else he needed to get them away. If his hunch was right about his attackers, he'd have to get far away indeed.

As he heard the sound of the electric garage door grind its way open and looked at the room one last time, he felt a pang of regret. They'd only had a brief time here, but it had been enjoyable. His wife had made friends with the neighbors, he'd started work and the children had settled in at school. Their cover had been perfect.

That meant there could only be one attacker: the Foundation.

He regretted having to leave, but in Chen's world, nothing was forever.

CHAPTER 19

Local police currently have made no arrest for the quadruple murder in Spring Green, Wisconsin. In a statement today, the Sauk County Police Department revealed that the dead men were involved in a home invasion gone wrong. They've appealed for the occupant of the house to hand himself in, stating it is highly likely he was defending himself and has little or nothing to fear. Channel 4 News spoke to neighbors in the street, who described the residents of the house as a quiet Asian couple and their young children. The neighbors added that they were baffled by the deadly episode.

  Frank Tait, Channel 4 News, October 21

J ack sat in his car across the road from the house. When he'd traced the number from Dominique's notepad, it had proven interesting enough to be worth a trip. He hadn't expected to arrive and find it surrounded by police tape and a smattering of media. Any hope he'd had of interviewing the person who lived here and somehow finding answers to Ernest's shooting now seemed lost.

He watched as Celeste walked away from one of the neighboring houses, shaking her head. She'd flown into Madison, Wisconsin, a day after him, and they'd made their own way to the town of Spring Green —population 1500. Since then, they'd joined the rest of the local media, and some national media, outside the house. Thankfully, the rest of the media had gone now. Most had left a few days ago, three days into the stakeout, and the last of them had gone the previous night. A small town couldn't hold the attention of the major city papers and networks for long, especially when the locals had no answers. They'd rely on subsidiary networks to cover any follow-up.

Jack was just glad he could finally get down to the real reason he was here—getting answers about the mysterious Chen. The murders just piqued his interest even more, given the sheer impossibility of one normal man taking out four armed intruders. That made Chen special.

Celeste reached the car, opened the door and got in. "Neighbors aren't talking, Jack. Just general gossip."

He found it hard to believe there was no clue about the character of a man who'd killed four home invaders. "No idea who he was?"

She grabbed his Big Gulp and took a long pull. "Not that they're sharing. Some real weirdos live here."

"They just don't like us city folk." He gave up on his best attempt at a redneck accent. "Plus they've probably had their fill of journos asking questions."

She laughed. "Doesn't change the fact that we might be too late."

"Let's go look." Jack already had the car door open.

Celeste followed him across the street. "What about the cops?"

Jack smiled as he looked around. With no neighbors in sight, he ducked under the police tape and tried the front door. It was securely locked, a rarity for this part of the country. He searched underneath the welcome mat, inside the dying pot plants and in the letterbox for a spare key, but came up empty.

Celeste kicked the door in frustration. "So much for stereotypes. A house in the quietest street in America and no spare key? Ram it, Jack. That works in the movies."

Jack rapped his knuckles on the door. It sounded solid, not that Jack knew a lot about wood. "It'll just give me a sore shoulder. Not so keen on that. Let's try around the back."

She laughed but walked with him. "Coward, I had you pegged as an action hero, Jack."

He snorted but didn't reply. They walked through the latched wooden gate and down the side of the house. Once they reached the backyard, Celeste walked over to investigate the fence and the shattered plants while Jack tried the door.

"There's been a struggle here! There's blood and a whole lot of broken flower pots."

He didn't respond, too engrossed in the door. Unlike the front, the back of the house had a screen door with no lock, which Jack opened with no trouble. Unfortunately, the back did have the same heavy wooden door he'd found at the front. With one notable exception—the lock was broken. He tried the handle and it opened.

He laughed and called out to Celeste, "Looks like the cops didn't want to wait around for the locksmith. Thanks, Sauk County PD."

Celeste came up beside him, shaking her head. "See, you're an action hero. Or at least the luckiest guy on the planet."

Jack was about to make a joke in reply when he pushed the door open. The joke disappeared, replaced by a sharp inhale as he took in the scene before him. There were bloodstains on the carpet and a large, crimson streak on the wall halfway down the corridor. The scene was worse than he'd anticipated.

Concrete floor. Blood. Fists and feet pounding him. Metal instruments. His bowels contributing to the miasma.

Celeste put her hand on his shoulder. "This place is creepy, Jack."

Jack shook his head, trying to clear away the flashbacks from China. "Yeah."

Celeste pushed past him. "Some evil shit happened here."

She was right. Jack had hoped that it wasn't him breaking into Dominique's house that had brought the hammer down on this place. But whoever this Chen guy was, he looked like he could handle himself. He was more convinced than ever that Chen was involved in Ernest's shooting.

He flicked on a light switch. "Let's see what we can find. The cops will have scoured the place clean, but it's worth a shot."

Celeste nodded and went to search one of the bedrooms. "You never know. They weren't thorough enough to lock the back door, so they might have missed something."

He went to the master bedroom and called quietly, "Ten minutes, then we're out of here."

Jack searched the room without result. While there was more blood and signs of a gunfight, he found nothing useful. The possessions of the house's occupants were still here, too. They'd probably left in a great hurry. Jack wished he knew where they'd gone.

"Going down to the basement, Jack!" Celeste called.

Jack was impressed. Celeste had already searched the kitchen and living room and made her way to the basement. Jack was creeped out and wanted to leave, but he went to join her. He walked down the stairs but stopped halfway. Something felt wrong. The light flicked on and he saw a large man pointing a pistol at Celeste.

"Stop right there." The man's voice was Eastern European. "Who're you?"

This was leading to no place Jack wanted to go. "We're journalists."

"Unlucky ones." Their captor waved his pistol at him. "Back up the stairs, please."

Jack had the distinct impression that the hulking foreigner wouldn't ask again. He walked up the steps from the basement, with Celeste and their captor behind. He gave some thought to running, but didn't think he could outrun a bullet. The man led them to the front door, which had a button on the back of the door knob to unlock it.

They were taken out to the front of the house. Jack looked back, and saw that their captor had put his gun discreetly inside his large jacket and was pointing at a large black SUV parked a few houses up the street. Jack approached it as slowly as he legitimately could. His mind raced. He knew that inside that car was death for both him and Celeste.

They edged closer, and Jack was about to do something desperate when a police cruiser turned the corner at the top of the street and drove toward them. Jack stopped and waited for either the cop car to pull alongside or to get a bullet in his back. The shot didn't come, but as the cop car rolled alongside, the cop looked straight at Jack.

The car braked and stopped. Jack would never know the officer's name, but he'd have to make sure never to slag off the fine men and women of the Sauk County Police Department ever again. He knew a lifeline when he saw one. He turned quickly to grab Celeste's hand and started to walk toward their car.

He snuck a glance at their captor, who looked back at them impassively as Jack led Celeste away from the SUV and back toward his own car. The man made no move to intercept them as he started the car, and Jack wasn't sticking around. He drove up the street, away from the house.

Jack looked in his rear-vision mirror and saw the cop car driving away. "We're safe now."

"That was too fucking close for my liking." Celeste was shaking and staring straight ahead, but was holding up a USB stick. "I found this."

He turned his head. "What is it?"

"A USB stick."

He shrugged. "Let's worry about it later. I want to get miles from this place."

～

CHEN CLOSED THE CUBICLE DOOR, turned the latch and then pushed on the back a few times to be certain it was locked.

He placed his bag on the floor, sat on the toilet seat and cradled his head in his hands. He took in a deep breath and let it out in a long, slow sigh. His heart was racing, but he knew this was the best way to calm down. He needed to regain his composure before he took any action, and kept reminding himself that he had time and was safe.

He'd flown from Wisconsin to Los Angeles, and was now in Hawaii on his way to Taiwan. His family was already in the air. He was panicking because he'd left his insurance policy—the USB that contained Anton Clark's file dump—at home in Wisconsin.

He'd spent a frantic few minutes in the terminal searching through his bag, but hadn't found the envelope. He'd cursed all of the gods and deities that he knew, from Allah to Zeus, unable to believe that he'd been stupid enough to lose it. He'd thought back and determined that it must have fallen out of his bag during the rushed departure.

If someone else found it, his identity and the safety of his family would be at risk. And with four dead bodies in full combat gear, he was sure that a diligent police search would find it. He just had to hope that the local police weren't smart enough to crack the encryption and recognize its importance.

As it was, he couldn't worry about the USB for now. He had little choice. He had to access the Darknet for the first time since he was contacted by Dominique, to finalize the arrangements for his return to Taiwan. There was one computer in the airport that had the Darknet browser he needed, but before he could use it he needed a credit card so he could pay for the internet kiosk time without being traced. He could have used cash, but he wanted the user log to point to someone else entirely.

Chen didn't move an inch as he waited, seated on the toilet, just breathed deeply and tried to slow his heart. After about ten minutes, he heard the bathroom door open with a squeal. As the door closed, he could hear the staccato beat of business shoes on the tiles. Chen sat in silence as the new arrival entered the cubicle next to his and closed the door bolt with a snap.

Importantly, once the door was locked, Chen heard a scraping sound as the man in the cubicle next door hung his jacket on the hook on the back of the door. Chen waited another few moments, until he heard the man's belt buckle rattle against the tiles and the beginning of his business.

Standing up from the toilet, Chen picked up his bag and unlatched the door of his cubicle. He stepped out and looked around, sure that nobody else was in the bathroom except his neighbor but wanting to double check. Satisfied they were alone, he stepped in front of the other occupied cubicle, swiftly reached over and stole the jacket.

He was already walking toward the exit when the man started shouting in German. Chen didn't understand what he was saying and ignored him as he searched through the pockets, hoping for some luck. He found the man's wallet in the inside pocket. He rummaged through it just as he heard the cubicle door unlock. He grabbed a few credit cards from the wallet, and as the cubicle door opened, threw the jacket and wallet behind him. He pulled open the door to the washroom and the man to pick up the contents of his wallet.

The door closed behind him and Chen was safe, just another Asian traveler. He walked the length of Terminal 5, past coffee shops and newsstands. He reached into his pocket and pulled out a business card. On the front were details of a dry cleaner, but it was the back that interested him: hastily scribbled instructions on how to find the one computer in Honolulu International Airport with the necessary browser to access the Darknet. He'd scrawled the instructions in the last frantic minutes before leaving Wisconsin.

He inserted the stolen credit card into the payment terminal and the computer lit up. He accessed the Darknet and started to make arrangements for his return to Taiwan. Though the island was under daily attack, it was still safer for him than the United States would be for a while.

He was on the move again. He also had somewhere to go.

CHAPTER 20

The inquiry of the UK Parliament into the conduct of EMCorp tabled its findings yesterday. The report recommended that EMCorp be forcibly divested from some of its UK interests and that Mr McDowell surrender his position on the board of the UK operation, should he regain consciousness. Though a severe blow to the company, the recommended measures are considerably more lenient than most analysts had expected, perhaps reflecting sympathy for the attempt on Mr McDowell's life. Prime Minister David Kennedy is expected to make a statement about the report today, and in particular about how the government will proceed.

Paul O'Brien, Financial Times, *October 22*

J ack sat in his pajamas. The heat of the laptop on his thighs had warmed things up downstairs a little too much for his liking. Next to him, Celeste was similarly clothed, but without the laptop threatening to burn a hole in her privates. He looked over, she smiled at him and gestured with her head at the screen. The message was clear—get on with it.

Jack was still uneasy about the events from the previous day. It had taken all his self-control not to crack open the motel minibar and neck a few beers to ease his nerves. He sensed that Celeste felt the same, but was conscious of encouraging his continued sobriety: she'd opened the fridge, looked longingly at the booze, then settled on a juice.

He sighed and leaned back on the sofa. Neither of them had slept the previous night, too wound up from the events at the house. Now, in the early hours of the morning, he resumed searching through the documents on the USB. The run-in with the Eastern European man was all the confirmation he needed that they were on the right track. They'd speculated on what could be on the USB during the drive back to the motel. They'd expected secret plans to bring down the government or the names and locations of dozens of master criminals. They'd come up with all sorts of wacky ideas, but the reality had been more disappointing than that.

He looked back at the screen and clicked on the next set of documents. It was a record of receipts with dates, items from a shopping list and a receipt code next to each—a series of letters and numbers. Another document was a budget, listing some fairly random items and a cost. Another was a copy of a receipt for a child's toy.

Celeste sighed. "This is all useless."

Jack had to concede she was right. He was interested in none of them. "Yeah, none of this makes nearly getting kidnapped worth it."

Celeste laughed. "A shopping list doesn't cut it. I'm buying a gun tomorrow, by the way."

Jack snorted and looked up at her. "I'm not sure that's the best idea."

"A big one." She smiled, but he wasn't sure if she was serious or not. "A shiny one."

"Actually, it's a stupid idea."

She frowned. "I don't care, there's no way I'm ever going to feel like that again."

Jack sighed. "You know, research shows that pulling a gun in a situation like that makes it more likely that you'll end up dead?"

"Don't care. What've I told you about facts?"

Jack laughed and turned back to the computer to scroll through the file names. He came to an .exe file and stopped. While he'd spent most of his life in peaceful, ignorant coexistence with technology, he knew that an .exe file made shit happen. He clicked the file and gasped at the same time as Celeste. They both leaned forward as a black box appeared on the screen, asking for a password.

Celeste punched his arm. "What've you done? Is that a virus or something?"

"Don't think so, it does something, though. Shame we don't know the password."

Jack tried a few obvious combinations, but had no luck. Thankfully, the program didn't appear to restrict the number of password tries; he knew he'd need a fair bit of luck to crack it. He was not looking forward to the flight between Wisconsin and New York, but at least it would give him something to do.

Celeste yawned. "I'm sleepy. What about one of the tech guys at the *Standard*? Or paying someone to do it?"

Jack looked at his watch. It was very late. Or, more accurately, very early. "Maybe, but I'd like to try to work it out first. There could be all sorts of funky stuff behind this password, or it could be completely innocuous. I'd rather we find out what we've got before we hand it over."

She raised an eyebrow. "I get the feeling it's something big."

"Me too." He handed the machine to her. "Keep trying?"

She nodded as he got to his feet, walked to the bathroom and closed the door. As he did his business, his mind wandered through the collection of documents on the USB—the budget, the grocery list, the receipt codes—it all felt like hundreds of pages of complete, meaningless gibberish.

As he was finishing up, he spotted the newspaper that Celeste had left on the floor. He read the date and something clicked. He flushed, washed his hands and rushed out of the bathroom. Celeste was mashing away at the keys and looking disinterested, trying to crack the password but having no more success than he'd had.

He flopped back on the sofa. "Hey, pull up that weird shopping list."

She turned and looked at him. "Pomegranates? Baked custard tarts? What about it?"

"It had dates, even into the future. And items next to the dates. But how can you have a receipt code for something you're buying in future? They're passwords."

He took the computer and looked at the shopping list, found the date and the particular shopping item for the day, then copied the receipt code. He opened the .exe file and the password box popped up again. Jack looked at Celeste and shrugged, then pasted in the code. The password box disappeared and a document browser appeared.

"Holy shit." Jack's eyes widened. "Seems like a lot of effort to hide some porn."

Celeste laughed. "Must be more to it than that. Open one of them."

Jack let out a hoot and clicked a random file. When it opened, another box appeared asking for another password. "Fucking hell, there's multiple layers of encryption. There's a meta password, then every file has individual protection. This is going to be a nightmare."

Celeste stared at him. "What?"

"It means we need some help with this." Jack sighed and ejected the USB. "We need to get it cracked, but it'll take some smart tech heads to do it."

~

MICHELLE SMILED as she pointed the remote at the television and hit the mute button. The talking head who'd been summing up the war between China and Taiwan was silenced immediately, though the picture continued to shift between the studio and highlights of the war coverage.

Michelle had realized days ago that she was addicted to footage of the war. It had a potent placebo effect, letting her see how much China was bleeding as well as the growing strength of the US and its allies in the region. That didn't mean she needed to love the reporters, most of whom annoyed her with their spoon-fed analysis.

The war was proceeding as well as she could have hoped. While China had bombed the crap out of Taiwan, they'd failed to mount a successful invasion. The US Navy and Air Force were duking it out with their Chinese counterparts, and both were more than capable of sea and air denial, but not of superiority.

This worked for Michelle. She was relying on a protracted US engagement that avoided the deployment of ground troops or nuclear weapons. At least until after the midterm election. After that, if the US won the day and China retreated from its claims over Taiwan, so much the better.

She was certain, deep down, that as long as the US didn't suffer a disastrous loss, things would be okay. The right Congress would be elected, full of Michelle and her colleagues. The right messages would be broadcast to Americans. The US would prosper. The decay that had set in would be reversed.

The country could look to the future in the knowledge that its power was unchallenged.

Her power would be similarly unchallenged.

Events closer to home weren't progressing as well. After the news that the hit team she'd sent after Chen were dead, she'd received a call from Andrei Shadd. He'd had a pair of snoops bailed up in Chen's house—more than likely it had included Michelle's mystery lover—but they'd gotten away. Her favorite vase hadn't survived the news.

She sighed, picked up her phone and dialed. She waited through the series of strange sounds that signified an encrypted line, then the line started to ring.

"Hello, Peter's Dry Cleaning." Erik Shadd played the role well. "Make sure you ask me about our five shirts for five dollars special. How can I help you today?"

"It's an encrypted line, Erik." Michelle had little patience, even as far as the Shadd brothers' cover was concerned. "I need you to come to my office and escort me tonight."

Erik didn't hesitate. "Where to?"

"An event for the campaign."

"No problem."

Michelle leaned back in her chair and took a deep breath. Her plans would unravel if she didn't get matters closer to home under control. Chen had slipped the net, had a head start and was probably halfway to Asia. In addition, the mystery man was turning into a major annoyance, popping up in inconvenient places. That was more manageable.

"And Erik?" She picked up the remote and turned the television off. "I need every asset looking for that man. If he sticks his head above the parapet, I want it shot off."

"I'll take care of it and see you tonight."

The line went dead.

Michelle stood and walked to the large bay windows. The view of the Mall was commanding, and she never got tired of it. As she locked her hands together and stretched them over her head, she heard several vertebrae in her back pop. She'd been working too much.

She looked at the Capitol building, off in the distance. The good judgment of the American people willing, she and other Foundation candidates would take their place in the Congress within a few months. Once there, she'd join a small group already in Congress and loyal to the Foundation. Others still would be bribed or blackmailed.

She'd have a great number of votes. She'd have power.

She walked to her desk, picked up the phone again and dialed.

"Hi, Michelle." Sarah McDowell clearly recognized the number.

"Hi, Sarah, how're things?"

"Bad. Dad isn't any better, the suitors won't fuck off, and I still have no interest in the company, no matter how much the board and my dad's advisors tell me I need to."

Michelle rolled her eyes. "Sorry, Sarah, I'm trying."

Sarah hesitated on the other end of the line. "I didn't mean to criticize you! You've been fantastic through the whole thing. It's all the other rent seekers that I hate."

She had her, Michelle realized then. She'd cultivated the relationship with Sarah McDowell to the point where she was now the girl's trusted friend and sounding board, particularly on matters concerning the company.

"It's going to get worse before it gets better, Sarah. The UK Parliamentary inquiry handed down its findings today. I'd expect a bit of blowback once the PM speaks."

Sarah sighed loudly but didn't answer. Michelle smiled and readied herself for an hour or so of gossip.

Some things were out of hand, but others were well under control.

JACK CURSED as he stepped into the full-body scanner, the only way past security and into the passenger terminal at Charlotte Douglas International Airport. He'd had his fill of airports lately, yet he had little choice but to wait as some security guard looked at an X-ray of his junk. After a moment, the TSA official waved him through. He scowled at Celeste, who'd already passed security and was waiting for him.

"Every fucking time. It's like I've got a tattoo on my head saying terrorist or something."

She smiled. "Get over it, we're through and we know your friend is here, so let's go have a chat to him."

"Right, come on then. Hickens won't wait for us if we're late."

After a bit of a sleep at the motel in Wisconsin, he'd called Peter and asked for help cracking the USB. Peter had called him back an hour or so later, with flights already booked for them to Washington via North Carolina, where he'd told them to meet up with a special friend at the airport. A special friend Jack hadn't seen in over a year—Simon Hickens.

As they walked in silence through the terminal, past sleeping travelers and ads for Swiss watches and expensive clothing, he hoped Hickens might help them. He was one of the smartest tech guys in the world, and EMCorp had used him exhaustively over the years. He'd been caught up in some of the UK mess, but managed to stay out of the worst of the trouble. Most of all, Jack trusted him completely.

"Jack fucking Emery!"

Jack knew the voice instantly and turned around. Hickens had placed his bag on the ground and opened his arms wide.

Jack closed the gap between them and wrapped the smaller man in a bear hug. "How are you, Simon? Good to see you."

Simon Hickens was the best hacker Jack knew, and the most difficult to work with. Despite having known him for a long while, he still had a lot of trouble understanding the surly thirty-something from Chelsea.

Hickens patted Jack on the back firmly, then backed out of the hug. "Good to see you too. Been too long. I was really sorry to hear about Erin, mate."

Jack felt a stab of pain in his heart. "Thanks. She rated you a lot, Simon."

Hickens laughed. "You're a liar. She hated my guts."

Jack shrugged. "Good to see you're still on the job, anyway."

"On the job? Not since this shit back home. Not a pound in it for an honest gent like myself. I'm having to spend more time in the States to find work. And who's this, then?"

Jack felt a little possessive as he watched Hickens look Celeste up and down. His gaze lingered on all of Celeste's curves, and she went red in response. Jack didn't take it personally, since he'd seen Hickens do the same to plenty of other women over the past few decades.

"Eyes up here, Simon. She's still got access to your HR department."

Hickens looked at Jack and seemed offended. "But she's packing heat, mate!"

Jack laughed and Celeste walked closer to them.

Hickens held out his hand to her. "Simon Hickens, at your service."

Celeste rolled her eyes as she shook his hand, and made a particular note of his ring finger. "Celeste Adams. How is it you don't have a wife? You're such a charmer."

"Standards. You see, the average woman just can't hope to live up to this." He gestured up and down. "I'm like the Chelsea FC of single guys. A challenger might come along, get some luck or buy themselves into contention, but everyone knows who'll last."

Jack laughed and Celeste rolled her eyes again. If there was one thing

Hickens was known for in addition to his skills with a computer, it was his big talk with the ladies.

Hickens grinned. "Now, your average woman, she's peaked at about twenty-eight, thirty tops. After that, it's all downhill. Give it another couple of years and you'll be all jiggle-jiggle yourself, love, and for a discerning sort like myself, that's just not cricket.

"Your average bloke, on the other hand, doesn't really hit his prime until later. Simple economics, and knowledge that the curls get the girls." Hickens ran a hand through his hair.

Celeste smiled. "You know, you're proof that at least some humans are just an overly complex transport method for an asshole."

"Thanks, love. And don't stress too badly, you're fine. Enjoy it while it lasts."

Celeste rolled her eyes, and Jack could see she was amused. He changed the subject. "We've got something that needs your particular set of skills, Simon."

Jack knew that if anyone could crack open the security on the USB and find what was inside, it was Hickens. Jack was certain the USB was the key to everything, and hoped that something with so much security might have some information he could use.

Hickens frowned and his features became serious. "Yeah, Peter mentioned it is encrypted to hell and back. I can do it, but it'll take time. I'm willing to help as long as it isn't going to be something that stokes this fucking war."

"I don't know about that, but it has everything to do with Ernest McDowell's shooting."

"Suits me. Don't understand the line the company has been taking lately, especially since he got shot. It's like we want half of Asia to be killing each other. If we can get to the bottom of his shooting, it might bring some fucking sanity back."

Jack held out the USB. "Here it is."

"Shouldn't be too hard to figure out." Hickens plucked the USB from Jack's hand, then nodded at Celeste. "And hey, miss, if you change your mind, your old mate here will be more than happy to provide room and board."

CHAPTER 21

As the midterm election campaign heats up, analysts are wondering just what effect the war with China will have on the balance of Congress. The White House freely admits that the President has had little time to campaign on behalf of Democratic candidates, and sources say that President Kurzon is banking on the goodwill and confidence of the electorate to stem the predicted landslide toward the Republicans. The wild cards for the GOP are the candidates aligned to the ultra-right Foundation for a New America, who have made no secret of their distaste for both the Democrats and the majority of Republicans in recent years. In a number of Congressional districts, hard-right, Foundation-aligned candidates have overthrown moderate Republicans. There remains talk in Washington about the potential for GOP leadership to cut ties with these fringe-dwellers.

    Hannah Naylor, The Soapbox, *October 23*

Michelle hummed as she drove along the Columbia Pike, returning to her office from a campaign event. Her latest polling numbers were excellent and her staff were convinced that she'd easily take her seat in Congress at the midterms. Though she had to keep up the effort of the campaign, the strong numbers let her focus energy on other problems.

She took a left, glanced for a moment at a pair of pedestrians on the sidewalk and almost rear-ended the car in front of her. She slammed on the brakes but never took her eyes off the men, even as she pulled the car over and drove it onto the sidewalk. A ticket was the last of her concerns.

She unbuckled her seatbelt and got out of the car as quickly as she could. The pair were seemingly oblivious to her interest and kept to their slow walk. She didn't even take the time to lock the car as she hurried after them at a brisk but casual walk.

One of the men was a consul at the Chinese embassy—Consul Li Guo—while the other was the man she'd slept with who'd tried to crack her iPad. Their pairing could be entirely coincidental, but she doubted it. The more she thought about it, the worse the range of possibilities seemed. She needed to know who'd breached her trust and attempted to learn her secrets, and why he was talking to the Chinese.

She pulled her cell phone out of her pocket and dialed Erik Shadd. "Erik, I'm near the Pentagon. I've found the bastard who tricked me."

"Need some help? I'm pretty close if you need me."

She kept her eyes locked on to the two men. "No, I'll sort him out myself. But he's with a consul from the Chinese embassy. Take care of that for me?"

"Which one?"

"Consul Li. Do what you need to do. I'm going after my friend personally."

Michelle clenched her teeth. Ever since the mystery man had ransacked her apartment and tried to discover her secrets, she'd felt less in control than she usually liked. He had found his way to Chen, and there was some chance that he had started to piece together the puzzle: Shanghai, the war, McDowell, the election. He had to go.

"You sure that's a good idea?" There was a note of concern in Erik's voice. "Are you armed?"

"Yeah." Michelle felt instinctively for her concealed pistol. "I've got some unfinished business I want to discuss with him."

"Okay, be careful though. We don't know the guy's story."

"That's what I want to discuss."

～

JACK HAD HAD to catch up fast. He hadn't seen Li Guo in a few years, but they were close from Jack's time in Afghanistan, where Li had been a

Chinese consul in Kabul—and a key source. Somehow Jack had missed that Li had been posted to the States at some point. Probably not surprising considering his recent issues.

Li had surprised him at a coffee shop, and it hadn't taken long for them to reacquaint. As they'd walked back to the Mall, they'd shared a laugh and discussed Li's work at the Chinese embassy. But the more they spoke, the more it became obvious that their chance meeting wasn't so random—Li had sought Jack out.

He stopped. "Li, what can I do for you?"

Li turned and looked into Jack's eyes for a moment. "I need your help, my friend."

Jack laughed. "Short on resources these days, but I'll do what I can. I owe you."

Li looked around, as if their every move was being watched and their every word monitored. "What I'm about to tell you is highly confidential, but it needs to be heard."

Jack frowned. "Sounds ominous."

Li nodded. "You were tortured by my government because of editorial concessions made by Ernest McDowell to the Foundation for a New America."

Jack stared at him, his mouth open. While he had suspected that Ernest had made a deal with the Chinese, and that Dominique and the Foundation had their claws right into him too, he had no idea that it was to such an extent that it worried the Chinese. It all made sense— and made Dominique more important than ever.

Li placed a hand on his shoulder. "Are you okay? I understand what I'm telling you is difficult to hear."

Jack shook his head. "Just a lot to process. Let me guess, Ernest made a deal with China to free us and then got himself stuck. Why tell me?"

Li smiled sadly. "The war."

"It's not going that badly for China, is it?"

"Not on the face of it. But while the missiles fly, our navy and airforce battle it out and the army sits on the southern coast, China is smoldering. The US Air Force has been relentless and my people are rising. They're frightened. They want freedom, not an island. The Party has kept it quiet, but it gets more difficult by the day."

Jack was shocked as the penny dropped. "So you want to stay in the United States?"

Li smiled. "Who says you're not an investigative journalist any more, my friend? The whole thing is smoke and mirrors, and the Party may well fall. I don't want to be on the wrong side of history. I can give you information about the initial deal between McDowell and the Foundation and the subsequent deal with China."

Jack smiled. "What's in it for you? And me?"

"The profile it gets me will help me stay safe. As for you, another Pulitzer?"

"And getting EMCorp out of hostile hands?" Jack thought for a moment. "Let's do it right now, then."

Li shook his head. "I need a day to conclude a few other matters. We'll do the interview tomorrow. I'll call you with the location an hour before."

Jack frowned. He never liked to delay big interviews like this, especially with a source as important as Li. If the slightest whisper of Li's intentions made it into the wrong ears, Jack doubted he'd ever get the chance to do the interview. He considered pressing the matter, but knew better. Li wouldn't budge.

"No problem, Li. Look forward to helping you on this."

～

MICHELLE HAD FOLLOWED them for a quarter of an hour and now watched the men talking from fifty yards away. She'd snapped some poor-quality pictures on her cell phone and sent a few to Erik. Impatient, she'd decided to go in for a closer look, but just as she started to move, the two men parted ways. She had no doubt who she should follow.

She sent a quick text to Erik, telling him that the targets had separated. She closed the distance to her target. He continued to walk with no great urgency and at one point pulled out his cell phone to make a call. She was determined to decipher his piece in the puzzle, but it was important to be patient. If she made a mistake and he got away, she might never get another chance to deal with him on her terms. Michelle edged closer, hoping to catch him unawares and subdue him with the threat of her pistol.

Michelle was about thirty feet away when he slid his phone back into his pocket. She groaned as he started to turn, knowing she'd made a mistake. She'd moved too close, sucked in by the chance to discover his secrets. There was nowhere for her to hide. She froze as his eyes locked on her, then widened in surprise before narrowing in apparent recognition. She held her breath and didn't move, waiting for whatever he might do next. He took the predictable option, turning around and walking briskly away from her.

She ground her teeth and followed him. Now he'd seen her, it was even more important that he not be allowed to get away. This was her one chance, and she'd be damned if she was going to let it slip.

~

JACK LOOKED STRAIGHT AHEAD and walked as fast as he could without breaking into a slow jog. He knew that if he panicked and ran, she'd be on him like a gazelle.

He'd never expected to see Michelle Dominique again, unless it was on his terms and preferably with her in prison orange and separated by a large slab of Perspex. But she'd found him, whether by dumb luck or a cunning plan—or more likely his own stupidity in returning to Washington so casually. Now he had to get away.

He struggled to control his breathing and he could feel his palms starting to sweat. He hoped that she hadn't spotted Li, or else the break he'd received less than an hour ago could be for nothing and he'd be back to square one.

His mind was racing, trying to think of a place close by where he might be safe. He could stay in the open, but she'd just need to keep sight of him and call in her goons. He could talk to any of the police officers nearby, but that would lead to all sorts of awkward questions about why he was so fearful of a slightly built woman.

He looked left and right, and his eyes settled on the National Museum of American History. It was as good a choice as any. At this time of day it would be teeming with tourists and school children, and if he could lose her in some of the more popular sections he could be at Dulles Airport and on a plane to anywhere by the end of the day.

~

MICHELLE CURSED as he entered the museum. She'd hoped he might make a run for it down some back streets, giving her a chance to strike. But clearly he was smart enough to stay in plain sight until he'd lost her, to give himself the safety of the crowd and from any weapon she might have. Like her pistol.

She saw the museum's metal detectors up ahead and, without breaking stride, dug the small weapon out of her pocket, wiped away any prints with her blouse and dropped it into a trash can. It gave a metallic clang as it hit the bottom of the empty can, but she wasn't concerned. The safety was on and the weapon couldn't be traced to her.

She entered the museum through the white automatic doors. There was no line, and she walked through the lobby and passed through the security scanner. She smiled at the guard as she collected her things and started her search. There was no sign of her target.

As she continued to search for him, she was rapidly downgrading her plans. While she'd wanted to find out who he was and then kill him, now she just hoped to learn who he was. She slowed only once, in the cafeteria, to pick up a steak knife that someone had left unattended on a table. With no other weapon to hand, it would have to suffice.

She moved as quickly as she could, contorting her body to squeeze past the crowds of school children marauding through the museum. She was getting frustrated, until she rounded a corner and caught a glimpse of him before he disappeared from sight again.

She moved faster, past countless treasures of the United States, and watched him duck into the 9/11 audiovisual room. He clearly thought he'd lost her and would be able to lay low in the theater for a short while before leaving. She had other ideas.

She entered and spotted him near the front, facing the screen. He was the only person in the room. If she hadn't seen him enter she was certain she'd have missed him. She smiled at the small stroke of luck, approached him and took a seat to his right.

"You've a very difficult man to track down." She kept her voice low and even. "Don't do anything stupid."

When he saw her he tried to get to his feet. Michelle dug the knife into his ribs just deep enough to stall his movements. She heard him take a sharp breath, and then he slowly sat back down again. She could tell he was frightened as he turned and faced her with a nervous smile.

"Look." His voice trembled. "If this is about the other day, I'm sorry, alright? I got spooked."

"Shut up and give me your wallet." Michelle kept the knife against his ribs.

He complied and she opened the wallet. There was just enough light in the room for her to see the name on his license—Jack Emery.

She stared at the name. An alarm in her head was ringing, but she was struggling to figure out why. She kept the knife pressed against him as she thought. Suddenly, she recognized the name, and a lot of different pieces of a difficult mental puzzle fell into place. It was both reassuring and frightening to finally know who he was.

She gave a small laugh. "Well, looks like I can cross fucking a Pulitzer Prize winner off the bucket list, and I didn't even know. How impolite."

He didn't speak until she dug the knife into his ribs a little harder. "Sorry to keep you in the dark, but so goes the lifestyle of the rich and the famous."

"You're becoming a pain in my ass, I'm just not quite sure why. Surely you've got better things to do than harass my organization?" She looked into his eyes.

He glared back with a look of hatred that surprised her. "Because you seem to have a whole lot of coincidental involvement in a whole lot of things that have gone wrong in my life lately, that's why. I can't prove anything, yet. But I'm certain you were involved in the shooting of Ernest McDowell, and probably the war in China."

She laughed, but her mind was racing. She wasn't sure how he'd caught her scent originally, but he was the sort of problem she didn't need. A journalist of his talent wouldn't relent until he found a chink in her armor. With McDowell still alive and Chen out of hand, this was one thing she could tidy up easily.

"I'm involved in a whole lot more than that, Mr Emery, and there's a good reason." With her spare hand she pointed to the screen, showing a video of the Twin Towers collapsing. "That's the moment America got kicked in the nuts, Mr Emery, and we never really got up off the mat."

He shrugged. "What are you going to do?"

"I'm afraid you're a loose end I'm going to have to tie up." She swiftly brought the knife to his throat. "I find this place fitting."

She thought he might struggle, but he waited, clearly aware of how easy it would be to cut his throat. She pressed harder and was about to strike when she heard a giggle. Her head snapped around and she saw two schoolgirls peeking through the curtain and into the theater room.

"They're kissing." The girls giggled again. "They saw us!"

"Hi girls, come on in." Michelle smiled as she lowered the knife, then brought her mouth to Emery's ear. "You're a very lucky man. I'm coming for you."

He didn't move an inch, even as a whole class of elementary schools students filled the room. She threw the knife onto the carpeted floor, stood and walked out of the theater.

Her cell phone was already in her hand.

CHAPTER 22

The prospects of peace between the United States and the People's Republic of China may have taken a turn for the worse with the death of Chinese Ambassador to the US, Mr Du Xiaoming, in a motor vehicle accident. Regarded as a voice of restraint in PRC–US relations, the ambassador was a long-serving diplomat with significant achievements in the US and elsewhere. The circumstances of his death are being treated as suspicious. One other embassy staff member, Consul Li Guo, also perished in the accident. Comment is being sought from the State Department.

Jan Fraser, DC News Central, October 24

An ambulance screeched its brakes near the emergency entrance. The driver killed the lights and hospital staff rushed the unfortunate passenger inside. Michelle had been parked near the entrance of New York Presbyterian Hospital for over an hour. While she'd killed some time watching the ambulances drop off their cargo, she was getting impatient. She looked again at the cell phone that was sitting in its cradle on the dashboard, waiting for the call that would change her fortunes.

Finally, it rang and she smiled and answered. "Hello, Andrei. Took your damn time."

Andrei Shadd grunted. "I've got confirmation from our source at the

Stock Exchange. Sarah McDowell has nominated you as proxy for all of her share holdings."

"Enough?" Her heart threatened to leap out of her chest. "Will it be enough?"

He didn't hesitate. "The eggheads say so."

"Okay. Get our man ready to purchase EMCorp shares as soon as the news strikes." She thought for a second, to be sure she'd covered everything. "And security?"

"Taken care of."

"Good enough for me." She hung up and took a deep breath to calm her nerves.

Now that she'd been nominated proxy for Sarah, it was time to act. Little did Ernest's daughter know that she was about to get a whole lot more shares. Michelle also had to trust that Andrei was ready to purchase bucketloads of EMCorp shares once they hit rock bottom. She smiled as she opened the car door, climbed out and crossed the car park, careful not to look too eager. Once she'd passed through the electric doors of the hospital, she found herself in a lobby even busier than the emergency bay. The place buzzed as people rushed around, visiting sick friends and family.

The staff were calmer, walking around in their uniforms with confidence, some clutching takeaway coffee cups. She looked down at her pant suit and brushed some imaginary lint off her jacket, then made sure the wig and glasses she was wearing were firmly in place. Combined with the heavy makeup she wore, she was unrecognizable. She followed the signs to intensive care. A disinterested-looking ward clerk held court at the reception desk, flicking through a magazine. She looked up as Michelle approached.

"Can I help you?"

Michelle smiled, pulled her identification out of her handbag and held it up for the clerk. "Jane Michelham, I'm with the Bureau. I'm here to check in on Mr McDowell."

The clerk stiffened, stared at the fake FBI identification badge then up at Michelle. "Okay. Are you on the visitor's list?"

"Should be." Michelle dropped the ID back in her bag. "My field office was supposed to call you."

The clerk gazed at Michelle for a few moments too long for her comfort before turning to her computer screen, but she eventually nodded. "Here it is."

Michelle smiled and did her best not to betray her relief. Andrei had assured her that she had been put on the list of authorized visitors, and the fictional Agent Michelham would have no trouble gaining entry to McDowell's intensive care suite. Now she hoped that the implied authority of an FBI agent would keep the clerk's questions to a minimum.

"Great. Can I go through?"

"Sure. Let me check you off. Are there any problems that we should be aware of with Mr McDowell's security?"

"No, nothing to worry about. This is just routine. I'll only be a few minutes."

"Okay, Agent Michelham." The clerk nodded and handed Michelle a keycard. "There's nothing much going on up there, but go through. It's room 402. The card will let you in."

Michelle nodded and masked her relief at not being recognized by the clerk. Though she didn't have a huge public profile outside of Washington, she had made more television appearances lately. As she walked to McDowell's room, she kept her head down, hidden from the security cameras. Andrei had briefed her on their locations. It wouldn't do to be careless.

She followed the signs to the right room. She could see through the window of the suite that McDowell's body was receiving significant technological assistance to stay alive. She thought again of Chen's failure and her anger spiked. But so too did her resolve to do this herself, rather than risk someone else making another mistake. She scanned the keycard and walked into the room. As she moved closer to the bed, she wondered if she'd been naive to trust McDowell. He was always a chance to get a better offer.

She approached the bed and touched him gently on the arm. "Oh, Ernest, we could have been so good together."

She reached into her handbag and pulled out a small case. Inside was a syringe already filled with a poison that had been organized for her. It was potent enough to do the job, but slow-acting, so it would take hours to stop Ernest's heart. By that time, she'd be a long way from the hospital. Best of all, it was undetectable. All she needed to do was inject it into one of the IV drips connected to him. The syringe gave a little squirt when she tested it, being careful not to let any of the mist touch her.

Michelle glanced at McDowell, ready to inject the syringe into an IV. His eyes opened.

She froze in place, all thoughts of the syringe leaving her mind as a million possible scenarios jostled for attention. He had the look of a caged animal, clearly confused about where he was. He was unable to move, under the influence of some pretty strong drugs, but there was no mistaking that his eyes were locked onto hers. Michelle took a deep breath and jabbed the syringe into the IV. She was morbidly curious about how the poison would work, but couldn't afford to stick around.

"Nothing personal." She pressed her thumb on the plunger. "I didn't think it would be as easy as they said it would be, Ernest."

There was no response. He gave no indication that his body had just been invaded by poison. His eyes continued their unblinking stare.

Without further delay, she removed the syringe from the IV and, careful not to let it prick her, put it back inside the protective case. She slid the case into her bag and allowed herself a nervous laugh. She knew that at this moment the poison was coursing through Ernest's system, and would soon start to shut down his body.

She needed to get away and be ready to console Sarah when the inevitable call came, even as the Foundation scooped up a motherlode of EMCorp shares once news of McDowell's death hit.

Things were looking up.

JACK SIGHED as he put down his cell phone. He sat up in bed, turned on the lamp and ran a hand through his hair. He glanced at the clock and wasn't impressed. He had been asleep for a few hours since he'd arrived back in New York and checked in to a shitty motel, but it was still well before midnight.

He'd have gone back to the Wellington Hotel, but didn't want to risk it given Dominique now knew who he was. He was afraid. Worse, he'd had to tell Celeste and Peter to go to a motel, unsure of how much Dominique knew. He'd also called Li to warn him, but clearly he'd been too late on that front. The news had come in a few hours later.

Now Ernest was dead too. He had no doubt that Dominique was involved, given how many pies she had her fingers in lately, but it still came as a shock. In hindsight, perhaps it shouldn't have. She'd shown herself so willing to go to nearly any length to consolidate her control that murder hardly seemed out of the question.

He picked the phone back up and called Celeste. She answered after a few moments.

"Jack? Everything okay?"

He sighed. "Sorry to wake you. I just heard from work. Ernest is dead, Celeste. "

"Fucking hell." Her voice was throaty and she was clearly struggling to wake up. "So now Ernest is gone, along with your lead at the embassy. I'm sorry, Jack."

Jack sighed again. In truth, he was more shocked by the death of Li. He'd slowly become used to the idea of Ernest not waking up, but Li had been the key to everything. Though he'd filled Celeste and Peter in on the threat from Dominique, he'd provided only basic details about the conversation with Li. With both dead, he spilled it all.

"Li was shaping up as a great source, linking Dominique to EMCorp and the war. He also told me that Ernest cut a deal with the Chinese to get us released. Looks like he was caught between the two of them and killed. But it's over, Celeste. We had them, now it's over. Li was the only real link. And now Dominique is free to do whatever she likes."

"She is." Celeste went silent for a moment. "Unless we get something off the USB. But I spoke to Hickens earlier. He's having some trouble. He's untangled some of the encryption but some of the information has been destroyed."

Jack frowned and laid back on the bed, keeping the phone to his ear. "Meanwhile, we're all in danger. You, me, Peter. None of us might survive this."

"I'm sure we'll be fine. With Ernest and the embassy staff dead the threat of anyone finding out about their control is now neutralized. She'll just forget about it."

Jack doubted it. "Stop kidding yourself. These people don't leave loose ends."

"Then I'll harass Hickens even harder to get me the contents of that USB and we'll go after Dominique. There's nothing else to be done."

"No. I want you and Peter to stay out of it. I'm going to take care of her."

She scoffed. "So you want me to hide while you act like some lone gunman? You need to let me help you, Jack. You need to let *others* help you."

"No, I don't."

He hung up and instantly regretted it. He knew that Celeste was right and that he should let her help him, but he wasn't prepared to risk her getting involved any deeper. They were in danger and it was his fault. Once more any good in his life, lovingly built, was crushed under the weight of circumstance.

He should have left it alone, let the police and the authorities deal with Ernest's shooting and moved on with his life. But he'd thrived on the game since finding the voicemail on Ernest's cell phone and had been playing with fire ever since. He'd pushed too hard and let Michelle Dominique force his move. He'd gambled and lost.

He pushed himself up from the bed and walked to the minibar. He opened the door and stared inside. He ignored the soft drink, instead eyeing off the bottles of beer waiting to be opened. They glistened and held the prospect of mental relaxation, at least for a night. For Jack, that was good enough.

As he cracked the first beer and slumped into the room's single armchair, he sighed deeply and tried to clear his thoughts. He wanted the world to go away, to leave him alone and for the carnage around him to stop. It was a forlorn hope, because as soon as one thought exited his head, it was replaced by a newer, darker one. He took a long swig of the beer and thought of the maelstrom of death and violence that had surrounded his life in recent months. Erin, Celeste, Ernest, the war in China, Li—his torture. In one way or another, it was all linked to one person, pursuing one agenda.

As he worked through the supply of beer, Jack wondered if it was worth fighting for anything anymore. He considered drinking until he couldn't lift a bottle, comforted by the thought of dark oblivion. He was not afraid of death, because he had nothing left to lose. He'd been on borrowed time since his release. Time granted to him by Ernest McDowell.

Long after he'd finished the final beer and moved on to the small bottles of hard liquor, he decided that it was time for redemption. He decided, whatever the cost and however much the odds were stacked against him, he'd go down swinging. He decided it was all or nothing. Everyone lost sometimes. And some people lost big. But he also knew that the difference was how well you fought back and recovered.

If he was sure of one thing, it was that he could get rid of Michelle Dominique from the world's throat.

ACT III

CHAPTER 23

"Thanks, Kim. As you mentioned, there's been a great deal of activity at the New York Presbyterian Hospital overnight, following the death of Ernest McDowell in his sleep yesterday. McDowell had been in a coma following his shooting. His death leaves considerable question marks over the control of EMCorp, with the company's share price taking another huge hit following the magnate's death. McDowell is survived by his daughter, Sarah. Back to you in the studio."

Dan Wilkins, CNN, *October 25*

Jack hated the phone. He hated its incessant buzz, face down on top of the wooden dresser. It had reverberated like a hammer drill against his skull several times now. When it had stopped, he'd fallen asleep again in seconds, but before long the pain would start over, punctuating the first hangover of an unreformed alcoholic. This one hurt more than most.

He'd tried a pillow over his head, then tried throwing the pillow at the phone, before, in desperation, he tried to will the phone into spontaneous combustion. None of these ideas had worked. Now, as he lay face down on the mattress, the springs of the cheap bedding cutting into his cheek, the phone started to buzz again. He pressed his face into the mattress and let out a shout of rage.

That didn't work either.

He stood uneasily and kept a grip on the furniture as he made his way to the dresser. He answered the phone, tried to talk and realized his throat was as dry as the Gobi Desert. He must have sounded like some sort of terrifying alien menace to whoever was on the other end.

"Jack? It's Peter." His tone was all business, without a hint of appreciation for the pain Jack was in. "Any sign of Dominique or her people?"

"Hello." Jack's attempt to force a word failed. He swallowed several times and tried to get some moisture into his throat, then tried again. He didn't appreciate the chuckle on the other end of the line.

"You sound like shit, Jack."

"Feel like it too." His stomach roared. "What do you want?"

"Just checking in. You're clearly alive, if a bit worse for wear."

Jack couldn't argue with that. He'd worked his way through the minibar with a vengeance, then called reception for a restock. The staff member who'd brought the fresh booze to his room could barely conceal her disdain as she spied the empty bottles. Jack had worked his way through most of the fresh stock as well.

But, for all that, he was alive. Deep down he wondered if they'd find him at the hotel anyway. If they did, it would make his experience in the Chinese prison seem like a Caribbean cruise. While the Chinese had tortured him, they'd deliberately kept him alive. Dominique had no reason to.

Blood everywhere. Cold, hard concrete. Fear for Celeste Adams. Confusion. Pain. Lots of pain. And shit. In his pants and on the floor.

"Jack?" Peter's voice cut through Jack's flashback.

"I'll live. How're you going?"

There was a long pause on the other end of the line. "Honestly? Don't think it has sunk in yet. I've worked for him for years. He was closer than family. It'll take a while."

"Sorry, mate." Jack didn't really know what to say to console Peter.

"Thanks. Got some good news for you, Jack. Hickens has been trying to call you. He couldn't get through and so he called me instead. He's cracked it."

Jack sat down on the edge of the bed, shook his head and tried to clear away some of the fog. "The USB? You'd better not be teasing."

"Kidding you about the key to all of this? I'm not. He's filled me in. We've cracked the USB. He lost a heap of information in the process, but he said what he opened was a treasure chest. It all points to this Chen guy, but there's stuff about it all: Dominique, the

Foundation, the attacks in Shanghai, the war, their run for Congress. Everything."

"Fucking hell. Peter, we might just have a fighting chance." Jack couldn't hide his excitement. He smiled; now he could do what he'd pledged to last night, the one thing that had the potential to return him from the precipice of self-destruction: send a swift kick right to the head of the person responsible for all of this, Michelle Dominique.

"More than a fighting chance." Peter laughed softly. "This deals us back into the game, and we're sitting on a great big stack of chips."

Jack didn't say anything right away. He considered what came next. He'd known that when he'd handed over the USB, it had been a long shot to produce a dividend even if Hickens could break it. Now, it seemed like he had. And unless Ernest's former assistant was exaggerating—something he wasn't known for—it changed everything.

"Will it be enough?"

"Maybe." Peter didn't hesitate. "But there's a catch. We've got fragments. We're going to need to talk to Chen to bolt all of this information together into a story that will make people listen. Clean yourself up, you've got a flight to catch."

"Where to?"

There was a pause. "That's the interesting thing. Taiwan. Hickens found a clue on the Darknet that Chen has fled there, but we've got nothing more concrete than that. It's not a great lead, but you've got to find him. I'll email you."

Peter hung up and Jack grunted and threw the phone on the bed. His head suddenly felt quite a bit better, but it would be improved by a few more hours' rest. He lay down again but doubted sleep would come. There was too much to think about, too much to do.

He was just dozing off when the phone rang again. This time, he reached for it as quickly as he could. He thought it must be Peter again, but he smiled when he saw the caller identification. He hadn't expected her to call. He took a deep breath, exhaled and then answered the phone.

"Hi."

"Jack? It's me." Celeste sounded cautious. She'd clearly cooled down since their last conversation. He was glad that she was talking to him. "Enjoy your drink?"

"Yep."

"Where are you? Peter told me you had a sore head."

"I'm at a motel. Come over and we'll go from there."

"Go where? There's nowhere we can run from these people."

Jack was relieved she recognized the danger. "There might be one place. I'm not sure any of them have heard of Yeppoon, Australia, let alone been there. We're going to fly home—to my home—and that will give us time to think and consider our next move."

She didn't talk for a minute, and despite the situation, he smiled at the look he knew she'd be making: there would be a frown in the ridge between her eyes, and her forehead would be wrinkled with worry.

"Okay, Jack. Okay. I'm out of ideas so I'm happy to go with yours. I'll be over there within the hour."

He hung up and took another long breath and let it out through gritted teeth. He hated lying to Celeste, but had no choice. If he was going on a wild-goose chase to find Chen in Taiwan, then he had to do it alone. And to do that, he had to know she was safe. He stood, still unsteady, and looked around the room. He had an hour to make himself respectable, get packed and ready to fly. All the while he had to try to stay upright and keep the contents of his stomach from exiting his body.

No sweat. For Jack, this was living.

～

MICHELLE HATED MEETINGS, but was looking forward to this one. She could have attended the extraordinary general meeting of the EMCorp board and significant shareholders via video link from Washington, but she gained particular satisfaction from slaying her enemies in person. Metaphorically, at least. She was not going to give this one up.

Seated around the table were the usual members of the EMCorp board, along with the top twenty significant private and institutional shareholders. The most prominent of these was Sarah McDowell, but Michelle also had a seat at the table, following the Foundation's purchase of a large amount of stock. The board had called them all together to determine control of the company moving forward. They'd resolved to sort the matter quickly.

She looked down the table to Sandra Cheng. She looked like she was about to drop dead on the spot, with heavy eyes and limp hair. After her divorce, she'd gained a board seat. Now Ernest was dead. It looked like the news had hit Sandra particularly hard. Michelle nearly sympathized with the stress the woman must be under—the death of her ex-husband

and the fact that Ernest's daughter had chosen to confide in Michelle rather than her stepmother. Sarah, for her part, just looked sad.

As if on cue, Peter Weston cleared his throat. "Good afternoon, ladies and gentlemen. We've got a lot to get through. Moving right into it—"

Michelle interrupted. "Excuse me, Peter, before we kick off, I'd like to ask that the meeting minutes record condolences to the family and friends of Ernest McDowell."

Weston could hardly hide his scowl. "Very well."

She smiled. "Ernest was a visionary. He's a terrible loss for all of us. Sarah and Sandra, let me offer my personal condolences for your loss."

Michelle looked down the table and saw several nods and sad smiles. Sarah gave her a warm smile. Sandra didn't even manage that, offering nothing but a half-hearted nod.

Weston waited for the small amount of chatter to die down and then continued. "First item of business: the ongoing leadership of the company."

Sandra leaned forward. "I hope you'll all be willing to support my bid for chairmanship, given the trauma we've all gone through."

Michelle chuckled as several outraged board members barked their disapproval. One she didn't know spoke. "Sandra, you're grieving. There's no need to be silly."

Sandra was unrepentant. She raised her hands, palms facing outward, to block any attempt at rebuttal and further flare ups of the argument. "My family and I hold enough of this company to retain the chairmanship. Ernest may be gone, but it's important that we keep things in the family."

Michelle cleared her throat. "Excuse me if I'm being too forward, but I do wonder what particular family you're referring to? The man who divorced you or the stepdaughter who hates you?"

As Sandra blustered, Weston spoke up. "Ernest's will specified that his entire portfolio go to his daughter. There's no correlation between Sarah's holding and your own, Sandra. I've invited her to this meeting to make her views known."

Anthony Tanner, a Foundation-aligned board member, spoke up. "Indeed, given the size of her holding, we should hear from her."

Michelle smiled. Tanner had been easy to buy off: a large amount of money and a small number of revealing photographs outside the Ruby Slipper. He was another piece of the EMCorp puzzle in her pocket, and also an effective mouthpiece in her current fight to gain total control. Michelle sat back as Sandra started to protest.

Tanner shook his head again. "You have the floor, Sarah."

Sarah looked nervous and unsure as she looked down the table. "Okay."

Sandra tried to steal the march. "Sarah, tell them that you want me to be chairwoman. It's ridiculous to consider any other possibility."

Michelle was fascinated by the interplay between the two as Sarah narrowed her eyes at Sandra.

"That's not what I want." Sarah's voice was haunting. "I'm combining the weight of my shareholding with Michelle's stock. I trust her to look after the best interests of my father's company."

Michelle felt a wave of relief wash over her. After having Ernest in her hand, then losing him, this was sweet vindication. McDowell had been a loose cannon, a man of such immense power and ego who had proved difficult to control. She wouldn't make the same mistake twice. She'd ensure her appointed chairman was completely loyal.

She smiled, aware the others were looking at her. "I thank you for the show of faith, Sarah. I'm sorry, Sandra."

Sandra bristled but kept her mouth shut, and Peter Weston leaned forward as though about to talk, a look of concern on his face.

He didn't get the chance, as Tanner forestalled any reply. "Right, who will it be, Ms Dominique?"

"Thanks, Anthony." Michelle nodded to Peter Weston and gestured toward the door.

Weston looked confused, but moved as instructed. Michelle waited as the doors to the boardroom were opened to admit a tall, well-dressed man—Michelle's answer to controlling EMCorp. She was not actually interested in the daily workings of the company, just in ensuring it was on message. Her flunkies would sort that out, so she could focus on her bigger problems: Chen, Jack Emery and the approaching election.

As the newcomer walked to the head of the table, Michelle kept talking. "I'd like to introduce Gavin Marles. He joins the board and assumes the chairmanship with a wealth of experience. He has the full support of Sarah McDowell, myself and several other significant shareholders. I hope you'll join me in endorsing his board appointment and chairmanship unanimously."

Michelle didn't add that Marles was also as pliable as they came and in utter lockstep with her agenda. As she looked up and down the table, there were no dissenting voices. She was impressed that the board members could read the situation. Even Sandra, who sat with her arms folded and a sour look on her face.

Marles smiled. "Good morning, all. It's a pleasure to be here. I intend to hit the ground running, with a review of all of our operations. I'm concerned that at times in recent months our focus erred slightly. I intend to rectify that."

Michelle smiled. Marles might be a patsy, but he was a capable one. Most importantly, he was her patsy. He'd ensure the war was covered properly. Just as importantly, he'd throw a wave of support behind the bid for Congress by the Foundation candidates.

"Now, with the chairmanship settled, I'd like to get onto the guts of the meeting." Marles paused. "Peter, could I ask that the shareholders be excused?"

Weston nodded, a sad look on his face. "I'll send minutes of this meeting to everyone in attendance. You have the company's thanks for taking the time today. There'll be light refreshments served in the executive dining room that you're all welcome to enjoy."

Michelle smiled and stood without a word. She walked toward the door and met Sarah McDowell. She placed a hand on the young woman's back and guided her through. Sarah turned her head and smiled, but kept quiet. The meeting had gone as they'd planned.

"I'll catch you in the dining room?" Michelle kept her voice low.

"Okay, see you there." Sarah nodded and kept walking.

As Sarah walked away, Michelle smiled. Things were traveling nicely. The war against China was kicking along, and there had been a positive increase in US economic figures. Most importantly, public sentiment had swung back in a conservative direction which gave Michelle and the other Foundation-aligned Congressional candidates a good chance to win a decent number of seats.

Once that happened, the fun would begin. Power. And rebirth.

As she started down the hall toward the dining room, she checked her cell phone. It had a message that needed her attention. It was confirmation that Jack Emery had boarded a flight at JFK Airport to Hawaii and on to Taiwan. There was only one plausible scenario—he had tracked down Chen and was on his way to find him. She frowned, less happy with the progress made in dealing with those two problems.

She knew that the end game was coming, and that if those two were allowed to meet, then there was a real chance that everything she'd fought for would be lost. She needed to terminate both of them, but knew that Emery was a far easier proposition than Chen. It was fortuitous that they'd both be in the same country at the same time. Or at least that's what her gut was saying. If Emery was going to Taiwan then Chen must be there.

She sent a simple message: *Send assets to Taiwan. Follow Emery until he leads us to Chen. Then sort it out.*

With luck, Emery and Chen would be dead in a gutter within a few days.

CHAPTER 24

The Chairman of the Joint Chiefs of Staff addressed media in Washington today, providing a comprehensive update on the progress of the conflict against China. Admiral Matt Glennon detailed the NATO and other allied assets that had arrived in theater, spearheaded by the French aircraft carrier Charles De Gaulle. The flotilla of forty-eight ships from nineteen countries will join the Japanese Navy's efforts to protect sea lanes in the ocean around the conflict. While their involvement in the conflict will be limited to defense of merchant shipping, the presence of such an international coalition is an important public relations win for the United States, further isolating China among the international community.

Lee Jordan, New York Standard, *October 27*

Jack knew that the Happy Kitchen and Bar wasn't everyone's cup of tea, but it suited him just fine at the moment. He'd left Celeste safe in Hawaii and boarded a flight to Taiwan. She hadn't taken it well, once she'd realized they weren't going to Australia, nor was she following him to Taiwan. At first she'd raised her eyebrows slightly, as if waiting for him to reveal it was a gag. But her expression had quickly changed to a frown. He'd told her that he was traveling to Taipei to finish this business.

She'd protested and refused to stay behind. He'd desperately wanted to concede and let her come, but he hadn't. He'd reviewed some of the information on the USB, and it was awesome. He just had to track down Chen and get the last lot of evidence they'd need to end the serpent-like grip of Dominique and the Foundation for a New America on EMCorp. He knew it was dangerous and he couldn't do what needed to be done if he was worrying about Celeste. She'd backed down only after he'd laid on a fairly heavy guilt trip on her about needing to know she was safe, and that he'd already lost too many people who were important to him. The end result was the same, though: she was safe in Oahu and he could get on with what needed to be done.

He sighed and got back to work. He'd spent countless hours trawling through the information on the USB that Hickens had managed to unlock, and it was scary shit. There were pieces linking the Foundation to everything, but Chen was the only glue that could bind all the bits together. Jack had no idea where Chen was, but Hickens had found a tiny fragment on the Darknet to show that Chen had returned to Taiwan after he'd been forced to flee America. It was also the logical place to go.

The only interruption to his trawl had been an email from EMCorp Human Resources, telling him he'd been fired at the request of the board. Jack couldn't explain it, and hadn't spent much time thinking about it, but he somehow knew Dominique was involved. He'd determined to worry about his employment situation once Chen and Dominique were dealt with. They were his priority at the moment, and the first step was finding Chen.

Jack heard raised voices and looked up at the bar. He hadn't noticed the entry of the four well-dressed Chinese men who were now harassing the barman. Jack did his best to keep cool, but the barman's occasional nervous glance toward him was enough to tell him the gig was up. He closed the browser window and hit the shutdown icon on the desktop. As the machine whirred and then went silent, he pulled the USB free from the slot.

He looked up as the group of new arrivals approached his booth, reaching behind where he was sitting to slide the USB between two cushions. It was a tight fit, but as they came to a stop before his table, he was confident that the device was hidden.

Jack smiled at the men as they crowded around the table. After another moment, one of them slid into the booth opposite Jack. One of the others stood facing him, while two more faced outwards. Jack glanced over to the bar and noticed that the barman had made himself scarce. He wouldn't be surprised if there were another couple of goons standing outside, directing pedestrians away from the bar. One way or another, it was clear that this meeting was on their terms and wasn't to be interrupted.

"Hello, Mr Emery. I'm sorry for this display, but it's quite necessary to ensure my safety—and yours." The man who'd sat opposite him spoke in decent English.

Jack scoffed. "I'm struggling to see the imminent threat to your person, quite honestly. Afraid I might put a fork through your eye?"

The other man laughed. "A fair point. My name is Wen and I represent Michelle Dominique. You're on a fool's errand that has placed you in grave danger."

Jack made an effort to keep his facial expression neutral. "I know this area is a bit seedy, but I'm only after a beer and a night with a warm body."

Wen laughed and waved his hand dismissively, clearly not buying Jack's version of events. "To ensure your safety, I require you to tell me where Chen is. We know you've traced him here. Once this information is provided, my colleagues and I will escort you to the airport. You may then go anywhere you want with our blessing."

Jack laughed. The Foundation were getting desperate. Though they'd traced him here, the fact that they were talking to him rather than putting a bullet in him showed they had less idea where Chen was than he did. If the Foundation knew where Chen was, they'd have no use for Jack. Their entry into the situation made it a three-way game of hide and seek. He hadn't expected finding Chen to be easy, but this made things significantly more difficult. He had to find Chen before they did.

"Sorry, mate, even if I knew what you were talking about, a good journalist doesn't reveal his sources." Jack started to stand when one of the Foundation men took a few steps toward him, reached out and pushed him forcefully back into his seat.

Wen's expression darkened. "Mr Emery, you'll give us any information you have about the whereabouts of Chen sooner or later. But the longer you delay, the greater the potential threat to your health."

Jack could have taken issue, but he had no doubt about the sincerity of their threat. "Look, you'll need to find another tree to bark up. I don't have any idea what you're talking about. So I'll pass, if it's all the same to you."

Wen's eyes narrowed menacingly. "Give me what I want, Mr Emery."

Jack sat in silence. The information on the USB and finding Chen were the only ways to bring McDowell's shooting and the subversion of EMCorp to the fore. If he surrendered it then he'd lose the key to justice for McDowell, and the company's influence would continue to be used to push an agenda.

After a few moments, Wen shrugged, stood and gestured for his men to leave ahead of him. Once they were out of earshot Wen put both hands on the table and leaned in close to Jack's face. Jack didn't flinch, even though he could smell the tobacco on Wen's breath and see the anger etched on his face.

"We will meet again, you and me. And when we do, I'll shit in your mouth and have my men force it closed until you choke on it."

Jack didn't get the chance to respond, as Wen turned on his heels and left. It was bad enough that Dominique knew about him, but now her men were on his heels, waiting to pounce the moment he found Chen. His life was in greater danger by the day.

He needed to find Chen. Soon.

❧

CHEN HAD SEEN his share of blood, but it had never seemed as important as this.

He stood with his mouth open and slack. His feet were planted like the roots of the mightiest tree, and refused to move despite signals from his mind. His entire consciousness worked furiously to process the sight of the thin ribbons of crimson that were interrupted only in a few places by small puddles. His training had abandoned him and he could focus on nothing else for several long moments.

He'd traveled the short distance from his hideaway in central Taipei to the luxury apartment his wife and children were living in. Chen had taken all necessary precautions: he'd checked that he hadn't been followed and discreetly entered the car park of the apartment building. He'd made his way cheerfully through the door and expected to be mobbed by his children and a relieved wife. It was to be their reunion.

He had been met with silence.

He'd first rushed to the master bedroom and found no sign of anyone. He'd shouted out and rushed to the next room in the apartment —the bathroom. There, near the entrance, he'd seen the blood. He'd looked inside the room and frozen. He knew, deep down, that he'd find a heavy toll at the end of the trail. The real mystery was how steep the price would be. Wife or children? Wife and children? Chen feared the answer.

He shook his head, reached into his pocket and pulled out a small flick knife—the only weapon he had on hand. Carrying a gun around in Taipei was far too risky at the moment. He doubted that whoever was responsible was within a hundred miles, but hoped there would be a hostile foe in the house to help him expunge his sorrow by plunging a blade into their throat.

He followed the trail of blood. As he did, the speed of his heartbeat increased and he struggled to keep his breathing even, despite his training. He knew the pattern of the blood—thin streaks along the carpet —meant someone had been moving quickly. But in some places there was a larger stain of blood, as well as handprints and streaks on the wall. Most concerning were the bloody footprints, bigger than any feet in his family.

The trail snaked up the stairs, to the top level of the apartment. Chen gripped the knife tightly as he followed, knowing that anyone waiting in the expansive living area at the top of the stairs would have a free shot at his head once he reached the top. He moved cautiously and listened for any sound, but he could hear none. Whoever had done this was long gone, or very good.

He peered over the lip of the stairs and felt his heart break. He gripped the knife tightly as the first tear rolled down his cheek. He climbed the last few stairs and rushed into the middle of the living room. On the large rug, with the debris of the living room splayed around her, his wife lay still and abused. Chen inhaled deeply, then let his training take over.

Though he found it difficult, it was important that he secure the room before moving to his wife's side. He scanned the area, knowing that there was only one possible hiding place from his current vantage point: the kitchen. He crossed the room, the small knife ready, but there was nobody there. Apart from his wife, the apartment was empty. That included his children. Whoever had killed her had most likely taken them.

He moved to his wife's side. Her face was barely recognizable. Her eyes were closed, but even if they weren't he doubted it would make any difference. Purple and puckered, her eyelids didn't reveal any hint of the black pearls he remembered. Her lips were cracked and cut. Her hair was matted and clumped together with her own blood. She had a nasty gash on her head, but what had killed her was a cut throat.

Defying logic and moving like an automaton, he fell to his knees beside her and felt for a pulse. There was none. He listened for sounds of breathing. She was silent. He scooped her into his arms and rocked her gently, his sobs coming in ragged and heavy fits. Her body was a dead weight, her clothes ripped and displaced. She'd been beaten nearly to death and then killed.

He rocked her back and forth, his tears falling to her broken body. He wasn't sure how long passed, with him simply holding her body and weeping, but slowly his senses returned and his vision broadened. It was only then that he looked up at the wall and saw a white piece of paper pinned there by a knife.

He placed her body gently back on the rug and stood. He walked slowly to the wall, not really wanting to read the message but hoping it might provide him with a hint of her fate. He pulled the knife from the wall and dropped to the floor, then opened the sheet of paper.

This is the interest charge on debts unpaid. No further payment is due unless you divulge anything about Shanghai. In such case, your children are your next best asset. They'll be kept safe and well for the next few months, while your loyalty is tested.

Chen screwed the note into a ball as he thought of his daughter and son. He threw it with as much force as he could muster, but it hit the wall and fell to the floor with nearly complete, unsatisfying silence. He picked it up and put it in his pocket. He ran a hand through his hair and moved back to his wife's side.

He'd taken every precaution after leaving the United States. He'd used the Darknet to reach out and secure safe passage and lodging in Taipei for him and his family. They'd traveled and been accommodated separately, and he'd thought it would be enough. Obviously someone had made a mistake. The Foundation had found his family. Now his children needed him.

He was thinking a bit clearer. He'd report this to the local police anonymously. His wife had no identification, her fingerprints weren't on file and his children were gone. She'd be a random, dead female in the middle of a country at war. He regretted enormously that she wouldn't have a proper funeral, nor would he attend, but it was the only way. He had to think of his children.

And vengeance.

∼

"GOOD MORNING, Mrs Hamilton, good morning, Ms Dominique."

Michelle stepped forward and smiled as the few dozen bright-eyed fourth graders chanted the greeting. As they stared back and forth between the school principal and her, Michelle lifted her hand and gave another wave, then moved aside as the principal gained the attention of the class.

The principal spoke. "We're very lucky to have a very special guest with us today, children. My friend Ms Dominique is running for Congress in two days."

The children continued to stare, clearly unmoved by Michelle's pending triumph. She knew that the media hacks would get enough to edit up a thirty-second video, so she relaxed and let the event take its course. She just had to nail the sound bites, flash a smile, avoid any problems and they'd do the rest.

Ms Hamilton continued. "Is there anything you'd like to ask Ms Dominique, children?"

Hands shot into the air, and Michelle made sure she flashed a wide smile.

The principal pointed at one doe-eyed girl, who looked down at the table as she spoke. "Why do you want to be a Congress?"

Michelle smiled warmly at the gaffe. She split her glances between the camera and the child as she answered. "Because, young lady, I want to make sure you grow up in an America that is exceptional, that leads the world in knowledge and innovation and is a beacon of freedom and prosperity."

The girl smiled nervously, and after a brief moment of silence the principal asked another child for their question.

A boy's hand shot into the air. "Why are we fighting China? My mom says it's bad to fight."

Michelle frowned, then walked over to where the boy was sitting. She kneeled down, and put her hands on his shoulders. "Unfortunately, sometimes countries do things that are wrong. China has attacked a place called Taiwan, like a giant bully. Have any of you ever been bullied?"

Michelle waited for the nods and then continued. "Well, like when a bully bothers you, you hope that there'll be someone to help you and look after you. Maybe your teachers or your parents. Now, our country,

America, has had to stand up to the bully and look after our Taiwanese friends."

Michelle flashed another smile. She loved children and their simple questions. They let her ram home any point she wanted without any backtalk or danger of going off message. She'd used the tactic liberally during her campaign, so it was fitting that her final public event would be at a school.

She took the boy's hand in hers. "Unfortunately, it shouldn't have become this bad. For many years, we've watched the bully get stronger, while we've become weaker. One of the things I want to do, if I'm allowed into Congress, is make sure bullies are never able to push us around again. I want America strong. Wouldn't that be nice?"

Ms Hamilton stepped forward with the smile. "Well, thank you, children, we'll keep moving along and let you get back to your class."

After a short tour of the rest of the school, Ms Hamilton farewelled Michelle at the front steps. Michelle was careful walking down them, lest the last televised moment of her campaign be her falling down stairs. The polls were showing a comfortable win for her and for many of the other Foundation candidates, as long as they avoided mistakes.

As she reached the final step, the two members of her security detail —also Foundation loyalists—stepped forward to intercept a man who was pushing through the crowd toward her. She backed away, but as he reached the front of the crowd he lifted his arm and threw something at her.

She cowered as the plastic cup sailed through the air and her security tackled him to the ground. She couldn't avoid a substance that smelled like urine splashing all over her.

The man shouted uncontrollably, even as he was wrestled into submission. "Do not vote for this woman, she's worse than Bush, she's a neo-con who will bring war to America and plunder our public services! Do the right thing, America, stand strong!"

"Alex, Grant." Michelle stood proud as her guards turned to look at her. "Let him go."

The two guards looked confused, but nowhere near as confused as the protestor, who gave her a quizzical look. Her words were even enough to stop his ranting. Michelle tried to mask her disgust as she stood tall, aware that the cameras were still rolling.

She gave the man the steeliest look she could muster. "While I don't condone your assault, I agree with your call for a strong America. I may not agree with your views, but I'll defend to my very last breath your right to hold those views. Our founding fathers would have expected nothing less."

Without another word, she resumed her walk to her car, which was waiting with its back door open.

The campaign had just been won.

CHAPTER 25

"There you have it, explosive footage that has emerged from China, despite the media blackout. While much is unclear, we do know that a large protest in Beijing's Tiananmen Square has been violently put down by elements of the People's Liberation Army. This is the latest of several such videos, showing at least a degree of dissent and an undercurrent of dissatisfaction inside China at the moment. We spoke to an analyst from Jane's Defence and Security earlier, who speculated that the protests are being sparked by the stalemate of the war, the damage caused by US strikes to energy and infrastructure, shortages of fuel and food, and the continuing harsh curfews."

Len Oakes, ABC Newsflash, *October 29*

Jack glanced at yet another table of baubles and miscellaneous shiny junk as he followed the flow of the crowd through the busy Taipei market. At least he had a good disguise: a pair of Levis and a New York Yankees cap. America and US citizens were fairly popular in Taiwan at the moment, given that the United States Armed Forces were the only thing separating the Chinese dragon from the Taiwanese lamb.

As he paused to look at a stall that sold second-hand books, his cell phone rang. He pulled it out of his pocket, and sighed at the caller ID. Celeste was still mad at him, but at least she was talking to him. She was safe in Hawaii, but he didn't want to talk to her right now. He let the call go to voicemail.

He continued to walk through the market, which was riotously busy considering the constant threat of Chinese rocket attack. Someone bumped into his shoulder. Jack turned his head and recoiled. The stranger who'd bumped into him was perhaps the ugliest man he'd ever seen. Though the man was well dressed in jeans and a collared shirt, he had burns and a shocking scar down the entire left side of his face.

"Out of the way, Yankee."

"Sorry, mate." Jack took a step back and overplayed his Australian accent, hoping the man would go away. He didn't need the attention right now. "My bad."

The man stepped closer and pushed his face closer to Jack. "You should come and see my shop, buy lots of things and atone for your assault."

"No, thanks." Jack turned and started to walk away.

The Taiwanese gentleman didn't give up, and started to walk after Jack. Before he knew it, he had a large, barrel-chested Pacific Islander in front of him, and the ugly, yammering salesman behind him.

Jack turned. "Look, I don't want any trouble, I'm just not interested in whatever you're selling."

"I was talking to you. You should listen to what I have to say or my boy will make you listen. Nobody walks away from me."

Jack turned back to the man mountain, just in time to hear bone crack. The Islander howled in pain and crumpled and the Chinese man who'd inflicted the damage aimed another vicious kick at the Islander's leg. The pain must have been immense, and the man screamed in agony. Jack stepped out of the way of the man's two hundred and eighty–pound bulk as he fell.

As onlookers screamed and ran, the Chinese man who'd delivered the kick spoke to the ugly man in decent English: "Walk away and don't do anything stupid."

Jack swallowed hard, knowing that was nearly the universal signal for someone to do something stupid. He took another step back as the man reached for a small knife in his boot. Jack's Chinese savior stepped forward, easily deflected the quick thrust of the blade, and caught the man in a wrist lock. Jack heard something snap, and the Chinese man gave his victim a punch to the throat for good measure.

Jack breathed a sigh of relief, the immediate threat gone. He stepped toward his Chinese benefactor and held out his hand. "Thanks a whole lot for that. I'm not quite sure what their problem was."

"You've been looking for Chen?" The man's whispered tone was harsh. "You've found me, but we need to get away from here. They're amateurs, but others are closing in. The next bunch might not be so sloppy."

Jack's eyes widened. He reached into his pocket and pulled out the knife he'd been carrying for exactly this eventuality. He hadn't expected Chen to find him, but Jack's approach was unchanged. He flipped open the knife and held it out. His hand was shaking.

Chen sighed. "Didn't you just see the futility of that? You have a strange way of thanking someone who just saved your life."

Jack ignored him as he held the knife out. "You're Chen Shubian."

Jack was disappointed by how calm the Chinese man seemed. "I am."

"Your bomb killed my wife."

Chen shrugged. "Did it? Unfortunate."

"That's it?"

"It was not deliberate. She could have just as easily been hit by a bus, or been stabbed and mugged. But I'd suggest neither of us have time for your vengeance at this moment. The Foundation want me dead, and my own wife is dead thanks to them, so we've something in common."

Jack didn't lower the knife. He hadn't expected to find Chen on quite these terms, and clearly someone had told the two idiots to attack him, yet he was still torn between a desire to rip Chen's throat out and the need for his evidence that only Chen could give him.

Chen sighed again. "Look, the only reason you're alive is because they think you can lead them to me. You're more useful next to me, and probably safer too. So if it's all the same to you, I'd like to get out of here."

After a second, Jack nodded, pocketed the knife and followed Chen at a brisk walk through the market. A few people looked sideways at them, and Jack worried that with every corner they turned, the next street was going to be filled with armed thugs.

They were near the edge of the market when, as Jack had feared, they were surrounded on all sides by large men armed with a mix of bats and blades. At once he wondered where the rest of the crowd had gone, and how many foes Chen could take down while he ran.

One of their assailants stepped forward. "Hello, Chen. Michelle

Dominique sends her regards. Hand over your friend, give yourself up and your children will be spared."

Chen laughed. "Spared what? The rape and murder of their mother? Being abducted? It's too late for that."

Jack looked sideways at Chen. But before events could proceed further, there were shouts and an ear-splitting whine. The ground shook with tremendous force and Jack was knocked off his feet. He landed hard and could taste dust and dirt, mixed with blood. He must have bitten his tongue. He rolled over onto his back and did a quick stocktake. He could see no injury. He was unhurt but dazed.

He rose to his feet involuntarily, as Chen grabbed him by the arm and pulled him up. Together they ran past screaming shoppers and away from the flames and rising plumes of smoke. The Chinese missile could have landed right on top of Jack's head, and he was glad to have a little luck for once. In all of the confusion, they lost their pursuers. He was thankful when they reached the edge of the market without further incident.

Jack stopped, trying to catch his breath when Chen turned to face him. "Now what do you want? It better be good, because you carried the vipers to my doorstep."

"How did you find me?"

"You're not as subtle as you think. Word of a Westerner asking questions about me made its way to my ear. It wasn't hard to find you. Now, what do you want?"

"I want to talk to you about Michelle Dominique and the Foundation, then kill you."

Chen laughed darkly. "I like honesty. You may hate me and want me dead, but there is one thing we both want. I can give you the rest of the information you need, and you can use it in a way I can't. Now if you're going to stab me, do it, because the noose tightens around our necks."

"How do you know what evidence I've got?"

"If you know who I am, then I know you're the one who found my USB. The fact you're here shows that you need me, and now I need you too. I'll help you."

"Okay. But why are you willing to give this to me?"

"Dominique has my children. I owe her."

∼

CHEN CRACKED the egg shell firmly and carefully let the insides spill into the frying pan. The egg gave a satisfying sizzle as it hit the hot oil beside the steak, and he repeated the act three more times. Chen hummed a nameless tune as he waited the few minutes until the food was done. He removed the pan from the heat and divided the meal evenly between two plates. He carried the plates over to the small dining table in the kitchen.

"You sure know how to impress on a first date." Emery's tone was dry.

"The war rationing makes these steaks worth more than diamonds."

They ate in silence except for the clink of ice in their water glasses. Within a few minutes the two of them had cleared their plates. Chen stood, gathered the dishes and placed them on the kitchen counter. When he returned, he sat and looked calmly at Emery. The journalist had kept his cards fairly close to his chest, but Chen could sense a fierce intellect and a burning anger.

"Okay. You've eaten. Now it's time to open your mouth with something that impresses me."

Emery's gaze didn't waver, and if he was intimidated, Chen couldn't tell. "As I said earlier, I know you're responsible for the deaths in Shanghai, including my wife, and for the attack on Ernest McDowell. While that burns me to the core, I also know you're probably the only one left alive who can give me what I need on Michelle Dominique."

He didn't mind that the journalist knew all of this. He was here because Chen had let him in. The major threat to him remained the Foundation. The threat was twofold: they had his children and were also hunting him. Assisting Emery expose Dominique could help with that, though he didn't need to tell Emery that.

He'd spent the last two days trying to locate his children, using every network he had at his disposal. He'd had no luck. It was quite possible that they were still in Taiwan, under guard, but it was just as likely that they'd been squirreled away by the Foundation and flown to America. The trail was cold.

Without any information about where his children were, he'd needed a different approach. He'd been alerted to the journalist getting too close for comfort, and had decided to bring matters to a head. If he could use Emery to flush out Dominique, or cause her some damage, she might reach out and negotiate the release of his children.

Chen shrugged. "Why do you care so much about all of this?"

"Vengeance, justice, repaying a debt." Emery balled his fists and placed them on the table. "Because she's behind a whole lot of bad shit that's gone on lately. I know you killed my wife and others, including Ernest McDowell, but there's more at stake. You were the weapon, not the wielder; the tool, not the tradesman. Dominique is the threat."

Chen nodded. He understood the pervasiveness of a personal crusade as well as any man. "Fine. My wife was murdered and she has my children. We want the same thing—to expose Dominique and to cripple her organization. But I don't need you for that."

"You do, actually. It has taken a lot for me to swallow my distaste for you, but now we're linked whether you like it or not. I need you to finish painting the picture, you need me because I have the networks and profile to expose her using the information."

Chen leaned back in his chair and folded his arms. The next move was his. The Foundation could—and had—hurt him, and still had his children. He wanted the same thing as Emery. While Emery had some information, Chen had it all and more—movements, transactions, records of contact, plus his confessions. Enough to destroy Dominique. If Chen was the ammunition, the man sitting in front of him was the gun that could fire it. Chen stared at Emery and nodded slowly.

"Okay." Emery leaned forward on his elbows. "I want information. All of it. Every scrap of paper, every single name, date, time, equipment manifest, motive."

"Go and get your notepad and tape recorder. Let's get to work."

CHAPTER 26

"America wakes this morning to the first midterm elections held during a significant war in over forty years. Despite an apparent shift in the strategic balance of the war in recent days toward the United States, most analysts and polls are predicting the Republican Party will sweep the field in a show of deep dissatisfaction at the Kurzon Administration's handling of the war. An interesting kink in the elections is the emerging scandal, which first appeared yesterday in an online blog post by Pulitzer Prize–winning journalist Jack Emery, implicating a number of hardline Republican candidates in corrupt and treasonous behavior."

Charlie Rattan, MSNBC News Hour, *November 1*

As he sat on the set of a CNN studio in Los Angeles waiting for his slot, Jack was frustrated by the constant attention of the makeup and hair stylists. He was trying to think, but the primping and preening of the two women made it difficult. He didn't believe it mattered what he looked like, and if he was writing this for the *Standard*, it definitely wouldn't. But he'd lost that avenue, so had to cooperate with the norms of television.

He'd spent a few days picking Chen's brain, along with getting access to the entire treasure trove of information on Chen's USB. Though Hickens had salvaged some information, Chen still had an original copy and everything on it. On the flight from Taiwan to Los Angeles, Jack had compiled everything into a workable story: the Foundation's role in the Shanghai attacks and the war, the control of EMCorp, the shooting of Ernest McDowell, their continued subversion of large parts of US society, and a huge effort to control a large slice of US Congress.

He'd traveled with one eye open, half expecting Dominique's goons to ambush him at the airport, on the plane or once he'd landed. But nobody had challenged him and Celeste had met him at the airport in Los Angeles, having flown in from Hawaii. From their hotel room they'd crafted the stories, listing no names and making no claims that couldn't be proven with certainty in court. He'd left himself plenty of room to maneuver. He'd put the lot into a blog post, and beamed it out through his Twitter feed, timed to ensure it hit the daily news cycle. It had been a bombshell.

In the hours that followed, what had begun as a trickle of calls, texts and emails became a torrent, then a tsunami. Half of them were concerned friends, Peter and Josefa included, while the rest were offers for interviews or publication. He'd smiled at the response to his blog post. It was nice to know he still had the touch. It had actually been Celeste who had organized the spot on CNN's *Insight* program.

"Thanks. Mr Emery." The makeup girl stepped back with a pearly white smile and finally left Jack to his own devices. "Andrea will be with you shortly."

Jack nodded. "Thanks."

He turned his head and looked straight at Celeste, who was standing just behind the cameras. She smiled and gave him the thumbs up. They'd rehearsed the interview for most of the morning, but Jack had no doubt that Andrea Serrenko would be a far tougher gig. She had an impressive reputation, but if there was one way to get his message against Dominique and the Foundation white hot, nailing this interview was it.

He was about to say something to Celeste when Serrenko appeared and approached the set. She was an impressive woman, over six feet tall and higher still in heels, with fiery red hair and a personality to match. She sat in the seat opposite him, placed her notes on the counter and made sure her water glass was full.

Only then did she look up at Jack. "Good evening, Mr Emery, thanks for coming in. How're things today?"

"Jack, please." He held out his hand. "Could be worse, I could be in the crosshairs of more than one very dangerous organization."

Serrenko laughed and shook his hand. "Well, Jack, for the sake of my audience, I'm glad you're in the sights of at least one of them. It's a hell of a story."

Jack smiled. "You don't know the half of it."

As they exchanged further small talk, an assistant approached and fitted a lapel mike to each of them. Jack was a veteran of the process, having done a few interviews over the years. While each network and studio had its quirks, for the most part it was the same. Finally, a producer spoke from behind the safety of the camera and told them there was one minute until the show.

Jack watched one of the many monitors around the studio as the program's splash graphic played. When it was finished, the shot panned around the studio before landing squarely on Serrenko and himself, seated on either side of the desk. Serrenko smiled straight down the camera as the intro music faded. Jack stayed still as she read her opening.

"Good evening. Welcome to *Insight*, I'm Andrea Serrenko." She turned to look into another camera as the shot shifted. "Tonight we have Jack Emery, former political editor for the *New York Standard* and Pulitzer Prize–winning journalist, in the studio. On the same day as the midterm elections, his blog post this morning about the corruption in and subversion of American politics threatens to rock the system to its core. Thank you for joining me, Mr Emery."

Jack took a deep breath, leaned forward and smiled. "Please, call me Jack. Great to be with you."

Serrenko gave a well-rehearsed smile. "Okay, Jack. The first thing I wanted to cover is why a journalist of your caliber is out of work at the moment. This all feels a bit too convenient."

Jack swallowed. He hadn't expected this to be easy. He still hadn't reached the bottom of his firing, but from a conversation with Peter, it was pretty clearly linked to Michelle Dominique's board push. He smiled. "Well, I'm open to offers, if you're hiring."

His attempt at humor fell on deaf ears, as Serrenko raised an eyebrow.

"Look, it's a tough industry, now more than ever. My views didn't match the direction of the paper, so they fired me. But this story is authentic, I've done the hard work. It stacks up."

That was something Jack was sure about. Between the contents of the USB and the information he'd gained from Chen, he had a slam-dunk story against Dominique and the Foundation. He was certain it was enough to bring her down. And once she was eliminated, he hoped her whole rancid organization would decay and collapse.

Serrenko nodded. "Okay then, can you summarize for our viewers what your contention is? Particularly for those who haven't yet read your blog."

Jack bit his lip. This was it. "Okay. In short, there's a politically cancerous think tank operating in Washington to undermine American democracy."

Serrenko laughed in a way that felt dismissive. "Aren't all think tanks doing that though, Jack? You're going to need more than that."

"Oh, of course, Andrea. But I've got clear evidence linking this group to the attacks in Shanghai, China—"

Serrenko interrupted. "You're saying an American organization *attacked China?*"

Jack nodded. "Not directly, but without them there would have been no attacks. They provided the funds and helped the mastermind—Chen Shubian—with the logistics."

"You have proof? Even more than what was on your blog today?" For the first time, Jack thought he might have her interested.

"Sure do—an interview with Chen Shubian. Along with documents and records that support his allegations."

"Wait a minute." Serrenko was incredulous. "You've *met* the main bomber? Wasn't your wife killed in Shanghai?"

"Yes, I have, and yes, she was. I had to put aside my personal grievances for the good of the story. So this organization has a highly complex cell structure that takes its orders from Washington. If one cell is compromised, it looks like a small group of nut jobs, but I've been able to blow the lid off the whole organization.

"Just recently, they've had involvement in Shanghai, the war, the shooting of Ernest McDowell and the subversion of his company. And this is the tip of the iceberg. They're now trying to get their members into Congress. If I had the resources, I'd have found more. I trust the FBI will have an easy time of it. I'd be more than happy to help."

Serrenko clearly knew a bombshell when she heard one, and when something was being held back. Her eyes narrowed. "Give me the name of the organization, Jack."

Jack stared straight down the camera. He had prepared most for this next part. He could have easily have dropped the Foundation for a New

America and Michelle Dominique in the deep end by naming them on his blog, but he'd needed the protection of being a national celebrity with a story that people wanted to hear.

"Michelle Dominique and the Foundation for a New America." Jack looked down at his cell phone. "And, according to the newsfeed, your next member of Congress."

~

MICHELLE SQUINTED but kept a smile on her face as the camera flashes rolled like a wave across her vision. She smiled again, then walked to the lectern. Her mind wasn't in the whole victory event, really, but she had to go through the motions. Jack Emery's blog post and subsequent interview on *Insight* had changed the focus of the day—from triumph at being elected to damage control. She had to do this then get to work.

She rushed through her speech, batting off the same lines that had been home runs with the voters and seen her elected with a massive margin. She paused for applause at the right times, smiled for the cameras and the crowd at the right times, and gave the speech only enough mental energy required to avoid blunders. She thanked her supporters, and congratulated the other Foundation-aligned candidates who'd won.

Most importantly, she denied the allegations Jack Emery had made and explained he was a bitter ex-employee with a drinking problem. The crowd had cheered her and booed him, but she knew that the room was full of her supporters. She'd have a much tougher time with the general public. Not to mention the FBI. She waved and walked backstage.

Waiting for her in the green room were Erik and Andrei Shadd. They stood impassively off to the side, in the exact same spots from which they'd delivered the news about Emery's interview, just before she took the stage for her speech. She walked over to the side table and poured herself a drink, then threw the pitcher across the room. It exploded in a spray of glass and painted the white wall with grapefruit juice. She didn't care. She was tempted to set the whole building on fire. She'd never felt anger like this.

"All this information!" She picked up her iPad and threw it across the room.

"All this power!" She moved to the window and ripped the curtains down.

"For what!" She kicked over a vase, which smashed with a satisfying spray of glass.

Andrei moved closer. "It's not that bad. You have a number of options."

She stared at him, tempted to punch his lights out, but after a few moments she exhaled deeply and sat on the arm of the sofa. "We need to turn this around or the FBI is going to come knocking. If that happens, it's only a matter of time before you're both being gang-banged at Rikers, and I'm giving some lady a little something to stay alive."

Andrei shrugged. "There were always bound to be setbacks. It's not possible to run an organization as ambitious and as large as ours without the odd problem. Look at all the messes Anton cleaned up over the years."

"This is more dangerous than anything he ever dealt with. We're named, gentlemen. That changes everything. In addition to the Feds, the other cells will be gunning for me too."

She thought for a moment. She was a student of politics, but equally adept at history. When things got desperate, it was the individual or the country that could be the most ruthless that generally won the day. An idea popped into her head. She mulled it over, then decided. It was her only option.

"We're going to take a leaf out of Stalin's book." She raised her head to look at the brothers, who winced at the reference to Uncle Joe. "Scorched earth."

Andrei frowned in thought, then smiled. "Let them have most of it, but protect the core."

Michelle smiled. The more she thought about it, the more it made sense. "Precisely."

The Foundation had a huge amount of influence in all sorts of areas. While it would hurt to give up some of her power and her people, by doing so she might have a fighting chance to stay alive and keep the core of the organization—and its influence—intact. The rest was expendable. It was the only way to survive. To recover. To succeed.

Michelle stood. "We need to inoculate our core. We need to totally cut off our central organs from the rest of the body. That's your job. Expose them, kill them. Whatever."

"Easier said than done, Michelle." Erik shook his head. "I doubt large parts of the organization will take kindly to being hung out to dry."

"I don't care. Do it. Today. I'll take care of protecting the important stuff."

Andrei's eyes narrowed. "How?"

Michelle smiled. "I've had something up our sleeve in case we needed it."

She picked up the phone and dialed her assistant. "Mallory, I'll need the Heisman file ready when I get back to the office. It's urgent, okay?"

She hung up without waiting for a response. Both of the brothers had confused looks on their faces, but it was Andrei who spoke first. "The Heisman file?"

Michelle smiled. "A dirt file on the President so large it will bring him down."

"Isn't using something like that a bit...final?"

"Yeah, it's like dropping the bomb on Hiroshima, but we don't have a choice. I'll meet with him and keep the government and the Bureau off our case. If we can use our leverage over Kurzon to keep the FBI off our backs long enough, we can feed most of the organization to the wolves, but protect the most important parts. We *can* recover."

The brothers nodded.

"Andrei, you take care of Emery. Erik, you handle the Foundation liquidation. When I drop this file on Kurzon's desk, he'll be eating out of our hands like a lamb and we'll be able to protect ourselves. And if he doesn't cooperate, we'll make it public and be yesterday's news."

CHAPTER 27

The results are in and Congress looks to be taking a decidedly hawkish tone, after an electoral bloodbath left Democratic hopes shattered. While Republicans carried the day in general, perhaps the most surprising development was the election of so many extreme right-wing candidates to Congress. Though nominally linked to the GOP, there is huge concern within Republican ranks about the new arrivals, and talks already of a potential schism between moderates and the new extreme arm of the party. At any rate, the new-look Congress promises to bring a new vigor to the war against China, with analysts predicting an even stronger push to end the conflict decisively. It may be a moot point, however, given American gains in recent days and the apparent slackening of Chinese assaults on Taiwan. Whether because of tactics, exhaustion, attrition or troubles at home, sources tell the New York Standard that the sum total of attacks has fallen by thirty percent in recent days.

   Phil Eaton, New York Standard, *November 2*

Jack smiled wearily at the flight attendant as he walked past her. "Thanks."

"Our pleasure, sir." The woman was far too perky for someone who flew for a living. "Thanks for flying with United."

Jack nodded then turned to Celeste. "Let's go."

She nodded. "Man, I can't wait for a shower and sleep."

He laughed but said nothing. He hefted his backpack over his shoulder and walked through the door of the aircraft and onto the sky bridge. It had been over two days since he'd slept properly, jetting from Taiwan, to Hawaii, to LA, to Washington. The entire time, he'd been getting word out about his story, which had gone all the more nuclear since his interview with Serrenko and Dominique's election win.

He wrapped an arm around Celeste as they walked. "I really appreciate your support through all this."

She leaned in and kissed him on the cheek. "My pleasure. But I don't think it's going to get any easier any time soon."

"I know." Once he stepped out of the artificial environment of the airport, things were going to get crazy.

He exhaled deeply and stepped into the terminal. As he looked around, he felt Celeste grab his arm and squeeze tight. He looked at her and her eyes were wide, locked on a group of men standing on the other side of the terminal. He looked at them and recognized only one of the four but still felt a spike of fear. Recognizing one was enough. It was the same man who'd bailed him and Celeste up at Chen's house in Wisconsin.

This wasn't good. He'd thought that in the wake of his release of the information, his public profile would be enough to prevent Dominique from moving against him. He'd been wrong.

Celeste seemed on the verge of complete panic. "Holy fuck, Jack. They're here. *He's here.*"

Jack grabbed Celeste's arm and they turned and started to walk toward the baggage claim. In his peripheral vision he could see the Foundation goons fall into an easy stroll behind him. Jack picked up his pace, pulled out his cell phone and dialed Peter Weston. He held the phone to his ear and increased the speed of his walking. The phone rang, time after time, but there was no answer.

He looked back. The men were getting closer. While he doubted they'd try anything at Dulles International Airport, with all the security in the world watching them, he had no doubt that as soon as he and Celeste left the building and got a fair distance away, they'd strike. He had to prevent that. He could approach the police, but they'd do nothing if there was no clear threat. There was only one way they'd pay attention.

He turned to Celeste as they kept walking. "As soon as we round this corner, stop and cry out for help. As loud as you can."

"Why?" She looked at him as they turned a corner, then shrugged. "HELP! HELP ME!"

Jack kept walking as Celeste stopped in her tracks. He waited a few moments before looking back. She had gathered a small crowd of airport staff and concerned travelers. Most importantly, the gentlemen trailing them had kept moving. He was their primary target, and they weren't interested in making a scene with a woman who was already shouting for help. Celeste was safe. Now he had to figure out something for himself.

He walked, mind racing for ideas but coming up blank. He looked down at his cell phone, thinking of who else to call, when he became vaguely aware of someone else getting in his way. He put the phone down and stopped walking, looking up at the pair of strangers with a mix of curiosity and dread. After all he'd been through, from the carrier to his torture to finding Chen, this was how it was going to end.

One of the suited man took a slight step forward. "Jack Emery?"

Jack cursed himself for not anticipating that the Foundation would send two teams—one to flush him out and one to scoop him up. Despite that, he saw no reason to make it easy for them. Whatever noise and fuss he could make as they dealt with him, he'd make. He turned around. The four men who'd initially pursued him had stopped dead in their tracks and were now doing their best to look completely disinterested.

"Are you Jack Emery? I won't ask again."

Jack relaxed slightly, turned back around and summed up the new arrival. Dark suit, dark sunglasses, a buddy dressed in exactly the same way. He nearly laughed. "Yeah?"

The other man was expressionless as he produced ID. "I'm Agent Brenner, FBI. This is Agent Vaughn. Looks like you could use a friend or two right now."

Jack looked back again. "Yeah, you could say that."

Brenner was impassive as he put a hand gently on Jack's back. "Come with us."

"Can you look after my colleague, Celeste Adams? She's back there near gate 6A."

Brenner turned to Vaughn. "Go get her and meet us at the café."

"Thanks." Jack smiled with relief as Vaughn peeled off and headed in the direction of Celeste. It had been far too close a call for his liking. He looked back at his pursuers. The one he recognized from Wisconsin seemed pissed.

He walked with Brenner in silence through the arrivals hall. He didn't really know what was in store, but the FBI would no doubt be better company than the Foundation. His interview with Serrenko had clearly had an impact, both on Dominique and on the Federal Government, now he just had to hope he had enough ammunition to keep the authorities interested.

After a few minutes, Brenner stopped next to one of the cafés in the airport. "Mr Emery, the director will see you in here. I'll keep the bad guys away."

"Thanks. And Celeste?"

"Sorted. I suggest you don't keep Director McGhinnist waiting."

Jack entered the cafeteria and stood next to the only occupied table. Seated there was a large African-American man, who looked as if he could crack Jack open like a walnut. Jack had done his research and knew that Bill McGhinnist, ex-Navy Seal, Director of the FBI, probably could. McGhinnist calmly took one last sip of his coffee, put the cup down then stood to face Jack.

"Good morning, Director McGhinnist." Jack held out his hand. "I'm Jack Emery."

"Bill will do, Mr Emery." McGhinnist shook his hand. "Thanks for agreeing to meet."

Jack laughed. "Your agents made a pretty compelling offer. And please, call me Jack."

"Glad they could save you a headache or two. I thought a little show of force might be helpful." McGhinnist laughed and sat down. "I won't even charge you for it, if your information is as good as you claim. Take a seat, Jack."

Jack did as he was told. "It is."

"You have made a lot of people nervous and you've hardly set about making friends in all of this. But I was intrigued by your blog and your interview. So I'm giving you the benefit of the doubt. You better not be wasting my time, Jack. It's a busy time for everyone."

Jack could tell that McGhinnist had a lot on his plate, no doubt because of the war. He'd also be nervous at the thought of Jack's information, which shed new light on the causes of the war and left many prominent Americans with question marks over their head, including a few brand-new members of Congress. Jack was going to have to show off his garter belt before the big dance if he had any hope of enlisting the Bureau's help.

"I've got a lot of evidence linking the Foundation and Michelle Dominique to prominent politicians, business interests, the media—you name it. It's more than lobbying and the odd long lunch. We're talking about endemic political corruption, insider trading, money laundering, perjury, fraud, blackmail, murder—and a whole lot more. They're a bunch of nasty fuckers."

Jack swallowed hard. "I've also got evidence linking them to the attacks on Shanghai and to the war with China. A Taiwanese national named Chen Shubian worked with Dominique and organized the attacks using a secure server the Foundation established. He was funded by a series of front companies that I've linked to the Foundation, plus Dominique was in Shanghai in the days before and immediately after the attacks."

McGhinnist frowned. "And there's more, I trust?"

Jack smiled. "Sure is. She's taken control of EMCorp and now Foundation-aligned candidates have been elected en masse into Congress. They're taking control, Bill."

Jack could clearly see the director tense, but he knew the man was interested. "Your allegations affect some very influential people, Mr Emery. Not to mention the war."

"Jack, remember? I've got the evidence to back it all up, both from Chen's confession and Anton Clark's computer files. Look, I know better than most the power of that organization and its people, but it changes nothing."

"Oh, it changes everything, Jack. Michelle Dominique has a large power base in Washington. I'm not sure you realize what you're asking me to do, Jack, to declare war on the entire Washington elite at the same time as we're at war with China."

Jack could see the man was torn. "That's about the sum of it, yeah."

McGhinnist sighed. "The war is going well, but we've lost a couple of carriers, countless air force birds and half of Taiwan has been flattened. The world is now a very different place. The last thing I want is to start a forest fire in Washington."

"I know. But you're my only hope."

He looked up at McGhinnist, who was silent. He'd given him everything except Ernest's links to the Foundation. He didn't quite know what he'd do if McGhinnist declined to help. He'd have to walk outside and into the arms of the Foundation thugs, having succeeded in releasing the story but failing to protect himself and those he cared about. Plus, it would likely save the Foundation from complete destruction.

His vengeance would be incomplete.

Jack dug into his pocket and pulled out the USB containing the evidence. He placed it on the table. "There are strings attached to the information. Some of it incriminates Ernest McDowell, and I want that particular part of it forgotten about. Also, Chen Shubian needs immunity. It was the price of his evidence."

McGhinnist looked down at the USB, then up at Jack with a smile. "You're a cheeky bastard, but I like that. I couldn't care less about a dead old man, so that's fine. As for Shubian, he blew up half of China, not Los Angeles or Chicago, so what do I care? You've got a deal."

Jack nodded. "The password is Erin."

McGhinnist exhaled, longer and louder than any man Jack had ever heard. "Okay, Jack. I just hope you know what you're getting us into. This is going to hurt, but I'll set up a task force and lead it personally. We'll wrap this network up in a matter of days."

Jack stood. "You have my number, if you need anything at all, or if the information isn't clear to your analysts, I'd be happy to help."

"Okay. In the meantime, I'll put you and your friend up at a hotel and put my guys on protection duty." McGhinnist stood as well, patted Jack's back then paused. "Tell me one thing, though. How did you begin to link all of this to Dominique and the Foundation?"

Jack paused, then decided it was best not to lie to the man. "Um... would you believe that I slept with her and ransacked her apartment?"

'Damn!" McGhinnist laughed, clearly impressed. "I've admired her from afar for years! I'm going to ignore the felony just to hear that story at a later date."

～

MICHELLE STEELED HERSELF, but kept her smile pristine. "Mr President."

President Kurzon didn't stand, but gestured her to a seat. "Congratulations on your election, Michelle. How was your flight?"

"Fine, Mr President." Michelle sat. "Thanks for agreeing to see me."

She'd flown the short distance from Washington to Maryland, then been driven to Camp David. She hadn't wanted to leave the capital with the FBI threatening to roll up on the Foundation's doorstep at any moment, but it was the only way to rein in the situation.

"You didn't give me much choice, given what you claim to possess. So what can I do for you? I've got a two o'clock with the Australian ambassador." Kurzon's tone was cold.

Michelle sat. "The Bureau is about to start arresting or harassing half of my people on charges that are trash. I want you to make it stop so we can get on with our business."

Kurzon waved his hand. "A nasty situation. I don't know the specifics, but it sounds like some of your people have been freelancing, to say nothing of yourself."

"The problem is a bit bigger than that."

"How so? Bill McGhinnist wouldn't be pursuing this if he didn't have reason. Just keep your hands clean and you'll be fine." Kurzon started to stand. "Is that all?"

Michelle remained where she was. "No."

Kurzon sat back down. "Right, let me have it."

Michelle reached into her handbag and pulled out her iPad. She unlocked it and hit play on the video that was ready to go. She turned the screen to Kurzon. She didn't have to watch it again to know what he was seeing: himself having sex with a young woman. She tried to hide her smile as he realized what this meant for his presidency.

"She really doesn't look sixteen, does she?"

Kurzon watched the whole thing. He had the look of a frightened child in his eyes. "Where did you get this?"

"That doesn't matter."

He sighed. "Fucking hell."

She was a bit surprised that he didn't deny his involvement or try to talk her out of releasing it. They both knew that this would end his presidency, ruin his legacy and probably send him to jail. She was relying on it. Only direct intervention by Kurzon would make the various arms of the Federal Government go away.

She prompted him. "This can go away, if you do what I ask."

He laughed darkly. "You think I can get McGhinnist and the others to call off an investigation against you and your colleagues? It doesn't work that way. Besides, what's stopping the journalist from releasing it all publicly? He's already named you, after all."

"I can deal with Jack Emery." Michelle lowered her voice menacingly. "I just want you to play your role."

For several minutes, Kurzon seemed to think through the ramifications of the situation, for himself, his family, the Foundation, the country. With a single stroke of a pen he could protect both of them. She was sure he'd make the right decision. She was surprised when he shook his head and sighed again. She waited patiently.

"Michelle, for a moment or two I considered your deal. But I'm afraid that, no matter the cost to my professional life, I will not work, collaborate or otherwise be involved in anything you're peddling."

"You're mad." She was shocked, but wouldn't show it. "May I ask why?"

"Because I spoke to McGhinnist prior to this meeting, and discovered that your organization was probably responsible for the death of my friend, that's why. Ernest was no saint, but he deserved a hell of a lot better than a bullet in the neck. I'll try my luck with the press, Ms Dominique."

"They'll crucify you, Mr President. Your administration will be destroyed."

Kurzon smiled. "Great thing, democracy. I'm a lame duck after the midterms anyway, and there's always someone else willing to step up. I'll already be regarded as the President who took America to war with China, but I'll be happy if history remembers me as the man who also stood up to the greatest ever threat to American freedom and stopped them getting away with terrible crimes and stacking Congress."

Michelle didn't reply. She turned the iPad back around and placed it in her lap. She sent an email she'd already prepared. It gave her no pleasure and got her no closer to solving the issue of Jack Emery and his evidence, but she had to follow through. The Foundation was only as powerful as the punishment backing up its threats. Not even the President was immune. She'd have to deal with Emery another way.

"It's done, Mr President." She stood. "I hope you don't live to regret your decision."

"Miss, I kindly regret I can't shove my telephone down your throat. Get out."

CHAPTER 28

"Addressing the nation, the President looked tired and beaten. He did his best to downplay the contents of the video and the allegations against him, revealed by the New York Standard, but had no answer for the damning nature of the vision. Kurzon has vowed to fight the allegations and any impeachment. At the same time, he commented on the allegations against Michelle Dominique and the Foundation for a New America, stating that while the investigation and arrests were ongoing, there was clear evidence showing that the organization was responsible for the attacks in Shanghai. As allegations continue to fly in Washington, following the release of the new information, the President has made a public and unconditional offer of a ceasefire with the People's Republic of China. Kurzon stressed the recent success of United States forces and noted that America had no desire to fight with China for years to come, especially given the Foundation's likely involvement in starting it. He stated that if China could accept the independence of Taiwan, peace could be had within hours. Considering their losses, and the ongoing domestic difficulties that Chinese authorities are facing in trying to maintain order, it is quite possible a deal could be on the cards."

Vanessa McKenzie, PBS News Hour, *November 3*

J ack breathed as deeply as he could, trying to calm his nerves. He twirled his pen and tapped his foot on the floor. There was nothing else to do. The television news had wall-to-wall coverage of the war and the scandal facing President Kurzon, and he was under strict orders not to use his phone. All the while, he couldn't help but think he'd made a mistake and that this would all end badly.

While the President's Suite of the Washington Marriott was a nice enough place to wait, he could think of a million other places he'd prefer to be. Earlier in the day, McGhinnist had called him with mixed news. He'd told Jack that the Bureau was rolling up Foundation for a New America cells all over the country, but still hadn't manage to locate Michelle Dominique since she'd left Camp David. Jack had convinced himself that Dominique had slipped the net, leaving him to walk the Earth as a hunted man. McGhinnist had said, when they'd first met, that the tendrils of her power base extended deeper than anyone could fathom. There was no way for him to stand up to that. So he had been forced to wait for a second day in the hotel, relying on McGhinnist, and with nobody but Celeste, Agent Brenner and Agent Vaughn for company.

His eyes were on the table when the door to the suite unlocked with a clunk. Jack looked up as it opened and he smiled with relief when Agent Brenner walked into the room, fresh from completing a security check of the hotel. Agent Vaughn had stayed in the room, silent, but he freaked Jack out a bit.

Jack held out his hands up with his palms facing outward. "Don't shoot."

Brenner raised an eyebrow. "Everything okay, Mr Emery?"

As Vaughn walked over to the window and pulled back the curtain, taking a peek outside, Jack felt like telling Brenner that, no, everything was not okay. In truth, he felt minutes away from needing a change of underwear, and that his faith in the competency of the FBI and its agents was being sorely tested. But he held his tongue and nodded. He felt exposed, and wanted the FBI to get on with arresting Dominique.

"Don't worry, there's more than a handful of decent shots between the lobby and you." Brenner clearly sensed he was uneasy. "Unless she brings an army, you're fine."

Jack smiled. "I know, I just feel a bit vulnerable. I'll be the happiest man on the planet when Dominique is in cuffs. Hell, I'll buy you guys a beer downstairs."

Brenner shrugged. "Just part of the job. You're the one who's put yourself on the line, can't say I understand why though."

"She killed my wife, started a war, ordered my boss murdered and tried to stab me in a museum. If that's not enough for you, she's also trying to stack Congress."

"Good enough, I suppose." Brenner laughed. "Quite amazing how deep this all goes, though. It's some serious shit you've uncorked."

Jack couldn't disagree. "Given the choice, I'd have preferred to be left out of it all. But once I pulled the first thread, her whole dress unraveled, and I couldn't walk away."

"Why not?" Brenner scoffed. "To use your analogy, just because a woman is undressed in front of you, doesn't mean you need to sleep with her."

Jack laughed, and the dark cloud hanging over his mood lifted. "I can't resist the lure of a beautiful woman."

Brenner opened his mouth to reply, but Jack heard nothing but a boom. Before his mind could process what was happening, Brenner's blood showered over him. Jack froze, until he heard a second boom, as Vaughn fired another shot into Brenner's skull. Jack dived to the floor and climbed under the table. Vaughn appeared to be in no hurry, slowly walking past Brenner's lifeless body toward him. The agent seemed as calm as the man in Chen's basement, but Jack had no police cruiser to save him this time.

Jack had nowhere to go as Vaughn bent down and peered at him. "Mr Emery, you've caused a whole lot of problems for a whole lot of people."

Jack's fear had gone, replaced by sheer and utter disbelief—and rage. "After all of this, *you're* the one who's going to get me? Just fucking do it."

Jack watched as the barrel of the pistol inched up. A wave of thoughts rushed through his mind, but he couldn't pin down any particular one as he waited for the inevitable. He wondered if he'd hear the shot or feel anything before it was over. Then his eyes widened as he saw a pair of legs run toward Vaughn.

Celeste. In his fear and anger, he'd forgotten about her.

She leaped and landed on Vaughn and the gun fired. Jack crawled as fast as he could from under the table. He was too late. Vaughn collapsed to the ground, a panting Celeste sitting on him and a steak knife protruding from his skull. Jack threw the gun away from Vaughn then struggled over to Celeste and hugged her.

Jack grabbed Vaughn's gun, then the cell phone in his pocket rang. "Hello?"

"McGhinnist speaking, we've found her, Jack. We're moving in at any moment."

"Good. One of your agents just tried to shoot me."

There was a pause. "Which one?"

"Vaughn."

"Fucking hell. He must have been one of Dominique's moles."

"Yep. And Brenner is dead."

There was another slight pause. "I'll get some more people up to you. Until then, take his gun and trust my other agents to keep you safe."

"Already taken care of the gun part." Jack was happy to have a weapon in his hands. "Where is she?"

"Dominique? An apartment in Baltimore. Off the grid."

"So this is it?" Jack held his breath, not willing to believe it just yet.

"Yep, we've got the place surrounded. There's a couple of large-looking dudes with her though. But we'll get her. Just wanted you to know."

Jack smiled and sighed with relief. "What about the rest of them? Doesn't seem like that particular snake will be killed by just chopping off the head."

"We've already beat it over the head a few times with a shovel. Their funds are frozen and we're rolling up their network. There'll be plenty of mop up, but this will just about finish it. We'll slice the organization into a million pieces and bring as many as we can rustle up into custody. I'll see you soon."

The line went dead. Jack gestured at Celeste to get Brenner's weapon. They resumed their hug as a pair of agents opened the door and entered. They had weapons raised and scanned the room, but could clearly see the damage was done. He spent the next few minutes explaining the ambush, and to their credit they let him keep the weapon.

It was over.

～

MICHELLE LIFTED the glass to her mouth and took a long pull of the whisky. She savored the burn of the liquid as it coursed down her throat and into the pit of her stomach. It temporarily replaced the empty feeling she'd had for the whole day, once she'd started to get reports of Foundation cells being assaulted by the FBI. The news was worse than she could have imagined.

Some of her people had been arrested, some killed. Losses were heavy and the Foundation was shattered. Scorched earth hadn't worked and there wasn't much left to save. She'd hoped to make a deal with Kurzon to prevent the complete collapse of the organization, but it hadn't happened. Her only consolation was that she was still breathing.

She pulled the glass away from her mouth and considered the last of the beautifully colored liquid, cut with just a splash of water. She threw it back with one flick of her wrist. She felt a momentary pang of regret. It was a shame to leave such a fine bottle here. Like the rest of the stuff in the secret apartment she kept in Baltimore, it'd make some FBI agent a very happy man.

She put the glass down on the table. "Time to go, boys."

She looked up to Andrei, who stood by the door. She stood as he started to turn the handle, but he didn't get the chance to open the door. There was the sound of cracking timber, and she took a step back as the door swung inward.

"They're here!" Erik's shout was barely audible over the explosion near the door. "Get down, Michelle!"

Michelle was surprised but reacted instantly. She started into a run for the other side of the room. Erik, who'd been standing by the window, already had his weapon out and had upturned her oak dining table for cover. He shouted something in Czech to his brother as she grabbed the hand he held out for her. She jumped over the table and joined him behind the impromptu shelter.

Several federal agents had already entered the room. She didn't need to see the lettering emblazoned on their vests to know they were FBI. She doubted they were pushovers, either. If Bill McGhinnist had enough balls to storm her hideout in Baltimore, he'd have sent his best crew, armed with the best gear and with backup on call. She ducked back behind the table.

"Federal agents! Give it up!"

They got their answer when the first shot boomed. Andrei was only able to get a single shot off before he was gunned down by a volley of return fire. That left Erik as the one thing standing between her and the agents. As she heard the chattering rumble of Erik's TeC-9 SMG, she reached over and pulled the M9 Beretta from the back of his pants, figuring he wouldn't need it while he was firing the machine pistol.

She looked over the table and extended her arm as shots boomed through the small apartment. She squeezed the trigger on the pistol several times and smiled with satisfaction as one of the agents fell, clutching his chest. He probably had a vest on, but it was enough to sting and take him out of the fight. She ducked back down.

Her situation was dire. She'd miscalculated the speed at which the FBI could get to her apartment. She'd wanted to clear out a few things and share one last drink with Erik and Andrei, but now they were here. Her choices were fight it out and die, surrender and go to prison, or try to escape. She didn't like any option.

But if she was to live, there was no going back for the Foundation, despite the success of her plan. She was a free agent, but she was determined to try. That meant getting far away from here, probably to the south, where she could regroup and consider her options.

As if Erik was reading her mind, she felt a pat on her backside. She looked at him and noticed tears in his eyes. The brothers had been close. He jerked his head toward the window. Her eyes widened, but he nodded. She knew him well enough not to protest his stupid chivalry, let alone when under fire. She nodded then raised her head over the table, squeezing off a few more shots. Without further thought she dropped and scurried toward the window. She heard bullets whiz over her head, but the shooters seemed more interested in silencing the return fire of Erik than in her.

From the sound of it, he was still firing as she reached the window. She looked back briefly as he loaded a fresh magazine, his last, then nodded and started to stand. Michelle got to her feet as Erik reached his full height and sprayed the far side of the room with his weapon.

The window had been destroyed by the gunfight and she was halfway through when Erik's fire stopped. A lesser team might have ducked against such a terrifying volley of fire, but this Bureau squad was better. They easily gunned him down. She grunted as she cut her hand on a jagged piece of glass, but didn't stop. She hurried down one level of the fire escape. Looking down, she saw an agent at ground level aiming his weapon at her. A pair of bullets ricocheted off the steel railings. She moved quickly, raising her weapon and firing off a few shots, but from this range it was useless.

When she spotted additional agents running to support the lone gunman, she decided she couldn't continue this way. With a grunt she hurled herself through the window to another apartment. The glass shattered around her and she landed heavily on the floor, but after the quickest check, she decided she was still intact.

She scrambled to her feet, glad that the apartment appeared to be empty. She raised the gun and moved quickly, half expecting a squad of agents to burst inside. Thoughts of escape and taking her vengeance on Jack Emery was all that kept her going, room by room. She reached the door to the apartment and opened it.

The corridor was empty. She pulled out her cell phone and dialed a number she knew by heart as she ran down the hall. "This is Dominique, change of plans, bring the car around and be ready to move it. We're under fire."

She reached the elevator and mashed the button. When it arrived, she rode it to the lobby and waited for the door to open, gun raised. Her mind was blank as she evaluated the threat—two Federal agents. She raised her weapon and fired at one. The agent went down as the other raised his weapon. They fired at about the same time.

The agent fell, but Michelle felt something impact her arm. She looked down as she ran for the exit. There was blood and an entry wound in her forearm, but she'd have to worry about it later. There was no sign of more agents as she ran outside. She'd finally caught a break.

She spotted the car and waved furiously at it. As it pulled up, she opened the door and dived in, the car never stopping. The driver gunned the engine as she took her seat and buckled in. She was safe, but if she was going to make good her escape, the driver would need to die at the end of the drive. She pressed her hand against her wound.

She rested back in the seat and after a few blocks she started to feel safe. The car pulled up at a red light. She heard the glass on the car window shatter before she was deafened by a large bang and blinded by a million shining lights. Her head was spinning as she closed her eyes and brought her hands up to her ears.

Her breathing quickened and her heart raced, even as her hearing started to return. She heard a gunshot, which meant her driver was dead. Then the door of the car open as she fumbled for her seatbelt and any chance at survival. Still too disoriented to move efficiently, she squealed as she sensed someone slide into the back seat beside her.

"I surrender." She could barely hear her own voice over the ringing in her ears. "If the Bureau wants me that badly, they've got me. Just don't shoot."

"It's not the FBI."

Fear gripped the pit of her stomach. While she still couldn't see as a result of the flashbang grenade, she knew the voice. "Chen."

His hand grabbed her by the throat. She squealed again.

"Where are my children? That is your only chance." There was malice in his voice.

She started to hyperventilate as her vision returned enough to see him. He wore a balaclava and there was no remorse in his eyes. Her mind scrambled for the answer he sought. The Foundation—or what was left of it—had his children, but she couldn't think of where.

Then it came to her. "Pennsylvania. They're in Philly. The address is in my phone. Leave me alone and you'll be with them in a few hours. But I need a deal."

"Give me the address and I'll determine what deal you get."

She had no choice. "The code to the phone is three one five six. The address is in the notes."

She felt pressure under her chin. Something poking into it.

This time she didn't hear the bang.

～

CHEN STEPPED BACK and crouched down. A second later, the small charge on the door handle hissed and flared white hot. The lock was breached. Chen looked around one last time and pulled the door open. It swung back on its hinges with only the slightest whine. He moved inside swiftly but silently, his pistol raised and alert for any sound or movement. He closed the door and was alone in the dark.

Using the information from Dominique's phone, he'd tracked his children to this address in Philadelphia. While he was elated to be so close to them, he was also mindful to keep his thoughts on the job. His children were still missing and in danger, and the FBI and the Foundation were engaged in a dangerous cat-and-mouse game all across America. They could arrive at any second. That would be complicated.

The first room in the office was dark, lit only by green emergency lighting. He could make out a reception area and front desk, but the room was remarkably sparse for any sort of active business. He didn't give the area another thought as he moved cautiously to the only other door in the room, which he assumed led to the main office area. He put his hand on the door handle and turned it slowly. When it was half turned, he waited for any sound, but there was only silence. He opened the door and stepped through.

He was faced with a long hallway with offices at evenly spaced intervals. At the end of the hall, slightly offset, was another room with no door. He moved quickly but as quietly as a snake toward it, checking each office for threats before moving on. Finally, he reached the doorless room at the end of the hallway.

He felt his breath catch in his throat when he saw his daughter, blindfolded, sitting at a steel table in what must be the lunchroom. A few more steps and he saw his son. They were both blindfolded, with ankles shackled to the table leg and uneaten sandwiches in front of them.

He raised his pistol an inch higher, but eased his finger away from the trigger. Despite his training, his emotions were on edge. He moved silently to the doorway, but kept to the side and out of sight. Finally, he saw the guard he knew had to be there. He doubted the overweight, middle-aged slob was among the Foundation's elite.

Chen moved quickly, his head clear of all thoughts except the threat to his children. He took four large steps between the door and the sleeping man, who was dozing with his chin on his chest and a newspaper in front of him. Chen placed the pistol against the man's head and squeezed the trigger as easily as turning off his television.

The pistol gave the slightest kick in response, which is more than the man in the chair offered. A fine spray of blood escaped from the other side of his head and only then did the children sense that someone else was in the room. They both raised their heads, and turned them from side to side, as if they expected their blindfolds to fall away.

When he saw his daughter grab her little brother's hand, Chen's heart nearly broke.

"Who's there?" His daughter spoke only broken English. "Please don't hurt us."

Chen crouched down to his knees and whispered, in case other threats were close by. "It's your father. Stay calm, climb under the table and uncover your eyes."

His children settled instantly. He stayed in position while they climbed under the table and removed their blindfolds, though he couldn't do anything about their shackles for the time being. Once they were in position, Chen removed the dead man's pistol from its holster and took out the clip.

There was one door left, on the opposite side to where he'd entered the break room. He moved toward the door and stood to the side. He put his hand on the door handle, but didn't get the chance to turn it fully, because a high-caliber pistol barked, blowing two large holes in the door. If he'd been standing in front of it, he'd be dead.

Chen's mind screamed with options: either advance through the door, fire back or find another way into the room.

A voice called out from the other side of the door, "I know who you are. Take the kids, leave me alive and we all walk away. The key is on the hook."

Chen processed what felt like thousands of small bits of information in a single second. He'd completed a hostile entry under fire a number of times, and it held no fear for him, but he'd never done it with two frightened children—his children—half-a-dozen feet away from him.

While every fiber of his being wanted to terminate the man on the other side of the door, he thought about the feeling he'd had when his father had been killed by the Chinese. He looked to his children, who stared up at him with wide eyes from under the table. The decision was an easy one.

He ground his teeth and took a step back. "You have a deal."

It was time to go home.

EPILOGUE

The Chairwoman of the Pulitzer Prize Board, Elizabeth Harley, smiled as she read off the autocue. "And for Best Commentary, the award goes to Jack Emery, for his incisive blogs and columns on the spread of corruption by the Foundation for a New America. Please welcome him up to the stage."

Jack smiled as he stood. He buttoned his jacket and brushed down the front of his suit, making sure no loose breadcrumbs would ruin the shot of him collecting the award. That would be perfect, end the threat of the Foundation, only to come undone at the hands of a nefarious cobb loaf. He started his walk to the stage.

Harley continued. "Jack's stories led to hundreds of arrests across the United States by the FBI, and Interpol is still executing dozens of arrest warrants overseas. Among the arrests were many prominent Americans. Most importantly, his work exposed the link between the Foundation and the war with China, and their attempts to stack Congress."

As he walked toward the stage Celeste smiled up at him, Peter and Josefa patted him on the back and some of the others he knew at his table and in the room offered words of encouragement as he passed. In many ways, this was the end of the craziest year of his life.

Jack reached the stage and walked up the handful of stairs and into the open arms of Harley, who hugged him politely and then shared a peck on the cheek. Jack broke the embrace and walked to the lectern. He searched his pocket for his notes and then thought better of it; he knew what he wanted to say.

He smiled, then leaned in close to the microphone on the lectern. "It's a pleasure to accept this award and be recognized by the prize board for the second time in my career."

More polite applause broke out from the room, and Jack was forced to wait while it dissipated. "I believe the stories I wrote about the Foundation were the most important of my career, because of the threat they posed to our freedom.

"Unfortunately, the story won't bring back some good people. Erin Emery, Ernest McDowell, Admiral Carl McCulloch, and lots of others. I'd like to dedicate this prize to their memory."

He backed away for a second, and felt a tear welling up in his eye. He smiled awkwardly and Harley placed a reassuring hand on his back. "Just take your time, Jack. The stage is yours for as long as you want it."

'Thanks." He stepped forward to the lectern again. "The last thing I want to say is that, more than anything, the last few months have shown me that we need to be vigilant. The people in this room are the last line."

Jack nodded and held up his hand, as long and sincere applause broke out around the room. The short speech felt entirely appropriate, and was about all Jack could give. He'd said more in private to those who were closest to him. It would do. He left the stage with a smile and returned to his seat.

"Nice job." Celeste leaned in to kiss him on the cheek as he sat. "Nice words."

'Thanks." He looked at the trophy: a solid glass paperweight, engraved with his name. "Something else to gather dust on the shelf."

She laughed. "Such a burden to be a success."

"You'll have to win one next year and start catching up. I think I'll be stuck on two for a bit."

The others at his table—Josefa, Peter Weston, Sarah McDowell, Simon Hickens—all laughed at that thought. While the crushing tentacles of Michelle Dominique's control over EMCorp had receded, there was still a lot of damage for the new management of the company to fix.

Peter Weston had taken control of the board at the behest of Sarah McDowell, and had set about purging the company of Marles and the others who'd made their way in during the period of Foundation rule.

The editors had control of content again and things were slowly getting back to normal.

"Want your job back now your price has just doubled, Jack?" Peter laughed. "I might get in trouble from the boss, but she did put me in charge."

Jack looked at Sarah, who flushed red and looked down at her wine glass. "Pretty sure you're doing better than the last person I chose, Peter."

Jack had to feel for her. While none of it was her fault, she'd put the woman who had murdered her father in charge of his company. Though Sarah had been expertly buttered up, it wouldn't be the finest hour when she got around to her memoirs in sixty years or so.

After Dominique's body had been found, the FBI had continued to scoop up the Foundation's entire network, the newly elected members of Congress among them. China, smarting from its losses and barely holding on to control, had accepted US overtures of peace after an apology from President Kurzon. The peace was holding.

Jack raised his glass of Coke. "A toast, everyone? To Ernest, Erin and all the others lost."

The others raised their glass into the air. Josefa broke the silence that followed. "You've got a job waiting for you at the *Standard* if you want one, Jack."

"No thanks, Jo. I'm starting something new."

STATE OF EMERGENCY

JACK EMERY 2

To all those who have resisted the excesses of tyrants in ways big and small and often at great personal cost.

PROLOGUE

"Twenty seconds." One pulled a balaclava over her head. "Gun it."

The driver nodded and put his foot to the floor, the engine roaring as the vehicle sped across the Harvard Bridge and onto Massachusetts Avenue. The windows were tinted, so the pedestrians who glanced at the vehicle as it sped past couldn't see the deadly cargo inside.

"Ten seconds. Everyone check in."

As the van took a hard right onto Vasser Street, the rest of One's team checked in. The team – four in the van with her and one located strategically on a rooftop near the campus – were as slick as ever. One smiled under her mask. She didn't need to do the check and knew they'd be ready, but fifteen years of habit was hard to break.

One was jolted in her seat as the van mounted the curb and then pulled to a stop. Two slid the door open, climbed out and broke into a run. She too was running as soon as her feet hit the ground. Three and Four would follow, while Five would stay at the wheel. As she moved, there were squeals of panic from nearby students. She ignored them. They were irrelevant unless they got in the way.

The team crossed the sidewalk and reached the entrance of the Massachusetts Institute of Technology Electrical Engineering and Computer Science Department in seconds. She pointed at Four and he moved into the building with his submachine gun raised. The others followed him in and they split into pairs.

"Remember, we're looking for Daryush Daneshgahi." She paused. "We need him alive."

From the foyer she went left with Two, while Three and Four went right. They had intelligence that Daneshgahi was a creature of habit and would either be in his office or his lab. She had her weapon raised and was moving briskly when an alarm started to wail. It was a surprise it had taken this long.

Her headset crackled. "One, this is Six. Campus police are starting to arrive."

One spoke into her voice-activated microphone. "Copy."

They reached Daneshgahi's office and took up positions on either side of the door. One waited as Two turned the handle and pushed the door open quickly. She entered the room and swept from side to side with her submachine gun, then quickly lowered the weapon. The office was well lit and empty. There was nowhere he could be hiding.

She cursed under her breath and the distant boom of a high-caliber rifle seemed to punctuate her profanity. Six was on the rooftop, tasked with keeping any police away from them, and he'd started the boom boom. While a few officers weren't a problem, with each passing second more would arrive.

She left the office with Two in tow as she spoke into her headset. "He's not in the office. Moving to check the cafeteria."

As she rounded a corner, a shot boomed. She flinched but kept moving toward an MIT police officer, who stood with his pistol drawn. He looked about fifty and very scared. Her silenced weapon barely made a sound as it delivered two rounds into the officer's chest. His eyes widened as crimson blossomed on his blue shirt. His pistol fell to the floor with a clattering sound and his body followed. One fired once into his face and didn't break stride as she stepped over him, with Two behind her.

Her headset crackled. "This is Three. We've got him. We have the target. He was in the lab."

"Good job." She felt a mix of relief and satisfaction. "Begin exfiltration."

She pictured the entirety of the exfiltration in her head as she moved. The snatch teams would move through the buildings and then onto the lawn, southeast across the campus. Five would drive to pick them up, while Six would shift position to cover Killian Court and their escape route before withdrawing. The whole team would be in and out with Daneshgahi in less than seven minutes, as planned.

She waved at Two and they moved south through the building and out into the courtyard. Once outside, they kept moving, scanning their surroundings and the top of buildings for shooters. The few students that remained ran when they spotted the armed commandos. Maybe MIT grads were intelligent after all. Smarter than their campus police, anyway.

She looked at her watch. By now Six would have taken his final shots. He'd be abseiling down the Maclaurin Building and moving to meet them at the extraction point. Radio silence meant no hitches. It had gone reasonably well so far and they were in the last minute of the operation. Nobody challenged One and Two as they reached the edge of the campus and crossed Memorial Drive.

She glanced at Three and Four, who were already crouched with weapons raised and facing outward. Two joined them in a covering position while she looked at Daneshgahi, face down on the lawn with his hands cuffed behind his back. She lifted him up. His face was the illustration of terror, but he kept quiet. It looked like he was pretty smart.

A shot drew her attention and she turned towards it. She needn't have bothered, because her team put down the police officer quickly. A few seconds later, Five pulled the van to a stop in front of them. She slid the door open, bundled Daneshgahi inside and climbed in. Their prisoner gave a small whimper of protest as the rest of the team joined them.

Six arrived at the van just as One was closing the door. The sniper's breathing was heavy and something had obviously taken longer than it should have, but he'd made it. She didn't need to ask and he didn't need to answer – if he hadn't made it, he'd have been cut loose. That was the business they were in.

As the door slammed shut and the engine roared, One looked over to Daneshgahi. The Iranian computer scientist was watching the floor and she could feel the fear radiating off him. She took the hood that Two was holding out to her and placed it over Daneshgahi's head. He started to cry.

ACT I

CHAPTER 1

FEMA would like to assure the public that, despite the recent terrorist attacks, its ability to provide disaster assistance remains intact. Staff are working hard to provide coordinated relief to all locations affected by these attacks. Citizens in need of support or those with something suspicious to report are encouraged to contact the new National Security Hotline.

Federal Emergency Management Agency
News Release

J ack Emery stared at the news bulletin as the massive Reuben sandwich in his hand continued to sag. Though he was meant to be on vacation, you couldn't take the news out of the newsman. He took a bite without taking his eyes off the screen, his brain working overtime to process the ramifications of what he was seeing. A half-dozen attackers – good ones – had gone to a lot of trouble to snatch one MIT student.

A chunk of corned beef and a dollop of sauerkraut breached the edges of his sandwich and fell onto his lap. He cursed, placed his lunch back on the plate and mopped at the mess with his napkin. It didn't help. He looked like a freshman who'd been touched in the nice place by a cheerleader. Jack shook his head and looked back at the screen as he picked up his Coke.

A hand on his shoulder made Jack jump and spill the drink. He looked around, angry, until he saw Josefa Tokaloka's smile beaming down at him. Though it had been only a year since they'd seen each other, the large Islander looked like he'd aged a decade. Jack grinned widely and stood to wrap his arms around Jo's enormous shoulders. It felt like hugging a bronze statue.

Jo crushed him in a bear hug. "Making a mess as usual."

Jack laughed and pulled away. "It's good to see you, Jo. Meeting up was a great idea."

"No problem, it's been a while." Jo's smile slackened slightly. "Plus, I figured you could do with some human contact that didn't involve people shooting at you."

Jack nodded and jerked a thumb at the screen. "Can you believe it?"

"Given recent events?" Jo frowned. "Yeah, Jack, I can."

Jo had a point. Jack had only been back in the US for a few weeks, but in that time there had been a dozen attacks across the country, all professional and brutally successful, targeting critical infrastructure and public gatherings. No group had claimed responsibility and no suspects had been identified. Casualties were mounting, panic was spreading and the authorities seemed impotent to stop the attacks.

"They're all connected, Jo. I'm sure of it. If I didn't know any better, I'd think it was the Foundation reborn." Jack hated thinking it, but even though over a year had passed it felt like just yesterday he'd been fighting to stop Michelle Dominique and her corrupt think tank. He'd gone to hell and back to stop her, but not before Dominique had sparked a war, taken control of the largest media empire in the world and almost gained control of Congress.

Jo shook his head. "Doesn't fit. The FBI tore them to shreds and their entire leadership is dead or before the courts."

"Yeah, you're right. But these are professional hits." Jack sat back down and gestured for Jo to sit on the lounge chair opposite. "Makes Syria seem almost civil."

Jo laughed softly as he sat. "How was it over there? You did some good work."

"Tough. There's not a lot of hope." Jack had spent the last three months in Syria covering the siege of Homs. It had been hard, but had also provided a rich vein of stories for his new site, which focused on long-form investigative journalism that the rest of the news media could bid on to broadcast. It was the perfect deal for everyone: he had the skill and not very much money, while they had the chequebooks but had cleared out most of the journalists with the skill.

"So why Vegas?" Jo looked around at the table games and the slot machines. "Given your particular vice, I figured this would be one of the last places you'd want to spend time."

Jack followed Jo's gaze. While the attacks – and the fear of more – had subdued Vegas a bit, you could never fully clear out the stags and hens, the corporate getaways, the tourists and the addicted. They were like moths to a flame. While there was gambling everywhere, it didn't interest him. The booze did, though he was more in control of those temptations these days. But what really drew him to this particular desert in Nevada was the fact that it was probably the least news-conscious place in America. Day and night passed without notice here and if it didn't involve gambling, sport or entertainment then it didn't rate a mention.

He thought he'd needed that time away from the news. After he'd won his second Pulitzer for the stories he'd written about the Foundation, he'd spent months working to get his estranged wife's body repatriated from Shanghai and organizing her funeral. He'd thought that watching her casket being lowered into the earth would be a release, an ending. He'd been wrong – more pain had come up inside him. After that, he'd tried burying himself in his work. He'd thrown all of his effort into the new site. Then, needing stories to tell and an escape, he'd traveled to Syria. Upon his return, he'd wanted some time away from the news. In theory.

"I like it here." He exhaled slowly. "Hell, I'm just glad to be back in the States, to tell you the truth. The site is going well and I've hired some other contributors. It was time for a break."

"Glad to hear it." Jo smiled slightly. His face looked gaunt and tired. "EMCorp wasn't the same when you left, you know that?"

Jack raised an eyebrow. "Wasn't?"

Jo's smile widened. "I retired a few weeks after you left, Jack. I'd love to say it was because you weren't there, but it was actually the love of my life who forced me to quit."

"Your wife?"

"My heart surgeon." Jo laughed and tapped his chest. "This fucking thing should have killed me, but the good people at New York Presbyterian kept me ticking a bit longer."

Jack couldn't believe it. Jo was the toughest hunk of meat he'd ever known. "Sorry I wasn't there, mate. Why didn't anyone let me know?"

"Well, I was too busy being cut open. I think Celeste wanted to tell you but Peter stopped her. He said you had to be left alone to heal. I don't think she was very happy about it."

Jack winced at the mention of her name, but before he could reply a drinks waitress approached. Given the length of her skirt, it was a good thing she had a beaming white smile and cute eyes, or else Jack might have struggled to look anywhere else. They made small talk for a moment before Jack ordered a beer. Jo went with ginger beer. As she shuffled off to get their orders, Jack's eyes were locked onto her legs.

Jo gave a long, booming laugh. "Fall off the horse, Jack?"

Jack turned back to Jo, feeling himself flush red. "I never stopped liking women, Jo."

"The booze, I mean."

"I limit it to a couple these days." He shrugged. "Hard to be a saint all the time."

～

"Good afternoon, Administrator." The young White House staffer held out her hands in apology. "The President has been delayed, but you're welcome to wait."

Richard Hall frowned. He reached up to his nose and slid his glasses back into place. "Okay, please let me know when they're ready."

He moved to a sofa and sat with a sigh, his back aching as he did. While Richard had lorded over the entirety of the Federal Emergency Management Agency for a decade, his boss was the most powerful woman on the planet, so delays were to be expected. But within a few moments he looked up to see the President striding down the hallway with members of her staff, each trying to get a word in. The scene was akin to hyenas stalking a wounded lion. The lion might be the most powerful, but the hyenas were legion. It made the lion vulnerable. The thought made him smile as he adjusted his tie.

President Helen Morris offered a tired smile as she approached. "Good to see you, Richard. I hope you haven't been waiting long?"

Richard stood. "Not at all, Madam President. Only a few minutes."

Morris didn't stop walking. "I'm heading to the Situation Room now. Care to join me?"

Richard nodded and followed her to the lift, where the staffers were repelled by some invisible force field. Apparently none of them were senior enough for a jersey in the big game. After a short ride and some small talk, they exited into the cavernous, 5000-square-foot Situation Room. Dominated by a mahogany table and leather chairs, the room was a high-tech dungeon used by the most senior members of government and the military to deal with any crisis abroad – or at home. The other members of the National Security Council were already seated as the President sat at the head of the table and Richard took a chair to her left.

"Thanks for coming in, everyone." Morris opened her leather folio and quickly perused her papers. "What do we know?"

Richard knew the answer: Nothing. He glanced up to the large screen at the far end of the table, which showed a map of the continental United States with digital pins marking the locations that had been attacked in recent weeks. When displayed in such a way the enormity of the situation revealed itself. Though the attacks had resulted in carnage, the authorities had identified no pattern, no logic, no leads and no suspects. He kept his mouth shut and others adopted the same strategy, though there were a few nervous coughs to punctuate the awkward silence. He sat back. The failure did not belong to him, though the solution might. Forty years of public administration had taught him patience.

Finally, Walt Clarke – the President's National Security Advisor – leaned forward to speak. "The attack on MIT was precise and astonishingly fast. They were in and out in less than eight minutes. Local police had only just started to arrive."

"That's it?" Morris peered over her glasses and down the table at Clarke. It wasn't a kind look. "I know all of that. I watch CNN and read my briefings. I want to know who? Why? Where next? What're we doing about it?"

There was a muted sense of tension in the room. While Morris was quite inexperienced, she wasn't regarded as a pushover. Richard doubted anybody in the room had seen her react this icily to their advice. Though she'd been in office for nearly a year and Richard had hardly been overwhelmed by her competence, this was the first time she'd seemed panicked. Richard knew there was opportunity for whoever could explain the attacks and provide a path forward to stopping them.

Clarke was visibly shaken by the President's bluntness. "I can't answer that. We have some footage, but it gives us nothing. We do know they kidnapped a computer scientist – Daryush Daneshgahi – and then swapped vehicles a number of times and disappeared."

Hayley Penbroke, the Director of National Intelligence, cleared her throat. "While I can't speculate on the who, the why is clear. Daneshgahi is a genius."

Clarke scoffed and turned towards Penbroke. "I doubt he grew up with running water. He can't be worth all that effort, surely?"

Penbroke glared at him, then turned back to the President. "We smuggled him out of Iran and gave him a full scholarship at MIT. He can pop the hardest encryption like it's bubble wrap. We keep a pretty close eye on him and he's never given us reason to doubt him. He's a good kid, really. Whoever has him is now a huge threat."

Morris frowned. "In practical terms?"

Penbroke didn't hesitate. "Any computer system is vulnerable. The Stock Exchange. Power grids. Air transportation safety systems. You name it, he can crack it."

General Mike Cooper, Chairman of the Joint Chiefs of Staff, raised his hand and interrupted. "Nuclear launch codes?"

"No, not those, General." Penbroke crossed her arms. "Pretty much everything else is in play though. This is more dangerous than some missing ammonium nitrate."

"Okay." Morris placed her hands flat on the table. "While everyone keeps trying to figure out who's behind all of this, what're our options? We can't just sit and wait."

Cooper spoke. "Madam President, give the word and we can have troops on the street in every major city in the country within twelve hours. We can also increase the cover at major infrastructure. I can't guarantee that these measures will stop the attacks, but they will make the bastards think twice."

"No." Morris's voice was sharp. "I don't want the army on Sixth Avenue. If there's one thing that'll panic people more than attacks across the country, it's a visible army presence. Besides, there's no possible way we have enough troops to cover everywhere that needs it. Deploying the military just gives these bastards a victory."

Richard gave a small smile. He'd underestimated the depth of the President's dissatisfaction with the other arms of the Federal Government. While she'd no choice but to rely on her advisors, she clearly wasn't putting much faith in them getting results. He couldn't blame her. The attacks had rocked America and her advisors weren't coping. They were overwhelmed and predictable, offering nothing that would work, nothing that would influence the situation or America.

It was time for him to speak. "Madam President, if I may?"

Morris gave a small nod. "Go ahead, Richard. That's why you're here."

He leaned forward. "While I agree with the desire for additional security, and concede that combat troops may be needed if this continues, there's another option. FEMA can use the State Guard to provide more security at key facilities. It's a middle ground – more protection, but without tanks on street corners."

Morris's face was expressionless. She seemed to consider his words for a few moments before she held her hands out. "Thoughts?"

Richard looked around. His plan earned a few nods and a lot of silence. Only Cooper seemed opposed, sitting with his arms folded. Most importantly, nobody raised any objections. Truth be told, they were all out of answers and probably happy for someone else to take the heat for a while. That suited Richard just fine. He was banking on the fact that he'd been in his job for a long time, while many of the people at the table had clocked less than a year in theirs. Rolling up the Foundation for a New America had taken a scythe through the upper ranks of government and the end of the Kurzon administration had removed more still. Richard had kept his head down and his hands clean, and was now considered a trusted broker by many, including Morris. He decided to press his luck.

"At the same time I can ramp up the support that FEMA is providing. All it will take to get this up and running quickly is a budget allocation." Richard sat back in his chair and looked at Morris. "That will take me to the limit of what FEMA is able to do, at least without the declaration of a state of emergency."

Morris sighed, removed her glasses and closed her eyes. While he knew she was a strong believer in civil liberties and loathed any discussion of the state taking more of a role in daily life – like deploying troops into cities – she also must know that doing nothing was not an option. Personally, Richard thought the choice was obvious – cut down on freedoms, ramp up surveillance, saturate the streets with assets and it just might be possible to win this thing. He could understand her hesitation, however. This was one of the largest decisions of her young administration so far and she was clearly fighting an internal struggle over it. She massaged her temples, looking every bit as old as her fifty-eight years. Finally, she opened her eyes again and ran a hand through her greying hair.

"Richard, make it happen. Dial it up as high as you can go without that declaration. Get the State Guard protecting our most important facilities and increase the relief FEMA is providing across the country." She exhaled heavily. "But I want FEMA talking to the rest of the administration. Protect us and help our people."

"Not a problem, Madam President." Richard nodded and sat back with a small smile. He'd won the hand, but in Washington things could go backward as quickly as they went forward. He knew when to gamble and when to take his winnings. He'd been trying for months to get FEMA dialed in to the main game as a legitimate player rather than just a mop-up agency at the call of others. He'd succeeded, now he kept quiet.

Morris stared down the table at the rest of the council. "Let me make this clear, ladies and gentlemen. While Richard beefs up our defense, I want the rest of you on offense. We have the most elaborate national security apparatus on the planet. I'd like to see some of it put to use. Find these bastards."

THE SOUND of the rotors slicing through the air was One's constant companion. Her team sat in silence as they edged closer to their target. The briefing, walk through and gear check had all been done on the ground and each member of the team knew their role, except for Daneshgahi. The Iranian computer scientist sat in his seat with his head downcast, with Two and Three seated on either side of him captive. It was all quite relaxed.

One looked down at her watch: 2159 hours. Right on time, the helicopter started to descend. She waved her hand at the rest of the team and held up one finger. The other five members of the team gave a thumbs-up in return. With thirty seconds to go, she lowered her night-vision goggles over her eyes and stood. The others joined her, Two and Three hauling Daneshgahi to his feet. The second her watch ticked over to 2200 hours, the helicopter touched down with a light thud.

She slid the door open and jumped the short distance from the helicopter to the ground. She took a deep breath. The cool evening air was both a shock and a thrill. It was her first time in Nevada and her first visit to the Hoover Dam. Once her team had finished disembarking she slid the door shut, raised her carbine and started to move along the causeway. Once they were clear of the helicopter it lifted off again, to take up station overhead and act as their eyes in the sky.

"This is Big Bird." The team was about halfway between the landing zone and their target when the helicopter reported in. "Three armed sighted targets ahead of you."

"Confirmed." One crouched and the rest of the team did the same. She kept her eyes peeled, but couldn't see the threat. "Move up."

She moved forward slowly with the others, leaving Three and Five to guard Daneshgahi. Losing the Iranian was not an option. Though she couldn't see any targets yet, they must be near the concrete structure that housed the entrance to the control room. Whoever was guarding the dam had hastily constructed some basic cover and fortifications. A boom broke the silence of the night – some sort of rifle.

"Three targets visible." Six's voice came over the network. He was slightly ahead of her.

"Get rid of them." One crouched and raised her carbine, but she didn't have a clear shot.

More shots roared from the other end of the causeway. Their foes weren't very good, shooting from extreme range and with no real accuracy. It was possible they didn't have night-vision gear and were shooting in hope, but she couldn't bank on that. She started to move forward, but was forced to drop low again when more fierce gunfire erupted. She heard a grunt in her earpiece.

"I'm hit." Six sounded like he was in pain. "My hand. Not too bad though."

She cursed under her breath. "Confirmed."

She heard a whoosh as Four – the squad's grenadier – fired the underslung grenade launcher on his carbine. A large explosion lit up the night and One heard a roar as the grenade struck home. Hardly stealthy, but effective. Flames licked at the cover that dam security was using and one of the guards staggered forward. She raised her carbine and fired a burst at the exposed guard. He dropped.

She hadn't expected much resistance and it was over and done with now. When nobody reported further hostiles, she started forward. "Move up."

They reached the large steel door that separated them from the command center, paying little attention to the three bodies scattered among the crates they'd used as cover. She knocked on the door and whistled softly to herself. The door was too thick to blow up and its electronics had recently been upgraded to make it independent from any network. Luckily her employer had provided the answer.

"Three, Five, move up with Daneshgahi." She turned to Four. "Do it."

Four nodded. He let his weapon hang by its strap and dug into a pocket on his combat vest. One smiled as he held the electronic access card to the reader until it beeped, flashed green and unlocked the door with a clunk. She'd half expected the card to fail, foiling their entire operation, but it turned out her employer could be trusted. Some dam employee somewhere would soon be very rich.

Four swung the heavy door open with a grunt and led the way inside with Two. One waited as Three and Five moved up with the scientist and followed the lead pair inside. She waited a few moments until she was satisfied things outside were under control, then followed with her carbine raised. She left the wounded Six on guard outside. He was hurt, but could hold their rear if any trouble came along.

They moved quickly through the corridor, alert for any threats. In a few moments they reached the expansive control room, which had a bank of computer terminals, large monitors and status boards on the walls. The capacity and flow of the Hoover Dam were managed from here, along with the key safety systems and contact with the outside world. One lowered her carbine as the team checked for any threats.

Five examined the terminals. "The systems are in lockdown."

Two's spoke up from across the room. "I've got a pair of civilians."

One walked to where Two was standing over a pair of workers, cowering under a terminal. She crouched. "You have five seconds to override the lockdown."

"Please, just leave us alone." A young woman shrank back further. "We just look after the systems in the evenings. I don't know how to do very much."

One stood, raised her carbine and fired a single silenced round into the woman's skull. A spray of blood escaped from the woman's head and she slumped to the ground as the shell casing pinged off the floor tiles. One believed her – she was just a console operator, unable to help the team out of their predicament. She turned to the older man, whom she had a hunch knew more than his dead companion. She pointed at him.

The man nodded and One stepped back as he crawled out from under the terminal. Without speaking, he took his seat and started to type. He was shaking like a leaf in the wind as a password command box appeared on the screen. One held her carbine to the back of his head as he typed the command in slowly, then hit Enter. The password box disappeared and the screen flashed red with a warning that an alarm had been triggered.

"How disappointing." She sighed and pulled the trigger.

As his body dropped to the floor, One let her carbine fall to her side. A quick glance at the terminals told her all she needed to know. The facility control room had now gone from being locked to completely inert – even if a member of staff wanted to unlock the systems, they'd be unable to. She hated heroes. With a sigh, she approached Daneshgahi and lifted his chin with her index finger.

"I can deal with the override, so long as you have the equipment I asked for." His voice had a tremor and his eyes kept flicking to the dead man. "Just promise I'll live."

She smiled and held out a small kit bag that had been on her combat vest. "You deliver on your promise and I'll deliver on mine."

He nodded frantically and snatched the bag from her hand. One was alert but curious as he opened it, drew out a small device and plugged it into a USB port. Daneshgahi's hands danced across the keyboard, command prompts and lines of code flashing on the screen at dizzying speed. She didn't understand it, but she didn't have to. Her employer had assured her that Daneshgahi had the skills to do what was needed.

After less than a minute, he stepped back from the terminal and smiled at her. "The lockdown is no longer in effect. The control panel is back to normal."

One looked at Three, who nodded as he held a carbine to Daneshgahi's side and whispered into his ear. Daneshgahi's eyes went wide and a deep look of worry crossed his furrowed brow. Finally, Daneshgahi looked down at the console, hit a few keys, turned to her and nodded. She stepped up to the terminal, where a box on the screen was asking for confirmation of the command.

"Everyone ready?" She looked at her team and saw nods in return. She hit the Enter key. Klaxons started to wail and lights flashed red. "It's time to go."

Daneshgahi looked as if he'd burst into tears at any moment. "I've done what you wanted. Please, I want to go home."

She ignored Daneshgahi and spoke into her headset. "Big Bird, we need extraction. Two minutes."

"Confirmed." The helicopter pilot's voice was calm. "No sign of further hostiles, but there's some radio noise coming out of Nellis Air Force Base. Suggest you hustle."

She jerked her head toward the door. Daneshgahi started to move and she followed him and the other four members of her team toward the main door and out into the cool night air. She looked over the side of the dam, and though she couldn't see the water in the darkness, she could hear it. As they waited for their ride, Daneshgahi moved a few steps closer to her, a look of frightened conviction on his face.

Four raised his carbine. "Back off, buddy."

The Iranian didn't buckle as he ignored Four and addressed One. "I gave you access. I've done what you wanted. I want to go back to Boston. You promised."

She smiled at Daneshgahi and nodded once. Without a second's delay, Three and Five grabbed him from behind. As they manhandled him closer to the edge, One followed. His eyes were frantic and kept flicking back and forth amongst the team as he fought to free himself from their grasp. She casually drew her pistol and placed it against his skull. His eyes widened as she pressed down with some force.

Daneshgahi became a dead weight in the arms of her men as he started to wail. "Please, I gave you what you wanted. You can't. You promised."

"You've been a great help, for whatever that's worth." She squeezed the trigger.

CHAPTER 2

With unprecedented flooding across several states following the attack on the Hoover Dam, FEMA has mobilized to assist cities, towns and rural areas in need of support. Until this support can reach affected locations, citizens are reminded to beware of areas that are flooded, to secure their home but be cautious of electricity around water, to avoid driving and conserve food.

Federal Emergency Management Agency
News Release

J ack looked out over the serene water contained by the Hoover Dam as he sipped his coffee. He found it difficult to comprehend the devastation it had caused just a day earlier. Though the dam wall was physically intact, the terrorists had opened a pair of spillways, freeing an enormous amount of water. Half-a-dozen large towns downstream had been flooded and thousands were missing, presumed dead.

Jack ran a hand through his hair and resumed his walk along the causeway. "They did a job on this place."

"It was surgical." Josefa frowned. "If they can pull an attack like this off, there's really not a safe location in the entire country."

Jack shrugged but said nothing as they neared the operations center. There was a score of maintenance staff on the causeway, repairing damage caused by the gunfight. Though they could do little to help the towns flooded and lives ruined downstream, they were doing a fair job of hosing away the blood. Milling around, far less busy, were some Nevada state troopers, police and some security contractors.

Josefa snorted. "Upping the security seems a bit pointless."

Jack laughed. "Like waiting until after the shot clock has expired before shooting."

They had already passed through a security cordon at the entrance to the dam, but there was another checkpoint near the entrance to the operations center. Jack was glad that, at times like this, he had friends in high places. Given he'd very publicly assisted US authorities to foil the Foundation for a New America, he was able to access areas that would be denied to others. It was time to make use of it.

He gave his widest smile and held up his press pass as he approached the two guards standing outside the operations center. "Hey, guys."

The security guards looked at each other and then one of them scrutinized the pass. "You've got no business inside."

Jack sighed. "Bill McGhinnist, Director, Federal Bureau of Investigation, would have something to say about that. Should we give him a call?"

"I don't care if you've got the King of England on speed dial, pal." The guard didn't seem impressed as he tapped the clipboard. "No name, no entry."

Jack was about to point out there was no male monarch currently straddling the British throne, but he saved his breath. Another man approached them, dressed in chinos and a polo shirt that bore the logo of the US Bureau of Reclamation. He had the look of someone deeply troubled, a guy pushed into the deep end and struggling not to drown – Jack knew a source when he saw one. He stepped forward.

"Good morning, sir. I'm Jack Emery." He flashed his pass. "I've been given permission to cover the story of the dam attack. This is Josefa Tokaloka, my... assistant."

"Eric Waterford." The other man smiled weakly and jerked a thumb toward the guards. "Don't mind these gentlemen. You're not on their list, but you are now."

"Thanks." Jack smiled at the guards. One of them glowered, as if resenting the challenge to his unassailable authority.

Jack snorted and followed Waterford and Jo inside. Though there were signs of conflict outside, there was no apparent damage to the inside of the facility. They walked in silence down a short corridor and into a cavernous room dominated by a few rows of computer terminals and wall-mounted screens. It was pretty clear that this room had been the focus of the attack. The scene of a mass murder.

"We're here." Waterford turned and held his arm out, showcasing the computer terminals. "This is what lives were lost for. This is where your story is, Mr Emery."

Jack took a few more steps into the room. "Can you tell us what happened?"

"They hacked in and compromised the spill gates." Waterford looked close to tears as he pointed at a terminal. "A lot of water rushed out of the dam very quickly."

Jack paused, then joined Waterford and put a hand on his back. It was time to change tack. "Why are you talking to us, Mr Waterford? Why give me the story?"

"I know who you are and what you did for this country. You'll call it fair." Waterford shrugged. "Plus, I owe it to the people who died here. I'm lucky to be alive myself."

"You saw the attacks? As in, eyeballs on what they were doing?" Jack was excited by the thought of an eyewitness account.

"No." Waterford cast his eyes downward. "But I heard it. There's a supply cupboard in the hallway. I hid in there once I heard the gunfire."

Jack nodded. Waterford's mess of emotions was clearer now. "There's no story here. You're not giving me anything CNN doesn't have. I need something exclusive."

Waterford gave a sad-looking smile. "I can do you one better. They cut our security camera feeds, but we've got a hard-wired network. We caught it on tape."

Jo whistled. "Can we see it?"

Waterford nodded and walked over to a cabinet against one of the walls. He chose a key on his oversized key ring and unlocked it. Inside the cabinet there was a small monitor. Jack watched with fierce curiosity as Waterford's hands danced across the keys and the wall-mounted monitors came to life with some dark but decent footage. He could barely contain his excitement at the size of this scoop.

"You got it. The whole thing." Jack couldn't believe such an elite team could be so careless.

The video showed six figures wearing balaclavas, weapons raised and alert as they led a seventh man – Daneshgahi – across the causeway. Before long, they'd paused and were exchanging fire with the security team. Jack watched in awe as they met the attack with cool professionalism.

Waterford pressed a key. The vision switched to above the external door, where three bodies were sprawled like dolls discarded by a raging toddler. Jack winced. The attackers were at the door and managed to unlock it easily. Five of them moved inside with Daneshgahi while a single figure remained outside.

"Wait a minute." Jack's eyes widened and he looked at Waterford in confusion. "How the hell did they get in so easily?"

"An inside man." Waterford shrugged. "I don't know who, or why, but it's the only way they could get through that door so quickly."

"Okay." Jack nodded. "I need these tapes and I need to get back to Chicago. This is going to explode."

~

CALLUM WATKINS CROUCHED low as he moved through the foliage, careful not to step on any dried twigs or knock his rifle against a tree or sapling. He held up a gloved hand, his fingers balled into a fist, to stop his companions from advancing any further. He listened, alert for any sound or sign of their target, but heard nothing. With a smile, he lowered his fist and edged forward slowly. He lived for this.

He winced when he heard a small crack from behind him, and turned his head to see one of the others holding up a hand in apology. Callum glowered, but moved on without further rebuke. They weren't in Fallujah this time and mistakes didn't mean death, but it still annoyed him when others screwed up. He brushed aside some shrubbery as quietly as he could, then inhaled deeply.

There he was. Callum crouched as low as he could and lifted his rifle. Square in front of him was the mother lode – the largest male stag he'd ever seen. It was an amazing beast. When its haunches were locked squarely in his iron gun sight, Callum breathed. In and out. In and out. He aimed, concentrated on his breathing then squeezed down on the trigger slightly.

The sound of a steam train whistle broke the serenity. Callum flinched involuntarily, just as the rifle boomed in response to his caress.

He'd missed and the deer was spooked by the barrage of sound. It broke into a run, crushing twigs underfoot as it disappeared deep into the forest. Callum stared at where the stag had been, his mouth agape, then lowered his weapon and looked around.

"What the hell?" Callum locked his eyes on one of his companions. Though Todd Bowles was a friend, right now Callum wanted to shove a branch down his throat until leaves sprouted from his ass. When the other man didn't look up from his iPhone, Callum placed his rifle against a tree and marched over to him.

Todd looked up from his phone. He gave no sign that he understood the enormity of his screw up. "What? It's important."

"So is the biggest deer this side of the Rocky Mountains. I had it lined up!" Callum pushed Todd off his feet and onto his back. "Who brings a phone hunting?"

"Hey, calm down!" Todd took a half-hearted swing at Callum as a few of their friends dragged him away. "I had the phone set to ring only for an emergency. It rang."

Callum fought off the hands of his friends and sat on the ground. "What do you mean? What's the matter?"

"It's from my buddy in the Secret Service. We were together in Kandahar. Word is that all the state defense forces are being mobilized."

Callum paused. It was no small deal if true. The Illinois State Guard had been reconstituted after the war between the United States and China, along with those from other states that had long ago abolished them. A rung below the National Guard, they were a small force under the command of the state governor. Every state in America now had one, armed with surplus military equipment.

Like many in the guard, Callum was ex-army and attracted to the pay and conditions that they offered for part-time work. It seemed a good way to keep in touch with the life and career he'd known for his whole adult life. He could keep his pension and work for them tax-free, which sure beat packing groceries at Wal-Mart or cleaning windows in the Illinois winter. He'd signed on and kept his sergeant rank.

"That's a big deal." Callum started to stand. "Must be because of the attack on the Hoover Dam yesterday."

While the attacks across the country had been severe and showed no sign of slowing, Callum hadn't expected them to lead to the mobilization of any arm of the military. Even the activation of the state defense forces showed that a large number of people in the highest levels of command were taking things pretty seriously. He wondered if there was more to it.

"Wait a minute." Mark Pettine looked up from the ground, deep in thought. "Who's doing the activating? We're under the governor's authority."

Callum and Todd looked at each other and shrugged, before Callum started to walk back to his rifle. "Doesn't matter. We better pull up camp. We'll get the call soon."

MARIPOSA ESPOSITO PAUSED BRIEFLY and then clicked confirm, sending thousands of pounds of relief supplies from warehouses across Illinois to towns devastated by the Hoover Dam flood. She stood, walked to a whiteboard near her cubicle and drew a line through a name on the board. She smiled, proud that she'd now helped all of the towns she'd been assigned to assist. It was a good thing, because while FEMA Area V had deep resources to call upon, most relief supplies in Illinois had now been trucked off. Mariposa walked back to her desk and sat heavily in her chair.

She struggled to stifle a yawn and looked to the left of her monitor. She'd pinned a photo of her seven-year-old son, Juan, on the cubicle wall. His close-cropped hair was ruffled from play and his smile was so wide that it plumped up his cheeks. Best of all were his chocolate brown eyes that made her heart melt. She looked back at the screen, but before she had the chance to do any work, one of her colleagues walked over and parked his rear on the edge of her desk. She looked up with a smile still on her face. Murray Devereaux looked as tired as she felt.

"You're cheery." He took a sip of his coffee and looked up to the board. "Nothing left to dispatch?"

"Just pressed go on the last lot." She patted his leg. "How're you holding up, Murray? How's Di?"

"One step closer to a divorce." He gave a tired shrug. "Things were going better until we had to start working these double shifts. Back to where we started now."

Mariposa gave a sympathetic nod. FEMA officers had been working hard since the beginning of the attacks a month ago. All leave had been canceled and many of the staff had been spending more time at the office than at home. She'd had to hire a sitter. But the attack on the Hoover Dam had nearly broken their backs, with the work stepping into overdrive in the past twenty-four hours.

"I don't know what to say, Murray." Mariposa grabbed his hand and gave it a squeeze. "Except that we're helping a lot of people."

His expression darkened. "Fat lot of good it's doing. As soon as we react to one attack they cause chaos elsewhere. Each time, our supplies run a little lower."

She nodded. "And it doesn't feel right that we're leeching all of our supplies, given Chicago hasn't been hit yet? I get it."

He exhaled for a long few seconds. "There's no point thinking about it – it's all on the back of trucks now. We better just hope the hammer doesn't fall here."

"Amen to that."

He raised his coffee cup in salute and then lowered it to consider its contents. "Running on empty, you want one?"

She glanced at her cup but didn't get the chance to answer as her computer made a sound that drew her attention. Only emails from a select few people made that sound, Murray among them. She leaned forward, clicked on the new arrival and scanned the contents of the email quickly. Murray read over her shoulder and let out a soft whistle.

"Big wigs incoming." He scoffed. "Arriving just in time to congratulate themselves."

Mariposa let out a short laugh then reached up to cover her mouth. "You're terrible."

"Not wrong though. Catch you later." He smiled and walked back toward his desk.

Mariposa put her headphones in and started answering the emails that had built up while she had been coordinating relief supplies. As she worked in rhythm with the music, the distractions of the rest of the office vanished. Most of the emails were routine and many were complete junk, but all had to be dealt with. She liked to go home with an empty inbox.

Something hit her in the head and she jumped with a start. She looked down at the eraser which had settled on her desk, then looked up to see Murray beaming a smile in her direction from his desk. She frowned, until he jerked his head toward the break area, where a bunch of men in suits were waiting and the rest of the staff had started to gather.

She checked the time and was shocked that a full hour had passed. She stood and stretched again, unsure about what could be so important that it required a full gathering of the staff. It was late, everyone was tired and the work was mostly done. People deserved the chance to finish up and go home for a while before it all started again tomorrow.

As she approached the break area, she sized up the two men from management: one of them was very slick but also very young, while the other had a few more laps on his tires. Yet the aura of power radiated off them both in a way that surprised her. These were very important people. She crossed her arms and waited for them to begin.

"Thanks, everyone." The older of the two, a completely bald man, smiled and held his hands together. "I'm Frank McCaskey, here on behalf of Administrator Hall."

That got everyone's attention. Richard Hall was a god to the men and women who worked for FEMA. He'd taken over the organization after Hurricane Katrina, when it had been smashed by criticism about the effectiveness of its response. Since then he'd quietly gone about fixing the problems, building morale among the staff and making FEMA more influential than ever.

McCaskey smiled. "The executive team wants to express our thanks for the incredible effort over the past month or so. If this were the private sector, we could give you bonuses, but it's not, so we can't. All I've got to offer is our thanks and the assurance that you're making a difference. You're saving lives and helping people.

"Unfortunately, we're going to need to ask more from you all. From tomorrow, FEMA is going to full mobilization. Code Red." McCaskey paused. "I know this sounds unusual, but it's in response to the unprecedented challenges that the country is currently facing. We have a huge role to play."

Mariposa looked around at her colleagues. They appeared as concerned as she felt. The last time the organization had gone to Code Red had been for Katrina, and that hadn't gone well. A full response to one geographic location was one thing, but to achieve it across the entire United States felt like an impossible dream. It would mean longer hours, more stress and more work.

"I'd like to introduce my colleague." McCaskey pointed to the young man. "This is Alan Benning, he's going to take charge of Area V for the duration of the emergency."

Benning offered a grin and a wave as half-hearted applause greeted the news. "As far as you'll all notice, not much will change."

Mariposa looked at Murray, who'd raised an eyebrow. She knew that look.

Everything was about to change.

CHAPTER 3

All available support has now been dispatched to the areas flooded following the attack on the Hoover Dam. FEMA is pleased to announce that all Critical 1 incidents have been responded to and the agency is working in collaboration with local authorities to respond to Critical 2 and Critical 3 cases. The President will address the media today at the White House and provide a full update on the situation.

Federal Emergency Management Agency
News Release

R ichard had never set foot inside the White House Briefing Room before, despite four decades of public service. It was testament to the type of work he did that, on the odd occasion he spoke to the media, it was from the site of some disaster or another. Yet here he was, seated alone and off to the side as he waited for President Morris to arrive. Circumstances had changed – for the very first time he had a place in the center of major conversations taking place in America.

Camera flashes and the low hum of conversation interrupted his daydreaming as President Morris arrived with her press secretary and a Secret Service agent. Morris was wearing a blood-red jacket that strongly contrasted her graying hair and pale skin. It had probably been chosen by her political handlers to project strength. The press secretary whispered into her ear and left her alone at the lectern, while the agent stood off to the side. Richard watched her intently.

"Good morning, everyone." The President looked straight ahead with as much conviction as Richard had ever seen from her. "Today I'm here to speak to the American people about the most severe threat we've faced this century."

Richard smiled as some of the journalists looked up. The White House press corps gathered here nearly every day to hear the routine affairs of state, but it was rare that a briefing would begin with such a blunt statement. Given the events during that time period – 9/11, wars with Afghanistan, Iraq and China and attempts by the Foundation for a New America to control the country – it was a bold claim. Yet Morris wasn't wrong.

"The terrorist attacks that have swept our nation are unprecedented. We've been attacked before on home soil, but we've never before seen a chain of coordinated assaults like the one that we're currently facing. The damage has been immense, from Cowboys Stadium to MIT to Walt Disney World. The attackers are well trained, well equipped and deadly. No group has claimed responsibility and we do not know their motive.

"It pains me to admit that while the authorities are doing their best, they've made little progress. While investigations continue, I've had to escalate our response, to provide more security for our critical installations and on our streets. In doing so, I've tried to balance security against the impact on the daily lives of Americans. But it's clear to me that traditional approaches aren't working to protect us."

Richard felt a surge of satisfaction. For Morris to publicly admit that her administration was powerless in the face of such assaults was huge, and he knew better than anyone how far away they were from results. Since she'd authorized the deployment of the State Guard at the NSC meeting, he'd been working overtime to get things moving. Since the meeting, the attack on the Hoover Dam had only escalated things further.

The previous evening he'd been working late into the night to get the State Guard deployed when Morris had called. She'd skirted around the issue at first, until she'd finally swallowed her pride and asked him what more could be done. It was the moment Richard had been waiting for. They'd talked for an hour about the possible contingencies and he imagined that her speech notes for this morning had been changed significantly after their conversation.

Morris gripped the lectern. "The atrocity at the Hoover Dam was the final straw for me. That attack looks to have killed thousands and is the latest sign that nothing we're trying is working. Given that, I've consulted with my advisors and searched deep into my soul to look for new ways, new ideas, to keep our people safe. We think we've come up with something, but it was a hard decision to make."

Richard snorted. Morris had been speaking to her advisors for weeks, since the commencement of the attacks. They'd come up blank and their inexperience and lack of imagination had cost the country dearly. In truth, he knew that he was the only one she'd consulted the previous evening, and was glad that his experience was finally being taken into serious consideration. He'd been available to her from the very start, but she'd neglected to seek out his advice. He'd served America for decades and only wanted it to be great.

He sighed. It was a shame so few Presidents were up to the challenge. Most floated through their time in office like so much driftwood on the high seas, achieving nothing except in occasional, deferential nods to the Constitution, the Bill of Rights and the founding fathers. They told Americans what they *deserved*, but not what was necessary for them to have it, or to keep the country safe and prosperous. They ignored the fact that, sometimes, foul-tasting medicine was needed to fix the body. Occasionally, a President was forced to face this fact.

Morris shifted her gaze and stared straight down the cameras. "Prior to entering this room, I signed orders declaring a state of emergency across America and executed a number of executive orders pertaining to our government, legal system, economy, media and critical infrastructure. The current situation necessitates this action and I don't take this step lightly. Actually, please come up here and join me, Richard."

Richard was surprised at the invitation, but composed himself quickly. He stood and walked to the front of the Briefing Room, going over their conversation from the previous night in his head. They'd discussed the mobilization of the State Guard and the extra options Richard had hinted at in the NSC meeting. He'd told her about a number of long standing executive orders that were on the books, ready to be activated in an emergency but an afterthought to nearly everyone in America. Nearly.

In the time it took him to reach the President, she had given the assembled media the highlights of his career. He was surprised with how gushing she was in her praise, but perhaps shouldn't have been, given he offered her a life raft to save her administration. The advisors she'd hand picked to be part of her inner circle had failed so she'd turned to him, a career bureaucrat with decades of service to a half-dozen presidents. He smiled. If he was her chance at absolution, she was the key to his legacy. If she could be persuaded.

"Thank you, Madam President." He stood beside Morris, adjusting his eyes to the lights and mentally preparing – for the first time – for the spotlight. "Good morning."

Morris smiled. "Richard is a colleague and friend with immense experience in disaster management. Commencing immediately, he's in charge of a coordinated response to these attacks. He's in charge of the basics – transportation, power supply, food distribution – as well as security and the investigation."

The assembled members of the press corps looked up from their notepads and tablets and just stared. Every set of eyes bored into him like a drill, as the realization of what they were witnessing sank in. He'd never actively sought the limelight, but to achieve his goals it was a necessary next step. Others had proven incapable of such responsibility, but he was up to the job.

Hands shot into the air and questions started to fly. Richard looked to the President, who smiled slightly and waited. She'd done this before. It was a process that Richard didn't quite understand, but it seemed to work. Morris waited patiently for the initial boilover to calm down to a low simmer before one journalist drowned out the others. Morris pointed to the man.

"Tim Gossinge, *Washington Post*. Madam President, you're handing over the reins to FEMA? How will it work and why are you taking action of such severity?"

The President smiled. "Thanks, Tim. The orders that allow me to place much of the administration of our country under the control of FEMA have been on the books for years. After much thought, I've decided that we need a new approach. We need everyone singing from the same sheet, and Richard is the finest conductor in the country. All arms of federal and state government will report to him."

Richard swallowed, shifted forward slightly and waited for the President's nod to speak. "If I could just add, coordinating all parts of our campaign against these terrorists will take a huge effort – from security to first response to disaster relief to investigation to arrest to prosecution. FEMA's involvement will get everyone pointed in the same direction and, when that happens, we can't be stopped."

Gossinge persisted. "That doesn't explain the need to take over things completely unrelated to the attacks though, does it?"

Morris frowned. "Come on, Tim, you're not that stupid. These attacks target our way of life and we must protect that way of life. Americans expect the lights to turn on, food on their supermarket shelves and gas in the pump. This reality is under threat. It's Richard's job to protect it. I don't back away from my decision."

"Madam President. Elena Winston, *Chicago Tribune.*" Another reporter cut in, as she tapped a pencil against her leg. "What resources will FEMA have to do this job?"

"Whatever they need." Morris's reply was blunt. "Pretty much the entirety of the federal government will be at Richard's disposal, except the military."

Winston scribbled furiously as she spoke. "Without the military, how do you expect to protect anything? Beat cops and private security too fat to chase anybody?"

Richard stayed silent. It was best for the President to fend away the shots at his authority, including questions that dealt with the extent of the new powers that FEMA had been granted. Given the enormity of the job, bringing the entire country under the administration of FEMA and the protection of the State Guard, he'd have enough threats and challenges in the coming days. He didn't need to step into the line of fire unnecessarily.

"The state defense forces will also be providing security at our most critical infrastructure and rapid response to any attacks that occur." Morris glanced at Richard and then continued. "These forces were recently beefed up following the war with China. It gives us the force we need at the right time."

"The right time?" Winston leaned forward in her chair. "And how long will these controls be in place? Isn't this a breach of our democracy?"

"No. I was elected to solve problems, and that's what I'm doing. As for how long? These orders are effective immediately. It's possible we may quickly reach a point where things can return to normal, but after a year of operation, the executive orders will be reviewed. You'll be briefed accordingly throughout this period."

The room erupted.

Morris held up her hands. "The orders also cover control of the news media. We're keen to ensure terrorists don't gain exposure for the attacks, so we must take this step."

The President's press secretary, clearly unhappy with the uproar, stepped forward. "That's all for today, ladies and gentleman. Thanks."

Morris started to step away from the lectern and put a hand on Richard's back. He went with her, the Secret Service agent in tow. As they approached the exit, Richard heard the press secretary deliver the final zinger – that the press briefing packs would detail the changes and how they would work, but that all reports from now on needed to be cleared by the Press Office before printing or publication on the internet.

The roar that filled the room was only silenced once the door closed behind them. Richard took a deep breath. He didn't like the chaos of the mass media and it would be one of the first things he'd get under control. It still amazed him that America could shift to virtual totalitarianism with a signed document and a press conference. The changes gave him the opportunity to bring order and stability back to America. It would be his lasting legacy.

He turned to the President. "Well, I think that went alright?"

JACK CURSED as the amber light switched to red just as he drove through it, causing a camera to flash. Though he was in no hurry, he'd been sucked into what he was listening to on the radio and hadn't been paying attention. He didn't look forward to a traffic fine from the good state of Illinois, though he did wonder how the executive orders applied to such things. He'd just have to wait and see if FEMA were as efficient at stamping out traffic offences as they were at taking control of society.

The more detail he heard about exactly what FEMA would be in charge of, the more worried he became. Worse, he suspected the stale reports were being read straight from approved media releases. He'd flown out of Las Vegas early after publishing his story on the Hoover Dam, so he had been in the air when the bombshell from the White House had dropped. By the time he'd landed, the screws were already starting to tighten.

Now, as he drove down West Adams Street toward his hotel, it was clear that FEMA had been prepared for kick-off. He tooted his horn as a black Illinois State Guard Humvee cut him off. The vehicle held four uniformed troopers with their weapons clearly visible, but Jack had seen enough men with guns in recent months to not be intimidated. It was for naught anyway – they didn't acknowledge his presence as they continued down the street. So much for courtesy among motorists.

He sighed and pulled the vehicle to the side of the road, right out the front of the Club Quarters Hotel. It had been his home away from home in Chicago since his return from Syria. It wasn't palatial, but it was cheap and comfortable until he found a place of his own. He'd thought about returning to New York to live, but there were too many memories there. Too much pain. He killed the engine, reached into the back seat for his duffel bag and climbed out of the car.

A valet rushed over to him. "Welcome back, Mr Emery. Good to see you, sir. Can I take your bag?"

"No need, Mo." Jack smiled at the familiar routine and handed over his keys. "Take care of the car though?"

"You got it." Mo took the keys and started toward the car. "Unlucky for you that you're so late. We've had issues with check-ins since noon."

Jack hefted the duffel bag over his shoulder, confused by Mo's words, and crossed the sidewalk to the hotel entrance. Once inside he slowed and then stopped entirely. A uniformed Illinois State Guardsman stood in the foyer sporting a bored expression. He didn't even look at Jack when he entered. Jack swallowed hard and approached the reception desk, behind which sat a cute brunette he knew well.

"How's it going, Maggie?" Jack rummaged around in his pocket. He pulled out a cigarette lighter and placed it on the counter. "I got you that lighter."

"Oh, thanks! I didn't think you'd remember." Her eyes lit up. "Did you have a good time in Vegas?"

"It was great until the Hoover Dam got attacked." Jack pulled out his wallet and extracted his credit card.

"Yeah, isn't it terrible? Those poor people." Her expression darkened. "I've organized your normal room, but I'm going to need to register you."

Jack frowned. "What do you mean?"

She jerked her head toward the guardsman and then lifted a piece of paper. "New rules. Everyone on this list has to go through enhanced check-in. You're on the list. I'm sorry."

Jack looked at the list. It contained names, occupations and contact details. He laughed at the simplicity of it all. On the back of the huge data trawl that the National Security Agency had been conducting over the past few decades, FEMA had clearly been able to produce a list of people it was interested in keeping track of. As a prominent journalist, he was a prime target for such treatment, though he did wonder how far the list extended.

"Okay, let's get on with it." He gave her a small smile. It wasn't her fault. "What do I need to do to be able to park my head on the pillow?"

Maggie smiled. "Oh, just the usual. But we've also been instructed to take copies of your license and all of your credit cards."

It took about ten minutes for Jack to fill in the paperwork and hand over every piece of ID he possessed. He shook his head as he took the elevator up – he had a bad feeling about where this was all heading. When society started to muzzle and track journalists, bad things tended to follow. He'd seen it in conflict zones overseas, but he'd never expected to see it in the United States.

Once he reached his room, he tossed the duffel bag onto the bed and pulled out his cell phone. He searched through his contacts until he found the name he was after: Celeste. He stared at it for a few long seconds, not sure that he wanted to make the call, and then pressed the green button. He put the phone to his ear and waited for what seemed like an eternity for her to answer.

"Hi Jack." Her voice was cold. "I think I hear from my dead grandmother more than you."

"I deserve that, but it's good to hear your voice." During the time he'd spent dealing with Erin's funeral, setting up the website and working in Syria, they'd barely spoken. He'd hoped she'd understand his need for distance, but clearly she'd taken it personally. He couldn't blame her. They'd gone through hell together, and as much as he'd needed space, it wasn't hard to imagine her needing something different. And he'd left her out in the cold.

Her sigh was drawn out. "What do you want, Jack?"

"I've just checked into my hotel and it seems there's a whole lot of shit that comes attached to being a journalist now. I wanted to make sure you're okay and let you know."

"It's happening here too, Jack." There was a pause. "There's New York State Guard troops on the streets. They're at Penn Station, Central Park, Yankee Stadium – you name it."

So it was happening all over America. It was amazing how quickly the executive orders were being implemented. The announcement had only been made four hours ago but already the troops were in the streets, the monitoring was in place and the tendrils of FEMA were expanding to embrace all of society.

"I reckon they've had this drawn up for a while." He sat on the edge of the bed with a sigh. "It's low key for the moment – dudes with rifles – but I wonder what comes next."

"It gets worse, Jack. The *Standard* offices got a visit from some FEMA employees an hour or so ago, explaining our place in the new world order."

"Oh?" He lay back on the bed, closed his eyes and did his best to imagine that she was in the room with him. He didn't dare say that though.

"Yeah. They basically told us to continue working, but that all stories must be submitted for approval prior to publication."

Jack was appalled. "Did Peter go for it?"

"Don't know. We haven't got a response from the company yet, but it's hard to see them resisting."

Jack couldn't picture it either – the company was likely to toe the line even with Peter Weston in charge. EMCorp had been through too much in the past few years to put up much of a fight. The company was traumatized and the shareholders were jumpy. Any journalists that strayed from the strict conditions were probably on their own.

"Just keep your head down, Celeste. This is a dangerous situation. Stay out of it."

"Oh, I plan to." She laughed softly. "I've had my turn at the hero game."

Jack felt the same way, deep down. A year ago he'd have been outraged by all of this, but he'd rocked the system enough and had the scars to prove it. The trauma both Celeste and Jack had suffered during the war with China and at the hands of Michelle Dominique would be a long time healing. It probably also gave them a free pass to sit out of this battle.

"How are you doing, Celeste?"

"Alright. Busy. You should be here, Jack."

"I can't." He ended the call.

∾

MARIPOSA FELT STRANGE, seated on a plastic chair on the grass of a high school football field while, in the bleachers, a few thousand people were gathered for a FEMA briefing about the executive orders. The same briefing was taking place in thousands of locations across the country. They were also being broadcast on television, radio and the internet. She wondered if the other briefings had the same feeling of tension as this one. She could feel the silent fury emanating from the mass of people as a Chicago Police Department lieutenant finished his briefing on the changes to law and order in the city. As he sat, there was silence from the crowd.

Mariposa tapped her lapel microphone to make sure it was on, then stood up and walked around the table. She wanted to project an air of calm and impress on these people that FEMA wasn't the enemy, talking from behind a desk. Following the police officer who'd laid down the law about curfew and potential punishments was a tough gig, but she needed to show them that FEMA were the guarantors of security, prosperity and order during this extraordinary time. As she moved toward the crowd, the State Guard troops and Chicago PD officers providing security tensed up, apparently uncomfortable with her proximity to the crowd.

She raised her hands, palms up. "Our final briefing concerns the impact on business. In short, we need to balance the maintenance of private enterprise with protecting essential services, social order and consumers. For the vast majority of you this will mean no change. You'll be able to run your businesses and make a profit."

She felt like a liar. The changes that had been announced and the restrictions to movement and activity would affect everyone. For most the changes were minimal, except for enhanced security and some restriction on accessing goods and services. But for business, the impact was enormous. Though there was no sense in causing panic before the measures were fully implemented, she was sure there'd be plenty of that anyway.

"However, for the minority of you involved in the production, distribution and retailing of certain goods and for those of you delivering essential services, there will be some changes. For starters, there will be price controls to protect consumers and prevent profiteering, along with random audits to ensure good conduct."

Her last few words were drowned out entirely as the stands exploded with outrage. She waited patiently, her hands clasped in front of her. The security detail inched forward slightly but kept their cool for the time being, though she noticed a few hands on weapons. The noise from the crowd started to subside after a minute or so, until a grossly obese man in the front of the bleachers got to his feet. His face was flushed red.

She knew what was coming and tried to cut him off. "There'll be time for questions at the end of the sessions, sir. We'd ask that—"

"Just who the fuck do you think you are, lady?" The man's voice was like rolling thunder. "This is America. I'll run my business however I like."

Mariposa did her best to keep calm, but she was scared. The security detail didn't reassure her. "I'm here to explain the changes, sir, and—"

He interrupted again. "Explain them, huh? You're going to cripple my business for no reason. Chicago hasn't even been attacked!"

Mariposa narrowed her eyes. She'd been briefed on the executive orders along with the rest of FEMA, but hadn't expected the changes to be so drastic. The outrage in the community was understandable. She felt some of the same reservations as the people in the crowd were expressing, but she trusted Richard Hall to get it right. "Let me be clear—"

Another man stood and interrupted her. "Oh, shove your bureaucratic bullshit, lady."

Mariposa needed to act. She couldn't allow this anger to overflow. She turned and looked at the police lieutenant, who gave a slight nod. Without warning, the State Guard troopers and local police stepped forward and raised their weapons. The men who'd been protesting stammered and then stopped speaking entirely. A stunned silence fell over the crowd. Peace at the end of a barrel. It had come to that.

"Let me be clear. These changes have been enacted across America until the attacks stop and order can be restored." She stepped forward and stopped a few feet away from the bleachers. "You don't have the ability to opt out. You'll comply or the police will shutter your business. Resist further and you'll be locked up."

She waited. The resistance was still there, but the appearance of guns had pushed it beneath the surface, hidden behind muttered comments and shaking heads. She couldn't shift the feeling that FEMA was trying to achieve something that was nearly impossible – bringing Americans to heel. But even though she didn't like it, she knew that it was the only way to stop the attacks.

She took a few steps back and walked toward the table as the roving microphones found the first person wishing to ask a question. An elderly woman stood and started to speak. Mariposa was worried she'd miss the question, given how much her hands were shaking under the table, but she caught the gist of it. As she started to answer, she hoped again that this was all worth it.

She hoped that Richard Hall knew what he was doing.

CHAPTER 4

The President has declared a state of emergency and enacted a number of executive orders. The orders grant FEMA emergency powers over critical infrastructure and normal civil liberties. FEMA is well prepared to respond to this new demand with the support of its State Guard colleagues. All citizens, businesses and media organizations are encouraged to check FEMA.gov to learn what the new restrictions mean for them.

Federal Emergency Management Agency
News Release

Callum lifted his canteen to his mouth and drank deeply.

It had been a hell of a couple of days since American life had been turned on its head. For Callum it had been even worse. He'd had to drop his day job for full-time State Guard deployment and had spent the last few days as a glorified security guard as FEMA put the changes in place. Callum had been deployed with a handful of guardsmen to Bartlett, Illinois – a postage stamp–sized town of about 40 000 people.

This took the cake though. He was standing with Mark Pettine and Todd Bowles by their Humvee, carbines at the ready, as the local liquor store opened for the day. A small queue had already formed in front of the store. People must be stocking up, given liquor stores could only open twice per week. But as the queue formed he could feel a strange buzz from the crowd. Tension. Anger.

"This blows, Cal." Bowles ran a hand through his hair. "Where the fuck else in the world would you need guys with carbines covering a liquor store?"

"Russia?" Callum shrugged. "It's because they had some trouble here last time they opened. The locals just need to get used to their booze being rationed."

"At least we didn't draw duty patrolling the old folks' home." Pettine laughed as he leaned against the Humvee.

Callum groaned. Since the FEMA controls had been enacted, it was the medium and small towns of America that had experienced the most trouble. The cities had enough guardsmen and police to keep the peace, but in towns like this there was usually only the cops and, if they were lucky, a small State Guard contingent to keep an eye on everything. It had boiled over on a couple of occasions already.

"Show time." Pettine stood at his full height, one hand on the barrel of his carbine. "Let's see how this goes."

Callum nodded grimly as the door opened and the owner stepped out. They watched in silence as the man explained that, under orders of FEMA, purchase of beer was being restricted to one six-pack and purchase of cigarettes to one packet. Callum winced when he heard that the sale of spirits was being restricted entirely on the weekend. That sure was one way to win hearts and minds.

The collective mood of the crowd seemed to change in seconds. Callum estimated that there were forty people in the line, ready to pounce on the booze for the hour that the shop was open. But as the owner finished speaking the crowd started to get vocal, jeering at the owner and shuffling forward. Callum sighed, walked to the back of the Humvee and opened the trunk. He dug around in the back, found the megaphone and turned it on.

He winced as the megaphone gave a squeal, then raised it to his mouth. "This is the Illinois State Guard. Stand down immediately."

His order seemed to have no impact. The crowd surged forward, pelting the shopfront with whatever they had at hand. Then, as if in slow motion, a member of the crowd reached into his jacket and pulled out a small pistol. Callum didn't have time to raise his own weapon before the gunman fired two shots. He glanced sideways at Bowles and Pettine, who had their carbines up.

"Firearm!" Bowles fired his carbine as the shopkeeper fell. "Put him down!"

The gunman was felled by the rubber rounds fired by his friends. Callum knew that rubber rounds had an equal chance of dispersing the crowd or enraging them further – he'd seen both reactions in Fallujah. As Bowles and Pettine moved forward slowly, Callum reached up to his vest for his radio.

"Command, this is Watkins. We've got a riot at our post. Shots fired. Requesting support."

The response was nearly instant. "Watkins, this is Command. There's no support nearby."

Callum couldn't believe what he was hearing. The command post had oversight of all FEMA operations for miles around and that was the best they could do? He found it nearly as hard to believe as rioting over restricted consumption of beer and smokes. But he had a job to do. He joined Bowles and Pettine and started to move forward, raising his carbine and firing into the crowd.

As he'd feared, the rubber rounds did little to dim the outrage of the crowd. Some people scattered and ran, but others surged towards the liquor store and trampled the body of the owner. The majority of the crowd was now inside the store, taking what they pleased from the shelves and making a mess in the process. But a few had forgotten about the booze and turned on Callum's squad with firearms visible.

"Stand down!" He hoped the crowd could hear him over the noise. They didn't stop. "Stand down! Now!"

It didn't work. This was going to hell quickly and would get worse if his team came under fire. As one member of the crowd raised his weapon, Callum crouched to one knee, aimed at the center of the man's chest and squeezed the trigger. The man staggered, but he didn't drop his weapon. Until Callum hit him with two more.

The crowd surged closer, and Callum could feel cold sweat on his back. He fired at another target, a man leaning down to pick up a bottle. Then another, a woman who snarled at them like some sort of horrible dog as she pelted a rock at them. He aimed at her and fired, but his weapon clicked. His carbine was empty.

"I'm out!" Callum looked left to Pettine.

Pettine nodded. "Me too."

He glanced back to the woman, who was leaning down to pick up the gun the other man had dropped. Callum made his decision. He was out of rubber rounds, and there was only one other way to end the riot. He ejected the magazine and loaded the real thing. As his finger caressed the trigger, he shouted for the woman to stop.

Then Pettine's carbine barked from right next to him, and the woman dropped to the ground, a small mist of blood escaping her head. The few left in the crowd slackened, as if they couldn't believe what they'd seen. More shots rang out. Once the rioters realised what was happening, the attack was reversed. They screamed and ran as one.

The others inside the store took a second or two longer to figure it out, but once they did they scrambled to follow the pack, running from the store. Given the blood now flowing onto the road, Callum didn't much care that a bunch of the looters had cases of beer and bottles of booze tucked under their arms.

Callum and his team immediately ceased fire, though they held their positions. After a minute, there was nobody in the parking lot except the dead and the wounded, who writhed on the ground in agony. From what he could tell, there were two dead – the shopkeeper and the woman – and six wounded.

It was an enormous toll for a riot at a suburban liquor store. He turned to his team. "Keep the live rounds loaded in case they come back."

"I think that's the least of our problems." Bowles shook his head. "CO is going to freak."

Callum didn't want to think about that, though he didn't see any alternative to what they'd done. "We'll need some cops and ambulances."

Pettine nodded and then looked down at the corpse of the shop owner. "Poor bastard."

Bowles glanced inside the shop. "I'll drink to that."

~

MARIPOSA HATED THE CHIME, and whoever had designed it. As she stood and stretched her muscles, she questioned the need to have it ring again and again to call staff to a meeting. She thought an email would do the trick just as well, but the hourly five-minute standup staff meetings had become routine since the commencement of the executive orders.

"Come on, Murray." Mariposa leaned over the cubicle partition, where her colleague was still typing away. "Let's get this over with."

He sighed as he stood. "Yeah, my doctor usually says the same about my prostate exam."

She smiled but didn't speak as they gathered with about a hundred other staff in the meeting space. Nothing better illustrated the growth in staff numbers at the FEMA Area V Clark Street offices since the attacks and the declaration of the state of emergency. They'd grown from 160 staff to nearly 500, and their office was barely large enough for everyone.

Alan Benning, the new director, held up his hand. "Okay, thanks everyone. I want to keep this one short. You guys know the drill."

Under the standing agenda, Mariposa was first to report. She cleared her throat. "The city is quiet. There's only been a few minor reports in the last twenty minutes."

A few of the others gave small nods or smiles of encouragement. Mariposa and her team had been handed the toughest job of all: coordinating the control orders in the city of Chicago. It had gone fairly smoothly and the systems they'd long had prepared had held up to the real-life test. Chicago was probably safer than ever, given the number of cops and State Guard troops deployed throughout the city. There had been a few scuffles and arrests, but things had settled down.

Once she was finished her report, she listened as the other team managers reported in. There were no major issues. The medium-sized cities and larger towns were less secure but not too bad. Public utilities and transportation were secure and operating. Though the media was fidgety and a few organizations had rebelled, examples had been made of a few high-profile holdouts and most were toeing the line. All in all, the entirety of FEMA Area V was looking okay.

Benning looked toward Murray. "How's our distribution network looking?"

Murray smiled. "No trouble. The only angst has been around the vice rations."

Mariposa winced. Lost in the fine detail of the FEMA crackdown had been a strict reduction in the amount of booze and cigarettes people were allowed to buy. She didn't really see the sense in it. Given people were restricted from going out after midnight, she saw no harm in letting people cool off at home with a bottle. As it was, there were a lot of bored people unable to go out and without much to help them loosen up at home. It was a bad recipe.

"Okay, great." Benning knocked his hand on the table. "See you all next hour. Until then, let me know if anything comes up."

Mariposa started to walk away when a junior staffer ran into the middle of the gathering. "Hey! There's been a shooting in Bartlett. It's the State Guard."

Noise erupted in the room. Mariposa looked over at Murray, who gave a shrug and stood in silence. She watched as Benning held his hands up and did his best to be heard. A shooting was a dramatic escalation on their patch of turf and she found herself shaking at the thought. There could just as easily have been a similar incident at one of the community briefings she'd led.

"Everyone calm down." Benning finally managed to be heard above the noise. "What happened?"

"Some State Guard put down a riot at a liquor store. There's a few people dead." The junior looked like he was about to cry. "It's all over the media, despite the bans."

Mariposa's eyes widened. While the media had been told in no uncertain terms what was acceptable to report, the restrictions clearly hadn't sunk in fully. While other FEMA areas had experienced more trouble than Area V had, as far as she knew this was the first incident anywhere in America in which the authorities had had to put down dissent with lethal force. Mariposa felt a lump rise in her throat. The game had just changed.

"Okay, we'll need to handle this. You all know the drill." Benning looked at the manager responsible for media relations. "Get your dogs under control, Jim."

The team dispersed but Mariposa waited behind, a million thoughts running through her head. Though things had been relatively calm to date, she had no doubt that people were being suppressed, rather than carried along with the changes until the attacks were dealt with. If people were pushed so hard that they resisted and started to die, things had gone too far. She was about to move back to her desk, but found her feet anchored to the floor.

She swallowed and then approached the director. "Alan, do you have a second?"

"Sure." He gave a weary smile. "What can I do for you?"

She leaned on the edge of the giant table. "I've got some concerns, Alan. I think some of the changes we're trying to force are unnecessary, attacks or not."

"Come on." Benning reached up to massage his temples. "I've –

we've got enough going on here without an attack of the morals, don't we?"

Mariposa wavered. She was not usually the one to speak out, but she felt she had an obligation to voice her concerns. "I don't agree. If we keep squeezing, there's going to be more issues that bubble up. I think we need to let things settle, not agitate them even more."

He sighed. "Things have been going fine here, Mariposa. But don't assume that's the case across the whole country. The south is ablaze. Let's keep our patch quiet."

"But—"

"No, Mariposa." Benning's eyes locked onto hers. "This is above your pay grade. Do your job and leave the rest to me. If you still want it, that is."

She wanted to fight, but Benning's threat was clear. She thought of Juan, at home with the sitter she could barely afford despite all the overtime. If nothing else, she had to make sure he was looked after. Others, more important than her, had put the country on this path. Who was she to argue? She sagged. "Okay, Alan."

He exhaled loudly and his posture softened. "I don't like running roughshod like this, but we've all got jobs to do. Go do yours."

She nodded and walked toward her desk with her head downcast, all fight gone from inside of her. She was still worried about the direction things were heading in, but felt that she'd pushed her luck about as far as she could with her boss. She sat down in front of her computer and reviewed her emails, which never seemed to cease. After a few emails she glanced at her phone, picked it up and dialed. It rang for a moment before being answered.

She mustered all the authority she could. "I want extra caution by city security forces. I only want live rounds in the hands of the rapid response squads."

She waited for the confirmation then hung up. She smiled. If there was no way she could impact the direction of the entire organization, she could at least make sure that the zone she was responsible for didn't go to hell. For now, she'd have to be satisfied that no police officer or State Guardsman inside the Chicago city limits would be firing off live rounds without her knowing, given the rapid response squads were under her direct command.

There was nothing else she could do.

~

RICHARD INDICATED, turned the wheel slightly and eased to a stop outside his home. As he killed the ignition, he looked out of the window and stared with pride at his house – a fashionable and perfectly restored colonial in the heart of Georgetown. After another second of indulgence he grabbed his briefcase from the passenger seat and climbed out of the car. He locked the vehicle and crossed the sidewalk.

"Evening, Administrator." The Metropolitan Police Department officer standing at the bottom of the stairs greeted him the same way as always.

Richard stopped at the base of the stairs. "Good evening, Frank. How are the wife and kids?"

The officer smiled beneath his cap. "They're great, Administrator."

Richard fumbled with his keys. "Good. I'll be staying in for the night."

"Okay, sir."

Richard nodded. He climbed the stairs, unlocked his door, entered the house and closed the door behind him. He knew that the police guard was probably unnecessary, but since the attacks had started all department heads in Washington had been given similar protection. From tomorrow, he'd also have an armed driver picking him up every day. He'd miss driving to the office himself.

He keyed in the code to the alarm and then pressed another button on the same console. On cue, the curtains started to close, the climate control fired up, some of the lighting came on and soft classical music started to play. He locked the door and hung his keys on a hook beside it, then walked through to the open-plan kitchen and living area.

He paused at the entry to the living area and smiled as he took in the scene before him: a large corkboard that covered two whole walls in his living room, which he otherwise kept sparse. He'd started the corkboard years ago. He couldn't remember when exactly, except to say that it was at the point when he'd started to feel like America was off the rails and careening out of control. It had been an outlet for frustrations he could share with nobody.

But it had become more than that. Since that moment, he'd watched the leadership of the country flounder and fail, being all too easily led by the nose or bought off or sidetracked. Instead of being a diligent servant of pragmatic governments, Republican or Democrat, he'd instead watched with dismay as good public administration made way for partisan bickering, a deadlocked Congress and federal debt and deficit nearing catastrophe.

One full wall of the board was covered in a color-coded history of the past few years – news clippings, FEMA briefings and a map. It told a story of American dysfunction. Many of the more recent clippings were the fault of Michelle Dominique and the Foundation for a New America. He'd hoped that the near miss America had experienced with that lunatic would recalibrate the system, but many of the same problems remained.

As the years passed and as Richard entered the twilight of his career, he'd come to realize that his hopes for a leader to emerge in the mould of Washington, Lincoln, Roosevelt or the other greats were false. No great politician was coming to wash away the filth that was clogging the gears of effective governance. The country just lurched on, served by mediocre government, as it ever gradually approached the precipice.

Once he'd decided he needed to act against – rather than just catalogue – the dysfunction, Richard had tried to make himself available to President Kurzon and, later, President Morris. He'd offered innovative solutions to some of the deadlocks facing the country and his experience in managing disasters should have made him an invaluable support to a president. But he'd been ignored and pigeon-holed as the guy who cleaned up after cyclones.

This had forced him to take matters into his own hands. It had become clear to Richard that if no leader stepped forward, and if the incompetents already in power wouldn't take his help to learn and improve, then something had to give. He'd decided that he could get the country moving on the right track again – if he got the chance. He couldn't do it through election and campaigning, but there were other ways.

No, the answer was seizing control and solving difficult problems, even if those solutions required some extreme measures – restricted freedom, mass surveillance, a compliant media. Only then would the attacks stop. If he achieved that, then history would look upon him kinder than the parade of squatters and incompetents who'd occupied positions of power in recent years. His legacy as a man of supreme integrity and enormous public service would be secure.

He shifted his gaze. The other wall of board featured columns filled with the steps he was taking in clear stages. It had started with months of research into the power he had at his disposal as the Administrator of FEMA, along with the power the position potentially held in the right circumstances. All he'd needed was a catalyst, in the form of the deadly attacks sweeping across the country. He sat on the sofa and stared at the board.

Now events were moving him toward the middle of the board, which featured the steps he'd take to bring order and stability to the governance of America. He'd tried serving incompetents, waiting for the right leader. When that had failed, he'd proactively made himself available to those same incompetents, to steer and guide, but they'd not listened. Now the opportunity had arrived. He'd take more control. He'd solve problems. He'd reshape America. He'd secure his legacy.

He woke with a start and realized that he must have dozed off. He reached up and massaged his temples with his index fingers. He was tired and pushing himself too hard, but saw no choice but to continue on the current path. He'd told nobody else about his plan, trusting others with only enough information to play the role he'd assigned them. With a shake of his head to remove the cobwebs, he rose and made his way into the kitchen.

A glance at the clock made him wince at how late it was. He opened his fridge and took the assigned meal – planned and prepared a week in advance – and heated it up in the microwave, then sat at the table to eat. The food wasn't spectacular, but it was nutritious. He didn't take pleasure from much other than his work, so had no qualms with the bland pumpkin soup. There was nothing wrong with it that some fresh pepper couldn't fix. He ate slowly, taking pleasure in the music playing.

After another glance at the clock, he placed his dishes in the dishwasher and then opened his briefcase. He removed a single news clipping, walked to his board and pinned it to the wall. Satisfied, he started up the stairs to bed. He undressed, hung his suit and placed his dirty laundry in the basket. As he climbed into bed, he reached over to press the button that would turn off all of the lights in the house. He smiled as he closed his eyes.

ACT II

CHAPTER 5

In the three months since the executive orders were enacted, the diligence of my staff and the cooperation of the American people have allowed these new powers to be introduced with a minimum of fuss. It is my hope that, for however long they're necessary to ensure security, the restrictions have the minimum possible impact on everyday people going about their lives and make the maximum contribution to our security and wellbeing.

Richard Hall, FEMA Administrator
Media statement

J ack's phone buzzed on the table. Unknown caller. He answered as he rushed to finish his bagel and wash it down with the dregs of his coffee. "Jack Emery."

"My name is Omega." The voice on the other end was being scrambled into an electronic mess. Jack swallowed hard and checked nobody was in earshot.

Captain Dan "Omega" Ortiz had been the commander of the squad of Marines that Jack had been embedded with in Afghanistan. Ortiz had saved Jack's life after Jack's exposure of isolated Marine Corps cooperation with a CIA torture operation. Though the full details had remained top secret, Ortiz had earned himself a chest of medals and a promotion and Jack had earned a Pulitzer for the story. If Omega was calling, something was wrong.

"I don't know anyone by that name." Jack was completely deadpan, not wanting to give away that he knew Ortiz to anyone tapping the call. "What can I do for you?"

"A lot. And soon. In the place my kids love." The line went dead.

Jack felt a bit of a buzz. For the three months since the commencement of the executive orders, he'd mostly kept his head down. Jo had flown home to New York and Jack had kept filing stories on his site, which were then purchased by national media. Despite temptation to do otherwise, he'd done the right thing and had everything vetted by the authorities before publishing. Though it grated on him, he had no desire to rock the boat.

Now he wondered what Ortiz had for him. He knew straight away where the meeting point was – Millennium Park. Ortiz had told Jack about the place on a long ride through the desert in Afghanistan. His kids loved the Millennium Dome, he'd said. Luckily Jack was close. He stood, exited the Starbucks and started to walk the few blocks to Millennium Park. He'd be there in a few minutes.

His heart was beating faster and he was uneasy about meeting his friend. Jack knew it was likely that he was being monitored – just as closely as Ortiz, probably, given the effort the other man was going to to avoid scrutiny. But despite the risk, Jack didn't hesitate. He owed Ortiz more than any other man alive and if he said jump, Jack asked how high.

He looked toward the park as he crossed North Michigan Avenue. He could see no sign of danger except for the armed State Guardsman scattered around, which was par for the course these days. He still found the sight of armed men on every second block off-putting. By the time he reached the Millennium Dome it felt like everyone was watching him as he paced back and forth next to it.

"Where is he?" Jack whispered, after he'd waited for about ten minutes. He was feeling as conspicuous as a pink battleship, until he spotted Ortiz approaching.

"Hi Jack." Ortiz held out his hand and sported a wide grin. "You've been busy since I saw you last."

"Yeah, tough gig, saving the world." Jack smiled as he shook the proffered hand and then pulled Ortiz into a hug. Jack was taller, but Ortiz was as solid as a tree trunk.

"I bet." They broke apart. "Good thing this humble one saved your not-so-humble ass."

Jack laughed. "Good to see you, Dan."

"I'm wearing a Cubs hat, in case you haven't noticed. I feel filthy."

"At least you've still got your quarterback good looks. How are you?"

"Just peachy." Ortiz nearly spat the words. "Get my ass shot at fighting for freedom only to find uniforms on the streets over here. I can't even buy a bottle of booze!"

"At least you can still work." Jack snorted. "I have to submit to Uncle Sam before I'm allowed to publish."

Ortiz laughed. "Pussy. What happens if you don't?"

"I'll get locked up. A journo I know tried that one on. Turns out FEMA isn't joking." Jack kept his voice low. "So what's going on in the world of the US Marine Corps?"

Ortiz shrugged. "Oh, about the same. The grunts are confined to base full time and the NCOs and officers can't scratch their ass without approval."

Jack was slightly surprised by this. Though he knew the troops on the streets weren't regular military – or even National Guard – it shocked him that the military was apparently on lockdown along with the rest of society. The situation stank, and Jack wasn't sure if there was any hope of a resolution any time soon. Though the attacks had slowed, they hadn't stopped entirely.

"So what can I do for you, Dan?" Jack looked around, paranoid they were being watched. "You've taken an almighty risk."

Ortiz shrugged. "Look, these pricks are clamping down on the country that I fought for. I want you to get the word out. There's regular citizens resisting all over the country, and even a couple of smaller military units, but they're isolated and being picked off by the State Guard."

Jack wasn't surprised. You couldn't just turn America into an armed camp and not have problems, but the government had kept news of the trouble quiet. "Where?"

"I need your promise that you'll report it."

Jack hesitated. "I can't promise anything, Dan. You know what I'm risking."

Ortiz smiled, a clear twinkle in his eyes. "You think I'd bust my way off base wearing this shit to meet with your sorry ass if I didn't have something decent for you?"

"Maybe?" Jack let it hang.

"Take this." Ortiz rummaged through the tote bag that he carried and held out a manila folder. "It's all the detail you'll need to cause at least a little bit of heartburn."

"How'd you get it?" Jack didn't take the folder right away.

Ortiz shrugged. "You don't need to know how. But it shows there's a bit happening across the country."

Jack looked at the folder for a few long seconds then let out a long sigh as he grabbed it. He owed Ortiz his life. "I'll do it. But I'm not sure it'll work."

"Just do your best." Ortiz gave a toothy smile. "It's no fun being a passive son of a bitch anyway, is it?"

Jack laughed at that thought for a long while as Ortiz turned and walked away. As his friend disappeared into the crowd, Jack mused that if he had any sense in the world, he'd keep within the boundaries – as he had for the last few months – and toss the folder in the nearest bin. But Jack Emery wasn't known for his sense. It's why he kept getting dragged into warzones and conspiracies.

～

ONE WATCHED through her binoculars like a patient hunter stalking prey. At this late hour, the FEMA distribution center was quiet. They'd watched it all day and it had been a hive of activity, with trucks coming and going. At night, however, there was little except silence and shadows. Just the way she liked it. She smiled as she swept her gaze across the entire facility one last time. A chain-link fence topped with razor wire surrounded the facility, which was lit up by floodlights. The only way in – or out – was through one of three gates, each guarded by a pair of armed State Guard troopers. Inside the facility, another handful of security personnel strolled around with no particular routine.

She lowered the binoculars with a smile. The security looked tough, but she knew better. For such a critical facility, it had some of the slackest security she'd ever seen. This would be easier than taking on the student police at MIT – the easiest job she'd had in months. She looked to her left. Three other members of her team were prone in the dirt, alert for any threat and ready for action. Positioned further away, on either side of the base and out of sight, Five and Six would provide sniper support. She smiled. Though it was a pleasure to command them, dealing with such talented people made her feel a little bit redundant sometimes.

"Everyone, confirm ready."

It took only a second for confirmations to come in over her earpiece.

"Okay, cut it."

The floodlights cut out instantly. Though from this distance she couldn't hear the inevitable alarmed shouts from the security, she could imagine the carnage. Within moments a few tiny pinpricks of light started to illuminate the darkness as the security turned on their flashlights – a poor substitute for the floodlights' angry yellow illumination.

One lowered the goggles that had been resting on her head, taking a second to adjust to the night vision before giving the order to proceed. One and her team moved low and fast across the flat grassland that led to the distribution facility, making a beeline straight for the closest gate. She knew they'd be close to invisible in the darkness.

When they were a hundred yards out, One held up a clenched fist. Looking through his large scope, Five would see her signal and radio Six, and together they'd begin the count.

Three Mississippi.

One raised her carbine as she approached the guardhouse. Thanks to the night-vision goggles, her target was as clear as the sun.

Two Mississippi.

Another target was on the periphery of her gun sights, but she couldn't think about him. She had to trust that her unit mates would do their job while she did hers.

One Mississippi.

She slowed and took smaller steps. The target filled her sights. Despite the blackout, things seemed calm. If they'd been spotted, the base would be a hell of a lot busier.

One squeezed the trigger as the count hit zero in her head. At the same time, she heard the dull thud of suppressed weaponry from nearby and the booming reports of the rifles used by Five and Six – the sound traveling slower than the death it signified. Both of the State Guard troops in One's assigned gatehouse fell. Five and Six were taking care of the other gates. On cue, she heard another pair of thunderclaps.

"Gate A clear." She spoke as she moved inside the gatehouse, kicking away the rifle lying next to one of the corpses. Neither guard was moving.

"B clear." Five's voice was soft.

"C…" Six sounded unsure, then she heard another boom. "C clear."

"Commence phase two." With the gates assaulted simultaneously, she didn't envy the four State Guardsman still alive inside the distribution center: they would be confused, scared shitless and know they were outgunned. One moved outside the gatehouse to where Three and Four had already cut through the chain-link gate. With the power out there was no other way to open it. She waved her hand and the three others followed her through the hole.

They moved quickly through the distribution center, weapons raised and covering each other. She'd hoped that Five and Six would be able to reach out and touch the four remaining State Guard troops, but the maze of shipping containers would likely block their line of sight beyond the gates. Unless the snipers received a bit of luck, her ground team would have to deal with the final defenders up close and personal. It didn't bother her, it just made the situation a bit messier.

She followed Four around a corner, then ducked instinctively as a weapon barked from somewhere. She heard a grunt in her earpiece as she crouched onto the hard concrete, her eyes searching for the shooter. The shooter's mistake was peering up to see if he'd hit anything – in her night-vision goggles his head was easy to spot above the wooden crates he was using for cover. She put a round straight through his skull, then stood and scrambled to where Four had gone down.

"Two, Three, keep going." She crouched beside Four. "You okay?"

The other man nodded, though he gripped at his chest and was sucking in quick breaths. "Took one on the Kevlar, but I'm good to go."

"Okay." She nodded and they followed Two and Three. She rounded a corner and discovered they'd put down the remaining State Guardsmen.

"Commence phase three." She was moving as she gave the order. "I want the explosives planted and ready in four minutes."

The team split and she jogged toward the base of the first container stack. She let her carbine hang from its strap as she removed her backpack, threw it on the ground and unzipped it. Inside were enough explosives to land her in prison for several lifetimes. She pulled one of the compact bombs from the bag and secured it to the side of the container. Once she was satisfied, she raised the small antenna and flicked the switch on the device. A green light glowed.

She picked up the bag and moved on to the next stack. The bombs her team was busy planting were a mix of high explosives and incendiary devices, so whatever didn't blow would hopefully burn.

They wouldn't destroy the entire facility or even all of the supplies, but they'd make a mess. It was all a small team could do to such a large facility. She was confident the result would be the same: a vital facility crippled, a state short of critical supplies further stretched and a nation stressed.

"Uh, incoming." Five's voice drawled in her ear. "A pair of State Guard Humvees are closing on gate B. They're a few minutes out."

She stopped in her tracks. They'd planned to be gone before any reinforcements arrived. The nearest State Guard units should have been over an hour away, and local law enforcement wouldn't respond to such a dangerous situation. It was a problem. Given the amount of explosives they'd had to haul along, the team had packed lightly: they certainly weren't geared up for a prolonged fire fight with any sort of capable foe. She considered her options for a moment and then decided.

"Okay, Five, Six, stay cool for now. The rest of you finish up, then find some cover just inside gate B and await my order. You've got one minute."

She planted her last bomb.

~

CALLUM DRUMMED his hands on the back of the passenger seat as the Humvee raced along the road. Pettine was at the wheel, singing along to the song at the top of his voice, while Bowles simply laughed and shook his head. The newest addition to their small squad – a small guy named Tony Harrington – didn't seem to know what to make of the situation, so simply smiled and cradled his carbine. A second Humvee followed them.

They were all in good spirits considering the lack of sleep they'd all had. The order had come through that afternoon to redeploy from Bartlett, where Callum had spent three uneventful months since the liquor store shooting. Their new assignment was to guard one of the large FEMA distribution centers. They were nearly there, but it was almost midnight. Callum knew he'd be paying for the lack of a full night's sleep for days.

The car started to slow. Pettine turned his head. "Hey, Cal, there's something wrong."

Callum sat higher, leaned to his left and looked through the windshield. Up ahead the Humvee's headlights brightened the gatehouse of the distribution facility. It should have been flooded with light, even at this hour, and there should have been a pair of State Guard troops looking to share a joke before they were relieved. Instead, all they saw was a closed chain-link gate and an empty hut with blood sprayed all over the glass.

"Heads up guys, I'm going to call it in." Callum held his carbine in one hand and reached for the radio with the other. "Command this is Mobile Four."

There was a brief pause before the radio squawked back. "Go, Four."

"We've reached Distribution Center Echo. The lights are out, nobody's around and there's blood. No visible bodies but they can't be far away. Any info for me?"

"Standby."

Callum placed the radio handset on the seat beside him and checked his weapon. The carbine was cradled between his legs, barrel facing the floor. Callum ejected then reloaded the magazine and checked the safety. Around him, Bowles and Harrington had their weapons ready, while Pettine had one hand on the wheel and the other on his sidearm. Callum hoped that the troops in the other Humvee were ready as well.

The radio crackled. "Mobile Four, we've no reports of power outages at that facility and the guards haven't reported any problems."

Callum tensed. "Well, I'm staring at a problem. They haven't reported anything because they're most likely all dead."

"Move in with Mobile Three to investigate. We're routing Mobile Seven, Mobile Twelve and Air One to you." The voice on the other end was dispassionate.

"ETA?"

"Unknown. Will advise. The facility is critical. Repeat order: Move in with Mobile Three to investigate."

Callum nearly managed to mask his fury. Nearly. "We'll ride into the darkness. See if you can do anything about the power situation?"

"Affirmative, Mobile Four. Command out."

Callum looked around the vehicle. In the dim interior light he could see enough on the faces of his squad – his friends – to know what they were thinking. None of them had signed on for hot combat or for driving into an ambush, but both seemed on the cards in the next few minutes if whoever had attacked the compound was still around. FEMA taking over had changed everything: they'd gone from being glorified militia to soldiers again, eight men driving into the unknown.

The radio sounded again. "Mobile Four? What's the play?"

Callum picked up the radio again. "Mobile Three, we've been told to check it out."

"Affirmative, Four. We'll follow you in. Stay frosty."

Callum didn't bother replying. He returned the radio to its position. "Hit the gas."

Pettine nodded and the vehicle edged forward, headlights showing the way. Callum turned his head and saw the second Humvee start to move forward as well. Though they provided some protection from small arms fire, he felt very vulnerable. He had two Humvees and eight men to secure an enormous facility against god knew what. He didn't like the odds.

The chain-link gate buckled then gave way under the pressure of the Humvee's bullbar. Callum winced at the high-pitched squeal the gate gave as it shifted off its railings, then the loud crash as it crumpled in a useless heap on the ground. If the bad guys didn't know they were at the base before, they certainly did now. Pettine hit the gas and the Humvee moved inside.

They drove in, overlooked by shipping containers and enveloped by shadows. Callum leaned forward, peering desperately out of the windshield for any sign of activity. A hundred yards inside, they rounded a shallow corner and found themselves in a large, open area used to house trucks. In the middle of the yard lay two State Guard troops in duty fatigues, unmoving on the ground.

"Fucking hell!" Bowles pounded his armrest as the vehicle ground to a halt. "They're dead, Callum."

Callum summed up the scene. It wasn't good. There was no sign of the attackers, even if they were still here, and limitless cover for a concealed foe. He had no tactical advantage and found it hard to believe that command had ordered them in, given the situation, but an order was an order and they had a job to do. He resisted the urge to tell Pettine to turn the Humvee around and get the hell out.

"Callum, we've got to pull back." Pettine's hands gripped the wheel. "We should wait for some light and some help."

Callum ignored Harrington's silent nod. "Our orders are to investigate. More than likely whoever made this mess is long gone. Probably just wanted some alcohol."

"And managed to take down ten armed guards and the entire base power grid to do so?" Pettine scoffed. "Come on, Cal."

"I don't want to hear it." Callum gripped the door handle of the Humvee. "We need to get out of these tin cans. Let's go."

Callum opened the door and climbed out of the vehicle. After a moment all eight Guardsmen stood outside the vehicles, scanning the surroundings. Then he heard a scream, followed by the impact of rounds hitting metal. Though Callum could see muzzle flashes from four different locations, he couldn't hear the shots being fired. It was as if he and his team were surrounded by phantoms.

He shouted at his team to find cover as he reviewed the situation: his foe had suppressed weapons, good visibility – probably aided by night vision – and excellent firing positions overlooking vulnerable and lightly protected targets. It all added up to a hopeless situation. Callum ducked low and started to move around to the back of the first Humvee, which seemed safe for now.

As he moved, more rounds knocked angry welts into the door he'd been in front of just a moment ago. A few of his men raised their weapons and returned fire in the general direction of the muzzle flashes. As he slid down against the rear of the Humvee, in the dim light provided Callum could see Harrington writhing in pain, Bowles sprawled on the ground and members of Mobile Three similarly placed. Pettine was crawling toward him.

All this carnage, and he hadn't fired a shot. Callum screamed out for the last man from Mobile Three to hustle, then rose from his haunches and fired his weapon to cover him. It was no good. The man took a round to the head and dropped. Callum cursed, ducked his head around the corner of the Humvee and fired into the darkness. He may as well be firing spitballs at a tank, though, because each round was met with a withering response.

He inched behind the vehicle again. The only consolation was that they didn't seem to have the vehicle completely surrounded. It might let him hold out for long enough for reinforcements to arrive. But that would just mean another eight dead. He ejected his magazine and replaced it with his only spare. He slammed it home as Pettine slid down alongside him. His face was covered in blood, probably from one of their colleagues.

"You got any spare magazines, Cal?" Pettine's expression was grim.

"Nope. Last one."

Pettine cursed, threw down his carbine and drew his pistol. "Seen Bowles?"

"He's dead, Mark. We could try to make a run for it?"

Pettine wiped his brow. "You're kidding. We're done, my friend. Been nice know—"

Callum ducked down instinctively as rounds pounded the back of the Humvee. The attackers had shifted position. As Pettine gripped his throat, Callum raised his weapon and fired blindly into the night, without even the headlights of the Humvee to guide him. He emptied his magazine then started to draw his pistol, but didn't get the chance. He screamed in pain as a round hit him in the foot, then another in the chest. He fell backward.

Despite the pain, he could feel the cold concrete against his skin. He tried to move but couldn't seem to coordinate his limbs. The blackness of the night had left the stars shining brightly. He wondered if he'd follow Pettine, Bowles and the other members of his team toward one of them.

CHAPTER 6

Following the attack on the FEMA distribution center in Illinois, the agency would like to express condolences to the families and friends of the following FEMA staff and State Guard troops, killed while performing their duty: Mark Pettine, Todd Bowles, Tony Harrington, Lamaar Price, John Fitzgerald, Stephen Welles, David Sales, Craig Anderson, Dean Worthington, Daniel Yee and Greg Laselle. The only surviving victim of the attack, Callum Watkins, remains in critical but stable condition in hospital.

Federal Emergency Management Agency
News Release

Jack turned his head to check for cars, thinking that if there was something to be said for an authoritarian crackdown, it was improved traffic. He crossed the street, getting ever further away from his hotel room. He'd spent the days since his meeting with Ortiz frustrated. He'd struggled to resist the allure of the information he'd been given – intelligence reports about a few units in the south going rogue, along with some reports about gun-nut militias. Resistance to FEMA control was a good story.

An hour ago, he'd tossed the folder onto the bed and gone for a walk. He'd made several attempts to circumvent the censorship and anonymously post details of the files he'd been given online, but all had failed spectacularly. He didn't know enough about navigating the darker shadows of the internet to get it out that way, meaning his only choices were to find someone who did or to put his name to the story and submit it for approval.

Jack stopped dead in the middle of the road. There he was again, the man in the green shirt, for the third time in the past half-hour, alongside a less conspicuous and better-dressed female companion. Jack started walking again. Unless the pair was walking as listlessly as he was, there was no explanation that would satisfy him that they weren't on his tail. Though he hadn't broadcast the information yet, maybe the authorities had noticed his attempts and put a tail on him.

He began to snake his way through the city randomly: he turned down a street, entered a shop, did a lap then walked out again. No matter what he tried, they followed. He reached up and wiped the sweat that was starting to bead on his forehead, then turned sharply and stared at his pursuers. The man in the green shirt looked away, but Jack locked eyes with the woman. He knew in a second that they were after him. He needed to get somewhere well populated and try to lose them. He turned and made his way to Navy Pier. It was the best he could come up with under pressure.

Jack entered the building, weaving past dawdling children and families. He looked over his shoulder and couldn't immediately see his pursuers. He tried to lose himself in the food court. Though it was after lunch, there were still enough people milling about to give him a chance. He left the cavernous building next to the *Spirit of Chicago*, a white cruise ship with several rows of windows, then cut left and walked further along the pier. It seemed counterintuitive to corner yourself at the end of a pier when being pursued, but he was counting on that assumption. He smiled with relief.

He walked, slower now, past another pair of cruise ships. He was just starting to think he might have evaded the pair when he looked behind him and saw that horrible green shirt. Jack turned, his anger building up like a tempest. Though the shirt was terrible, the man inside it was a good size. Jack could see no sign of a weapon, but that didn't mean there wasn't one. Even if he was unarmed, Jack doubted he could take the guy. His only chance was escape.

Jack looked around frantically and eyed a tour boat about to depart. He started to walk toward it when the woman stepped into his path. She wore a serious look and had a hand inside her purse. He guessed she had a weapon, but hadn't produced it because there were kids about.

Jack sighed and held up both hands. "I don't want any trouble and I don't want to scare the children. Let's take it easy."

The pair looked at each other, then the man in the green shirt smiled slightly as he spoke. "I don't know what you think is happening here, Jack, but that's not it."

"Well, if it's all the same to you guys, I'm going to get out of here. I've had quite enough of spy versus spy." He started to walk away but the man reached out and grabbed him by the wrist. Jack didn't hesitate. He caught the man's hand and stepped into the hold, twisting behind him and yanking the man's arm up.

Jack was about to ease off, his warning heeded, when the woman had stepped forward and held a flick knife at his throat. "Let go of him."

Jack's eyes widened and he eased off on the pressure slightly. "Get that away or I'm going to break his arm."

"That's worth a slit throat." Her voice was deadpan and her emerald eyes flashed naked fury. "Let go of him."

"If you think you intimidate me, you're sorely mistaken." Jack twisted a little harder, causing lime green to inhale sharply. "Tell me why I shouldn't break his arm."

She took a deep breath, but the knife didn't move an inch. "I can't tell you who we are, not yet, but you need to trust us."

"No, I really don't." Jack applied slightly more pressure.

The man gave a yelp and spoke through gritted teeth. "We're from Guerrilla Radio."

Jack laughed, but he did relax the pressure slightly. Amateurs. "From where?"

"Guerrilla Radio. We're part of the resistance that's forming. We're trying to get the word out, report the truth and support others opposed to FEMA control."

"Using *actual* radios?" Jack released the man's arm. "What sort of name is Guerrilla Radio, anyway? Been listening to a bit too much Rage Against The Machine, guys?"

"We can't tell you much just yet." The woman glared as she lowered her knife. "But it's just a name. We're—"

"Forget it." Jack held up his hands. "I don't care. I shouldn't have asked. Just leave me alone."

The man rubbed his arm. "We saw your report from the Hoover Dam. It must have raised questions."

"We need help." The woman had a hint of desperation in her voice. Jack couldn't figure out her angle. "We need *you*, Jack."

He ignored them, turning away. The last thing he wanted was to be involved in trying to topple the authorities. Battling Michelle Dominique and the Foundation for a New America had nearly cost him his life – *had* cost the lives of some dear to him. He was uneasy about the control being exercised by FEMA, but he was still a far cry from getting involved in a two-bit resistance movement.

"We've got your friend Simon Hickens helping us." The woman's voice called from behind him, tempting. "He said you're not the sort to walk away."

Jack stopped dead and closed his eyes. First Ortiz now Simon Hickens. She might be lying, but if he was involved it changed things. "Why me?"

Lime green spoke this time. "We admire your work. You need an outlet, we need another reporter. We don't know everything but we know some, and it's critical we find out more. People have started to die. The attacks are just the start. FEMA has started to flex its muscles and enjoys the President's unqualified support."

The woman gave a cheeky smile. "You're too much of a newsman to walk away. I'm Elena Winston. This is Matt Barker. Let's get a beer and you can hear us out."

Jack stood for a long few moments. Every ounce of good sense told him to walk away, but his feet remained rooted in place. Barker had a genuine smile on his face, despite his terrible taste in shirts. Winston intrigued him more. She had a fierceness about her and her name was familiar for some reason, though he couldn't place it.

He turned to her. "I know your name. Where are you from?"

"I was a White House Press Corps reporter for the *Tribune*, but I quit the moment the paper agreed that all stories would go through the FEMA censor."

Jack nodded. At least she was a journalist. "Fine. A beer. And you're paying. And you're also going to use your networks to distribute some info I'm sitting on."

~

MARIPOSA NURSED her coffee mug with both hands, glad for its warmth and the fact that, with her hands occupied, she was less likely to fidget.

Across the table from her sat Alan Benning, eyes glued to his tablet as he swiped and zigged and zagged with his finger, his work never done. They were in one of the few enclosed meeting rooms that had been retained in the cubicle jungle that was the Clark Street home of FEMA Area V Command.

"He's late." Benning didn't look up from his tablet. "His prerogative, I suppose, but hardly the best use of our time, is it?"

Mariposa muttered something to the affirmative. She wasn't in the business of gossiping about her superiors, especially Richard Hall. He was in town and his assistant had organized a meeting with Benning and herself. Now he was late and Benning was irritated. For her own part, she winced at the thought of how much work was building up while she waited here. It just meant more hours in the office and fewer at home with Juan.

Before she could say anything else, Administrator Hall strode into the meeting room. He was an old and foppish-looking man, but his reputation and the power he now held was undeniable. She stood a moment faster than Benning, who'd been distracted by his tablet. Hall gave them a curt nod and stared for just a moment too long at Benning. As she sat back down, Hall took the vacant seat at the head of the table.

He looked up. "Thanks for meeting with me, both of you."

"No problem at all, Administrator. Mariposa and I were just discussing how much of a pleasure it is to be able to show you the great work we—"

Hall held up a hand. "This isn't the time. We've got seventeen dead on your watch. I want to know what happened."

Mariposa was shocked by his bluntness. She looked to Benning, who reached up and stuck a finger between the collar of his shirt and his neck. He pulled, loosening it a bit. It was an obvious gesture, but a mistake. It showed both the administrator and her that he was nervous. Already unimpressed, Hall's eyes narrowed at the delay, as if he was making an assessment of Benning. If Mariposa was a betting woman, she wouldn't wager on it being a positive one.

Mariposa spoke first. "I think there's been a misunderstanding, I look after Chicago. The incident happened—"

Hall glanced at her. "You're here because I want you here. But first I want to know exactly what happened."

Benning finally managed to find his words. "Uh, that one was on me, Administrator. We changed the duty rosters but there was an oversight.

The distribution center sent half of their security detail on to the new posting at the correct time, but the changeover was very late. By the time help arrived, it was too late."

"I'm aware of the details, Alan." Hall's glare could have obliterated concrete. "I want to know *why*."

"It's my fault. I didn't make sure the order was followed through." Benning looked down at the table. "It was just a mistake."

Hall seethed. "A mistake that led to one of my most critical facilities going up like a bonfire? A mistake that left seventeen State Guard men dead and another critical?"

Benning stammered. "Yes, Administrator, but—"

Hall slammed the table. "It's hard enough for me to keep the country united as we deal with this threat. Mistakes like this sap my ability to do so."

Mariposa had heard that Richard Hall was a level headed man, but he was showing he had a temper. She couldn't blame him. State Guard casualties had always been a possibility with an undertaking of this scale, but this was more than that. It was a wipe out of several squads. Hall needed the Guard ready to jump into burning buildings, but already she'd heard whispers about their capacity and new restrictions on their operations.

Benning looked shellshocked. "All I can offer is my apology."

"No, it's not." Hall stared straight at Benning. "I had high hopes for you, but you've let me down. You're resigning, Alan."

"But—"

"This isn't a conversation. You're resigning. Immediately. Get out."

Benning looked like he might protest, but the administrator's stare put a halt to that. Benning went pale and gripped his tablet like a life raft, not looking at either of them as he stood and moved to the door. Mariposa started to stand as well, more confused than ever about why she'd been in this meeting, when Hall cleared his throat. She glanced at him and he shook his head slightly. She paused then sat back down and waited.

Hall ran a hand through his hair as Benning left. Once it was just the two of them he spoke. "I've heard good things about you."

"I'm just trying to keep things as stable as possible, despite the restrictions." Mariposa looked at her hands, then up. "It's a hard situation for everyone."

Hall smiled thinly, no hint of teeth. "That it is. I'm appointing you to replace Benning in charge of Area V. I need someone who considers their actions and is thorough."

Mariposa didn't know what to say. She squeezed out her words. "Thank you, sir. Alan is a good man, but I won't let you down."

Hall sighed, finally seeming to cool down. "We're stepping up our timetable. Most of the country is now compliant with the orders, but the south is ablaze. A resistance is rising and there's underground media. The attacks have slowed, but not stopped, and each additional niggle we get makes it harder to achieve our core mission."

Mariposa nodded, but kept quiet. The rise of a resistance and underground media was not surprising, given the scale of the changes involved. But it was also a set of problems that Hall seemed willing to apply force to to stop. The underground media was probably the more difficult to deal with. They could be anonymous, dispersed and effective. As damaging as poison; as elusive as quicksilver. A problem.

Hall continued. "I was hoping some low level enforcement would be enough to deal with these problems, but they're growing nonetheless. The President is getting very impatient and I'm going to start leaning harder on my area commanders for results. That includes you from now on."

"I understand, sir. I'll do my best." Mariposa swallowed hard. "We've had some success here, but there's more we could be doing."

Hall smiled like a hyena. "That's exactly what I had in mind. The great thing about the executive orders is the level of autonomy they allow us to get the things that need doing done. I'm always available for a call if you have new ideas on how we can achieve this. Now, come with me."

She stood and followed Hall out. Promotion had been the last thing she'd thought about when she'd walked into the meeting room. She knew about the distribution center attack, but it was the latest attack among many. It seemed strange that the Administrator of FEMA would take such exception to this one that he'd promote her in its wake.

Once outside the meeting room, she saw the entire staff gathered. Murray Devereaux gave her the thumbs-up as Hall gestured for her to stand alongside him. Mariposa kept her head down as the conversation buzzed. A hundred whispers with a thousand different theories swirled around the room, but to most it would be obvious – Benning was gone and Mariposa was standing next to Hall.

"The incident at Distribution Center Echo was unforgiveable." Hall spoke over the chatter, which died down. "While we can't completely prevent these terrorist attacks, at least not yet, nor tie down our bases so tightly that they're impregnable, a mistake by this office contributed to the death of seventeen of our people."

Mariposa noticed the shuffling of bodies and the sideways glances. It wasn't every day an organization head was quite so blunt. Richard Hall was clearly not a man who suffered failure. He was a legend within FEMA, so he'd earned that right. It made her dread the idea that the buck now stopped with her. If a firecracker went off it would be her fault.

Hall shifted on the balls of his feet. "We now don't have critical supplies for half the Area. Your colleague, Mariposa Esposito, has performed admirably in her duties in securing the downtown area of Chicago over the past few months. By all reports, there have been few issues with the administration of her area of responsibility.

"This is no small feat, given the potential for conflict in dense urban environments – as we've seen in Salt Lake City and other places. As a result, after Alan Benning's resignation, I'm promoting her to leadership of FEMA Area V. I expect her to bring the same level of professionalism, diligence and results to her new role."

There was a buzz from among the staff, until Murray guffawed. "Go on, don't keep the boss waiting."

Mariposa shook her head and stood slightly taller. "I'd like to thank the administrator for the faith placed in me. While the incident at the distribution center was terrible, it's a blemish on an otherwise faultless performance by our office. I strongly believe we can get back on track."

She paused. This was her opportunity to speak out, to tell the administrator in front of a large number of their colleagues of the wrongs being done in his name. That the restrictions, the violence and the oppression were just making things worse and that they were lucky there hadn't been worse incidents. That the changes taking place in America weren't ones that she wanted for her son, terrorism or not.

She didn't get the chance, as Hall started to speak again. "I'd like to thank Mariposa for agreeing to take on this responsibility. It won't be easy, but with such a fantastic team around her, I've no doubt you'll get the results that are needed. The way we stop these attacks and restore order is through doing our jobs well.

"I'm spending the next few weeks traveling around the country, to oversee the response to problems in many of our areas. While, by and large, the entire organization has done a great job in securing America, there have been patches of bad performance. I intend to rectify these. Personally."

If Hall's ruthless treatment of Benning were any sign, then whoever was causing Hall problems would be best to quit before he arrived. He'd taken over a shattered organization and within a decade was leading the response to the largest wave of terrorism in US history. To Mariposa, he didn't seem to be the kind of man who let a problem go unsolved, but more the kind who'd beat one into submission.

~

JACK WIDENED his eyes and blinked a few times, trying to will away the tiredness that threatened to make him a car accident statistic. He'd never realized how dull driving on straight, empty roads at night could be. He'd been going the same speed in the same direction with nothing but the reflector strips on the road for company for hours now. He couldn't even play the radio or wind down the window, lest he wake up his passenger.

Elena Winston was curled up in a ball on the seat beside him. He admired her ability to sleep in a moving vehicle. He remembered such effortless sleep – these days, his sleep was interspersed with nightmares about Erin, his torture at the hands of the Chinese or the other pain inflicted upon him by Michelle Dominique. Yet Elena seemed undisturbed by the world or her mind. He sighed and drummed softly on the steering wheel.

They'd left Chicago just prior to the city being locked down for the evening curfew. Elena had arrived at his hotel with mixed news: Guerrilla Radio had broadcast Ortiz's information successfully, but because of Jack's earlier attempts to disseminate the report it was important that he leave town. She'd offered him a car and now, less than twelve hours after meeting her, he was leaving Chicago with her, bound for New York.

One of the things FEMA had outlawed but couldn't really police was travel on interstate roads at night – America had too many roads for that. It was a risk, but they were trying to get the hell out of Dodge before some flunky figured out that Jack was behind Guerilla Radio's story about the nascent resistance. He cursed himself again for trying to post the story. While he wasn't safe anywhere, he would be safer elsewhere.

He failed to completely stifle a yawn as a truck approached from the other direction. The amount of light that filled the car increased until, right at the point of passing, the inside of Elena's Chevy was lit up like day. It turned out Elena was human after all, as she stirred and sat up beside him. The darkness enveloped them again, but she was already awake. She sucked in a deep breath and scratched her head for a moment.

"Welcome back."

"Did I fall asleep?" She ran her hands over her face.

He laughed. "The minute we left the city."

She pulled down the visor, which had a small light and a mirror. "Sorry. Tired."

He cast a glance sideways and smiled at the hair matted to her face. "Classy."

"That's me." She fixed her hair.

"Tell me how you got that story out."

She looked at him as if she were summing up whether she could trust him or not and then shrugged. "Easy. We release everything we gather and can verify through all of our channels: shortwave radio, the Darknet, underground lectures. Even printed pamphlets, in some places where it makes sense."

"Why not just use the Darknet exclusively?"

"Could do, but there's not enough people using it. We need a mass movement of organized resistance. What we're trying is nothing that hasn't been done before when the shadow of totalitarianism casts itself over society. We have to try. Our reach is modest, but growing. Thanks to people like you."

Jack let that one go. He still wasn't entirely comfortable with helping Elena. If he'd been thinking straight, the issues he'd had while trying to disseminate Ortiz's information and the danger Elena had put him in by broadcasting it herself would have sent him running in the other direction. Instead, here he was, digging himself deeper. But at least he was asking questions. He didn't get a chance to probe her further, because her phone started to ring.

"It's my fiancé." The pride in her voice was palpable as she looked down at the screen. "Do you mind?"

Jack smiled and shook his head, but struggled to suppress the darkness that rose from the pit of his stomach. Losing Erin still hurt, though less these days. Despite her cheating and the distance between them in the final months of her life, he still felt like he'd been robbed of something. He didn't begrudge anyone their happiness, he just found it hard not to think of what he'd lost.

She answered the phone. "Hey, babe, how're you?"

Jack listened to the conversation, though he tried not to. She sounded so in love, so committed to the man on the other end. Yet she also seemed to have another passion – reporting against the menace that was creeping across America and recruiting others to do so. He admired her resolve. He'd felt the same once, a passion for both his wife and for fighting injustice. He wasn't sure he still had it in him, but he liked to see it in others.

Finally she hung up and turned to him with a smile. "Sorry, hope I wasn't too soppy. It's been a while since we've seen each other."

Jack smiled slightly and turned his head to glance at her. "It's fine. What's his name? What does he do?"

"Brad." She beamed. "He works deep in the physics dungeons at UCal Berkley. I don't really understand what he does, but he's a great guy."

"Sounds wonderful." Jack turned his eyes back to the road.

"He's the only reason I hesitate to do what we're doing." She sighed.

"What do you mean?"

She laughed softly. "If we make a mistake and we're exposed, they'll go after us hard. Is there anyone they can use to get to you?"

Jack thought about it, and conceded that Elena was probably right. FEMA were clearly growing restless and intervening into American society with an increasing vigor. So far journalists had been some of the worse treated, and growing dissent increased not only the risk for the journalist but also their loved ones. Guerilla Radio and the fledgling resistance were the very definition of such dissent.

"No, my wife died last year." Jack thought of Erin again, then his mind flicked to Celeste. Did she count? He wasn't sure.

"That doesn't protect you. All it will take is one mistake and you'll be exposed. It nearly happened in Chicago. If you're joining us, think hard."

He considered her words. His entire family was in Australia – out of reach. The majority of his friends were journalists and, while he had feelings for Celeste, he wasn't sure what to call whatever they had.

Regardless, if his friends were keeping their heads down, they'd be completely fine. If not, he couldn't help them anyway. But he had no way of knowing if they were wrapped up in all of this. No phone call was safe from interception.

"If you're in, *really* in, I'll need your help in New York. We need people we can trust. Hickens trusts you, so you're in."

"I've committed to going as far as New York. I need to think about anything more than that."

A few seconds passed in awkward silence before Elena turned to him. "We've got a few stops to make along the way."

"Don't trust me enough to tell me where?"

She laughed. "You've got plenty of time to make the right decision."

CHAPTER 7

FEMA has issued a cease and desist order to a number of media organizations around the country. These organizations have been complicit in reporting mistruths that aid terrorists and other agitators in making life and the administration of the country more difficult. These orders require the immediate removal of all censored material and carry with them significant financial and custodial penalties for any proprietor, editor or journalist in breach into the future.

Federal Emergency Management Agency
News Release

Jack kept his eyes closed as his ears strained to confirm what he'd heard. He knew the sound of light machine-gun fire like he knew the bottom of a whisky glass. He looked at the alarm clock beside his bed. It was early and they'd arrived in Indianapolis late. Despite wanting nothing more than to go back to sleep, he lay awake for a few minutes, waiting for the sound, until he chuckled and decided he was crazy. Then, just as he was about to try to go back to sleep, he heard it again.

He kicked off the covers, climbed out of the bed and pulled on his jeans and a T-shirt. He was staying with Elena in an apartment that apparently belonged to her mother, but Jack was skeptical. He didn't know too many people who kept a fully furnished but otherwise vacant apartment just in case their visiting children needed it. He hadn't argued though – they couldn't stay in a hotel and it sure beat curling up in a Chevy.

He rushed to the master bedroom and shook her firmly. "Elena. Wake up. We need to get moving."

She mumbled something that rhymed with duck.

He shook her again and then turned on the lamp. "Come on, there's fighting in the streets."

"I know." She groaned loudly as she squinted against the light. "A bit early, but yeah. I know. It'll be fine."

He stared at her, waiting for an explanation. None was forthcoming. His synapses were firing on all cylinders, sending a million thoughts rushing through his head. Every single one of them was telling him that he'd been played. He just wasn't sure why. She'd brought him here deliberately and had known there would be conflict. He wasn't sure what she was playing at.

"Elena?" He sat on the edge of her bed. "I've come a long fucking way to be kept in the dark."

"It's not dark. You made sure of that." She snorted. "Spare me. If I hadn't pulled you out of Chicago you'd be in prison right now, or worse."

Furious, he grabbed the covers and pulled as hard as he could. If he'd have thought about it before acting, he'd have considered the possibility of her not wearing very much under them. As it was, he saw plenty of her in her underwear. His cheeks flushed and his anger subsided nearly instantly. She ripped at the covers in his hands, pure rage burning in her eyes.

"What the fuck? Why are you being an asshole?" Her voice was vicious. "No wonder you got a divorce."

He didn't rise to her bait. "I know machine-gun fire. By my figuring, we should be leaving here right now, in the complete opposite direction."

"No can do." She exhaled long and hard, apparently letting some of her fury subside with it. "I told you we were stopping a few places along the way."

"Why?"

"We've got work to do, though it's a few hours sooner than I'd expected. You should have caught some zees while you had the chance. Turn around."

He turned around and felt movement behind him as she got out of bed. She stood and moved past him, and he shifted his gaze away from her as she gathered up her clothes and started to dress. He'd had more than an eyeful of her, and despite the gravity of the situation and his anger, he felt it was polite to give her at least some privacy.

"We're here to cover the first strike of the resistance. The gunfire is a couple of brigades of the 38th Infantry Division. This is where we start to take the country back."

"You're joking."

"Afraid not. It's happening. There'll be tanks in the streets soon. The underground media and a handful of southern militia aren't really enough to overcome all of this, Jack. We need some big guns. This is the birth of the resistance. The 38th is taking back their city." She paused and gave a long sigh. "Come on, you didn't really think we were just going to New York to have a chat?"

He turned around. She'd put on the same clothes as the day before. "Well, the thought did cross my mind. The State Guard in town—"

"Will surrender." She sat on the edge of the bed and started to slide on her shoes. "They're weekend warriors.

"And if they don't?"

"Why wouldn't they? They're all puffed up and tough in their black Humvees, but nothing against real army."

"You're mad."

"Maybe, but it doesn't matter. It's happening, we're just here to report it. If it works, and we can get the message out, the whole country will know. Come on."

Without waiting for him to follow, she grabbed her backpack and walked to the front door. He sighed, returned to his own room and grabbed his bag. Postings in a lot of dangerous places had taught him to be ready to go with all possessions of importance at a moment's notice, but he'd never had to, not even in Afghanistan or Syria. He ran out the door and followed her down the hall.

"Keep up!"

"Where the fuck are we going, Elena? New York, I hope."

"Sure." She bolted down the staircase, taking them two at a time. "Eventually."

They burst onto the street through the fire door. The alleyway seemed quiet enough and Jack decided it was time to steal back some of the initiative from her. He rushed to the end of the alleyway, stopping at the brick wall with Elena only a step behind. He held his breath and peered around the corner. His eyes widened. There was something large and squat and tan that made for a very bad day.

"Um, we might want to go back."

"Why?" Elena grabbed his shoulder and started to edge around.

"We both must have slept through the tank rolling into the park!"

"Well, they're ahead of schedule. This is perfect!"

He shook his head, exasperated. As he watched, the tank's turret rotated, but because of the darkness he couldn't see what it was targeting. Less than a second after its cannon boomed, a fireball roared into the air off into the distance. He hid back behind the corner and was horrified to see Elena, phone in hand, filming the whole lot. He glared at her, not quite believing it.

"What?" She spoke without turning around to look at him as she kept filming. "Don't stare."

"What're you doing?"

"My job."

He took a few steps back into the alley. "Remind me again why I'm hiding in the middle of fucking nowhere while tanks roll through the streets?"

She kept filming, but turned and flashed him a smile. "Because you're turned on by adventure?"

"I had plenty of that in Afghanistan…and China…and Syria. I never thought I'd get another dose in downtown Indianapolis!"

When he'd left Syria, Jack had thought he'd seen the last of his time as a conflict reporter. The siege of Homs had been brutal and it had taken a great toll on him, to see both the Syrian government of Bashar Al-Assad and the rebels who opposed him fight with such blatant disregard for civilians. They'd ground whole cities to dust between them. He wondered if the same thing would happen here.

The boom of the tank's cannon drowned out Elena's reply, but he saw her visibly tense.

"What?" He heard a gun shot from nearby, then another.

"The turret's turning."

Jack pushed her deeper into the alley, then looked back around the corner. The tank's cannon was pointed at the building they were hiding behind. From above them came small arms fire, which was being returned by infantry beyond the tank. They were in the middle of a warzone. He started walking away and then turned back to her. She was rooted to the spot.

"Elena, we need to move—"

"I was told we'd be safe here."

"Guess not." Jack glanced back around the corner. The tank turret was now pointed at the base of the building. "*Fuck!* We have to move, *now!*"

He grabbed her hand and broke into a run. He pulled her down the alleyway as fast as he could, but they hadn't made it to the far end when the deafening roar from the Abrams' cannon sounded. The building shook with the impact and he heard the front of the building start to collapse. In the aftermath, he heard the tank's engine rev and the grinding sound of its treads as it moved.

"Come on. This is getting nasty." He increased the pace, away from the tank and deeper into the city.

Elena jogged behind him. "Jack, I'm sorry. I was told—"

"I get it. Apologize later, we need to focus on getting out of this alive."

~

THE NOISE of the machines filled Callum's ears. His mind was foggy as he tried to open his eyes. Achieving that one thing consumed him.

Beep...Beep...

He managed to flick them open briefly but, unprepared for the assault of the light, he closed them again.

Beep...Beep...

Eventually he managed to keep them open if he squinted. The ceiling was white with harsh fluorescents.

Beep...Beep...

He had no idea where he was. The only clues were the noises of the machine and the white lights.

Beep...Beep...

The last thing he could remember was being shot several times at the distribution center and hitting the ground. His friends had been shot, too.

Beep...Beep...

He lifted his right arm off the bed about an inch, though it felt like he was trying to powerlift 400 lbs. He shifted his head a little. IV drips were hooked to him.

Beep…Beep…

His mind slowly started to unfog. He could barely shuffle an inch to the right, but he did manage to turn his head sideways.

Beep…Beep…

He wasn't sure there were plastic pink drink bottles in the afterlife. Suddenly, getting hold of the bottle from the side table was the only thing he wanted.

Beep…Be—

"Ah, you're finally awake. Good. Good." A nurse appeared in his vision then leaned in with a soft smile.

He tried to speak but didn't recognize his voice. He closed his eyes again and then felt something press against his lips, something moist. Water dribbled into his mouth. It was the best thing he'd ever tasted. He sucked at it fiercely and then coughed heavily as he tried to swallow too much. His eyes felt heavy. He tried to keep them open.

When he woke, some time later, smiling down at him was another nurse with a kind smile. He tried to speak. "Where am—"

"Mr Watkins, you're okay. You're at Mount Sinai Hospital. You're safe and you're going to be okay. The doctor will be around to see you soon."

Callum tried to speak again but she shushed him. She stayed with him for a few minutes, while the cloudy haze of the medication lifted, then left Callum to his thoughts. He began to slowly piece everything together, though it seemed harder than it should have been. He was alive. Somehow. He'd been wounded, but he'd woken up. His team had been shot to hell.

Callum's eyes flew open. Someone was touching his shoulder and shaking him slightly. He must have dozed off again. This time, he managed to keep his eyes open fully, though his head still felt heavy. A doctor in a white coat stared down at him, but lacked the same cheer the nurses had offered. He picked up Callum's chart and studied it.

"How's it looking, doc?" Callum had one million questions, but started with the most obvious.

"It'll take a few more hours for the sedatives to clear your system entirely." The doctor didn't look up from the chart. "Your vitals are good. You'll be fine. You're lucky."

"What happened to me?"

"That I don't know." The doctor paused and looked up. "You came in with three bullet wounds. We asked what happened and got told not to. We patched you up."

The answer was thoroughly unsatisfying, but it wasn't the doctor's fault. "Am I going to be alright?"

The doctor shrugged. "You'll be weak for a bit. You took one in the foot, one in the shoulder and a third in the chest, but it bounced off a rib. You'll have some rehab."

"How long until I'm out of here?"

"It'll take time." The doctor looked back down at the chart. "A week, if we have our way, sooner if the gentleman outside has his. I'll leave you to it."

"What do you mean?"

"There are some journalists who want to speak to you." The doctor smiled sympathetically. "I refused on your behalf, but you've got a friend out there who's insisted."

"You can't make him go away?"

The doctor laughed. "Like the rest of us these days, I serve at the pleasure of FEMA. You'll have to excuse me."

Callum tried to say more, to ask more questions, but the doctor didn't respond and left the room. It was only a few seconds before the door slid open again, admitting an impeccably dressed man in a business suit. He wore glasses and had slightly longer hair than would have been allowed in the military. Bureaucrat, the sort Callum hated.

"Glad you're awake, Callum." The man approached the bed with a slimy smile. "I'm Tim Dobbins."

"Can you tell me what happened at the distribution center?"

"I sure can, but there's more to—"

"I'm not discussing anything until I know what happened to the rest of my unit." Callum turned his head away from the bureaucrat.

Dobbins sighed. "Fine. Everyone in Mobile Three was KIA. Same story for Mobile Four except for you and Todd Bowles, but—"

"Wait a second, Todd is alive?"

Dobbins shook his head slightly. "No, he didn't make it. You very nearly joined him, but your injuries were less critical. You're a lucky man, Sergeant."

"So people keep telling me."

"When our reinforcements arrived they secured the scene and aided the casualties. You were evacuated, but things got a bit hairy after that.

The center was blown sky high. Timed explosives. It killed more and has disrupted our supply chain massively."

Callum didn't care about toilet paper and razor blades. Or even about the other dead, if he was being honest. He turned his head away from Dobbins, to hide the tear that streaked down his face. Though he wasn't so clichéd to say he'd rather be dead, he'd known Bowles and Pettine for a long time. He struggled to understand how he could be alive.

Dobbins cleared his throat. "I've been sitting here a long while waiting for you to wake up, you know? You've got an interview to do. As soon as possible."

"Not interested. Thanks for letting me know about what happened, but I'd like to be alone now if you don't mind." Callum closed his eyes.

"I don't, but my superiors would. It's not a request. You're a uniformed serviceman. You don't have an option here."

Callum sighed and opened his eyes. He'd been fed shit sandwiches by command before, but this one was a double whopper. He knew when he was beaten. The best way to get some peace was to give them a line or two that they could beam out nationally in support of the cause. Then they'd cast him as a hero and pin a medal on his chest.

"Fine." He scooted up the bed, managing to get himself slightly elevated. It felt a bit more dignified than lying on his back.

"I'm glad you've seen the value in what we're trying to do." Dobbins smiled as he pulled out his cell phone and walked back to the door. "You're going to be a star."

~

"PLEASE, BUDDY." Jack held out his hands, pleading for the other man to listen. "We just found out that my girlfriend is pregnant and our home is rubble."

The man had his hands gripped tightly around the bars of the security gate as if it were a life raft. His eyes narrowed. "What's it worth to you?"

Jack looked back over his shoulder, half expecting to see troops. He dug into his pocket and counted his cash. "Seventy bucks and my watch?"

With a nod, the other man unlocked the security gate, opened it and held out his hand. Jack unclasped his Tissot and handed it over with the cash. Once he had the loot in hand, the man stepped aside and let them past. Jack led the way inside and Elena followed as they took the stairs two at a time, racing for the rooftop. He hoped the position was worth the price of admission, but figured the rooftop of the five-story low-rise was the best view they'd get.

He still couldn't believe he was back in the middle of a warzone. As soon as they'd escaped the tank at the apartment, he'd demanded answers. She hadn't blanched and had explained how Major General Anthony Stern and the leadership of the 38th Infantry Division had chosen to liberate Indianapolis. Guerrilla Radio was to cover it all and Elena firmly believed that it was the birthing of the resistance. The conflict had been brutally brief as it rolled across the city and they'd filmed some of it.

Jack reached the roof and ran toward the edge. It gave a commanding view of the streets surrounding Indianapolis State House. "This is perfect."

"Brilliant spot, Jack." Elena's breathing was heavy as she stopped beside him. "I reckon you might have done this before?"

"Couple of times, yeah." Jack smiled and looked back to the street. "This is my personal best, though."

The State House held the headquarters and administration hub for FEMA in the city. Elena had wanted to film the minute the last defenders surrendered, to put the final flourish on the footage they'd collected. Jack had agreed and they'd lucked across the guy at the entrance to the building. It was a good thing for two reasons: Jack preferred to be above the action to get better quality footage, and they were less likely to be shot at.

He leaned down and rummaged around in his pack, pulling out his camera. As he looked out from the roof, the final act was drawing to a close. While the result hadn't been in doubt – the 38th had cut through the State Guard like balsawood – the final act still needed to play out. With the conflict confined to isolated skirmishes there hadn't been a mass exodus of civilians from the city and, as far as Jack knew, the only remaining State Guard defensive positions in the city were at the State House.

Now he had a better view of those defenses, he was unimpressed. Sandbags and a few hard points were about as complicated as it got. Jack knew it wouldn't hold up against the attackers and he'd found it hard to understand why they were still fighting, until he'd turned on the radio and heard over the broadcast that the army was executing anyone who surrendered. Jack didn't believe it, but the average guardsman might.

Elena stood and pointed. "Here comes the army, Jack. They're not messing around, are they?"

Jack lifted the binoculars he'd stolen from a camping store from around his neck. Army units were advancing from three directions. "It's a ton of hardware."

Elena nodded and crouched lower behind the safety wall on the roof of the building. "We're safe up here, right?"

Jack laughed, despite the situation. "As safe as it gets in the middle of two groups of combat troo—"

"Fucking hell!" Elena ducked in response to the boom of a tank's cannon less than a mile away.

An explosion flared near the State House. Jack swung the binoculars toward it and could see several State Guard troops scattered and unmoving among their defensive positions. "Don't they know there're civilians inside? That old stone building won't hold up against this kind of pounding."

Elena checked her phone, which she'd been using to patch into some sort of feed of information relating to the attack. "Um. The army doesn't know that. Stern has demanded they surrender, but they've refused. FEMA is saying that 'terrorists' are executing all prisoners."

Jack started to stand. "Keep filming."

Elena looked at him with wide eyes. "Where the hell are you going?"

"To stop a slaughter and prevent a stake through the heart of your rebellion."

"But—"

"You think it's good vision for your friends to flatten an iconic building full of civilians? Just keep filming! And tell the army to cool their heels!"

He broke into a run toward the edge of the rooftop, not waiting for her response. He started down the fire escape, a stream of thoughts rushing through his head, mostly involving how stupid an idea this was. He didn't even have anything identifying him as a member of the press. As he descended the stairs two at a time, he unzipped his jacket and tore at his T-shirt. It would make a passable white flag.

He reached the street and broke into a sprint across the park, towards the State House. As he drew closer, he took some solace from the fact that the tanks had stopped firing. He didn't know whether the advance had stopped or not, but as he came to the attention of the State Guardsmen behind the sandbags, he was suddenly aware of several weapons pointing in his direction.

"Whoa! Whoa! Fellas!" Jack held up his hands, his voice as loud as he could make it. "I'm neutral."

One of the Guardsman spoke from down his sights. "What do you want, pal? You got a death wish or something? Army is hitting us hard. Go back to your home."

"You guys don't have a chance." Jack stood firm. "There're two brigades gunning for you."

"You don't think we know that?" The same trooper sounded angry now. "We're boxed in and they're not taking prisoners."

Jack thought about arguing, but thought better of it. "If I can negotiate a release, will you consider it?"

They paused and looked at each other. Finally, the leader of the unit shrugged. "You get us a guarantee of safety and we'll withdraw with our civilian staff."

Jack nodded. He doubted the army was interested in killing any more State Guardsman than necessary to take the city, but knew they wouldn't stop until their foes were rooted out and the city was theirs. Jack saw a chance to save lives and also give Guerrilla Radio and the resistance a huge public relations victory. Now he just had to make it happen.

He raised his hands into the air again and walked toward the army forces encircling the State House. He half expected to be met with gunfire, but he inched closer, one foot in front of the other, until finally he reached the forward elements of the army. He was ushered away by soldiers to a Humvee in the rear. Jack kept his arms high as an older officer climbed out of the Humvee.

The officer rubbed his salt and pepper moustache. "Who the fuck are you, son? I see you walking out on your own and I get a message telling me that you're a friendly?"

"I'm Jack Emery." Jack kept deathly still. "The forces guarding the State House want to walk out of the city, but think you'll kill them if they surrender."

"That explains a few things, then." The old soldier removed his hat and ran a hand through his hair. "You're sure they'll budge without me having to kick the door in?"

"Yep." Jack hoped he was right. "Make them an offer and they'll take it. I've got a colleague up on the rooftops ready to film the withdrawal."

The officer considered Jack's words for a moment, nodded and then walked back to the Humvee. Jack swallowed. The air was electric. He thought back to the scared men behind the sandbags. These were two groups of angry and tense men – one stray shot and hot lead would start flying. He wished he could see the State House, but he was too far away.

He just hoped for an outcome that he and Elena could work with.

CHAPTER 8

FEMA has announced that all travel in and out of Indianapolis, Indiana, is restricted until further notice following an attack on the city. Elements of the 38th Infantry Division of the US Army appear to be working in concert with terrorists and other agitators. While FEMA and the State Guard respond, those inside the city should stay indoors. FEMA would like to join the President and other authorities in calling for a peaceful surrender by these individuals.

Federal Emergency Management Agency

News Release

"Administrator Hall?"

Richard was instantly alert. He rolled over on the sofa as he rubbed his eyes and reached for his glasses. He felt like he'd been awake for days. There was just too much to do. "What is it?"

Rebecca Bianco smiled down at him sympathetically. His chief liaison with the State Guard looked as fresh as morning dew. "I've received confirmation that all elements are in place and ready."

"What time is it?" He sighed and sat up. He was in a small office on the outskirts of Indianapolis. Since the city had fallen and the remaining State Guard had withdrawn, he'd flown in to take control of the situation personally.

"Early, sir. I'll give you a minute." Bianco turned and walked out of the room.

Richard ran his hands across his face a few times, trying to wake up. As he did, he thought about the situation. The occupation of Indianapolis was the greatest challenge to his authority yet, given the extent to which Guerrilla Radio and the resistance were claiming it as a victory. He wasn't worried by general friction – gun-nut militias in the south and protestors waving placards in Washington – because he'd expected such agitation.

What he hadn't expected was elements of the US military rebelling. Had they no respect for order and stability? Couldn't they see the merit in what he was doing? His entire effort to bring peace to America was based on the removal of some individual rights to the greater benefit of everyone. It also relied on the authorities doing their jobs, no matter what was asked of them, in order to get results. The assault by the 38th contravened both of these. It was a cigarette flicked into dry grass, igniting a wildfire.

He'd called in a huge number of State Guard from all over Indiana and neighboring states to surround the city and, if necessary, retake it. It had left other parts of the country bare, but this situation had to be put down. If the 38th were allowed to dictate terms here, and Guerrilla Radio were able to claim it as a victory against the express will and authority of Richard and FEMA, chaos would break out across the country. But he'd hoped it wouldn't come to this.

He climbed to his feet and walked out of the small office. Bianco was waiting. "They haven't responded to our ultimatum?"

"Not quite, sir." She paused.

"Tell me."

"It came in a few minutes ago." Bianco looked down at her papers. "I'm told that the formal response was 'Tell that little tin Hitler to fuck himself', sir."

Richard laughed. "I thought it might be along those lines. Very well. Issue one final ultimatum: The 38th Infantry Division has thirty minutes to surrender. If they don't, order all drone commands to execute their orders. At that point we'll re-evaluate and decide whether to send in ground troops."

Bianco's sharp intake of breath told him his chance of a nap was lost. "They let our people walk out of the city. You're going to flatten the whole lot?"

Richard stared at her. "I'm giving them one more chance to

surrender. That's one more than terrorists deserve. We can't let them hold this city."

"It's the United States Army, Administrator!"

Richard sighed and stared at the wall. He didn't understand why some of his junior staff found it so difficult to comprehend the necessity of action like this. An agenda as ambitious as the one he was pursuing required extreme action. The quicker others fell into line, the quicker life would get back to normal, and the less extreme his measures had to be.

"I don't enjoy doing this, Rebecca. Indianapolis should be safe from unmanned drones raining Hellfire missiles on it. But they've left me no choice!" She didn't looked convinced. Richard didn't care. He started to talk again, but paused briefly. He smiled. "Actually, I've changed my mind."

Her eyes widened, then she exhaled deeply and smiled back at him. "I'm so glad, sir. I think it would have been a mistake to—"

"You misunderstand."

"Wh—"

"No ultimatum. No opportunity for surrender." He talked over her. "Give the go ahead to drone commanders. I want the 38th Infantry Division destroyed."

She seemed to be on the verge of refusing him, but eventually nodded and picked up a radio. "General? This is Rebecca Bianco. The administrator has given the order."

Richard was under no illusion that this would be painless – there would obviously be casualties, but they concerned him less than the public relations issues. The continued success of Guerrilla Radio and its role in the growth of the resistance was becoming a real problem. It concerned him far more than rooting the army out of Indianapolis. It needed to be crushed.

After a few moments, Bianco spoke into the radio again. "Affirmative, General. No final warning. The order is correct."

Richard reached into his pocket and pulled out his tin of breath mints. He popped the lid, shook one into his hand and put it in his mouth. As he started to suck on the mint, he held the container out to Bianco. She shook her head and watched him in silence, with a look he was sure was disgust. But she maintained her professionalism and kept her feelings to herself. He appreciated that and smiled at her gently. She was young. She still had the luxury of a conscience.

He didn't require everyone to believe in what was being done.

Though it was preferable, so many government employees had become so used to mediocre leadership that they didn't recognize the decisive, inspired kind when they saw it. FEMA had been the same when he'd taken over, after Katrina. Shellshocked staff had hated him at first, but grown to regard him as a legend. The same would happen across America once he solved this crisis. It would be his legacy.

No, he didn't need everyone to love him. He just needed them to do their jobs.

~

JACK WAS STANDING at the front of the State House chambers, watching as General Stern and his senior officers held an impromptu staff meeting inside the beautiful rooms. The midday sun was peeking through the windows, causing hell with his attempts to film the meeting. It was a good problem to have, though. Being inside the building meant they'd won the battle. Afterwards it had taken less than an hour for General Stern and his staff to take up residence in the building and begin planning the next phase of their operation: the spread of their area of control to the towns of Anderson, Franklin and Martinsville.

Jack had been allowed inside the chambers with Elena to film the opening few minutes of the meeting. It was nothing but platitudes and backslapping, but it was important to broadcast to America that the adults were back in charge, at least in this small part of the country. It felt like, with the capture of Indianapolis, the first strike had been made in getting things back to normal. He hoped a proper resistance might start to form in place of a few tin-pot militias and Guerrilla Radio. For Jack, it was also the first time he felt part of it all.

He kept filming as Stern looked straight at him and spoke. "Finally, I'd like to say that freedom is our birth right as citizens of this country. We must take it back."

Jack stopped recording. "Thanks, General, that should play well. You've done good work here."

Stern nodded. "We're about to discuss things that aren't fit for public consumption, so we'll need some privacy."

"No problem, General. We might make a nuisance of ourselves talking to some of your troops."

The general looked down at his papers and started talking to his officers. As Jack and Elena packed up and moved toward the exit, Jack reached out and placed a hand on her shoulder. She looked at him and smiled warmly. He was about to open his mouth to say something when a thunderclap filled his ears and a flash of light seared his eyes. He was thrown forward several feet and landed hard on the carpeted floor.

He could see a glow and hear more explosions. *Explosions. Trying to stay low, behind cover. Others not so lucky. Fire.*

He felt heat. *People burning. Screaming.*

He heard someone shout his name. *A child in his mother's arms. Crying.*

He felt someone touch him. *A hand reaches out to help the mother. She falls, limp. The hand catches the child.*

He was being shaken. The shouting was right in his ear. *The hand is his. He turns the child over. He's already dead.*

Jack rolled onto his back and shook his head, finally recognizing what was happening. The explosions weren't in Homs, they were in Indianapolis – the Indianapolis State House. He looked up at Elena, who had a mix of fear and relief painted on her features. She held out a hand. Jack took it, using her help to get up off the ground. His entire body was sore, the numb replaced by a deep ache.

"Thanks."

"We need to go, Jack. We need to go now." She started to jog.

He looked back. Where the general and his staff had been there was now only death and fire. He followed her as quickly as he could, trying to figure out what was happening as the building was rocked by another explosion. Stern had been the most senior military officer in the local rebellion and a chance to become the figurehead of the entire resistance. His success would have led to others taking notice. Asking questions. Now he was dead.

Jack flinched and ducked instinctively as more explosions boomed in the distance, adding to the cacophony now rolling through the city. Whoever was attacking had started with the command and control of Stern's army and was now attacking the secondary targets. He pushed himself to catch up with Elena. She was out of sight, but when he rounded a corner she was standing near the exit.

"They're hitting the city, Jack." Her voice cracked. "Are you okay now? What was all that back there?"

"The result of too many close calls like this." He held her gaze. "Sorry, I'm fine now. We need to go."

He'd thought his flashback days were finished, but Homs had

obviously stayed with him. That was a problem for later. For now, they had to get the hell out of Indianapolis, because if the hammer was coming down on the city then the State House was the head of the nail. They'd delayed too long and had nearly paid the ultimate price. He doubted the 38th would be in control of the city for very much longer under this sort of bombardment.

The two soldiers guarding the foyer didn't try to stop them as they ran past and pushed the heavy wooden doors open. Outside, Jack stopped on the steps and stared, mouth agape. The city was ablaze. The missile through the window of the council chambers looked to be the least of their problems, with explosions blooming and smoke rising from three dozen places. A tank in the street ahead burned. He ran, away from the State House and back into the city, with Elena right behind him.

They covered a mile before they were back among the buildings, explosions all around but safe for the time being. He couldn't hear aircraft, so it was clearly drones doing the damage. He couldn't believe FEMA and the State Guard would attack a city so indiscriminately. After another hundred yards, he slowed then stopped. His breath came in ragged chunks and Elena panted next to him, hands on her knees as she tried to catch her breath.

"Jack." Her voice was strained. "This has all gone to shit. I don't know what to do. Where are we going?"

"To get the car and get out of here. Any troops left in this city will be dead within the day. We don't want to be here when FEMA rolls back into town."

"Okay. Let's do that." She looked up at him, and despite her words he saw doubt on her face.

"This place was a false hope. We're going to New York. It's where we should have gone in the first place."

～

"THANKS SO MUCH, STEPHANIE." Mariposa handed the sitter a handful of notes. "Same time tomorrow, if that's okay?"

The other woman gave a weary smile and then turned and walked away. Mariposa closed the door behind her and placed her keys in the bowl next to the front door. She sighed as she kicked her shoes off then leaned with her back against the door, feeling as if that was all that was holding her up. She closed her eyes for several seconds, then opened them and walked to Juan's room.

She eased the door open, careful to make sure it didn't screech, then entered the room. In the illumination provided by Juan's nightlight, she scooped up a few toys between the door and the bed and deposited them in the corner. The sitter could worry about them tomorrow – she was here for one reason. She sat on the edge of the bed and smiled, reaching out and running her thumb down her son's cheek.

Juan was asleep, curled up on his side and hugging his teddy. She stroked his cheek again, then his hair. Guilt hit her like a wave and she fought back tears. She felt like she'd missed the last few months of his life, spending eighty hours a week at the office and relying exclusively on a sitter. She told herself it was necessary and that her job was important, but the guilt threatened to overwhelm her.

She made sure he was tucked in, determined that she'd spend breakfast with him before going into the office. She flicked off the nightlight and crept back through the door. Walking to her own bedroom, she emptied her pockets onto the bed. Amid the usual dross of her day – crumpled-up post-its and a few pens – she found a pamphlet she'd been handed on her way to lunch. She opened it.

It was a small A5 brochure with black and white lettering. It had a small map with a circle around Indianapolis, Indiana, with the words liberation starts here across the top, and guerilla radio along the bottom. She screwed it up and went to work unbuttoning her blouse. She wasn't much interested in propaganda. From either side. Nobody had come out of the mess in Indianapolis looking good.

Given Area V took in Indiana, she'd been briefed on the incident in the city. Though Administrator Hall and the State Guard were overseeing the response, she still took an interest. She was patched into the national command network and received reports about issues and setbacks across the whole country. It was a level of information that most people had been starved of since the clampdown.

She removed her skirt. With this new information, she'd seen the whole picture for the first time. Parts of the country were ablaze in conflict. Southern militias were ambushing supply convoys. Army units across the country were agitating. The terrorist attacks had lessened, but not ceased entirely. FEMA responded more harshly every day.

She was about to collapse into bed when her cell phone started to ring. She stared at her purse, willing the whole thing to combust and give her some peace, but the phone kept ringing. One of the struggles of leadership, she'd discovered, was having to always be available. Decision makers were expected to sort problems out, even when they were dead tired and standing in their underwear.

She reached for her purse, dug around inside and answered the phone. "This is Mariposa Esposito."

"Ms Esposito?" The man's voice was unfamiliar to her. "This is Ray Felton calling from headquarters."

She sat on the bed, wishing he'd just go away. "What can I do for you, Ray? I've had a long day."

"I understand." His tone suggested he probably didn't. "Administrator Hall has asked me to brief you on developments in Indiana."

She lay back on the bed and closed her eyes. "I've read the reports on the incident. I don't think I nee—"

"We've retaken the city. But casualties among the rebels and civilians were immense. The administrator oversaw the operation personally and wanted you to be aware. A full report is being sent to your inbox. There'll be a teleconference with all areas at seven tomorrow morning to discuss recovery."

Her mind screamed with fury. "Okay, thanks, Ray. I appreciate the heads up. Have a good night."

She hung up. Not for the first time she considered calling in to resign, crawling under the covers and letting the world pass her by. The violence and the mayhem was not what she'd signed up for. She'd been with FEMA for years, yet she barely recognized the organization or believed in its purpose anymore. It was supposed to protect, to save and to build. Instead, it seemed to be doing little more than destroying and suppressing.

While she didn't doubt the threat that the terrorist attacks represented, she didn't think it was any more disastrous than a cyclone or wildfire. That FEMA had been given such power irked her more with each passing day, with all that she saw and heard – hell, the more she *ordered*. Things were getting out of hand. Apparently, FEMA could do anything. Even attack a city, bomb an army into submission and slaughter civilians in the crossfire.

She shook her head. As bad as things were – and no matter how terrible they became – she was tied to FEMA. If working too much and being responsible for some morally questionable acts was the cost she had to pay to keep a roof over her child's head, then there was no decision to make. They paid well and working for FEMA meant extra rations for her son. If she couldn't be here for him, she at least could make sure he had a full stomach.

If she was laid off, or quit, her situation would be desperate. She had no savings and hardly any support network in Chicago to speak of. Worse, chances were, given the executive orders, she'd be unable to get work with the companies that now loathed FEMA. Nor would she likely to get any work with other government agencies. She opened her eyes and looked at the clock: 3.00 am. She counted back in her head from the meeting in four hours. She'd have time to read over the briefing and then call the sitter at dawn.

She could shower at the office.

CHAPTER 9

Following recent tragic events, FEMA and the State Guard are pleased to announce that Sergeant Callum Watkins, the sole survivor the attack on FEMA Distribution Center Echo, has today been downgraded from critical condition to stable. Sergeant Watkins made a brief statement to the media, in which he thanked the medical professionals who saved his life and expressed huge grief at the loss of his colleagues. In closing, Sergeant Watkins called for unity across America while the threat is dealt with. He will be discharged from hospital today.

Federal Emergency Management Agency

News Release

Callum woke with a scream.

He was covered in sweat and tangled in his bed linen, but he slowly realized the nightmare had been just that. He sat up and rubbed a hand over his face before releasing a growl. Since waking up in hospital, the nights had been full of such moments. The nightmare always began with him stepping out of the Humvee at the distribution center, then flashed forward to the moment he was shot, then ended in darkness. At that point, he woke up.

He shook his head and looked at the clock. 8:30 am. He smiled slightly. He'd actually forgotten to set his alarm, so the timing of the dream was fortunate. He had a meeting in half an hour with a State Guard psychologist. Along with his physical rehabilitation, the psychologist's report was just another step in the long path back to active duty. Or so the theory went. In reality, Callum had a very different purpose in mind for the meeting.

It was just good to be home. He climbed out of bed, showered and dressed while trying not to dwell on the nightmare. He sat at his kitchen table in silence, preparing his mind for the meeting to come. As the clock struck the hour his doorbell rang. The guy was punctual, if nothing else. Callum stood up, walked to the door and opened it. He was immediately forced to revaluate his chances of getting what he wanted when he saw the man waiting outside.

"Sergeant Watkins? I'm Major John Bainbridge." Bainbridge stood as straight as a board. "Illinois State Guard Chief Psychologist."

Callum had hoped he might get someone a bit softer, a bit more open to the case he was about to make, but Major Bainbridge appeared to be the consummate hardass: his uniform was sharp and his features were hard. Once he removed his sunglasses, Callum could see his eyes held little sympathy. He wouldn't back down and would still try to make his case, but it looked more difficult than he'd expected even before he'd started.

"Good morning, Major." Callum saluted and then waited while Bainbridge returned it. He walked inside and gestured toward the table. "Take a seat."

"Thanks, Sergeant." Bainbridge removed his hat and placed it on the table, appearing to size up Callum while he did. "I appreciate you meeting with me."

"No problem, sir." Callum sat alert, waiting for Bainbridge to begin. "Where do you want to start, Major?"

Bainbridge's smile was thin and without any hint of warmth. "Before you're cleared to return to duty, I need to check there are no lasting ill-effects from the incident."

"The incident?" Callum was immediately incensed. "The *incident?*"

Bainbridge's eyes were hard as diamonds. "You getting shot and—"

"And my team being killed." Callum regretted interrupting the major, but he was that angry. "Sorry, Major, but is that the one you mean?"

Bainbridge's blank expression didn't change. "Yes, that one."

Callum closed his eyes for a second and forced the anger down. It wouldn't help. He sat forward. "My intention is to resign from the State Guard."

This time Bainbridge raised an eyebrow and gave the slightest hint of a smirk. "Is that so, Sergeant?"

"Yes. I'd like to get back to my normal job." Callum knew he was screwed, but he had to try. "I've been involved in two fatal incidents now. I think that's enough."

Bainbridge said nothing. Callum had been through enough therapy following his troubles in Iraq to know that the major was leaving space for him to fill. He was being assessed and analyzed. Bainbridge didn't have a notepad, but Callum knew that he was building a file nonetheless. Callum just had to make sure that the other man was logging the right information.

Callum sighed. "I saw my friends get shot to death, sir. I think I've done my duty for my country overseas and now at home as well. I've had enough."

"Nobody would argue that you haven't, Sergeant." Bainbridge paused and leaned forward slightly. "Look, Callum, I can't sign off on a discharge. You know that."

Callum scoffed. "I'm a volunteer. I haven't signed any contract binding me to the guard. You can't keep me."

Bainbridge shrugged. "The executive orders granting FEMA authority over the guard also prohibits resignation except in cases approved by the Administrator of FEMA."

Callum felt his dream slipping away, and the nightmare coming back. "Please. I don't want to do this anymore."

Bainbridge was unmoved. "Sergeant, it's time to stop thinking about something that's impossible—"

Callum slammed the table. "It's not impossible."

Bainbridge waited for a second and then continued. "And start thinking about what can be achieved."

Callum looked up at Bainbridge, suddenly sensing that the game had changed. The major was dangling something in front of him, but he couldn't figure out what. Either way, he wasn't well served by his anger. He eased back in his chair, crossed his arms and took a few deep breaths. He kept his eyes locked onto Bainbridge, waiting to see what the other man had to offer.

"Now, you know I can't give you a discharge. Our forces are spread thin and we've taken some losses. But that doesn't necessarily mean you need to go back on patrol."

"Okay, I like the sound of that."

Bainbridge smiled and nodded. "Okay. You're a hero for surviving the distribution center attack and you helped us to tell the world about the atrocities these thugs are committing. More importantly, you showed America that we can survive and endure with the right people in charge."

Callum sighed. He sensed whatever was coming had been cooked up before Bainbridge had even walked in the door. He just wasn't sure what it was. "Okay."

"I'm ordering that you be transferred to a security detail to guard some of the individuals being detained on suspicion of aiding the terrorists." Bainbridge smiled. "It's a hell of a lot better than driving into firefights and getting your ass shot off, don't you think?"

Callum wasn't sure he agreed, but he kept his mouth shut. If he couldn't walk out the door, then he supposed this was a decent compromise. It was hard to imagine a scenario in which guarding a camp would be a problem, but he still wasn't thrilled by the idea. On the other hand, while he'd still have a gun, others wouldn't be trying to shoot at him. The camp was good enough for now, but what if it didn't last?

"You've got yourself a deal, Major."

RICHARD LIFTED the coffee cup to his mouth and took a long sip, savoring the heat that coursed down into his stomach. This was his third coffee for the day and he was well on the way to an all nighter, an all too common occurrence since the activation of the executive orders. He'd never worked so hard in his life, but had no right to complain. He'd wanted this – the chance to lead – and with that came hard work and long hours. Hotspots and flashpoints had stolen his attention, forcing him to focus on putting out fires instead of the direction of the country, but he was intending to change that. He put the cup back on the table, sighed and then went back to work on the smallest mountain of paperwork on his desk – the items his staff considered most critical.

He was glad to be back in Washington. With the issues in Illinois and Indiana sorted, he'd flown back to the capital to get things back on course, take care of paperwork and meet with his senior staff. Though he was still committed to handling the larger spot fires personally, the worst of them were under control. His next problem was dealing with one of the root causes of those spot fires. He picked up another briefing and read the title: *NSA metadata analysis of suspected Guerrilla Radio members.* While crushing the rebellion in Indianapolis would give pause to any further organized armed resistance, it had only dealt with the head of the beast. Its beating heart was the amount of bootleg media that had been allowed to flourish, the so-called Guerrilla Radio.

Though his plan for the administrative takeover of America had included provision for setbacks, he'd not properly considered the strength of an underground media. He'd thought that the media could be handled like any other issue, but he was wrong. The influence and spread of such reporting was growing daily, and was a direct threat to his efforts to bring order and stability to the country. He'd mentally added the crushing of bootleg reporting to his other key priorities: the erosion of personal freedoms that made group cohesion and security difficult, the enforcement of additional control over society, a state controlled media and a strong surveillance state. Combined, these were the only way to ensure no more attacks occurred on home soil.

He flicked through the report, skimming the background information and going straight for the recommendation: that to stop the flouting of the law by Guerrilla Radio and its supporters, all confirmed or suspected members should be detained immediately and indefinitely. Richard tossed the report across the desk with disgust. Whoever was being paid for this analysis had no idea. The problem with journalists was that they were martyrs, the lot of them. Start jailing them and they'd treat it like a badge of honor, meaning the problem would just spread as more reporters became outraged enough to join the cause. More members would lead to more coverage, which would lead to more fires that needed to be put out. Enough of those could cause an inferno he couldn't control.

He picked up his phone and waited for his receptionist to pick up. "Sandra? Get me Rick Sullivan at the NSA."

Despite the hour, he was certain that Sullivan would be available. Finally, the hold music stopped, replaced by a quiet voice. "Hi, Richard."

"Not too late I hope, Rick?" Richard lifted the report again. "I'm looking at the report about Guerrilla Radio that you guys sent over. It's a piece of work."

"Yeah, one of my best guys put it together."

"Hire new guys. It's garbage." There was silence on the other end.

Richard exhaled slowly. There was no point in further mocking one of his key allies in government. "Tell me what we know, Rick."

"Given the apparent importance of Guerrilla Radio to the broader resistance, we've used intercepts to establish the network of Guerrilla Radio members. Our working theory is that if we can deal with the communications side of things then we can kill any further armed resistance in utero. But we needed to know who's involved first."

"And do we?"

There was a slight pause. "The list isn't complete and anyone using a VPN or decent encryption will be invisible to us, but it's a decent start. We estimate that scooping up the known suspects will reduce Guerilla Radio membership by sixty-two per cent and degrade their capacity by somewhere in the vicinity of eighty per cent."

Richard was silent for a moment. He'd learned to be suspicious of the intelligence community whenever he had to make a decision based on their analysis. They always painted a complete picture with clear recommendations, but it was a mirage. There was always more to the picture, something untold. He treated their information as one factor in his decision-making. He trusted only his own analysis and his own decisions.

"Richard?"

He took another sip of his coffee. "I'm here. Are we able to track the most common associates of the Guerrilla Radio members? Family, close friends, that kind of thing?"

"Of course." Sullivan sounded confused. "Easy. Our interns could do that."

Richard was surprised. "You have interns?"

"Figure of speech."

Richard didn't laugh. "Okay. I want a list showing me the two most important social links for each member on your initial list. If you're unsure, make your best guess."

"To what end?"

"We're going to send some people to prison."

"It'll be thousands of people." Sullivan scoffed. "How will you detain them?"

"Let me worry about that. You just get me that list. You have six hours."

Richard hung up the phone, stood and stretched his back. He walked over to the floor-to-ceiling window that offered a commanding view of the Mall. When he wavered in his conviction, he just had to stare at it for long enough to know that it was all worth it. Great men had led the country from Washington, and he'd grown tired of waiting for another one to step forward. The country had decayed and chaos had become the norm. He was determined. Order would be brought to America, whatever the cost. It would be his gift to the American people.

But first he had to deal with the problems getting in his way. He was not worried about the resistance, yet, but he was concerned by Guerrilla Radio. They had to be crushed.

While journalists may be martyrs, they were still people. By taking away the ones they loved and giving them an ultimatum, most would fall into line. The ones that didn't could then be dealt with directly. He'd be able to starve the existing members of their motivation and, more importantly, targeting the loved ones of existing members made it far less likely that new recruits would be in a hurry to join. Though he'd authorized a few arrests so far and ordered camps be built to detain people, it was time to scale up.

He'd tried being subtle, but it hadn't worked. It was time to swing a sledgehammer. It was just a shame all the highly paid analysts in the world couldn't come with an idea half as good as his own.

∾

THE CHEVY PULLED to a stop with the screech of well-worn brakes as Jack turned to Elena. "We're here."

She nodded and gestured out the window, toward the house they'd pulled up in front of. "Time to meet your girlfriend."

Jack winced. "She's not my girlfriend."

She winked. "Sure."

Jack groaned as she opened the door and climbed out. They'd left Indianapolis with a stream of other civilian refugees. Luckily, the State Guard hadn't targeted them as overwhelming force was brought to bear on the 38th Infantry Division. The civilian casualties had been immense, as had damage to the city, but Jack and Elena had been lucky enough to make it to New York without further incident.

Now they were at Celeste's house. He sighed and turned off the ignition. Part of him preferred the idea of being in combat to what was to come. He and Celeste hadn't exactly parted on the best of terms. He'd fled his responsibilities and shut her out, along with everyone else, and he was sure their relationship had been damaged. But he'd driven halfway across the country and it was time to front up to her.

He opened the door, climbed out of the car and locked it. As Elena fell in behind him he climbed the steps and knocked on the door. He wondered if Celeste was on the other side, sizing him up through the peephole and deciding whether to let him in. There was a roughly even chance of her opening the door armed with a handgun as there was of her not answering at all. The door opened. Turns out he was wrong.

"Good to see you, Jack." Peter smiled.

Peter Weston had been Ernest McDowell's assistant for a decade, prior to McDowell's death. Now he was the Managing Director of EMCorp, appointed by Ernest's daughter in her stead. The stresses of the new job looked to have aged Peter, but his smile was no less warm than Jack remembered. He'd expected him to be here, but it was still nice to see the other man, if only to have a witness present if Celeste came at him with a cleaver.

"Hi Peter." He held out his arms and gave Peter a quick hug. "Been a rough time trying to get here. Thanks for coming."

"Not a problem." Peter's eyes twinkled in the streetlight. "I thought the reporting from Indianapolis might be your handiwork."

"You saw that?" Jack winked, but didn't confirm anything.

"We still have some connection to the outside world, you know."

Jack bit the bullet. "Celeste around?"

Peter's features hardened. "She's inside."

"Okay." Jack started to walk inside, past Peter, when he felt a hand on his shoulder.

"Take it easy, Jack." Peter's voice was heavy with warning. "She's still upset at you."

"I know. Give me five?"

"Sure." Peter nodded. "I'll keep your friend company."

"Thanks."

He walked down the hall until he reached the open-plan kitchen and living room at the back of the house. He pulled up short when he saw her sitting on the sofa, a glass of wine in her hand and lit only by a lamp. As she stared at him, a wave of emotions hit him: guilt, fear, lust. He hadn't seen her in a long time – this meeting would determine if he got to see her much into the future. Suddenly he realized that he wanted that very much.

"Nice of you to drop in." Her British accent somehow made her sound all the more icy.

"Hi." He walked across the room and moved to sit next to her on the sofa.

She held up a hand, her face a picture of darkness. "You don't get to sit."

He nodded and backed off, feeling awkward. He could feel the waves of pain and anger radiating off her. He couldn't blame her. While he'd hoped that once they were together in the same place again things wouldn't be so bad between them, it looked like a false hope. It was looking unlikely that she'd speak to him, let alone forgive him. He needed to have another shot at explaining the reasons for his absence, though it might not satisfy her.

"I'm sorry, Celeste." He held his hands out, palms facing upward. "No reservations."

She stood, her wine glass still in her hand. He waited and watched as she came closer, then in one quick flick of her wrist sprayed him with the remnants of her drink. He felt the moisture on his face but resisted the urge to reach up and wipe it off. She tossed the glass onto the floor, smashing it on the tiles, then sat back down again. He stood, unmoving, and waited for whatever happened next.

"Now you can explain." Her voice was barely a whisper. "You've got one chance."

He felt the wine slowly drip from his face, but he ignored it. "I needed to heal, Celeste. After we stopped the Foundation and I won the Pulitzer, things—"

She scoffed. "Things started to happen between us. Things you were a willing participant in, Jack. Then, just as I was starting to have feelings for you, you ran."

"I know." He shrugged. "I don't have an answer, not one to fix my mistake or satisfy you. I thought I could heal and stay in New York, but I was wrong. It was too much."

She continued to stare up at him, and he thought he could see a tear in her eye. "You don't think I had healing to do? I was okay being friends but you pressed for more."

"I know."

"Then you ran."

"I know."

She curled her legs underneath her and hugged her knees. "You know what hurt most?"

He braced himself. "Go on."

"After all the shit we went through, you didn't just say 'let's cool it' and go to Florida. You jumped on a flight and crossed the globe. I didn't think I'd ever see you alive again." She closed her eyes for a second, then opened them again. "You cultivated feelings in me, then ran as far away as you could once we started to grow close."

"I know." Jack put his hands in his pocket. "I'm sorry. There's no justification. I felt something for you that I wasn't ready for, so I ran."

He watched as she sized him up. Her eyes narrowed and she stared at him for several long moments. He'd known for months that when this moment came it would be a close call. He could have done more, had more phone conversations with her, but he'd been an idiot. Seeing her in front of him, he was now certain that he wanted her in his life. He just hoped he hadn't screwed it up.

He stepped forward a little. "I want to give this a try, if you'll let me. But I understand the damage I've caused. The crime is mine, the verdict is yours."

"I need to think." She let out a long sigh. "Go and get Peter."

He nodded, stood and went to the front of the house, where Peter and Elena were making small talk. By the time he returned, Celeste had turned some lights on and he could see the kitchen table was already covered with platters of food. When Elena entered the larger room, Jack felt the temperature drop as Celeste summed her up. He wondered if Celeste was getting the wrong message from Elena's presence, so soon after he'd apologized.

For her part, Elena was standing awkwardly in the entrance to the living area, as if some invisible force had stopped her in her tracks. He'd never seen her looking like she lacked confidence, but on the other hand, their time together had been brief. You could never tell how someone would react to being the outsider in a social situation, especially when the insiders had shared as much as Jack, Celeste and Peter had. He had to do something.

Jack waved Elena over. "Celeste? I want you to meet Elena Winston."

Elena lifted a hand up and offered a weak smile. "Hi."

"Nice to meet you." Celeste's voice remained cold. "Come in. Eat if you want."

They sat around the dining table. Peter did his best to lighten the mood as the two women remained reserved. Jack and Peter chatted about the crackdown, the terrorist attacks, the FEMA atrocities and gossip they'd heard about the situation in other places. Jack shared his and Elena's experience in Indianapolis and when it was their turn, Peter and Celeste shared insight into what was happening on the east coast, including the extent and limits of FEMA control. Though both Peter and Celeste were still at EMCorp, they were horribly constrained in what could be reported. Jack sensed frustration, but saw no obvious sign that they'd be in a hurry to join the resistance.

Finally, he decided it was time. "Ah, so guys? Elena is one of the leaders of Guerrilla Radio. I'm working with her to get word of FEMA overreach out."

Elena gave a small laugh, but there was silence from the others. He wondered if he'd gotten it wrong, as Peter's eyes widened and Celeste crossed her arms.

Finally, Peter broke the silence. "Why are you involved, Jack?"

"I wasn't at first. I wanted nothing to do with it."

"What happened?" Peter seemed genuinely interested. "What changed?"

"A friend I owe everything to asked for my help. Elena helped me to help him, and it meant I had to get out of Chicago. We were doing the filming in Indianapolis."

"Indianapolis." Celeste cut in, her voice sharp.

"Yes." He stared straight at her. "Indianapolis."

"She nearly got you killed, Jack." She stared back.

"I did a pretty good job of that myself." He shrugged. "I was actually hoping you guys might be willing to help us out in New York."

Celeste shook her head and stood, bringing the conversation to an abrupt close. She picked up her wine glass and walked to the back door. She slid it open, stepped outside then closed it again. Jack could see her outline, staring out into the night. Every inch of him ached to join her and to comfort her, but there was larger business to complete. Or so he thought.

Peter cleared his throat. "I think we're all tired. A few of us in particular."

Jack smiled. "Sorry, Peter. It's good to see you, anyway."

"Jack, I'm not opposed to helping you. I actually respect what you're trying to do. But you need to get your house in order with Celeste before anything else."

"I know."

"And another thing." Peter frowned. "I want Jo Tokaloka left out of this, whether or not Celeste and I end up helping. His heart won't stand up to it."

Jack nodded. "Okay."

Peter stood. "Why don't I show you to one of the guest bedrooms, Elena?"

"I don't know." Elena looked unsure. "She doesn't seem thrilled that I'm here."

"Good thing I pay her salary." Peter patted Elena on the shoulder.

"Go on." Jack smiled at Elena, trying to reassure her. "It'll be fine."

Elena nodded, but Jack could see the doubt on her face. She stood and followed Peter without further word, leaving Jack sitting at the table with his thoughts. He sipped his own wine, ate a few biscuits and delayed the inevitable until, eventually, he stood. He walked to the back door, slid it open and stepped outside. He closed the door and stood just behind Celeste. She was sobbing quietly.

"It wasn't so long ago you were standing behind me on the *George Washington* when I was upset." His voice was barely a whisper. "A lot has changed."

"You didn't even know about Jo's heart attack! I wanted to tell you, but Peter wouldn't let me. You disappeared." Celeste turned to face him, tears streaming down her face. "You were a fucking coward. Others needed you and you weren't here. That's not Jack Emery. Not the Jack Emery I know, anyway!"

Her words felt like a jab to his stomach. "I'm sorry. I let you down."

She let out a long sigh. "It's a long way back for you."

"I know."

"And I may not be able to forgive you."

"Fair enough."

Her features lightened for the first time. "But I think I'd like to try."

CHAPTER 10

FEMA is pleased to announce that increased restrictions on movement in Indianapolis, Indiana, will be lifted. The restrictions, in place since the city was liberated from rebellious elements of the military, were required to ensure the threat to the city was fully dealt with. Administrator Hall has praised the patience of residents in Indianapolis, noting that although their city was violently assaulted things are now back to normal. Administrator Hall also expressed the need to be vigilant against those who wish us harm, noting that some FEMA staff and State Guard troops remain in conflict with terrorists in other parts of the country.

    Federal Emergency Management Agency
    News Release

J ack enjoyed the rhythm. He lay on his back with his hands behind his head, taking in the view with hunger. Celeste's features looked wonderful in the lamplight, moving slowly back and forth as she ran both hands through her mess of shoulder-length red hair. She offered a cautious smile, which he returned, then continued to allow his gaze to devour her entire body.

They'd talked into the early hours of the morning, agreeing that they still had feelings for each other but the potential for hurt was enormous. Celeste had made no promises, but had asked to go to bed together.

She'd told him that, after a delay of over a year, she wanted to be with him, to be held by him. They'd slept like that, but woken up to more.

She writhed on top of him and her breathing became heavier. He felt his own pace quicken and a soft moan escaped from each of them. He felt his hunger turn to desperation and they pressed closer together, until his abdominals tightened. He reached out and gripped her tightly. A second later her quiet, brief moans became more sustained and he had to put his hand over her mouth.

He smiled up at her. "The others might hear."

Her eyes narrowed as she continued to press down onto him. She kissed his palm, then sucked one of his fingers and bit it playfully. Slowly her pleasure seemed to subside and he rolled sideways with her, into an easy embrace. She snuggled in close and they said nothing for several minutes, as their breathing returned to normal.

"I'm glad you're here, Jack." Her voice was a mix of satisfaction and sleepiness. "Don't make me regret this."

He kissed her head and pulled her closer. He started to doze as she roamed his body, stopping occasionally on his scars, examining them then moving on. He knew that her scars weren't visible, and his knowledge of what had happened to her in China – her rape – had made him hesitant. He'd let her take the lead and the result had been spectacular.

"So, what do you need from us out here, Jack?" Celeste's voice was thick with sleep when they stirred, hours later.

"What do you mean?"

"Guerrilla Radio." She pulled away from him and put her head on the pillow, her eyes boring into him. "I want to help. What do you need?"

He thought for a moment, trying to clear his mind from the hazy mix of sex and sleep. "The failure in Indianapolis showed us a few things. We need to develop a proper national network before we let it loose. Once that's done properly we can discuss the growth of the resistance more broadly."

Celeste smiled. "I can start to sound out some EMCorp colleagues. I'm sure there are some who'll help. Peter, for starters."

"Yeah, I spoke to him briefly last night. He's on board."

An enormous bang from the other end of the house interrupted their conversation. Celeste immediately sat bolt upright. "What was that?"

Jack remained still, listening. He wondered if Elena had done something to cause the noise, but couldn't immediately think what. But when he heard a second bang and the sound of cracking timber, he had a fair idea what it was. He rushed out of bed and started to rummage around for his clothing, which was scattered around on the floor.

"What's going on?" Celeste's voice was an higher than usual.

"Trouble."

"What are you doing?" She hugged the covers.

"Getting dressed." He smiled sadly as he pulled on his underwear. "You should too."

She didn't get the chance and he only had his jeans half on when the shouts started. *"NYPD! All occupants need to stay where they are."*

The door to the bedroom was kicked in a second later and four officers dressed in Kevlar vests poured through, pointing pistols at the two of them. One of them flicked a switch and the quiet solitude of dawn was broken. Jack blinked a few times to help his eyes adjust to the light as Celeste pulled the covers higher. Jack raised his arms as he thought about Elena, who'd been sleeping at the front of the house. They must have scooped her up.

"Get down. Get down now!" An officer shouted as he moved around the bed, keeping the pistol trained on Jack. "On the floor."

Jack complied. He immediately raised his hands and dropped to his knees. "No need to wave the guns around, fellas."

"Keep your mouth shut." The officer pulled Jack's hands together roughly behind his back and cuffed them. "Up."

Jack started to stand, helped by the officer. Another officer had his pistol trained on Jack while the final two were focused on Celeste. He'd been arrested before – once in Australia for taking a drunken swing at someone and a few times overseas for reporting on various stories – but he'd never been assaulted by storm troopers in such a way. He thought this might be Celeste's first experience with police, though not with the authorities.

"Take it easy, guys." He looked down at Celeste, who was cowering in fear, and he thought back to their experiences in China. "This doesn't need to happen like this."

The officers ignored him and one of them stepped toward the bed and addressed Celeste. "I need you to show me your hands, miss, then I'm going to pull back the covers and you're going to climb out of the bed and get dressed. It's important that you make no sudden movements."

Jack started to protest, but was pulled back by the officer holding him. The one with the pistol trained on him stepped forward an inch. "You need to calm down."

He took a breath to compose himself. "You're here for me, fellas. This is stupid."

"Calm down."

Jack watched as Celeste pulled her hands out over the covers, then placed them down slowly. She sobbed. "I'm naked under here, guys, can I have a minute?"

"Negative. I'm going to pull back the covers and you're going to climb out of the bed." The officer repeated himself. "Remember, no sudden movements."

She nodded and bit her lip as the officer held his pistol in one hand and ripped the covers off the bed with the other. Jack felt the anger well inside of him as he watched Celeste start to sob harder. She kept her hands exactly where they'd been, not even daring to cover up, though she did press her legs together. His face burned red at her humiliation, but any protest he made would just make things worse. He kept his mouth shut.

"Okay, get up." The officer reached onto the floor and tossed her a blouse. He then spoke into the radio that was mounted on his shoulder. "All clear. Suspect located and detained."

Jack found his voice again. "What now?"

"Look, pal." The officer holding the pistol on him spoke. "We're not here for you, but if you don't pipe down, you're coming in too. Okay?"

"Who are you here for, then?" Celeste, now dressed, turned to the officer. "Me?"

"You."

To her credit, she sensed that further protest was pointless. "Okay."

Jack had no such sense. "Come on. She's a journalist, not a terrorist."

The only officer who hadn't spoken yet piped in. "I don't care. One more word and you'll be sitting next to her in the van."

Jack started forward, causing the officer with the pistol on him to tense slightly. Celeste locked eyes with him and shook her head very slightly. She was clearly thinking that there was no point both of them being locked up. He rocked back on the balls of his feet and didn't move any further as the officer relaxed and Celeste was led from the room. Only then did they uncuff him and leave.

~

"ONE *THOUSAND* IN ILLINOIS ALONE?" Mariposa looked up from the report that Murray Devereaux had handed her.

Murray chewed on his gum. "Yeah, and they picked up some doozies. Everything from an eighteen-year-old to a ninety-three-year-old. Real threats to security."

"Seems a bit ridiculous, doesn't it?" She shook her head and placed the report on the table.

He shrugged and placed his coffee on top of the document, showing what he thought of its value. It was a hundred pages long, a dossier of every Guerrilla Radio sympathizer who'd been picked up across Illinois by a mix of police and State Guard. She knew the same action had taken place in other states as well, in an attempt by the administrator to clamp down on the activity of Guerrilla Radio and, in turn, stem the growth of the resistance.

She sighed. "Command tells me it's to wrap up the Guerrilla Radio network that's popped up, but it seems like a big show of force and an awful lot of people to detain."

"Fuck command. They've screwed the pooch on this whole episode. Why attack the friends and family?" He snorted, his disdain for what had happened clear on his face. "That's some Stasi-type shit right there. If you know who's breaking the law, take them down, but as far as I can see these folks are innocent."

She nodded and left it at that. He was right. Her new job gave her huge access to information she'd previously been denied and most of it disgusted her. It told her that they were no closer to stopping the attacks around the whole country, that the presence of Guerrilla Radio was growing, and that FEMA's actions were getting increasingly desperate – and violent – to keep order. The detention of thousands of people was the latest attempt.

"I wonder what the story is in other states." He raised an eyebrow.

"Classified."

He rolled his eyes. "Of course."

"Thanks, Murray."

She was glad he took the hint. He picked up his coffee and left her office. She leaned back in her chair and looked at the ceiling. Every negative thought she'd had about FEMA and the path it was on came crashing back. She'd done her best to busy herself with work, trying to hide away her larger concerns, but even that dam was starting to crack and spew out negative thoughts. Her career. Her pay check. Her colleagues. Her safety. Her son. All were reasons to will away the ill-feeling she had about everything that was happening. But it wasn't enough. With each draconian measure she signed off on, the further into the maw of evil she felt herself slipping.

Sooner or later, she knew that the Nuremberg defense wouldn't hold up against her conscience. Doing something that she disagreed with because she was ordered to, even if she spoke out against it occasionally, was not acceptable. She was as culpable as the drone pilots firing on Indianapolis or the SWAT teams who'd kicked in doors and arrested thousands of innocent people around the country. She made her decision. She stood up, walked out of her office and toward the central meeting point where they held the staff briefings. She pressed the button that started the chime, then she waited in silence while the whole staff came together.

"Thanks, everyone." She smiled, wanting to convey as normal an impression as possible. "We're not doing a briefing, unless anyone has anything critical?"

She looked to each of the managers, who looked to their staff in turn. There were a few confused faces, but mostly a lot of shaking heads. Illinois was buttoned up pretty tight. Incidents like the arrests aside, there wasn't much happening. Her team was doing a great job at what they'd been ordered to do, which broke her heart all the more. It was all wrong. She steeled herself for the path she was about to start down.

"Okay, given everything is under control, I've informed command that I'm sending you all home early for the day." She smiled at the lie, and as faces around the room brightened she caught sight of Murray looking at her carefully. "It's been a long time since any of you spent some real time with your families, so off you go."

"What about our work?" Murray spoke up, asking what everyone else was likely thinking.

She lied again. "Area IV is going to take care of any non-essential overflow for the day and we'll be doing the same for them next week. If anything comes up, you'll be contacted. Enjoy yourselves."

She smiled one last time then returned to her office. She left the door open and sat down, busying herself with paperwork as the staff cleared out quickly – it was as if they thought the bubble might burst or she might change her mind. She kept her head down and tried her best to ward off the doubts that were creeping in. The minute the last staff member walked out, there was no turning back.

She closed the manila folder that held the file she was reading and walked from her office. She needed to make sure everyone had left. Her heart nearly jumped out of her chest when she saw Murray leaning against one of the cubicle partitions right outside her office, blowing bubbles with his gum. She punched him in the arm and he responded with a smile and another bubble.

"What's the story?" His voice was firm. "Sending everyone home for a little R and R? Right after we discussed how much of a joke those arrests were?"

"It's fine, Murray. Really. I just think we're all spread a bit too thinly right now and I wanted to give everyone a break." She wasn't lying, technically. "You should go too."

"Okay, I'll walk out with you?" He crossed his arms and raised an eyebrow when she didn't move. "Didn't think so. I want a piece of whatever you're up to."

She sighed. Now that she'd finally made a decision and put in place the first part of it, the last thing she wanted was to have an argument with Murray. He was her best friend at the office and she didn't want him caught up in what she was about to do. Worse, if he wouldn't budge, not only would he be implicated but she wouldn't achieve what she had to either. He had to go.

"Murray, I want you to go home now. Please." She turned back into her office, and nearly roared with frustration when he followed her.

"Nope." He moved closer to her, standing inches away as she backed up against the desk. "Tell me what you're up to."

She sighed. It was time to fight dirty. "Murray, this is your last chance. We're friends, but now I'm giving you an order as your superior. You need to leave."

"No." He crossed his arms. "Not until I know what you're doing."

"I'm doing my job. But if you keep it up and continue to disobey my instructions, I'm going to issue you with a formal warning. That'd be your third, wouldn't it?"

"You wouldn't!" He backed away, fury in his eyes. "I'd lose my job! You know that!"

She did know that. She kept her voice sharp. "I do. Now I want you to go home."

Her heart broke as he looked at the floor. His fists were balled at his sides and he started to say something, then shook his head. He turned and left the room without saying anything further. She sighed and felt the tension drain out of her, but knew that she'd crossed a much more final precipice than the treason she was about to commit. Her friendship with Murray was damaged, perhaps destroyed.

She dug through the paperwork on her desk, picking out the most important pieces. A few tears splashed against the papers as she gathered them together, but she ignored them. She was no expert in the release of information, but she was going to photocopy and scan the heck out of anything she could find that she considered to be a breach of FEMA's mandate.

If she was successful in distributing the information, she might begin to end the organization's vice-like grip on the country. If nothing else, she was confident she could have some success locally and make life for the residents of Illinois a bit easier. She picked up the stack of hastily gathered paperwork and moved towards the photocopier. It was all about to change.

～

RICHARD SMILED at the White House staffer as she opened the door leading into the Oval Office. He adjusted his tie absentmindedly and then walked inside. On the other side of the room, President Helen Morris was consumed by paperwork, a feeling he knew all too well. He'd only just reached the bottom of his pile. It surprised him that she had so much to do, considering he was running the country.

She was concentrating and hadn't noticed him enter. She had her head resting in one hand and a pen in the other. He stopped and coughed quietly. She looked up and her eyes blinked a couple of times, as if he'd pulled her out of a deep trance. She appeared tired and drawn, but a broad smile cracked through the gloom on her face like sun on an overcast day.

"Madam President." Richard stood as tall as he could. "It's wonderful to see you again."

"Hi Richard." She held the smile and gestured him toward the sofa. "Thanks for coming in."

"No problem. I was surprised though." He knew as he sat that he shouldn't have said it, but couldn't resist. What had once been a rarity for him – meeting alone with the President – had become common since the state of emergency was declared. He had a mountain of work and no time for this, but he knew that with power came the need to reassure the person who'd given it to him and who, if pushed, could theoretically take it away again.

"Why?" She winced as she sat heavily on the lounge opposite him, obviously in pain from too many hours at a desk. "I want an update on our efforts to stop the attacks."

Richard caught his sigh before it showed obvious disrespect. He didn't have time for this. "Did you see the latest report?"

She raised an eyebrow, but he held her gaze. "I don't want paperwork, Richard. I gave you the responsibility to end this, and I want to hear it from your mouth."

He wondered why he bothered to have his staff compile enormous reports of FEMA's operations and successes if she was just going to cast them aside. He had a preferred way of working, a *proven* way of working, and by asking for a verbal update she was shitting all over that. This was one of the reasons he'd grown tired of waiting for a great leader to come along, the reason he'd had to take over. Why couldn't she recognize that things were under control and just sit back and watch?

Sitting in front of him was a pale caricature of a President. Morris had been a fierce woman. She'd roared through the Washington establishment like a firestorm following the revelations about the Foundation for a New America. No corner of government had been spared the excision of corruption. All had felt her wrath equally and Richard had gained an enormous respect for the woman's sense of order. That had been the high point.

Now she was a frightened shell. She'd proven to be the same disappointment that most of her predecessors had ended up being. She'd been unable to grapple with the dysfunction, unable to fend off the rent seekers, unable to bend the country to her will and do what was needed to save it. The attacks had overwhelmed her ability to lead, and she'd looked for someone – anyone – to save her. Richard would provide that salvation. It would be his legacy.

"I see." He kept his voice level. "In short, the number of major terrorist attacks has fallen significantly since the commencement of the special arrangements. We're not out of the woods yet, but the steps we've taken are working."

Morris looked over her glasses, then sighed and removed them.

"Don't play me for the fool, Richard. Indianapolis. The agitation in the south. Though they were dealt with, all were serious."

"Different matters." He shrugged. "Those were the work of traitors and rebellious elements who don't want to toe the line, not terrorists. They're reacting to our movements to end the bigger threat."

"What's the difference?" Morris looked unconvinced. "An attack is an attack."

Richard frowned. "I disagree. Terrorism is an attempt to instill chaos. These attacks are quite different – they're a response to order, a rebellion against the effort we're making to stabilize our country."

She seemed to consider his words carefully. "Okay, assuming I accept your proposition, what're we doing about it?"

He smiled. "The worst of the rebellious activity is being fuelled by the underground media. I've countered it."

"Will it be enough?"

"I think so." He was counting on it.

"Fine. I'm not thrilled though. I hate seeing us kill civilians and members of the military like in Indianapolis – rebellious or not." She rubbed a hand over her face. "Beyond that, if the attacks have stopped – the real attacks – then we can look to pull the plug on the state of emergency and the executive orders."

"That would be a mistake, I'm afraid." He'd seen this coming – she was so predictable. He rattled off his rehearsed lines. "Even though the attacks have stopped, it's more because of the increased security than anything else. We haven't yet apprehended any of those responsible for the attacks."

"Sorry, Richard. You said it yourself, the attacks have slowed. It's time to end the emergency measures and get things back to normal. The rest will melt away."

He kept his features even. "I'm not certain that's true. If we revoke the state of emergency, we're likely to see more attacks and carnage."

"More deaths." She sighed and paused, apparently deep in thought. "So what do you need to smoke out those responsible for the attacks and to defeat this rebellion? I'm of a mind to mobilize the military to end this thing once and for all. Maybe the Joint Chiefs were right all along."

He leaned forward, resting his elbows on his knees but with his hands held out. "I can assure you that things are under control, Madam President. FEMA and the State Guard are preventing many attacks, and those that do occur are being contained and cleaned up as best as we can."

"Okay, and finding those responsible? Dealing with the resistance?"

"I'm in the process of taking care of the resistance and our efforts to find the original attackers continue. Our operations haven't been perfect, but close to it. My strong advice is to stay the course as planned." He knew she'd go with it. To revoke his powers and risk reigniting the worst of the attacks seen months ago was a chance she wouldn't take.

She sat back in the chair with her arms crossed, stared at him for a few long moments, then exhaled deeply. "Look, Richard, I'm going to be blunt. The reason I turned to you is that you're a lot more effective than the rest of the blowhards. I'm not entirely satisfied, but you've made a good start. But I want no more civilian casualties from FEMA operations."

He nodded, though he had no intention of complying. "I'll continue to get results."

CHAPTER 11

FEMA, the State Guard and police across the country have arrested a large number of individuals on terror-related charges. The operation was the result of much hard work and investigation, aimed at disrupting the propaganda machine and communications networks of the perpetrators of recent terror attacks. Administrator Hall praised the work of all involved.

Federal Emergency Management Agency

News Release

C allum hocked and spat over the safety rail. He watched it sail toward the ground and then began the short lap of the guard tower for what felt like the thousandth time. Down below, a few of the inmates in the yard looked up briefly then down again. They tended to stay away from the tower and the fenced off walkways at ground level that let the security staff move through the camp securely. They knew better than to tempt bored guards, even if Callum wasn't the sort to bust chops just for the fun of it.

Following his meeting with Bainbridge, he'd received a letter posting him to the security detail at a subversive internment camp near Effingham, Illinois. The facility housed around two thousand, with the capacity for more. He was still resentful that he hadn't received his discharge, but if there was an easier posting in America right now, he wasn't sure where. The major had been good to his word: Callum had stayed in the State Guard and in return he'd been posted as far away as possible from places where he was likely to be shot at.

Callum approached one of the other guards stationed in the tower, Staff Sergeant Micah Hill, who was busy reading a magazine. "Good to see you working hard."

The large black man smiled as he looked up from his magazine, something with cars and tits on it. "You're too stupid for sarcasm, Callum."

"That's fair." Callum laughed. "Doubt we'll be putting down any riots though. This lot can barely look sideways without pissing their pants."

Hill's smile vanished. "Fine by me. I had buddies in Indianapolis. We got the golden ticket right here. Don't jinx it."

Callum grunted in response. Dusk was starting to settle and as he looked out over the yard he reflected again on the size of the camp. Twelve pre-fabricated sheds dominated most of the space, though there was also a central recreation area and a well-guarded sub-complex along the western side of the facility which housed the hospital and administration wing. It was all divided by razor wire–topped cyclone fences and walkways for the guards. The prison was testament to how much could be built quickly if you put your mind to it.

"Hey, Micah?" He turned his head to Hill. "Just heading downstairs for a walk around and to make sure they all get to dinner. On the radio if you need."

"No problem, Cal." Hill didn't look up from his titty magazine. "Make sure you leave the rifle behind though."

Callum nodded and racked his rifle. Leaving it behind was a small price to pay for some freedom from the tower. Besides, he still had his pistol and Taser. He walked to the circular staircase. Lately he'd found himself taking these leisurely walks at least once a day, just to break up the drudgery of guarding people who posed no threat to anyone at all. Hell, most of them still seemed in shock that they were here at all. He appreciated that – they moved, ate and slept when told to, and were unlikely to try to shiv him or steal his weapon.

He reached the ground and swiped his access card on the reader. The gate unlocked with a clunk and he pushed it open and walked into the yard, protected on either side by the fence. He walked twenty feet before he was among the first inmates. They was a mix of gender, race and age. The only thing they appeared to have in common was loving the wrong person. That wasn't the official line, of course, but it was whispered enough among the inmates for him to believe. Most or all of them were guilty of no crime.

When he was halfway between the tower and the first pre-fab building, a bell started to blare over the PA system. Dinner time. The inmates around him started to walk toward the dining hall, except for one woman who moved towards him instead. He caressed his pistol, but the fact that she was alone made the threat tolerable. As she drew closer he could see her eyes were puffy and red from too much crying. Despite that, she was very beautiful, with pretty features and nice curves.

"Slow it down, inmate." He turned to face her straight on and called out. "I need you to think a bit harder about what you're doing and stay away from the fence."

"What the *fuck* do you think I'm doing?" She was visibly shaking as she approached. "I'm in jail for having a journalist for a husband. I need to get home to my children."

He lifted one hand, palm facing outward and trying to calm her down. "This isn't the way to do it. Don't come any closer to this fence."

"What is the way to do it then?" As she walked, she removed the top of her orange prison garb, exposing a tan-colored bra and a flat stomach. "Like what you see?"

Callum struggled to look away as he drew his pistol. "Inmate, stop where you are and put your clothes back on."

He got one out of two. The woman stopped in her tracks, then started lowering her shapeless orange pants. He mused darkly that this was the issue with having the yard segregated from the paths the guards walked – he couldn't quickly end this. Once her pants hit the grass, she reached behind her back and unclasped her bra. She didn't immediately let it fall, however, but held her hands over the front as she took a few more steps forward. He wasn't going to shoot her, but this mischief had to end.

"Last warning before you find yourself in isolation." He leaned in to the radio mounted on his shoulder in a deliberate enough warning.

She laughed. "Isolation? What do you call being stuck in prison for doing nothing, away from my family and without knowing a single soul in here?"

He pressed the button down on the radio. "Hey, Micah? Can you send a team down to me, I've—"

She raised her hands in mock surrender. The bra fell. "Look, all I want to do is get out of here. I'll do whatever you and your buddies need doing, if that's what it takes."

"Callum, you okay?" The radio crackled. Micah's voice had a slight hint of concern. "View looks good from here."

"Not interested." He looked away from the woman then leaned back in to the radio. "Micah, send someone to collect the naked princess for a day in isolation."

He turned and kept walking. Once he'd walked a few yards down the path he glanced back to see the half-naked woman slumped on her knees on the lawn. She'd gathered her orange clothing and now hugged it to herself, her sobs audible even over the dinner chime. He shook his head. It wasn't his job to question the decision to imprison these people. But he did wonder how long it would be until someone *was* trying to shiv him, rather than offering her body in return for freedom. He let out a long, slow sigh.

Being in combat might be dangerous, but Callum understood it a hell of a lot more than here.

RICHARD FELT ONLY a slight bump as the helicopter touched down softly on the rooftop, and he wasted no time sliding the door open and climbing out. He was here for one reason – this was one conversation he couldn't have by phone or email – and the helicopter's engine would barely have time to cool before he was in the air again. He glanced at the pilot, who stared ahead minding his own business. Good. He crossed the rooftop, entered the stairwell, walked down several flights and then placed his hand on the door handle. He took a deep breath, turned it and walked through.

The floor was vacant and painted a sterile white that wouldn't have been out of place in a hospital. Plastic sheeting covered the cubicles and other assorted furniture that might one day house federal employees. But for now the entire building was empty, except for one table. She sat there with her back to him, her blond curls flowing down just past her shoulders. It was odd. For someone so deadly, she clearly trusted him not to stick a knife in her back. Or, more likely, her men were close enough to prevent that.

He could sense the anger radiating off her. She'd told him that the distribution center attack would be her last, that her team had taken on enough high profile jobs for him. She'd wanted to bank the enormous amount of money she'd earned and sit on a beach in South America for a few years, while the heat died down. But Richard couldn't have that. He'd cultivated her for too long to lose her as an asset. He'd twisted her arm to accept one last job, to make one last attack, to help keep Morris convinced of the need for the state of emergency.

She'd attacked Times Square and the attack had gone well, but at a cost.

They'd lost one commando. *Her* commando.

He stopped five yards from her. If she was feeling violent, a little distance wouldn't hurt. Not that he could do anything to stop her anyway. He was a bureaucrat. A skilled one, with a great deal of power, but still a bureaucrat. His power was in bringing the sledgehammer of government to bear. She wielded a more surgical type of power. Both were vital to his plans. She hadn't been behind all of the attacks, but she'd been behind many. She'd helped whip the country into such hysteria about terorrism that Morris had declared a state of emergency and put Richard in charge.

Now he had to soothe her. "I'm sorry about M—"

"Names." The fury rolled off her in waves and her voice was barbed.

"Oh, don't be so paranoid. The building is safe."

"Remember who you're talking to." Her voice had pure menace as she stood and turned. "I told you I wanted to take a break. I told you Times Square was too hot."

"It was." Richard started to say more, bit his tongue, then continued. "I'm sorry."

"I lost a man."

"I know, and—"

"I don't care." Her hands were balled into fists. "I'd worked with him for a long time."

"I know." Richard was growing tired of this, but he needed to humour her.

"This is it. I'm out. I don't work for you any more and neither does my team."

He laughed, despite the fact that he was slightly afraid of her. One was not a woman to be mocked lightly. Even if her team wasn't present, of which there could be no guarantee, she could kill him with her bare hands. On the other hand, the whole reason he knew her, and the whole reason she was willing to work for him, was the past they shared. Richard had saved One from a terrible situation. They didn't talk about it anymore, but they both knew about it. He held the whip hand and, despite her bravado, she knew it.

"You don't get that choice." He kept his voice even. "You're out when I say you are."

She snarled and her eyes narrowed. "I've repaid my debt."

"We'll have to agree to disagree." Richard smiled. "But you have earned a break."

Her eyes narrowed. "Go on."

He brushed some imaginary lint off his suit jacket. "I don't believe it will be necessary to stage any further attacks. You've done enough."

Richard smiled at her look of surprise. While it was true that more attacks would make it easier to keep the pressure on Morris and keep the state of emergency in place, he'd known this moment would come sooner or later. At some point, FEMA's control would inevitably reach its zenith. At that point, it was imperative that the attacks began to slow. While this might be occuring a little earlier than he'd hoped, the risk of having One pissed off was too great. The attacks to date would have to be enough.

She nodded. He knew that his words had been accepted. She probably didn't trust him to keep his word, but she didn't have a choice. If push came to shove, he had the leverage to get her to do whatever needed doing. In the meantime, she'd be quiet and away from the eyes of authorities, and he could start making the case that he had brought peace to America. Or at least the start of it. He knew this might be the last time he saw her, or needed her.

But probably not.

～

JACK PULLED the baseball cap a bit lower, to hide as much of his face as possible from the State Guard troopers walking on the other side of the street. He stared straight ahead as he walked, but kept the patrol in his peripheral vision. He had no reason to think they were after him, but he didn't know what to expect from FEMA and their minions since Celeste and the others had been taken. Yet this lot didn't even look at him, too busy talking among themselves and strolling along.

Once he was out of their sight, he leaned against the side of a building and composed himself. New York had been saturated with uniforms for the past few days as FEMA, the State Guard and the NYPD made noise about the detention of terrorists, supporters and sympathizers. Now the point had been made and with their targets in custody, he hoped that the tide would start to recede. Only then could they count the cost.

Since Celeste had been taken he'd kept a low profile, trying to decipher where she was, who else had been taken, and what was left of his support network. It was bleak. None of his old sources in New York had been any help: most had vanished, others claimed to know nothing and some refused to talk. Only Peter remained free. As for Guerrilla Radio, he'd had no word from Elena and he had to assume the resistance was stillborn.

Best he could figure, Celeste must have been sent to one of the camps that FEMA had erected, though he had no way of finding out which one. Worse still, the detentions had everyone on the edge of a razorblade. Nobody knew if they'd be arrested and detained for talking to the wrong person, or even who those people were. It meant people kept their mouths shut and their ears closed. It was exactly what FEMA wanted.

He took a left off 51st Street and onto 8th Avenue. He had to find something to eat and get back to Celeste's house by curfew. He had no idea what to do or where to go, so he focused on nothing but living. He kicked at a loose piece of pavement, then watched it skid down the street and nearly hit a woman who was standing against a stop sign in a trench and boots. He squinted, then his eyes widened in realization. Elena.

He balled his fists by his side and huffed as he walked closer, ready to confront her, but he never got the chance. As he drew closer, she pushed herself off the pole. She'd clearly been waiting for him and there were tears in her eyes. While he'd lost Celeste, he hadn't yet discovered what Elena had lost. She probably knew dozens of others scooped up in the raids. His anger subsided just a bit, but he still wanted answers.

"Hi Jack. It's good to see you." Her voice was soft, weak.

"How did you get out of the house?" His fingernails dug into the his palms. "You were in the front room. Where did you go?"

"What?" She wiped at her face, which contained tears mixed with a look of confusion. "I was out front. They rolled up in a SWAT van so I stayed where I was."

Jack was speechless. He'd like to think that if he was in a similar situation he'd try to intervene, to help his friends or at the least make sure there were enough witnesses to keep the cops honest. The fact that she'd stood back and watched it happen – watched Celeste be taken – shocked him. It drove home the fact that he barely knew her at all, despite all that they'd shared in Chicago and Indianapolis and at the kitchen table in Celeste's house in New York.

"Look, Jack, cool your jets, okay?" The conviction in her voice increased. "A lot of people important to me have been locked up too, just like Celeste."

Jack huffed. "But—"

"No Jack." She held up her hand. "You've lost one person, I've lost everything. While you were inside the house dealing with Celeste's arrest, my phone was lighting up. A lot of people got picked up all over the country. A lot of colleagues, friends and allies – and their families – got locked up or killed."

He tried to hold his anger, but it dissipated. She had a point. He let out a long breath. "Okay."

Her face crumpled. "They arrested Brad as well."

"Your fiancé?" Jack stepped closer and hugged her. "Why? Where—"

"It doesn't matter!" Her voice was a little louder than she'd probably intended.

He backed away from the hug. "We'll get them back."

Her eyes were squeezed shut and her hands balled into fists. "It's not just family and friends, Jack. We've lost people as well. Matt Barker got shot dead trying to protect his sister. The south-east was hardest hit. We've lost good people there. They know we're not toeing the line, so they've targeted our loved ones."

"I know." Jack shrugged. "We can go back to Chicago if you—"

"No." She opened her eyes and her eyes locked onto his. "That's what they want."

"What do you mean?"

"If they wanted me, or you, they could have scooped us up. But doing that would only embolden more of us, right?"

He wasn't convinced. "Maybe."

"They want to twist our arms. For each of us that gives in there'll be one less voice speaking out and trying to recruit for our cause."

"I understand." Jack reached out and grabbed her hand. He gave it a squeeze then let go again. "I just wondered where you'd been."

"Catching up with an old friend. I needed to figure out how they tracked down all our supporters." She stopped in front of a café and opened the door. "After you."

Confused, he walked inside. The café was tiny, with only four small tables along the left side and a breakfast bar with eight stools. Only one table was occupied, by a man with his back to the door. Jack turned to Elena. She had a broad smile on her face, a strange contrast to her tears. Given the news she'd just shared, he couldn't understand why. She gestured toward the seated man. He turned around and saw a face he could nearly kiss.

"Jack! Mate!"

The hug was high impact. Jack and Simon Hickens wrapped their arms around each other and slapped each other's back hard. Though he hadn't seen the surly IT pro from Chelsea for over a year, it was like they'd never been separated. More importantly, if he was standing here then there was at least one person who hadn't been scooped up by FEMA. Simon had a habit of helping Jack out of binds, so it felt good to have him here.

"Sorry to hear about Celeste, mate." Hickens backed away and gestured them over to his table. "She's being held in Illinois by FEMA, but I can't get an exact location."

Jack didn't even ask how he knew. Knowing which state she was in didn't change much. "Doesn't matter, we can't get her out of a prison camp."

"No." Hickens shrugged then dug into his pocket. He placed a couple of small flip phones on the table. "Take these."

Jack sat and looked down at the phone, then something clicked into place in his mind. He looked back up at Hickens. "NSA?"

Hickens nodded. "They tracked all of your mates down. All of everyone's mates. Celeste included, given I'm sure you couldn't resist calling to kiss her goodnight."

Jack could kick himself. It was so obvious. While Guerrilla Radio might have been growing in influence, with that influence came an increase in membership, communication and activity. Like a spider's web, the further out from the center the network spread, the less it could be watched and protected by the core membership. FEMA, through the NSA, had taken advantage of that, scooping up the details of any known Guerrilla Radio member and the people important to them.

"The mass detentions were designed to shut Guerrilla Radio down." Jack shook his head, then turned to Elena. "Detain supporters, scare off the less committed."

"Then isolate and attack the core." Her features were grim. "In sum, stem the growth of the resistance."

"That's where these come in." Hickens smiled and pushed the phones toward them. "Think of that phone like the rubber that protects your giant cock when it's doing the dirty work. Most of the time, you're fine, but when you need it you'll be glad you've got it."

"This will hide us?" Jack raised an eyebrow.

Hickens shrugged. "They know who you are, but they won't be able to find you using electronic means if you're careful with these."

"Thanks." Jack hefted the phone. It was heavy and square. It felt like a trip back to the mid-'90s. "Vintage."

"Pre-PRISM, with a few of my personal modifications." Hickens shrugged. "They can't be tracked or listened in on. Don't let them out of your sight."

Jack stared. "Simon, I could kiss you."

"Nah, mate, but thanks." Simon winked. "Save it until we end these bastards."

Jack smiled. He was glad to have Hickens on board. More importantly, he now had an idea about what was happening, where Celeste was and how to fight back. His network of friends and allies was shrinking and he was fighting the government he'd worked so hard to protect, but it was a start. The hopelessness and desperation of an hour before had been replaced by a seething, angry determination. He was back among friends.

"We need to make a move." Jack pocketed the phone, his gaze shifting between Hickens and Elena. "They think they've won, that we'll just sit on our hands in fear."

"Most people will, mate. Don't kid yourself." Hickens shrugged. "You lock up someone's friends or spouse, they'll shut up well enough."

Jack slammed his fist down on the table. "There's enough shit going on around the country that people will act, if they're given the confidence and support they need."

Elena put a hand on his fist. "What're you up to?"

"I'm going to talk to some old friends." He smiled. "I'd love you to meet them. I'm taking charge of this shit. We're not just getting information out now."

Elena and Simon spoke in unison. "What then?"

"We're forming the goddamn resistance ourselves."

CHAPTER 12

Together we remain committed to staying the course against the threats that plague our country, whether the original terrorist threat or the new threat of those dissenting and taking actions against the common good. A number of internment camps have been established to house those suspected of such crimes, to remove this cancer from our society faster than our legal system can. These camps, and all other extraordinary measures, will remain in place for however long they are necessary and until the attacks and the dissent cease. As always, good and law-abiding citizens have nothing to fear.

President Morris and Administrator Hall

Joint statement

Mariposa pressed the button on the Xerox and waited as the yellow light ran across the gap. Once the light went out she lifted the lid and removed the document, as the machine whirred and spat out the copy. As she grabbed the pile of papers out of the hopper she wished again that her office had a faster machine, but it would have to do. She looked around, satisfied that the office was still empty.

This was the best material she'd been able to get her hands on yet – evidence showing that the orders for attacks on Guerrilla Radio members in the south-east had originated from this office, when Richard Hall had been in town. She'd copied documents showing the attackers had been given orders to kill any journalists not willing to identify the leadership of the organization. Along with the information about the attacks, she had information about the immunity granted to State Guard troopers charged with crimes. The charges ranged from petty theft and assault, right through to rape and a murder. None of the charges had proceeded, nor had there been any coverage in the media.

FEMA's involvement with the atrocities was a serious matter needing air and sunlight to disinfect. She had no idea how to get the information out, but she'd compiled a dossier large enough to sink FEMA – thousands of pages of classified documents. She'd figure out a way to get it out, but first she needed to get through the day. She stifled a yawn. The doubt that had clouded her thinking had dissipated. She'd also started to feel better about her role in the administration of the executive orders, the crackdowns and, if she had to admit it, the brutalities. She wasn't innocent, but she was doing her best to make amends. She smiled at the thought and hummed a tune as she walked to her office.

A squeal caught in her throat and she stopped dead in her tracks. Two men in suits were waiting for her. The larger and younger of the two was perched against her desk, staring at his cell phone. The older man, forty or so, simply stood with his arms crossed. She felt a flutter of fear, but forced it down. She wanted to run, but if she acted guilty she was doomed. She gripped the documents tightly.

"Who're you?" She raised her voice and mustered all the outrage she could bring to bear. "You've no right to be in this office unsupervised."

"Ms Esposito." The older man raised an eyebrow and ignored her bluster. "May I ask that you sit down?"

"You may not. I'm the supervisor in this office and I've got work to do. My staff will be here soon, including my secretary. You're welcome to make an appointment."

The younger man laughed, pushed himself off the desk and stepped forward inside her comfort zone. "We don't make appointments."

Mariposa felt a chill down her spine as the younger man's blue eyes stared at her from his expressionless face. He was apparently waiting for her to act. She felt trapped in her own office with a pair of large predators stalking her. Though she didn't know what they wanted, she could guess. The door was at her back and she could try to run, but doing so would only confirm everything they were here to accuse her of.

"Very well." She crossed her arms. "What can I do for you?"

"We need you to come with us." The older man shrugged. "Voluntarily."

"You're joking?" She stepped back. "I'm not going anywhere. Who are you?"

"Classified."

She took another step back and started to turn. She didn't get the chance. The older man lunged at her, grabbed an arm and held it tightly. She pulled her arm. "Let go!"

The younger man spoke. "This is your last chance, Ms Esposito. Voluntarily or in cuffs. Your decision."

"Go fuck yourself!" She screamed as loudly as she could as the older man grabbed her other arm. She struggled but failed to escape his tight grip. "*Help!*"

The younger man smiled. With her arms held she spat at him and did her best to kick out at him as he drew closer, but it was difficult in heels. He laughed as he pulled a hood from his jacket, dodged her blows and placed it over her head. She kept screaming as the blackness descended and breathing became harder. With each shout she sucked in a breath, but the hood prevented much air from entering her lungs. She needed to get it off her.

"Let me *go!*" She gritted her teeth against the pain. The hood was suffocating. Her heart pounded in her chest. "Let me *go!*"

"Stop struggling and you won't be hurt." The older man's voice was strained. "You need to recognize the situation and look after yourself here. Think about your son."

"Okay. Okay." She stopped struggling. "I'll come with you."

"Wasn't that easy? Give us the answers we need. You'll see your boy soon."

She nodded and did her best to breathe. She let them lead her out of the office, through the cubicle farm and out of the building. She hoped that one of her staff members would arrive and take issue with her abduction, but they'd probably thought of that. She was marched down steps, bundled into a car and driven for about fifteen minutes. As they drove, neither of her captors said a thing. It added to her worry. She tried her best to calm herself and concentrate on breathing.

Then the process reversed. Out of the car, into a building, onto a seat, hands cuffed in front of her. All the while she tried to quash her fears and prepare for the questions. Light pierced the darkness like a supernova as the hood was lifted off her head. She squeezed her eyes shut then blinked repeatedly, waiting for them to adjust to the brightness. When they did, she saw the older man seated across from her, hands steepled in front of him. There was a manila folder on the table.

"Please." Mariposa leaned forward. "There's been a huge mistake. I—"

He stopped her by holding up his hand, then tapped the folder in front of him with his index finger. "I don't care. I just need you to admit that you're responsible for the illegal copying of 11 734 hard copy and electronic documents belonging to the Federal Emergency Management Agency."

"I—"

He didn't let her interrupt. "Some of these documents are classified and have the potential to cause great harm and embarrassment to the organization. If they were made public, they'd severely endanger public confidence in the organization and our current mission to fight terrorism."

Mariposa was fucked. She could think of no way to stop them. She'd done her very best to trawl as much information as possible, but hadn't released a single page. If she had it might have gained her some public profile and protection. As it was, they knew what she'd done but nobody else did. She'd been careless. In her rush to stop the atrocities, she'd given little thought to the consequences or her own safety.

Somebody had clearly noticed and informed the authorities. She regretted now that she hadn't taken more precautions and also started the release. She'd wanted to have a complete dossier before taking that step, but maybe she'd delayed because she was afraid. Now she had a mountain of information that had been wasted. She was on her way to prison and the information would never be seen. She'd failed.

"I've nothing to hide." She started to sob and a tear rolled down her face. She was terrified, but all she could do was deny. "I want my lawyer."

The man smiled. A second later she heard a whoosh of air from behind her. She started to turn her head toward it when her vision exploded with stars. She screamed, fell forward off the chair and hit her head on the table and the ground on the way down. She instinctively grabbed at her head, but it was made difficult by the handcuffs. She heard laughter.

"You don't get a lawyer here."

Mariposa inhaled deeply, coughing as she tried to catch her breath. She crawled to her hands and knees then spat out the blood that was pooling in her mouth, leaving a metallic tang. She'd bitten her tongue on the way down. She ran her swollen, split tongue along the front of her teeth, probing. Several of the teeth on the left side were gone. But worse than the pain was the fear.

"Get up, Ms Esposito."

She spat again and shook her head, trying to clear the fog. She rolled onto her side. She had no chance of getting up while cuffed, but did her best. The guard who'd hit her in the head stepped into her view. It was the younger man, with a jet black baton held limp by his side. He'd hit her and also been at her to get up off the floor. She'd never been more afraid of someone in her life.

"Had your fill?" He hit the baton against his open palm several times. "Ready to admit what you've done and get on with it?"

She coughed and spat again. "Okay."

"This is your last chance. If you don't give us what we want I'll need to interrogate you." He lifted her from under her arms. "Do you understand?"

She nodded. "I think so."

He frowned. "You'd better, or social workers will take young Juan. If you cooperate we'll hose your blood down the drain and you'll be back with him tonight."

The mention of her son hit her harder than the baton had. She nodded. The game was up. She had to think about Juan now. The younger man helped her back to her seat with a tenderness that confused her, given the violence. After that, the questions came thick and fast. Mariposa answered each honestly. It took hours, but by the end of it they had everything.

"So you confirm that you copied the documents and built an enormous cache of classified material that you intended to release?" The older man slid a piece of paper and a pen toward her, hours later.

"Yes."

"Sign this declaration and we're done here, Ms Esposito. You'll be able to go home."

Mariposa picked up the pen and signed the document.

"We're done here." The older man stood.

She stared up at him, exhausted and terrified. "What now?"

"You'll be detained. I thank you for your honesty."

Mariposa flared with rage. "You promised I'd be able to go home to my son."

"I lied." He shrugged. "I appreciate the cooperation you've given us, but you need to get used to the idea that you're never going to see your son again. It's only because of your service to FEMA and your cooperation that you're making it out of this room at all. If you're free before you're ninety, you can consider yourself lucky."

She started to stand, but the younger man pressed the baton down on her shoulder. She kept trying to rise, but the pressure increased. The message was clear: give it up. She wanted more than anything to keep pushing, but she'd had enough. She sat back down in the seat and fought back sobs. The tears rushed out of her, a torrent of regret. Her moans became deep and long.

JACK LOOKED down the table and felt the memories come flooding back. Though the building was different and so was the boardroom, it was the first time he'd been around a corporate table in a long while. Sitting at its head, he felt both excited and exhausted at what was to come. Some of the most prominent figures on the east coast were in the room, all looking to him for answers. They were captains of industry, senior bureaucrats, emergency services chiefs and even a few military men and women. Half had been selected by Peter Weston, one of the few people in the world Jack felt he could still trust.

The rest had been chosen by Bill McGhinnist. The former Director of the FBI had been a casualty of Richard Hall's takeover, a lone voice of reason around the National Security Council table. Jack had reached out to him, they'd met, and discussed what he was planning to do. McGhinnist was dubious it would work, but was pleased to contribute. They'd worked together to end the threat of Michelle Dominique and the Foundation for a New America, only to find themselves back in another fight for America's future less than two years later.

Jack hoped that everyone in the room would form the nucleus of the organized resistance, if they could be persuaded to join. To get them all here without attracting the attention of FEMA had been an enormous challenge. If they were true to their word, there wasn't a cell phone or electronic device in the room, they'd all swapped modes of transport at least three times before making their way to the building and told none of their staff, family or friends about the meeting. The precautions weren't foolproof, but were the best that could be done at short notice.

Jack took a deep breath. He wasn't really sure how to start. It wasn't every day you asked people you barely knew to commit treason. "Thanks for coming in, everyone. You've all placed yourselves in incredible danger coming here."

"No shit. So why don't you get on with it, son?" Cormac Thomas was the gray-haired, ten gallon hat-wearing chief of the largest broker on Wall Street, about the only sector untouched by the executive order. He had been dragged here by Peter Weston.

"Okay, let's skip the niceties, then." Jack nodded. "You're all aware of the draconian regime we're currently living under. It started bad and it's getting worse, and you wouldn't be here unless you agreed that something needed to be done."

"You bet my granddaddy wouldn't have stood by while the government fucked everyone up the ass and told them to smile." Thomas pounded the table. "But I'm going to need some convincing before I put my nuts on the chopping block for you."

The comment drew a few smirks and nods, but Jack could still see a lot of skeptical faces at the table. A degree of concern about the situation and the influence of others had brought most of them here, but he knew that wasn't enough to keep them involved or to compel them to act. He'd made a career out of telling powerful stories. Now he had to do it again, to the most influential audience he'd ever had. He'd had precious little time to prepare, and it looked as if this group was going to need every last ounce of convincing. He hoped he was up to it.

"Look." He scratched his head. "Elena and I were involved with a group that was trying to get the word out, but it's been decimated. FEMA has rounded up the loved ones of just about every member and flat out killed a bunch of us.

"We tried our best, but FEMA is too entrenched and has too much power. Our only chance is to get active: smarter with how we communicate, stronger in the action we take to resist, faster in how we respond to attempts to shut us down."

Jane Fulton, head of public affairs at the New York Police Department, held up her hand. "You're asking us to risk our positions. Our lives. Our loved ones. Who are you to make such a demand of me? I've got kids."

Jack shrugged. "You're right, I'm no one. I'm not even American. But

I don't like what's happening, and I also don't think the President and legislature would either if they knew. *Really* knew."

"But if we just get the word out, we—"

Jack held up a hand. "No, sorry. Publicity isn't enough. Leaflets aren't enough. We need real influencers to start turning the tables. That's why you're all here. I need your help to get this country back."

Elena coughed. *"We* need your help."

Jack nodded. "The short of it is that there's a whole lot of shit that's gone on since FEMA's watch started. With your help, we'll find the evidence and get ready to act."

"Resist." Elena smiled.

Fulton leaned back in her chair with a shake of her head and her arms crossed. She clearly wasn't convinced. Jack didn't know where to go next, until Bill McGhinnist cleared his throat. The room fell silent as he locked his gaze on Fulton. She held it, then flicked a look nervously toward Jack, then looked down at her fingernails. Jack was aware of the molten fury that was about to spew from McGhinnist's core.

"Jack Emery has done more for this country than any person seated in this room." McGhinnist's voice was like rolling thunder. "Even though he's not a citizen, he took on the greatest threat we've seen since the collapse of the Twin Towers."

Fulton finally nodded. "I don't mean to cause any—"

McGhinnist smiled. "Good. Because Jack is asking you, asking us, for our help. He's asking us to join together to resist an authority that is stealing our basic freedoms and imprisoning innocent people. That is not the America I stand for. You might hide in your jobs or under your beds, but none of it is going away. Unless people of influence and power unite to fight this thing, the America we know will ebb away to nothing and we'll be picked off one by one."

Jack felt a tingle down his spine at McGhinnist's words. He held his arms out. "Bill has nailed it. If we don't stand up, despite the risk, then who will? If we cower, then the average Joe has no chance and no choice."

"Well I do." Fulton cut into the end of Jack's speech, causing everyone to stare at her. "I'm not going to risk everything in my life for a half-baked plan by a journalist playing hero one time too many. Sorry."

Jack's heart pounded as Fulton stood and moved towards the door. None of them had been forced to attend, and they were free to go. He sighed as a few of the others stood and followed her out without speaking. He should have expected it, really, but it was still hard to see so many people walk away from what he was trying to achieve.

"Fucking cowards." McGhinnist's voice was pure poison. "We're better without them."

"Okay, anyone else?" Jack looked at everyone left in turn. "To be clear, I don't want to do this. None of us does. I'm terrified and you should be too. But they've already locked up the one woman in America who I love. I've got nothing to lose."

"Okay, son." Thomas's guffaw cut through the tension in the room like a knife. "Want to get to the point?"

Jack laughed, feeling the pressure on his shoulders ease slightly. He'd hoped to convince some of them, to begin to form a nucleus, and it looked like he had. "I'm asking you all to risk your freedom, if not your life. Once you're in, there's no turning back. Who's in?"

His heart was pounding. He knew that to set up this sort of network across the entire country would be a massive effort. But if he couldn't achieve it in New York, where many of his most influential friends were, then it would be an impossible task. His heart nearly leaped from his chest when he saw nods up and down the table. He also received a few affirmations and more than a few pledges of support.

He looked over to Elena, who was taking notes on a pad. She looked up and gave him a warm smile. He knew she was still fragile following the arrest of her fiancé, the detention of her friends and the death of colleagues. He wondered where she found the energy reserves to keep going. It was inspiring. He hoped he could mirror her effort and, together, spoil FEMA's agenda and free their loved ones. Free Celeste.

He turned back to the others. "Okay. You all need to convince others. You all need to be ready to speak out and act strongly when the time is right."

"Fuckin' A." Thomas's voice boomed. "Try and stop me."

Jack smiled as cheers rang out down the table. Already they were discussing ideas, ways to resist and people to recruit. Jack looked over at Simon Hickens, nodded and then watched as Hickens stood and started to hand out cell phones up and down the table. Hickens explained the phones and what exactly was safe to do. Nobody seemed opposed to having technology the NSA couldn't hit.

Jack leaned forward. "Okay, first we build the network. Then, when we're ready, we act."

~

CALLUM WINCED as the horn from the yellow school bus gave a long blast. The sound reverberated through his skull and gave his already tortured brain hell. He held his shotgun in his left hand as he lifted his right and flipped the bird. That earned him another short honk and a grin from the bus driver, who obviously had no respect for camp guards with a hangover. The convoy kept rolling.

Callum shook his head as the buses drove inside the gates, like they had every hour for the past few days. It was incredible. The hastily engineered dirt and gravel road had been turned mostly to mud and a detail of detainees had to constantly cover the road with more gravel to stop the vehicles from getting bogged. FEMA hadn't thought of everything when constructing these camps, it seemed.

"Record number of buses today." Micah Hill scoffed as he walked up next to Callum, his eyes hidden behind Aviators and a toothpick protruding from his lips.

"It's crazy." Callum turned to face Hill. "How's the head after last night?"

"Fine, man." Hill smiled slightly and looked down at Callum. "Yours?"

"Fuck you."

Callum ignored Hill's deep laugh and turned back to the busses. A State Guard trooper positioned at the door of each bus held up a hand and, in unison, the doors on the yellow school buses squealed open. A police officer stepped off each bus, followed by a steady stream of fresh meat for the camp. Men and women, old and young, a broad mix of race and class – all in cuffs and looking terrified.

The process ran like clockwork. The human tide flowed from the buses and was forced into a straight line parallel to their bus. The doors closed, the buses drove off, the new detainees had instructions shouted at them and then were marched toward the camp one group at a time. The design of the fencing forced the groups to walk in single file, with cover provided by the escorts, guard towers and the few State Guard troops not assigned to a group, like Callum and Hill. The process ran smoothly for the first couple of groups, but as the numbers going through the gate grew, there were delays. It had been like this every day, a giant case of administrative constipation as the staff struggled to get all the new inmates inside and processed before the next lot arrived.

Callum frowned. "This group doesn't even have Guerrilla Radio sympathizers. Not entirely, anyway."

Hill shrugged. "Whatever, man. FEMA has its panties in a twist about all sorts of people. Why question it?"

Callum sighed as he watched a man the size of a line-backer push past two women who were chatting and waiting patiently for the line to advance. One of the women moved aside willingly, but the other turned around and fronted up to him. It was a comical sight, really, a thin red head blazing anger at a brick of a man who was a foot taller and covered with tattoos. He knew trouble when he saw it.

"Come on." Callum started to walk toward the disruption, which was barely thirty yards away. Hill followed.

The woman gave the large man a shove to the chest, but without the force required to move him. "Who the fuck do you think you are, asshole? You don't talk to her like that."

He laughed. "If they're going to let women inside with us, you'd better get used to a few unkind words. Or worse. I might protect you, if you keep me warm at night."

As Callum walked closer, the woman hissed and charged forward. Her hands were cuffed in front of her and she used them as a club to wail on the man's torso. He was cuffed behind, so couldn't strike back, but he didn't seem interested in that anyway. He laughed as she flailed madly – until she hit him in the balls. At that point he roared and threw a kick that put her on her rear, then slumped over in pain.

"Detainees! Enough!" Callum shouted as loudly as he could, just as the woman was regaining her feet. He raised the shotgun and pointed it at the man. "Micah, got the lady?"

"Sure do. Not sure about the lady bit, though."

Callum snorted and inched toward the man. He really was a beast, even with cuffs on and after a nut shot. He was a big dude with a shaved head and neck tattoos. "Take it easy."

"What the fuck do you want?" The man spat at Callum's feet. "I fought for this country, now they're locking me up on no charge."

"So did I." Callum was deadpan. "Here's what's going to happen. You'll take five steps back, slowly, with no sudden moves. You'll re-join the line. Behind the ladies."

"Fuck you." The man clearly didn't want to budge.

Callum pressed the shotgun into his chest. "Move."

The man snarled, but took one step backward, then another. He seemed less keen to tangle with a 12-gauge than a woman who'd weigh hardly anything soaking wet. When Callum had him back in the line, under the watchful eye of some other State Guard colleagues, he lowered the shotgun and left the giant with a smile and a wave. Only then did he turn to Hill, who had the woman quiet ten yards away.

"All good, Cal?" Hill asked, as Callum approached. "Can we let little miss back in the queue yet?"

"Why not?" Callum smiled, and turned to the woman. She had an impressive mop of red hair that had been messed up in the scuffle. "You okay?"

"No, I'm not okay." She was puffed and clearly still angry. "I don't understand why I'm being detained on no charge. Or why I was moved from the other camp."

"That's not my business. Your safety is. I'd advise you against trying to pick fights with men three times your size." Callum shrugged. "What was that all about?"

"He pushed past a dozen people, shoved me, shoved her over there." She gestured toward the other woman. "Then he called us both whores."

Callum sighed. "Okay. Cool down. And get back in the line."

She nodded and walked back to her position in the line. Callum doubted she'd be much more of a problem, she'd just been standing up for herself. Like the rest of them, she was here on no charge. He admired her spunk and doubted he'd be willing to go toe to toe with the guy like she had. As she re-joined the line, he exhaled slowly and held the shotgun casually by his side.

"That sure was fun." Hill laughed. "I thought you'd have to shoot the dickhead."

"Me too. Not sure one shell would have done the job."

"Yeah." Hill laughed and then flicked his chin toward the female detainees. "She's alright, isn't she? Her friend is too. Looks like she's been roughed up a bit. Might be fun."

Callum frowned but said nothing.

CHAPTER 13

FEMA Administrator Richard Hall today announced the first relaxation of the emergency measures since their enactment nearly six months ago. Speaking to the assembled media, Administrator Hall thanked Americans for their patience and for their forbearance, and noted that gatherings larger than six would now be permitted, with the new cap on non-family gatherings set at ten. He cited this as a sign of progress in returning the country to normal.

Federal Emergency Management Agency
News Release

Mariposa closed her eyes and raised her face to the showerhead. The near scalding water felt amazing as it ran over her skin, still black and blue from the beating she'd taken at the hands of her interrogators. It took her mind off her situation and off her son, just for a moment. She was finding it hard to adjust to being away from Juan. She tried not to think about him too much because it just made her cry, but the idea of him living with some random family organized by a social worker terrified her. She reached up and wiped away a tear, then gave a hollow laugh when she realized the water would take care of it. She was tired, both physically and mentally.

After a few minutes of just standing there, letting the water soak over her, she looked to her left. Celeste was looking straight at her, concern in her eyes. She'd been Mariposa's saving grace since helping her in the line outside the camp gates. She'd stood up for the both of them when the tattooed giant had tried to push in. Mariposa would have let him past, but Celeste had confronted him and the guards had intervened. Mariposa wasn't sure why she had, but she was thankful. Since then, they'd become fast friends. They'd shared meals and gossip as they tried to cling to some amount of normalcy. She smiled at the other woman.

"How're you holding up?" Celeste reached out and touched her on the shoulder gently, the concern clear in her eyes. "You were a million miles away."

"I just miss my son." Mariposa gave a sad smile, feeling self-conscious. She wasn't the only person missing loved ones. "You worry too much. You know that?"

The concern in Celeste's eyes was replaced by a frown. "Sorry. Force of habit when I'm locked up. It's happened all too often lately."

Mariposa started to say something, then stopped, as a dark look crossed the other woman's face. The previous night Celeste had shared a fraction of her Chinese prison experience, speaking until she'd ended up in tears. She'd explained that this was a cakewalk in comparison, but it also showed why she was so determined to stand up for herself and for others. She'd no right to ask Celeste to dwell on it further.

"Let's get dressed and get something to eat." Mariposa jerked her head towards the benches outside the shower.

Celeste nodded and they both stepped out from under the water. They walked over to their towels and bright orange clothing. Mariposa had just slipped on her underwear when there was a series of fast taps against the tiles. She looked at the door, where a large, black guard was standing in the way. He was smiling like a hyena as he watched the women, his baton beating softly against the wall to draw their attention.

"Detainees!" His smile was replaced by a frown. "Out!"

Mariposa felt a tinge of fear. He was one of the guards who'd intervened to help in the line outside the camp. But her gratitude toward him had been misplaced and the other women had warned her about Micah Hill. They'd warned everyone about him. He liked to catch an eyeful in the shower block. Harmless, apparently, unless you spoke back to him. They'd told her that it was best to just keep your eyes down and ignore it.

She suppressed her revulsion as best she could as she pulled her towel up to cover herself. She looked over at Celeste, who already had her bright orange pants on and made no attempt to cover up, despite wearing nothing else but a bra. Mariposa jerked her head toward the door and they joined the other women in various states of undress shuffling out of the shower room. The guard inspected each of them as they passed.

Mariposa was near the exit when the guard held out his nightstick, blocking the path. She stopped in her tracks and the guard gestured to the wall. His intent was clear. Mariposa dropped her head and stepped to the side. Once she was against the wall the guard dropped his arm and the exit was clear again. Mariposa looked up. Celeste was standing there, free to exit but as still as if she was cemented to the floor.

"Go, Celeste." Her voice cracked as she spoke. "I don't want you in trouble. It'll be okay. I'm sure."

Celeste shook her head and stayed rooted in place, with her fists balled at her side. Mariposa was ashamed that, again, she was unable to help as Celeste protected her. She watched, standing helpless against the wall, as the guard took a step forward with his palm facing outward and the baton raised to strike. Celeste gave ground, backed away and found herself against the wall alongside Mariposa.

"You an idiot?" The guard's voice was laced with menace. "You nearly got your skull caved in the other day and now I'm noticing you again. I don't like noticing people."

"Let us walk out of here then." Celeste's voice started to waiver. "I'm not after any trouble. *We're* not after any trouble. I'm sure you've got better things to do than harass us."

"Oh, you'd be surprised." He patted the baton against his hand hard enough to produce a clapping sound. He took a few steps straight at Mariposa.

She sunk against the wall as the man reached out to touch her face. His hand brushed against her cheek and kept moving upward to her hair. She wanted to fight back, to be worthy of Celeste's defense of her, but she was frozen with fear. If anything happened to her, if she resisted, she'd be in here longer and there would be far less chance of getting Juan out of state care. She had to take what was coming.

She shrieked as he gripped her hair and pulled her up harshly. She reached up for his hand and screamed again as her towel fell away. "Let me go!"

"I knew I liked you." He reached out with the nightstick and pressed it firmly into her exposed breast. "We're going to have some fun."

Mariposa tried to ease the pain, reaching her tiptoes, but the more she compensated the higher he pulled her. It was excruciating. She clawed at his hands but it was no good. She closed her eyes and cleared her thoughts of everything but Juan. If she complied, it would be over sooner. He kept hold of her hair as he separated her legs roughly and reached up inside of her. She winced at the pain but kept her mouth shut, squeezing her eyes tightly.

She felt his breath against her neck. His mouth was an inch from her ear. "I knew you'd be up for it, once you gave me a chance."

A whisper escaped her lips. "Please don't."

"This is *not* going to happen here, you fuck!" Celeste voice was shrill as she jumped on the guard's back.

Mariposa cried out in pain as the guard fell to the tiles, yanking her hair on the way down. As she hit the ground beside him, she struck his hands as hard as she could with her fists, trying to break his grip. It was no good. After that, she did her best to push the guard away. She kept her left palm over his face while punching out at every part of him with her right hand. It was pointless. He was twice her size and as strong as an ox.

At some point in the rolling melee he let go, distancing himself from Mariposa and Celeste, who'd been wailing on him from behind. He scampered away on the tiles then stood up, panting and heaving. His hat was on the tiles and he was glistening with sweat. His eyes were menacing and his mouth twisted with rage as he reached down for the nightstick. Celeste was already standing as Mariposa struggled to her feet.

"Stay away from us!" Mariposa didn't recognize her own voice, hoarse and guttural. "Leave us alone."

"You can lock us up, but you can't rape us, you fucking asshole." Celeste was panting, her sweat-soaked red hair matted over her face.

Mariposa did her best to stay brave as he advanced on her again. Celeste stepped between them. Her fists were at her side but her knuckles were white. The guard smiled darkly. Blood covered his teeth, the legacy of some blow or another. He advanced further and raised the baton. Celeste gave an ear-curdling scream as the baton connected with the side of her knee. She crumpled to the wet tiles.

As if snapped out of her paralysis, Mariposa shuffled forward to help, her heart torn in half as the younger woman shrieked in pain and held her knee. Mariposa placed a hand on her head and stroked her hair.

She looked up at the guard, waiting for him to strike her. The blow didn't come. Whichever emotion had driven him to rape and violence was apparently satiated for now. He took a step back.

"Cock teases, the fucking lot of you." He shook his head and then spat at them, the fury draining from his eyes. "You're both in here for a long time. Your life just got harder."

As the guard turned away, Mariposa cradled Celeste's head in her lap and watched as blood, tears and the guard's spittle mixed with the water on the tiles.

~

JACK HELD his arms out as the Secret Service agent ran a metal detecting wand along his arms, down his torso and his legs. Though the device made an occasional squealing noise, none were apparently large enough to cause any concern. The metal detector completed the trifecta after they'd patted him down and scanned him for bomb residue. He was glad he'd left his Swiss army knife at home.

The agent stepped back and gestured Jack forward. "Follow me, sir. Please stay close and display your tag at all times."

Jack felt for his temporary security pass, hanging by a lanyard around his neck, and did his best not to be overawed by the West Wing of the White House. While he walked, he reflected on the events that had carried him here. He'd thought he was done with all of this, the politics, the intrigue, the danger. He wanted nothing more than to opt out and wait for it all to blow over, but he had too much skin in the game to do that now.

He'd made a start on leading the resistance: the first cells had been established, resourced and equipped. Hickens had come through with the technology, Cormac Thomas had come through with the dollars, McGhinnist had helped Jack to configure the ever expanding operation in a way that was less likely to be exposed, and everyone had helped with contacts, friends and influencers in government, media, law enforcement, the military – anyone fed up with things. Elena had been the star. She was recruiting all over the place.

The Secret Service stopped and held out his hand towards a sofa. "We're here."

Jack nodded. "Okay, thanks. What now?"

The agent smiled. "You sit just over there until the President is ready to see you, then you say 'Hello, Madam President' and go from there."

Jack took a seat and settled in. He knew that it could be a while, and thought again that he shouldn't even be here. The others had advised against it, but he had to try. He had the celebrity and the credits in the bank to get an audience with a grateful President. He had to know if the belief in what FEMA was doing went all the way to the top. He owed it to everyone he was asking to risk their life to try the direct route. Before he flicked the switch on open rebellion, he needed to be sure that the takeover couldn't be reversed by negotiation between reasonable people. It was a risk, but one he needed to take. He gently drummed his knuckles on the armrest of the sofa, until the President's secretary approached and invited him inside the Oval Office.

"Mr Emery." President Helen Morris stood and rounded her desk to greet him just inside the door. She held out her hand. "It's a pleasure."

Jack shook her hand. "Thanks for meeting with me, Madam President."

"Come and sit." She smiled as they walked over to the couches.

Jack was a little surprised by the warm reception. "Thanks."

She sat opposite him, leaned forward and rested her elbows on her knees. "Now, what can I do for you? I was surprised to see you in my diary."

Even though she'd largely been sidelined by FEMA, Morris was still the President. He needed to make each word count, because he wasn't likely to get many. "Madam President, I've come here to implore you to revoke the executive order granting FEMA extensive control over the country. The consequences have been enormous."

Morris considered him for a few moments. "Mr Emery, while I respect your impressive career and the help you've provided this country, I disagree."

"But—"

Morris held up a hand, frowning. "We've taken the actions necessary to safeguard the country and the measures are working, more or less."

Jack shook his head. Though he'd considered the chances of changing Morris's mind to be remote, he'd been entirely unprepared for the strength of her convictions. She seemed confident in the decisions she'd taken and that the response was proportional to the threat. It defied belief. She apparently had no problem with the abuses taking place. Or she didn't know about them. The leadership of the country had been bubble wrapped by FEMA.

"Madam President. You need to get outside the Oval Office more often. Your country is burning around you."

Morris laughed softly. Her continued smile didn't hide the frostiness in her eyes. "Don't mistake me welcoming you here as an invitation to flippancy, Mr Emery. Let me be clear. Administrator Hall has my complete support. Your past service was exceptional, indeed, exemplary, but you don't know what you're talking about."

Jack nodded, even though he didn't agree. The conversation was over. He stood. "Madam President, thank you for your time."

She nodded, but stayed seated. "I hope you'll think carefully about your next move. America needs patriots, not more loose cannons."

Jack nodded and turned to leave the office. He'd tried staying out of the situation, then been dragged in. He'd tried resisting with information, and his friends had suffered. He'd tried to directly question those in power, then been threatened. Deep down, he knew there was only one course of action left open to him, one he was prepared for but loath to commence. He saw no other way.

It was time to go to war.

～

"I see. Thanks for letting me know." Richard frowned, trying to process the information being fed down the phone line. Then he made a decision. "Pick him up. I want a chat."

He hung up and tossed his cell phone onto the desk, where it found a place among the mountains of paperwork. He leaned back in his chair and looked up at the ceiling. The call had been from his mole in the Secret Service, who'd escorted journalist Jack Emery through the West Wing to meet with the President. His man couldn't tell him what they'd discussed, only that the meeting had been brief. While Richard doubted anything Emery could say would impact too heavily upon his efforts, to have another bird chirping in Morris's ear was not something he needed. When that particular bird was Jack Emery, it was all the worse.

Emery's successes in exposing the corruption in Washington by Michelle Dominique and the Foundation for a New America were legend. Dominique had been an egotistical sociopath who'd caused havoc throughout the world in an attempt to control the political agenda in the United States and stack Congress. She'd also been an idiot, trying to influence events from outside of halls of power, thrashing madly to control those inside and trying to join them as equals. It had brought her unstuck. Richard knew that true power, true influence, was wielded from the inside. Anonymous. Sudden. Final. He'd been glad to see her go.

Jack Emery wasn't his enemy, or shouldn't be. He should be a natural ally in bringing peace and stability to America, yet somehow he doubted Emery had met with the President to express faith in the administration. With Emery circling, there was no telling what was coming next. On top of that, there were rumors that a more organized resistance was being established, which made him furious. He'd wanted the dismantling of the journalist network to be the end of it, but they clearly couldn't take a hint. It was possible that a new, more dangerous beast could rise from the ashes of Guerrilla Radio like a phoenix. He was going to have a chat with Jack Emery.

He let out a long sigh and was about to start back on his pile of paperwork when the phone rang again. He answered. "Hello?"

"Good morning, Administrator, this is Ashley Madigan at the Effingham Detention Center. We've had an incident with Mariposa Esposito. You asked to be notified in such a case."

"Yes." Richard closed his eyes. "What is it?"

There was a pause on the other end. "She was assaulted by one of our guards. Another detainee was hospitalized."

"I see." He reached for a file and flicked through it. It had Mariposa's photo clipped to a series of copied pages. "Tell me what happened."

As the news filled his ear, he only partially listened. With the rest of his attention he flicked through Mariposa's file, trying to answer a question that had plagued his mind for several days. Though she'd betrayed him badly and been detained, she was still one of his people. Where possible, he looked after staff at FEMA. They were his foot soldiers in the war to achieve stability. That's why he'd been so hurt by her betrayal. The young woman he'd entrusted with FEMA's Area V command had copied classified documents with the intention of leaking them. She'd been interrogated, out of necessity, but he hoped that she could be rehabilitated once the crisis was over.

He searched through the file, his eyes scanning the pages. He wanted badly to find a reason to let her out of detention, but her crimes were serious. If she was smart, she'd keep her head down and stay out of trouble, despite the issue with the guards. But he was concerned by her apparent lack of remorse. He could free her, under the right circumstances, but he wasn't able to abide the risk of her spreading more information, telling more secrets, riling up more dissent. There was no telling what she still knew, gleaned from her time spent in his inner sanctum. If she was to ever see the light of day, she had to repent and he had to be convinced that it was safe to release her.

He was about to close the file, his decision deferred for now, when his eyes grew wider. He stared at the sheet for several moments, the voice in his ear becoming so much noise as his mind worked frantically to understand the ramifications. He cursed himself for not looking more closely earlier. Richard pounded the table with his fist. "*Fuck!*"

"Excuse me, Administrator?"

He was surprised that the woman was still on the phone. He ignored her, enraged that he hadn't put two and two together. For someone in such immense command of his organization, his people and most of America, he'd missed a critical detail. Mariposa Esposito had documents linking FEMA to supplies that had been provided to One and her team. It had all occurred through back channels, of course, but with enough analysis the documents could be used to prove his link to One. A list of documents she'd copied – many damning – had been inside the folder on his desk for days. But he'd delayed looking at it, wanting to find a way to free her. He'd been careless.

"I want her dealt with." He pressed the button to terminate the call.

He hadn't wanted to keep her detained, but by trying to find a way to free her he'd exposed himself. No more. She'd be dead within twenty-four hours.

CHAPTER 14

As arrests continue across the country and the first of the detainees start to face justice, FEMA can announce the resumption of some private internet service to approved families. Households with no criminal convictions and with no web history of searching for prohibited topics will be provided with a login to the FEMA administered gateway, which allows access to a large number of websites.

Federal Emergency Management Agency

News Release

J ack felt his stomach rise to somewhere near his throat as the helicopter started to descend. He mumbled a curse under his breath and gripped the overhead rail so tightly that his knuckles went white. It was irrational, given he was seated and strapped in, but the last time he'd been aboard a helicopter he'd thought safe it had crashed into the South China Sea. His heart was pounding when the helicopter touched down with a light bump. He waited. When there was no hint of fiery explosion, he opened his eyes. He realized he'd been holding his breath and exhaled slowly. It had taken a lot of convincing and coercion to get him aboard. He'd never make the mistake again. He was done with helicopters.

"Mr Emery? You can let go of the rail now, sir. We don't want you to damage it." The pilot's mocking in Jack's headset was made worse by his southern drawl. "We're here."

Jack looked up. The pilot and co-pilot both had their necks craned to watch him, doing their best to conceal their smiles. He gave them a thumbs-up and removed the headset as one of the ground staff slid the door open and gestured for him to exit. He unbuckled and climbed out, keeping his head ducked low as he walked to the waiting convoy of vehicles. Or golf carts, anyway.

He approached a crowd of men and women surrounding one older man, who appeared to be sipping iced tea. This man was the whole reason he'd ventured onto the helicopter – despite his better judgment – and agreed to be flown right to the tee of the third hole at the East Potomac Golf Course. He was hardly able to refuse the invitation of FEMA in the current climate.

After his meeting with the President he'd checked in to a Washington hotel, given it had been too late to fly. He'd slept soundly and woken early, only to find Hall's people waiting for him the minute he reached the lobby. They'd obviously known about his meeting with the President. They'd asked him to join them for a helicopter flight to meet with Richard Hall. He'd hardly had a choice.

As he reached Hall and his entourage, he lifted a hand in a lazy greeting. "Good morning for it."

Richard Hall took one last sip of his iced tea, handed the glass to an assistant then pushed himself off the golf cart he'd been leaning on. "Good to meet you, Jack."

"Likewise." Jack kept his expression neutral, but was unable to resist the chance for a jab. "Didn't think a man of your stature would have to work so hard to make friends, though."

Hall's lips thinned in what Jack gathered was a smile. "You've become a person of interest. I wanted to meet before you disappeared down your hole again."

Jack doubted Hall would have any trouble finding him down any hole and suspected the timing of their meeting had been calculated for maximum impact. Though Hall might know he'd been involved in Guerrilla Radio and that he'd met with the President, Jack felt for sure that Hall was trying to work him out and intimidate him. Jack nearly laughed at the thought. Hall may have a lot of power, but he was an elderly career bureaucrat. He was hardly tough as nails.

Hall reached out and placed a hand on Jack's back, directing him gently toward the tee. "Walk with me, Jack. I need to have a discussion with you."

"Okay."

"I need you to understand the bind I'm in." Hall looked pained as he reached the tee. "Against every fiber of my being, I've given you a degree of special treatment already."

"You have?"

"Yes, I have." Hall sighed and selected a driver from the bag of clubs that was waiting next to the tee. "What's your handicap, Jack?"

"My swing." Jack gave a small laugh. "I'm not much of a golfer, Administrator. I tend to whack and pray."

Hall smiled, a twinkle in his eye. "I respect a man who appreciates his own limitations enough to make light of them."

Jack watched as Hall reached down and placed the ball on the tee then stood up straight. He seemed transfixed on the ball. He lined his shot up, drew the club back high and gave it his full swing. It was an exceptional shot. Hall held the club still as he watched the ball sail straight and true down the fairway. Jack doubted he could do better in a hundred tries. Hell, even a thousand tries.

"As I mentioned, I've given you a degree of special favor already." Hall turned back to him, his face a picture of seriousness. "My bind, Jack, is that I know your agenda."

Jack showed no emotion, though he did inch closer towards the golf bag. If this was an ambush it might help to have some iron in his hands. "I have no agenda, Administrator."

Hall sighed. "Can we be honest? I know of your involvement in Guerrilla Radio. I know you were helping to stir up events in Indianapolis. I know you met with the President. I also know you're not the kind of man to be easily dissuaded, but I need to try anyway. I owe you that much, out of respect for your achievements."

Jack's eyes narrowed, as his mind struggled to find Hall's angle. Then, it hit him like a brick. He nearly laughed. "My achievement against the Foundation? That was a long time ago. And you'd be surprised by the number of times I heard that right before people tell me something I don't want to hear."

"I'd like to hear your side of it first." Hall placed his club back in the bag and faced Jack front on. "Then I'll give you mine."

Jack shrugged. He had nothing to lose. "Look, cards on the table, I don't agree with the executive orders and I have huge concerns about what you and FEMA are doing. It stinks."

Hall frowned. "You seem to deny me the respect I'm affording you. I think I'm being incredibly reasonable here, Jack. The President has made a number of decisions in the interests of protecting the country and I'm responsible for implementing those decisions. I'm doing my job. Surely you can respect that."

"You've got a job to do, sure." Jack wasn't buying the tortured bureaucrat act. Hall knew what he was doing and the impact of his actions. Jack chose his words carefully, being sure not to mention Celeste. "But the same justification has been used by tyrants for centuries. I'm struggling to see the difference."

"Sorry, I—"

Jack held up his hand, feeling the anger well up inside of him. "I was in Indianapolis. You've locked innocent people up. You've killed civilians. You may have a job to do, but I don't think I like where things are heading or where it all ends. So forgive me if I don't buy the shit you're selling, Administrator."

Hall's eyes narrowed, his face flushed red and his mouth opened and closed a few times, in a way that reminded Jack of a floundering fish. Jack wondered if he'd pushed the administrator too far. He'd definitely lost his cool, if nothing else. He wondered if he'd soon be joining Celeste in one of the camps. He took another step closer to the golf bag, now just a few feet away. A nine-iron might just hit the smug off Hall.

Finally, Hall began to speak. "Very well. I was hoping I'd be able to convince you to keep your head down while the trouble passes, but you've made your position clear. I won't waste your time or my breath. You're a hero, Jack, and I regret that it's come to this, but your special treatment is at an end. You've been warned."

"I understand." Jack's voice was barely a whisper and he was surprised by the menace in his voice.

Hall gave a short, sharp laugh. "I don't think you do. The next time you slip up, the next time you pop up on my radar, your precious Celeste will begin to feel pain."

Jack flared. He took a single, final step towards the golf bag and grabbed a club. He flicked it up into his hand and held it, with both hands, ready to strike Hall. "Do not threaten her!"

Jack heard a commotion and shouts from behind him, but he kept his eyes locked on the administrator. Hall, surprisingly, didn't move. He stared at Jack as he might a stray cat that had strolled into his yard. Jack gripped the club tighter, wanting to swing it and cave in Hall's head, decapitating FEMA at the same time. But he knew that doing so would sign Celeste's death warrant.

"Freeze!" A voice behind Jack shouted with authority. "Drop the club or we shoot."

Jack flicked a glance behind him. Several suited men were pointing pistols at him. Every fiber in his being wanted to take the shot, to swing the thing at Hall's head, to end this.

Hall coughed. "Done? If you were going to swing that thing, you'd have done it by now."

Jack closed his eyes as his grip on the club slackened. He knew that the only way forward was organized resistance. He lowered the club and tossed it on the ground. "Fuck you."

Hall gave the same laugh. "I don't want to hurt you, Jack, or your girlfriend. As I said, I respect you. You achieved a great deal for our country. My reaction will be directly proportional to your action. There's no simpler way for me to say it and you'll need to decide what comes next."

Jack seethed. "I'd like to go back now."

Hall's features lightened and he cracked a smile. "Sure you wouldn't like to join us for a game? The sixth is a killer."

Jack balled his fists by his side. "I'd like to go back."

Hall shrugged. "Okay, it was nice to meet you and I hope that you'll consider my words. My helicopter will take you back."

Hall picked up the club Jack had tossed and replaced it in the bag. Without looking at Jack, he turned and started off down the fairway. Jack fumed, fists clenched, for several long moments as the other man walked away. He tried to calm down, but was struggling. He'd expected Hall to be a tyrant, a maniac. He'd expected threats of violence and bribes to get Jack to stop doing what he was doing.

Instead, Jack had met a normal man, a bureaucrat who believed in what he was doing and would squeeze Jack – and Celeste – as hard as needed to get the desired result. To Hall, this wasn't personal. It was just another problem faced by a man who was used to dealing with them. His position was crystal clear: back off, or Celeste will start to become mightily uncomfortable in FEMA custody.

Jack was more committed than ever to ending him.

～

CALLUM CLOSED his eyes for the first time in sixteen hours. It wasn't quite as good as having his head on a pillow, but a comfortable chair and his feet on the desk was the best he could manage for the moment. He was on duty for another half-hour and for once there was nothing happening that required his attention. He hoped his luck would hold. He'd been on desk duty for the past few days, as part of a rotating shift involving all of the guards. Everyone took a turn on the towers, in the yard and in the administration. The latter was the most boring slot on the duty roster. It also had the longest shifts.

He hated himself for thinking it, but he wondered whether it would be a better idea to return to active duty. He hated the politics of the camp: management to guard, guard to guard, guard to prisoner, prisoner to prisoner. With the politics came the issues: maintenance, overcrowding, complaints. The thought of being back in a unit of soldiers, all working toward the same goal, suddenly seemed very appealing, if not for the carnage and violence it risked. He couldn't deal with that. Not yet.

There was a soft knock on the door. His eyes shot open and he nearly fell off the chair, but he managed to grab the desk before he made a fool of himself. "Come in."

The door opened and one of the few civilian staff in the detention center entered. Callum couldn't remember her name, but she flashed him a shy smile. "Hi, sorry to bother you."

"No problem." He waved her inside. She walked towards his desk and placed a single sheet of paper on it. He looked at it, then up at her. "What's that? Can't wait until next shift?"

"I don't think so, Sergeant. It's a, um—"

"It's okay." He smiled at her and held up a hand. "I'll take a look."

Relief spread like a rash across her face. Whatever the document was, it was something she was uncomfortable with. She nodded and backed toward the door. He shook his head, amazed that they'd recruited such a wilting flower to work in a place like this. He glanced at the sheet of paper, hoping he'd be able to palm it off on the next person to warm the chair, then sighed. It had the FEMA and State Guard logos side by side at the top. That made it important. He removed his feet from the desk and started to read the document.

He had to read it through four times before he processed and believed what was on the piece of paper. It was astonishing, to the point where he suspected fraud or some sort of practical joke. Except that this was no laughing matter. He flipped through the papers on his desk until he found a post-it with the number he was looking for. He picked up the phone, but paused before dialing. He looked once more at the newly arrived sheet of paper then dialed with a shake of his head.

The call was picked up quickly. "Operations, Nancy speaking."

"Hi Nancy, it's Callum Watkins out at Effingham."

"Hi Callum, how can I help?"

Callum leaned in to look at the sheet. "Can you confirm that correspondence Alpha-Hotel-Four-One-Five is legitimate?"

"Just give me a minute." He heard the sound of fast typing in the background. "Looks like it's legit. It has all the requisite approvals."

Callum's eyes widened as she spoke. "Okay. Thanks."

He hung up the phone and stared at the sheet for a few long moments. A detainee was to be executed for treason. The order was clear. Now it was confirmed as well. There was nothing else to do but act. He climbed to his feet and grabbed his shotgun from the rack on the wall. He checked the load and made sure the safety was on. If he was to detain a woman for execution, it meant separation from the other detainees. It could mean trouble.

He'd nearly reached the door when Micah Hill appeared on the other side. Callum winced, then regretted it – the other man had seen. He'd tried to avoid Micah since the incident in the shower block with the female detainees. Callum would prefer not to be associated with Hill's lack of professionalism and borderline criminal behavior, if he could, but they worked so closely together that it was hard to avoid the other man entirely.

Callum forced a smile. "How's it going, Micah?"

The other man ignored his greeting and glanced down at the shotgun. "Where you going, Cal? Your shift doesn't end for another twenty minutes."

Callum bit his tongue. He had to be careful. Despite his issues, Hill was still a superior. Callum waved the paper. "Orders."

"Oh yeah?" Hill reached out and grabbed the piece of paper.

Callum didn't resist or speak up as the other man read it. His eyes flicked back and forth rapidly, as a grin grew slowly on his face. When he finished reading, he resembled a wolf that had just been handed the key to the chicken coop. "You've checked it out? It's legit? Damn."

"Yep." Callum shrugged. "It checks out."

"Well I guess that little bitch is going to get what's coming to her." The grin turned cold. "I'll take care of this one, Cal. You take it easy."

"But—"

"Don't worry about it." Hill's tone was sharp. "You take the next one."

Even though Callum doubted there would be a next one, and the other man made his skin crawl, he could hardly resist the order. In truth, Callum was glad to avoid the job. He needed, and wanted, to keep his hands clean – that was the deal with Bainbridge. If Callum could hand this over to someone else, he had to take the chance. Hill would handle the prep for the execution. If he fucked up, it was on him.

He nodded. "Okay."

"Later, man." Hill turned and stalked after his prey.

Callum shook his head as he closed the door. He placed the shotgun back on its rack and then walked back to the desk. Before he closed his eyes, he glanced at the clock. Another thirteen minutes and he was in the clear. He did all he could to avoid thinking about the unfortunate woman, whatever her crime. But no matter how hard he thought about other things, the order haunted him.

And she would haunt his dreams.

MARIPOSA WINCED as she watched Celeste struggle to shift her position in the bed slightly. Though she offered a brave smile, the woman was clearly in a lot of pain. It was hardly surprising. The guard's nightstick had shattered her kneecap and she'd also done some damage to the ligaments in the knee when she'd fallen. It was a combination of injuries that would take a while to heal.

Mariposa looked around. There was only one other patient in the small detention center hospital. She'd heard that the guards were quite hesitant to permit a trip to the hospital for most people, but they could hardly argue a shattered kneecap. It was more surprising that she'd been allowed to keep Celeste company, though. They'd spent the time chatting, getting to know each other more.

"Can I get you anything?"

"A frozen Margarita?" Celeste's smile was contagious.

"No, unfortunately." Mariposa laughed softly. "But I could get you—"

"Seriously, I'm fine." Celeste reached out and gripped Mariposa's hand. "Stop worrying. I'm just glad I've got someone to talk to."

Mariposa felt her face flush. She felt like she owed Celeste so much. Twice now she'd saved her, this time at great personal cost. "Do you have a boyfriend?"

"No." Celeste gave a tired looking frown. "Well, maybe. I don't know. It's complicated. Absurdly so."

"What do you mean?"

"It's a really long story." She shook her head in near disbelief. "I hadn't seen him for a long time, then our first night together was the night I was arrested."

Mariposa didn't know what to say. "What happens if you get out of here?"

"I don't know. Hopefully a hug and a smile. But I'm not sure. This is the second time we've spent a lot of time apart in less than eighteen months. It might be too late."

Mariposa nodded and Celeste went quiet. They sat in silence until she noticed Celeste blinking a few times, as if trying to ward off sleep. Mariposa reached out and gave her hand a squeeze. As if she'd pressed a button, Celeste's eyes closed and before long she'd started to breathe heavily. Mariposa could have left, but she kept holding the other woman's hand.

Mariposa woke when she heard a noise behind her, shocked by the noise as much as the by the fact she'd fallen asleep. She turned around and felt her heart jump into her throat as she saw him – the black man who'd assaulted them in the bathroom. There was no doubt who he was here for. Mariposa let go of Celeste's hand and held her hands up slightly, showing him she was no threat.

He approached the bed, shotgun held casually. "On your feet."

Mariposa kept her voice to a whisper. "Please be quiet. She's only just gone to sleep."

"Detainee, on your feet. I've got orders to take you to a different wing."

"What wing? My friend—"

"I'm not asking." He yanked her back, away from the bed.

She squealed but didn't resist. She'd had her fill of fighting authority, it had done nothing but lead her here. She was going to be assaulted by the man, but she couldn't ask Celeste for help this time, even if the other woman was capable of providing it. She would fight, for all that she was worth, but she'd do it away from Celeste Adams.

"Please let me say a few words?" Mariposa looked him straight in the eyes. "Then I'll come with you."

"You better." His eyes narrowed and something in his voice seemed very final as he backed away. "You've got two minutes."

Mariposa nodded and walked over to Celeste. She wasn't thinking clearly, but she didn't have time to fix that. She shook the woman's arm. Celeste stirred and mumbled something. Mariposa shook her some more, and Celeste's eyes flickered open. She looked up at Mariposa, confused. Celeste winced in pain as she tried to move.

"What's up?" Celeste blinked a few more times. "I just need to sleep, Mari."

"I know." Mariposa smiled sadly as she squeezed Celeste's hand. "I have to talk to you."

"Okay." Celeste's eyes started to close again.

Mariposa pinched Celeste's chin and shook her head slightly. "Celeste, you need to stay awake. Just a few more minutes."

"Okay."

"If you ever get out of here and something has happened to me, I want you to go to my home. Just look it up."

"Okay. I'll say hi to your son."

"Good." Mariposa smiled sadly. "There's a spare key under the ceramic cat out the back. I want you to go inside and find my mother."

Celeste fell silent and started to snore softly again. Mariposa cursed under her breath and tried to shake her. She was about to try harder when the guard grabbed her again and pulled her away from the bed. She'd clearly had all the time she was going to get. She let herself be led outside, hoping her final words to Celeste had registered.

As they walked along the path, surrounded on either side by a high chain-link fence, she started to get a sinking feeling. In an overcrowded camp where there was no privacy or free space, she was amazed by the lack of people around. The lack of witnesses. She walked for another dozen steps and then turned around.

She looked him straight in the eye. He stared back. There was nothing in his eyes, no spark, no warmth. She tried her luck. "Where are we going?"

He raised an eyebrow and gripped his weapon tighter. "I like that you think you have a right to question me, detainee."

"Please." Mariposa fought back tears. "I know you're going to rape me, but please. I have a son. You don't have to do this."

"That's where you're wrong." He shrugged. "You're not going to be raped. But you should start praying to whichever god is your thing."

"No!" Her eyes widened. Ten minutes ago she'd been talking to her friend, now she was facing her end. She fell to her knees, prostrating herself before him as tears flowed down her face.

He sighed. "Get up."

"I have a son! I don't want to die, you bastard! There's no reason for this. I have a son!"

She'd lost it all. Her job, her freedom. Her son. The thought of Juan growing up without her was devastating. She collapsed into the dirt and couldn't stop the sobs. She struggled to breathe. Her chest hurt. She wanted to talk, but no words came. She gripped the small crushed rocks on the pathway, grabbed a handful and threw it at him.

It didn't help. She knew this was a one way trip.

ACT III

CHAPTER 15

At a morning tea with State Guard troops wounded in the line of duty, President Morris, Administrator Hall and a number of cabinet secretaries celebrated three full months without a terrorist attack on American soil. President Morris presented each of the wounded men and women with a newly struck medal, the Peace Cross, noting that America has pushed through the darker clouds and that rays of sunshine were ahead. Administrator Hall was unavailable for comment.

Federal Emergency Management Agency
News Release

Callum squinted and shook his head as he looked down from the guard tower with his binoculars. He could see Micah Hill walking alongside a detainee, down the same path he walked every day at about this time. This detainee looked young, a scrawny twenty-something with a shaved head. Hill gripped his shotgun casually by his side. He was headed for the motor pool, where the prisoner would be hauled into a van and off to his death.

Callum lowered the binoculars and ran a hand through his hair as he exhaled slowly. He'd watched the same thing dozens of times over the past few months, and knew there'd been about one per day. Mariposa Esposito had been the first, shot by Hill against protocol. Hill had claimed she'd resisted on the way to the motorpool. Since then orders had come in for more. The only thing that prevented the prisoners from rioting was secrecy. They were told they'd been transferred.

Callum had refused to participate, citing Bainbridge's psychological report as sufficient reason why. When a guard officer had called Bainbridge to take issue, the psychologist had given the officer an earful. Though Callum had been spared the need to take part in the executions, he'd still had to stand and watch as more and more detainees were led to their death. He didn't know if the same situation was taking place in other camps, but figured it must have.

But today the order had come in that he'd feared. It was the first time that there'd been two executions ordered on the one day and his name had been put down to transport one of them. Apparently not even Bainbridge had the pull to get Callum out of the duty, or else he'd changed his mind. Callum wasn't sure. But whatever had happened, the order was clear and he had a job to do. He was posted in the guard tower until the time came to drive the young woman to her death.

As if on cue, the camp's PA system gave a loud squeal and then Callum heard the words he dreaded. "Detainee Celeste Adams, please report to the B wing courtyard immediately."

He sighed loudly, gripped the shotgun and patted his holster to make sure his pistol was in place. As ready as he could ever be, he descended the stairs from the guard tower. It was a short walk through the compound to where the motor pool was located. As he walked, he tried to deal with the conflicting thoughts racing around his head.

"Reporting as ordered, sir." Celeste Adams was already waiting for him.

Callum jerked a thumb towards the nearby van. "I need to head into Effingham and I'm hung over. You're going to drive."

Her lips pursed and he thought she might mouth off, but after a moment she nodded and walked toward the van. He watched as she opened the door and climbed in. This all seemed so pointless, orders be damned. He'd read her file. She was the detainee he'd helped in the intake line. Her knee had only just recovered from being shattered by Hill's baton months ago in the shower block. She'd certainly had an eventful stay. He climbed into the van.

She started the engine, keeping her eyes ahead. "There's no need for this charade. If you're going to do it, just do it."

"Just drive the vehicle, detainee."

She kept quiet as he entered the address of the town into the GPS and hit start. He cradled the shotgun between his legs and eased back into the chair. The van picked up pace, until they reached the guardhouse to the only gate out of the camp. Adams pulled the vehicle up next to it and wound the window down when prompted by a guard, who strolled out of the guardhouse and over to their vehicle with a clipboard in hand.

"Hey, Callum." The gate guard leaned his head inside the van with a smile. "Where y'all heading?"

"Hi Andy. Just have to head to Effingham. Too hung over to drive, so thought I'd take fuck up over here."

"Not a bad fuck up, if you're going to take one, if you catch my drift." Andy Ward gave a long laugh, as if Adams wasn't even there. "Okay. Enjoy your drive."

Callum forced a laugh as Adams wound up the window and they started to move again. They drove in silence for nearly an hour. He'd usually listen to the radio, but he needed time to think and process what he was about to do: drop a woman off for execution. It violated every inch of his moral code. He gripped the shotgun tighter and wished there was some other way. As they drove further, the sun disappeared behind a large, dark cloud. It seemed like fitting symbolism.

He looked over at her. "Pull over."

She glanced at him, indicated and pulled over to the side of the road. He sat in silence as he thought hard. She wasn't stupid. He could sense her looking at the shotgun in between his legs, probably weighing up whether she could grab for it, escape or do something else before the hammer came down. He let out a breath, lifted the gun and opened the door. He climbed out of the van.

She looked at him quizzically. "What are you doing?"

"Go." He slammed the door shut and held the shotgun casually at his side.

The electric window on his side wound down and when he looked inside she was staring at him. "What the fuck?"

He took a step back from the vehicle. When she made no move to depart, he raised an eyebrow. "Go. That's an order."

"Um, no?" She took her hands off the wheel and crossed her arm. "You're suggesting a sure-fire way to end up dead or in a real prison."

Callum glared. "You may end up in prison, yes. But I've been ordered to drop you off to be executed. Even if you eventually end up dead, you break even. This is your chance. Go!"

She looked at him for a moment or two and then nodded. She started the van, wound up the window and glanced at him again. It was as if she expected him to change his mind, but he'd never been surer about anything in his whole life. She placed her hands on the wheel and inched the van forward. He laughed when she thought to indicate as she pulled away, kicking up a small plume of dust.

He hadn't known which way his mind would take him, which choice he'd make. It was against every fiber of his being to help execute a civilian, despite whatever puffed-up crime they'd been accused of. On the other hand, carrying out those orders would have been easier than what faced him now his decision was made. He waited until the van was a speck in the distance. Whatever. He'd done the right thing. Damn Hill, Bainbridge or anyone else who tried to bust him for it.

He stretched his neck, rotating it left and right, and then sighed as he unsafed the shotgun. He raised it to his shoulder, pointed it in the air and squeezed the trigger. The gun roared and kicked into his shoulder. He lowered it, pumped it and then repeated the action. Done, he safed the weapon and threw it onto the ground. Now there were a couple of spent shells to prove he'd tried to stop her. He pulled his cell phone from his pocket, dialed and waited for an answer.

"This is Major Bainbridge."

"Major? It's Sergeant Callum Watkins. There's been an incident. I need some help."

~

JACK GLANCED up at the four-story heritage building with some pride. In the heart of Chicago's Old Town, it was far enough from downtown to avoid FEMA saturation, but in a convenient enough location to suit his needs. It was discreet and low key – absolutely perfect. He'd been surprised when Elena had revealed that she'd arranged for the resistance to use the building as its headquarters.

It had been a busy couple of months. Since he'd met with the initial members of the resistance in New York, the movement had grown at great pace. They hadn't commenced operations, but had been busy gathering information and readying themselves to agitate and resist when the time came. After his meetings with Morris and Hall, Jack had wanted to make sure they were ready before acting. The time was now.

He'd traveled to Chicago with Peter Weston the previous day. It was risky to move so far across the country, but Jack had seen no alternative.

New York was too close to Washington, and there was a strong cell established there now. He had to trust others to maintain the operations there while he prepared to kick off their activity. Though he'd half expected to be detained a dozen times on the road, he'd made it.

"Just the trick, I'd say." Peter patted him on the shoulder and looked up at the building. "Looks good, doesn't it?"

"Sure does. Elena has done a great job." Jack smiled and jerked his head toward the door. "Let's go in and check it out?"

They rode the elevator to the top floor. It opened with a chime and a pair of burly-looking men met them at the door. He shouldn't have been surprised that Elena had organized some security to protect the inner sanctum of the resistance from prying eyes. She'd apparently thought of everything. One of the guards stepped forward, a clipboard in hand, while the other maintained a watchful distance.

Jack smiled. He was certain they'd know who he was, given he was the nominal leader of the resistance. "Good to see you, fellas."

"Need to get your names, gentlemen." There was no warmth from clipboard man. "Please also keep your movements slow and your hands where we can see them."

"Not a problem." Jack sighed and tapped his leg. "I'm Jack Emery and this is Peter Weston. Elena Winston is expecting both of us. Can we make this quick?"

"It'll take as long as it takes, sir." Clipboard man looked down at his list.

Jack crossed his arms and turned to Peter. He kept his voice low. "Can you believe this?"

Peter gave a pained look. "Bunch of little dictators, aren't they?"

Clipboard man looked up at them. "Okay, you're alright to head on through."

Jack didn't give them another second of his time. He walked down the corridor, which opened up into a large, open-plan space with some desks and meeting spaces, but only a single office at the back of the room. There was a handful of people scattered about, but for the most part the room was empty. Jack didn't know any of them except for one – Elena. She was leaning against a doorframe, a broad smile on her face.

Jack smiled and crossed the distance quickly, as the others in the cubicle farm stared at him strangely. He didn't care. Elena was one of the few people who understood what was happening, what he was going through and what he was trying to do. When he reached her, they hugged tightly. The friendship they shared still surprised him a little, but they'd become allies under fire.

"I'm glad you're okay, Jack." Her voice wavered slightly. "I was worried you wouldn't make it. It's really good to see you."

He backed away from her. "I've kept my streak going. I think FEMA likes having me around."

"Is that so?" She smirked. "Meeting the President, golf with Hall, months underground – shame you couldn't get them to change their mind, with all that popularity."

"It would make all this unnecessary." Peter gestured around the office.

Elena jerked a thumb behind her. "Come inside."

Jack nodded and the three of them stepped inside the office. He used the spare moment to gather his thoughts. Something felt wrong. It was odd that Elena had mentioned the meetings with Morris and Hall from months ago. They'd been the final straw for Jack, proof that the balance of power in America had shifted massively. It had been his last attempt to use reason and argument to free the country from FEMA's web.

In the preceding months, a network of influential Americans had sprung up using the technology Hickens had provided to block electronic eavesdropping. Jack had been in hiding, along with most of the leadership, waiting patiently as their power grew. Though there had been setbacks, for the first time there were people in place across nearly the whole country. The resistance was ready to move.

"This is perfect, Elena." Jack smiled as he closed the door, then walked over to sit on one of the chairs. "Your office, I presume?"

"No, nothing of the sort." She shook her head. "It hasn't been assigned yet. I want to know what comes next, Jack. The network is ready."

"Guerrilla Radio was all about information." Jack patted her shoulder. "Now we've spent months building something a little bit more potent than that."

"And what're we doing?" Elena stared at him, a strange look in her eyes. "I want to know, Jack. I've earned that."

"We're taking the country back. They have control of civilian government and a paramilitary force to back them up. We've gathered a bunch of influential people around us to speak out, act out, advocate, resist, provide finance and sustenance. Thousands. All we need to do is tip the scales and the people will follow. They have to."

"But—"

Peter stepped forward. "I know you're worried, but we've evolved, Elena. They think they've shut us down, Hall included, but there'll be eyes on us waiting for us to do something wrong. We just have to be careful and hope Hickens' technology keeps us off their radar for long enough to do what needs doing."

"Don't worry just yet, Elena." Jack walked over to her and placed his hands on her shoulders. "You've got a role to play, just like everybody else."

She sighed and squirmed away from his touch. "Jack, I really need to speak with you in private about something."

He shook his head and smiled. "Can it wait? I've got to call Bill McGhinnist. He only has a small window. Catch you later?"

"No." She was jittery. "It's important. It really can't—"

He was surprised by how on edge she seemed. He'd never seen her act like this before, not even at their most desperate, in Indianapolis. Perhaps she was just nervous that things were close to kicking off, given how poorly that had gone with Guerrilla Radio. But he couldn't indulge her now. He thought about how much work he had to do – a dozen calls to make and so much to organize.

"Please, Elena. Peter. I just need a few minutes." He didn't wait for them to leave the room, but turned away and started to dial. He lifted the phone to his ear.

He had to speak to McGhinnist and check in on efforts on the east coast. After that, he had to check in on the other cells. One of the problems of a tight cell structure and a small leadership was the amount of work each member had to do. It was critical to limit information to those in the inner sanctum, to reduce the risk of exposure and protect those close to him, but it took a heavy toll.

He turned around as McGhinnist picked up, just as the door closed behind Peter and Elena. He let out a deep breath. It was time to unleash the beast.

~

THE BIRD IS *in the nest.*

Richard smiled like a hyena as he read the text message, taking a moment to enjoy the words. He looked up from his phone. His was the only occupied table at the 1789 Restaurant, which had been cleared by his security detail prior. He picked up his glass and drained the last of the pinot. He sloshed the wine around in his mouth, savoring the taste, before swallowing. Along with pleasure came relief. It had been months since Jack Emery had been spotted, but since their meeting at the golf course Richard had kept an eye on him. He'd received intelligence that Emery had been central to the revitalization of the resistance. He'd miscalculated often when dealing with these individuals, but he was determined to get it right this time. He was glad he'd have the chance.

He'd first tried to smash the resistance by making an example out of the agitators in Indianapolis. But in hindsight he'd been too heavy handed. In trying to dampen down one crisis, all he'd done was make martyrs out of the dead and imprisoned. It had vindicated the resistance against FEMA control in the eyes of the neutral observer and emboldened the fanatics. His next miscalculation had been detention of loved ones and surgical strikes. Those hadn't worked either. Neither the journalists or other members of the resistance had been dissuaded, instead all he'd been left with was thousands of people to detain at enormous cost to the taxpayer. It hadn't gone down well with Morris. Finally, he'd hoped an appeal to the resistance's nominal leader, Jack Emery, would work. It hadn't.

At every step he'd miscalculated. He'd secured the country, but failed to eradicate the termites nibbling away at the base of that control. They'd gorged themselves, grown stronger and smarter, and now posed a greater threat to his agenda. But against all temptation to strike again, Richard had waited. He'd learned that not everything could be planned on a corkboard. He'd backed his gut, halted all offensive operations against the resistance and waited for Emery to emerge from hiding. As he did, he'd gradually begun to relinquish some minor elements of control, to show the public that with cooperation came increased freedoms.

Letting the resistance grow had been a huge risk, but he knew that if he couldn't get Emery, he couldn't truly end the resistance. If he'd waited much longer, the resistance would have been in a position to pose a serious threat. But the gamble had paid off. Richard now knew where Jack Emery was. On the eve of the commencement of resistance operations, he was in a position to smash them once and for all. Not only Emery, but a large number of prominent and affluent Americans. It would be a coup de grâce in every possible sense.

He let out a long sigh of relief and stood to stretch his muscles, then picked up his briefcase and walked to the entrance of the restaurant, all thoughts of dinner forgotten. A few of the staff looked at him with confusion, but didn't speak. They were probably appalled that Washington DC's most well regarded restaurant had been cleared out for the evening so he could eat there, and he hadn't even stayed for his second course. He didn't care. He had work to do and his people would fix up the bill. He left the restaurant and climbed into the car that was waiting.

He leaned forward to speak to the driver. "Take me to FEMA headquarters, please."

"Yes, Administrator." The driver fired the engine. "Everything okay with dinner, sir?"

"Lost my appetite." Richard sat back, making it clear he didn't want any more small talk.

As the car inched forward and the lights of the police escort started to flash, he picked up the phone and looked back at the original message. He keyed a response and let his finger hover over the phone for a moment, as his mind processed the situation one more time, looking for any holes in his plan. With a smile and a shake of his head, he hit send. Once she read it, the woman he'd come to rely on would terminate the threat of Jack Emery, bringing a giant hammer down on his resistance. The endgame had arrived. He dialed Rebecca Bianco.

After a moment Bianco answered. "Hello, sir."

"Good evening, Rebecca. Proceed with Operation Barghest."

There was a pause. "Are you sure, Administrator? The cost will be enormous and once the order is given it will be difficult to recall."

He sighed. His underlings continued to disappoint. He was astounded that Bianco had to ask if he was sure, after her hesitation in the face of his orders in Indianapolis. Though the pinot had been fantastic, it was as if she thought he'd made the decision to green light the most ambitious law enforcement operation on American soil in history after a few too many red wines. The weight of the whole country rested on his shoulders, yet stupid questions were still asked and answered. He let it go. She'd been a good operator for the most part. He had precious few of those.

"Yes, I'm sure." His voice was unintentionally sharp. "I'm on my way to headquarters, I expect you to be there when I arrive."

"That only gives me—"

"Sixteen minutes." Richard terminated the call.

He put the phone beside him on the seat and closed his eyes. He'd underestimated Jack Emery and the resistance from the beginning. It was time to act, to cut off the head of the resistance and crush its membership into dust. Eyes still closed, he allowed himself a small smile. Tomorrow was going to be a good day.

CHAPTER 16

In line with the raising of the Homeland Security Advisory System threat level to Severe (Red), FEMA has announced that all emergency measures that have previously been loosened will immediately be reinstated to their original status. All citizens will have a 24-hour grace period to adjust to these measures, after which penalties for breaches will apply. FEMA echoes the calls from President Morris and Administrator Hall for everyone to remain calm.

Federal Emergency Management Agency

News Release

Jack smiled as he looked around the table at the result of months of work. He'd returned to the Old Town office to meet with the team handpicked by Elena to handle all day-to-day coordination of the resistance. Alongside Elena and Peter were about a dozen others united in the same cause. The small group would be responsible for a tectonic shift in American politics, as the resistance began a concerted push against FEMA control across the whole country.

He'd been on the phone until the early hours of the morning, checking in with every cell leader. The people were in place and Jack was as happy as he could be with the preparations. This was their best chance to disrupt FEMA, expose their atrocities, influence neutral decision makers and take back the streets. It mightn't work, but it wouldn't be for lack of trying. Jack considered this network to be his masterpiece, an achievement far beyond what he thought possible.

"Last of all, I just wanted to thank each and every one of you for the risk you're taking by being here and doing this work." He glanced at Elena, then at Peter. "It's all too easy for us, individually, to turn away when we're faced with a situation like this. Hell, I nearly did. But an extraordinary person got me involved. Elena."

Elena flashed beet red. "Jack, I..."

"You're modest." Jack smiled, held out a hand toward her, then started to clap. The others joined him in applause for a moment or two. "You've all built this. It's important we acknowledge the work everyone has put in, but tomorrow the real work starts. We light the first sparks in what'll become a roaring bonfire. Thanks."

Jack nodded and walked away from the table. He could hear Elena telling the staff to go home, take a day for themselves, get some sleep and stay safe. That had been her idea, and he'd taken some convincing, but he'd swallowed his reservations. While he didn't like the idea of a day of inertia, she was right. Everything was in place and it was important his people were rested before they hit the switch.

He moved to the office, closed the door and collapsed into the chair. He was exhausted. For all the talk of letting the team have a break, he hadn't slept properly in a week. He closed his eyes and felt himself start to drift off, despite his mind protesting that he had work to do. His eyes shot back open when the door opened and Elena and Peter walked in chatting. He must have fallen asleep for a moment. They stopped in their tracks.

"Jack, sorry." Peter held up a hand in apology. "Thought you could use a coffee. The others have all gone home."

"Should have grabbed me a double shot." Jack smiled as Peter placed the tray of coffees down on the desk. He stood and took one of them. "Thanks."

Peter patted him on the back then looked to Elena. "And for madam, a soy—"

"Jack, I'm sorry." Elena's voice was pained.

Jack was confused by the shift in conversation. He looked over at her, the coffee cup still held to his mouth. Elena had a pistol trained on Peter. A tear streaked down her face. Jack's cup fell to the carpet and his mouth fell open. A thousand thoughts and a million questions battled for primacy in his head, but they were overwhelmed by far too many memories of being held at gunpoint. One thing won out.

"Help!" Jack's voice pierced the silence.

Elena didn't move. She kept the gun trained on Peter as a single sob added to her tears. Jack held out his hands and tried to talk her down, to get her to lower the weapon, but she just shook her head vigorously. To his credit, Peter didn't move an inch, merely held his hands up. He couldn't comprehend what was happening, but Elena's tears and hesitation gave hope for a peaceful resolution.

The two security goons ran into the office. Jack sighed with relief. The man who'd checked his name off the clipboard on his first visit scanned the room, his hand squeezing a revolver tightly, as his similarly armed colleague used his bulk to block the door. Elena looked over her shoulder at the men, sighed deeply and lowered her weapon. Jack relaxed a little, satisfied that the immediate danger had passed.

"Thanks, fellas." Jack sighed with relief. "Elena, what the fuck?"

"Fucking hell, Jack." Peter's eyes were wide. Jack followed his gaze to clipboard man, whose knuckles were white from squeezing the pistol tightly. "This whole thing is a setu—"

In the small office, the boom sounded like planets colliding. Peter fell to the floor, his blood spraying all over the wall. Jack screamed, fell to his knees and scrambled toward his friend, lifeless and face down on the ground. He cradled the head of the man he'd been to hell and back with. There was no point. There was a hole the size of a small fist in the back of Peter's skull, which oozed blood.

He turned and looked up at Elena. Multiple weapons were trained on him. "Why?"

"This was the only way." Her voice cracked. "They've got my fiancé."

"They've had him for months!" Jack's scream was full of anguish and anger, but she didn't react beyond another small sob. "Why now?"

"These guys are going to have a chat with you." She looked down at the ground. "I'm sorry, Jack."

"Fuck you." He snarled as his head ached, trying to process this. "I assume this means the rest of the resistance is being fucked in the same way right now?"

"Yes." She stared at the ground. "I'm sorry."

Jack climbed slowly to his feet. His legs were wobbly. He spat in

Elena's face, his spittle mixing with her tears, then turned to clipboard man. "Let's get this over with."

~

A VOICE SQUAWKED in Callum's earpiece. "All teams stand by."

Callum nearly laughed at the absurdity of a command staffer having to warn them that the stroke of the hour was approaching. Every man and woman in his small unit had their eyes glued to their watches. He supposed it was good to let some commanding officer, somewhere, prove that he could tell the time at least as well as the people under his command. On the other hand, his operation was part of a countrywide effort, so maybe there was some logic in having an inane countdown.

Callum had no idea where the other targets were located, but he hadn't been part of an operation of this scale since he'd been in Iraq. More than 120 guard troops had been mobilized to assault a single hotel. It was excessive force, but it would be effective. Shock and awe. He doubted the resistance posed enough of a threat to warrant such a hammering, but not much had been normal lately.

He checked his shotgun once more. There was no need, but he did it out of habit. It felt strange conducting an offensive again, but the weapon felt comfortable in his hand – more comfortable than his presence on the mission, anyway. He'd thought he was done with this business, now he was back in charge of a squad of State Guard troopers about to assault a resistance stronghold in the middle of downtown Chicago. He'd gone from one extreme to the other and then back again.

He let out a sigh. After he'd let Celeste Adams drive off, there had been a brief investigation. Callum doubted that the commanding officer of the detention center had wanted to be associated with an escapee *and* the guard who'd let it happen, so the incident had been brushed under the carpet. He'd been quietly reassigned to one of the active guard battalions. His call to Bainbridge had probably helped with that and, though he hated active duty, he'd hated being a prison guard even more.

That was how he found himself leaning against a concrete wall outside the Club Quarters Hotel in downtown Chicago. Much of the hotel had been booked for months in the name of an influential businessman and State Guard command suspected that much of the hotel was being used as a front for the resistance. Now, Callum's squad had been assigned the task of assaulting the third floor while other squads hit other floors.

"Show time guys." Callum pushed himself off the concrete wall. "Let's go."

His team moved in single file into the hotel lobby. The teams that had been assigned to the upper floors were already moving up the stairs. Once it was their turn, Callum led his team up the stairs and they exited on the third floor, taking up covering positions along either side of the corridor. After a few moments, a buzz sounded in his earpiece. It was time to make some noise. He gave his team thumbs up.

His team started moving in pairs to the door of each room on the floor they'd been ordered to hit. Callum was paired with Paddy Carlisle, a quiet kid from Boston he'd known for less than a day. He took up position on the left side of the door, while Carlisle took up his spot on the right. When his team was in place, Callum shouted for them to go and watched as Carlisle stepped forward with a ram. The soldier didn't hesitate, smashing into the door once, then again. It gave a loud, tortured cracking sound as its timbers protested then gave way.

Carlisle dropped the ram and moved inside with his pistol drawn, followed by Callum with the heavy artillery. Callum scanned the room. There were no targets and only two possible hiding places: behind the bed on the far side of the wall or the bathroom. He gestured for Carlisle to take the bed, while Callum checked the bathroom. He edged forward, until he heard the tell-tale pop of a small caliber handgun. He turned around. A gunman had shot Carlisle from behind the bed, the exact spot Callum had been worried about.

"Freeze!" Callum raised the weapon as Carlisle fell to the ground. "Don't do anything stupid!"

The gunman swung the pistol around. Callum reacted instantly. The shotgun barked and a dozen crimson stains appeared on the man's white T-shirt as he fell. Callum moved over to where Paddy Carlisle lay motionless. The pistol round had hit him in the head. Callum checked his pulse. Nothing. He'd probably been dead before he'd hit the floor. Callum slammed a fist into the ground. With a growl of frustration he ripped the quilt off the bed, threw it over Carlisle's body and then walked out to the corridor. Within two minutes, his entire unit had finished its work. Some prisoners had been taken, and some had fought back.

Callum gathered a detailed picture before he radioed in. "Command, this is Watkins. Third floor is secure. One Guard KIA. Three suspects killed and seventeen in custody. All clear."

He ignored the confirmation from command as he returned to the room he'd cleared, placed his back against the wall and slid down until he was seated on the carpet. He let out a long breath and rested his head in his hands. He couldn't believe he was back here, doing this work again, watching more young men go to their graves. He thought of Celeste Adams. He'd saved her life, but the price may very well have been his own. He wondered if he'd crack and have to have Bainbridge testify on his behalf at some trial or another. He didn't get the chance to finish the thought, as heard a noise and looked up.

"You okay, Sarge?" One of his men was peering in with a strange look on his face.

"Fine, Private. Just a long day." Callum climbed to his feet again. "Let's move out."

The private nodded. "I'll gather the guys."

Callum sighed. He wondered how many more people – Americans – had died today.

~

JACK'S HEAD THROBBED. He could barely open his left eye, it was that badly swollen. Every time he moved, his chest screamed in pain. He had cuts and lacerations all over body and his blood stained the carpet, mixed with the dried mess of Peter's final moment. He kept his eyes closed as he felt around his body and inspected the damage further. He'd chipped a tooth on a leather boot and was pretty sure he had a broken rib. He wondered if the swollen left eye might have some permanent damage.

He rolled onto his side with a groan. They'd beaten him in the hours since Elena's betrayal. But if there was one saving grace to having the shit kicked out of you by relative amateurs instead of the Chinese military, it was the fact that he'd managed to get some sleep in the early evening when they took a break. It was a small victory, but he'd take it. On the other hand, their lack of finesse also meant they lacked the skill necessary to extract maximum information for minimum damage

He pushed himself up with both hands and an enormous groan. His head spun and a wave of nausea hit him. He forced it down and shook his head, trying to clear the haze. He wondered if he had a concussion on top of the other injures. He did his best to squeeze his eyes open and looked over to where Peter had been shot dead. If nothing else, he was pleased that they'd dragged the body out at some point, though Peter's blood had left a wide red stain on the carpet. He missed his friend already.

He sighed as he leaned forward and hugged his knees, wincing in pain. More painful was the knowledge that he'd fucked everything up and probably gotten everyone killed. He'd been so stupid, blinded by his trust toward Elena and oblivious to the signs of treachery. She'd been absent when Celeste's home was raided. She'd probably betrayed the location of the Guerrilla Radio leadership. She'd leaked other information for god knew how long. She'd caused Peter's death. Worse, she'd probably ended any chance of defeating FEMA.

He didn't know the extent of the damage, but it had to be immense. She'd been at the heart of both Guerrilla Radio and the rebooted resistance effort. If she'd set up an attack in Chicago, chances were good that the other resistance cells had been hit as well. Jack didn't know if anyone was left alive, but from what he'd seen in Indianapolis, Richard Hall would strike hard and aim at the head. Once that was done, the FEMA administrator would grind the body of the movement to a pulp. He wouldn't chance another rebirth.

A small cough behind him startled him, and he growled in frustration at the pain in his ribs. He did his best to turn, but the movement was nearly comical. It was Elena, seated on an office chair with her elbows resting on her knees and her chin cupped in her hands. Make up stained her face and made her look like a panda. Her hair fell across her shoulders in a mess. What surprised him was the satisfaction he felt at the fact that she looked like shit. Fury rumbled in the pit of his stomach, despite the condition he was in.

"Jack." Her voice was soft, full of sadness.

He roared as he tried to push himself forward onto his hands and knees. "I'll kill—"

He heard a pistol cock. She was pointing it at him. "Don't."

Jack paused. He was enraged, but he had no desire to die. He rested back on his knees and laughed darkly. "I never thought in a million years that this would happen."

"Me either." She held the pistol on him for a second longer and then lowered it, apparently satisfied that he wasn't going to charge her. "We need to talk."

"No, we don't." Jack held his hands out wide. "Fucking hell, Elena. Was all of this worth it, you fucking Judas? I hope you enjoy the thirty pieces of silver."

She stood and took a step toward him, then paused. He saw the pain in her eyes and the tears streaking down her face. They fed his anger. "Jack, I—"

"No!" He shook his head and pointed a finger at her. "You brought the hammer down on me. On *us*. How many of us did you betray? Everyone?"

She staggered back as if he'd struck her. One step, then another, then she caught herself on the edge of a desk. She stared at her feet "Hall said he'd kill my fiancé if I didn't help."

"I just don't want to fucking hear it, Elena. They're going to kill me. I—"

"Nice little love-in we've got here."

He saw Elena look up at the door and followed her gaze to see clipboard man standing in the doorway. He had a broad smile on his face and his offsider leaned against the door frame. They both had pistols drawn. Jack looked back at Elena, who had her weapon held loosely by her side. She dropped it when instructed to. If nothing else, it looked like she mightn't survive her treachery either.

"Looks like you might have changed your mind, young lady." Clipboard man's voice was loaded with sarcasm. "Can't say I'm surprised."

The offsider laughed. "Hey, Mike? After we kill him, I'd like a piece of her. Nothing in the orders said we couldn't have a little fun with her once the job is done."

Clipboard man turned and let out a long laugh. "Sure. It might be fun, even though she looks a bit like a clown."

Jack snarled. His ribs screamed at him as he lunged at clipboard man, who heard the noise and started to turn just as Jack reached him. Jack lowered his shoulder and the force of the tackle pushed the two of them through the office window. The pistol boom mixed with the sound of the glass shattering to form a terrible crescendo. Jack landed heavily on top of the larger man as glass crashed down on top of them.

Clipboard man wasn't idle. He bucked and did his best to dislodge Jack as he pounded his fist into the other man's face. At the same time, clipboard man reached for the pistol that had slipped from his grip. Jack couldn't let that happen. He brought down his clasped hands on clipboard man's arm. He heard a crack and the other man screamed. Jack swung punches wildly as clipboard man changed tactics and started to aim blows at Jack.

Jack winced in pain as he took one glancing hit to the head, then a second to his nose. Stars exploded in his vision and he fell backward. His face felt like it was on fire. He blindly swung another punch as he fell, but hit air. He grunted and heard a crunch as he landed on his back, but didn't have time to consider the glass he'd landed on because the other man threw himself on top of him.

"I was going kill you quickly." Clipboard man wrapped his hands around Jack's neck. "Now I'm going to crush your fucking throat."

Jack struggled to breathe and to dislodge the other man. He clawed at the hands gripping his neck, then attempted to buck the other man off. But it was no good. Clipboard man had fifty pounds on him and the strength of an ox. He started to black out. His vision narrowed. His body screamed in agony. His muscles burned. He lost the strength to struggle against the man, who had his thumbs dug into Jack's throat.

He closed his fingers into a fist and used the last of his strength to swing his hand toward clipboard man's throat. He heard a gurgle and the pressure on his own throat was immediately gone. Jack wheezed and coughed, sucking at air but struggling to breathe even as a torrent of blood sprayed over him. Clipboard man fell off him, clutching his throat, trying to stem the bleeding from his severed artery. Jack rolled over, gripped the piece of glass in his hand tighter and stabbed it into the man's face several times.

Jack kept sucking in air and, as his peripheral vision started to return, he saw the other man struggling with Elena. He must have left clipboard man to finish off Jack and moved in to claim his prize. Her top was ripped and he raised a fist to strike her. Jack dropped the glass and propped himself up onto an elbow. He was surrounded by glass, covered in blood and struggling to stay conscious. He looked at his hands. They were bloody and cut open from the glass. Then he saw the revolver.

He reached out. It was so close, yet the effort required to grab it seemed superhuman. When his hands wrapped around the grip, he pointed the barrel to the floor and used it to push himself off the ground. He coughed hard as he struggled to his feet. He staggered forward, bracing himself on the frame of the door as he raised the revolver unsteadily and fired. Miss. As the other man started to swing around

Jack accounted for the recoil and fired again. The second shot hit true. He fell to one knee and dropped the revolver.

He steadied himself then looked up as Elena walked toward him, a step or two away from the body of her attacker. Jack wasn't the best shot, but it was hard to miss from six feet away. The dead man had never seen it coming. She fell to her knees and wrapped Jack in a hug. His mind screamed in protest, despite the battering he'd taken. He pushed her away and struggled to his feet. It took an eternity, but he made it. He said nothing else as he started to walk to the elevator.

"I'm sorry, Jack!" She was crying. "I'm going to fix this."

He didn't look back.

CHAPTER 17

Terrorist cells in more than forty cities have been disrupted or destroyed in simultaneous operations by the State Guard and other federal and local authorities. Administrator Hall called it the most significant development since the onset of the crisis, and also released details of the group's leader: Mr Jack Emery. Mr Emery is wanted on a range of terrorism-related charges, which center on a conspiracy to disrupt and degrade the capacity of FEMA and the United States Government. Anyone with information should contact the National Security Hotline.

Federal Emergency Management Agency

News Release

R ichard approached the President, who held her arms wide and sported a broad smile on her face. Though he usually didn't like physical contact, he moved in closer and hugged her. She slapped him on the back a few times and then backed away. Richard took a moment to compose himself, then sat in the chair she was gesturing toward. It was probably worth more than he earned in a week on his government salary.

"Richard, hell of a job." She beamed as she took a seat on the sofa opposite him. "Sorry for calling you in, but I read your briefing and couldn't quite believe it."

He'd never been to Camp David before and, as he looked around the

President's office, he felt a wave of relief wash over him. The patience to get the resistance in exactly the right spot hadn't been without risk, but it had paid off handsomely. Clearly Morris felt the same way. Usually she was reserved, critical and very sparing in her praise, but from the moment he'd walked in the mood had felt festive.

He sat a little bit taller. "Not a problem, Madam President. The operation was without setback and was a complete success."

She frowned. "As simple as that?"

"As simple as that." He smiled again, so widely his cheeks hurt. "This is the coup we've been waiting for. The resistance has been annihilated. It's over."

"Run me through it."

"Okay." He tried not to show his displeasure – it had all been in the report. "Under FEMA direction, the State Guard and local police forces undertook operations across forty cities in thirty-one states. All known locations of resistance activity were assaulted and the perpetrators arrested or killed. It's as complete a decapitation as possible."

It was true. With Elena Winston's information and the combined resources of the Federal Government, he'd managed to locate nearly the entire network of the resistance: Jack Emery and the leadership, the influencers, the cell leaders and the foot soldiers. His forces had crushed them all. His only mistake had been trusting Winston and the two agents he'd assigned to kill Emery. They'd failed.

"If it's not a complete lopping off of the head, to use your parlance, then what's left hanging from the neck, Richard? I've been burned by your assurances before. If I'm going to close the book on this, I want to know that I'm at the end of the story, and not just starting another chapter."

Richard sighed. He'd hoped to avoid this. "Jack Emery, their leader, is alive. But he's now irrelevant. He has no power base and he's on the run. We'll catch Emery and mop up the remains of his mess in the next few days. There's nothing else left to worry about regarding the resistance in its current form."

"Excellent. Thanks for coming in, Richard." Morris smiled as she got to her feet and extended her hand. "I'm going to ask my chief of staff to prepare for the rescinding of the executive orders. Our regular structure can sort things from here. I can't thank you enough for all you've done. You've been a great help to this administration. Stay the night."

Richard frowned and remained seated as alarm bells rang in his head. He'd waited for the right leader and been disappointed each time. Now he'd taken matters into his own hands, he'd grown accustomed to the power and the ability to shape the country. The last thing he'd expected was for Morris to attempt to seize back the initiative moments after his greatest success. He needed time to secure his legacy before handing back the reins.

"Richard?" Morris raised an eyebrow, the smile still on her face. "Is something wrong?"

Richard shook his head. "Madam President, that would be a mistake."

She hesitated and her smile vanished. "I'm sorry?"

"Rescinding the orders would be a mistake. The state of emergency isn't over."

She sighed and shook her head. "Richard, I know you might have come to like some of this extra power, but the work is done. There hasn't been an attack for a while now, the resistance is smashed – you said so yourself – and order has been restored. I can't ask the American people to continue to live restricted lives. I won't."

Richard had never felt this way about a meeting with the President before. She'd resisted at times, had concerns at others, but for the most part she'd been malleable. He'd come to expect her to swallow her pride and let him do what was necessary to stabilize the country. Morris asserting herself was a new development. An unwelcome one. He laughed. Long and slow and cruel.

"Something funny?" She crossed her arms, displeasure clear on her face.

"With respect. I'm honestly shocked by your lack of understanding."

Her eyes became glaciers and the temperature in the room dropped as she leaned forward, towering over him. "You're staring down the barrel, Richard."

"I understand that." He stood, removing her height advantage. "I've given everything for this country during the crisis, yet you're ready to discard me before my work is complete."

"No. Things need to return to normal and—"

"Normal?" He hissed the words. "The only reason there's order is because of the control FEMA has managed to exert. And the minute we have a comprehensive success you want to give up all of our hard won gains. I'm not convinced that this is over, not by a long shot. I want to continue to have the tools to protect our society for a while longer yet."

"It's over, Richard." She shook her head. "There's no reason to keep a superagency that crushes the liberty of America and its people for no good reason?"

"No good reason? Safety. Order. Those are the reasons, Madam President." Richard scoffed and started to walk toward the door. He paused and turned, feeling the anger surge inside of him. "I came here to report on our greatest success and you propose to pull the rug out. You should hang for treason."

Her face flushed red as her iciness was replaced by rage and fury. She pointed her index finger at him and started to talk, but he didn't want to hear it. She'd made up her mind, and he was wasting his breath and his time. She'd been a patsy, sure, but now she was dangerous. An enemy. If she wasn't prepared to let him do what was needed, she was of no use to him. Or anyone.

He took no notice as she continued to vomit words at him. If the air had been festive a moment ago, it had now become flammable. Morris's stupidity had created a conflagration that would consume everything if it was allowed to. He turned and walked to the door, in no doubt that under her leadership the orders would be revoked and he'd be out of a job within a day.

JACK WOKE with a start and winced at the shot of pain from the sudden movement. His eyes opened in time to see the pigeon that had been resting on top of him take flight. He sat up and rubbed his eyes, then hugged his torso to try to warm up a little. He wasn't surprised to discover that sleeping on a metal park bench was not good for the retention of body heat. It was the best he'd been able to manage.

He sighed and placed his head in his hands. Everything had gone to shit. On his way out of the Old Town office building he'd grabbed his phone and his wallet and then stumbled as far away as he could, given the pain and his exhaustion. He'd thought about a hospital, but that was the first place FEMA would look. He'd tried to think of somewhere smart to hide, but in the end, exhausted and needing sleep, he'd settled on a park bench.

He thought hard, trying to forge some sort of plan, but his mind had abandoned him. He'd lost a friend, been betrayed by another and, to the best of his knowledge, the resistance had been crushed. Losing had been a possibility, but not this way. Of all the scenarios he'd imagined might befall the resistance, this hadn't been one of them. It was over. No smart plan or twist of fate could undo the strategic Armageddon that faced him.

But he needed to know how bad it was. He swung his legs to the ground, stood unsteadily and started to walk. He shuffled, in great pain, to where a mother and young son had their backs turned and were having a picnic. He nearly laughed at the sight of two people so carefree, eating sandwiches on a rug despite the disaster that had played out in the last 24 hours. They weren't to know though.

He kept some distance away from them and cleared his throat. "Excuse me."

The mother turned. She was a cute blond with bright eyes, but her kindness and warm smile evaporated when she looked up at him. Her eyes widened as she reached for her son and her purse simultaneously. She gripped both with the ferocity of a lioness. "Please just leave us alone."

Jack held up his hands. She obviously thought he was a beggar or some kind of creep. "No, you don't—"

"Just *go*." Her voice was cold, far beyond what Jack would have expected. He must look worse than he thought. "I know who you are. Please go."

He rubbed his face and ran a hand through his hair. He was confused by the woman's reaction. He'd only wanted to ask her about the media coverage of the resistance, but she wanted no piece of it. He complied and walked away, determined to check the news the old fashioned way. Since Hickens had expressly told him not to check the news on his phone, he rummaged through a trash can and found a newspaper.

It was bleak. Though the coverage was heavily influenced by FEMA, it was reporting that a large number of operations had been conducted against terrorists all over the country. It reported that casualties were high and that the threat had been obliterated. Jack winced at the next line. Though the majority of the threat had been dealt with, it said, terrorist leader Jack Emery was still at large. His photo was splashed everywhere and there was a reward.

He cursed. That explained the behavior of the woman. It also told him everything he needed to know about his chance of survival and the future of the resistance. He threw the phone onto the grass, collapsed to his knees and then fell to his side. Months of effort and conflict had finally caught up with him. He was spent and on the run, with no resources and no support. The woman might have called and FEMA could already be on their way. He struggled to care.

He wasn't sure how long he laid there, eyes closed and despondent, before his cell phone started to ring. He opened his eyes and stared at it, confused. Everyone who had the number to the phone should be dead or detained by FEMA. Every part of him wanted to let it ring out, but he owed it to the people who'd been smashed because of his carelessness to answer. If just one of them was alive, he'd help them with everything he had left in his body.

He answered. "Hello?"

"Jack? Fucking hell. Jack?"

"Hi Celeste." His head felt light at the sound of her voice, and a few moments passed before he could comprehend what she was saying. He'd never expected to hear her voice again, either because she was dead or he soon would be. An overload of emotion coursed through his body.

"I thought you were dead, Jack." She laughed and he heard her sniff and choke back tears. "I thought I'd escaped only for you to be taken away."

"Afraid not. May as well be, though. It's all gone." He rolled onto his back and looked up at the sky. "I'm glad you're out, though, Celeste. How? And how did you get this number?"

"A guard let me escape." There was a pause. "As for the number, I saw the news and that you were alive, so I called Hickens."

Jack smiled. "Simon is alive?"

"Sure is. He's a broken man, though. I don't know what you guys were cooking, but he tells me most of the rest are dead or in custody, Jack."

"I know. Well, I'm glad he's alive. We need to stay separate, Celeste. They're after me. I'll be lucky to last a day now I'm all over the news."

"No way." Her voice was pure, cold fury. "I didn't get out of there, thinking you're dead then finding out you're alive, only to be told to stay away. I want to help."

"But—"

"You are not sidelining me again, Jack. You are not cutting me off."

He laughed despite the seriousness of the situation. She'd been furious at him for going to Taiwan to confront Chen Shubian and get what he needed to expose the Foundation. She'd been even madder when he'd retreated to Syria to escape from his life. He'd been forgiven, they'd made love and he thought he'd lost her for good. Now, staring into oblivion, he was faced with a choice: to let her in or lose her.

"Jack, I'm a fugitive as well." She was persistent, that was for sure. "If they capture me on the road or hiding or with you it's the same result."

"Okay, Celeste." He shook his head, not quite believing what he was doing. "But being with me is dange—"

"I know." Her voice was sharp.

"I mean it, Celeste. I—"

"Jack, I know."

He wasn't sure that their reunion was a good idea, given the likelihood he'd be dead or in cuffs by the end of the day, but he was done trying to protect Celeste by pushing her away. All that did was enrage her and undermine the feelings they shared. It might end poorly, but it'd end together. His heart thumped, his head screamed, his veins burned with energy and his muscles twitched for him to get up. To see her. To act.

"Plus you really want to see me, right? Pick up where we left off?" Her voice was a little playful, clearly trying to break the awkward silence.

"Okay." He smiled as he pictured her naked body on top of him, despite everything else that was at stake. "I look forward to it."

She laughed. "I bet. But we've got some business to take care of too. You're not going to believe what I've found."

He got to his feet. "What do you mean?"

"I'll explain when I see you, but it's dynamite. I've linked FEMA to the attacks. All of them."

He was confused. "Just how long have you been out, Celeste?"

There was a pause. "Oh, three months or so."

"And you're only just getting in touch now? And you say *I* drop out of contact!"

"I needed to get to the bottom of it, Jack." Her voice had an edge. "I owed it to someone."

He couldn't hold it against her, given his past. "Okay."

"I'll text you an address, meet me there tomorrow. I love you, Jack."

The call ended and Jack looked around. He'd thought she was dead and that all hope was lost. Now, Celeste was alive and was sitting on something that might give him one last chance. The phone beeped. He looked down at it. He didn't recognize the address, but it wasn't far away. He'd go there, reunite with Celeste and see what she'd got her hands on. He'd never been much of a gambler, preferring his vice in liquid form, but he had played poker and could recognize when it was time to play his final hand.

He was all in. He was done running.

~

ONE KEPT the night-vision binoculars steady on the road, as she had for the last hour. Not a single vehicle had passed in that time. Her mind had started to wander and, inevitably, question what she was doing. It had been months since she'd spoken to Richard Hall, but he'd called her unexpectedly and offered her a job. She should have declined. She'd enjoyed the break and thought herself done with him, but the challenge had sold her. If she could pull this one off she could do anything.

He'd given her only a moment to accept the job. She'd agreed on the spot. It had been a struggle to get her team together in time, chopper them out and get them into position, but they'd successfully inserted without raising the ire of the authorities. Now all she needed was for the target to appear. If she was honest, it was a strange mission and a strange target, but she was the axe, not the wielder. Whatever reason Hall had for green-lighting the mission was his own. Her job was to pull it off.

The first Chevy Suburban came into sight, rounding the bend with headlights beaming and engine roaring. She waited, breathing deeply as the second, third and final vehicles followed barely ten yards apart. Hall had been as good as his word. Intelligence of a clear and present danger to the President had flushed Morris from Camp David. Though she'd usually fly, the weather did not permit it, so the Secret Service had bundled her into the car. All according to the book. All very predictable. All very A to B.

One lowered the binoculars and put her night-vision goggles into place, then nodded at Two. A second later Two fired his RPG. It whooshed and the rocket covered the distance between the tree line and the lead vehicle in a moment. As the other members of her team fired their rockets, the first hit the lead Chevy squarely on the engine grille. An explosion flashed and a fireball blossomed, followed by a secondary explosion as the fuel tank blew. The devastated vehicle came to a halt, alight and oozing smoke.

She took her eyes off the lead vehicle and looked down the line of the motorcade, where two of the other vehicles had been dealt with in a similar way. Only the third vehicle was still intact, and it picked up speed as it swerved around the destroyed vehicles. The Secret Service driver had to have veins of ice, given his colleagues had just been annihilated, but he had no answer for the rifle that roared and destroyed the vehicle's engine block with a high caliber, armor piercing round. The car slowed and then stopped.

"Go!" One lifted her carbine and started to move through the trees, closer to the road but still concealed. She closed in on the President's vehicle with single-minded purpose.

She was within twenty yards of the President's vehicle, weapon raised, when an agent appeared. She tried to get a shot off but the gunman dropped suddenly. A millisecond later she heard the telltale report of one of Five or Six's rifles. They were on overwatch and taking care of stragglers while the rest of the team stalked larger game. One kept moving, around the trunk of the car. The agent was lying dead on the road.

She smiled like a wolf at the door of a hen house at the vehicle in front of her, the only one untouched by the RPGs. The President's vehicle was designed to withstand all sorts of attack. But it was still just a car, not a tank. It had vulnerabilities against a well-equipped foe. That was why the President usually had a dozen Secret Service agents on hand to protect her. When they fell, however, she was vulnerable.

She turned to Two. "You got it?"

"Yep." Two nodded, reached into his combat vest and pulled out a piece of paper.

One took the sheet, unfolded it and walked up to the window of the presidential vehicle as Two, Three and Four took up covering positions. In addition, she knew that Five and Six were also covering her, now that any last Secret Service survivors had been dealt with. She placed the note against the window and waited. She waited a minute or so, but there was no huge hurry. Though reinforcements were on the way, they wouldn't arrive in time.

After a moment, the cell phone in her pocket started to vibrate. She pulled it out and answered. "Good evening, Madam President."

"Who are you?"

"That doesn't matter." One kept her weapon down. If any of the Secret Service agents tried anything, her team would sort it. "We're short on time. I'm glad you see sense."

"I see inevitability. I've called the House Speaker and Senate President and transferred executive power to the Vice President."

"Wonderful." One didn't care. "You have ten seconds to step out of your vehicle. The agents stay inside."

Morris sighed on the other end of the line. "And my daughter will be spared? You give me your word?"

"Yes. And the other agents. Nobody else needs to die."

The phone call ended and the rear door of the vehicle opened. One stood in place, relaxed, even as she saw the Secret Service agents inside gripping their weapons. They wouldn't like it, but with executive power transferred the agents had no further interest in the former President if she ordered otherwise. One was pleased that Morris wasn't stupid. She took a step back as Morris climbed out of the car.

One smiled once Morris was finally out and standing on the road with her hands by her side. "Thanks for being sensible, Madam President."

"It's just Helen, now. And fuck you." Morris scowled. "My car might be tough, but it can't stop an RPG. I shouldn't trust your word, but I have to hope you'll spare my daughter."

"Of course."

"I also hope you know that this is a waste of time. There's nothing you can extort out of me. It's clear to me there's no coincidence between my meeting with Richard Hall and the circumstances I now find myself in. Unusually for Richard, he's fucked this one up in a big way."

"I couldn't comment." One raised her weapon. "Now, I just need you to sign something and we can get this over with."

"This will never be over with. I've made the gravest mistake of my life trusting that man, to the detriment of us all and our country." She slammed a fist against the car door. "I should have seen it. It was all too neat. But I was caught up in the narrative. Just do me a favor and tell Richard I'll keep a seat warm in hell for him."

One said nothing as she held a second piece of paper in front of the former President, along with a pen. Morris looked at her with disgust clear on her face and then snatched at the pen and paper. She read it over briefly in the dim light and her eyes widened. She looked like she might refuse, until she glanced back at the car. She sighed, signed the paperwork and then handed it to Two, who had his hand outstretched.

One fired a single round into the President's head, then turned and started to walk back to the tree line. She heard the whoosh of an RPG round, followed by an explosion. Though she felt the heat of the flames, she didn't look back. She'd wanted to help Morris's daughter, but orders were orders: not a single person was allowed to walk away from the Presidential motorcade.

CHAPTER 18

Following the assassination of President Helen Morris and the murder of her daughter and security detail, President Newbold has reiterated his support for the emergency measures. He noted that the attack on the Presidential motorcade signals a new and dark chapter in the country's fight against extremists, and that he would not shirk from doing whatever was necessary to find those responsible. Administrator Hall will speak this morning in Chicago.

Federal Emergency Management Agency

News Release

Callum looked down from the nosebleed seats of Soldier Field. He was standing with his carbine, waiting for Richard Hall to take to the stage that had been hastily erected in the south end zone prior to the Bears game. The stadium was nearly at capacity and Callum was one of the State Guard troops assigned to security.

He scanned the crowd from behind sunglasses, looking for any suspicious movements or overt threats. Nothing jumped out at him, but it was tough to keep tabs on such a large crowd. He was up high, but there were others scattered around the stadium, each looking for the same thing he was. Video cameras all around the stadium would be using facial recognition technology to try to find any problems before they became deadly, while a couple of FEMA helicopters hovered up high. His earpiece was silent as well.

Since the assault on the President's motorcade less than twenty-four hours ago, the whole city had felt on a knife edge. Callum doubted it was different anywhere else. For his own part, he'd felt like someone had punched him in the chest. After everything he'd gone through, he'd thought his latest mission was also his last. But clearly whatever success FEMA and the State Guard had achieved against the terrorists was not complete.

"Sector 37, report." The voice in his earpiece was all business.

Callum took one hand off his carbine and pressed a button on his headset. "37, all clear."

"Confirmed." The voice paused for a second. "All sectors report clear. Proceeding."

Callum chuckled at the charade of it all. With a crowd of around 50 000, spotting a threat before it manifested would be difficult at the best of times. In an angry, frightened nation full of guns, the day after the President has been shot, it would be next to impossible. If the Secret Service couldn't stop a determined attack, Callum doubted a handful of State Guard could.

He watched as Hall approached the stage, climbed the stairs and stopped at the podium. He was probably the only prominent person to visit and be announced at Soldier Field in history to be met by silence. Then a low murmur began, until Hall held out his hands toward the crowd. The gesture was lost from this distance, but the giant scoreboard screens magnified it.

"I'll not take much of your time." Hall smiled. "I understand there's an age-old score to settle today."

"Get this clown off!" The crack from a man near Callum earned a few laughs from those near him. Callum's grip tightened on the carbine but the guy sat down.

Hall ignored the catcalls and booing he was being subjected to. "I, like the rest of the country, was shocked to learn that President Morris's motorcade had been attacked and that she'd been murdered, along with her entire security detail and her daughter. While we're still piecing things together, the attack is unquestionably an escalation by the terrorists who've rocked America for a year."

Callum tuned out as Hall gave all the usual platitudes. The President's death was a huge loss for America and so on. He'd heard it all so many times, usually for friends and fellow soldiers, that it had lost its meaning. He focused on the crowd, but it was a waste of time – there was more danger of spectators falling asleep and hurting themselves than one having a shot at the administrator. Then something Hall said grabbed Callum's attention.

"FEMA is determined that these attacks won't disrupt our operations, or divert us from the correct path." Hall paused. "It's important to remember that."

Callum's eyes narrowed. Hall had used the exact same words when discussing the attack on the distribution center in public. It was a rehearsed line, completely out of place for a man supposedly in shock and dealing with the President's assassination, in unison with the rest of the country. Was the attack a surprise to Hall at all? Callum started to pay close attention to the speech again. Close attention to Hall.

"Though we've had some success against these terrorists, there have been setbacks. To combat this, I met with President Morris yesterday, hours before the attack on her motorcade. She was resolute in her commitment to the path we're traveling." Hall looked straight down the camera. "My staff at FEMA are doing a wonderful job of keeping our society functioning, and their State Guard colleagues are keeping us safe.

"But it hasn't been enough. I came to an agreement with President Morris along these lines." Hall held up a piece of paper. "This document is an executive order authorizing FEMA to take command of elements of the United States Military on home soil. It doesn't apply to overseas forces, or our strategic assets, but it's a necessary next step to help us combat the ongoing threat."

There was a murmur among the crowd. Callum looked around. The civilians were restless in their seats and it felt like the mood in the stadium had switched from mourning to suspicion. Callum's mood was shifting too. For the first time, he felt that Richard Hall was one of the things wrong in America. But he still had a job to do. He scanned the crowd but there was no obvious threat. He looked back to Hall.

Hall placed the sheet of paper down. "I've already spoken to President Newbold. He's as committed as his predecessor was to doing what's necessary to combat this scourge. He's re-affirmed all executive orders that the former President signed. The country will endure, despite these most testing of circumstances."

Callum clenched his jaw. He considered raising his weapon and aiming at Hall. He'd stare down the iron sights as he breathed, in and out, in and out, and prepared himself for the shot. Though the range would be extreme, he wondered if it was worth a try. He shook his head. It was a shot he'd never take. While he regretted some of the things he'd done in Iraq and on his home soil, he wasn't a murderer. He let out a long sigh.

"I want to be clear." Hall's voice was filled with aggression. "The ability of the terrorists to hit the presidential motorcade is unacceptable. With these new powers, we will make our streets and people safe. We will bring order to America. God help anyone in our way. God bless America."

~

JACK WOULD HAVE LAUGHED if not for the seriousness of the situation. The house was a cliché: white picket fence in front of a red brick home. He looked down at the phone again, then up at the house. He repeated the process a couple of times to be sure the address was right and then opened the gate.

As he approached, he thought for the millionth time that this story all felt a little bit too convenient: Celeste getting out, then calling him months later and begging to meet. He was running to her like a puppy and he knew there was a chance that Celeste was being used to capture him. It was possible. Probable. But he had little left to lose by giving it a shot. He reached the door and knocked twice. There was no answer. He frowned. She had said she'd be here. He tried to peer in the window next to the door, but the curtains were drawn. He knocked again. He could wait a few more moments, on the chance she was in the shower or something, but he felt exposed on the porch.

As he waited, his enthusiasm faded and then evaporated into despair. Since the call, he'd thought of a reunion with Celeste as a second chance, but it was a dead end. He'd never see her again. She was dead or in prison and this was some sort of ruse. He started to turn around, ready to leave the house, when someone's arms encircled his waist. He stiffened and recoiled at the touch, then relaxed as the feminine arms completed their movement and pulled him as tight as a boa constrictor. He felt lightning pass between them as Celeste pulled him closer. He raised his hands and placed them over the top of hers as a broad smile crossed his face.

"Hey." Her voice was a whisper in his ear. "Got you."

He wriggled in her grip, turned around and wrapped her in his arms. He pulled her close and they kissed deeply, fuelled by their relief at the most unlikely of reunions. He should have been concerned that they'd be spotted, two of the most wanted fugitives in America, but all he wanted was to hold her and expunge months of loneliness and guilt and worry. They kissed for nearly a minute until she pulled away. She smiled and he mirrored it.

"We should get inside." He jerked his head toward the door. "I assume you have the key? You had me worried."

"Sorry." Her cunning smile matched the playful gleam in her eye. "I had to make you sweat a little."

Jack smiled as they broke their embrace and she unlocked the door. They stepped inside and Jack was shocked by the broken furniture and stained floors. "Who pissed FEMA off?"

"The owner."

He gave a small laugh, but when he saw the look on her face he changed the topic. "I couldn't believe it when the phone rang and it was you."

"I never thought I'd get out of there." She shrugged and placed a hand on his shoulder. "It's good to see you, Jack. What happened?"

He barely knew where to start. They walked into the dark living room and sat on the sofa, lights off and curtains drawn. He explained everything in as much detail as he could, from the moment they'd been separated in New York. She knew about much of it: the new attacks, the scale of detentions, the atrocities. She gasped and squeezed his hand at key points in his story. She cried when he told her about Peter.

"How the hell did it happen, Jack?" Her voice cracked.

"Elena betrayed us." He gripped her hand, which was trembling. Peter and Celeste had grown close while he was in Syria. He explained the story, fury radiating off him in waves.

Finally, she spoke. "They had her fiancé, Jack. I can't comprehend the damage she's caused, but I understand why she did it."

"That doesn't excuse—"

"No, it doesn't. But I might have done the same. She saw the light in the end."

He shook his head. "But—"

"She let you go." Her voice was firm as she leaned in to kiss him. "I've got you back. You've had your turn, now it's mine."

"What do you mean?"

"Come with me." She stood. "I have to show you. You're not going to believe it."

He didn't think it could be as good as she was claiming. He didn't really care what it was, but he wanted nothing more than to be close to her so he followed. He figured it must be good if she'd sat on it for months and then called him here at great risk to both of them. They walked down the hallway and down the steps to the basement. She turned on the lights and he was amazed by the piles of documents around the room.

She smiled and held her hand out like a game show host presenting a prize. "It's all we need. It's all we've ever needed."

His eyes narrowed, not wanting to believe she'd found a treasure trove. "Is any of it any good?"

"It's better than good." She wrapped an arm around him and ushered him downstairs. "Take a look."

He chose a random pile, picking up a piece of paper concerning the attack on the Hoover Dam. It was a supply manifest of weaponry sent to a warehouse near the Hoover Dam on the eve of the attack. He replaced it and moved to another pile and picked a document. This pile was all about an attack in Phoenix. He whistled. Someone had gone to a lot of trouble and had an awfully high level of access. No wonder it had taken Celeste months.

"Where did this all come from?" Jack turned to her, his eyes wide. "If we can get this out, it's over."

Her features hardened. "Mariposa, a friend inside the camp. She used to be a senior employee at FEMA. She gathered it all. They imprisoned and killed her because of it."

Jack moved closer to her and hugged her again. They embraced for a couple of moments, then she seemed to gather herself. "She never released any of it?"

"Never got the chance. This is why I've stayed off the grid all this time, Jack. It took some effort to get through it all. You should see how many printer cartridges I went through."

"I can imagine." He laughed and looked around again. "Why the hell didn't FEMA find all of this when they arrested her?"

"Looks like they found the hard copies she'd made, but she left it all on a flash drive in the urn containing her mother's ashes. They flipped the whole house but missed it."

He smiled. "Have you looked at it all?"

She nodded. "It's a paper trail linking FEMA to nearly everything, linking Richard Hall to everything. Or a lot, anyway. If this isn't enough to bring him down then he's bulletproof."

"The attack on the President?" Jack raised an eyebrow. The news that President Helen Morris had been gunned down shocked him, not that he'd had any huge love for her.

She shrugged. "Mariposa couldn't see that far into the future and none of the documents I've seen mentions it. But everything else is here."

"It'll do." He couldn't quite believe it, but was unable to deny what was in front of him. He laughed. "I'm impressed. Looks like it's time to pass the baton. Who needs me anymore?"

She nestled in closer. "I do, Jack."

∾

JACK LOOKED up at Celeste and smiled as she placed the coffee cup in front of him. He took a sip, then put it down and rubbed his eyes. Though Celeste had sorted most of it, they'd been reviewing the documents all afternoon and evening. The work made him feel like he was back at university or in the early years of his career, when all-nighters spent poring over reams of documents weren't uncommon. He was too old for it now, though.

They'd struck gold. The story was damning and Jack had reached the conclusion that Richard Hall was the most dangerous man in the history of America. Though he was still technically subordinate to the President, he'd shown that meant nothing. He'd monopolized institutional power and the use of force in America, using it to keep the entire country suppressed and compliant. Only J. Edgar Hoover's FBI came close.

"You look tired." Celeste sat down next to him and took a sip from her own coffee. "Why don't you take a break?"

"Yeah, okay." Jack nodded and leaned back on the sofa. It was a ratty old thing, a castoff that had been exiled to live the last of its useful life in basement purgatory.

She touched the bruises on his face. "I wonder if we should just burn these documents and hide here for a year or two."

Jack smiled and stroked her hair. "I'd love to, but we'd run out of tinned tuna before too long. Besides, I hate this décor too much to call it home. We'll just have to stop Hall."

While the US had seen its share of lunatics, extremists with poisonous ideology, Jack felt that Hall was the first with the unfettered power to back him up. In a year he'd created a police state without parallel in recent history, with more sophisticated surveillance than the East German Stasi and more military might than any regime in history. He had to be stopped.

She pursed her lips. "Easier said than done."

"Totalitarianism and oppression only last as long as there's a threat to make people afraid. Once there's nothing to fear they want their rights back. Plus, if we don't fight, nobody will. I've seen a lot of good people die this year, trying to do the right thing, some of them because of my mistakes. It needs to end."

He was about to say more when there was a knock at the front door, a pounding that they could barely hear in the basement. Jack tensed and wished he had a weapon, but found it strange that the authorities would knock. That wasn't FEMA's style. They were more the 'have goons kick in your door and shoot you in the face' type. He looked at Celeste. She seemed relaxed as she stood. She smiled and gave him a single nod as she started up the stairs.

He thought briefly about trying to hide the papers, but there was no point. They were both fugitives, and there were so many classified documents in the basement that if it was the authorities at the door then they'd have ample evidence of wrongdoing. He sat back on the sofa and sipped his coffee, waiting for whoever Celeste had invited into the house. He wondered if it was a relative of the owner, Mariposa, or a straggler from the resistance.

It turned out to be neither. Jack gasped when he saw who was following Celeste down the stairs. He flared with anger and pitched his coffee cup across the room toward her. Elena flinched and cowered as the cup sailed past her head and shattered on the brick wall behind her. She held up both hands as he looked for something else to arm himself with. He stood and lifted the ashtray in the middle of the coffee table. He hefted it.

He didn't get the chance to throw it before Celeste was in front of him, wrapping her arms around him and saying words he couldn't process. Slowly, the red mist receded and he could hear her telling him it was okay, that she'd planned it, and that Elena was here to help. He growled in frustration and stepped backward, which seemed to satisfy

Celeste. She let go, but remained between Jack and Elena, who was still on the stairs.

"Jack, please." Elena's voice was soft with emotion. He wondered what she'd been doing in the days since she'd sold him out. It had probably involved champagne and caviar.

"Elena, if you were on fire I wouldn't piss on you." He exhaled strongly through his nose and looked at Celeste. "Why did you bring her here?"

Celeste stepped close to him again, took hold of his hands and smiled. "Because she can help us, Jack. She's scared, just like us. She wants to act, just like us."

"The resistance is in tatters because of her!"

"You're wrong." Elena shrugged. "While I may have sold you out, the only other thing I did was confirm some information FEMA already had about the resistance and its members."

"So they could kill them."

"They'd have done that months ago, Jack, if you hadn't been hiding. Hall was waiting for you to re-emerge. Once you did, he struck."

Jack didn't care what role she'd played in the dismantling of the resistance, either central coordinator or bit player. She'd betrayed him, betrayed their cause and helped to get a lot of people killed in the meantime. Personally, he'd never felt a punch to the guts like the moment she'd shown her true colors. It had been worse than the beating he'd taken. Worse than any beating he'd ever taken.

He was about to say more when Celeste put a hand on his shoulder. She leaned in close to his ear. "Jack, give her a chance. I think you should hear her out."

He sighed. If he wasn't so happy to be alongside Celeste, against all odds, he'd have resisted her advice. He clamped his teeth together. "Why are you here, Elena?"

She smiled sadly and started to walk down the stairs again. He put down the ashtray and stood with his fists balled by his side as she joined them, and they all took a seat on one of the two sofas. She crossed her legs in front of her and seemed to consider her words carefully before she spoke. He waited, impatiently, while she seemed to struggle to find what she wanted to say.

Finally, she spoke. "Jack, I just want to say that I'm sorry. Beyond sorry. Hall imprisoned my fiancé, as you know, and he's been used as leverage against me."

"Sorry, but I don't care." He stared straight at her. "A whole lot of my friends are dead now because of the action you took."

"I know." She smiled sadly. "And I'm sorry. I made the wrong choices. But I knew you wouldn't be giving up. That's why I'm here."

"How did you find us?" Jack's eyes flicked to Celeste, then back to Elena, when finally the realization hit him. "Hickens."

She nodded. "He's been my friend for a long time, Jack. I didn't sell him out. He tracked your phone to this location, though he assures me the NSA can't do the same."

"Fuck me, did he give my number or location to everyone who asked?" He sighed and rubbed his face. "Just go, Elena. There's nothing you can do that I'd trust you to do."

"I can get a message to Hall." She dropped the revelation like a bomb. "I can tell him where you are. That must be a massive opportunity in some way."

Jack paused. A plan began to form in his head. Several times the women asked him what was going on and if he was okay, but he ignored them. It would be a long shot, but if Elena really could get a message to Hall, then it might work. He closed his eyes and turned the fledgling plan over in his head, probing for flaws and trouble spots. Hall had proven to be a detailed planner, but consistent in his habits. Predictable. It just might work.

He opened his eyes and smiled. They had to stop Hall, who now had the entire apparatus of the US government and military at his disposal. If they failed, there wouldn't be a country worth living in. It was time to take a final stand. He spent the next hour explaining the plan to them. At first, they doubted him, then they started to come around to his thinking.

When he was finished, Elena laughed. "More than happy to do my part in that, Jack."

"Wait a minute." Celeste looked concerned. "He's got the military, Jack. It's impossible."

"Not impossible, just difficult." He shared her grim expression. "We win or we die."

CHAPTER 19

FEMA has today released footage of a man believed to be wanted fugitive Jack Emery, taken on a camera near a gas station in Chicago. The Agency and other federal authorities believe that Emery is still located in Illinois. Emery, wanted on dozens of terror-related charges, is considered to be highly dangerous and may be armed. He should not be approached by members of the public.

Federal Emergency Management Agency
News Release

Jack sat on the bench, a baseball cap covering his head and his eyes hidden behind dark sunglasses. His disguise wouldn't deter a keen observer, but he had to hope that his efforts would hold up to a casual glance by a passer by. For extra concealment, he had his back to the road. He stared out into the distance, enjoying the fact that he had little but the giant mass of Lake Michigan for company.

"Jack Emery. I knew they couldn't fucking kill you!"

Jack smiled when he heard the voice. It was barely a loud whisper, but the speaker was close enough that Jack could hear every word. He'd know that voice underwater. He turned and his smile only grew wider. Dan Ortiz was standing there in uniform, looking a lot less scruffy than the last time Jack had seen him. The meeting they'd had in Millennium Park felt like it was a century ago.

"Good to see you, Dan." Jack reached out a hand and they shook. "You're late."

Ortiz laughed. "They had bacon in the mess this morning."

Jack scoffed. "Take a seat, Dan. I need to talk to you. I need your help."

Ortiz nodded, rounded the bench and sat down. He pulled out a cigarette, saw the look Jack gave him and then put the packet away. He shook his head. "Don't judge me."

"Didn't say a word." Jack smiled.

"Like hell." Ortiz sparked the cigarette and took a long drag, then blew it out slowly.

"Thanks for meeting with me. I know it's not safe."

"You're telling me it's not safe? I'm the one got you involved in all of this shit, Jack. I reckon we're even in the danger stakes." Ortiz shrugged. "So what do you need?"

Jack had considered his next words for the past week, but they still didn't come easily. He'd spent that time working up the plan with Elena and Celeste. They'd concluded that while it had a theoretical chance, there was a high likelihood that they'd end up dead. They'd all come to terms with that fact, but asking Ortiz to help – a man with a career and a family largely untouched by the takeover – troubled him.

More troubling still was the idea of Richard Hall continuing to tighten his grip on a country that was nearly exhausted. Whatever the risk, whatever the threat, he knew the plan and what it could achieve was worth it. Between them, Jack, Celeste and Elena had considerable talents in analyzing information and telling a story, but without the means to broadcast it they were toothless. Jack knew a solution.

"We've got everything we need to bring down Hall and FEMA. It's as simple as that."

"No, it's not, or I wouldn't be here." Ortiz slapped Jack on the leg. "Get on with it."

Jack stared down at his feet. "I have information, but no way to broadcast it."

If only Ortiz knew the half of it. He dug into his pocket, pulled out a few folded sheets of paper and handed them over. The sheets were a typed summary of events between the start of the attacks and now, with highlighter marks next to the events that Jack had managed to link to FEMA. He waited as the other man scanned the documents, a range of emotions rolling across his face. Mostly anger.

After a while, Ortiz handed them back and looked squarely at him, his eyes probing for any hint of mistruth. "I'm listening, Jack."

Jack stared back at the lake. "What's the feeling inside the Marines?"

"People are shitty we're taking orders from FEMA now." Ortiz's voice dripped with disdain. "From the same guy that shot up the 38th Infantry in Indianapolis."

"So, big fans then."

"Yeah, the boys are getting their tits out for autographs. But why do you ask?"

Jack smiled. "I have a mountain of stuff. If I can get it out, it'll topple Hall, FEMA and the State Guard. It has to. But I need your help. Lots of it."

"OK." Ortiz tapped his foot. "I'll play along. If I help you out with that, what happens? We take back the country?"

"Something like that." Jack nodded. He didn't need to tell Ortiz that his ambitions were a hell of a lot bigger than that. "But there'll only be one chance. If we fail, we die."

"I'm used to those sort of odds." Ortiz smiled. "But how can some grunts help with what you need? They're blocking our comms, so it's not like you can use the Marine network."

"Well, that's the thing." Jack turned his head to look at Ortiz, whose gaze was locked on him. "Have you ever heard of the Emergency Alert System?"

~

RICHARD WATCHED with interest as the man's eyes bulged and his body fought hard against the restraints. The medical professionals kept their distance from the gurney, even as the guard and priest did their best to calm the man down. Richard couldn't hear what they were saying through the glass, but guessed it had something to do with the futility of the struggle. Though the man was strapped in tight, Richard respected the effort.

He leaned forward, his face inches from the glass. He'd never seen a man die and the process of a state-sanctioned killing – calculated, clinical and just – fascinated him. It was the ultimate manifestation of the power of the state over the individual, the ultimate upholder of order against the worst crimes: in this case, the efforts by rebels to undermine his important work. He didn't like having to do this, but nor could he cower from it.

Eventually, the staff inside the room calmed the man down enough for the two orderlies to go to work. Richard was amused by the fact that they still swabbed the man's arm with alcohol, considering infection was probably a moot point for someone who'd be dead in an hour. They then inserted a pair of IV tubes into his arm, attached the line and secured the whole setup. After a saline drip and a heart monitor were attached, it was ready.

As the priest did his work, the prison officer keyed the intercom. "Administrator Hall, we're about to begin."

Richard smiled. Even though he had no role to play, the staff were clearly unnerved by his presence. He pressed the button on his own intercom panel. "Don't let me stop you."

"Okay, sir."

Richard sat back and waited as the final spiritual preparations were made. Though there had been other executions under FEMA's watch, this was the first he'd watched. He cursed as his phone suddenly started to blare. He stared down at it and felt faint as soon as he read the message. It was as if all of his Christmases had come at once. Elena Winston had texted him that Jack Emery was alive and was planning a major broadcast of information against FEMA. Most importantly, she knew where he was.

Richard's lips peeled back into a smile. He glanced up at the man doomed to die, pleased that the process had started. But his attention was now elsewhere, on Elena Winston and Jack Emery. Richard had thought she'd gone rogue, but it sounded like she was just where he needed her. He was glad that the room to witness the execution was empty. This was the opportunity to put the final piece in the puzzle. He dialed her number and waited until she picked up, then waited again while the encryption technology on his phone did its thing.

Finally able to speak, he took a deep breath. "Elena? It's Richard Hall. You've got some explaining to do."

To her credit, she didn't hide from his accusation. "I've been held up. When the two you sent failed to do the job, I was worried you'd blame me. But I know where Jack Emery is."

Emery was the last piece in a very large puzzle. "Tell me."

"He's at a house. It's just a regular, suburban place. He's sitting on a mountain of information that was leaked by one of your staff. Mariposa Esposito?"

Richard's eyes widened and his mind screamed. Somehow Emery had got his hands on the Holy Grail. Elena couldn't be lying because she had no way of knowing. In the blink of an eye Emery had graduated from washed-up minor annoyance to the most dangerous man on the planet. With the information that Mariposa had trawled, Emery would have all he needed to put the pieces together on nearly everything Richard had been doing. As much as those actions had been necessary, they wouldn't resonate well with the broader public. Crucially, Emery had shown through the saga with the Foundation for a New America that he had the ingenuity to get the word out. He had to be dealt with.

"Give me the address, Elena."

She paused. It betrayed her nerves. "For a price, sure."

He rolled his eyes. "Name it."

"You release my fiancé." Her voice was angry. He couldn't blame her, given how badly he'd played her. He regretted it, slightly, but it had been necessary. "And leave us alone."

"Done." Richard knew the deal even before she'd asked for it. The release of one man was a trifling matter. "Your information better be good."

"The release first."

Richard sighed. "The address first. You've got precious little credit left with me, Elena. You can be smart and alive or dumb and dead. Make your decision."

She gave him the address and Richard hung up the call. He sent out a message to have Elena's fiancé released, then quickly dialed another number. Time was of the essence. As he waited, he watched as drugs were pumped into the man on the gurney. Where he might have expected spectacular convulsions, blood – *something* – instead the man's heart slowed, betrayed only by the heart rate monitor that showed it was done. As he watched the priest close the man's eyes, Richard considered that his work in fixing America was nearly done. There was only one more thing to do.

Jack Emery had to die.

∾

ONE FELT A SENSE OF CLOSURE. Barring a major surprise, this would be her last mission for Richard Hall – the assassination of Jack Emery, the man responsible for the resistance that had kept her busy for months. She'd thought the attack on the President's convoy would signal the end of their arrangement, but Hall had contacted her with blunt instructions: kill Jack Emery, no matter how loud or costly. Loud and costly her team could do, especially for a large pile of cash.

She nodded at Two. "Go."

The small ram that Two swung at the door took just a couple of hard strikes to send the flimsy wooden thing swinging back on its hinges. As he backed away and threw the ram onto the lawn, the rest of her team surged inside. She'd left nobody on guard, this job was going to be done quickly, brutally and by the numbers. She let her team move inside before following, with Two bringing up the rear to keep their exit clear.

She moved through the house with the rest of her team. With each room they reached, a member of the team split off to make sure it was clear. She kept her weapon raised as she entered the kitchen when it came to her turn. The flash light on the end of her weapon illuminated the room. As the rest of the team started to report in, she scanned the kitchen a few times back and forth, then added her call to the mix.

The house was small, so it didn't take long. She'd made a decision to enter with maximum aggression, one member of her team per room, given it was unlikely that Emery was expecting an assault. He also probably didn't have the capacity to fight back, even if he was. While she wouldn't usually go in so loud, she hadn't had time to plan properly or get hold of the floor plans. That meant speed was their best protection.

As the last member of her team reported in, having checked the yard, she paused near the entrance to the basement, the only possible place for Emery to be hiding. Either that or Hall's information was incorrect and Emery wasn't here. But Hall had been right about nearly everything else since she'd been working with him, so she figured the likelihood of bad intelligence was fairly low.

She keyed her mic. "Okay, basement it is."

The order was confirmed in her headset. Three and Four reached for the handle, opened the door and then moved down the stairs. One followed, leaving the others upstairs. She reached the bottom of the stairs and her eyes widened as she saw the mountains of paper stacked in the middle of the room. She walked over to it as Three and Four stood alert. She gave the material a cursory glance. She'd found the information, but not Emery.

"Fucking hell, guys." She scoffed. The shock at finding so much information and the frustration at not finding Emery struck home. "Would you look at all of this?"

Three broke into a broad grin. "I wonder if there's—"

A single thud from upstairs interrupted him mid-sentence. It was a sound akin to a sack of potatoes hitting the floor. They looked to the ceiling and raised their weapons. One's mind screamed with possibilities as she froze, waiting for another sound or for one of her team to open the door, stick their heads in the basement and tell her it was okay – that someone had made a mistake. Her team didn't make mistakes. There were two more thuds.

"Move guys." She took one step toward the stairs, weapon raised, when the door at the top opened. A pair of small metal canisters bounced down the stairs and she heard the distinctive rattle of metal on concrete. She knew the green canisters well. "Oh, fuck."

The flash bangs exploded with light and noise. One tried to shield her eyes, but it was far too late. She staggered and dropped to one knee. She was blinded and couldn't hear anything around her. A few seconds later she felt a blow against her temple. She fell to the ground and screamed in pain as a boot found her midsection, again and again, until she was against something – a wall or some sort of furniture. Then she felt a barrel press against her skull.

It took some time for her vision to clear. When it did, she was lying on her side, able to see the brutal consequences of Richard Hall's miscalculation in full technicolor. It burned in her vision worse than the stun grenades. Three and Four were splayed out in front of her, a pair of corpses who minutes ago had been highly skilled men she'd considered friends and colleagues. The story would be the same upstairs.

After another moment, someone ducked down to her level and tried to speak with her, she couldn't shift her eyes from the bodies, but nor would she show emotion. She'd taken hundreds of lives, but the human mind – no matter how hard and conditioned to the trade of death – had no answer for grief when loved ones were taken. Like the finest sports stars and musicians, she'd fallen for the classic trap: trying to stay on top for a little bit too long.

She glanced at the man in front of her for just a moment, then back at her dead team members. In the recesses of her mind, the fact that the man was in uniform registered. It was a strange development, but she had neither the time nor the mental capacity to fully process the information before a hard blow hit her in the back of the head. She barely stayed conscious, then a second blow hit home.

"*Hey.*" The voice sounded like it was underwater. Underwater. And far away. "*Hey, shitbag.*"

She blacked out again.

"*Who do you work for?*" The same voice. Deep underwater.

More questions followed, but she registered only every second word and couldn't follow. Her head felt light and she had a pounding headache. She tried to sit up, but failed and retched. The two standing in front of her as she lay on the ground stepped backward as she puked and then blacked out again. She woke a few more times and briefly resisted their questioning. Then she blacked out for good.

CHAPTER 20

Authorities are no closer to identifying or locating the six terrorists responsible for the attack on President Helen Morris, though it appears to be the same group that previously attacked the Hoover Dam. Also released today, FEMA polling data shows that, broadly, the public supports the emergency measures that are in place and that 79.2% of Americans feel safer than they did six months ago.

Federal Emergency Management Agency

News Release

J ack looked at his watch and wondered again how the Marines did this every day. It was early and the sun hadn't come up, yet as Jack stood and waited for the caffeine to kick in Fort Sheridan was a hive of activity. All around him soldiers readied their equipment and vehicles as he slurped down the last of his coffee. Truth be told, he felt a bit useless, watching as the men and women on the base worked.

Ortiz and his officer colleagues had delivered. The two battalions of the 24th Marine Regiment had made their way to Chicago under the guise of exercises, but now approximately 2000 men and women were gathered and ready to move. It wasn't an overwhelming force – a drop in the ocean against what Hall could command between the military and the State Guard – but Jack had to hope it would be enough to get the job done.

"Time to go?" He smiled as Ortiz approached in his combat fatigues. "Guess I don't have time for a second coffee?"

Ortiz nodded. "Our scouts are reporting that there's very little between us and the target. We're lucky. If they knew its importance it'd be fortified further."

"Will it work?"

"It might." Ortiz ran a hand through his hair and scratched his head. "We'll surprise them, and we'll have decoy attacks going on all over the city during the main push."

"Just have to hope we're in business before they realize what's happening, I guess." Jack shrugged. "Shame we don't have that terrorist bitch to parade around though."

Ortiz grunted. Both Jack and Ortiz had been furious at the marine who'd hit the woman in the back of the head with his carbine. The blow had concussed her and rendered her useless. Though Jack had some cell phone footage of her mentioning Richard Hall and the other attacks, he hadn't managed to get to the bottom of who she was or why she'd cooperated with Hall before she'd died. The ambush hadn't gone as well as he'd hoped, but at least Elena's fiancé had been freed. If nothing else, if the plan failed, Jack would die knowing that he'd stopped a nasty woman and her friends from further acts of terror. He'd wanted more information to hang Hall with, but anything she could have given him would have been a cherry on top of the greatest cake ever made. He had enough to crucify Hall, if he could get the word out.

"Showtime." Ortiz walked toward the main vehicle convoy. "Let's go."

Jack passed dozens of men and women hard at work as he approached the Humvee he'd been assigned to. Some nodded, some stared, some ignored him – but all of them had a crazy day ahead. He was glad that Mariposa's information had apparently convinced enough of Ortiz's fellow officers to mobilize the entire regiment. So much force didn't guarantee success, but it was more than he'd hoped for.

"This is where I leave you, Jack. You got everything you need?" Ortiz looked at him with some skepticism.

Jack couldn't blame Ortiz for any doubt he harbored. Jack had been through a lot and was about to ride into a firestorm once again. From Afghanistan to the battle against the Foundation for a New America to Syria to the struggle against FEMA, he'd seen more conflict and experienced more pain than most. Now he was asking Ortiz and his comrades to risk their lives. Ortiz wasn't saying anything, but Jack knew he had doubts.

He patted the satchel that he carried on his shoulder. "Mariposa Esposito made sure of it. I'm ready, Omega."

"Okay." Ortiz slapped him on the back. "See you on the other side, Jack. You stay frosty, buddy."

Jack nodded. His mouth was dry and he wanted more than anything to turn around, but the time for second thoughts had passed. He put his hand on the door, opened it and smiled when he saw who was inside. The shapeless combat fatigues and her combat vest did nothing to hide her attractiveness. From the flame-colored hair downward, she was a sight he was grateful to have back in his life. He smiled and climbed in.

"Howdy stranger." Celeste smiled at him. "I thought I'd surprise you."

"Hey."

"You alright?" She could clearly read his concern. When he was seated and settled, she placed a hand on his knee and squeezed it. "It's going to be okay."

He nodded, smiled as bravely as he could and placed his hand on top of hers. As the driver gunned the engine, he shifted slightly in his seat to face her. "One for the road?"

Celeste beamed. They held each other as tightly as they could in the confines of the armored vehicle and kissed deeply. His hands started to explore her body, despite the unflattering battle gear, until the driver of the vehicle turned around and cleared his throat. It was as if a trance was broken. They separated and straightened themselves out. The driver turned back to the front, focused on getting the vehicle ready.

Jack smiled. "Sorry, got carried away."

Celeste gave him one more peck on the lips. "Until later."

The driver looked at him in the mirror and laughed. Jack flushed red. He wasn't usually easy to embarrass, but the thought of career soldiers seeing his flirtations was a little much. They settled in, ready for the ride, their clasped hands the only sign that they'd shared such an embrace just a moment earlier. If he'd had his way, she wouldn't be here at all, but they all had a role to play. Jack turned and watched as the convoy prepared to head toward his assignment and his destiny.

"Comms check." He heard Ortiz's voice over the radio network.

For the next few minutes, he was distracted by vehicles checking in and diesel engines starting. It was funny, the last time he'd been inside a

Humvee he'd nearly died, but now all this hardware was on his side, the crews were fighting for the same thing he was and he was alongside the woman he thought he might love. He just hoped he made it to the other side of the firestorm that was to come.

He hoped they'd all make it.

～

"Fucking hell." Callum raised his binoculars. "Fucking hell."

He'd thought his mind was playing tricks on him, but the powerful binoculars showed him the truth: there was a convoy of a dozen or so US Marine Corps vehicles rolling down the street. He lowered his binoculars, gripped his carbine and then gave a quick shout for his men to get ready. He had ten men to defend the position. Nowhere near enough.

Callum keyed his headset. "Command, this is post 457, we've got a situation here."

There was a long pause. In the time it took for a response to come in, the convoy grew from a speck in the distance to being highly visible. He could count at least twelve Humvees, enough to carry more men than he could handle. He nearly considered keying the radio again and repeating the report when, finally, it chirped in his ear.

"Be advised, 457, the entire 24th Marine Regiment has entered Chicago and elements are approaching a dozen different targets. You're to hold your position and await orders."

"Understood." The radio went silent and Callum shook his head. He called out to one of his men. "Bring me the horn!"

He gripped his carbine tightly as one of his men ran over with the megaphone. He had no idea what the 24th Marines were up to, but doubted they were on a tour of the city. He was astonished that they hadn't learned from Hall's response to Indianapolis, which had involved a far larger unit than a few thousand Marines. But he had to deal with the situation.

He waited until they closed to within a block, then lifted the megaphone. "This is Sergeant Callum Watkins, Illinois State Guard. Stand down!"

The response was swift. Callum instinctively ducked as the machine gunners on the Humvees all zeroed in on his position, but held their fire. He knew the difficult truth, that his men would lose a fire fight against the approaching convoy. They had no heavy equipment and were staring down the barrel of armored vehicles and better armed Marines.

He keyed the megaphone again. "Last chance before I have to order my men to open fire. Please, brothers."

He doubted they'd comply. Even if they stood down, their march on this building made them outlaws. They'd taken up arms against FEMA and the guard, which meant Richard Hall would crush them. Callum knew they had reasons to be concerned: the executions, the imprisonments, the squeezing of average Americans. But he didn't think this was the way to bring about change.

When his second plea achieved nothing he put down the megaphone, raised his carbine and ordered his men to do the same. Certain that fighting would erupt at any second, he was astounded when a flame-haired woman pushed her way past the Marines and held her hands up. His eyes widened as he made the connection in his mind. It was the woman he'd freed. Celeste Adams.

"Don't shoot." Her plea was laced with fear and doubt. "Please, I'm coming up the stairs."

Callum kept his weapon trained on her, even as she advanced on their defensive position and as the doubts ricocheted around his head. If he'd lacked the resolve to shoot her in the detention center, there was next to no chance he was going to do it now and spark a fire fight between the State Guard and the US Marine Corps. He gave a guttural growl and lowered his weapon.

"Let her approach!" Callum radioed to his squad. "Repeat, let her through."

Confirmation came in from his other soldiers. None of them sounded convinced, or particularly happy, but there wasn't any protest. Nobody fancied the prospect of going toe to toe with what was in front of them. Though Callum and his squad were entrenched enough that they'd cause some damage, it would be futile. There was nothing inside the building worth dying over.

Celeste Adams reached the top of the stairs and waited a few feet from Callum's position. He put his carbine down and stood, confident that his men would keep him covered. When no shots were unleashed from the Marine column, he started to hope that maybe there was a resolution to this mess. He moved slowly, walked over to her and shook her hand.

"You're mad, you know that?" Callum sighed and shook his head. "You were half a chance to get your head blown off just there."

"I know." She smiled wider. "But once I heard your voice, I had to try. I'd heard it enough times over the camp intercom."

He smiled, despite the tension. "What can I do for you?"

She shrugged. "I'm trying to save the lives of you and your men. I owe you that much. It's up to you what happens next."

Callum reached up and scratched his chin, shocked that it had come to this. He thought back to when he'd been hunting in the forest with Todd and Mike. They'd been naive then. It was hard to believe he'd allowed himself to be so corrupted by the State Guard. He'd signed up originally for some nice cash once he left the army, not to be the hammer that smashed the American people against the FEMA anvil. He didn't want to do this anymore.

He stood taller and lifted his carbine high over his head. He hoped that there wasn't a trigger-happy kid among the Marines, because that's all it would take to start a fire fight. But a shot never came. Slowly, as Callum looked around, he could see the others in the unit adopt a similar posture. The message was clear: Come and get it, but leave us alone while you do. He looked back down the stairs. The Marines were already bounding up them.

As the Marines reached the top, one unarmed man raced up to Celeste and kissed her deeply. When they broke their embrace, he laughed. "You're crazy, do you know that?"

Callum laughed hard. In front of him was the most wanted man in America. His eyes flicked between Celeste Adams and the new arrival. "Just my luck you'd end up here."

Celeste stepped between them. "Jack Emery, this man saved my life, whose name I don't actually know."

"Callum Watkins."

Emery's eyes narrowed and he said nothing for a few moments. He seemed to be considering what she'd told him against the other misdeeds he no doubt assumed Callum had committed in the State Guard uniform. Eventually, Emery nodded and held out his hand. Callum shook it. Emery seemed to be in charge of the assault and Callum could nearly feel the collective sigh of relief from his men when peace appeared to be made.

"Celeste has told me the story about you freeing her from

Effingham." Emery's voice had a sharpness to it. "I don't condone anything your side has done, but thanks."

Callum nodded. "I can't expect anything else. So what now?"

"What now?" Emery laughed. "We start to end this thing."

"Here? There's nothing in here." Callum paused. "Is there?"

Emery just laughed again and shook his head. He turned and gestured to one of his companions, a Marine captain who appeared to be in command. As the troops moved forward to detain him, Callum looked to the bottom of the stairs, where vehicles sat like giant sentinels, warning that the game was up. Marines poured over the State Guard defensive positions and took his men captive.

He nearly jumped into the air when the radio in his headset chirped. "Post 457, this is command. If it proves impossible to hold your facility, you're to destroy it."

Callum laughed. He laughed hard, and couldn't stop.

His war was over.

～

"Jack?" Ortiz stuck his head into the office. "We're out of time. We need to go. Now."

Jack looked up from the computer. "But I'm—"

Ortiz held up a hand. "Aircraft incoming. We haven't got the gear to defend this position."

Jack knew better than to argue with Ortiz over issues such as these. The vehicles had bugged out an hour ago, moving on to the next target and hoping to sow confusion in FEMA Command about what they were dealing with. He was glad they'd been able to take the broadcast center without any bloodshed, but it was folly to think that luck could last. Two dozen feint attacks by the Marines across Chicago had opened the door for Jack and the others to do what was needed. The military force had been the can opener and Jack had found what he'd needed inside.

But even now, reports were coming in of 24th Marine Regiment forces being harassed by drones and of State Guard forces closing in on Chicago. The entire operation had hinged on this moment. Jack had hoped he'd get a bit more time, but it would have to do. He nodded, removed the headset and held his finger over the transmit button for a moment. A million things could have gone wrong, but it had worked flawlessly until now. With a smile, he pressed the button. There were no fireworks, just a light on a console that changed from red to green.

The Emergency Alert System had been switched on in 1997 and upgraded continuously since. It was designed to allow the President to speak to the entire nation for ten minutes, or to disseminate information about more localized events such as disasters and extreme weather. Following the FEMA takeover, it had been further upgraded still, with one primary transmission center commissioned in each state capital and many other major cities. Jack was thankful that Chicago made the cut. He'd received a crash course in the system from Hickens over the telephone, prior to the assault on the station. He hoped he'd done everything right. The green light flashing on the console gave him hope he had, that the information he'd prepped for broadcast had been successfully beamed out. Out of the masses of information that Mariposa Esposito had gathered, he'd broadcast the best of it. It was enough to crucify FEMA.

Or so he hoped. He'd done all he could. It was time to go. "Okay, let's go."

Ortiz nodded and walked toward the door. Jack looked back for a second, satisfied that the green light was still flashing on the broadcast panel. Over the next few minutes, the information he'd uploaded would beam its way to every radio, television, computer and tablet in the country. The information would damn FEMA using the very system they'd used to spew their lies. It would continue to operate until someone reached the broadcast room and turned it off, but by then it would be too late.

He followed behind Ortiz and they descended to the basement, where a dozen or so marines were waiting. They were the last of the 24th Marines still here. "What now?"

Ortiz placed his carbine on the ground then pulled out his pistol and stepped closer. "Now? You're going to learn how to use this. If we get into trouble, it might save your life."

"But—"

"Turn the safety off." Ortiz ignored Jack's protests as he held the weapon out and flicked the safety off.

"Okay." Jack nodded.

"Cock it." Ortiz pulled back the slide on the handgun and let it spring back, loading a round with a satisfying click.

Jack felt like he was being taught how to drive for the first time. "Okay."

"Hold it like this." Ortiz held the weapon out in front of him with two hands. "And none of that sideways, one-handed gangsta shit, either. If I see that, I'll shoot you myself."

"Okay."

"Squeeze the trigger." Ortiz tapped the trigger with his index finger, then reset the safety and then he held the weapon out to Jack. "Take it."

Jack looked down at the weapon in horror. "I don't want it. If you're relying on me to take out bad guys, then chances are you're all dead."

"That's why you need this." Ortiz thrust the weapon forward into his chest. "I'd rather you know how to use it before the rest of us are down."

Every synapse in his brain was telling him to refuse. He didn't want to hold the weapon, fire the weapon or be responsible for the weapon. But he didn't seem to have a choice in the matter. As he looked around, there were a dozen Marines with eyes on him, apparently waiting to see if he'd stand alongside them in the conflict to come. He couldn't ask them to take up arms for the final battle if he wasn't willing to. He took the gun from Ortiz.

Jack had been in the shit plenty of times, but he'd never been in the sewers before. Ortiz had dreamed it up. Heading down there was a way to escape the airstrikes and ground forces that would be bearing down upon the city, just like they had in Indianapolis. But Jack had learnt something else in that unfortunate city. He'd learnt that Richard Hall liked to handle things personally.

The first job was done, and Ortiz had given the bug out order to all 24th Marine Regiment forces. Jack just had to hope that the first attack would open up the second.

For that, they needed far fewer men.

CHAPTER 21

In a teleconference with reporters, Administrator Hall expressed his confidence in the ability of authorities to apprehend wanted fugitive Jack Emery, but stressed that he was a dangerous and potentially violent man, with a significant support network. FEMA would like to advise all residents of Chicago to remain in their homes, as the State Guard pursues Mr Emery and the small number of rebel United States Marines currently aiding him.

Federal Emergency Management Agency
News Release

As soon as the helicopter touched down, Richard unbuckled and climbed out. As he did, he reflected on how much things had changed in only a handful of hours. He'd thought he was flying in to deal with the attack on Chicago by the marines. But instead he faced a different issue: the hijacking of the Emergency Broadcast System by Jack Emery. Though his forces had retaken the facility, the damage had been done. Half of America had now seen some of the evidence against FEMA. It would take a huge effort to deal with the blowback. If he could.

Outside the helicopter he was met by a five-strong armed security detail. It was excessive, but the local FEMA office had insisted. The commander of the security forces nodded. "Good morning,

Administrator, we've secured the building and the Area V Command Center is ready to welcome you."

Richard nodded and as walked across the roof to the waiting elevator, he wanted to kick himself. He'd underestimated Jack Emery so much. Though Richard had whipped Emery and the resistance furiously, the man had clearly learned from each setback and each lump Richard took from his hide. He'd figured out that it wasn't the people you controlled, or the information you held, or the distribution method you had at your fingertips. Those were irrelevant.

No, real power came from those with the drive, the sense of moment – of *gravitas* – and the ruthlessness to do what needed to be done. Once Richard had decided he needed to seize power, to be the leader he'd waited decades to serve, he'd taken over America and imposed the order he considered so vital. It was also how he'd deliver the final mailed fist right to the teeth of Emery's supporters. He hoped it would be how he'd finally finish Emery, if he could find him.

They reached the main work area and Richard waited as the staff of the FEMA Area V Command Center were summoned. When they had gathered, he grasped the edge of the table with both hands. "Are we certain that all elements of the 24th Marines have now been eliminated or driven from the city?"

The State Guard attaché to the office, whose name Richard hadn't learned, nodded. "The last troops were eliminated thirty minutes ago. Airstrikes took care of the last of them. Our forces have regained control of the city, though unfortunately there was some collateral damage—"

"There always is." Richard tapped his hand on the table. "Have we found Jack Emery?"

The local supervisor coughed softly. "That's our next highest priority, Administrator."

"Wrong." Richard stood up straight. "It's your *only* priority. I don't want this office doing anything else until Emery is found."

The supervisor swallowed hard as he nodded. "You'll understand that amid so much carnage, it can be easy to lose one man. We'll inform you once we have him."

Richard smiled thinly. "I don't plan on departing until he's been located."

Richard turned and walked away from the table. He'd given them a fright, now it was time to let them work. Though his power in the organization was absolute and his word was god, there were downsides.

If he was hovering where his staff worked, very little would get done. He'd made his point. He went to the staff lounge and poured a coffee from the communal pot, took a sip, grimaced at the quality and then sat.

He used the time to make some calls to his subordinates. Though Emery was the only thing on his mind, some other business wouldn't wait for a resolution to that particular headache. He was thankful that none of the individuals he called, nor anyone in the Command Center, had mentioned the information dump that Emery was responsible for leaking. He was certain they knew about it, but they'd kept quiet.

The calls were the standard time killers he dealt with every day: the President, to re-assure him that everything was under control and that the executive orders would be needed for just a little while longer. Various lobbyists and influential Americans, protesting this or that or FEMA control in general. The State Guard general staff, begging for more manpower and resources. It was all a distraction.

"Administrator?" A woman spoke from across the room.

He looked up at the distraction. "Yes?"

"We've found Jack Emery, sir. We've alerted the State Guard in the building."

"Alerted them about what?"

"Emery, sir." The woman paused. "Radio triangulation confirms he's here."

JACK NEVER THOUGHT the darkness would be worse than the smell. Even though it was a line-ball decision, he could overcome the stink of shit. But hours of moving underground with only the powerful shafts of light provided by the Marines' flashlights had made him anxious. The blackness was suffocating, akin to the cell he'd very briefly called home in China. He was tired and wet. Most of all, he missed Celeste and was worried about her.

They'd moved for blocks through the sewers underneath Chicago. As they did, the elements of 24th Marines still in the city should have started to pull back or, if they were cut off, dug in for a protracted defense. Jack had no idea if that had gone to plan or not, but the broadcast had gone out and the little band of sewer rats had gone off the radar. As far as FEMA and the State Guard were concerned, they were phantoms.

In the wake of the 24th's departure, they'd left spotters in civilian clothes to monitor dozens of locations around Chicago, possible areas where Richard Hall would arrive to coordinate the defense of the city and the search for Jack. Less than twenty minutes ago, one of those scouts had sent word: Hall was at the Clark Street building that FEMA used as its area command in the city. Hall had gone to the most obvious location. Now they just had to reach him.

Jack sighed with relief as he watched a man at the top of the ladder give the cover a firm push. He was clearly doing his best to be quiet, but it was hard to shift the heavy steel manhole cover with any sort of stealth. The man stuck his head above ground, and Jack found it odd to see nothing above the man's waist for several moments. Eventually, the Marine ducked down and gave the all clear.

Jack exhaled heavily. Ortiz had said that this would be the hardest part. If there'd been guards outside the building, it would have been nearly impossible for the Marines to force their way inside. As it was, even as they climbed the ladder one after another and he waited his turn, Jack kept his hand on his weapon. He felt stupid for doubting its necessity when Ortiz had tried to hand it to him earlier. Jack was the last to climb to the top of the ladder and pull himself up to the street.

Once he was above ground, he saw the defensive perimeter that Ortiz and his men had formed, their weapons pointed outward. He stayed in the middle of the group and followed as Ortiz's men fanned out and covered all possible directions, moving as one toward the building. They reached it with no incident, then waited as two of the soldiers scouted the lobby and returned with a report that it was all clear. Jack looked at Ortiz. He seemed disturbed by the lack of civilians, but said nothing. They moved inside.

Jack looked around the lobby. As the scouts had reported, it was dark and deserted. He frowned and felt for the gun again. A large government building such as this should have been bustling, especially given it was home to the FEMA Area Command. It should also have been guarded. All he could hope was that, with Marines assaulting the city, all non-essential workers had been sent home and the building locked down. It seemed a forlorn hope, but it had to be true. The alternative was too terrible to contemplate.

Jack was directed to wait near the door as the team started to move more quickly, waved forward by Ortiz. They had to reach the fire stairs on the other side of the lobby. He watched as the marines scanned their surrounds, including the mezzanine balcony above. When they were halfway across the lobby, every light in the area flared white hot. Jack raised his forearm to shield his eyes, even as he heard shouts and the tapping sound of boots on tiles all around. He backed away.

"*Put down your weapons!*" The shout echoed around the lobby. "*Weapons down, now!*"

Jack backed further against the wall as Ortiz's soldiers kept their weapons trained on the State Guard soldiers above them on the mezzanine level. They were outnumbered and outpositioned, but their assailants were obviously waiting on something before opening fire. Given what he knew of Richard Hall, that seemed strange. Maybe the information he'd broadcast had soothed some of the itchy trigger fingers.

"*I won't tell you again.*" Jack couldn't see the man who was shouting. "*We want your weapons and the location of Jack Emery.*"

"I'm Captain Daniel Ortiz, 24th Marines." Ortiz's voice boomed in response, with no hint of fear. "I ask you to stand down and hand over Richard Hall."

Ortiz kept his weapon raised but turned his head away from it. He caught Jack's eye, hidden from the view of the attackers, and winked once. The message was clear: they can't see you, so stay hidden. Jack wanted nothing more than to shout out, to give himself up and save these lives, but every man here had known their fate in the event of capture. Whether it was in a fire fight or in a FEMA detention center, death was certain.

"*Last chance, Captain Ortiz.*"

"Fuck yourself!" Ortiz fired.

Jack screamed as the world exploded in front of him. There was no way his voice could be heard over the roar of gunfire, the screams of combat troops and the cries of wounded men. Ortiz's team got some shots of their own off, but it was a drop against an ocean. Jack had never seen anything like it. In action movies, the heroes win regardless of numbers or positioning. Not this time. This time they were slaughtered.

He turned and ran back across the street, toward the sewer, with tears streaming down his cheeks. He fought hard to stay composed. With three steps to go, he tripped and fell, landing hard on the road. He sucked at the air, but none entered his lungs. He started to panic until, after a few moments, his breathing returned. He scrambled to his feet and to the manhole. He hauled it open and climbed down, replacing the cover.

Darkness was the only ally he had left.

RICHARD STRODE FORWARD from the elevator and inspected the carnage from moments earlier. He'd ridden down as soon as the fire fight was over, but could still smell the smoke. The scene was chaos. Around a dozen dead men in marine uniforms were sprawled in tight formation in the middle of the lobby. Their guns had been taken but no other effort had been made to move them. Emery was not among them.

He growled in frustration as he took in the scene. "How fucking hard can it be to catch one man?"

The State Guard attaché to FEMA Area V, who'd ridden down with him, did his best to soothe Richard's anger. "All attention has shifted to finding Emery, sir."

Richard turned, grabbed the man by his collar and looked him straight in the eyes. "I'm sick of this. Find him. Kill him."

The man nodded. Richard let go and turned back to the dead soldiers. He took a few steps toward them, then stopped when he heard a cough. One of the soldiers he'd thought dead a moment ago was apparently still alive. Yet another fuck up from the State Guard troopers. He approached the wounded man, just as a guardsman hovered over the Marine and prepared to finish him.

"Don't you dare." Richard grabbed the man from behind and pulled him back. "Give me your weapon."

The young trooper looked confused, but handed over his rifle. "Sir, be careful, if you're not careful he'll—"

"Be quiet." Richard crouched down to the dying soldier. "What's your name, young man?"

"Daniel Ortiz." The soldier coughed hard once, then again. Blood dribbled down his chin.

"Here's the situation, Daniel." Richard leaned on the rifle as he crouched. "I have you and a lot of your comrades. To help all of you, I need you to tell me where Emery is."

"Go fuck yourself." Ortiz smiled. His teeth were bloody. "Just kill me. I'm not telling you shit. Neither will any of the others you've captured around the city."

Richard sighed and stood. He looked around. The State Guard troopers were searching the ground level of the building, as well as the basement and the stairs, but he had no faith in their ability to find Emery. He looked down at Ortiz again, struggling for breath and clearly fighting the pain. He pressed the barrel of the rifle into the man's stomach, right where he could see a bullet wound. Ortiz gasped and cried out.

"Where. Is. He." Richard pressed the barrel harder and ignored the man's shrieks. But the effort was hopeless. Ortiz bled out. Richard roared with rage. "Just *find* him!"

Richard threw the weapon onto the tiled floor then stalked back toward the elevator. There was no point in him staying here much longer, among the slugs crawling around trying to please him. He could do more back in the Command Center, coordinating effort across the city to find Jack Emery. He rode the elevator on his own, using the time to think about what he'd missed, where Emery could be.

Hours passed as Richard waited futilely for his people to get results. Without Emery's head on a pike, he'd have no enemy to parade before the public, to take the attention off the information that had briefly leaked. With Emery, he could torture the other man to say the evidence was all fabricated. He made his way through four coffees and eight fingernails. He'd never felt like this before, his future so contingent on something so completely out of his control.

After yet more hours, his phone rang. He nearly screamed. He was not in the right frame of mind for this phone call, but had no choice but to take it. "Mr President."

"Administrator Hall." The President's tone was cold. "This is a courtesy call to inform you that I've revoked all executive orders relating to FEMA and the State Guard. My attorney general has also informed me that you're to be arrested on a long list of charges. I suggest you wait where you are prior to being taken into custody."

"Mr—" Richard stopped speaking when the line went dead.

He threw the phone across the room. He'd known this might be coming, but had hoped to fight it off by capturing Emery. The information that had been leaked had obviously run wild in Washington. Richard had hoped to turn the tide, but now it had washed over his head. He turned and made his way to the elevator and toward the roof. He didn't even wait for his guards. Now he had to think about survival. All he needed was his helicopter pilot.

Once he reached the roof, he was pleased that the helicopter was still there, sitting like an old friend in the night. He called out. "John! Fire it up! We're out of here."

"Hall." The voice came from beside him.

Richard knew it instantly. He turned to his left. Though the roof was only dimly lit, he could see Jack Emery emerge from behind an air-conditioning unit. He looked like hell, but he held a pistol in his hand. Emery raised the weapon and took a few quick steps toward Richard. With a shake of his head, Richard raised his hands lazily. He steeled himself for the inevitable, the irony of finally having found Emery not lost on him.

"Turn around." Emery's voice was all business. "Back to me."

Richard laughed as he turned. "Just how the hell did you get up here?"

"That's the thing with absolute dictators, isn't it? You think you control everything, but miss the detail." Emery jammed the gun into the back of his head. "Down."

Richard fell to his knees. His best chance at survival had shifted. "You realize that I'm about to be arrested? That I'm powerless? Your little vigilante job is too late."

"I don't care. This ends here." Emery's voice was cold as he pressed the weapon into the back of his head. "This ends now, you cunt."

❧

THE PISTOL WAS SHAKING in Jack's hand as he held it to Hall's head. The other man said nothing else, apparently at peace with what was to come.

So much emotion and fury was flooding through him, he was unsure what to feel. He'd waited for hours in the sewers, unsure about what to do. He'd thought about fumbling through the sewers, until he found daylight and freedom, but that would have wasted the lives of the marines who'd fallen. He'd known he still had a role to play, even if there was nobody else left to help him and very little chance of success.

When he'd fought the Foundation for a New America, he'd been content to sit in a hotel room while the FBI wrapped up the threat. But this time was different. Even though the choicest pieces of Mariposa's information were now percolating around the country, and he was certain it would be enough to topple Hall, he still had a score to settle. He had to be sure that this was the end of it.

He'd waited until night, then climbed out of the sewer and crossed the street. Then, instead of going upstairs, he'd spotted something – a window-cleaning rig outside the building. Silently and in darkness, he'd enjoyed the wind through his hair as he rode it to the top. On the roof, he'd waited, hoping that Hall would emerge and head for his helicopter.

Now, he had the administrator right where he wanted him. Right where he'd wanted him for months. His finger squeezed the trigger slightly, but Jack held off when he heard the *thock-thock-thock* sound of helicopters drawing closer. They moved quickly and soon there were two circling above. Jack could barely hear himself think over the noise.

"My name is Special Agent Roberto Garcia, FBI." A voice boomed over the sound of the choppers. *"Richard Hall is to be arrested and charged with treason and multiple counts of first-degree murder. Put down your weapon."*

Jack shook his head at the irony. He'd fought so hard for nearly a year to fight Hall's control and got nowhere, but now he had a choice about how to do it. Whether his inner circle was breached or not, Hall still had a great deal of power all across the country. There was no guarantee that Hall would end up in the slammer if Jack let him live.

"Listen to him, Jack." Hall's shout could barely be heard over the noise. "Put your faith in the people, in the justice system. You don't need to do this."

Jack had been a reporter for ten years and had covered enough injustice to know the system got it wrong sometimes. On the other hand, if America was to have a chance of rediscovering itself, its freedoms and its moral purpose, then men like Richard Hall needed to be brought to justice, not executed.

Jack lowered the weapon, tossed it aside and stepped back, even as FBI agents began to rappel down onto the roof. He closed his eyes and took a deep breath.

It was over.

EPILOGUE

"**A**ttention passengers, this is your captain. We're about to enter a small patch of turbulence. I'd ask that you return to your seat and buckle up for a few minutes."

Jack sighed and opened his eyes as the aircraft started to shake. He was already in his seat and buckled up, but after the pilot's announcement, he was no longer asleep. He'd been sleeping fairly lightly recently – the slightest noise or flash of light enough to wake him – much to his annoyance. While this wasn't surprising, given the events of the past few years, what he'd never considered before was how many minor irritations could be found on a plane flight.

Even Air Force One.

He was flying from Los Angeles to Washington DC in time for the State of the Union address. The President's chief of staff had invited Jack along. He'd buttered Jack up, telling him that the President wanted him as an honored guest and that the President would be pleased to share a meal with him on board the aircraft. It hadn't happened. The turbulence lessened and he turned to Celeste. She was still asleep. Jack closed his eyes and started to drift off again.

Just as he was nearly out the cursed chime sounded again. "Jack Emery, please report to the President's office for your appointment."

Jack's eyes shot open, more quickly than the last time. He prodded

Celeste and she woke with a start. Jack leaned in to kiss her on the cheek. "Just going to meet with McGhinnist."

"Okay." Her voice was groggy, and he knew she was no good in the moments after waking. "Good luck."

Jack made his way through the aircraft. Once he arrived at the office, he exchanged a few pleasantries with the Secret Service agent stationed outside, even as the agent used his radio to report Jack had arrived. He obviously heard what he wanted to in his earpiece, because the lock on the door give a heavy *clunk* and the agent pushed the door open and stood aside to let Jack inside.

President Bill McGhinnist was seated behind his desk. Though this was not the first time he'd met world leaders, or even Bill McGhinnist, it was the first time he was both one on one with the President and also likely to be the major topic of conversation. Jack waited nervously as McGhinnist finished signing some paperwork, then looked up with a broad smile.

"Mr President?" Jack had planned what he'd say to the most powerful man in the world, but it had escaped him. "Thanks for inviting me to meet with you."

"Come on, Jack." McGhinnist stood, walked around the desk and slapped him on the back. "How many times do we need to save the country before you'll start calling me Bill in private?"

"A few more times yet, given your new job, sir." Jack laughed.

One of the pleasant surprises in the aftermath of the arrest of Richard Hall and the return to normalcy had been finding out Bill McGhinnist was alive. Somehow he'd survived the assault on the New York resistance cell and gone to ground. Along with Celeste, he was one of the few involved who'd survived Hall's decapitation of the resistance. A lot of good people hadn't. Jack mourned them all.

Hall was still on trial, but the daily court reports showed little chance of him being freed. Though he'd had a mandate to take over the country, he'd gone a mile beyond it. Every day new information emerged about the atrocities Hall and his organization had committed in the name of order and safety, and it sickened him. FEMA had already been gutted and the State Guard abolished.

In the aftermath, Jack had traveled to Europe with Celeste, to visit her family in the UK and get as far away from the States as he could while it healed. At the first elections following the collapse of FEMA control, Bill McGhinnist had been elected in a landslide for the

Republican Party. Though he'd seemed a reluctant candidate, the public had bonded with his call for a whole lot of fresh air through Washington.

Jack had worked closely with McGhinnist to end the threat of both the Foundation for a New America and FEMA, but those interactions had been brief and for a sharp purpose. He'd had no real time to get to know the man beneath the bureaucrat, who now happened to be President. Jack couldn't guess what McGhinnist had up his sleeve, but he wasn't sure he'd like it.

McGhinnist gestured toward a lounge chair, then took a seat himself. "I've got to be upfront. I didn't just ask you along for the ride."

Jack kept his features even. "What can I do for you?"

"I need you to come work for me, Jack."

Jack didn't hesitate. "Not interested."

"I'm not asking, Jack." McGhinnist's features hardened. "Your co—"

"I'm Australian, don't forget."

McGhinnist laughed and his face softened. "Fine, *the* country needs you. While I think we've purged most of the cancers, I can't be completely sure."

"Well, I did try to shoot Hall." Jack shrugged. "The FBI stopped me. Even given that, I still nearly pulled the trigger."

"A shame, if you ask me. But don't worry about Hall. He's sorted." McGhinnist sipped his coffee. "I need you, Jack. I need you on my side full time."

Jack leaned forward in his chair. "Why me, though? There're better people for the job."

"No, there aren't. You've got a knack for this stuff. But more importantly, you're also above reproach. You've saved America from itself and its leaders twice. I need you on the payroll."

Jack stayed silent.

"The first time, it took us to war with China and we nearly had a large chunk of Congress controlled by maniacs. You put a stop to that, though not without cost. The second time, it was our own agencies attacking America while pretending to save it, using the very laws designed the safeguard us all. Again, you stopped it."

"At great personal cost." Jack's voice was soft.

"I know that."

Jack sighed. "Okay, so theoretically, what's the job?"

McGhinnist smiled. "Winding back the clock twenty years. While terrorism is a serious threat, it pales in comparison to the loss of our freedoms over the past few decades. To sleep soundly at night and keep the shadows at bay, we've unshackled a much greater darkness. It is too open to abuse and must be put right."

Jack didn't disagree. Since 9/11, the Patriot Act and its various add-ons had combined to form a miasma of abuse. Civil rights had been curtailed. Bureaucracy and red tape had been allowed to stifle good sense. A minor increase in security from the unlikeliest of events had been given primacy over everything that made America what it is. And, while he doubted it could be unwound entirely, there were definitely improvements that could be made.

"Put right..." Jack's voice trailed off.

"Reviewed and abolished where sensible. I'm talking about a full, independent inquiry into the laws, regulations and actions of government that have gone too far, and a combined effort of my entire administration to fix it."

Jack would have doubted the words if they came from the mouth of any other person on the planet. Governments the world over were pleased to take more power on the slightest pretext, but didn't like to give it up. Curing the addiction of America's government to this power would be difficult, if not impossible, but Bill McGhinnist had done his absolute best to fight both the Foundation and FEMA. He mightn't succeed, but Jack knew he'd try.

"You don't need me for that."

"You're wrong, I do." McGhinnist sighed. "I'm the former Director of the FBI, I helped to devise and enact some of the laws. Others? They're too blinkered to see what needs doing. I need someone who has been proven to have America's best interests at heart, who's smart and who can lead this change."

"Me."

"You, Jack."

"Okay." Jack stood after a moment and held out his hand. "I'm in. But I think you're crazy brave. If you pull this off, they'll need to make some space on Mount Rushmore."

McGhinnist stood, beaming, and shook Jack's hand with vigor. "When I agreed to run, I hoped you might agree to join the team. You won't regret this."

"So, what's that make me?"

"Special Advisor to the President of the United States of America. It'll look good on your CV, though it's not quite a third Pulitzer."

"Two are enough."

"Indeed." McGhinnist laughed. "Keeping an eye on the review will be your first job, but after that I've got some other things in mind."

"Fine. When do I start?"

"Well, I'd actually planned to announce it in about..." McGhinnist checked his watch. "An hour? I have to say *something* at the State of the Union."

Jack stared. He hadn't expected his appointment to be quite so public, quite so soon. "Okay, sir."

"Bill."

"Okay, Bill." Jack laughed.

"Plus I've got a medal or two to pin on your chest."

NATIONS DIVIDED

JACK EMERY 3

For those fighting for peace with words,
rather than guns

PROLOGUE

Rashid Sirhan opened his eyes at the sound of her voice, blinking quickly as he tried to adjust to the harsh overhead lighting. "Sorry, just napping."

The nurse smiled kindly, the usual twinkle in her eyes. "I've got your pills, Mr. Sirhan. I'm glad you finally got some sleep."

The young nurse filled his palm with a rainbow assortment of drugs, like his father used to with candy when he was a child. He shook his head at the thought, stuffed the pills into his mouth and washed them down with some water. The pills certainly didn't taste like his childhood, but instead felt like one more insult heaped upon many others as he'd grown old.

"All done?" Her voice had an edge of menace. She'd probably had problems with other patients today.

"Mission accomplished." Rashid opened his mouth to show her, then closed it. "I'll look forward to my lollipop."

She ignored the jibe and he closed his eyes again. As he relaxed and tried to ease back into sleep, Rashid heard the nurse push the drug cart to the next bed. Before he had the chance to drift off, he was gripped by a coughing fit, a dry and raspy reminder that he was down to one lung. The cancer that had plagued his body also destroyed his rest.

Just as his coughing subsided, Rashid heard a loud chattering sound from a few rooms away. The sound was unmistakable, akin to a half-dozen small firecrackers exploding in quick succession. Even before the squeals and shouts had started, he'd figured out what was happening: a standard-issue Israeli assault rifle was firing on full automatic. The IDF was here.

Rashid kicked off the covers and rolled out of bed, bracing as he landed hard on the ground. He'd be damned if he'd make himself an easy target or let the shrapnel from a frag grenade catch him in bed. Coughing again, he ducked low and listened. The gunfire relented for a moment, ripped off again, then stopped once more. The pattern – shoot and pause – hinted at one gunman.

Glancing around for a weapon, any kind, he ignored the noise and chaos around him as others fled the gunfire. He settled on a metal kidney dish and struggled to his feet, knowing this would be his last stand. Refusing to die on his knees, Rashid stood tall as the sound of the gunfire moved closer.

The door to the ward swung open. Rashid squeezed the kidney dish tighter as a male patient and a nurse ran through the door and towards him. The woman fell as gunfire found her, leaving a spray of blood in her wake. A second later, the man dropped as well.

The gunman walked through the door, dressed from head to toe in the uniform of the Israeli army and the triple chevron that revealed him to be a samal – a sergeant. Rashid stood as proud as he could, unwilling to let the Israeli see him take a backward step.

While Rashid had launched rockets into Israel before, likely killing civilians, he figured you had to be a special kind of killer to shoot up a hospital. Or the closest thing Gaza had to a hospital, anyway. He wasn't sure how many had died, but as he lifted the kidney dish Rashid felt anger course through him.

The Israeli sergeant's features betrayed no emotion as he brought the assault rifle up. Rashid swallowed hard and threw the kidney dish at the Israeli. The projectile hit the other man on the chest and then clattered to the tiles, the lamest possible resistance. Rashid didn't care. He hadn't run away.

It wasn't much fun living with cancer anyway.

ACT I

CHAPTER 1

As dignitaries descend on New York City for the signing of the historic peace agreement between Israel and Palestine, many remain skeptical that a deal will be finalized. Though both camps say that all issues are close to being fully resolved and that the massacre at Gaza's Al Amal Hospital has brought the parties closer to a deal, the world has seen too many false starts on this issue to be certain of an agreement. Until pen touches paper, the stakes will remain high and nobody has more to gain, or lose, from the agreement than President Bill McGhinnist, who has worked tirelessly to resolve this issue before the end of his first term.

New York Standard

J ack Emery's eyes darted back and forth across the page, consuming the news for the day. He licked his finger and turned a page with one hand while he fumbled for his coffee with the other. The shock from the story on page five caused him to knock over his coffee cup, drowning the *Post*'s scoop about a Supreme Court justice being photographed at a titty bar.

"Damn it." Jack reached for a napkin and mopped at the spill, trying his best to save the rest of the newspaper.

"Nice work." Celeste Adams' voice was heavy with sleep. "Good thing you never listen to me about the advantages of reading the news on your iPad."

Jack looked up. Despite the mess, he couldn't resist a smile as she leaned against the doorframe, wearing panties and a tank top. "Hey."

"Hey." She pushed herself off, walked toward him and reached for his plate. "Why'd you let me sleep so late?"

He swatted at her hand and his smile turned into a frown when she stole the remains of his bagel, biting into the last morsel. A smear of cream cheese remained on her lip. He stood, took her hands in his and kissed her deeply, using his tongue to lick at the cheese. She laughed and pulled away. They looked at each other for a second and then shared another kiss.

"Too cute to wake." Jack gave her hands a squeeze, pulled away and made a show of eyeing her up and down.

She gave him a gentle slap on the rear, then rounded the table and took a seat. "Any of the papers survive your drenching?"

He considered the mess. "Not sure. They all look a bit moist."

"Gross. That word should only be used to describe cake."

Jack laughed as she grabbed the *New York Standard* and started to flick through it with the practiced eye of someone who'd edited the paper the previous afternoon. She never knew how to disconnect from her work, though it wasn't like he could talk. He left her with the paper, walked to the kitchen and put a bagel into the toaster for her.

He thought about the strange situation that existed between them. Though Jack felt their relationship was equal to the one he'd had with his ex-wife – loving and supportive and exciting – sometimes it felt neither of them ever switched off from work enough to enjoy it. Celeste was living in a townhouse in New York and working as managing editor at the *Standard*, while he was living in Washington and working for President Bill McGhinnist. It had been that way for three years. He traveled to New York every second weekend, where they spent their time together feigning normalcy until he caught a late flight out of JFK on Sunday night. It was hard, but worth it.

The bagel popped. He gave it a liberal spread of cream cheese then picked up the plate and walked back into the dining room, stealing a glance over her shoulder at the story she was reading as he placed the plate down. It was yet another story about Israel and Palestine. The papers had been full of them for weeks.

"It'll work." Jack placed a hand on her shoulder.

"I'm not sure." She grabbed his hand and held it to her body as she finished reading the story. Then she reached for the bagel, took a bite and started to talk with her mouth full. "There have been so many letdowns it's hard to get too excited. Bringing them all into town was a ballsy move."

He nodded and sat beside her. They'd discussed the Israeli–Palestinian peace agreement deep into the night. Both of them were hopeful – but neither convinced – that the two sides would agree on the final few sticking points and get it done. Things had moved a long way since the massacre at the hospital in Gaza a few months prior, but the deal was a complicated one to negotiate.

"It'd be huge for McGhinnist. It's been a slog these past few years. He needs a big win leading up to the election."

"Plenty of presidents have tried, and failed, to crack the Israel–Palestine nut in their time, Jack." Celeste squeezed his hand gently. "If he's relying on this to get him over the line then it might be best to start preparing for life after the White House."

"He'll win." Jack's tone made it clear he didn't want to discuss the possibility of Bill McGhinnist losing the presidency.

"Just don't get too invested, okay?"

Jack nodded. It wasn't the first time she'd told him to be careful since he'd taken the job as special advisor to the President. While McGhinnist had no shortage of big ideas and a decent record of steering them through Congress, his popularity had taken a hit in recent months. Given America was still healing from the near takeover of the country by the Foundation for a New America and the full takeover by FEMA, Jack couldn't blame the public for some political fatigue. Yet he still felt the situation was unfair. McGhinnist had halted the blanket monitoring of US citizens and limited other impositions in place since 9/11, but those successes were yesterday's news – McGhinnist needed a new win.

The peace would be that.

Jack had spent nearly a year working with McGhinnist and US negotiator Karl Long to help shepherd the peace agreement between Israel and Palestine through complex negotiations and, at times, fraught decisions. Over countless meetings and phone calls, the sides had worked out problems large and small until, finally, they'd reached agreement on all issues but one: Israeli settlements on land claimed by Palestine. Despite this, McGhinnist had made the gutsy decision to schedule a date for the signing, hoping it would help to force a resolution on the last issue. McGhinnist had even authorized Long to throw out a few carrots if it meant getting a deal.

He'd be lying if he pretended not to care about the politics of it, given part of his job was to leverage wins like this into political gain for the President. But Jack's primary responsibility, and the sole reason he'd agreed to work for McGhinnist in the first place, was achieving good policy outcomes. The peace agreement was one of those. Any political benefits were a bonus.

"McGhinnist needs this to show he can build something positive. He needs to prove he can do more than just remove the excesses of others. This feels different. It feels good. He's going to get it done."

"Well, I hope you're right. He's proven before that he can take on big policy issues and win." Celeste pushed her plate aside. "Do you have much work to do today?"

"Not particularly. The President flies in later tonight, but he's straight into meetings with Karl." Jack thought hard to make sure he hadn't forgotten any appointments. "All clear."

"Glad to hear it. I get the feeling this might be the last break you get for a while, so I want you to make the most of it." She stood. "Now, are you coming or not?"

Jack's eyes widened as she walked slowly out of the kitchen. With each step, she exaggerated the movement of her hips slightly. She raised her tank top over her head and tossed it on the floor, then paused and dropped her panties. As he watched her walk to the bedroom, Jack grabbed the last bite of the bagel left on her plate, stood and followed her.

It was good to be home.

～

SAMIH KHALADI WAITED at the crossing as dozens of cars blitzed through the intersection. He loved New York City, though not for the reasons most people did. It wasn't about the skyscrapers, the bustle or the attractions. What moved him was that so many people – all kinds of people – could live so closely together in relative harmony and safety. It was chaotic, but it worked.

The lights changed and he crossed the street with his pair of security guards in tow, doing his best to stay a step or two ahead. If he had the choice, he'd go without the security entirely, but President McGhinnist had insisted the negotiators be escorted at all times when they were outside. Given Samih was representing Palestine in the peace negotiations, he had little choice.

He slowed as he caught sight of a Starbucks, then smiled and turned to his security. "I'm just going to get a—"

"Mr. Khaladi?" One of the guards interrupted, as the other looked at his watch. "We need to return to the UN building, sir. The lunch hour ends soon."

Samih sighed. He hated being on a schedule. It wasn't the guard's fault, but it was annoying. "Okay, but first let me grab a coffee."

"There's coffee back at the meeting, sir." The guard was insistent. "I really must insist that we turn back."

Samih felt his face flush. "The entire world will wait for me today if they have to. I'm one of the people trying to end the most intractable political conflict on the planet. I want a coffee, from here, so please wait outside for me while I go inside to get one."

Samih exhaled loudly and the door to the Starbucks felt his displeasure, as he pushed it open with some force. His security didn't seem happy and Samih didn't like throwing his weight around, but he wanted a few more minutes before returning to the pressure cooker. He waited in line for just a moment and then he reached the front.

"How're you today, sir?" An attendant struggled to feign interest. "What can I get for you?"

Samih swallowed his irritation and did his best to smile. "I would like a coffee please."

The man stared at him blankly. "Which kind, sir? You're supposed to know your order by the time you reach the front."

Samih's eyes narrowed as he considered the menu. "An Americano. A large one."

Samih paid and moved to the end of the counter, struggling not to laugh at the inanity of the exchange. After being involved in negotiations over land borders, migration of peoples and security issues – all incredibly high stakes – he'd had to be stepped through ordering a coffee by a college kid. Thinking about it cheered him up.

As he closed his wallet, he glanced at the photo he kept inside and felt a pang of regret. All he wanted for his people was peace, for them to be able to enjoy fast food, entertainment, shopping malls and sporting games without the threat of extremist violence or Israeli gunships. He wanted a nation for them. All that remained was closing the deal and hoping it was accepted. Only a few short years ago, Samih would have been at the front of the line of Palestinians decrying this agreement. Worse, he'd have advocated and committed violence to stop it from being signed. He'd been caught in a cycle of hate that served nobody and only left people dead. It was why he kept the photo of his brother close.

After his brother had been killed by an Israeli airstrike in retaliation for an attack Samih had ordered, Samih had faced a choice. In his anger, he'd considered further attacks, but he'd mourned and seen another way. Forming a breakaway group of Hamas, he'd banded with the Palestinian Liberation Organization to take the battle to the unreformed extremists. The conflict had been bloody – moderates and hardliners engaged in open warfare on the streets, with Israeli gunships occasionally adding their own fire and noise to the mess. The moderates had won, at huge cost. Samih had been offered leadership of the new, unified Palestinian authority but had declined in order to focus on helping to secure a lasting peace.

"Sir?" A Starbucks staff member touched Samih on the arm. "Sir? Your coffee is ready."

Samih shook his head. He was always prone to deep reflection on the past, but it seemed to be happening more often lately. He took the coffee. "Thank you."

He walked outside and didn't wait for his security to fall into line. The walk back to the UN building was uneventful. As he walked, he thought about the draft agreement. Though it didn't give his people everything they wanted, or deserved, it was the best deal that could be achieved. A good deal, peace and a state were better than waiting forever for the perfect deal.

The agreement had to succeed.

Back inside the building, Samih juggled his coffee as he returned to his seat with the other delegates. Everyone had the same goal: resolving the last issue. Samih represented the Palestinians and Ben Ebron represented the Israelis, as they'd done for years, aided in the negotiations by the US Special Envoy for Israeli–Palestinian Relations, Karl Long.

The last person to enter the room was in some ways the most important – Liliana Garza, Secretary-General of the United Nations. She'd obliged US President Bill McGhinnist's demands for the signing ceremony to be scheduled and for the talks to be finalized. Samih watched Garza as she walked to the head of the table.

"Gentlemen, I trust you enjoyed lunch?" She held her arms wide, a typically welcoming gesture from her during the tough negotiations. "If we're to sign an agreement tomorrow, we have this session to resolve the final issue. We left off at—"

"Compensation for displaced Israeli settlers." Ebron cut the pleasantries short, his voice sharp. "Israel is committed to finding a way through this issue and finalizing the agreement, but it mustn't be at the expense of our own people. There needs to be a strong package that I can take to my government."

Samih's lips pressed together but he kept quiet. Though he found it hard to comprehend that the final sticking point after three years of negotiations could be payments to Israelis who'd annexed the lands of his people, he knew that without compensation there would be no peace. He'd learned the hard way that one wrong word could destroy much painstaking work.

Garza took the interruption in her stride. "I've had my staff working the phones during the lunch hour. United Nations member states have agreed to contribute forty percent of the compensation amount. The rest of the world has done its part, now it's the turn of the others in this room."

Samih was surprised by the news, but smiled sadly. "This is an area where the Palestinian people can make little contribution. We are not a rich people."

Ebron flared. "Unacceptable. The Palestinians must contribute—"

Samih held up his hand. "However, upon achieving statehood, Palestine will set aside one percent of government revenue until one-tenth of the total is paid."

Ebron's mouth fell open slightly, before he seemed to catch himself and right his composure. "That's a welcome gesture, Mr. Khaladi, and one I didn't expect."

Samih smiled. He'd planned on just that and the effect had been powerful. For the diminutive state of Palestine to make a financial contribution to resettling Israelis was a game changer. Samih had long argued the presence of the settlers was illegal and that no compensation should be paid, but in the interests of peace a concession had to be made. He hoped it would be enough.

Long tapped his signet ring on the table. It had stopped bothering Samih, because it appeared be a habit. "The President has authorized me to increase the contribution of the United States to twenty-five percent, but that's as high as we're going to go."

"A very generous offer." Samih nodded.

"Twenty-five percent remains." Ebron sighed as he looked at each of them, as if the pressure of expectation was too much.

"Mr. Ebron?" Garza's voice was gentle. "Do you need a recess to consult with your government and consider Israel's position?"

"No, that won't be necessary." Ebron sighed. "It burns me to my core that Israel must contribute financially to the displacement of its own citizens, but the pressure of tomorrow's deadline and the aftermath of the Al Amal massacre leave me little choice. I agree."

"Wonderful." Garza beamed. "Any costs borne out of this agreement will be more than paid for by the peace and prosperity that also flows from it."

"It's agreed then?" Long's eyes widened as they flicked between Samih and Ebron. "We have something to sign?"

"The agreement is suitable for Israel, if a little expensive." Ebron placed his palms flat on the table. "I hope this can be the end of it."

Now Samih felt the weight of expectation. He looked down at his notes, trying to think of any negatives for his people that he might have missed. He'd already gained the agreement of his leadership on the draft text, with the exception of the issues worked out during this final day. There was nothing in the last few resolutions that would prevent the deal being closed. It was good enough.

"Well?" Long's voice had an edge.

Samih looked up. He rested his elbows on the table with a smile. "My friends, this is an important day. We've achieved peace."

The ever-serious Ebron leaned back and spun around on his chair, while Long slapped the table and sported a wide grin. Samih closed his eyes and allowed himself a moment of reflection. This occasion had been so long in coming, he never thought he'd see it. Thousands dead, generations ruined, years wasted. He hoped his people would welcome the peace on offer.

"Excuse me, Mr. Khaladi?"

Samih opened his eyes. Ebron was standing in front of him. "Yes?"

"I'd like to shake your hand."

Samih stood, feeling all the weight of his sixty years, then shook the proffered hand. "This is a momentous day, my friend."

"It is." Ebron nodded and pulled his hand away, clearly not used to being so personable.

"We will sign the agreement tomorrow." Garza joined them, the relief in her voice clear. "Twenty-eight days after that, there will be peace."

~

"Zed Eshkol is professor of history at Yeshiva University, a position he's held for nearly forty years. He lectures in Jewish history and his specialty is the politics surrounding the creation of Israel following the Second World War. He's considered one of the world's leading thinkers on the causes and consequences of conflict between Israel and its neighbors, including the Palestinian people."

When the crowd started its applause, Zed planted his cane on the ground, pushed on it heavily and climbed to his feet. Letting the cane support him, he shuffled slowly to the stage. At the bottom of the stairs he paused, making a mental note to talk to the staffer who'd selected the venue. Zed wasn't as spry as he used to be.

"Thank you, Ariel." Zed spoke softly, short of breath, once he'd reached the top of the stairs. He patted the man on the shoulder.

Ariel beamed. "No problem, professor. Good luck with your lecture."

As Zed moved to the lectern, he reflected that, while Ariel had promise, he needed to be molded. He adjusted the microphone, handed his cane to another staffer and gripped the sides of the lectern as if his life depended on it. After checking his notes were in place, he looked up to the packed theatre. That audiences still came to see him speak was a thrill to him.

"Thank you all for coming. My thanks also to Ariel, who's organized a great program for us." Zed smiled. "I do wish I wasn't here tonight, though, or that we at least had a better reason to come together, but here we are. I'll speak for just a few moments, then we'll enjoy supper and reconvene for questions and discussion."

Zed looked down at his notes and used the pause to catch his breath before speaking again. "Quite simply, my friends, the peace agreement that will be signed tomorrow is a betrayal of Israel and the Jewish people, who gained their freedom and a state of their own after one of the darkest episodes in human history."

Zed looked up at the crowd. He usually didn't like mentioning the Holocaust, but there was no way to avoid it this evening. "I'll not speak of the Holocaust again, though many of you know that I survived it, but please be clear that the situation facing us tomorrow is the most desperate since that terrible chapter in our history.

"Israel has existed and grown despite being under the dark cloud of conflict. Every citizen has military training, its armed forces are potent, Mossad is rightly feared and a nuclear stockpile is the ultimate deterrent. Indeed, Israel has defended itself against aggression many times, often in desperate circumstances. It has never been belligerent, but always vigilant."

Zed paused and looked around the theatre. For a hastily convened event, the turnout was excellent. It gave him hope that, while the vast majority of the world and the American public wanted a deal between Israel and Palestine, there was still a cohort of the faithful. Over nine decades, he'd learned that where there was a glimmer of hope, there was the possibility of deliverance.

He continued. "Through it all, Israel has showed remarkable restraint in dealing with this aggression. Sometimes against better judgment, it has tolerated and negotiated when others would have struck, resorting to retaliation only when it's absolutely necessary. Israel invested in the Iron Dome, to stop rocket attacks, rather than spending more on jets and rockets to flatten the attackers."

Zed started to cough. Turning away from the lectern, he raised one hand to cover his mouth, but made sure to keep the other in place. He felt as if knives were stabbing him in the chest as his body clenched with each cough, though he did his best to calm himself and bring it under control. A few members of the crowd shouted out for someone to help him.

Someone gripped his arm and he heard Ariel's voice. "Professor, are you okay? I'll ask for an early recess."

"No!" Zed coughed again and then looked up to Ariel, his voice sharp. "Just give me a moment."

"Okay, professor. Take your time, at least."

Zed kept his back to the audience as he brought the coughing under control. Finally, the worst of it subsided and he returned to the lectern. "My apologies for the interruption, ladies and gentlemen. I frequently find that my body is my toughest critic these days."

The crowd offered sympathetic smiles and laughs. He continued. "Israel's restraint hasn't been enough. For decades the world has judged and threatened Israel, twisting the arm of its leaders to show ever more restraint, make deals and repudiate its right to exist, peacefully, within its own borders.

"Yet while Israel has attempted to co-exist with its neighbors and the Palestinians in the hope of peace, it's never enough. Israel's enemies aim for total annihilation while the world expects capitulation to the demands of cutthroats and criminals.

"Thankfully, strong Israeli leaders long resisted those demands. But now, weak leaders are happily slitting their own throats. A massacre perpetrated by a madman, sad though it was, has pressured Israel's leaders into signing an agreement that is evil. It will split an Israeli state that should always be strong."

Zed paused. He'd thought long and hard about the next part of his speech. "The United Nations and the USA are revisionists who helped to grant Israel its freedom only to convince the country's leaders, now, to abandon much of that freedom – to act, to defend itself, to exist within its own borders.

"This agreement mustn't be signed. It represents the eradication of an Israeli state at the height of its power, the betrayal of our people and a disgrace before God. Every free-thinking Jew the world over needs to stand against this travesty, or history will judge this generation as the one that killed the dream of Israel!"

Zed felt an enormous wave of pleasure and relief wash over him as applause roared. He smiled slightly and gripped the lectern until the noise receded, then waved a hand lazily in the air and signaled for a staffer to bring his cane. It would take him an eternity to get down the stairs again.

By the time he'd managed the journey and taken a seat, most of the rest of the crowd was busy getting supper in the foyer. Zed wasn't interested in making small talk. Instead, he wanted time to himself before the questions started and other eminent speakers joined him on stage. But he never got the chance.

A man approached and leaned down to speak to Zed. "Professor Eshkol? I'm David Kahlon. May I have a moment?"

Zed smiled softly, unable to help himself but careful to hide it. Men like these were as regular as clockwork. "Of course."

Kahlon nodded and sat. "Professor, I wanted to pay my respects on behalf of the Jewish Home. Many of my colleagues share your views."

Zed laughed. He'd closely followed the statements of Jewish Home – one of Israel's major conservative political parties – about the peace agreement. "It's a shame the government does not. I think it's important that those with a public voice continue to advocate sanity."

"Couldn't agree more, professor. I've been asked to sound you out, again, for your interest in becoming a citizen of Israel and running to join the Knesset."

Zed shook his head softly. This felt like the thousandth time he'd been asked to join the Israeli parliament. But he was old, tired and comfortable. He'd had his chance at the spotlight after surviving the Holocaust and helping to establish Israel, but had chosen instead to make his contribution in academia.

"Professor?" Kahlon pressed.

"Your request just takes me back some years." Zed smiled. "I think you know my answer. I'm an old man."

"But—"

Zed held up his hand. "No. Please respect my decision. I'll continue doing all I can to speak against this peace process, and to support the right conservatives with my voice during Israeli elections, but that's the sum of my contribution. I'm not a man for the limelight, Mr. Kahlon. Now, please excuse me."

There was a tinge of regret in Kahlon's smile, but they shook hands and he left. Zed forgot about him quickly. He had a lecture to finish.

CHAPTER 2

On the day the peace agreement between Israel and Palestine is to be signed, sources from inside the White House have revealed that the United States is considering an unprecedented level of military support to Israel over the next month. The same source stated that the President is nervous about the agreement holding over the twenty-eight–day countdown period. Following the leak, several key Republicans have spoken in favor of the deployment, though others joined with Democrats to condemn yet another US military adventure in the Middle East. Despite the mixed views, it appears that the McGhinnist administration will let nothing stand between the division of Israel and Palestine into two states.

New York Standard

Jack stared at the croissant, tempted to devour it against all protocol and his better judgment. He'd been sitting in the New York Grand Hyatt dining room with a half-dozen others for nearly an hour, waiting for the President and his guests to finish their private meeting and arrive for breakfast. Polite group conversation had devolved into a series of rolling battles, with existing acquaintances talking quietly among themselves while they waited. Jack was struggling not to contemplate his empty stomach and the pastry that promised so much.

The President had ordered the entire hotel booked for VIP attendees at the peace conference. McGhinnist was also staying at the hotel, leaving no doubt as to how seriously he was taking the event. The Secret Service and NYPD had locked down the building, with only official vehicles and a select number of credentialed visitors allowed inside the cordon. The security was extreme, but then so to was the event. Jack knew that one bomb or crazed gunman would be all it took to end this thing.

"Reckon we'll hit an hour?" Jack turned to the President's National Security Advisor, James Tipping, doing his best to get his mind off food.

Tipping turned to Jack and smiled, as if his mind was returning from considering some deep question. "I'm going to eat the table soon."

Jack laughed. Though they'd been friends since Jack had joined McGhinnist's administration, Tipping was a man of few words – a very private guy. Tipping lived in Georgetown and McGhinnist had brought him over from the Bureau upon becoming president. Jack respected Tipping's intellect deeply and the other man was good for a drink. He couldn't say the same about all of his colleagues.

"How's Celeste?"

"Busy. This agreement is as much work for her as it is for us." Jack let out a long sigh. "It'll be good to see it done, though Celeste might sell less papers."

"Should have stayed in that game." Tipping frowned. "I'm not really sure why you left journalism to join our merry band. What exactly is your role, Jack?"

Jack had heard it all before and knew where this was heading. Tipping had a sharp sense of humor. "Special Advisor to the President."

Tipping snorted. "I advise on national security. Others advise on economics, foreign relations – all sorts of things. What do you do, Jack?"

Jack kept his voice flat. "I advise."

Tipping guffawed and Jack shared the laugh, knowing there was some truth to the other man's jokes. As McGhinnist's fixer and sounding board, Jack's role description was fairly vague and he was constantly stepping on toes. It meant a few people were just waiting for him to slip up, even some of those inside the White House.

Jack was about to speak again when the woman sitting one along from Tipping, Republican senator Diane Yates, craned her head toward them.

"Excuse me."

Jack sighed but did his best to smile. He wasn't in the mood for the senator or her opinions, but such was the price of a compliant Senate. "Yes, senator?"

Yates glanced at Tipping and then locked eyes on Jack, her features cold and sharp. "I couldn't help but overhear your conversation. I understand your role in the administration, Jack, unlike some of your colleagues, but I can't fathom how you can think the path the President is taking with Israel is wise."

Yates had been dead against the peace from the start, demanding America walk away from any solution that displaced Israelis. Given her status as Senate Majority Leader, she had to be listened to, humored and invited to the important dinners. She hadn't gotten her way, but she'd gone down swinging. Luckily, Jack knew which buttons to push.

"State Department and DOD analysis shows that if we can secure the peace, then we'll be able to reduce our military and diplomatic footprint in the region by forty percent." Jack looked to Tipping, who nodded. "Given the President's commitment to tackling the deficit, I think you'll agree that's a handy saving."

Yates shook her head. "Well, that's true, but—"

"Not to mention the way we've been able to use this deal to get Iran on side." Tipping completed the one-two alley-oop. "We've got Tehran eating out of our hand right now, which is something the Democrats never managed. They let Iran acquire nukes, which we've managed to keep them from using."

Yates harrumphed and turned away. With a shake of his head, Jack smirked slightly at Tipping, thankful for the save. Yates could go on for hours if she built up enough steam, but having the National Security Advisor shoot down her protests had prevented that.

The door to the dining room opened and Jack stood with the other guests as McGhinnist walked in, joined by Ben Ebron, the Israeli negotiator, Samih Khaladi, the Palestinian negotiator and Karl Long, the US Special Envoy for Israeli–Palestinian Relations. They appeared in good spirits after McGhinnist had insisted on a morning meeting with the negotiators, prior to the signing.

"Sorry everyone, we were held up." McGhinnist's voice boomed in the enormous dining room. "Sit, please."

Despite McGhinnist's words, protocol dictated that every guest stand until the President was seated. Once he was, everyone sat and polite conversation resumed. Jack scanned the new arrivals for any hint of stress or gripe, but Ebron, Khaladi and Long seemed fine. Jack had been concerned when McGhinnist had told him about the unscheduled meeting, but it appeared to have gone well.

McGhinnist cleared his throat softly. "Before we eat, I wanted to express my sincere pleasure at having our guests here, along with some of my colleagues. Everyone here has had a part to play in negotiating peace, though we have not yet achieved it.

"In private, we've discussed the pressure on everyone to walk away from this deal. Israel faces political backlash and Palestine still has militants in its midst who may try to derail the peace. But we must remain strong as allies and as friends, because we've come too far to fail."

Jack's eyes narrowed. Even though there'd been a huge breakthrough in the negotiations and the deal was ready to be signed, McGhinnist was still urging vigilance and caution. After the signing, there was to be a twenty-eight–day countdown to peace, after which the state of Palestine would exist. Jack knew the President was nervous, but he wasn't sure where the speech was heading.

McGhinnist stared straight down the table. "After discussion, and after all parties reiterated their unbridled commitment to this agreement, I've signed off on the US force deployments that had previously been discussed. These measures will bolster the chances of the agreement surviving the next month."

Jack thought he could feel the steam from Senator Yates's ears as he caught Tipping's eye. The National Security Advisor nodded slightly, indicating that he'd tried to talk the President out of the deployment, but that McGhinnist had won out. They both turned back to the President, eager to hear the details of what was going to happen in the coming weeks.

"Significant naval assets will be deployed into the Mediterranean to warn off Israel's neighbors from trying to thwart the process. As well, American theater missile defense assets will be deployed inside Israel, to prevent any rockets launched by rogue Palestinians from landing and derailing this agreement.

"In return for these measures, I've gained agreement from Israel that it will hold an entirely defensive military posture, while Palestine will redouble its efforts to keep militants in check. All sides must work at this, because one incident could destroy all of our efforts."

McGhinnist sat back and there were nods all around the table. As the food was served, Jack couldn't help but think it was going to be a good day.

~

JACK CLAPPED HALF-HEARTEDLY with the rest of the dignitaries as Samih Khaladi finished his remarks and stepped back from the lectern. The Palestinian chief negotiator had given a stupid speech about how, while buying a coffee, he'd reflected on the simple pleasure that statehood conferred on citizens. Jack had tuned out, bored and focused on his own problems, but clapped when required.

He let out a long, slow breath, realizing that he needed to cool down. As soon as he'd finished at the breakfast he'd logged on to the *Standard* online, only to find that Celeste had written a story confirming the US deployments to Israel, even before McGhinnist had announced it at the breakfast. Someone from inside the White House had leaked the President's decision.

Not that a leak within the White House was necessarily a problem. There were plenty every day, most of them intentional, but this one wasn't and the downstream reporting had painted the deployments as a sign that the President had doubts about the durability of the agreement. The peace process didn't need any more kindling on a bonfire that was piled high, waiting to be sparked.

It had made him furious at Celeste. But instead of recognizing the danger, he'd called her, ranted, and lost his cool about the leaks and her decision to publish confirmation of the deployments. Her voice had been cold when she'd told him, in no uncertain terms, to mind his own job while she minded hers. He'd hung up in a huff and not really cooled down since.

As Jack sighed again, the Israeli negotiator, Ben Ebron, stepped forward. He placed his notes on the lectern and adjusted the microphone.

"I'll be brief, because everything I wish to say is contained within the pages on that table over there. Israel wants peace and we want Palestine as a neighbor."

Jack was glad that Ebron left it at that. The more that was said and the longer it took, the more chance there was that a loose thread would be pulled and the whole thing would unravel. Jack wanted the agreement signed and for the next month to pass in boring normalcy.

This issue had taken up way too much of the administration's attention. It was time for the payoff.

He watched as Ebron and Khaladi walked to the signing table. As they sat and posed for photographs, Jack spotted Celeste across the room. She was standing with some of her staff, eyes glued to the signing and unaware that he was watching her. He knew she'd only done her job, but he was still furious at her for printing the leak. He knew he shouldn't, but he stalked over to her anyway.

"Got a minute?"

She turned, a look of surprise on her face, then frowned. "Can it wait?"

"Not really." Jack gestured with his head away from the group.

She nodded and followed him to the back of the room, clearly annoyed, but that was nothing compared to his pent-up anger. Jack glanced up at the stage, where Khaladi and Ebron were preparing to sign. Once they were on their own, Jack turned around and faced Celeste, who had her arms crossed over her chest and a look of irritation on her face. This was going to be a street fight.

"What's the problem? You just embarrassed me." Her voice was a low hiss. "It's hard enough having my boyfriend on staff at the White House, now this?"

Jack kept his voice low even as his temper flared. "You don't think you're making *my* job harder? You're printing leaks from inside the White House! Half of the administration now thinks I'm whispering sweet somethings into your ear for a blowjob, Celeste!"

Her eyes narrowed and Jack felt the temperature between them drop to below freezing. "You're embarrassing yourself. I'm walking away now."

Jack wanted to keep talking, but he let her go. He stalked his way back to the front of the room, where Ebron was signing the document. He couldn't take his mind off Celeste. Though he'd known that confronting her would achieve nothing, it was too late for second thoughts. He'd be able to patch it up, but it might take some time.

As Samih Khaladi lifted his pen and put it to paper, he looked up to the crowd with a wide smile. Despite his anger, Jack smiled as Khaladi turned to Ebron and shook the Israeli's hand, even as camera flashes bathed the men in light. At their insistence, McGhinnist joined the pair, forming a formidable triad of influence. It was hard not to appreciate history in the making.

Once the flashes started to die down, the President moved to the lectern. Jack was surprised – McGhinnist wasn't scheduled to speak and, though McGhinnist sometimes liked to freelance, Jack would prefer he didn't do it during one of the most sensitive political events in the history of the planet. He looked around and caught James Tipping's eye. The other man shrugged.

"I don't want to take the limelight, because this day very much belongs to Israel and, in twenty-eight days, the state of Palestine. But I do want to congratulate my friends Ben and Samih for achieving what many people considered impossible." McGhinnist beamed and held his arms out wide. "You're all witnesses to—"

"Gun! Gun!"

Jack's mind raced and his eyes swept the room, as Secret Service agents continued to shout over the top of the President's speech. A moment later a gunshot boomed from somewhere near the stage, well in front of Jack. Though Jack couldn't see the gunman, he could see McGhinnist wince and grip his arm as a second shot sounded.

Chaos erupted as several agents jumped on the President and brought him to the ground, heralded by the shots of Secret Service agents and the shouts of others in the room. Jack inched forward as those near the front turned and surged away from the stage. Fighting the crowd, Jack joined Secret Service agents and NYPD officers in pushing toward the President, needing to know if he was alive.

By now the gunfire had ceased, but the scene was still manic. When he reached the stage, the President and the negotiators were nowhere to be seen, having been evacuated, but several Secret Service agents remained, weapons drawn. Jack glanced at the front of the stage, where a man was lying dead, blood starting to pool around his corpse.

Jack made his way to the table, where the signed peace agreement was still in its leather folder. A small speck of McGhinnist's blood flecked the edge of the paper, which was otherwise untouched – the scratchy signature of Ben Ebron intact next to the elegant curves of Samih Khaladi. With a smile of relief, Jack closed the cover, lifted the folder and moved to the edge of the stage.

"You shouldn't be here, sir." One of the agents peeled off and grabbed Jack by the arm. "Come with me, I'll help you keep that thing safe."

Jack nodded and let himself be dragged forward. It was hard to believe that only moments before the room had been filled with celebration and goodwill. Now it was abandoned, except for men with guns and the detritus of those who'd fled: paper, water bottles and other trash. He shivered involuntarily. He needed to find Celeste.

The Secret Service agent led him outside, where NYPD officers were gathering everyone into a guarded area. He knew without asking that all would remain here until there was certainty that the threat had been contained. The thought of being inside a ring of serious-looking people with guns was fine with Jack at the moment.

Jack caught sight of Celeste. He thanked the agent and moved closer, hugging her tightly as she collapsed into his embrace. "You okay?"

"I thought we were done with getting blown up and shot at." She nestled into his chest. "At least this time the guys with guns are on our side."

Jack laughed, despite the seriousness of the situation. He broke the embrace and turned to the agent. "Any word from the President?"

The agent nodded. "He took one in the hand. They're evacuating him to New York Presbyterian to get it dealt with. We're lucky the guy was a terrible shot."

"He'll be okay." Jack smiled and clutched the folder, which had the peace agreement inside.

It was going to be a long twenty-eight days.

∼

ARON BRAFF SHIELDED himself against the wind and rain as it whipped at his face. Taking the final few steps toward the cellar, he grunted as he pulled open the heavy door. The wind conspired against his effort, howling in apparent protest as he stepped into the cellar and eased the door closed, bracing to stop the wind from slamming it shut.

The stairs were in near darkness. Though his eyes adjusted as he descended, he'd been here so many times that he could do it blindfolded. When he reached the bottom of the small staircase, it opened into an expansive room lit by dozens of candles of all shapes and sizes and dominated by a hardwood table, at which the others were already seated.

"Please excuse my tardiness." Aron strode forward and took his place at the head of the table. "It's this cursed weather."

"It doesn't matter." Miri Shaked smiled warmly, her features as bright as the candles. "We have twenty-eight days, what difference will twenty minutes make?"

"Well put." Aron stared at his hands for a few moments. He never thought he'd have to convene the meeting. He looked up again. "So, it's done."

The others offered a mix of reactions. A few were stone-faced, resolute and ready. Others seemed angry. A few were upset. After so much effort to safeguard Israel by thousands of individuals over decades, its final guardians were now needed: a mix of loyalists who'd each given much during their official service to Israel and would give more still in the next month.

This was the inner circle. Though Aron didn't know everything, he knew that there were other cells just like this one all around the world. Some were lackeys, ready to do the grunt work of their mission, while others were very senior – experts and influencers in different fields, with different expertise and one unifying goal.

"I don't need to tell any of you how serious this situation is. It threatens the death of Israel as we know it." Aron looked at each of them in turn, trying to spot any weak links in the chain. He doubted there were, but he had to be sure. "You all know what we're about to commence. If you have issue, you may leave."

"We're here for the same reason you are, Aron." David Lubelsky's voice had an edge and his shaved head seemed to glow in the candlelight.

Aron swallowed hard. These individuals had been selected, prepared and now activated in the same way he had and it was unfair of him to question their resolve. He'd take exception at his own being challenged, so it was no surprise that Lubelsky had taken issue with his words.

"Of course. Forgive me. I'm still astounded that it's come to this." Aron ran a hand through his hair. "I thought someone would walk away from the table."

"We all did, as has happened a million times before." Shaked shrugged. "But it's done. The agreement is signed and we have our orders."

Aron nodded and glanced at each of them. The scene was eerie and potentially overly dramatic – a candlelit basement in the middle of the countryside. But theirs was a high-stakes game against adversaries capable of finding small needles in large haystacks. Preventing that required the utmost care, considerable expertise and techniques long thought outdated.

"You're right." Aron held out his hands to encompass the group. "We must invoke the Samson Option."

Shaked nodded. "Yes."

"Regretfully." Lubelsky closed his eyes.

The discussion moved down the table and each of them had a say, but it was a formality. They knew what needed doing. The Samson Option had never been intended for use, designed instead to threaten potential enemies and show them that no matter how hard you hit Israel, no matter how beaten she was, she'd always win.

The doctrine was simple – any threat to the territorial integrity of Israel sufficient enough to compromise its existence must be met with indiscriminate nuclear fire. The Jewish people understood their past and the Samson Option was insurance against the future. If the Jewish state ever faced extinction, it had the power to destroy the world.

Aron and his colleagues considered the peace agreement such doom, and they would make sure to take the world down with them before Israel went meekly into history. That Israeli politicians had been conspiring in the death of their own state complicated matters, but it didn't matter and their doctrine was clear: massive destruction targeted at any threat to Israel. Even Israelis.

"Very well." Aron placed his elbow on the table and rested his head in his hands. "We should get started."

"I'll get the equipment." Shaked stood and moved toward a locked metal crate at the side of the room, which she busied herself with opening.

As he waited, Aron sat in silence with his eyes downcast. Though he knew what had to be done and that he had the most important role to play, he felt the enormity of the weight on his shoulders. In a short while they'd become the most wanted people on Earth. He knew that the treacherous government in Jerusalem would hunt them. As would others.

"It's ready." Shaked flicked a few switches. "It's not the most high-tech setup, but it will do the job."

"And it won't be able to be identified? We can't be traced here or tracked once we distribute this?" Aron needed to be sure.

"No."

"Okay." Aron nodded. He picked up a balaclava from the table and slid it over his head. "Everyone ready?"

The others donned their own masks and then stood. They crowded around his chair, facing the camera. When the group was loosely assembled, Shaked made sure everyone was in shot before pressing a few buttons and moving quickly to join the group. As she moved past him, Aron felt a pat on the shoulder. He interpreted it both as a message of good luck and to get on with it.

He looked straight down the camera and spoke clearly. "I'm a former Mossad agent. The others around me served Israel or the Jewish people in one form or another. We speak as one to a nation of many and a world of more, who don't realize the gross mistake that's about to be committed."

Aron paused and swallowed hard, making sure he kept his voice even and his pace slow. "We are the final bastion against any who'd destroy the Jewish state. Long a home, a refuge, to its people, that state is soon to be carved up by smiling traitors and enemies who conspire to destroy that home.

"My colleagues and I will ensure the survival of Israel, or the destruction of its enemies: the Palestinians who want to steal Israel's land and prosperity; the Knesset and the administration of Prime Minister Schiller who are in a hurry to abandon their people; and other states who are ready to pick the bones."

Aron leaned forward. "To the Israeli Government, we demand that you abandon this false peace, which spits on the sacrifice that generations of Jewish people have made to form and protect Israel. If the government won't act, it's up to Israelis to make them listen. Take to the streets and show your displeasure.

"To the Palestinian people, skulk from your holes and shout to the world to abandon this peace. Though we have problems with Israel, our anger is also directed at you. If it goes ahead, you will all feel the sweet taste of peace turn to ashes in your mouth.

"Finally, to the United States Government. You're as much to blame as anyone for this. You've used your influence to push Israel in one direction, now you must use that same influence to push it right back in the other. In gambling terms, you're committed. You're all in."

Aron looked left and right at his colleagues, watching them nod, before he continued. "Our demand is simple: that the deal be abandoned and that the status quo be maintained. If this occurs, we won't be heard from again. If it doesn't, the consequences will be devastating.

"Jerusalem. Mecca. New York City. Each location will be attacked with nuclear weapons should our demand not be met. There will be no negotiation or communication. Trying to find us would waste resources and time better spent unwinding the agreement. We're invisible. Until the countdown strikes zero."

Aron went silent and stared at the camera. As Shaked walked over and stopped the recording, Aron took several deep breaths. It wasn't every day you started the countdown clock on a nuclear attack. Several of the others patted him on the back or offered words of encouragement, but he barely heard them. He was lost in his own head for several moments.

Finally, he stood, walked over to Shaked and tapped her on the shoulder. She nearly jumped at the interruption and then turned and smiled.

"Okay?"

"Perfect." She beamed. "I'll cut it right away and get it ready to go. We can then release it to the world. An hour of work, at most."

"Wonderful." Aron smiled and spoke loudly to the whole group. "We carry the fate of our homeland in our hands, though what we're doing won't be easy."

Aron just hoped it would be enough.

CHAPTER 3

Just one day after the signing of the peace agreement between Israel and Palestine and the process appears to be in tatters. United States President McGhinnist was wounded in an attempt on his life at the signing ceremony, for which no group has yet claimed responsibility. In addition, last night, a group of extremist Zionists threatened to use nuclear devices to destroy Jerusalem, Mecca and New York City if the agreement is enacted. These events have sapped much enthusiasm for the peace process, sparking protests across America and the Middle East. Despite these pressures, the signatories have so far remained resolute in their support for the agreement.

New York Standard

Jack had felt uncomfortable about his place at National Security Council meetings for the past three years. Though it was part of the job, his status on the council was murky. He was an advisor – not a formal member – who attended at the behest of the President. While some of the permanent members had welcomed him, others barely tolerated his presence.

Given McGhinnist was absent following the shooting, Jack felt even more out of place. He cleared his throat. "How seriously do we have to take the threat?"

Frank Howard, Director of National Intelligence, glanced at Jack with barely restrained contempt and then addressed the whole group.

"Seriously enough, given the stakes. While we have no intelligence on this group, if they do have access to Israeli nukes the shit could fly. We need to find out if they do."

James Tipping gave Jack a small nod of support and then turned to Howard. "We don't know *anything* about these guys?"

"Nope. They're new on the radar. Monitoring Jewish extremists hasn't been a priority in recent years." Howard's eyes narrowed and he glared at Jack. "Though I should note that if we hadn't done such a thorough job of dismantling our intelligence eyes and ears in the past little while, we might know more."

Jack couldn't resist. "If those eyes and ears hadn't been monitoring American citizens en masse, we may have avoided that outcome."

Howard hissed. "Why exactly are you here, Ja—"

"That's enough!" Bill McGhinnist's voice boomed.

Jack's eyes shot to the door. As everyone stood, the President approached the table with the help of an aide, anger radiating off him. That he was here at all was incredible, given he'd been shot less than a day earlier. It showed the severity of the Zionist threat and how important McGhinnist considered the peace agreement.

Howard started to stammer something. "Mr. President, I—"

"Jack is here because I want him to be. I may be wounded, but I'm still the President. Now, can we focus?"

Jack smiled as McGhinnist sat. In the aftermath of the United Nations attack, he'd been evacuated to the New York Grand Hyatt with other members of the administration and the negotiators. He'd flown back to Washington overnight and an NSC meeting had been called for the morning. McGhinnist's presence was a surprise, though apart from a heavily dressed hand he appeared fine.

"So what do we know?" McGhinnist looked down the table, his tone making it clear he wanted to focus on business, not squabbles between his staff. "James?"

Tipping nodded. "After the attack on you at the signing ceremony, there was no increase in global flagged chatter. However, near midnight eastern time, every major news channel in the world received a video file containing a threat from a group of self-styled Zionist extremists."

"I saw that." McGhinnist sighed. "So let me see if I've caught up: The peace agreement is bad because it takes away Israeli territory, is the death of Israel itself and an attack on Israeli Jews? If the agreement stands, they'll hit Jerusalem, Mecca and New York with nukes. If we abandon the deal, all is well. How'd I do?"

Tipping smiled. "Perfect, sir."

"Okay, let's park that for a minute. Anyone claiming responsibility for the attack on me?" McGhinnist shifted in his seat and winced in pain.

Tipping shrugged. "We can't be sure the Zionists are behind your shooting, but it would be a pretty big coincidence if the events aren't connected."

"So one assault – on me – and one threat. They're wanting us to look at what they did and listen to what more they can do."

Jack leaned forward. "They've certainly made a statement."

"Where to from here?" McGhinnist eyed each member of the council.

"It's questionable whether this group has the clout they claim to, Mr. President." Howard spoke carefully. "We need to substantiate the threat."

Jan Wilson – the White House Chief of Staff – scoffed. "We've got twenty-seven days. We don't have time to substantiate it, we just need to stop it."

Howard started to protest, but Tipping chimed in, "Jan is right. We need to assume they have access to the weapons. The most likely source is Israel."

Jack winced at the thought of Israeli nukes blowing up Mecca. Whatever damage the nukes caused would pale in comparison to the shitstorm that was unleashed on whatever remained of Israel. It mightn't be a world war, but it'd make anything recent look like a fireworks display. It was moments like this he felt the weight of his job. He couldn't imagine how McGhinnist felt.

"Right, that's a fair assumption. So our first job is making sure all nuclear weapons – particularly those in Israel – are doubly secured." McGhinnist looked to the secretary of defense, who nodded and then pressed a button on the phone in front of him to put it on speaker. "Get me the Israeli PM."

It took a few moments for the council secretary to speak over the phone. "Mr. President, I'm told that the PM is in bed. His assistant asked us to make a time."

McGhinnist sighed. "I need to speak with him now, Madeleine."

There was another pause before she spoke again. "Connecting, sir."

"This is Mikael Schiller speaking." His voice sounded heavy with sleep, surprising given the events of the past few days.

McGhinnist smiled "Mr. Prime Minister, you're on the line with the members of my National Security Council. Thanks for taking our call."

"It's fine, Mr. President." The voice on the other sounded a bit reserved. A bit cautious. "How are you feeling?"

"My hand hurts like a bitch, but I'm on my feet and it could have been worse, thanks for asking."

The warmth in McGhinnist's voice when he was talking to others always surprised Jack. Though he was a former FBI Director and had a reputation as a bit of a hard ass, in conversation with others he had a wonderful rapport. Jack didn't doubt that McGhinnist's temperament had contributed to the negotiation of the agreement that now threatened to unravel.

Schiller coughed lightly. "What can I do for you?"

McGhinnist seemed to steel himself. "Mr. Prime Minister, we're enormously concerned about the Zionist threat."

"As are we. But rest assured that Israel remains committed to the agreement at the same time as we attempt to eradicate this cancer."

"We may not need to go on the offensive, Mr. Prime Minister, if we can ensure they never get their hands on nuclear weapons."

There was a pause. "Can you explain what you mean?"

"My National Security Council is convinced that the Zionists' likely source of weapons is from Israeli stockpiles. If we can safeguard those until the countdown expires, then the threat will be mostly dealt with. Unless, of course, they already have the weapons or an alternative supply."

Schiller spoke carefully. "We've no evidence of such. In fact, we have very little intelligence on this group, though we're working to get it."

"Same story over here." McGhinnist sighed. "It appears the best form of offense may be a good defense."

"Israel's stockpiles are safe. We've done a full audit." Schiller was speaking slowly, carefully, as if he had something to hide or was feeling his way through the conversation. "We've doubled security at all installations and are conducting enhanced background checks on anyone with access to the weapons."

Jack still found it incredible that Israel had revealed its nuclear stockpiles as part of the peace process. Israel had been pressured on the issue throughout the negotiations and, while Schiller hadn't taken a backward step in maintaining his country's right to the weapons, he'd made public more information about Israel's capability than any leader in its history. It had been a sign of goodwill.

"Hold for a second please, Mr. Prime Minister?" McGhinnist muted the call as he scratched his forehead. "I'm not convinced he's telling us the truth. Even if he is, it's not quite enough to reassure me that the nukes are wrapped up tightly. But what can we do?"

There was silence around the table, no one keen to offer a solution to a very high-stakes problem. Short of spying on the Israeli Prime Minister, there was no way to be certain that his country's nuclear stockpiles were safe. But taking Schiller's assurances at face value was a gamble and Manhattan was a large pile of chips to lose if they got it wrong.

Howard leaned forward. "There's not much we can do, sir. If we were getting questions about our weapons, we'd politely tell the questioner to fuck off."

As he looked at the pursed lips around the table and the silence rang like a bell, Jack was astounded at the lack of imagination. "Why can't we offer US troops? We're already deploying some to puff our chests and make sure both sides play nice. Just extend the protection to the nuclear stockpiles."

McGhinnist smiled and pressed mute on the phone again. "Mr. Prime Minister? Thanks for your patience. I've got an offer for you. I think you'll find it's one you shouldn't refuse."

~

ZED MOVED his pawn slowly and deliberately, glancing up at his opponent. "Your move, Ariel."

Ariel looked down at the board with a smile on his face. "Lame move, professor. You're usually better competition than this."

Zed closed his eyes. He was unbelievably tired from the excitement of the past week or two. The peace agreement between Israel and Palestine had been signed, despite his best efforts and the shooting of the President of the United States. Now the world was on a countdown to peace between the two peoples. The two nations. He'd invited Ariel to play chess to get his mind off it.

He really was a good student. He'd taken his censure after the lecture Zed had given with a smile and no ill feeling. This was the part that Zed enjoyed, the reason he didn't retire: he couldn't give up the chance to shape bright and inquisitive young minds. It was the source of his joy and the secret to his professional success.

"Professor?" Ariel spoke softly and placed a hand on Zed's knee.

Zed opened his eyes. "Sorry, I'm very tired. Can you repeat your move?"

Ariel smiled and pointed at the board. "Of course – rook takes pawn."

Zed nodded and gave a thin-lipped smile, though in truth he was a bit disappointed. Ariel had been lured into the exact move that Zed had hoped he'd make, putting one of his most important pieces in danger to take out a marginal one. He'd taught the young man for two years now and he had great potential, but he was still prone to making simple, hotheaded mistakes during chess games.

"You still have some to learn, Ariel. Each piece plays a part, from the king to the lowly pawn." Zed waved a hand across the board. "Each soldier wants to make his mark, without necessarily seeing the whole situation. The general, on the other hand, must weigh risk and reward of all moves. Without emotion."

Ariel started to speak. "I—"

Zed held up a hand as he looked up from the game. "Wait a moment."

His assistant had peered into the office. "Professor Eshkol?"

"Yes?"

"You've got a call on the private line. Should I ask them to call back?"

"No, that's alright." He looked back at the board, moved his rook and smiled at Ariel. "Knight takes queen, checkmate."

"Nice one, professor." Ariel shook his head. "Do you want me to leave so you can take your phone call?"

"I trust you, Ariel. Reset the board. This shouldn't take long."

Ariel smiled and started to replace the pieces as Zed stood. He walked to his desk, picked up the phone and pressed the button for the private line. He knew who'd be calling. It was odd to have Ariel in the room while he took the call, and he'd have to be careful about what he said, but it was important to show the young man that he was trusted.

"Professor?" His contact's voice was garbled by the electronics that made him anonymous to everyone but Zed – a necessary precaution. "Is it safe to speak?"

"Safe enough, my friend." Zed collapsed into his office chair with a long sigh. "What can I do for you?"

"A quick update, that's all. The United States is going to use the forces they're deploying inside Israel as extra security for nuclear sites. The original plan was for a very public show of force, but now they'll actually be defending critical sites – including the nukes."

As his contact detailed where and what forces would be deployed, Zed felt cold anger lump in the pit of his stomach. He'd known about the deployment, but assumed it would be bluster. This was another symbol of the loss of Israeli sovereignty. It was one more insult heaped upon a people being asked to suffer so much already.

"That is most disappointing." Zed waited until the other man had finished speaking. "Thank you for letting me know."

"No problem, professor." He thought he could hear a hint of warmth through the electronic mess of a voice. "I'll speak to you soon."

Zed hung up the phone without further word. There was no need for any pleasantries. He leaned back in the chair slightly and closed his eyes again. The US deployment was the final exclamation mark on the shout of outrage being perpetuated on Israeli Jews. He'd thought of the Zionist threats and he wondered how the deployment would impact their plan.

He opened his eyes again and reached for the phone, casting a glance at Ariel as he spoke. "Get me Celeste Adams at the *New York Standard*."

After a moment, a warm-sounding British woman spoke. "This is Celeste Adams."

"This is Professor Zed Eshkol, professor of history at Yeshiva University." Zed paused briefly. "I was hoping to share some information. Anonymously."

"Go ahead, professor. Anything you tell me will be in confidence, though whether we print it or not depends on the evidence."

Zed smiled. He knew as much. Following the attacks on democracy and the media in America in recent years, many of the country's leading news outlets had developed a fresh zeal for factual reporting and strict verification. He supposed they were tired of being used as mouthpieces for powerful individuals and corporations. Most of them, anyway.

"Professor?" Adams prompted.

"Excuse me." Zed chuckled. "The US military is deploying inside Israel to protect against rocket launches and discourage any incursions."

"I know all of this, professor. I—"

"Do you know they're also deploying to defend Israeli nuclear sites, following the Zionist threat?"

She inhaled sharply. "Do you have the details of units, locations or timelines that I could print?"

"I do, but it's best you get them from the horse's mouth. You'll receive a call from your usual source inside the administration at the turn of the hour."

"Okay, professor." There was a pause. "Say, I've got a gap in my opinion page for tomorrow. How'd you like to fill it to go alongside the exclusive?"

Zed thought for a second. Though he wanted to stay at arm's length from the story, if he took up the offer he wouldn't have to discuss the deployments specifically. He could reiterate again that the peace process is an unfair imposition on Israel. He'd promised the conservatives who'd approached him at the lecture nothing less.

"Okay, Ms. Adams. I respect the influence and the veracity of your newspaper. I'll write you a piece in the next few hours. My assistant will email it through."

"Wonderful, professor. Look forward to reading it. Goodbye."

Zed returned the phone to its cradle and scribbled a few notes on his notepad. When he was finished, he raised his voice.

"Louise?"

"Yes, professor?" His assistant stuck her head inside the office. "Something I can help with?"

"Take this note." He tore it from the pad. "I need it typed up quickly and ready when I leave this afternoon."

She looked down at the paper. "Uh, professor? I can't read it. It's just a combination of letters and numbers."

"Don't concern yourself with that." He smiled. The message was code, using a cypher that had been unbreakable for thirty years.

As she shrugged and walked off, he struggled to his feet. With a deep breath, he moved slowly back to the chess board, thinking about the piece he had to write. It needed to be sympathetic to the Zionist cause. He'd reiterate – again – that the sensible course of action would be abandonment of the agreement and maintenance of the status quo. Nothing else would maintain the integrity of Israel.

But first, he had another game to win.

～

JACK REACHED UP, stuck a finger into his necktie and gave it a tug. He let out a long sigh as he pulled the restrictive silk away from his neck and then undid the top button of his shirt. Taking off his tie was one of his favorite moments of the day, but when you worked at the White House you had to play by the rules, and the rules said suit and tie. He was just glad that, in Bill McGhinnist, he'd found a boss who felt largely the same way.

Jack raised an eyebrow at the President, who was in the process of removing his own tie and had his feet up on the Resolute desk. "Beer?"

"Love one."

Jack nodded and walked out of the Oval Office. He made it as far as the desk of the President's senior secretary, who kept a bar fridge stocked for exactly these moments. He opened the fridge, perused the bottles and selected some Hawthorn Brewing Company Amber Ale he'd ordered from Australia. He cracked them open, returned to the office and placed one in front of McGhinnist.

"Thanks, Jack." McGhinnist raised the bottle in salute. "Here's to twenty-seven more days before this thing is clear of our desks."

"Cheers." Jack smiled and then took a long pull of the beer.

McGhinnist sipped his own beer, then put it down. "This one is pretty good."

"There's some advantages of having a slightly troubled drinker on staff."

McGhinnist laughed and then, somehow, it turned into a sigh. "You know, every night when we do this, I remember what it's like to be a normal guy."

"You're not a normal guy, Mr. President."

"Thanks for ruining it." McGhinnist smiled. "If you keep calling me that in private, I'll need to put an end to these sessions."

Jack chuckled. "What else would I do with my evenings in Washington? I don't like many of the other people here."

They shared a laugh and settled into a comfortable silence. Their evening beer had become an important way for them to blow off steam after what were always manic days. Jack felt his role often led to disagreements with the President or other senior members of the administration, so he was sure these sessions were a message from McGhinnist.

"I don't think I could get rid of you if I tried." McGhinnist took another sip of beer, then gestured toward his injured hand. "Besides, I need someone to open the beers for me while this thing is broken. And to tell me to put American troops in the middle of all this."

Jack laughed. McGhinnist had taken a huge risk in using US troops to defend Israeli nuclear sites. If there were casualties, or if the Zionists squirrelled the nukes out from under US guns, then the pressure on the President would be immense. If one of those bombs actually went off, the shit would really fly, but it still seemed like the best way to safeguard the nukes.

Jack was about to speak again when there was a slight knock on the open door. Both of them looked up at once to see the President's press secretary, Janice Gilbride, standing by the door with a frown on her face and a piece of paper in her hand. Jack wasn't sure how long she'd been listening to their friendly banter. Not that it mattered. His closeness to the President was no secret.

Besides, it looked like she had bigger things on her mind. She coughed lightly. "Mr. President, do you have a few minutes?"

McGhinnist smiled and waved her in. "Of course, take a seat and Jack will get you a beer. He was just going to get more."

Jack laughed. "I was?"

"Sure." McGhinnist shrugged.

"I'll pass on the beer, thanks." Gilbride pursed her lips. "I've got some bad news, Mr. President. You're not going to like it either, Jack."

Jack looked to McGhinnist in time to see his eyes narrow and then looked back at Gilbride. "What's the problem?"

She clasped her hands together in front of her. "The *New York Standard* has an exclusive on the deployment of US forces to guard Israeli nuclear sites."

Jack's hand loosened on his beer and he cursed as it fell onto the carpet. He leaned down to pick up the bottle to prevent further spillage, not concerned about the liquid. He was too outraged at Gilbride's revelation, so convinced that she must be wrong, that he found himself speechless for a moment. She'd clearly guessed correctly that this would be a big deal.

"This is above my pay grade, guys." Gilbride smiled in sympathy. "But I sort of need to know if it's true."

"It is. We've got a leaky faucet in here." McGhinnist's voice had an edge. "The deployments weren't secret, but using the troops to defend nuke sites is."

"Right." Gilbride nodded.

McGhinnist sighed. "Your girlfriend likes ruining my day, Jack. We need to do something about that."

Jack faked a laugh. "Any suggestions?"

"Take her to a secluded getaway and ravish her for the next twenty-seven days? Ask her nicely? The hell if I care."

"I think the threat of extremists with nuclear weapons outranks a leak to the *Standard*." Jack bit his tongue and held back the rest of what he wanted to say.

"True, but I don't like having my every move to resolve the former chewed up and spat out by the latter. These leaks are restricting my ability to act, Jack."

"There's more." Gilbride took a seat on the sofa. "A senior Yeshiva University history professor has written an opinion piece slamming the deployment. He's a leading voice within the Jewish lobby, so you can expect some more heat from that front, if there wasn't enough already."

"I'm not worried about that so much. I'm worried that anything I say or decide is being leaked."

Jack saw a hint of vulnerability in McGhinnist, as if the weight of the office was pressing down on his shoulders. "Any idea who is doing it?"

"None." McGhinnist shrugged. "If I knew, it'd be taken care of already."

"Anyway, I'll leave you guys to chew over this one, didn't mean to interrupt." Gilbride handed McGhinnist the printout and stood. "Goodnight."

"Oh, sit down, Janice." McGhinnist nearly spat, then his face softened. He started to read the article, then screwed it into a ball and threw it onto the carpet.

"We'll need to respond in the morning." Jack leaned forward and rested his elbows on his knees. "But it shouldn't matter. The defense of the Israeli nukes is the key and the boots will be on the ground by tomorrow. The leak and the criticism is a minor annoyance that's worth wearing if we can safeguard those."

"I'm not convinced." McGhinnist stared at him. "We need to respond strongly to defend our actions."

"Okay—"

"In fact, Janice? I want to go to New York in a few days to defend the decisions we've taken. I want to shove my point down this guy's throat in person."

"I don't think that's a—"

"Don't want to hear it, Jack." McGhinnist shook his head. "Make it happen, Janice."

Gilbride winced at the damage control that would be required. "Of course, Mr. President. I'll make the arrangements. Do you want the press corps there?"

"Every last one of them." McGhinnist sighed and jerked a thumb at Jack. "Including his girlfriend."

Jack nodded, taking the hint. Even though he'd had some tough moments with McGhinnist, it had never felt this personal. Celeste was just doing her job and he was just doing his, but it was making things tough. Someone in the White House was leaking against the peace agreement and those leaks were flowing straight to her. He hoped New York would put the issue to bed.

He doubted it.

CHAPTER 4

The first United States troops have started to arrive in Israel, as large protests sweep across the Middle East and America. The troops have been stationed at a dozen locations across Israel, including several nuclear sites, in a very public display of force. Any benefit or stability the US hoped to gain from the deployments looks to have been quashed, with an estimated 100,000 Israelis taking to the streets in protest against the peace agreement and the US deployment. Meanwhile, US President Bill McGhinnist will speak this morning at Yeshiva University in New York about the peace agreement, the deployment, the protests and the damaging White House leaks.

New York Standard

Jack winced as he sipped the terrible campus coffee, which was too hot and had all the flavor of bubble wrap. As he peered out from the side of the stage, he figured that the Yeshiva University student theater was nearly at capacity. Scanning the crowd, he spotted Professor Zed Eshkol in the front row making small talk with colleagues.

"Desiccated old fossil, isn't he?" Gilbride spoke softly. "Hard to believe he can cause such a stir. He's become a lightning rod for the crazies."

Jack gave a short laugh. "Hopefully the boss can get a knockout, or at least go the distance out there. Is he ready?"

"Yep." She smiled.

McGhinnist strode past them to the lectern flanked by American, Israeli and Palestinian flags, a clear sign that Yeshiva University didn't necessarily agree with the views of its controversial professor. Fat lot of good such gestures made, though, when Eshkol was given a platform to spout his rhetoric. It was a mistake for the President to be here, but McGhinnist had insisted.

Jack looked at Gilbride. "Fingers crossed, Janice."

"And toes."

Jack nodded and turned to McGhinnist. The President had started his speech, acknowledged the VIPs and made some opening remarks. He was standing, tall and proud, like he owned the room. His arm, still in a sling, did nothing to detract from the sense of gravitas that his booming voice created. Jack could hear the anger at the leaks and Eshkol's opinion piece in McGhinnist's voice.

"Let me be clear." McGhinnist's voice thundered. "The United States unequivocally supports the peace agreement. America has a proud history of resisting extremist ideology and I reject the threats and demands of the Zionists outright. We won't waver in our support for this cause."

Jack nodded at the high notes in the speech. He hoped McGhinnist could leave the stage with the matter settled, the peace agreement stable and any support – tacit or otherwise – for the Zionist cause destroyed. The President would give a powerful performance, like always, but Jack wondered if this issue could be put to bed so easily. Nobody could blame McGhinnist for trying.

"America's interest in this agreement is solely to help secure a lasting peace and a sustainable arrangement between Israelis and Palestinians, which respects the former's right to exist but also recognizes the legitimate claim on statehood by the latter.

"The deployment of US forces was to encourage stability over the next month. But following the Zionist threat, it has become all the more vital. Those troops are now an essential protection against extremists getting their hands on nuclear weapons. Our troops will be the first line of protection against an atrocity.

"I should add, also, that these deployments have the full support of the Israeli and Palestinian leaders. To prove our intent, I've authorized for the media to be given access to all US assets in the region during the countdown to this agreement. The US has nothing to hide."

Jack grimaced. He wasn't sure that giving the international press access to the troops would calm things down, but it might help show the crazies that the deployment wasn't a covert invasion of Israel and the Middle East. Such a step wouldn't be necessary if Celeste hadn't printed the leak, but Jack couldn't blame her. That he'd have done the same thing didn't make it easier to swallow.

As McGhinnist concluded the speech, Jack sighed with relief. The President had nailed it. He watched as Gilbride went on stage and called for questions from the assembled media and students. A wave of nostalgia hit him as he reflected on the number of times he'd been on the other side of the equation – the journalist asking the hard question.

A young man took the microphone for the first question. "Mr. President, I'm a student here. I appreciate you talking straight. I'm in favor of the agreement, but not at the cost of Jerusalem and New York City. Why aren't you taking the nuclear threat more seriously?"

McGhinnist started to answer, amidst a few boos directed at the questioner. "Thanks for your question and let me be clear: while we're guarding Israel's stockpiles we'll also be actively looking for these terrorists. If we find them, we will deal with them."

Jack nodded and listened to the next question, something about Israel being robbed of its nukes as well as its land. He sighed and tuned out. His years in the White House and in the press had given him an eye for a story, and there was nothing here. McGhinnist and Gilbride could handle this. His time was better spent assessing the mood in the crowd.

He moved to the back of the theatre and took a seat. The questions continued to roll, but he was only half listening. He was more interested in the fear and distrust that charged the room like a superconductor. This wasn't a friendly crowd and it had been a mistake to come here. As the President finished up and Jack prepared to stand and leave, someone sat beside him.

"Hi."

He turned to face her, a thin smile on his lips. "Hi, Elena."

"Spotted you skulking about." She reached over and grabbed his arm, her voice barely a whisper as she gave it a squeeze. "It's good to see you, Jack."

He felt a range of emotions battle it out in his head. Though she'd acted under threat of harm to her fiancé, now husband, it had taken Jack a long time to forgive Elena Winston for her betrayal. Under duress, she'd given up information about Jack's resistance to Richard Hall.

FEMA had used Elena's disclosure to crush the resistance, leaving many of its members dead or in prison. At the last, though, she'd been a vital ally in revealing Hall's atrocities. She'd walked a long road since, a hard journey Jack understood well. Deep down, despite the hurt he still harbored, he was glad she was well and working.

"You too." He gently pulled away from her grasp. "What did you think of the speech?"

She shrugged. "I thought the speech was fine. But I don't think it will change any minds in this room."

"I can't disagree with you." Jack sighed, running a hand through his hair. "Where are you working these days?"

"With Celeste at the *Standard*." Elena's eyes narrowed. "I'm surprised she hasn't mentioned it."

He grimaced. "She might have. It's been a busy few months."

She gave him a quizzical look. "Ah, trouble in paradise?"

Jack just stared at her for a moment, then shifted his gaze to the stage. A pair of staff members from Yeshiva were wrapping up, but he paid them no attention. Elena had put him in a dark mood, despite the success of the President's speech and through no fault of her own. He'd never felt worse about the current job he had, his relationship with Celeste or the prospects of either surviving.

For the first time, he felt as if the countdown that the signed peace agreement had heralded wasn't just toward peace and potential nuclear devastation. It felt like a doomsday clock for Jack as well.

∾

ZED WATCHED as the university staff left the stage, ending the formal part of the event. McGhinnist's speech had been fine – as usual – but that was hardly surprising given he was a moderate and well-spoken. A competent administrator, he'd also proven to be a likeable man who could show policy vision and form coalitions for change. He was what America had needed as a balm to its traumas.

No, the only thing that made the President dislikable to Zed was his fascination with Israel and Palestine. Zed had thought a few times that, in another life, the two of them might have been friends and McGhinnist could have been a political ally, but it wasn't to be. They had competing visions for Israeli–Palestinian relations, an issue Zed could not compromise on.

Zed kept his face passive, but inside he was smiling at the thought of the intellectual differences. It had led their paths to cross in a way that Zed couldn't abide, which made the President a foe. McGhinnist had come to the wolf's den dressed as a rabbit, trying to convince the wolves that it was a good idea for them to cut off their own tails and stop eating meat.

It hadn't worked. Trying to persuade a room full of Jews that Israel should cede territory to people who'd tried to blow them up for decades was fruitless. Though some present might sympathize with the Palestinians, Zed felt confident that the vast majority in the theatre would fall on the side of common sense – maintaining the status quo.

Zed leaned on his cane heavily and groaned with determination as he struggled to his feet. As he moved toward the President, Zed could see McGhinnist speaking to senior university officials. The sycophants – many of whom shared Zed's views in private – were too busy sucking up to the President to prosecute the agenda that everyone at Yeshiva and all Jews should share.

Zed was just glad he was old enough to ignore all that rubbish. His roots went so deep at Yeshiva that even the strongest storm would leave him standing. He joined the group and coughed loudly. The dean of the history faculty turned in alarm and then made space for Zed, doing his best to suppress a frown at being interrupted.

"Thank you, Dean Benski." Zed smiled as he joined the group. "I must have missed the note that we'd be meeting with the President after his speech."

The dean took the interruption in his stride. "President McGhinnist, this is Professor Zed Eshkol. He's one of our stars."

McGhinnist smiled broadly, his famous white veneers shining bright. "Pleased to meet you, professor. Glad you were here to listen."

Zed nodded. "Mr. President, I'd like to thank you for coming here to defend your position on the peace agreement and your troop deployment."

McGhinnist held the smile, but any warmth disappeared from his eyes. "*Our* deployment, Professor Eshkol. America's."

"Of course, forgive me." Zed nodded and waved a hand. "That's what I meant. Though many of us don't agree with it."

"Or the agreement that will finally bring peace between Israelis and the Palestinians, apparently."

Either McGhinnist had deliberately invited him to dissent, or the

President didn't possess half the intellect that Zed had previously credited him with. Zed smiled. "The so-called 'peace' will be a tragedy, Mr. President, which will do more to harm the Jewish people than any foe has managed since the creation of Israel."

"Is land really that important to your people, Professor Eshkol?" McGhinnist raised an eyebrow. "So important that you'd risk peace and accept more rockets raining down on Israel, more suicide bombings and more deaths of women and children? Both sides have some to lose but more to gain."

Zed felt anger rise inside him. "You don't know how hard 'my people' fought to gain a homeland, Mr. President, or how much they suffered. You could rain a thousand rockets a day on Israel and it wouldn't compare. I don't agree with the extremist threats, but I do support their goal."

Dean Benski coughed lightly. "Even though some might disagree with the agreement, Mr. President, it was wonderful to have you here today."

Zed shook his head as the dean and the university president cut into the conversation, obviously trying to suspend any further bristling. It took all his self-control not to laugh in their faces. They were bureaucrats, concerned about public image and politics, but not the guillotine hanging over the heads of their people. They weren't even worthy of contempt.

He took a step back and left the university officials to their campaign. There was nothing else to be gained by pressing further. He was about to turn away and shuffle back to his office when he saw someone else approaching from the corner of his eye. It was almost enough to make Zed smile, given how much he knew of the other man's exploits.

"Mr. Emery." Zed took a pained step toward the younger man. "It's a pleasure to meet you."

Zed had done his research. In many ways, Jack Emery was the lynchpin of President McGhinnist's administration. It was clear that he was handed the hard nuts to crack, and so far every job Emery had been entrusted with seemed to have been sorted to the satisfaction of the President. Usually Zed wouldn't care, but Emery's attention was on the peace process and he could be a problem.

Emery's eyes narrowed slightly and flicked between Zed and the President, who remained in conversation with university officials. "Professor."

Zed held out his hand. "Please, it would be a pleasure to shake the hand of the man who's saved this country from itself several times."

Emery looked down at his hand, clearly suspicious, but eventually shook it. "I wouldn't go that far, professor. I just played my part."

"You're modest. You've played an enormous role in protecting America, which isn't even your home country."

Emery smiled. "So you say, professor. You'll have to excuse me, I've got some work to do. It was so nice to meet you."

Zed held his gaze. "It was nice to meet you, Jack. Please also thank your girlfriend for allowing me the opportunity to write about the peace process."

Emery's eyes went from cold to flaming hot in the space of a second. It seemed like he might say something emotional and let his anger out, but after another moment Emery nodded and walked toward the President. Zed smiled. He knew he was being petty, but he had enjoyed the indulgence. Living was no good if you couldn't have fun once in a while.

~

JACK HELD the precariously balanced trio of drinks as Celeste and Elena each took a cocktail, then he sat and raised his beer bottle. "Cheers."

They clinked and he took a pull of the beer. It had been a long day in New York, spent riding shotgun to McGhinnist at Yeshiva and other engagements, so he'd decided to have a night off with Celeste. He hadn't expected that she'd invite Elena as well, since he was due to fly back to Washington in the morning. He didn't mind, but it showed that Celeste was irritated at him.

"Good job today, Jack." Elena took a sip of her martini. "The President handled himself well. I think it'll calm things a little."

Jack nodded. "The diehards will still think we're invading Israel and selling it to the Palestinians, but I think we might sway some of the moderates."

Jack hoped so, anyway, if only to shove it down the good professor's throat. He still felt a little bitter about his run-in with Eshkol, whose views had gained quite a bit of attention and caused the President all sorts of trouble. Amid the nuclear threat and the stress of the countdown, Eshkol's agitation and the leaks were a thorn that stuck in Jack's craw.

Worse was Celeste's decision to print both. He turned to her. She had her drink to her mouth and her eyes on him. When he smiled she turned away, so he rolled his eyes, took another swig of beer and sat back in his chair. He wondered why she'd agreed to go out if she was still mad, but clearly Elena had been invited to mitigate that.

Elena seemed to be doing her best to carry the conversation. "How seriously should we take the nuclear threat? Do we need to head for the hills?"

"Hills? Near Manhattan? Fat chance." Jack gave a laugh. "We're concerned, but there's no proof the Zionists have a nuke. We're working to find out, though."

The conversation continued in pained fashion. They discussed the day at Yeshiva, plans for the weekend, the weather – everything except the elephant in the room. Jack didn't want to bring it up and was trying hard to swallow his anger, but he was finding it difficult. He loved her and understood being a reporter, but he'd never had the two cross with his business in such a way.

A cell phone started to buzz and Jack's eyes darted to the table. Both of the women looked as well, clearly hungry for some way to extricate themselves from the conversation. Celeste won the lottery and picked up her phone. She looked at the caller ID, smiled and stood to answer it. Jack tried to hear some of what she was saying, but she'd stepped too far away and the music in the bar was too loud.

Elena laughed. "Your ears burning or something?"

His eyes shot away from Celeste to Elena. "Sorry?"

"You're acting as if you can glean who she's talking to by intensity of stare."

Jack groaned. "Sorry."

"Now you're repeating yourself." Another laugh. "It's not me you need to apologize to. You're both being idiots, but someone needs to break the impasse."

Jack nodded and looked away. She was right, but his anger at the leaks and Celeste's decision to publish them were clouding his judgment. It took some effort to remind himself, just like he used to with Erin, that work was a means to an end. As obsessed and caught up as he got with his jobs, it was only worth doing if there was someone to share it with. He looked at Celeste, who was walking back.

"Sorry." Celeste placed her phone on the table as she sat. She turned to Elena. "Francine has a great story in her hands."

"Awesome."

"Something good?" Jack offered.

Celeste turned to him with narrowed eyes, clearly trying to figure him out. "Yeah. Might be on the front page."

Jack tried to resist, and nearly succeeded. "Need a quote from the White House?"

Her eyes narrowed further and she gave a barely perceptible shake of her head. "You're unbelievable."

"Sorry, I shouldn't have said that." He held out both hands with palms facing outward.

"Hey, Jack? Fuck you." She bathed him in the remains of her cocktail, balled her fists and stormed off.

Jack took the cocktail napkin that Elena was holding out for him. "Sorry about that."

"There you are with that word again." Elena laughed and patted him on the back. "Nice work, charmer."

As he wiped his face, he surveyed the damage. His white shirt was splashed with color and his face felt hot. "That was dumb."

"Yep."

Jack sighed again as he reached for his beer, took another swig and then started to peel the label off. The crack had been stupid and he'd be paying for the comment for days, but sometimes he couldn't help himself. He laughed quietly to himself and shook his head. The relationship he had with Celeste was far more caustic than the one he'd had with Erin before she died.

"What's so funny?" Elena took a sip of her wine.

"Just thinking about my wife." Jack looked at her. "It's been five years now."

"You've found someone else now, Jack. A keeper at that." She smiled.

"Yeah."

"You just need to recognize when you're on dangerous footing."

"That's what everyone tells me." He laughed. "It's funny, I'm dealing with terrorist threats by day and relationship ones by night."

"Which one is the more dangerous, Jack?" She had a look of concern. "Just how at risk are you guys?"

"I don't know." Jack shrugged. "You want another drink?"

"Sounds good. On one condition."

Jack raised an eyebrow. "What's that?"

"I help you find a clean shirt at Macy's once we're finished."

CHAPTER 5

Several days after the announcement of US troop deployments to Israel and as the last boots arrive on the ground, the world's media is being given an unprecedented look inside Israel's nuclear facilities. The Israeli Government has stated repeatedly that it has nothing to hide and that US troops are a welcome addition to their own security. All sides remain united in support for the agreement and it's hard to criticize the media access being granted to Israeli bases, US fleet assets and to the leadership of the US, Israel and Palestine. The sum result is a clear attempt to safeguard Israel's nuclear weapons, prevent any rogue elements from causing mischief and ensure the success of the peace agreement.

New York Standard

Samih smiled at the United States Army Ranger in charge and pointed at a security point that had been erected outside the base. "Is all of this necessary?"

The ranger – a captain – smiled. "Probably not, sir. But our orders were to beef up the defences. We've done that. We could hold up an army."

The Israeli prime minister, Mikael Schiller, wore a grim expression in spite of the captain's easygoing nature. "It won't be an army, captain. Any attacks will come from extremist elements within the Israeli

Government, army or security services who've aligned themselves with the Zionists. That's why you're here."

The captain nodded. "If they attempt to touch those weapons, my men and I will take care of it."

"A worthy objective, captain." Samih stopped and took in the enormity of the facility. "My people thank you for your service in helping to secure this peace."

The captain grinned. "All in a day's work, sir."

Samih smiled at the ranger's bravado, though he did not doubt that the US forces had the muscle to back up their words. The tour had just begun, yet standing inside the nuclear facility already felt extremely awkward. Until recently, Israel had denied it had nuclear weapons or that this facility existed, but the exposure of the nuclear assets had been one step on the long path to peace.

Now, Samih was walking a path through well-manicured lawns on a base containing weapons of disastrous potential. He'd nearly refused the invitation, content to let Israel deal with its extremist threat with the support of America, but after some reflection he'd decided it was important to show Palestinian support. His own people had been plagued by such elements, after all.

There was another reason for him to be here. The US deployment was a big deal – 5000 troops – and its purpose could easily be misconstrued. The only way to avoid that was to show support for the deployment and maintain consistency in referring to it as temporary. Once the countdown expired, the troops would depart, leaving Israel and Palestine to determine their own fate as neighbors.

"Thank you for your time, captain. We'll continue on alone." Schiller nodded at the young captain. "I hope you enjoy your time here."

"You've got a beautiful country, Mr. Prime Minister." The captain smiled. "We'll help make sure it will still be here in a month."

Samih winced as he resumed his walk with Schiller. Once they were out of earshot, he spoke. "Will all of these men be enough?"

He sensed Schiller assessing him, but Samih kept his eyes forward.

"The Americans? They've certainly given us a lot of support."

Samih nodded. He'd thought the scale of US deployment complete overkill, but overwhelming force was clearly McGhinnist's intent. In addition to the special forces troops, significant air and naval assets had been deployed to Israel. As well, the famed Iron Dome missile defense shield had been bolstered by US anti-missile interceptors. The President clearly wanted to leave no doubt that America took the protection of the nuclear weapons and the agreement seriously.

He hoped the show of force would also stifle any ambition – by Israelis, Palestinians or any of their neighbors – to cause trouble. Truth be told, Samih had been more worried about a few stray rockets fired by his own people derailing the peace than a fanciful threat to steal nuclear weapons, but it was nice to have the security blanket. With luck, the countdown to enactment of the agreement would be peaceful and the two-state solution would finally be realized.

"I hope we can both spend the next twenty-two days fretting about potential threats, rather than dealing with real ones, Mr. Prime Minister." Samih ceased his walk and turned to Schiller. "The Zionists are as much a threat as the last rogue members of Hamas, but we must resist both."

"A hard task." Schiller rubbed his head. "Though your extremists are in hiding, at least you know who you're dealing with: their names, their doctrine, their capability. The collective knowledge about the Zionists appears to be zero, and I can't be entirely sure they lack the capability to carry out their threats."

"I understand." Samih placed a hand on the other man's shoulder. "If you need any support that is within Palestine's meager resources, we will help."

Schiller smiled and spoke after a long pause. "Interesting concept, isn't it? Helping each other? After how much treasure has been expended blowing each other up, I really do wonder whether Israelis will still fear Palestinian rockets and whether Palestinians will still fear helicopter gunships when all of this settles."

"I hope that we can focus on the more mundane – education, healthcare, housing, economic development." Samih smiled. "Reconciliation."

"What do you mean?"

Samih sighed. "The righting of decades of wrongdoing by both sides. I hope we might finally resolve that."

"A worthy sentiment, Mr. Khaladi." Schiller's smile froze in place. "Both sides have made sacrifices for this peace. I hope it's all worth it."

Samih nodded as they resumed the walk. He cast a glance at a second US security post, and decided to leave the point at that. Though he'd negotiated the deal with Ben Ebron, Mikael Schiller was another beast entirely. Samih had his doubts about the Prime Minister and thought he might try to walk away from the peace at the first opportunity, so it was vital to keep reinforcing its importance.

He'd held his own people in check, despite some of them still wanting to lob rockets at Israel. It had taken bullying, bribery and cutthroat politics to convince most of them. For the rest, he'd simply reverted to threats. But it had worked. He doubted that any Palestinians would go against a unified leadership, risking Palestinian statehood and making themselves a pariah.

No, he was more concerned about the Zionist threats. Despite his doubts about their ability to follow through, he had to admit that it felt good to see the nukes secured by the United States. Though many of his people called him a fool for trusting America, nobody could deny the role President McGhinnist and his administration had played in negotiating the peace.

For the first time in a large number of years, Samih felt he could relax.

~

JACK SMILED at the chirping of the birds and the gentle touch of the breeze blowing through an open window. It was a rare luxury for him to wake up with nature, rather than the ringing of a phone or the morning news bulletin that was his alarm, and it felt nice. Rarer still was Celeste nestled against his chest, still asleep as he dozed. He'd never known her to sleep so soundly.

He'd forgotten about the simple pleasures of home. Yeppoon was a postage stamp–sized town in the middle of Queensland, Australia, but it was warm for most of the year and you could sleep with the bedroom window open. He couldn't think of a better place to get away from the pressure cooker of Washington and the bustle of New York City.

The holiday was aimed at patching up their issues. The incident at the bar had been the catalyst. He'd returned home to Celeste crying and with her knees hugged to her chest. She'd thrown a tissue box at him and unloaded on him about the impossible situation he'd placed her in. At the end of it, she'd given him an ultimatum: they had to resolve their problems or they were through.

They'd quickly plotted a trip away. Celeste had taken leave, while Jack had approached McGhinnist, hoping for something similar. He'd been surprised when the President had agreed, saying he'd caught wind of their fight and that he could afford to go without Jack for a while. The hard work on the privacy legislation and the peace agreement had been done.

Jack was uncomfortable about being away, but with broad support for the looming peace, US forces in Israel and no sign that the Zionists had any weapons, he'd swallowed his doubts. At home, in Australia, he hoped they might be able to iron out some of the creases that had appeared in their relationship. It was going well so far.

He hugged Celeste tight as she started to wriggle in his arms. "Not a bad way to wake up, is it?"

"Hey. Not bad at all." Celeste pulled away, opened her eyes and smiled at him. Her eyes were bright and her face seemed clear of stress. "It's nice to be back."

"Under better circumstances this time." He laughed. Years ago, while battling the Foundation for a New America, Jack had sent Celeste to Yeppoon to protect her. His parents had taken her in for several weeks while he'd fought Michelle Dominique. They'd never really spoken about her experiences in Australia.

"Yeah, with you, for starters. And without a psycho chasing me across the globe." She smiled. "This doesn't mean I forgive you, I hope you realize?"

"No?" Jack propped himself up onto one elbow. "I thought business-class airfares and some time away would be just the ticket."

She laughed. "I'm not that cheap."

Jack smiled. He sat up, pulled back the covers and shuffled to the end of the bed, then took Celeste's left foot in his hands and started to rub. "Now?"

"That's a start." She closed her eyes and moaned softly with pleasure as he kneaded. "It was nice of you to bring me here, Jack. Thanks."

He grunted and kept rubbing her feet. Coming home hadn't been his first plan, but she'd told him it was the best. The visit had surprised his parents. Though he called them once every few weeks, they'd long ago stopped asking when he'd visit. His father hadn't even mentioned how long it had been when he'd picked them up from the airport.

They'd drawn the line at staying with his parents, so he'd shelled out for the most expensive rental apartment in Yeppoon, inches from the water. They'd shared a few meals with his parents but spent more time together at the beach or shacked up in their apartment. The TV had stayed off and they'd focused on little but each other. It had been great. He'd felt the tension melt away.

"What do you want to do today? I've pretty much shown you all the sights, unless you want more beach time."

"Well, I—"

He looked over at the nightstand as his phone blared, interrupting her. It was a text message, not a call, and there were only two people whose messages would override the do-not-disturb setting – the President and the woman naked in bed with him. He kept his eyes on the phone for a split second too long, feeling Celeste tense and the mood in the room chill.

"Jack?" There was a hint of warning in her voice.

Though they were working at their relationship, they were still relatively vital players in two important endeavors. They'd agreed to avoid all but the most important calls from work, given they couldn't completely inoculate themselves from some of the necessary ones. While McGhinnist could still get hold of Jack and Celeste's staff could get her, the phones had been mostly silent. Until now.

"One second." He stood, walked over to his phone and checked the message. "Looks like US forces are now in place at all sites."

"Great." Her voice was flat. "You've had your fun, now come back to bed. You've still got to do the right foot."

"I can give all my attention to you now I know all the nukes are safe." He let out a long sigh as he stared at the phone, relief flooding through him.

"You're surprised?"

He turned to her, a playful smile on his face. "Look, you may have heard it from your man on the inside already, but some of us have to hear it officially."

She rolled her eyes and threw a pillow at him. He dodged it and returned to the bed, this time at the top end. They nestled close to each other, all thoughts of the day cast aside. She let out a long, slow breath. It was a clear sign that she'd dropped her annoyance at him answering the phone. He smiled and squeezed her tighter.

He woke up a while later. As his eyes flickered open, he realized that they'd fallen asleep and started to snooze again. He shifted slightly in place and coughed. She moved at the same time, turned onto her side and let out a short, sharp laugh when she felt him pressing into her.

Before Jack could respond, her hands were roaming and forcing him onto his back.

He locked his hands behind his head. "This is nice. I think we're safe."

∼

ARON BRAFF PULLED his trench coat closed at the front, did up the buttons and raised the collar. Satisfied, he buried his hands deep into his pockets, the heat from his breath leaving a trail in the crisp evening air. The cold had been bearable earlier in the evening, but as the hour grew later, the iciness in the air had increased. He could handle the cold, but this was something else.

He'd never been to Russia before and would be in no hurry to return. It was cold and drab. Everywhere. And the only thing worse than the surroundings was the people, who were as dark as their country. He'd known some Russian Jews in his time, fellow citizens of Israel, and he now understood a great deal about their makeup. No, Russia's only redeeming feature was the quality of the shopping.

He ran his gaze along the windows and rooftops on both sides of the narrow alley. The squat, Soviet-era apartment buildings that surrounded him rose to four or five stories, but he could see no sign of anyone watching him. Russians had learned centuries ago not to come to the window when there was a strange sound or muted conversation outside their homes late at night.

Satisfied, Aron looked down at his watch with a sigh. They should have been here by now. The delay was unacceptable, but he was a captive buyer. Quite simply, there was nowhere else on earth he could purchase the three nuclear weapons he needed. Whether he liked it or not, he was beholden to his supplier's timetable and their tardiness.

Luckily, he didn't have to wait long. He heard the low rumble of a powerful engine long before he had to raise his hand to shield his eyes from the headlights. He kept his hand in place as he heard doors open and then slam shut, unable to see because of the headlights shining in his eyes. The ice underfoot crunched with approaching footsteps and the van headlights finally switched off.

Aron lowered his hand. Without the headlights the alley was lit in dim streetlight, but it was enough to see the men in front of him. "Mr. Kotvas?"

"Yes." The older man standing behind three larger, younger Russians spoke with a rough voice. "Please be quiet for a moment."

Aron nodded, held his arms wide and waited as one of the Russians stepped forward to frisk him. As he did, the other two kept their weapons raised, but it was no sweat. He wasn't carrying a weapon and he'd been told about the procedure. Apart from them being a few minutes late, the meeting was going to plan. When the Russian finished he barked something in his native tongue.

"Okay. Now we do business." Kotvas nodded. "Are you sure you can afford the price, Mr. Braff? Things will be not fun for you if you're wasting my time."

"Three devices for eight million dollars." Aron waved a hand toward the four metal briefcases stacked at his feet. "Four million paid, the balance at my feet."

"Good." Kotvas's voice was as coarse as gravel in a cement mixer. "I don't appreciate time wasters."

Aron was tempted to point out that his own time had been wasted by their lateness to the meeting, but refrained. They were armed and there was no point complicating a straightforward meeting. Moving slowly, he kept his eyes on the Russians and they kept their weapons trained on him. He lifted the first briefcase and handed it to Kotvas. The Russian supported the case while Aron unlocked it.

"One million dollars?" Kotvas glanced inside the case when Aron opened it.

Aron nodded. "Count it if you like."

"Not necessary. We're all professionals. This way."

Aron nodded and followed Kotvas to the rear of the van. Two of the goons followed, while the other stayed with the cases. One of Kotvas's men opened the van, then Aron peered inside and smiled. Though they were old, each RA-115 device was the size of a backpack and very powerful. Each could level about twenty city blocks in Manhattan, cause chaos in Jerusalem or flatten Mecca.

"Fully functioning." Kotvas's voice was now cheerful. "As promised."

"Excellent." Aron smiled. "I think our business is concluded."

They walked back to the front of the van. Aron cast a glance at his cases, which were exactly where he'd left them. Kotvas's men were professional, if nothing else. He held out his hand to Kotvas, prepared to conclude their business, but had to wait as the other man stared down at

Aron's hand. Kotvas was clearly unable to mask his slight distaste, but he eventually shook.

"Suicidal Jews." Kotvas laughed as he took his hand back. "I'd have thought your people would have had their fill of violence."

Aron stared at Kotvas but said nothing. Eventually the other man shrugged and waved lazily to his men. Aron turned his head and saw they were scooping up the briefcases and carrying them out of the alley. The cash had bought him the van as well as the nuclear weapons inside, a bargain really. He took a step toward the van, ready to hit the road and get out of Russia.

"Not so fast, Mr. Braff."

Aron turned. Kotvas had a pistol trained on him, as did another of his men. The other two Russians and the briefcases were gone.

"You don't want to do this."

"We're taking your money, Mr. Braff, and the weapons." Kotvas laughed. "There's no way I'm placing these weapons in your hands. Crazy fucking Jews."

"We had a deal." Aron took a step toward the two armed Russians. "Please don't waste my time. You were already late to our meeting."

"Not another step." Kotvas shouted. "Come quietly, we'll take you out of the city and you'll get a quick ending. Nice and clean."

Aron took another step. "No, I—"

"Resist, Mr. Braff, and we'll make it hurt." Kotvas fired a shot at Aron's feet. "Choose."

Aron sighed. He'd come here to conduct a business transaction – clean and hassle free. He'd paid the deposit, arrived with the balance and had intended to drive away with the product. In return, Kotvas had been late and now he was trying to double cross Aron. It was a gross breach of faith. Rage burned in the pit of his stomach.

Aron kept his eyes on Kotvas as he whistled loudly. Less than a second later the alleyway exploded with noise. Aron ducked low then surged forward as a series of loud booms sounded from overheard, followed by several smaller pops as the Russians returned fire. The younger of the armed Russians dropped and Aron grunted as he took a hit to the chest. He kept moving, despite the pain.

He heard several additional booms. The two Russians carrying the cases would be down now, victims of the rifles that his colleagues were well versed in using. Only Aron and Kotvas were left. The old Russian snarled as he squeezed the trigger and Aron felt another round hit him. He gasped for air but took the last step toward the Russian.

Aron brought his fist down on Kotvas's arm. The gun fell to the ground with barely a whisper, a contrast to the scream from the Russian's mouth when Aron's knee connected with testicles. The Russian bent over slightly and Aron brought his elbow up to slam into Kotvas's face. Kotvas's eyes went glassy and Aron used his momentum to push the Russian onto his back and leap onto him.

As he straddled his prey, Aron pinned Kotvas's arms with his knees and gripped his throat. Though the Russian was old, he made every effort to dislodge Aron. Every ounce of Aron's strength went into squeezing the throat, even as Kotvas bucked and tried to free himself. Aron cast a glance around, making sure the gun was safely out of reach. Only then did he look at Kotvas's face.

The Russian's eyes were bulging as Aron drove his thumbs harder into the man's esophagus. Aron saw the pain and the fury and the surprise at the fact his plan had gone south. Kotvas started to go purple as he thrashed, but he was too old and Aron was too experienced. Aron's fury manifested in a cold, steely focus to bring death to this man.

When it came, Aron climbed off Kotvas, wincing at the smell of the man's evacuated bowels. He could already see his colleagues gathering up the bodies of the Russians, kicking fresh snow over the blood and cleaning up the scene. The police had been well paid to stay away, Aron was sure, but never would the Russians have expected this. It would make an interesting tale in the newspaper.

Aron let out a long sigh as his colleagues completed their work. As they did, he slowly undid the buttons on his trenchcoat, pulled it open and inspected the damage. The two rounds he'd taken had impacted the vest but not penetrated, though he felt like a horse had kicked him. He wondered if he'd cracked a rib or two.

He waved at one of his colleagues. "Ready to go?"

The other man nodded. "Cargo secure."

Aron walked over to the van. His colleagues had retrieved the cash and the nukes. As he climbed inside and the ignition fired, Aron cast a quick glance back at the alleyway. He closed his eyes and felt around his ribs as the vehicle started to move. It hadn't exactly gone to plan, but it was good enough. He'd done his job and the fate of his people was still in his hands.

CHAPTER 6

The New York Standard Online is attempting to confirm claims on social media that Zionist extremists are in possession of three nuclear weapons. The tweets, which claim to be from representatives of the group, contain pictures of what appear to be small 'backpack nukes' alongside a Russian newspaper that confirms the date. Comment is being sought from the White House, the Pentagon and the State Department, as well as from Russian, Israeli and Palestinian officials. To date no comment has been forthcoming.

New York Standard

Jack forked a heap of bacon, ran it through the drizzle of egg yolk and delivered it to his mouth. If there was one thing he missed from his childhood, it was his mother's breakfasts. They even made the company tolerable. He put down his knife and fork as he chewed, slipped a hand under the table and squeezed Celeste's leg. She patted his hand and they smiled at each other.

"You should eat better, Jack." His mother's voice broke their moment. "You're both leaving it late to have children, so nutrition is very important."

Jack squeezed Celeste's leg again, in apology, and then shot his mother a look. "I told you, there's no certainty we're going to have kids. That's not our lives."

His mother bristled at what he'd said. She pursed her lips, clearly wanting to say something, but kept quiet. He'd heard it all before, about working too hard and living too little, but this wasn't the time. He and Celeste were having one last meal with them before heading down to Sydney for a couple of days. Celeste wanted to see the bridge.

They ate in silence before Celeste's cell phone rang. Jack glanced at her as she looked at the caller ID and then up at him. She gestured with her head toward the living room and he nodded. It was important, whoever it was. Or maybe she'd asked a friend to call her to bail her out of breakfast with his parents. Either way, he wasn't going to try to stop her.

"I'll just be a minute. Sorry. It's work." Celeste smiled at his parents and stood as she answered.

He locked eyes on his mother, daring her to speak even as Celeste's voice grew faint as she vanished into the other room. "What?"

"She's a nice girl." Joan smiled. "We liked her when she visited a few years ago, and we like her now."

"Yeah, I—"

His mother held up a hand. "But we're not sure you understand the importance of family, Jack. You missed the boat with Erin. Don't do it again."

He sighed and looked to his father for support, but received nothing. His mother was like a broken record. Whatever your achievements, if you failed to spit out kids then watch out. He shrugged. "If it happens, it happens. We've discussed our options but we're not on a timetable. It has to be right."

"You are on a timetable, Jack." Joan's eyes narrowed. "I know you lost Erin and that that was hard, but you're both in your mid-thirties."

"Look—" He never got the chance to finish. His own phone started to ring. It was the President. Jack pointed at it. "Sorry."

He ignored the look on his parents' faces and moved into one of the bedrooms. As he walked, a series of beeps played in his ear. It took about ten seconds for the phone to do its thing and the beeps were followed by a long bleeping tone. He'd been told upon commencing his job with McGhinnist to always wait for that sound, because it meant the call he was on was encrypted.

"Hi Jack." McGhinnist's voice was tense and he sounded tired. "Hope it's not a bad time?"

"Your timing is perfect." Jack sat heavily on the bed and cast a glance around, habitually checking to make sure he was alone. "What's up?"

"I've got bad news." McGhinnist's voice cracked a little with stress. "We have confirmation that the Zionists have three small nuclear devices."

Jack's eyes widened. Coming directly from the President, it was as good as fact. "Are we sure?"

"The CIA got word thirty minutes ago." McGhinnist snorted. "Not that it matters, but the Kremlin reached out and told our people."

"They did?" Jack was surprised. America hadn't exactly been on great terms with Russia for a long while.

"Yeah. President Ivanov called me a half-hour ago. He wanted to make it clear that the Russian state had nothing to do with the exchange." McGhinnist paused. "The Zionists made the deal with some Russian mafia guys, the deal went bad and they escaped. The Russians are trying to find the bombs."

"Makes sense. Ivanov doesn't want us thinking it's him and raising hell." Jack changed tack. "How big are we talking?"

"Big enough to take a chunk out of Manhattan, I'm told." McGhinnist paused. "This thing just got a whole lot harder."

"Ivanov will find the nukes before they leave Russia." Jack wasn't confident, despite his words. "Or we will."

"Neither Russia nor the NSC are hopeful of that outcome, Jack. The Zionist posts about the bombs on social media were an estimated ten hours after the exchange. They could be anywhere. I'm surprised your girlfriend hasn't got the scoop already. Whoever is leaking to her must be slipping."

Jack ignored the jibe and stood. "Need me back stateside? Though I think I know the answer."

"Yep, it's going to be all hands on deck." McGhinnist gave a small laugh. "Hell of a way to ruin a vacation, huh?"

"I'll be back as soon as I can."

Jack hung up the phone, stood and walked back to the dining room. Celeste was just returning with her phone in hand. Her face was ghost white. "You too?"

Her eyes were glassy. "Yeah, I have to get back."

"What do you know?"

"Enough." She shrugged. "We're running the confirmation."

Jack frowned. The leaker, again. McGhinnist hadn't been far off. How the fuck could her source find out and called her minutes before the President had let him know? Whoever was leaking was close to the action. He nearly said something, but took a few deep breaths and let his anger subside. Now wasn't the time. They had a long flight back together.

"It was nice to see both of you again." Celeste addressed his parents. "I hope next time we can stay longer."

"Us too, dear." Jack's father ran a hand through his hair and patted his wife on the arm. "Safe travels."

Jack nodded as his parents stood, their breakfast not yet finished. He hugged his mother tightly for several seconds. Once they were finished he held out a hand and his father shook it with a nod and a smile. The farewells complete, Jack stood back as Celeste and his parents hugged and then they all walked out to Jack's hire car.

"Jack, mate." His father spoke softly. "I know you don't like it here, but we still care about you, your mum and I."

"I—"

"Just listen. You can come back as often as you like or not at all, but I want you to look after her. She's stuck by you."

"I know, Dad."

"Okay." His father nodded. He'd said his piece.

Jack and Celeste climbed into their car. They'd return to their apartment, quickly collect their things and then drive to the airport. With luck, they could book some flights for later in the day. It was a long way back to the east coast of the United States, and the jetlag would be a killer, but at least they'd get to fly at the front of the plane.

Celeste gripped his leg. "Jack, I'm publishing the story. I don't want to hear anything about it. I have to do my job. That's it."

"I know." Jack smiled. "I wasn't going to say a word."

He didn't say that he was done arguing. While he mightn't yet be ready to propose to her, like his parents so clearly wanted, he valued his relationship too much to keep beating his head against a wall. Instead, he was going to put all of his energy into catching the leaker. He glanced over at Celeste. She was clearly unconvinced, staring at him with narrowed eyes, but she nodded. That was it.

"Shame I won't get to see Sydney Harbour." She sighed. "Seems a waste to come all this way and miss it for a second time."

Jack looked over at her once more and flashed a sly smile. "Third time's a charm?"

~

ZED POUNDED the lectern with his fist. "It's impossible to reconcile the utterly meek surrender we're currently seeing with the history of the Jewish people!"

He coughed violently, took a step back and reached for a glass of water. Silently cursing himself, he took a sip, realizing that he'd pushed it again. He was giving one of his most well-known lectures and, as always, it made him emotional. For a middle-aged man that was fine, but he was old man with mobility issues and a bad heart and needed to take it easy. Or so his doctor said.

"So, the last thing to note is that—"

"Excuse me, professor?" Ariel spoke softly behind him.

Zed frowned and turned. There was nothing he hated more than being interrupted mid-lecture. It deflated the entire exercise. Though Ariel was one of his students, Zed glared at him. Even if Zed resumed speaking within a moment, the students wouldn't remember the finely crafted narrative, laden with evidence and capped off with a compelling ending. They'd remember the interruption.

"What is it, Ariel? This had better be important."

"I think you'll want to see this, professor." Ariel approached the lectern and held an iPad in front of Zed.

He took the device. He hated them, these tombstones to the decline of the daily newspaper. The news used to have impact – gravitas – as the sole point of truth for the intelligent man for hours worth of current events. Now, more information was being created every few hours than in the entire history of humankind. It made comprehensive understanding and reflection impossible.

Zed read the screen and his eyes widened. His anger melted away and he felt silly for being angry at all. It was a great day and Ariel had done precisely the right thing. He looked up at his younger student and gave him a broad smile and a pat on the back. Ariel frowned, clearly confused, but nodded and walked away from the lectern even as Zed's mind started to spin. He turned back to the class.

"I'm sorry." Zed wasn't really looking at them, his mind racing. "An urgent matter has come up. You're dismissed. We'll pick up tomorrow."

There were murmurs from the students, but Zed's mind had already moved on. Though he was in his twilight years, he was still an institution at Yeshiva. A few complaints would wash away like grease from Teflon. He had bigger things to worry about, if what Ariel had shown him was true. But given the *Standard* was reporting it, Zed believed it was.

He grabbed his cane and waved at Ariel to collect the rest of his things. He moved as quickly as he could back to his office, thinking the whole time about what he'd read. The Zionists having nuclear weapons was a game changer. Even if they were only small devices, it was still enough potential devastation to put the Samson Option into play.

Zed reached his office, closed the door and slumped in his office chair, exhausted. After a few long breaths to steady himself and ward off any coughing, he reached over for the only photo that sat on his desk. Thousands of people had asked him about it over the years, who the men in the photo were and when it was taken, but he'd never divulged the secret to anyone. Not even his wife.

He was the architect of the Samson Option, the last defense of Israel. Its purpose was complete destruction of any attacker, even if Israel itself had to be flattened to achieve it. Only through foes having complete certainty that Israel was committed to this policy could it work. In recent decades, weak leaders had prevaricated and opened the hen house just a crack. Zed had seen the potential for the wolf to peer inside nearly half a century ago. He'd convinced others – fellow Samson architects and other influential Israelis and Jews. They'd made a pact to do whatever was necessary to invoke the Samson Option if and when it was needed, whether or not it was government policy.

Though Zed was the last of those in the photo left alive, each of the original members had recruited others. Nobody knew everybody, or even many, which was the whole point. One of the men Zed had taught, and then recruited, was Aron Braff. He'd gone on to have a career with Mossad before joining the private sector, but they'd never lost contact. It warmed his heart that Aron had succeeded and that at least some people were prepared to fight for Israel and against the stupidity of the agreement. He'd been hoping that Braff would succeed, but it had been a long shot. Zed didn't want Braff to have to use the nuclear weapons, but it was important that the world knew the stakes.

He checked his watch. The timing was not quite perfect, but it was close enough. Braff had left it late, but he could be forgiven for some tardiness, given his success. Zed reached over and thumbed his way through his Rolodex. When he found the right number, he picked up his phone, dialed and waited. It rang for a long time until eventually it was answered by a groggy female voice.

"Hello?"

"This is Zed Eshkol calling Captain Cohen."

There was a pause and a sigh. "Professor, Joseph is sleeping. It's early."

Zed smiled. "Oh, of course, of course. Please excuse my waking you."

Another sigh. "It's okay. Looking after yourself?"

"Of course, my dear. Now I won't keep you any longer. Pass on my best."

"Goodnight, professor."

Zed hung up the phone. He'd introduced Joseph Cohen and his wife when they'd both studied at Yeshiva. Another of his recruits, Cohen had gone on to have a great career in the military. Zed regretted he was unable to speak to the man, but the message would do. Sometimes playing the doddering old fool got the message across fine.

He was counting on it.

~

CAPTAIN JOSEPH COHEN clasped his hands behind his back as he stared at his professional future – HMS *Vigilant*. He was a disciplined man, but considering the rarity of the circumstances, he allowed himself a moment of pride and a wide smile. It wasn't every day you prepared to set sail in a Vanguard-class nuclear submarine under your command.

"It's all yours, Joseph." Admiral Graham Sinclair gave Joseph's shoulder a friendly squeeze. "I told you it would be."

Joseph's first assignment in the Royal Navy had been aboard an attack submarine commanded by Sinclair. Though they'd served apart at times, Sinclair had risen through the ranks and Joseph had followed, serving diligently wherever he was posted. It was patronage, but Joseph wouldn't have it any other way. He'd based his entire career plan on it.

He turned and saluted the admiral. "Thank you, sir, for your kind words and for the trust placed in me. I won't let you down."

"I know you won't, Joseph." The admiral returned the salute briefly before lowering his hand. "We're in tough times, but you'll do just fine."

Joseph nodded and Sinclair gave one more smile, then turned on his heels. Nothing else needed to be said. He had no doubt that Sinclair had played a large part in him gaining this posting, which also reflected well on the admiral. It was how the game worked. He'd waited many years for a command, working his way up and serving for nearly a decade as an executive officer aboard HMS *Vanguard* until, finally, he'd been sent the papers. Now he had his own command.

He turned back to the submarine, *his* submarine, and let out a long breath. He'd spent some time with the crew working up the boat and readying it for sea, but this was his first time stepping aboard as an operational commander. He started to walk up the gangplank. Once aboard he made his way to the bridge, where the crew all stood at sharp attention. He returned their salutes, glad that the boat was formally his.

"Welcome, captain." His executive officer, Tim Jennings, smiled broadly. "The ship is ready to sail."

Joseph matched the smile and nodded, before starting to work on getting his boat out to sea. The process was automatic and he didn't have to think about it. It was his first time as captain, but his thousandth as a submariner. As they ran through the procedure, he couldn't help but beam with pride. He was joining an exclusive club – the four men in charge of Britain's nuclear deterrent.

The *Vigilant* would relieve another submarine and Joseph would sail his boat to the middle of the Atlantic. There, he'd remain under the waves, waiting for the order to launch and end the world. It was the notification that no submariner aboard a boomer ever hoped to receive, though they'd trained all their professional lives for the moment.

Joseph wasn't quite so bleak about it. Such doomsday weaponry was useful, if only to remind everyone that certain actions were above the laws of man and necessitated a god-like retaliation. He'd insisted on a religious man as his executive officer. It was vital that he could trust his second-in-command to follow the orders of men and the will of God. Even if it was a different brand of God.

He turned to Jennings. "Ready?"

"Ship uncoupled and crew at stations, captain."

"Away with it then."

Jennings nodded, barked orders at several of the crew and then turned back to Joseph and spoke with a low voice: "No escape now, sir."

Joseph gave a small, throaty laugh. "Hell of a time to be sailing on my first command, given this stuff in the Middle East. But I'm glad you're beside me, Tim."

They shared a look and a nod, then turned as one to watch the crew going about their work. The submarine was sailing slowly, above water, out to the ocean. Only there would it dive below the surface and assume its deadly station, as Royal Navy submarines had done since accepting the role of nuclear deterrence from Bomber Command in 1969.

"I need to go to my quarters for a moment." Joseph spoke softly to Jennings then raised his voice to address the whole bridge crew. "XO has the deck."

"XO has the deck."

When Joseph reached the door of his quarters, he entered his passcode. The door unlocked with a click and he pushed it open. The captain's quarters were hardly luxurious, but there was a decent bed, a small dining table, some storage space and even his own bathroom facilities. It would take a while to get used to all the extra space, no matter how modest.

For now he ignored it all, except for the safe on the wall, used to house his orders and any personal valuables. He quickly opened it, took some papers out of his pocket, placed them in the safe and then locked it. As he did, he thought about another safe, which was in the operations room and housed the main nuclear launch codes.

Inside *that* safe was *another* safe, dedicated to one thing: holding the Dead Man Letter. Joseph had never read the letter. Nobody had. The British Prime Minister wrote one to each ballistic missile submarine captain. In the event that the PM and her designated second were killed, and certain other conditions fulfilled, the letter contained orders from beyond the grave to retaliate, submit to an allied navy for orders, or to use his own discretion in responding to an attack.

Joseph couldn't open the safe containing the Dead Man Letter without Jennings' assistance. Chances were he'd never have to, either. The safe remained locked until it was needed. If a new PM was elected, or a new captain appointed, the letter was destroyed and the process started again. Over and over until, one day, one captain in one submarine would be forced to tear it open and ponder the end of the world.

He sighed deeply and closed his eyes. Though he was excited by his first Royal Navy submarine command, going out of contact with the world also daunted him. Though he'd be undersea with 134 other sailors as company, it felt like he was alone. It felt different. While he'd lived in the UK and served in its navy for decades, he had other loyalties. As a Briton, he was excited. As a Jew, he was scared.

He just had to trust others above the ocean to do what was necessary to safeguard Israel and the world from the countdown to madness. If that occurred, nobody would be any the wiser to his dual loyalty. If it didn't, the consequences would be dire.

ACT II

CHAPTER 7

Twelve days into the countdown to peace between Israel and Palestine and, so far,
the agreement is holding. The United States is doing all it can to keep the
situation calm, but with agitation from all sides increasing and Zionist
extremists in possession of nuclear weapons, the chances of holding the fragile
peace together for two more weeks appear slim. So far the United States has
resisted calls for the deployment of more troops to Israel, stating that those
protecting nuclear assets and providing missile defense are sufficient.

New York Standard

J ack reached into his wallet and handed seventy bucks to the
driver. "Thanks buddy, keep the change."

When he opened the door and walked around to the trunk,
he saw that Celeste already had it open and was grabbing her
bag. Jack caught her eye and smiled as he hefted his own case. She
smiled back as she extended the handle on her case and took his hand.
He wheeled his case alongside her as they crossed the street.

"I'm glad we both got some sleep on the plane." Jack sighed. "Going
back to work after that sort of flight is tough."

"Yeah. And you've still got to get to Washington in the morning. I've
just got to get downtown."

They'd flown out of Brisbane, Australia, and spent just over a day in
transit, lasting the whole flight without any tension. He was about to

speak but the words caught in his throat when he felt Celeste tense. Looking at her then following her eyes, he pulled up short as the door to her townhouse opened and a man in a black suit and sunglasses walked out.

Jack didn't sense danger, but he'd worked around Federal agents enough to know their swagger. "I'll see what this is about."

She clearly wasn't impressed, but she nodded as she let go of his hand. "I'll look after our cases."

He took the steps two at a time and stood in front of the suited man. "I'm Jack Emery. What's this?"

"I know who you are, sir." The agent made no move to get out of the way. "This is a joint Secret Service and FBI investigation. You'll need to wait outside."

Jack took a deep breath. He had to keep his cool. "What's the investigation looking at?"

"Classified."

Jack should have seen that coming. "Who ordered it?"

"Classified, sir."

"Then I'm going to need to see your warrant, Agent ..."

"McClellan, sir." The agent dug into his pocket, flashed his FBI badge and handed Jack the warrant. "We good here?"

It had to be about the leak. Warrant in hand, Jack took a step back and pulled out his cell phone. "Excuse me, Agent McClellan, I need to call the President."

McClellan's expression didn't change. "Do what you need to do, sir. We're nearly done in here."

Jack took a step back and dialed. The phone was answered in seconds by the President's secretary. "Clara, it's Jack, I need to speak with him."

"One moment, Mr. Emery. I'll see if he's available." Her voice was pure sugar, as always.

Jack tapped his foot impatiently while the hold music played in his ear. As he waited, Jack tried to peer past Agent McClellan, who was blocking the door. He also looked down at Celeste, still waiting with their bags at the bottom of the stairs. A look of grave concern clouded her features. He flashed her a smile as the call finally connected.

"Jack? What is it? I'm in with Senate leadership in five minutes." McGhinnist sounded as tired as when Jack had last spoken to him. And irritated.

"My house is being searched by the FBI and Secret Service."

"I know. Everyone is getting the same treatment, Jack."

"But—"

"No." McGhinnist interrupted. "Everyone is getting the same treatment. I want to find out who it is and crush them. I don't think it's you, for what it's worth."

"Fine." Jack sighed. "But can you at least tell them to let me inside? Celeste is worried they're searching her stuff too."

"They know all about the First Amendment." McGhinnist paused. "Put one of the agents on."

"The President wants to talk to you."

Jack handed the phone to McClellan and after a moment the agent glowered and moved aside. Jack stepped into chaos. All the drawers in the hallway hutch had been rifled through and there were papers scattered up and down the hall. He froze in place, even as he felt Celeste's arm slip around his waist. He squeezed her hand and then turned to her. Her face was a mix of anger and shock.

He walked into the master bedroom, where several men in suits were rifling through their things. They paid him no heed until he spoke. "Having fun guys?"

"We're nearly finished, sir. This is the last room." One of the agents paused and looked up at Jack with a smile. "We'll be out of your hair in a minute."

Jack nodded and stood with his arms crossed, until one of the agents opened Celeste's underwear draw. He took a step forward. "Hey, come on, I—"

"*Do not move.*"

Jack turned. The agent who'd smiled at him a second ago now had a pistol trained on him. "What the—"

"Sir, you need to take a step back. You can stay inside the room, if you like, but you're not to impede our search in any way."

Jack nodded and raised his hands as he took a step back, his heart beating fast. The agents searched through Celeste's smalls with no further protest, but when she entered the room, Celeste looked at the agent and then at Jack with pure venom. She kept her mouth shut, despite the outrage that he was sure she felt. This was the second time she'd had her home raided by the police.

Finally, as suddenly as a sharp gust of wind, the agents nodded to each other and headed for the front door, taking with them a small box filled with some of the contents of the house. Worse, the agents had Celeste's laptop. She started to protest but they simply kept on walking. A black SUV pulled up in front of the house, they climbed in and the vehicle drove off.

Jack and Celeste were left hugging each other in the detritus of their home.

"I'm not super happy with your boss right now." She had her fists balled by her side. "They took my computer. They might get the identity of my source."

"They might." He took a step toward her, wrapped her in a hug and they squeezed each other tightly.

She shook her head. "If they do, my person inside the White House will be exposed."

Jack couldn't resist. He smirked. "Your *other* man inside the White House will expose himself any time for you, my love."

She punched him softly on the arm, a smile breaking out across her face. "I'm being serious. They'll be locked up."

"Yep."

"What can I do?" She pulled away. "You're probably excited that you're about to catch them, but I need to help protect my source."

"Nothing, except reporting this search on your front page tomorrow. That's the best you can do." Jack paused. "I've got to get back to Washington."

SAMIH DOUBLED over and winced at the pain. It felt like every muscle along his spine was being pulled, making him crooked, even though he knew he'd been standing up straight. With hands on his knees, he took a few deep breaths. If there was one thing worse than getting old, it was getting old with back pain. He cursed himself for forgetting to take his medication this morning.

"Are you okay?" Ben Ebron leaned in and placed a hand on Samih's back. "Do we need to return to the hotel?"

Samih turned to the Israeli negotiator and smiled, even as a few of their security detail shot them a look. "No, I'm fine."

"Okay." Ben smiled. "Shall we continue?"

"Of course." Samih stood taller and sucked in a sharp breath.

"You're a soldier, my friend."

Samih laughed. "Those days are long over. For good reasons – the peace we've signed won't allow it and my body isn't up to it."

He'd spent years shooting at Ben and his countrymen, thinking that was the only way to fight, to rebel, to achieve. Only later in life had he come to see the incredible power of politics. Now he knew that sustainable change came from iterative improvement, not revolution. From compromise, not demands. It had been a hard pill to swallow.

As fears of the nuclear threat had grown, so too had agitation in the streets. It had started with protests and escalated into near rioting in some places. Samih and Ben Ebron had been discussing the growing tension privately for the past few days. Though politicians could call for calm, both negotiators felt they had a special responsibility to inform the public about the peace.

Samih didn't blame the protestors. They were scared. They were worried about nuclear fire being unleashed by Zionist extremists. Identical protests were taking place in Mecca and New York City. Here, in Jerusalem, there was an extra level of fear even assuming the Zionists could be stopped. The protestors were confused about what the future would hold next to a newly constituted Palestine.

As the men walked, their security detail ringed them at a respectful distance and local police kept the protestors behind the barriers that divided the street. It was a microcosm of Israel and Palestine. One side calm, safe and orderly and the other chaotic, suppressed and crowded. The one other constant, along with the security, was the camera flashes of the assembled media.

Samih took a few steps closer to the protestors behind the barrier. They cried out and shouted at him, but he stood calmly as several tossed empty bottles at him. When one man took it further still, Samih calmly wiped the spittle from his face. He knew that – because of his role in the negotiations – everyone was watching him, looking for proof that Palestinians couldn't be trusted.

He saw a couple, young and beautiful, with a little girl eating an ice-cream on her father's shoulders. The venom they shouted at Samih and the signs they waved with fury ruined their picture-perfect image. Samih decided at that moment that, more important than the peace agreement and statehood, he had to convince that one family that he and his people wanted peace.

"Careful, my friend." Ben Ebron walked beside him and put a hand on Samih's arm. "You should stay back a little bit. It's not safe."

"It's okay." Samih shook his head. He walked up to the family, ignoring the violence that threatened to explode. He looked at the mother. "Hello."

She started to wave her placard even more furiously in his face. "Go back to your home and don't steal ours! Don't steal from my child! You've no right!"

Samih smiled as her sadly. "I don't want to steal from your child, just achieve peace and a future for the children of Palestine."

Samih took a half-step back when the father thrust forward. The crowd gave a roar and the fence started to buckle. Samih glanced up at the girl on her father's shoulders. She was no longer sucking on her ice-cream, and she looked terrified. Samih reached out to her protectively, but the father slapped Samih's hand away. The police and security detail were shouting.

"Samih, come on, they're surging!" Ben's shout could barely be heard over the noise of the crowd. "Let security do their job!"

Samih kept his eyes locked on the family, even as the fence buckled. He wouldn't be intimidated. He balled his fists and closed his eyes, ready to be attacked by the crowd. If his best wishes and peace wasn't enough for them, there was nothing else he could offer. He counted one second, then two, and was surprised when instead of a punch or a kick, he felt a hand clasp his.

He opened his eyes, looked to his right and smiled when he saw Ben Ebron standing beside him. The two men clasped hands and raised them over their heads. Some of the protestors stopped, but others pushed forward harder. When they were less than three feet away, Samih winced. The first of the security detail had thrown themselves into the fray, and local police were close as well.

The crowd came to within a foot of Samih and Ben before they started to turn, less keen on charging trained police and armed security guards than a pair of old men. Samih found the family in the crowd, his eyes locking onto them as they tried to remain calm in the push. Samih let go of Ben's hand when he saw the child drop her ice-cream cone and then reach out for it. When she fell he moved.

He was among the crowd in a second. The police saw him and did their best to stop him, but he paid them no heed as he made a beeline for the child. He felt one blow on his back, winced, but kept moving. Finally, he reached the girl. Her mother was screaming hysterically a few yards away, unable to reach her daughter. The girl's father was nowhere to be seen, swept up in the crowd.

Samih stood over the girl as the police and his security detail kept the other protestors away. The child looked up at Samih with wide, moist eyes, which nearly broke his heart. Camera flashes from the gathered media sparkled like stars. Samih leaned down to the girl's level. As the noise and the fury swirled around them, he had eyes for nobody but her.

Though tears streaked down her cheeks, she seemed only dazed by the fall from her father's shoulders, though she did have some grazes and cuts. He helped her to sit up. She searched around frantically and finally saw the object of her obsession: her ruined ice-cream cone, spilled on the ground and trodden on by dozens of feet.

"Here you go." He dug into the pocket of his pants and pulled out his tin of breath mints. He popped the lid and held them out for the girl.

Her eyes widened as she looked down at his hand, then up at Samih and back down at his mints. Quick as a viper, she snatched the tin from his hand. She removed one of the mints from the container and held it out to him. As the cameras continued to flash, Samih reached out and took hold of her hand. He closed it around the tin, making it clear it was hers.

She beamed. "Thank you."

"You're welcome, little one."

~

JACK TOSSED his White House staff ID onto McGhinnist's desk. "Well, my security pass still works. I assume I'm not the leaker?"

"Don't be dramatic." McGhinnist stood with a sigh, picked up the pass and shoved it into Jack's chest. Hard. "Everyone was checked."

Jack pocketed the pass and did his best to swallow his anger. He couldn't blame McGhinnist for ordering extra checks and trying to pry loose the leaker, who'd grown from a minor political annoyance into a major national security threat. Nevertheless, Jack's understanding didn't extend as far as tolerating secret searches of his home.

He'd flown from New York to Washington at noon. Though he'd intended to resign, the time in transit had cooled his head a little and now he was satisfied that he'd made his point to McGhinnist. The suggestion that he might be the leak made him laugh, but it also infuriated him after how much he – an Australian citizen – had done for this country.

"You done?" McGhinnist raised an eyebrow.

"Sure." Jack paused, but was unable to resist. "So, did my girlfriend's underwear drawer hold any secrets?"

McGhinnist smirked. "I hear she has some fantastic lingerie."

Jack rolled his eyes. "Did we at least find something for all that effort?"

McGhinnist shrugged. "They're still sifting through what was seized, but there's no smoking gun. I want to strangle whoever it is."

Jack nodded. McGhinnist was clearly as furious as he was with the leaker, but while Jack was angry because it had impacted his personal life, McGhinnist must be pissed because of the effect on every decision he was making. It was hard enough being president without the additional guarantee that everything you did would be on the front page.

Jack followed McGhinnist to the Situation Room, where the members of the NSC were already gathered. They stood as the President entered the room. McGhinnist moved to the head of the table while Jack took his place among the rank and file. He knew that McGhinnist had given the council twenty-four hours to come up with options to deal with the Zionists. Their time was up.

"What're our options?" McGhinnist remained standing and leaned on his fists, impatience clear on his face.

"Mr. President, unfortunately the Zionists escaped Russia. We don't know where they went and we don't know who they are." James Tipping paused. "We *do* know that they have three devices and their timetable and list of targets has been made fairly clear. We need to work back from there."

"We may not find them at all." McGhinnist sighed and sat. "Two weeks isn't much time to find a few tiny needles in a huge haystack."

Tipping nodded. "We've tasked all assets globally to finding them: satellites, humint, sigint. Anything not already engaged in a critical task will be devoted to finding them. But I'd say the chances of success are low. We should begin to consider other options."

"We could up our DEFCON level." Admiral Bryson Tannenbaum – Chairman of the Joint Chiefs – chimed in. "It'd increase our readiness to respond to any attack by the Zionists, but it'd also panic the public."

McGhinnist shook his head. "Maybe, but I don't want to go to a war footing just yet. We have time to power up our shields later. For now, our activity needs to be measured and aimed at finding them."

"Or we could just suspend the peace process?" Jack shrugged. "The stakes are high, but we can wait until the Zionists have been dealt with and then restart the clock, with the agreement of the Israelis and Palestinians."

McGhinnist stared down the table and straight at Jack. "The agreement is enacted in eighteen days. That gives us two weeks to find the nukes, deal with the agitation and prepare for the worst if an attack does happen."

Jack couldn't begrudge the President his refusal to delay. The negotiations had taken years, on top of the decades of groundwork. Achieving peace would be the crowning foreign policy achievement of the McGhinnist administration and a great step forward for the Middle East. Apparently nothing, not even the threat of nuclear devastation, would derail the President from this track.

Jack tuned out as the discussion of various options continued. This wasn't where he made his money. McGhinnist had military and intelligence experts to chew over those issues with him, as well as a fair mind for that stuff himself. No, Jack helped the President in other ways – outside the strict lines of responsibility inside the administration. He did what others couldn't.

"Excuse me, Mr. President." Jack stood suddenly, thoughts rushing through his head.

"Okay, Jack." McGhinnist nodded. He was used to Jack's occasionally weird hunches and gave him the space to follow them. Sometimes they panned out.

Jack left the meeting room. In the time it took to return to his office – a hundred yards from the Oval Office – he pored over the plan in his head. He thought about what he knew: the leaker was smart, they'd remained hidden despite efforts to discover their identity and they'd made no mistakes. He was convinced that law enforcement would never figure out who it was. Not in time.

But he might. If there was one thing the leaker had shown, it was speed. Whenever the administration made a decision it was communicated to Celeste and the *Standard* in no time. He smiled. It was perfect. He only wished he'd thought of it sooner. He booted his computer and started working on a briefing note for McGhinnist and the rest of the administration.

McGhinnist stuck his head into Jack's office just as he finished keying in the final point, hours later. "What got into you back there?"

Jack looked up from his computer, dazed. He took a sip of water and leaned back in his chair with a smile. "I think I've figured out how to catch the leaker."

"Is that so?" McGhinnist stepped inside and closed the door. "That would be great, because I didn't get much to help fix our other problem."

Jack nodded and hit print on the briefing. Once it spat out of the printer, he handed it to McGhinnist. As the President read the document, Jack paced the room and explained his plan in detail. McGhinnist was used to reading and listening at the same time, but he looked up when Jack reached the juicy bit. He glanced at the ceiling and then let out a long smile.

"You like it?" Jack sat on the edge of his desk. "It may not work, but I think it's got a pretty damn good chance."

"I like it." McGhinnist handed the paper back to Jack. "Send it to Clara and she'll distribute it to the council."

"It's a risk, sir. The media will be in a lather if this leaks." Jack took the paper and moved back around to the other side of the desk.

McGhinnist shrugged. "If a nuke goes off in Times Square, we're done for anyway. We need to focus on solving problems, not PR. Do it."

CHAPTER 8

The President's National Security Council received a briefing yesterday on the threat posed by nuclear-armed Zionists, a copy of which has been obtained by the Standard. Inside the briefing was a range of options to be considered by the council to deal with the threat. These options included: delaying the implementation of the peace agreement, attempting to negotiate with the Zionists, or conducting pre-emptive strikes on the Zionists if their physical location or that of their nuclear weapons can be determined. The White House declined to comment on the leak or on the contents of the briefing.

New York Standard

J ack smiled as the sun started to rise, a cup of coffee in one hand and the newspaper in the other. He lifted the cup to his mouth as he scanned the front page of the *New York Standard*. He'd read it upon waking and it was a bombshell. He didn't need to read it again, but wanted to double check before he took action that was irreversible.

As he read, he took a few more sips of coffee. Once he was done, Jack let out a long sigh. It was true. It was time. After he'd laid some bait, the rat had chomped down on the cheese for a second or two before the trap had decapitated him. He'd had a feeling that his plan would work, but he'd been shocked by the outcome. It just proved that nothing was for sure in this business.

He sighed and turned back to the barista manning the coffee cart. "Thanks, Ramez. I'll see you tomorrow."

Jack tossed the paper into the trash, gulped down the rest of the coffee and trashed the cup too. He waved to Ramez, turned and crossed the street to his car. As he climbed inside and drove the short distance to the White House, he dialed a number on his cell phone and put it to speaker. The phone rang for a short while, then a man with a deep voice answered.

"This is Mike Seccombe."

"Mike? It's Jack Emery."

"Hi, Jack." Seccombe sounded surprised. It wasn't often that Jack reached out to the head of the Secret Service. "What's up? You okay?"

"I'm fine." Jack paused as he tooted the horn at a car. "Listen, Mike, I need you to have a word to the President and then detain James Tipping until I get in."

Seccombe laughed. "Sure, Jack, no problem. I'll just slap some cuffs on the National Security Advisor because of some prank."

Jack sharpened his voice. "It's no joke, Mike. He's the leak. We need to do this quietly before he figures out we're onto him. If I'm wrong, it's on my head."

"Damn right." Seccombe paused for a long few moments, then Jack could hear him exhale loudly. "Okay, Jack. I'll talk to the President."

The line went dead and Jack let out a long sigh. When he'd drafted the briefings the previous afternoon and had them distributed to all the members of the NSC, he'd inserted a small difference in each brief, stamped them Top Secret and waited. He'd known the *Standard* would pick up on the story, and the identifying detail would reveal the leaker.

He hadn't expected this morning's article to point at Tipping, but Jack had triple-checked the leak had the same detail as the briefing handed to the National Security Advisor – his friend. There was no doubt. As he pulled into the White House entrance, waved his pass and waited as his car was checked for explosives, his thoughts shifted from the betrayal to containing any further damage.

Jack pulled into the staff carpark, climbed out of the car and walked briskly toward his office. Seccombe and the Secret Service should have Tipping in custody by now, so Jack was keen to brief McGhinnist before their detainee kicked up a stink. The President wouldn't like it, but when Jack showed him the evidence, it would be undeniable.

He made it fifty feet inside the building when he turned a corner to see Seccombe and two agents. He pulled up short. "What?"

"He's gone, Jack." Seccombe's face was flushed red. He'd obviously lost it at his men, who stood around looking sheepish.

"Fuck!" Jack kicked at a potted plant, which toppled over. "When was he last seen?"

"Talking to Admiral Tannenbaum over breakfast." Seccombe shrugged. "Not sure what spooked him, but he's fled."

Jack knew. Tipping and Tannenbaum would have discussed the newspaper story. Tannenbaum would have revealed, confused, that his briefing lacked some of the detail of what was reported and Jack's game would have been revealed. Tipping was smart and would have realized then that he'd been played. Jack wouldn't be surprised if the other man was long gone by now.

Jack clenched his fists and his gaze fell upon Seccombe. "I need you to find him, Mike."

"We'll do our best. I'll be in touch." Seccombe nodded and then stalked off with his men in tow.

Jack let out a long sigh as he considered the art on the wall. He reflected that the beauty of this place sometimes outshone the dark shadows within its walls. The hard decisions, conflicting agendas and, occasionally, the acts of outright bastardry that were committed in the name of power. Tipping had committed several such acts. Jack needed to find him.

He went to the Oval Office and pushed the door open. Jack was one of the few with a standing invite to interrupt the President for matters of great importance. This was one of those. McGhinnist looked up from his desk, surprised at the interruption, and raised an eyebrow when he saw the look on Jack's face. He waved Jack toward a chair as he pressed a button on his telephone.

"Clara, we'll need something stiff to drink in here, please." McGhinnist cut the intercom. "What's wrong, Jack?"

"It's Tipping." Jack sat heavily on one of the sofas and then pounded a cushion with his fist.

"Mike said you'd found out it was him." McGhinnist sat opposite him and frowned, processing what Jack had said. "So your plan worked?"

"Yep." Jack shook his head. "He leaked it, Celeste published it and I asked Mike to detain him. But the fox has already fled the henhouse. He's gone."

"How?"

Jack was about to say more but they were interrupted by the President's assistant, opening the door with a tray of glasses and a bottle of Lagavulin – a favorite of McGhinnist's. She didn't pour, but simply left the tray on the coffee table in front of them and left. Jack poured drinks for both of them and then handed McGhinnist a glass.

"I don't know how he got away, but it looks like he's up to his neck in it." Jack took a sip and savored the sharpness. "He might even be with the Zionists."

"It's possible." McGhinnist shrugged. "If nothing else, I'd say it's damn likely that he's worth having a chat to about some missing nukes."

Jack felt hot anger rising inside of him. An hour ago, he'd felt betrayed by Tipping. To discover that his friend was behind the leaks, the trouble in his relationship and maybe had something to do with nuclear-armed Zionists was nearly too much. But the fact that he'd escaped made it even worse. Jack couldn't sit around. He needed to act.

"What's on your mind, Jack?" McGhinnist stared at him as he took a sip of his own drink. "Spill it."

"I want to go after him, sir."

"You're kidding." McGhinnist put down his drink and shook his head.

He certainly wasn't. He felt personally betrayed by Tipping's actions and wanted nothing more than to find the man and confront him. Though there might be some danger, Jack doubted it. Tipping was flushed out and on the run, without resources or support. Jack had been in more dangerous situations over the past few years and come out unscathed. Besides, he was good at chasing down clues.

"I'm dead serious."

McGhinnist rubbed his chin. "Okay. But there's conditions."

"Name it."

McGhinnist opened his eyes. "You don't move anywhere until we have a solid understanding of where he is or where he's going to be."

"Fine." Jack shrugged. "Easy."

"And the whole reason I'm sending you is because it will be quiet. While you're looking, keep out of trouble. I'll have some covert teams doing the same, but I want to keep this as low-key as I can. The last thing I need is more headaches to deal with, like you getting arrested or something."

"Done, I—"

"There's one more condition." McGhinnist's face was as hard as granite. "And you're not going to like it."

～

Aron paused and glanced around for what felt like the hundredth time since he'd landed in Saudi Arabia. It was all for naught – there was nobody looking at him and he'd checked that he didn't have a tail – but he was feeling unusually conspicuous. He wasn't a nervous person, but he felt out of place this close to the most holy Islamic location on the planet, with a nuke strapped to his back.

Though he'd made it out of Russia with the rest of his team easily enough, this time he had no support and had to be very careful. Posing as a tourist was the easiest way to get around, aided by fake travel documents and a cheap camera to hang around his neck. The tourist angle also helped to explain the giant backpack he was carrying around.

He hefted the sixty-pound backpack with a grunt. His body was still in great shape, despite the fact he'd left Mossad several years ago, but the weight of the bag was testing his frame as much as the paranoia was taxing his mind. He felt as if a giant neon arrow was pointing at him, telling others that he didn't belong here. He just had to hope that his training and his body held up.

The sooner he reached his destination, the less likely it was that he'd be captured. But it was still important to fit in. He lowered the hood of his sweater, lifted the camera from around his neck and took a few shots. If he was stopped at the airport, it would be useful to have some photos to show a nosy officer. He was a diligent tourist, after all.

He reviewed the photos, smiled and pulled the hood back over his head, then walked the short distance to the home of his contact. It was a rendered concrete building of four stories and zero elevators and, of course, his contact lived on the top floor. He sighed, walked through the entrance and started to climb the stairs.

By the time he reached the top, sweat was starting to bead on his brow and the straps from the backpack were cutting into his shoulders. He removed the hood, wiped his forehead and knocked on the door. He heard movement from inside the house, heavy boots walking on a wooden floor. He kept still, his hands in clear sight as one lock after another clicked and the door opened slowly.

"Who are you?" The barrel of a shotgun appeared through the crack of the door. "What do you want?"

Aron had expected such treatment. He was an outsider. "A friend sent me to deliver a package. It's quite urgent."

The shotgun stayed pointed at him for a split second longer than he felt comfortable with and Aron was just starting to wonder if he'd been betrayed when the weapon dropped and the door opened fully. A man pulled Aron inside, slammed the door shut behind them and bolted the five locks. Only when he was finished did he place the shotgun down.

Aron eased the backpack to the ground and then walked over to the man with his hand outstretched. "It's wonderful to meet you."

The other man grunted. He shook Aron's hand, but didn't appear thrilled to be doing so. "You're late."

Aron checked his watch. It was true, though barely. "Not a hanging offense, I hope."

The other man glared. "When you're floating on a tiny yacht in a giant storm, precision is everything."

Aron nodded. Given he had been told the other man was completely trustworthy, he could excuse some odd behavior if assured of results. Not that it was Aron's place to consider such guarantees. He played a small part in an enormous game of strategy, and this man played an even smaller part. They were moved around the board by a master.

He remembered his time at Yeshiva University, where Professor Zed Eshkol first captured his attention. Over several years, Aron had come to agree with the professor's views and with his sincerity of belief in Israel. Finally, the professor had taken Aron under his wing, confided in him about the special work of the Zionists and granted Aron his place in it all. He trusted Eshkol's leadership.

He just hoped the professor had chosen his men wisely, because this man from Mecca was one of three being entrusted with the future of Israel.

"Here it is."

The other man moved toward the bag and peered inside. "Armed?"

Aron smiled back. "Of course. It's set to go off one minute after the expiry of the peace agreement countdown. If the parties decide to step back from the agreement, then we disarm them. The bombs have been modified to allow remote disarming by satellite. There's nothing you have to do except keep it safe."

Secretly, Aron hoped the bomb would never go off, because it would mean that some wonderful historical treasures were saved, millions of lives were spared and sanity had prevailed. All it would take was for several powerful men to determine that the status quo was acceptable. If Israel was saved, then Aron was happy and so were the Zionists. The bombs would stay silent.

The decision to detonate the bombs wasn't Aron's, nor were the conditions placed on their use, but he fully supported the man tasked with such impossible decisions. He was done here. There was plenty to do without worrying about parts in the plan that weren't his responsibility. In his mind, he'd already moved on to the next target.

"Very well." The other man seemed satisfied. He closed the backpack and hefted it over to the corner of the room, out of the way.

They shook hands again. If the clock expired, then this apartment would join the priceless historical assets and hundreds of thousands of people vaporized to pay the price for the folly of Israeli and Palestinian leadership. If the agreement was abandoned, like Aron expected, then his man would bury the weapon in the desert.

He pulled the hood back over his head.

~

ZED LOCKED his hands together and laid them at the top edge of his desk. With a shout, he dragged them along the entire surface, reveling in every piece of stationery or other office paraphernalia that hit the floor. Some items smashed, while others just formed part of the messy chaos that achieved nothing but helped to soothe his rage.

Once he reached the end of the desk, he collapsed into his chair, exhausted. Lungs burning, he closed his eyes, trying to bring his anger, his breathing and his blood pressure under control. He was not an angry man, prone to these outbursts, but the message he'd received from James Tipping before he'd boarded a flight bound for the United Kingdom had sent him into a blind rage.

When he'd calmed himself a little, Zed opened his eyes and surveyed his office. A lifetime of treasured possessions were strewn like so much rubble and there was little left untouched by his anger. The bookshelves and coffee table had been given a similar treatment. Whatever Zed's tornado of destruction had lacked in speed had been more than made up for by blind fury.

His eyes paused for a second in the middle of the room, where his walking cane lay. There was nothing left to destroy unless Zed wanted to take his campaign beyond his office, though not even his legendary standing with university administration could survive that. He picked up the last thing on his desk – a pen – and dropped it onto the floor with a sigh.

Zed was mad that he'd lost his man inside the White House. While he didn't know how, he assumed that Tipping's latest leak must have contained some kind of poison pill. Tipping was alive, sure, but his usefulness to Zed was now zero. Tipping was the piece that had helped Zed to reach check against the peace agreement, but had been removed from the board before achieving checkmate.

Although it was impossible for any leader to not suffer a few losses over nearly fifty years of such work, Zed considered Tipping a larger loss. He'd risen higher than most and his mother had been Zed's lifelong friend until her death. Losing Tipping was like losing a son. He hadn't anticipated the loss, nor had he prepared himself for the personal consequences.

Zed wiped the single tear from his eye then staggered to his feet and used the edge of the desk to steady himself. He supported himself using furniture as he moved slowly to the door. While he did, he thought hard about what came next. He needed to cool down, despite his every instinct telling him to destroy and pillage to soothe his anger.

In truth, he was mad at himself. He'd overused Tipping's access and it had burned the young man. Zed had wanted to ramp up the media pressure on the signatories to the peace agreement to make them walk away or delay implementation, but so far he'd failed to achieve either. Tipping was gone and now it looked as if the only way to destroy the peace was to nuke three cities.

He'd seen the Samson Option as a last resort, but now he wondered if it was the only option left. The Israelis and the Palestinians had proven surprisingly resilient in the face of great pressure, while the response of the McGhinnist administration had been baffling. Zed had expected some degree of retreat by the US, but the President had escalated matters instead.

Zed reached the door to his office, opened it and stuck his head out the door. "I'd like you to head home early today."

His assistant looked up from her computer, the confusion on her face clear. "Is everything okay, professor?"

Zed nodded but kept quiet. She clearly knew something was wrong and had probably heard the noise, but knew better than to ask. She smiled at him and started to gather her things. Zed waited, propped against the doorframe and breathing heavily while she made her way out of the office. Soon he was alone and Zed returned to his office, picking up his phone from the floor.

He collapsed back into his chair, as exhausted from his journey as he was by his campaign of destruction. It had been many years since he'd moved without his walking stick. He waited a moment or two while he gathered himself, then dialed a number from memory, raised the phone to his ear and waited for the call to be picked up. When it was, there was the single beep of a voicemail.

"This is Zed." He spoke softly, trying not to let his sadness and the gravity of the situation divert him from the correct decision. "Knight 2 is off the board."

The message was enough for business to be taken care of. Zed knew that if Tipping was captured anywhere in a Western country he'd be arrested, extradited to the US and questioned. If that happened, Zed's place in the Zionist hierarchy could be revealed. He didn't care about his own freedom or his own life, given no court would jail a man of his age. He did fear that the authorities would figure out how to stop the Zionists in their holy cause.

There were cells, dozens of them, which faced exposure or destruction. But his ability to conduct the orchestra would be lost if he was caught. It wouldn't do. Tipping had to die and Zed had just ordered it. The decision was like a lance through his heart. But it was necessary for the safety of the entire Zionist cause and their important mission.

He'd honestly thought the nuclear option was the last resort and that the peace agreement would unravel against such a threat. But it had proven resilient. He'd been prepared for the use of the weapons, but given the exposure of Tipping, he wondered now if it was best to issue one final ultimatum and then use the weapons if his demands weren't met. He dialed another number.

"Hello?" The voice on the other end of the line didn't have any of the stress that Zed had coiled up inside of him. "Ariel speaking."

"Ariel." Zed smiled. Just hearing the young man's voice was proof that his work was not yet done, his campaign hadn't yet concluded. "How are you?"

"Fine, professor." Ariel paused. "Is everything okay? Do you need me to call someone?"

Zed nearly laughed at the success of his charade. Though his body was failing him, clearly the act that his mind was doing the same was proving wildly successful. He had everyone fooled, even his secretary and one of his closest students. A student he was also grooming to form part of his network. A minor part, at first, but with some potential.

"I'd like you to come to my office, Ariel. I've had a bit of an issue here and I could use your help cleaning it up." Zed sighed. "But only if you don't mind."

There was no hesitation. "Of course, professor, give me half an hour and I'll be over."

"Excellent. Thank you, Ariel. I'll see you soon." Zed hung up the phone and placed it on the desk.

He allowed himself one last flicker of anger before he dampened down the flame. Tipping had to die, but not in vain. He was determined that there would be retaliation, but he still needed to decide on the form of it. It could come in the form of another nuclear ultimatum or he could come up with something else.

The choice was his, but he needed to decide before Ariel arrived.

CHAPTER 9

The White House is in damage control after the shock resignation of National Security Advisor James Tipping. Washington is awash with speculation that Tipping, a three-year veteran of the McGhinnist administration, was the leak inside the White House that has plagued the President for weeks now. The timing of the resignation isn't ideal, with less than two weeks to go before peace between Israel and Palestine, nuclear-armed Zionist extremists threatening major cities and other states in the Middle East starting to talk tough. Though a White House spokesperson this morning claimed the resignation was an amicable, mutually agreed parting of ways, it's quite possible that Tipping walked before he was forced out.

New York Standard

C aptain Joseph Cohen nodded as the printer began its urgent clatter. When the message was complete, the operator ripped the printout from the machine and read it. Satisfied that the message was genuine, she passed it to Tim Jennings – Joseph's executive officer – who turned and immediately left the radio room, arm held high.

Joseph followed a few steps behind Jennings and the other officer with him, whose job it was to make sure the message wasn't substituted on the way to the control room. Joseph didn't say a word or interrupt them. It was important that the process play out, without interference from him. His crew knew what they were doing.

Only once they reached the operations room did Joseph step closer to Jennings. "Open the safe, XO."

"Yes, sir."

Leaning in close to the code panel, Joseph entered the eight-digits that made up his part of the code. He looked left to Jennings, who was a little slower, but within a few seconds the other half of the code was in and the safe unlocked with a click. Joseph opened it and pulled out the cryptographic codes that would tell them whether the order to launch was legitimate.

Before he closed the safe, he glanced quickly at the second safe, inside the first. It contained the Dead Man Letter – a weapon potentially far more destructive than the codes that he'd just extracted. With a quick shake of his head, he closed the safe and put his mind back on the job. There was time later to think about other matters.

Joseph handed one code sheet to Jennings and the other to the Weapons Engineering Officer, Ray Burroughs, who stepped forward to receive it. They looked down at their crypto sheets and compared them against the message that had come in from the boomer command bunker at Northwood, deep under the Chilterns.

"XO!" Jennings' shout reverberated around the interior of the operations room. "My half authenticates, sir!"

"WEO!" Burroughs' voice was deeper but not as loud, the rolling thunder after a lightning strike. "My half authenticates, sir!"

Joseph looked at them both. Their faces were stern, uncompromising. "The message authenticates correctly. XO, bring the submarine to launch station."

He stood back again, watching. His role was complete for the time being, and it was important that he allowed both men the space to complete theirs. He let out a long exhale, calming himself. Though he'd trained for this moment for years, it was his first time doing it in command of a boat. He needed to be stone. He needed to *show* that he was in command.

"Ship control. Pipe the boat to launch station." Jennings' voice was quieter now.

The crewman pressed a button and spoke loudly into the microphone. "Action stations! Missile for strategic launch!"

"Very good." Jennings nodded. "Full rise on the fore planes. Two up. Stop engine."

Joseph watched as the submarine – his submarine – was brought to its launch position closer to the surface. One of his crew held out a small earpiece, and Joseph placed it into his ear and nodded. Just as the submarine reached position, Burroughs left the operations center and moved to take his place in the missile center.

"Boat at launch position." Jennings' voice broke the silence.

"WEO in the missile control center." Burroughs' voice crackled in Joseph's earpiece. "Stand by, operations."

"Check." Jennings reached up and scratched the back of his neck.

Joseph knew that in the missile center, the target package would be being shifted onto target, the right number of missiles readied and coordinates confirmed. Only once the weapons were ready would the weapons officer unlock a safe above his console, open it and remove the trigger that fired the weapons. It had always amused Joseph that the trigger was the handle of a Colt .45 pistol.

The mood in the operations center was of intense concentration, as men and women stared at their screens and worked complex controls. Joseph found that, despite being the captain of the ship, he actually had very little to do when it came to launching the weapons. He carried the pressure – the load on his shoulder – but it was his crew who pressed the buttons in the leadup.

Finally, after another few moments, Burroughs spoke. "Command, weapons systems in condition one for strategic launch."

Joseph nodded, stepped forward and leaned in to the microphone on one of the consoles. "This is the captain, the WEO has my permission to fire."

Joseph stepped back and crossed his arms as Burroughs' voice crackled in his headset again. "Supervisor WEO, initiate fire one."

Joseph waited one more second, then nodded at a member of crew who so far had done nothing. She pressed a button and every light in the operations center – and the entire submarine – flashed on, breaking the strange trance that the drill had created among the crew. Joseph reached into his pocket as his eyes adjusted, then looked down at the old gold fob watch, a gift from his father.

"Too long." Joseph shook his head and closed the watch before returning it to his pocket. "Better, but still too slow on the verification."

The crew sagged as one as Jennings nodded and started the debriefing in the observation room, pointing out where they could improve and where they'd done well. Joseph turned on his heel and started the walk back to his cabin. He needed to freshen up, but he also needed to reflect on where things could be improved or where they could go wrong.

It was quite possible that in a few weeks he'd have to do the exercise for real. He was glad his crew was well oiled and knew their jobs. When the order came down from command, they'd follow his instructions. He'd drill them several times over the coming weeks, because in the event of a launch, he wanted things to move faster and he knew that events didn't always work out easily.

He thought again of the Dead Man Letter and wondered if, when the letter was opened, his crew would follow him.

JACK FOUND it a bit insulting that, after all he'd been through in helping the United States fight extremists and terrorists, Delta Airlines didn't trust him to use a real knife and fork. It was just one of the problems with being stuck on a commercial flight instead of an official one – a condition that the President had placed on sending Jack overseas to find Tipping in order to keep attention off him.

He stabbed at the small piece of overcooked beef with his plastic knife. Though the meat was slicked with some kind of congealed brown sauce, the knife bent as if repelled by steel armor plating. Jack held the knife in front of him and frowned at the ninety-degree bend of the blade. Taking over the plane with the dead cow would be more dangerous to the flight crew than proper cutlery.

"Should have gone for the salad." He gave up on the food and placed it on the vacant tray table next to him.

With a sigh, he pulled out his iPad. If nothing else, the flight had wifi. He downloaded his emails and started to work through them. It was autopilot. If you worked a white-collar job for long enough, wading through emails became as easy as a carpenter hammering a nail, if less enjoyable. It was actually a great time to think about the days ahead.

McGhinnist had finally agreed to let him chase Tipping after he'd been caught on CCTV footage at Heathrow Airport in the United Kingdom. Tipping was traveling on false papers, so he'd waltzed through immigration, but a bright kid at the CIA had spotted him on the footage a few hours after Tipping had entered the country. Jack was now flying to that same airport, hoping he could catch up.

"You're fussy."

Jack laughed and looked up at Chen Shubian, who gestured with his chin toward the food Jack had left aside. "I might have chipped a tooth on that beef."

Chen smiled. "When I finished my special forces training in Taiwan, I had to survive for two days in the Dawu Mountains with a tin of beans and my wits."

Jack dismissed Chen's statement with a wave of his hand. "Well, if you survive the White House press corps you can survive anything except airline food."

Chen shook his head and picked up his magazine. The conversation was over. The man remained an enigma to Jack and their relationship was complicated. Chen was a special forces soldier-turned-terrorist who'd blown up a fair amount of Shanghai and killed Jack's wife in the process. He'd also shot Jack's old boss and friend, Ernest McDowell. On the other hand, just like Jack, Chen had been duped, threatened and nearly killed by the Foundation for a New America, and he'd lost his own wife. Only Jack's efforts to convince Chen to provide evidence against the Foundation's leader, Michelle Dominique, had saved Jack's life and kept her from controlling Congress and a large portion of the world's media.

After stopping Dominique, they'd gone their separate ways. Jack hadn't thought much about Chen during the years following, until he'd joined McGhinnist's administration and learned that Chen was still in the United States. It made sense, given Chen's native Taiwan was a no-go zone for him, but Jack had assumed he'd left America. Instead, the FBI had kept him on retainer, probably as much to keep an eye on him as to occasionally extract information from him. Or to make use of his skillset, as Jack now was. He'd spoken to the other man at the airport and, though the details were scarce, it was clear Chen had been undertaking some work for the United States on American soil. He'd shrugged his shoulders and simply said that it was the cost to keep his children safe.

Having Chen along as an escort had been McGhinnist's other condition for approving Jack's request to go after Tipping. Jack was still a United States Government employee and, as such, he was unarmed. That made Chen useful. If they ran into any trouble with rampaging

Zionists the ex-Taiwanese special forces soldier had skills that didn't require a firearm.

Jack's eyes shot open. He must have dozed off and now the plane was rattling in some fairly severe turbulence. He looked at Chen. "You okay?"

Chen was gripping his armrests with both hands, his knuckles white. He turned to Jack. "I'm not a fan of flying."

Jack laughed, loud and long, to the extent that several other passengers cast a glance their way. "So Mr. Special Forces is human. Why agree to come?"

Chen gritted his teeth. "My children are in New York. Their school. Their friends. I could move them, but I'd just as rather save the city."

Jack nodded at Chen's words. He was as dry and as self-motivated as ever, yet on rare occasions Jack had found it possible to work with Chen toward a mutual goal. It was quite possible that Tipping was in with the Zionists, who'd proven they had a fairly decent ability to break shit and blow it up, so it was nice to have Chen along.

Jack looked across the aisle and locked eyes with Chen. "I'm doing this for Celeste, but we'll make sure your kids are okay too."

"I nearly blew her up once, I hear, so I probably owe her one." Chen's face was impassive. "We'll catch your man and find the bombs."

SAMIH HELD his hand high in the air and kept a wide smile on his face, even though his cheeks were starting to hurt. The applause was rapturous. His arm was linked with Ben Ebron's, who had his other arm linked with Karl Long. The triad in charge of the peace negotiations were receiving a rock-star reception in a community hall in Jerusalem – the latest event to build support for the peace.

Finally, the applause started to subside. Samih gave one last wave and then moved with Long to take his seat slightly behind the lectern, leaving Ebron at the front to speak. It was the same format they'd used a dozen times at events in the past few days. Samih had never smiled and waved so much, nor felt as welcome in Israel after the initial trouble with the protestors.

The vision of him handing his mints to the Israeli girl had gone viral. Suddenly, he'd been thrust into the popular imagination far more prominently than at any time during his career fighting for Palestine or, later, attempting to negotiate a political settlement with Israel. He was now a celebrity. It gave him hope that the world had some interest in what they were trying to achieve.

He'd felt the balance begin to tip. Since broadcasting their threats, the Zionists had gone quiet. Samih knew they were serious and that they had the weapons they claimed, but he felt they were losing the public imagination. It was hard not to worry, but he knew there was no point: the CIA, Mossad and plenty of others were looking for the group and their bombs. He couldn't help with that.

What he could do was try to build public support for the agreement and keep minds on the positives – for Israel, Palestine and the whole world. He shook his head and tuned in to what Ebron was saying. Though Samih had heard it several times already today, it was important to pay attention in case the Israeli negotiator changed his message and required Samih to do the same.

"I call on those Zionists, who call themselves Jews and say they're acting in the interests of Israel, to listen." Ebron held his hands out. "Listen to me. Listen to your people. You save nothing by threatening to destroy cities and kill millions. All you'll do is bring ruin to your spiritual homeland.

"Peace with the Palestinians will secure Israel a long-term, sustainable future in the region. We will no longer have to live with one hand on our guns. We can talk." Ebron shook his head. "Or, if you go through with your threats, we will be fighting for our very existence, against neighbors who'll rightly wish us gone."

On it went, until Ebron was finished and Long stood to make his speech. He spoke the usual lines about the level of US support for the agreement, that America was doing everything in its power to support the peace and catch the Zionists, and that the normal citizens of Israel and Palestine had the most to gain from peace. He was not a commanding speaker but his message was strong.

As more applause rang out, Samih stood and took his turn at the lectern. "Thank you. I want to be brief here today, because I agree with my dear friends and colleagues behind me. My people have fought for their freedom for decades. Despite violence on both sides, we've achieved peace. It's inevitable."

A commotion in the crowd prevented Samih from continuing. It only took a second to find the source. A man in the front row had stood and ripped his shirt open, revealing some strange rig of explosives strapped to his chest. Security had been tight, but somehow the man had found his way in. Samih raised his hand and screamed, his voice shrill, but the man ignored him as he raised a remote.

"This is a fool's peace!" The man's voice was high and laced with fear as he pressed his thumb down on the button.

Samih turned and dived, taking Ebron down to the floor just as the explosion tore through the small hall. A wave of pressure impacted him even as he hit the ground with Ebron. Dust filled his mouth and nostrils. His ears were ringing, drowning out all other sound around him. He pushed himself off the Israeli and looked around.

The hall was carnage. There were scorch marks on the wooden floor where the man had been. Bodies lay scattered, unmoving and broken. Others writhed in agony like experiments in some strange human abattoir. Samih's eyes were locked on the scene, unblinking, until he felt someone pulling on his shirt. He turned his head and blinked twice.

"We have to go!" Long had one hand gripped on Ebron's arm and the other on Samih's shirt. He let go and held out his hand. "Now!"

Samih grabbed Long's hand, using it as leverage as he started to struggle to his feet. He didn't get the chance, because a gunman approached the American and fired a shotgun blast into his head. As blood and gore sprayed Samih, Long's grip went limp and Samih stumbled back. He looked up, screamed and tried to shuffle away from the gunman.

The attacker turned to Ebron, pumped his shotgun and raised it at the Israeli. Samih watched in horror, frozen, as the barrel slowly came up. His hearing was still muffled, but he could hear other gunshots, booms that sounded to him as if they were underwater and distant rather than in close, lethal proximity. He glanced sideways. Two other gunmen were walking through the hall, terminating anyone who moved. He turned back to the first gunman, who was struggling to unjam his shotgun.

The gunman threw down the shotgun and drew a pistol. Samih scrambled to his feet, shouting, but was too late. The gunman fired a single shot into Ebron's skull and Samih let out a scream as the man he'd been through so much hard, honest negotiations with fell to the floor. Samih surged forward as the gunman started to turn, then leaped onto his back. The man tensed instantly as he tried to buck Samih off. Samih wrapped his arm around the gunman's neck, trying to strangle him, until he felt a hard punch into his side.

He staggered, confused, then turned and saw another man gripping a blade that was protruding from his side. Samih looked down in shock. His eyes narrowed as he tried to comprehend how a blade could enter his side and yet cause no pain. He tried to grip the blade, but his attacker withdrew it before he could grab it. Pressing his hand against the wound did nothing to stem the bleeding, even as he looked up at the other man. The look of hatred on his face was shocking as he thrust the knife into Samih again and again.

Samih's last thought was a prayer that the peace would endure. Ebron, Long and Samih had worked so hard for it. And given their lives.

CHAPTER 10

Israeli, Palestinian and American political leaders have released a joint statement condemning the Zionist attack on the lead negotiators for the Palestinian–Israeli peace treaty. Fifty-eight people were killed in the massacre, including the negotiators, in one of the worst ever terrorist attacks on Israeli soil. The Zionist terrorist group has claimed responsibility and downplayed the security camera footage of the Palestinian lead negotiator, Samih Khaladi, leaping to the defense of Israeli negotiator Ben Ebron. The footage has gone viral, with over seventeen million YouTube views.

New York Standard

Zed's eyes scanned the screen, lapping up the news like a cat with milk. The analysis was shoddy, but he was used to that. Gunmen had attacked an event spruiking the peace agreement and shot the negotiators and the crowd to pieces. Each of the negotiators had been killed, along with many members of the crowd. It had gone perfectly. Just as he'd planned.

He allowed himself an indulgent smile, pleased that the Israeli negotiator had been dealt with. Though the agreement was signed and he had no further formal role to play, Ben Ebron's cheerleading on behalf of the peace had made Zed's efforts to destroy it harder. Zed would have ordered him killed sooner or later under any circumstances, but Ebron's advocacy had forced his hand.

Unfortunately, the news wasn't all positive and one aspect of the attack had backfired. As he reached the bottom of the article he saw a link to a video he couldn't resist clicking on again. He ground his teeth as he watched the Palestinian, Samih Khaladi, doing his best to protect Ebron from the gunmen. A killing Zed hoped would help to destroy public support for the agreement had instead bolstered it. It was the internet, always the cursed internet. Thirty years ago, the headline would have read 58 dead in massacre in Israel, including peace negotiators. Now? Massacre in peace meeting – you won't believe what happens next!

Things used to be a lot easier. Organize a killing, the media reported it for a day and then the problem went away. He sighed. As much as he was in control of his network, he knew he was kidding himself if he thought he could totally control events. The world didn't work that way. All he could do was keep playing the game, using his pieces and recruiting more to ensure that he won in the end.

He picked up his phone and dialed. "I want the team in Israel dealt with."

Without waiting for confirmation, he hung up. He leaned down with a pained groan, opened the bottom drawer and pulled out a leather-bound folder. He placed it on his desk and slowly flicked through the pages. The names and photos caused memories and regrets to wash over him. So many men and some women – game pieces – expended to protect Israel and the Jewish people.

He finally found the right names and photos. He picked up a marker and sighed as he crossed out each man. They'd been loyal servants, but limited. Thugs. Pawns. They'd played their part and now more capable pieces would end their involvement. It wasn't a question. A move had been ordered and now it would be done. It was how he played the game.

Besides, there were always more pawns. He pressed the intercom to summon his assistant. "Please ask Ariel to come and see me."

"At once, professor."

Zed woke with a start at the knock on the door. He smiled slightly and rubbed his face. He hadn't been sleeping much, which wasn't unusual for him, but the older he got, the less he found he could take the long days and sleepless nights. He found himself dozing off in the strangest places, though thankfully this time it had been in his office and not in public.

"Come!"

The door cracked open and Ariel peered inside. "You asked for me, Zed?"

Zed smiled at Ariel finally using his name. He was one step closer. "Come in."

He struggled to his feet and walked to the chessboard at which they always held their meetings. As he shuffled over, he considered the growth of the young man. He'd made a decision, but he'd play the game first. By the time he'd reached his armchair and eased himself into it, Ariel had made the first move. Zed looked at the board and reached out to move a pawn.

"You're well, professor?"

"Yes, why?"

"No reason." Ariel shrugged. "There's just been some talk about you retiring."

Zed scoffed. "There's been talk about that for twenty years, Ariel. But I'm still here and they're still trying to get rid of me. For as long as I can continue to get up the nose of the administration, and beat students like you at this game, I'll be around. After that I'll haunt the place, mark my words."

Ariel laughed and looked back down at the board. "Of course you will."

While his student considered his move, Zed considered his student. He'd been working on Ariel for several years now. At first, he'd simply been the young man's teacher. Then, his mentor. Now, perhaps, his friend. While Zed didn't see any great potential in Ariel, he was loyal and smart enough to serve. Everyone had a place and a use.

"Your move, professor."

Zed shook his head. "My apologies, I was just thinking about you."

"Me?" Ariel looked at him quizzically. "What do you mean?"

"You graduate soon." Zed fixed his eyes on his student, who fidgeted under his gaze. "Have you considered your future? It's tough for graduates right now."

"Sure." Ariel shrugged. "I'd thought about doing some post-graduate study, but with the situation in Israel, I feel I might have something to offer as a citizen."

Zed smiled. Though he'd never been a citizen of Israel, everything he'd done as a professional had been aimed at protecting it. Part of that was recruiting the pieces for his board. He'd never expected to need to utilize his army or the great work of his life – the Samson Option – but he was twelve days away from needing both. The destruction of Israel was close.

"You're a remarkable young man, Ariel. I think becoming a citizen and serving in the military would be a wonderful choice for you."

"I've thought about it. But I'm not sure. I don't want to end up as a grunt in the West Bank."

Zed laughed. Maybe the boy wasn't a pawn after all. "I have some contacts in the IDF. I can make some calls and probably work out something better."

"That would be wonderful, professor." Ariel beamed. "Even if I don't sign up, it would be good to know my options."

Zed nodded. Ariel was now his. Though he'd been carefully cultivated over years, there had been no guarantee until now. But the minute Zed made the call to his man inside the Israeli Defense Forces, Ariel would be in his pocket. Zed would make him an offer too good to refuse and then the boy would be in his debt. A piece on the board. Limited, but useful.

He moved another pawn. Though some of his recruits went on to greatness, others fizzled out and some weren't used at all. Though he wasn't sure what he had in Ariel, he was obliged to keep adding pieces. With the stakes so grave and so many pieces being lost, it was nice to add a new one. He wondered how many would be left in a month.

JACK STOOD with his hands tucked into the pockets of his coat as he watched the ferry slowly inch up to the dock and come to a stop. When the ship was still, its air horn let out a long, droning blast. To Jack, it felt like his own personal wail of triumph, a shout to Tipping that his time was up and that he was about to face the consequences of his betrayal.

That betrayal seemed all the more serious now. After landing, Jack had spent several fruitless days searching the United Kingdom for Tipping, even as the pieces fell into place back in the States. Jack had received an email from Mike Seccombe, head of the Secret Service, which informed him that definitive proof had been found of Tipping's involvement with the Zionists.

Though the proof provided no clue as to who their leader was, it was enough to ratchet up the importance of the search by a few hundred percent. Tipping had to be found. Luckily, Tipping had been spotted boarding a ferry to cross the English Channel that morning. Though tempted to ask the British Special Air Service to nab him, the NSC had picked a different approach.

Jack and Chen had flown by helicopter to Calais, where they now waited with around fifty French police officers, braving the cold and the squally, biting wind in order to get their man. Jack felt an extra sense of urgency, given the negotiators had been killed. It felt like their deaths had frayed the chances of peace even further. The good guys needed a win. They needed Tipping.

Jack looked over at Chen. Icy breath escaped his mouth and he looked miserable. "Like the cold then?"

Chen grimaced. "Winter is winter anywhere, but winter with jetlag is a special kind of miserable."

Jack laughed and turned back to the ferry. By now, the ramp was in place and a large number of people had started to gather on deck. Jack watched as the man in charge of the police detachment ordered his officers forward, ready to foil any attempt by passengers to use the ramp. Their orders were clear: nobody leaves the ferry until Tipping is in cuffs.

When the ramp was finally readied for the police to board, they marched up it five abreast with batons drawn in an obvious show of force. The passengers who'd expected to disembark stood aside, confused, as the phalanx marched past them. Five officers remained at the bottom of the ramp to make sure Tipping couldn't escape.

"Let's go."

Jack and Chen walked up the ramp and onto the deck of the ferry. They waited as the police conducted their search, checking each passenger against a photograph of Tipping. Minutes passed, then more, and Jack began to lose hope of catching their man, when finally the senior police officer told them in broken English that the former National Security Advisor was not on board the ferry.

"Fucking hell!" Jack kicked the wall of the ferry and immediately regretted it. He winced in pain for a couple of seconds, before calming down. "What now?"

"It's no surprise." Chen sighed. "He didn't escape the Secret Service, fly to the UK and board a ferry across the Channel by being stupid."

Jack opened his mouth to respond, but then closed it again. He reached up, scratched his head and turned to face the guardrail on the outside of the ferry. He looked out to the ocean and smiled. Tipping may no longer be his friend, but Jack found it hard to stifle a laugh. He'd been stupid and overconfident. He'd marched in with an army of police officers on the assumption that it'd be enough.

He turned back to one of the crew. "Is there CCTV on board this ferry? Do you have easy access to it?"

The sailor shrugged. "Sure. But you'll need to convince the captain to let you access the tapes."

Jack nodded and gestured for the sailor to lead the way. Another sailor radioed the captain to let him know they were on their way. The small band made their way to the bridge, where the captain had already gathered a handful of laptop computers, ready to stream the footage from the server. He had a grim look on his face.

"Captain." Jack held out his hand. "I'm so sorry for all of this disruption, but we have to find this man."

The captain shook his hand. "So I keep being told. If we can find your man on the camera footage, will you let my passengers off?"

"Of course."

The captain gestured for them to get started. Jack watched one computer, Chen another, and the two police officers took one each. They watched at ten times the normal speed until Jack saw something. He hit the space bar on the machine, causing it to play at normal speed. There was Tipping, jumping overboard with nothing but a backpack and a bright orange floatation device.

Jack shook his head, turning to the others. Everyone except Chen seemed stunned. Jack turned back to the screen and rewound it. He needed to be certain before he could report to McGhinnist and the authorities. Not pretty sure, certain. But the footage was crisp and clear and the person he was looking at was undoubtedly James Tipping.

Jack cursed and slammed the lid of the laptop shut. He turned to the captain.

"You're good to let your passengers off. That's him."

"Thanks. Bad luck." The captain turned and walked away. His concern was clearly for his boat, not the international security crisis playing out on it.

Jack closed his eyes and gripped the table. When he'd scammed the National Security Council with the fake briefing, he'd known there was a chance the gambit would fail: perhaps it wasn't a member of the council leaking, perhaps the leaker would spot the trick, or perhaps

Celeste wouldn't print it. But it had worked. Yet Tipping had escaped the White House, America and now the UK.

Who knew where Tipping had swum?

~

ARON PUSHED the sporty convertible hard out of the corner and drove the final hundred yards to the Jerusalem office of UNICEF, where he braked hard right outside. He gripped the wheel for a moment to compose himself and then killed the engine. Checking his mirrors, he made sure the truck that was following him had pulled up, then climbed out.

"Mr. Yosef!" A well-dressed man greeted him outside the office, a broad smile on his face. "Welcome! I'm Levi Eban, I manage this office."

"Thank you." Aron gave a curt nod. "My apologies for being late, I was delayed slightly by the roadblocks."

"No problem at all. These are troubled times." Eban was clearly doing his best at small talk. "Pleasant drive apart from that, I hope?"

Aron grunted. He'd traveled from Jeddah, near Mecca, to Tel Aviv, where he'd been picked up at the airport by someone in his network. They'd traveled to a warehouse, where Aron had dressed in a suit and taken possession of the sports car. From there, he'd driven the car while two others drove the truck to the office. He wanted this done, given he still had a flight to New York to make today.

"Do you have staff available to help my men unload the truck? I'm afraid there's quite a lot of supplies and I'm keen to do it quickly."

"And what a generous donation!" Eban patted him on the back. "Of course we can help."

"Excellent."

Eban gestured some of the waiting staff forward. "They'll take care of it. Now, if you'd like to come inside, we can have some refresh—"

"I'll wait and watch, if you don't mind." Aron smiled. "My donors were quite insistent that I make sure these supplies reach your hands."

"Of course, of course." Eban waved a hand. "Bring the truck inside and we'll see it unloaded."

Aron nodded and waved at the truck. Its engine roared and it started to move again, directed to the parking bay by a UNICEF staff member. Aron was glad the truck was finally off the main road and inside the grounds of the UNICEF facility, a vital step in what he had planned. He gave Eban another nod. The man shouted orders at members of his staff, who got to work unloading it.

The truck contained dozens of boxes of donated goods for distribution to needy Palestinian children and families. The UNICEF team were joined by Aron's own men – other Zionists – in unloading boxes from the back of the truck for storage at the office. He wasn't sure how often UNICEF received donated goods rather than money, but they hadn't declined the support.

A smirk crossed Aron's lips as he watched them work. Given the money saved on the nuke transaction with the Russians, the cost of the ruse had been a simple affair: an old but reliable truck, a flashy sports car and a few dozens boxes of relief supplies. Not cheap, but nowhere near the cost of a nuclear weapon, especially if he could guarantee the success of the ruse.

The boxes were unloaded onto the ground. It didn't take long, and in ten minutes the back of the truck was empty and the boxes were stacked high, ready for distribution to the needy. Keeping his face passive, he watched as one of the Zionists closed the door at the back of the vehicle while the other moved back to the cabin. A second later, the truck's engine squealed.

"That doesn't sound good." Eban winced as the sound from the truck assaulted their ears.

Aron cursed. "I keep telling them we need to replace that truck. Every time it breaks down, it's out of action for weeks."

Eban's head rotated slightly. "So long?"

"Eastern European truck." Aron shrugged. "Takes that long to get the parts."

"I see." Eban clearly didn't understand, or care to. "Can we help?"

Aron paused for a moment, pretending to consider the office manager's words. "Well, if you don't mind, we could leave the truck parked here until the part arrives in a few weeks. I'd prefer to avoid the cost of towing it, given it reduces the money we're able to donate."

"No problem! We have plenty of space. It's the least I can do."

"Excellent!"

As the other Zionists gave up on starting the truck – an impossible job given they'd sabotaged it – Aron reassured himself that they'd covered everything. He pictured the backpack hidden in the cabin of the truck. The countdown was underway and the device was armed and fully functioning. Only a dedicated search would find the weapon, and that was unlikely.

Two out of three devices were now in place and he had plenty of time left to place the third. He turned to Eban. "I'll be in touch once we hear from the mechanic."

"Not a problem."

Aron stepped away toward his car. "Yes, thanks to you and your staff for taking such fine care of me."

"Our pleasure, Mr. Yosef, but hold on a second." Eban touched Aron's arm gently. "While my staff move the supplies inside, would you join me for lunch?"

Aron was about to refuse, but then he checked his watch. He thought for a second and decided it would be better to eat here than at the airport. "Sure."

Eban beamed. "Do you like curry? There's an excellent Indian place just down the road."

"Sounds fine." When you'd eaten from tins for many years, any restaurant meal was acceptable. He glanced at the sports car. "But I'm driving."

"Excellent! They have a vindaloo that's explosive!"

CHAPTER 11

French police were left red-faced yesterday when a large number of officers raided a Channel ferry at the Calais docks but came up empty-handed. The police have refused to comment on the purpose of the raid, except that they were looking to apprehend a suspect believed to be on board. The police left less than an hour after they boarded, leaving passengers and crew concerned about a possible connection between the raids and the Zionist terrorists currently being sought by authorities around the world.

New York Standard

Jack clenched his jaw tightly as he smiled at the cop, declining to say anything else given how close he'd already come to being arrested. Tapping the car's window frame impatiently, he waited for the Belgian officer to finish writing the ticket, taking it silently when it was handed to him. He watched as the officer walked back to his police car.

"You don't learn, do you?" Chen laughed from the seat beside him. "I can see the headline now: White House staffer busted for speeding. Again."

Jack exhaled loudly through his nose. "We've got a job to do. Treasury will sort out the bills we rack up along the way."

"Well, that's three fines and counting." Chen laughed again. "You sound very much like someone leading an authoritarian state."

"What's the saying? Omelettes and eggshells and all that?" Jack turned to Chen and smiled.

Chen grunted as, for the third time since they'd left Calais, Jack screwed up the ticket and tossed it in the back seat. They'd hired a car and driven after Tipping, following intelligence that he had come ashore in Belgium and was headed inland on the continent. The occasional piece of intelligence was enough to keep them on the trail, but the lack of any specific knowledge about where Tipping was headed was starting to bother Jack. He had the resources of the United States government on his side, but that didn't seem to be enough.

Jack sighed, started the car and pulled back onto the highway. Though it felt like they were traveling blind, onward they went, because if they didn't find Tipping then there was no chance of stopping the Zionists. His teleconference a few hours ago with the NSC had said as much. More evidence of Tipping's support for the Zionists had been found on the former staffer's computer, but there were few other leads to help with tracking down the backpack bombs. It seemed like it was Tipping or bust.

Minutes passed, then hours. Jack listened to the one English radio station he'd found, at least until Chen reached to switch it off.

"Hey! I was listening to that!"

Chen's face was impassive. "My life is too short for bad radio."

Jack let it go as his phone started to ring. He glanced at it in the cradle and waited for it to pick up automatically. "Hello?"

"Hi, Jack." Celeste sounded stressed. "Chen there too?"

"Yep." Jack smiled at the sound of her voice.

"Okay." Her voice told him it wasn't, but she kept talking. "How are you both?"

Chen turned his head and looked out the window.

"We're good. Chasing a phantom, though."

Jack probably shouldn't have told her, but he was too tired to care. Tipping had been a valuable source for Celeste, yet as far as he knew, she hadn't connected with him since he'd gone on the run. Though Tipping probably had stories left to tell, there was every chance a signals intercept would find him the minute he reached out. Until then, they were searching blind.

"Well, I might be able to help with that."

The strange tone of her voice made Jack sit up, while Chen also turned his attention back to the phone. "What do you mean?"

"I know where he is, Jack. I know where Tipping is." Celeste paused. He knew she'd be weighing up each word carefully. "I've got a choice to make."

"Okay."

"He's given me a beast of a story, Jack. The Zionists are trying to kill him and he knows you're on his tail."

Jack looked over at Chen, who shrugged. "What's he offering? What does he want in return?"

"He's offered me a one-hour meeting where he'll answer any questions. On the table are details on anything that's happened inside the White House for the entirety of the McGhinnist administration, Jack, as well as anything I want to know about the Zionists." She sighed. "He's scared and wants money. In cash."

Jack tried to process the different angles on this news. Tipping could give Celeste a torrent of information – most classified, some embarrassing – that would swamp the President's entire agenda, including the peace agreement. And giving him cash would allow him to disappear, removing the best and possibly only chance of finding the leadership of the Zionists and the nuclear weapons.

"You can't do it, Celeste." He swallowed hard. "I know we've argued about it, but you're putting whole cities and millions of lives at risk."

There was a long pause. "I know."

He was surprised by her words. Though she'd rightfully dug her heels in on this matter so many times, something had changed. "What's your move?"

"I've given him a meeting time and place. I've told him a journalist will meet him with a bag of cash and all the questions I need answered in return for it."

Jack looked at Chen again, who nodded. "We'll intercept him. Give me the details and this is a step closer to ending."

She laughed. "I've told him there's a journalist coming. I bet he'll lay an egg when he sees you. The meeting is at the lobby of the Grand Hyatt in Berlin at 7pm tonight."

"I'll take care of it, Celeste."

"Be careful." She paused again. "I love you."

"I love you too."

Jack grinned as Celeste ended the call. Berlin. They were about seven hours away from the city and within striking distance of Tipping. He looked at his watch and did the math in his head. They could be there with just enough time to spare. There was risk, not the least of which was a Zionist hit team in the vicinity, but it was their only chance.

Jack was a reporter and could play the part, but Tipping would recognize him instantly. He turned to Chen. "You're not going to like this."

"What?" Chen's eyes narrowed.

"I've got a few hours to teach you how to be a convincing reporter."

~

ANNA FOWLER KNOCKED on the door and waited. Within a second, a gruff voice called for her to enter. She opened the door and stepped inside the office of Sir Andrew Cunningham, Director-General of the British Security Intelligence Service – MI6. While it wasn't the first time she'd met him, it was her first time in his office. It was dour, full of hardwood and portraits of royals, living and dead.

"Agent Fowler." Cunningham was all business as he indicated the other man in the room. "This is Admiral Fraser."

"I know, sir." Anna smiled a fraction. "Nice to meet you, admiral."

"And you, Ms. Fowler." Fraser nodded at her. "Sit."

Anna sat attentively, opening her notepad and waiting for the briefing to begin. She usually received her assignments from her section commander and wasn't used to this sort of treatment. It meant that, whatever the assignment, it was big. Sitting down with the head of MI6 and Admiral Duncan Fraser, First Sea Lord and Chief of the Naval Staff, was a huge step up for her.

"Ms. Fowler." The admiral turned in his seat to face her with his whole body. "What I'm about to tell you is restricted to three people in the United Kingdom: the two of us in this room with you and the Prime Minister. You'll be the fourth and final. I trust you understand how sensitive this matter is?"

Anna nodded with some frustration, given she'd signed the Official Secrets Act and had no need for the lecture. The halls of the SIS building were never the most humorous place on earth, but this was taking it to a new level. Whatever had happened, whatever job she was about to be given, it had both men stressed. As much as she couldn't wait to receive the assignment, part of her dreaded it.

Cunningham leaned forward, rested his elbows on his desk and stared straight at Anna. "One of our Vanguard-class ballistic missile submarines – HMS *Vigilant* – is currently at sea, captained by someone we believe may be a deep cover Mossad agent."

Anna's eyes widened. "Surely not, sir. I think—"

"This isn't up for debate, Ms. Fowler." Cunningham spoke over her. "We believe, further, that said Mossad agent may have recently left their service, but maintained his links to the Zionist group currently threatening to attack several cities in the Middle East and the United States using nuclear weapons."

Fraser cut in deftly, holding a hand up to forestall Cunningham. "Our problem is greater than you might think, though, Agent Fowler. As you know, and as is on the public record, we're relatively certain the Zionists have stolen Russian weapons, which your service and many others are trying to find."

Anna inhaled sharply, connecting the dots. "But even if we manage to track down those weapons, the Zionists having a nuclear submarine makes it all moot. And worse, the damage the boat could cause would be far greater than the backpack devices, and the finger would be pointed right at us."

"Precisely." Cunningham nodded. "And then the missiles would really start flying. All over the world. "

Anna had been an MI6 agent since leaving Oxford. A week after her graduation, she'd responded to an ad offering adventure and work. In post-GFC Britain, those opportunities were few and far between for arts graduates. The years she'd spent inside the organization had been professionally and personally rewarding, though none of her assignments had been as explosive as this one.

"Not to ask the silly question, sirs, but why can't we just call the sub back?" Anna looked at Cunningham, whose faced remained impassive. "Even if the captain is crooked, surely the crew will turn around if a direct order comes down the line from command?"

Cunningham's lips pursed slightly before he spoke. "Usually, that would work, but it turns out the Zionists had moles higher up the chain. Admiral Graham Sinclair, until recently in charge of our submarine forces, ordered the boat to remain at sea regardless of countervailing orders until the end of its tour."

"The submarine is at sea for three months, unless they suffer mechanical failure, there's no point thinking otherwise." Fraser sighed. "Sinclair has been arrested, but the damage is done. We need to find out who the leader of the Zionists is, and confirm whether or not Captain Cohen is one of their number."

"Can't we just ask Admiral Sinclair?" Amy felt stupid for asking. "He'd know, wouldn't he?"

The two men looked at each other. Cunningham gave a small nod and Fraser sighed. "The admiral is dead."

Anna groaned. It would have been all too simple. "So where and when do I start then?"

"There's no 'start' on this mission." Cunningham's eyes bored into her. "We have a small number of days to avert disaster for Britain and the world."

"Okay." She nodded.

"Your mission is to track down Mr. James Tipping, former National Security Advisor to the President of the United States. He's currently somewhere in continental Europe. The Americans have sent assets to track him down, but I need you to find him first."

She nodded again. It all sounded pretty straightforward, if she could move quickly enough. "What's the catch?"

Cunningham smiled. "We believe James Tipping is an active member of the Zionist group. Our hope – our *only* hope – is that we can catch him and he can point us at their leader. We thought we had him in London, but he boarded a Channel ferry and escaped. We need to locate and acquire him."

Anna crossed her arms. "Will there be any other assets working on this, either with me or independently? It could get hot."

"You'll be operating alone." Cunningham shrugged. "Any associated action being taken is classified, as you well know, Agent Fowler."

She smiled and nodded. "I—"

She was surprised by a large bang behind her. She turned in her chair and was shocked to see the door open and Prime Minister Katherine Huxley moving into the room. Anna's mouth opened slightly, but she caught herself before it became an embarrassment. She shot to her feet and looked around, not surprised to see Cunningham and Fraser already standing.

"Sit down, you lot." Huxley eased herself in to the last vacant seat around the desk. She then turned to Anna. "Are you Fowler?"

"Yes, Prime Minister."

"Good, good. I've heard good things." She turned back to the broader group. "I've just hung up the phone from the Americans. They still haven't contained Tipping, so there's a chance we might get to him first. Until we can do that and find the head of the Zionists, news about the submarine doesn't leave this room."

"How do I find him?" Anna looked at each of the others in turn.

Cunningham smiled. "Have you heard of Jack Emery?"

Anna nodded. Emery was well known in the United States – the Australian who'd foiled several deep plots against the United States and then been invited into the inner sanctum of the McGhinnist administration. His exploits were known to MI6 as well, but he was regarded as a surprisingly successful amateur with some chutzpah.

"Emery tried to detain Tipping in Calais, with French help, but he escaped." Cunningham sighed. "The best way to find Tipping is to track Emery. He's headed toward Berlin in a French car, which we're tracking. Tipping was Emery's friend. It's personal between those two."

"Now, it's time for you to get going." Fraser leaned in and placed a hand on her knee. "How do you feel about very fast aircraft?"

∾

JACK KEPT HIS HEAD DOWN, facing the bar, his back to the room. It was taking all his willpower not to turn around and stare at Chen, but he made do with the occasional glance in the reflection of the mirrored sunglasses he'd placed on the bar. It was risky to be here at all, given how easily he'd be recognized by Tipping, but Jack had been unwilling to let Chen fly solo. There was too much at stake.

They were in the Vox Bar of the Grand Hyatt in Berlin, which boasted 300 whiskies that Jack wished he had the time to sample. Chen was posing as a *New York Standard* reporter and waiting for Tipping to appear while Jack, for his part, was seated at the far end of the bar. He occasionally sipped his whisky, but was taking it easy because he needed to keep a clear head.

"Show time." Jack kept his voice soft as he spied Tipping approaching Chen in the reflection of the sunglasses.

Tipping looked sharp, suited up like any other well-dressed professional. It took all of Jack's self-control to resist turning around, crossing the bar and punching the other man in the mouth. He had to wait another few minutes, at least, to find out whether Tipping would reveal anything. Then Jack would help to detain him.

They'd deliberately kept the police out of it. When they took Tipping into custody, they'd drive straight to the US Embassy in Berlin, where assets were in place to question him immediately. If the German police were allowed to arrest him it would be weeks before he could be questioned by US authorities or extradited, which would leave cities glowing in the dark.

It was also imperative that they scoop Tipping up quietly. While the US could send some Navy SEALs into Africa, or a CIA agent into Southeast Asia, operations on allied soil needed to be done with a little more care. Germany had the means to give America a hard time if its assets were caught misbehaving, including Jack and Chen.

Jack's eyes narrowed as he stared at them. Chen stood and shook hands with Tipping. Both men sat and started to talk, until a waiter came to take their order. They spoke for a minute or two and Chen wrote down the lot. Jack didn't take his eyes off Chen's pen. The minute the Taiwanese man put it down it would be time for them to strike.

They never got the chance. Jack's eyes widened as he saw four men closing in on Chen and Tipping from behind. He turned in his chair and shouted, "Chen!"

As Chen looked up at him, Jack rushed forward. Tipping glanced at him, surprised, and they locked eyes for only a second. Jack's lips curled up in fury, while Tipping smiled sadly and then turned to run. He didn't get far. One of the four men wrapped him up in a bear hug and another pulled a hood over his head. The two others moved to deal with Chen.

Adrenaline pushed Jack on and he made it to the sofas in a few long strides. He pushed down his fear as he vaulted an armchair, aiming straight at one of the black-clad men. Though the man Jack leaped at tried to dodge out of the way, he failed, and Jack landed a solid tackle. They crashed to the ground and Jack heard the other man heave as the oxygen was forced out of him.

The man beneath him hissed as he punched out at Jack. Jack tried to fend off the blows, while swinging a few of his own at the midsection of the other man. He felt the rage caused by Tipping's betrayal fuel his punches and he landed several on the man, including one great blow to the jaw. The man's eyes went glassy and Jack was about to finish the job when he felt a blow to the side of his head.

He fell to the floor and curled into a ball as several kicks punished him in the midsection. With each kick, Jack realized that charging into four-to-two odds hadn't been the smartest move. He let out a sharp cry and felt the breath go out of him as one particularly hard kick landed.

Finally, the blows stopped and Jack opened his eyes to try to make sense of it.

Chen had stunned the wannabe David Beckham, and things were now quiet in the bar, except for the staff who were cowering in the corner. He looked around. The two who'd stayed to deal with Jack and Chen were down, and Tipping was nowhere to be seen. Unfortunately, the two attackers who'd detained him had re-entered the bar and didn't look to be in the mood for a little *mano a mano*.

As the new arrivals reached into their coats and drew pistols, Chen grabbed his arm and yanked on it. Jack didn't have to be told twice, and they ran through the bar and into the hotel lobby as several shots boomed from behind them. They rushed toward the elevator bay, where one had just opened with a chime. The smiling guests inside fled the violence like panicked sheep.

"What now?" Jack's breath was heaving as he mashed the button to close the door. "I couldn't see Tipping, could you?"

"He got away." Chen tossed one of the bags abandoned by the tourists into the gap between the doors, leaving them open about a foot.

"How? There were four of them!"

"Five, actually." Chen shrugged. "We saw four initially, but there was a sweeper as well. When we took down the first two, the other pair approached to help and Tipping managed to cheap shot the one left to guard him. He ran off just as I started to get the kicker off you. That means there's several waiting for us."

"Fuck!" Jack pounded the elevator wall. "What now? We were so close to scooping him up!"

"Now?" Chen smiled. "You've got a choice to make. We either go up in the elevator and call for help or we try to fight our way out."

"We need to find him!"

"Okay." Chen pulled Jack's collar until they were facing. "But first you need to cool down. We survive and get past those guys out there, then we find him."

Jack stared into Chen's eyes for several long seconds, unable to believe that the two of them were in a gunfight in a five-star hotel in Germany. But the Taiwanese man was right. Jack had been so fixated on finding Tipping that he'd been ready to charge right at hot lead. There had to be a better way, and if anyone could figure it out, it was the man next to him.

Chen let go of his collar and peered through the small gap in the elevator doors, Jack staying low and to the side. As he watched, gunfire barked from outside the elevator, and the metal door sounded as if the largest hailstones ever seen were hitting it. None of it seemed to bother Chen, who did what he needed to do with complete calm.

"Well?" Jack prompted.

"Three shooters. Luckily they're not too heavily armed."

"Right." Jack scoffed. "Just a machine gun or two, is it?"

"Nine-millimeter Berettas." Chen reached behind his back, pulled out a pistol and hefted it. "Nothing to worry about."

"Where the hell did you get a weapon from?" Jack was incredulous. The Taiwanese man's resourcefulness always surprised him.

"I went for a walk last night and happened across a trustworthy merchant." Chen shrugged. "Thought it might be needed."

"You bloody genius."

Jack regretted not involving the German police, or at least some local US assets. He'd had tunnel vision, expecting that Chen's presence and set of skills would be enough to subdue Tipping. But in truth, Jack and Chen had walked into a bear trap. Now they needed to fight their way out of it. Or Chen had to, anyway.

"Stay there." Chen pointed at the corner of the elevator.

Jack nodded and watched Chen glide into the gap, weapon raised and firing in a flash. He fired three rounds before he was safely on the other side. The enemy gunmen responded again, more hailstones pinging against the elevator doors, though none of the shots penetrated. Chen did the same thing again, moving faster than the attackers could accurately track.

"I hit one of them." Chen looked down at Jack. "That's the good news."

Jack swallowed hard. "And the bad?"

"There's still two more of them. We should surrender and then try to make a break for it. We're in public."

Jack shook his head and stood. "I've got a better idea."

His finger reached toward the elevator panel, ready to press the button for another floor, when the bark of more pistol fire caused him to flinch. But instead of the sound of hailstones against the elevator door, Jack could hear shouting. He looked at Chen, who stared back quizzically then approached the panel. Before Jack could stop him, Chen pressed the button to open the doors.

"Come on." Chen jerked his head toward the door as it groaned open, clearly the worse for wear after being pounded by bullets. "They're gone."

"Okay." Jack followed Chen outside, but was immediately confronted with German police with their weapons drawn. He turned to Chen. "Nice work."

"No other choice." Chen made a show of lowering his pistol to the ground, then raised his hands. "Be careful. They look upset."

Jack nodded and raised his hands. The police swarmed them and in seconds they were both on the ground. Jack winced as they cuffed him roughly, exacerbating the pain from the kicking he'd received. The officers rushed them both outside, past the body of one of the attackers. Jack wondered if the others had escaped, as he was bundled into the back of a police van and the door slammed shut.

"That didn't go to plan." Chen's voice was barely a whisper.

"You're telling me. Tipping is on the run and knows we're after him."

"And we're in here."

Jack grunted but said nothing. They sat in silence for at least an hour. None of the police informed them what was happening, but the sound of sirens told them everything they needed to know – Jack and Chen had been involved in a major international fuckup. Jack could only imagine McGhinnist's reaction when he found out.

Jack's eyes shot open as the door of the van opened, revealing a woman in her late twenties. She wore civilian clothes, but stood too straight and alert to be one. She gestured for them to climb out. Jack and Chen did so. Whoever she was, taking the offer of help and freedom was better than spending time in a German lockup.

"Gents, you're just the men I'm after." Her accent was so overwhelmingly British she had to be an Oxford or Cambridge graduate. "You're Jack?"

"I am." Jack shrugged. "And you are?"

She ignored him and pointed at Chen. "Who's your friend?"

Chen addressed her. "Chen."

"Chen what?"

"Chen."

She shrugged. "I'm Anna. You boys are free to go."

Jack scoffed, not believing that this woman could exonerate them of anything, let alone have them walk completely free. But when she gestured for the German cops to remove their cuffs – and they complied – Jack started to believe. Soon they were out of custody and in possession of their things, even Chen's pistol. It was some kind of miracle, except Jack didn't believe in those.

He walked over to where Anna was talking to several of the German police officers. "Excuse me, but who are you?

"A friend."

"Why are you helping us?"

"I'm not." Anna smiled. "Her Majesty's government just had a word in the ear of our German friends. You're free to go."

Jack wanted to press her some more, but didn't get the chance. The woman turned her back on them, returned to the German police and dived right into conversation with them. Whoever she was, she had some pull. Getting Jack and Chen out of custody would have taken the State Department days, but it had taken her a few minutes.

Jack walked to his car. Chen had the engine idling and when Jack climbed inside the other man was smiling. Jack raised an eyebrow.

"What?"

"I got these from the pockets of one of the men I injured." Chen held up some papers. "The hit team knew where he was going."

"Dare I ask?" Jack closed his eyes.

"You don't have to." Chen shrugged. "But I know where Tipping is."

CHAPTER 12

The shootout in the lobby of the Grand Hyatt Hotel in Berlin is believed to have been the work of Zionist extremists. German police have so far remained tight-lipped about the incident, citing national security reasons, but sources have revealed that a high-ranking member of the Zionist organization was present in the hotel at the time of the attack. Police have not apprehended any additional suspects, but with a man dead and little information forthcoming, there are questions to be answered.

New York Standard

Jack cast his eyes ahead and settled on a lamppost as his finishing line, having reached his limit after running a small handful of miles through Prague. Though he did his best to stay fit, Jack's lungs were burning. He felt good for the effort, despite the bruises he'd suffered from the brawl at the hotel, but would be glad to reach his target.

As he ran the last little bit, he focused his mind on Tipping, trying to find a new angle. Even though Jack and Chen had missed their chance to scoop him up, at least they'd managed to foil the attempts of the Zionist gunmen to do the same. Better, Chen had nabbed information from one of the Zionists alluding to Tipping's ultimate location – Prague.

With that known, it hadn't taken much to task the apparatus of

American intelligence with finding Tipping. The trick was doing it quietly. While Jack had left Washington hoping to find Tipping with little public attention, since the shootout there'd been a heap of it. An Interpol Red Notice had been issued for Tipping's arrest and he was now wanted by every police officer on the continent.

That made things tricky for Jack and Chen, given they wanted to grab him and question him quickly. The search was now a race: Jack, Chen and US authorities versus everyone else. It was likely there was another Zionist hit team nearby, making the stakes even higher for Jack and Chen. They needed a break, but he didn't see where it was going to come from.

Jack started to wheeze as he slowed and after a few more moments he made it to the lamppost. He used the metal column to support himself as he heaved for air, slowly catching his breath. The run had helped clear his head, including the knowledge that, for the third time, Tipping had slipped from his grasp like a salmon from a bear. It was tough to stay calm knowing how close he'd been.

Jack started to stretch. When he was done, he pulled his phone out of his pocket and checked messages and emails. It took a moment to sift through the dross until one message – an update on Tipping's whereabouts – jumped out at him. Best of all, it was less than two minutes old. He read it and then exited his messages and dialed Chen.

"What?" Chen's voice was groggy. He'd still been in bed when Jack had started out on his run.

"I need you to meet me at the Charles Bridge."

"Why?" Chen still didn't sound impressed. "I don't want to sightsee. I need to sleep for another few hours."

"Tipping." Jack's voice was louder than he'd intended. More desperate. "An Interpol alert just blazed over the network. The police will be heading there."

"Let them."

Jack spoke through gritted teeth. "We need to speak with him before the cops get him. Once he's in a Czech cell, we'll lose access to him for weeks."

"Okay."

The phone started to beep. Jack pulled it away from his ear and stared down at the screen. Chen had hung up on him. Worse, Jack had no idea if Chen was going to meet him at the bridge or roll over and go back to sleep. But there was no time to waste. If Jack wanted to get to Tipping before the Czech police or another Zionist hit team, he had to move quickly.

He started into the fastest jog his fatigued body would allow. The few moments of cooldown had done little to help his endurance, and although the Charles Bridge was barely a mile from his location, each step felt like his last and each breath felt like a knife in his lungs. He'd make it, though, no matter what he had to push through.

There were so many things he was outraged about – the betrayal of McGhinnist and their friendship; the danger Tipping had placed Jack's relationship in; the threat to the peace agreement. The greatest insult of all, however, was that Tipping was involved with a group and a plot that had placed the world in grave danger of nuclear annihilation.

Finally, Jack turned onto the bridge and slowed to a stop. Tipping was standing in the middle of the bridge, arms propped against the railing and staring out at the water like any other tourist. Though wearing a jacket and cap, Jack had no doubt it was his former friend, deep in thought and not expecting to be found. Jack balled his fists by his side and strode over to Tipping.

"James." Jack spoke with ragged, heaving breath. "Nice of you to pick a picturesque spot."

Tipping turned quickly, startled, then smiled at Jack in a way that looked nearly like a grimace. "Hi Jack. Sorry I missed you in Berlin."

"Had a bit of a run in with some people trying to shoot me." Jack kept a few feet between the two of them, taking no chances.

"Yeah, sorry about that. There's some dangerous people after me." This time Tipping's smile was genuine. Sad, but genuine. "It's good to see you."

"You bastard." Jack lifted a fist and swung it at Tipping's jaw. The other man backed away, easily dodging the swing.

"Yeah."

"Do you realize what you've done?" Jack stepped closer to Tipping, the rage coursing through his veins like molten fury. "How many lives you've put at risk?"

"Yeah." Tipping didn't break eye contact. "I was working toward something I believe in, Jack. I still am."

"You were my friend. I don't understand." Jack exhaled slowly. "And you had to leak to my girlfriend's paper?"

Another shrug. "It's the best paper in the country and I knew she'd run the story. I assume the cops are on their way?"

Jack snarled. "Not because of me. I wanted you for myself. You've got some mighty fucking hard work to do redeeming yourself."

Tipping glanced over Jack's shoulder and Jack followed his gaze. There were police cars pulling up. Tipping sighed. "It's too late, Jack."

Jack had half expected Tipping to deny the link with the Zionists, to repent for the leaks and to apologize for all the damage he'd caused. If that had occurred, and Tipping had cooperated, it may have been possible to work out some kind of deal once they returned home. But Tipping wasn't playing that game. It didn't do much to help Jack's anger.

"There's time." Jack did his best to swallow his emotions. "Who is the leader of the Zionists? Tell me and help me fix this before it turns into a catastrophe."

"I'm a dead man. I supported a cause and now I'm no longer useful. I'll be lucky to see out the week." Tipping turned and gripped the stone wall of the bridge, casting his gaze over the water. "I know you want to believe I was conned, Jack, or that I wasn't a real player in the game, but I was."

"Who's the leader?" Jack pressed. "Tell me, James."

"You don't get it. It's too late." Tipping turned back to him, sighed and then opened his mouth. "The Samson Option is live and I—"

Jack bellowed as Tipping's head exploded before his eyes. A split second later Jack heard the tell-tale boom of a high-calibre rifle. As blood sprayed over him, Jack's mind shrieked with fear. He let out a guttural howl and reached out to catch Tipping as he fell. Though he knew it was pointless, he eased Tipping's body to the cobblestoned ground.

Jack looked up, trying to locate the direction of the shooter. He heard something pound into the stones behind him, followed by another boom of the rifle. He ducked his head instinctively and searched for cover, but he was completely exposed in the middle of the bridge. He looked to either end – the police cars had pulled up but the officers were taking cover from the shooter.

Jack started to move but didn't get far, grunting as something heavy hit him in the midsection and pushed him to the ground. He landed hard as his mind registered another shot. Whoever was doing the shooting had missed him twice now. He climbed up onto his hands and knees and looked up. Chen was staring at him. The Taiwanese man had taken him to the ground and probably saved his life.

"You're not very good at staying low when the shooting starts!" Chen was panting and sweaty. "Did you get a name?"

"No." Jack coughed and shook his head, trying to clear his vision. "They shot him before I could get the info."

Chen nodded as he crouched low, gripped Jack's arm and tugged. "We need to go. Now."

Jack shook off the other man's grip. "No! We need to find the shooter and get some answers!"

"No point. The shooter is a long way out." Chen gripped his arm again, tighter this time. "We need to go before the cops over there start asking questions."

Jack nodded and let himself be pulled to his feet. "We just lost our only link to the Zionist leadership. It's over."

∾

ARON DRANK in the view like the finest wine as the wind howled in fury and lashed out at him. He wasn't bothered by heights, but there was something about the view from the Rockefeller Center – Top of the Rock – that awed him. It was a spectacular way to view New York City, spread for miles as far as the eye could see. It made him feel like God.

It was hard to believe that in ten days anyone within ten city blocks of the building would be vaporized. He lifted his camera and took his time framing the shot – given he'd likely never have another chance at it – and then pressed the button. He took a second shot, just to be sure, then lowered the camera with a long sigh.

He looked out at block after block of offices and apartment buildings one last time. If Mecca was one of the spiritual capitals of the world, New York City was one of the temples to human ingenuity. It was a shame to lose the heart of it to the hubris and foolishness of American political leaders who were so intent on crippling a vital ally, but that was on them.

He sighed again and walked back inside the building. Earlier, he'd watched a video about a pioneering man who'd staked his fortune and his reputation on its construction. Aron respected a man who'd believed in something so much that he'd have ruined himself for it. He could think of no more fitting way to farewell New York than placing his bomb near here.

As he took a short elevator ride to the bottom of the building, he sent a text message to his driver. Once at the bottom he made his way outside and waited for the black sedan to pull up. After it did, he opened the trunk to check that his package was safe, then cast one last look at the Rockefeller Center and climbed inside the car.

Getting the backpack nuke here had been hardest of all. From Russia it had been driven to the German port of Bremen, loaded onto a ship bound for Mexico and then smuggled across the border. That had all been taken care of by others, who could be trusted with transport but not with placement. Aron had taken possession of the weapon in Charlotte and driven the ten hours to New York City.

They drove in silence for less than five minutes – in traffic – before Aron was deposited with his bag on the sidewalk in front of the Waldorf Astoria Hotel. He entered and made his way to the room he'd checked in to earlier, pausing only to dig through his wallet for his access card. He swiped the card, pushed down on the handle, opened the door, flicked on the lights and stepped inside.

He walked over to the bed and placed the bag down gently, glad to be rid of its weight. He briefly checked that the weapon was functioning and the countdown clock was ticking, and then opened the front compartment of the backpack and removed a small zip lock bag. Just like that, he had a fresh passport, a wad of Euros and a brand new cell phone. He was born again.

Aron had shed three identities in as many weeks as a precaution against one of the bombs being found. It was difficult to do this kind of work in the modern world, with all-pervasive electronic intelligence and large counter-terrorism budgets, and the last thing he needed was some lucky cop stumbling upon one of the weapons. All it took was one loose thread and the whole skirt could unravel.

Now it was time to wear his final skin. He pocketed the cash and the passport and turned on the cell phone. It had one number loaded into it – the only number he needed. He stared at it for a long few moments. In his head he worked through every detail of each bomb drop, making certain that there was nothing he'd missed.

He glanced again at the backpack on the bed and then turned his back and walked to the door. Once outside, he placed the do not disturb sign on the handle. He had no doubt that the sign would be heeded.

This wasn't the sort of hotel that asked too many questions of its guests, so long as the bill was paid and no fires were lit. He dialed a number.

~

ZED SMILED as a wave of relief washed over him. "Well done, Aron. You've done incredible work for our cause under very trying circumstances."

"Thank you, professor."

Zed closed his eyes and smiled. Aron had struck an almighty blow for their cause. The devices were now in place in New York, Jerusalem and Mecca. He could guarantee that those cities would be destroyed if the peace wasn't abandoned before the countdown reached zero. The preparations to enact the Samson Option, which he'd designed but hoped never to have to use, were complete.

"Now I need you to move on to the final piece of work." Zed opened his eyes and ran his hand over his face. "You understand what I need you to do?"

"My flight is already booked, professor." Aron's voice was soft, almost tender. "Don't worry about my assignment. I won't let you down."

"You never do, Aron." Zed smiled slightly. "This is quite possibly the last time we'll ever speak. Good luck and goodbye."

Zed reached over and placed the handset back in its cradle. He stared at it for a moment, sad that he'd probably just spoken to Aron Braff for the final time. The young man had always been his favorite student and Aron had repaid that favoritism in spades. He'd risen through the ranks of Mossad like a soaring eagle, all the while silently waiting for the time when Zed might need to make use of his skills for their greater purpose.

When the time had come, he'd entrusted Aron with the most difficult role of the grand game they played. If Zed was the king – slow moving, vulnerable but in command of a vast army – then Aron was the knight, possessing skills few others had, and an ability to move in special ways. He'd been charged with the impossible, acquiring three nuclear devices and then planting them in three different locations, yet he'd had succeeded beyond Zed's wildest hopes.

Now, between the bombs planted by Aron and the British submarine waiting silently under the sea, Zed's ability to execute the Samson Option was guaranteed. There was no doubt in his mind that if the peace wasn't abandoned the world would glow. He'd designed the doctrine with little subtlety – if Israel was destroyed then so too would its enemies be. The force had to match the threat to be taken seriously.

He reached over for his cane, propped against the desk. He felt ancient as he moved, but for the first time in the last couple of years he felt less weight on his shoulders. The announcement of the peace agreement had sent him into a mad rage. Its signing had led him to a coughing fit, where he'd spat up blood. Now he felt like he might actually see the other side of this fiasco intact. Decades of work would all be worthwhile.

He was halfway to his feet when his phone rang again. With a sigh, he eased himself back into his chair and picked it up.

"Hello?"

"The matter in Prague has been dealt with." The man's voice was coarse, like gravel in a cement mixer or a smoker with throat cancer.

Zed glanced at the drawer where he kept his photo album. Another of his students – another piece – had been taken off the board. He'd sent a hit team after James Tipping with a heavy heart, but it had been a necessary step. There had been a setback in Berlin, where one of the team had been killed, but they'd succeeded in Prague. The final weak link in the chain had been dealt with. His pieces were now fully in place, and nothing could be linked to him. He'd won.

"Good work." Zed spoke softly, his heartburn starting to give him trouble. "Go to ground for a few weeks. I'll speak with you once this is over."

Zed's arm went limp and the phone fell from his grasp. He was vaguely aware of it slamming on the desk and of the voice on the other end, still slightly audible. Zed clasped his chest. He'd never felt pain like it. He held out a hand, trying to reach for his cane, but he couldn't get close enough. He gritted his teeth against the pain and tried harder, grazing it with one finger before it slipped and fell to the carpet.

He cried out in pain as he fell to the floor. All the breath left his body as he landed hard. He tried to call for help, but no sound escaped his mouth. The pain in his chest intensified. It felt as if someone had plunged a fist into his chest, gripped his heart and was squeezing. He knew he should call an ambulance, get up and try to make it out of the room or do *something*, but he could barely move an inch.

Zed pushed his feet against the carpet, getting enough purchase to push himself upright against the base of the desk. He clutched his chest, wanting to live but knowing it was his time. It was fitting, really, that God would wait for the Samson Option to be ready before taking him. The clock was ticking, the threat was clear and the ultimate destruction just days away. Either Israel would be saved or retribution for her death would be swift. Zed closed his eyes.

It was time to go.

CHAPTER 13

A sad chapter in the history of United States politics has come to a tragic end, with former National Security Advisor James Tipping gunned down on the Charles Bridge in Prague, Czech Republic. Mr. Tipping, wanted on multiple charges relating to several high-profile leaks to this newspaper, was on the run from US authorities. His killers remain at large and no group has claimed responsibility, though several prominent Americans have claimed that the CIA was responsible for his death.

New York Standard

Anna clasped her bra at the front, twisted it around her torso and adjusted it. As always, doing so made her think of the ex-boyfriend who used to mock her for not being able to do it up from behind. It annoyed her that she thought of him at all – how far she'd come since ditching that bastard – but it was hard not to when he messaged her once a week. She snorted and shook her head. Fuck him.

Her hair was freshly washed and she'd chosen the best outfit she'd packed, but a quick glance in the mirror showed she looked tired, with large bags under her eyes. It wasn't ideal, given the job she had to do. She rummaged through her bag and found some concealer. It would have to do. She put on her blouse, completing her outfit.

After a quick final scan of the room, she grabbed her purse and slid her pistol and a silencer inside. She whistled a soft tune as she walked to the front of the townhouse, opened the door and stepped out with a smile on her face, the result of a job well done. What had seemed like an impossible mission when she'd been briefed had actually gone well.

She'd managed to get to James Tipping in Prague before Emery or the Zionists. After that, she'd simply had to play on his desperation for protection. He'd given her answers to the one question she had in return for all sorts of promises. At precisely the moment Tipping had mouthed the words "Professor Zed Eshkol" he'd become useless to her but potentially very valuable to others.

Despite her promises, she'd left Tipping to the mercy of the Zionist hit team. Though leaving him alive had been a risk, her superiors had thought it better to let others take the blame for murdering the former US National Security Advisor, giving Britain all the information it needed with none of the consequences. The success of the hit would also keep the Zionists confident and dumb.

Now she only had one more piece of business to conduct in Prague. She hailed a cab, climbed into the back seat and spoke in Czech. "Four Seasons Hotel."

The driver grunted, clearly surprised she spoke the language. She checked her emails while they drove. There was a message from Cunningham, noting that as soon as she was done on the continent she was to fly to New York City to complete the job. He made it clear that all options were on the table to get the information about the submarine confirmed. Good. She liked flexibility.

At the end of the trip she paid and climbed out of the vehicle. As she walked into the hotel lobby, she laughed at the thought of hardened killers staying in a hotel room with spa baths and high thread-count sheets. Just before the elevator bay she passed the restaurant, where guests were busy with breakfast. If any of them knew what was about to happen upstairs, they'd choke on their eggs.

Anna pressed the button for the elevator then rummaged around in her purse for a key card, which she used to swipe herself access to the eleventh floor. She took a deep breath before she exited, trying to stay calm as she found her way to one of the housekeeping closets. She used her key card on the door, opened it and stepped inside. Only then did she relax.

"Showtime." Her voice was barely a whisper as she used the light on her cell phone to illuminate the room.

Anna changed into a housekeeping uniform and removed the pistol from her purse. She attached the silencer then placed the bag and her regular clothes into one of the housekeeping trolleys. She gripped the pistol tightly and covered it with a cleaning cloth, then opened the door and pushed the trolley to door 1107. She knocked.

There were footsteps from inside and a few moments later the door cracked open only slightly and an eye peered out. "Who are you?"

Anna flashed her best smile. "Housekeeping."

The eye narrowed. A second later, the door opened fully and Anna had a large revolver in her face. Behind the gun was a member of the Zionist hit team who'd killed Tipping. She let out a small squeal and did her best to show fear, but said nothing. Her muscles stiffened and her hand gripped the pistol tighter, ready to work, but she made no move. She didn't yet have him where she wanted him.

"No sudden movements." The Zionist jerked his head inside the room. "Come inside. Bring the trolley."

She gave a nod and wheeled the trolley forward. The gunman moved aside but kept the weapon trained on her as the door slammed shut. As she inched inside, Anna did her best to sum up the situation. There were three men, one with a gun on her and two others preparing their bags to leave, who both cast a quick glance at her. She could hear the shower, which meant another target.

She slowed to a stop, the trolley inches from the feet of the man with the gun, and grimaced. "Please don't hurt me."

"You're not housekeeping." The Zionist spoke slowly and calmly. "I need you to tell me who you are."

Anna flicked her eyes between his face and the barrel of the gun. "I'm from housekeeping."

"No, you're not." His finger tightened on the trigger only slightly, the message clear. "We asked not to be disturbed."

Anna squeezed the trigger on her pistol four times in quick succession. It kicked slightly and made a sound akin to a champagne cork popping with each shot. She dropped to a crouch as four crimson splotches darkened the man's white shirt. His eyes widened in surprise and the revolver fell to the soft carpet before Anna lifted her pistol and fired one last shot into the man's head.

As his corpse hit the carpet, Anna propelled herself toward the two other men. They'd only just started to turn toward the unexpected sound, but given one had a weapon in hand, she had to prioritize her targets. As she moved, she raised her pistol and fired a single round into the head of the armed Zionist. A perfect shot. Blood and brain matter exited the back of his head.

Two down, two to go. The third Zionist had reached his weapon, but she fired first. Or tried to. Her pistol jammed as she pulled the trigger so she tossed it at him, vaulted up onto the bed and leaped at him. The jump carried her higher and faster than his weapon could track in time. She tackled him to the ground, earning a grunt from him. Most importantly, he'd dropped the weapon on the way down.

Anna struggled to her feet and reached for his weapon, but as she did, he grabbed her hand and twisted her wrist. A sharp pain shot up her arm and she lost her grip on the pistol, which fell from her hand. She didn't have the chance to pick it up again, because he lowered his head and tackled her in the midriff, using his size and weight advantage to lift her and push her back. He slammed her into the wall and then onto the ground.

She grunted as he sat on top of her and all of the air was forced from her lungs. Her eyes on his, she used one hand to fend off blows as the other felt around for something, anything, to strike back with. Then he connected with a right hook and stars exploded in her vision, just as her hand gripped a leather shoe. As she fended off another hook with her left hand, she shifted her body and brought the shoe swinging hard up into his face.

His nose gave a sickening crunch as the shoe slammed into it. He staggered back and reached up to cover his face, but Anna didn't give him the chance. She swung the shoe at his head again, then dropped it and thrust into his chest with both of her fists, shifting his weight backward. She bucked and slid out from under him as he fell. She looked for his pistol, but it was behind him and he was already climbing to his feet, a look of rage contorting his features.

"Who are you?" He spat the words as he raised his bloodied hands and balled them into fists. "You're meddling in events that you have no understanding of."

She laughed and advanced on him. He threw a series of quick jabs – which she dodged with ease – then tried to kick out at her. Anna moved to his left slightly and kicked out at his leg. The knee buckled at a strange angle and the Zionist let out a vicious scream as he fell to the carpet, clutching his ruined leg. As he writhed in agony and tried to climb back to his feet, she reached for the pistol. It was an unfamiliar model, but it would shoot him dead just fine.

"I'm housekeeping." She raised the pistol and fired into his head, leaving the Zionist dead in a pool of blood on the carpet.

She turned as she heard the shower stop. Her time was nearly up and there was a final player in the game. She moved toward the bathroom, where danger still waited. She pushed down on the handle and kicked the door inward, hard. It bounced back after it hit something and she heard a sharp cry – a mix of alarm and pain. Anna barged her way inside, where the last Zionist was standing in the nude, dripping wet and with his hands to his face as blood spurted from his nose.

She raised the pistol and stayed a few feet back from him, aware that despite his injuries he had a greater reach than her. "Kneel on the tiles, now."

He lowered his hands from his face and held them out, palms upward. "I can give you who you want."

"Not interested. Kneel."

"Very well." The Zionist spoke as he dropped to his knees, never taking his eyes off her. "But please, we can work something—"

Anna pulled the trigger the minute his knees hit the tiles. The weapon popped and kicked slightly. As he fell forward, she emptied the last of her clip into him, just to be sure. She looked in the mirror and let out a long sigh. She'd expected this to be messy, but she'd be feeling that hook to the jaw for days. Her cheek was already starting to swell. She ran the tap, tried her best to wipe the blood from her face and then dried herself.

She walked out of the bathroom and surveyed the bedroom, just to make sure she'd taken care of everything. Three bodies lay lifeless in the bedroom, and one in the bathroom, and there was no hint that anyone outside the room had heard the disturbance. She didn't bother to clean up – she'd be out of Prague before anyone found the bodies. She collected her own pistol, went to the housekeeping trolley, stripped to her underwear and changed back into her regular clothes.

As she dressed, she considered the situation in her head: she knew who the Zionist leader was, Emery was in the dark and both Tipping and the hit team had been eliminated, in case they got arrested and spilled the beans about Eshkol's identity. Her next stop was the United States, where she'd confront the professor and figure out if the submarine was under his control. If it was, things were about to get very bad for the good professor.

Her last act was to use the bloodied housekeeping uniform to wipe the prints off the trolley, the other man's pistol, the bathroom door handle and the tap handle. Her prints weren't in any system, but this simple precaution helped to make sure that remained the case. When she was done, she walked to the door and opened it. She stepped out into the hallway. Nobody else on the floor was visible and MI6 would fry the security footage.

If she hurried, she'd have time for breakfast at the airport before her flight.

~

JACK HELD his arms wide as McGhinnist approached and the two of them embraced for a second or two. Despite Tipping's betrayal, they were both feeling the loss. Tipping had been a friend and a colleague but ended up a traitor and dead. This was the first time they'd seen each other since Jack had arrived home from Prague, and it looked like McGhinnist was struggling as much as he was.

"How are you, Jack?" McGhinnist's gaze was intense, as if assessing whether Jack was going to fall apart on the spot. "You look tired."

"You'd be amazed what coffee and Red Bull can achieve." Jack shrugged. "There's too much work to do to rest."

"I'd call bullshit on that, but I fear you're right." McGhinnist frowned. "Are you getting anywhere with the digging?"

Jack gestured behind him, where dozens of research staff pulled in from across the entire Federal Government were digging into the life of James Tipping. The clues they had to go on – a reference to something called the Samson Option and that the leader of the Zionists was someone Tipping had history with – were enough to get the wheels of a giant research apparatus turning.

"It might not be enough people or enough time." Jack sighed. "I'm not sure we're going to get what we need before the deadline, but we have to try."

He'd left Prague after Tipping had been shot, flying back by private jet with Chen. He'd briefed the President and the NSC from the air and, while everyone had made the right noises about how close Jack had come to succeeding, he knew he'd failed. He'd been a moment away from getting the name, but instead he'd got Tipping's incomplete, dying whisper.

"And there's been nothing come up yet?" McGhinnist was disappointed. He clearly wasn't used to his people coming up short.

"Nothing so far." Jack shook his head, turning back to McGhinnist. "We'll do our best, but I wouldn't be betting the house on it."

"Can't anyway. Taxpayers pay for my house." McGhinnist sighed. "We've got to work with what we have – a single lead from a dying man's lips."

"Which leads to one needle in a haystack of 321 million people – the entire population of the United States." Jack sighed. "It looks impossible."

"Unless you can find an obvious link."

"Unless we can find an obvious link." Jack nodded. "I need to get back to work. It's not fair to ask these people to give up their evenings if I stand and talk."

"Of course, Jack. Keep me posted." McGhinnist patted him on the shoulder. "Get some rest, too. Red Bull only gives you wings for so long."

Jack gave a short laugh as they turned to go their separate ways – Jack back to the desk he'd commandeered and McGhinnist back to the Oval Office. As he sat in the chair heavily, Jack punched in his password then picked up his takeaway coffee, one among many scattered on his desk. While he waited for his computer to complete its login script he took a sip of coffee then nearly spat it out. It was as cold as a Chicago winter.

He put down the cup and resumed chasing the line of inquiry he'd been working on when McGhinnist had called to say he was coming down – the Samson Option. Tipping had said something about it on the bridge, and Jack had had no idea what it meant until friendly Professor Google had enlightened him. In fifteen minutes of reading, he'd deduced that the Samson Option was an Israeli defensive doctrine that was terrifying but also fit the Zionist rhetoric.

He got lost in the information. The background of the doctrine, its theoretical uses, the times its use hadn't been considered quite so theoretical and when it had been a live option. It spoke to Israel's unique sense of danger and the unique history of the Jewish people that they'd come up with such a no-holds-barred defensive doctrine. The more he read, the more he was convinced that the Samson Option was exactly the playbook the Zionists were working from.

He'd never heard of anything like it, but one thing nagged at the back of Jack's mind. If the Samson Option called for the complete eradication of the foe, even if it meant self-destruction, then the Zionists stashing a few suitcase nukes around the place wouldn't be enough. They'd put a sizeable dent in New York, Mecca and Jerusalem, but it wouldn't be the knockout punch that the Samson Option called for: overwhelming force to destroy the foe.

He shook his head. Whoever devised it had a screw loose, that was for sure, but whoever was applying the Samson Option on behalf of the Zionists was even crazier. It wasn't mutually assured destruction, it was simply popping off a few nukes to achieve something that was impossible. McGhinnist had shown no signs of buckling under the threat, nor had the Israelis or the Palestinians. No, the Zionist leader – whoever it was – had badly applied the Samson Option.

"Mr. Emery?"

Jack nearly jumped out of his seat. A junior researcher was holding out a fresh cup of coffee for him, which he took. "Sorry, I was a mile away. Thanks."

She gave a shy smile. "Thought you could use a recharge, sir. You haven't slept since you got off the plane. I guess this is the next best thing?"

He nodded. "Thanks. You're dead right, too…"

"Dana."

"Dana, right. Whoever made this is a lifesaver." Jack paused with the cup halfway to his mouth. "Do me a favor?"

She nodded. "Of course."

"I need your entire team to stop what they're doing – no matter how important – and get to work researching the Samson Option. I need to know who created it and if that person has links to Tipping." Jack couldn't believe he'd been so stupid as to not ask the question earlier. It compounded his failure in Prague.

She nodded. "We'll get on to it."

Jack thanked her and turned back to his computer. He sipped his coffee as the wheels turned in his head. The Zionists were following a playbook and had assets in place as well, even if those assets weren't sufficient to fully complete the job. What Jack hadn't been able to do was link the players to the playbook. It was a long shot, but he was desperate and starting to hope that one of those would pay off. It had to.

Jack's phone beeped and he reached for it, then cursed as he knocked his coffee cup over and onto the floor. He glanced down at the mess, then back at the phone. The message was from Celeste. They'd barely spoken since his return from Prague and he'd promised to call her hours ago. Though she was usually understanding of work pressures, she'd been making noises about him looking after himself. He dialed and tapped the desk while he waited for her to pick up.

"Hi, Jack."

"Hey gorgeous." He smiled at the sound of her voice. "How are you?"

"Missing you and trying to help run the major paper in a city that's nine days away from being nuked, reportedly. You?"

"Sore, tired, frustrated. It feels like I'm close to winning a hand but I keep coming up with a pair of twos. I really need a royal flush."

"You'll come up with it. You always do. You've got a good team working for you." She paused. "Are you looking after yourself?"

"There's too much work for that."

"Jack—"

"Next question."

"Jack." Her voice had an edge. "You need to get eight hours sleep."

"I—"

"Listen to someone who cares about you for once, would you?"

"Okay."

As she started to speak, to tell him how much rest he needed and what he should be eating, Dana returned to his desk with a printout in her hand and a smile on her face. He raised his eyebrows at her, and she offered a giant thumbs-up and an even wider smile in return. She'd uncovered something. He nodded at Dana and returned his attention to the phone just a moment too late, having missed whatever question she'd asked him.

"Jack?" Celeste's voice was approaching pissed off. "Are you even listening?"

"Sorry, what was the question?"

She sighed. "I asked if you'd eaten."

"Sure, a Snickers bar, coffee and Red Bull. And I ate on the plane."

"Seven hours ago."

"Yep. Look, I have to go, Celeste." Saying each word felt like passing a kidney stone, because he knew the likely effect. "Something has come up."

"Bye."

The phone went dead in his ear. He closed his eyes, let out a long sigh, then looked up at Dana. "I hope this is worth it."

"It is." She smiled and placed the paper down on his desk. "Your wife will forgive you."

"Girlfriend."

She blushed. "Sorry."

Jack looked down at the sheet of paper and his eyes widened. He pounded his fist on the desk. "It was so bloody simple? Why did I need to go to Prague?"

"I—"

"Never mind. We've been too busy chasing after Tipping's future rather than looking into his past. Could you excuse me?"

She nodded. "Good luck."

Jack's hands raced across the keyboard. He searched through the staff database until he found Tipping's file. It was classified, but he had the access to crack it open. He keyed in the code and waited as the large file loaded. Once it did, he skimmed it until he found what he was after. He had to read it twice, and it was like a punch to his face. He pounded the desk again, picked up his phone and dialed. The President's secretary answered and he asked to be put through.

"What's up, Jack?" McGhinnist sounded surprised. It wasn't often someone demanded that he come to the phone right after he'd seen them in person.

"Did you know Tipping was a practicing Jew his entire life?" The words sounded like an accusation, but it was too late to reel them in.

McGhinnist paused. "He never seemed to make a big deal about it in the time I've known him. I thought he was non-practicing."

Jack nodded. "Right, that's why it was such a surprise that he'd joined the Zionists."

"Yes." McGhinnist's voice was cautious, impatient. "So why did you need to interrupt my meeting with the Ghanaian Ambassador, Jack? Where's this going?"

"Sorry. The only thing we know about his faith and the only thing connecting him to active Judaism, at all, is where he went to school."

"Where would that be?" McGhinnist sounded cautious.

"Yeshiva University, where he studied under Professor Zed Eshkol."

There was a pause. "Wait a minute, that pain in the ass from earlier in the month?"

"The very one." Jack leaned back in his chair and spun around. "And, according to the research team, the father of the Samson Option."

~

JOSEPH COHEN FINISHED FILLING one of the fine bone china cups, then filled the other, careful not to spill any of the tea. When he was done, he placed the pot back on the table and lifted both cups. He handed one to Tim Jennings with a smile and kept the other for himself. He lifted the cup to his mouth and took a small sip, though in truth fresh tea was too hot for him to drink right away.

Jennings had no such problem. He took a long sip, gave a satisfied sigh and then placed the cup down. "Thanks, captain. Makes a nice change to teabags."

"There has to be some perks to command." Joseph laughed. "Not much else to do down here anyway, is there?"

"Suits me." Jennings' face clouded over. "There's plenty going on above the water that makes me want to stay below it."

Joseph nodded, lifted his cup and took another sip of his tea. He couldn't appear eager to pry, though, in truth, he knew plenty about Jennings' gambling and the marital problems that had followed. It was part of the reason he'd hand selected Jennings to serve on the submarine. He took one more sip then placed the cup gently back down on its saucer.

"Need to talk about it, Tim?" Joseph looked straight at the other man, who seemed to wither under the glare.

Jennings ran a hand through his close-cropped brown hair. "It's okay, sir. I won't put you through a psych session."

"No shame in it." Joseph spoke softly. "This life is hard on sailors, let alone their family. We serve our country and hope our family are there at the end of it. I never managed to even meet someone, let alone get married, so you won't get any judgment from me, Tim."

It was a plain lie, but Jennings had no way of knowing that. Joseph's rise through the ranks had been the result of hard work, but he'd had plenty of time to find a life partner if he'd wanted to. In truth, it hadn't been in the plan he'd constructed for his future with Zed Eshkol. He had no interest in settling down and spending his life with someone. Secrets were hard enough to keep alone.

But the lie appeared to work – Jennings' features softened. "It's not all it's cracked up to be. I have a few gambling problems, sure, but I earn a good salary."

"So what's the problem?"

"Well, while I serve my country, she served herself up to her doctor." Jennings sighed. "They've got a good lawyer, too, so she'll clean me out."

"I'm a strong believer that people who serve together need to stick together." Joseph placed his hand on top of Jennings' for just a brief moment and then removed it. "If you need some extra leave when we're back on shore, just say the word."

"Thanks, captain, but I'll be okay." Jennings gave a weak smile. "While I'm down here I'm good to go. I'll do my job."

Joseph was relying on exactly that. Zed Eshkol's Samson Option had so many moving pieces that Joseph worried something would slip between the cracks. The most important were the triggers that he would need to begin the launch procedure, to convince a crew of submariners that things above the waves had gone to hell. All he could do was focus on things he could control.

Things like Jennings. Even if the crew went along with the launch, he still needed his executive officer to co-authorize any strike. He'd spent quite a bit of effort buttering Jennings up in the event that he was required to launch the nukes. He wasn't certain that the other man would support the process, even if it was all above board, but he'd done everything he could to connect with the man.

He leaned forward slightly. "I know you will, Tim, and if all this Israel and Palestine stuff goes to shit, I may just need you to. I need you strong."

While hoping to connect with the man, Joseph had also started putting in place contingencies in the event that Jennings cracked and refused to follow Joseph's legal orders. He'd told the boat's third officer about his concerns and started to document them, so that if Joseph needed to relieve Jennings of his position there was a fair chance his effort would succeed.

Jennings smiled. "Not a problem, captain. I'll do what needs doing. Have to keep the salary coming in so she can take it, don't I?"

Joseph smiled but said nothing else. Jennings took the hint, finished his tea, stood and replaced his hat. He saluted crisply, but smiled as he did. Joseph remained seated as he fired off a quick salute, then watched as Jennings turned on his heel and left the room. Only when the door was closed did Joseph raise his tea again and take another sip.

In a few days, there mightn't even be time for that.

CHAPTER 14

With less than a week before the enacting of the peace agreement, Israeli, Saudi and American authorities are no closer to locating the nuclear weapons placed in their countries. In New York, the NYPD and FBI have responded to over 500 leads purporting to have information about the bombs, all of which have amounted to nothing. Saudi and Israeli authorities are more tight-lipped, but sources reveal that they've also made little progress.

New York Standard

Zed sighed.

"Professor, are you saying that, with a week to go and a nuclear weapon placed somewhere in this very city, you support the Zionist extremists in their efforts to unwind the peace deal between Israel and Palestine?"

Zed sighed again. "Not quite. I—"

The dean held up a hand. "Because, if that were the case, then this university would have to reconsider your employment, regardless of your health issues. Such views would be utterly incompatible with our values."

Zed closed his eyes for a moment. Despite there still being a week until the peace agreement deadline, it was hard not to wish it would come sooner. Sitting across from the dean and two of his flunkies, Zed nearly hoped that Israeli, American and Palestinian leadership would

stay resolute in the face of his threats, just so he could have the pleasure
of nuking this city, this university and the men opposite him.

Zed opened his eyes. "Excuse me, but I'm very tired. The angina
attack has taken a lot out of me."

The dean smiled for the first time. "Completely understandable,
Professor Eshkol. How is your health?"

Zed expected they'd be thrilled if he just dropped dead, but he wasn't
ready to give them that pleasure. "The doctor tells me the angina attack was
brought on by stress. But I'm scheduled in for more tests later this week.
They're quite concerned, but God willing I'll be around for a while yet."

The dean nodded. "You've had quite the ordeal. But I must insist on
knowing your position before we can agree to your continued tenure."

"I understand and support the position of the administration." Zed
fiddled with his walking cane, which he gripped in his right hand
despite being seated. "However, I have made no secret of the fact that I
do have some sympathy for the Zionist message, if not their methods."

Zed nearly laughed at the looks that crossed their faces. They were
peacocks, puffing out their feathers in an impressive but ultimately
useless form of theatre. They could be placated with lies and feigned
deference to their position, but if they knew the truth of Zed's role
they'd probably have larger heart attacks than the scare he'd just had.
For men in charge of a large Jewish university, their lack of vision for
their people and courage to see what needed doing was appalling.

"Very well, professor." The dean nodded, then looked to his
colleagues, who mimicked the gesture. "As long as you understand our
concerns. Things could get very hairy for Jews in this city."

Zed smiled and pressed down on his cane, using it to help him to
stand. "Of course, of course. Now, if you'll excuse me, I have an awful
lot of work to catch up on today. I was hoping to get a lot of it done this
morning."

"Of course, professor. Don't push it too hard though."

Zed left the dean's meeting room and struggled back to his office. As
he walked, he let his anger at being summoned before them simmer
down and then cool. While he'd never show them they'd gotten to him,
the outrage at being called to such a meeting to have the riot act read to
him burned to his core. If it weren't for the easy stream of recruits that
the university provided for his work, he'd resign.

When he made it to his office, ten minutes later, his assistant was nowhere to be seen. It was quite early in the morning, but she'd usually be at her desk outside of his office by now. It was unacceptable. He'd expressly told her he needed her close, each and every minute of the day, in case he had another episode with his heart. There was no guarantee that the next one wouldn't be a big one, and he wouldn't survive without help close to hand.

He sighed, started to open the door to his office and then paused. The lights were on. From home, he'd gone straight to the meeting with the dean. It was his first day back at work, his assistant was nowhere to be seen, he hadn't been inside his office and yet the lights were on. It could be a coincidence, but he didn't really believe in those. He took a deep breath, pushed the door open and wasn't surprised to see someone sitting on one of the sofas inside.

"Hi, professor." The woman flashed a pearly smile, stood and approached with an outstretched hand. "I hope you don't mind me waiting in here?"

He stepped inside. "I—"

"Your assistant said it would be fine."

Zed grunted and moved slowly around her, declining to shake her hand and using the time to sum her up. He made his way to the chair behind his desk, his mind racing with possibilities – none of them good. He doubted very much that this woman was interested in studying at Yeshiva, and doubted even more that his assistant would let a stranger into his office in such a manner. Particularly since she wasn't here. It meant trouble.

He collapsed into his chair with relief and then gripped the desk with his thumbs on top and his fingers underneath. Only then did he look at the woman again. He studied her for several moments, but nothing he saw changed his mind. She was a wolf in sheep's clothing, if a sheep wore ballet flats and a pastel dress with shoestring straps. She was dressed to kill and could probably kill in that dress. He could think of no other explanation.

"Professor?"

Zed shook his head and kept his grip on the desk. "Look, I don't know who you are, but you're not one of my students and I'm certain my assistant didn't let you in. I've been alive for a long time and I've learned to recognise the scent of the secret police when they come knocking, so just get on with it."

She tried to maintain her composure, but there was a flash of doubt that let him catch a glimpse of the wolf. "Professor, I—"

"Get on with it or get out. I'm old, sick and tired. And I have a lot of work to do this morning."

"Fine." She stood and opened her purse, then drew a pistol and pointed it at him. "Guess I need to go back to acting school."

Zed was not surprised she was here to kill him. "If you expect me to beg, you'll be disappointed. I'm a man well in tune with my own mortality."

She laughed and took a step toward him. "I'm after a simple transaction – information for your life."

Zed's eyes narrowed. There were a lot of things she could ask, and some questions he'd provide answers to, but only a few that mattered. "I'm listening."

She reached the other side of the desk and sat in one of the visitor chairs, never taking the pistol off him. "Tell me about HMS *Vigilant*."

So she knew. Zed kept his features even, but inside he was panicking for the first time. He'd known that there was every chance that Aron Braff's nuclear weapons would be found or otherwise compromised, but he'd been certain that his insurance policy – HMS *Vigilant* and Captain Joseph Cohen – would remain in play. A British woman with a pistol asking questions about the British submarine didn't bode well.

"I assume it's a ship in the Royal Navy?"

"Smart guy." She waved the pistol lazily in his direction. "Work with me. The game is up. I know you lead the Zionists. Tell me all about the submarine."

"I was just in a room defending my academic position against claims I supported the Zionists, now you claim I'm their leader." Zed laughed. "I never thought I'd be working this much in my old age."

"I need confirmation of the link between you and Captain Joseph Cohen, the submarine captain." Her voice was as calm, with a hint of menacing authority. "Give me what I need before I have to ruin those nice curtains behind you."

Zed closed his eyes and let out a long, slow sigh. To come so close and not see the result of his work struck him as a tragedy, but it had always been a chance. He just had to hope that the preparations he'd made to destroy either the peace process or the world would be enough. It needed to be, or else the doctrine he'd developed and advocated for would be for naught. He was staring down the barrel of his death and intellectual irrelevance at the same time.

She grew tired of waiting. "If you've got anything to say to me, Professor Eshkol, you've only got a few seconds."

"Get on with it." Without opening his eyes, he pressed the button on the underside of his desk.

~

JACK GRIPPED the overhead handle of the Chevy Suburban as its brakes squealed and the vehicle came to a sudden stop.

Agent Warner, commander of the FBI detail he was riding with, turned from the front seat. "Wait here, Mr. Emery."

Jack nodded and watched as Warner and the other agents spewed out of the SUV, a scene repeated in the two other vehicles that had pulled up as well. A total of ten agents armed with carbines swarmed forward in perfect choreography. Jack knew the same scene would be playing out on other parts of the campus, as the entire forty-six–member FBI New York Field Office SWAT force deployed around the university. Not on the front line – but no less important – were the NYPD officers running interference and keeping a two-block radius around the university clear while, up in the air, two NYPD choppers hovered and watched, ready to route the reserve NYPD SWAT teams toward any location requiring extra muscle.

It was a ridiculous show of force to subdue one old man, but given the influence of that old man and the potential he had to cause harm, Jack and McGhinnist had declined to take any chances. Jack had flown in from Washington soon after he'd discovered Tipping's connection to Eshkol and the Samson Option, and when he'd landed he'd been briefed on the operation that had been worked up while he was in the air. Jack was pleased that the NYPD had had no trouble creating a traffic-free path through the city, with uniforms on every street corner and green lights the entire way. The convoy had covered the distance between Federal Plaza in Lower Manhattan all the way up to Yeshiva University in Hudson Heights at record speed.

When Warner turned back to the vehicle and nodded, Jack knew it was safe. He took a deep breath, opened the door and climbed out. As he did, he wondered if this was the beginning of the end. He slammed the door behind him and moved quickly toward where the agents had formed a perimeter around this entrance to the building. As he ran, the pistol he carried in a shoulder holster bounced against his torso. While he'd never had a great love for guns, he'd been licensed to carry since he'd come down from the rooftop after confronting Richard Hall. It was nice to have the option if you needed it, like storming a building with an FBI SWAT team. As always, though, if he needed to use the weapon then he knew the forces of good were having an awfully bad day.

"What's the story?"

"Exits secured and air cover in place." Warner jerked his head toward the university building. "If your information is good and he's in there, we've got him."

"The information is good."

Warner shrugged. "Give the word then."

"Do it."

Warner nodded and fired off orders into his helmet mike. As he did, his team moved toward the entrance and Jack followed as instructed. They streamed up the stairs with weapons raised, shouting at students to stand aside as they moved. He knew that the same scene was playing out across the rest of the campus. Jack's team would advance straight to Eshkol's scheduled lecture, another would go to his office and another would go to the cafeteria. The other assets would remain in reserve, in case there was any blow up. If all went to plan, they'd have Eshkol in the bag and the nukes secured within hours.

Jack jogged behind the team as they approached the lecture theatre, scanning the hallways and rooms but with no real threat sighted. A few students squealed but most stood aside and got out of the way. The agents didn't seem to notice, given they were focused on Eshkol and any potential threats. After a few turns and some more jogging, they reached the lecture theatre. Jack stood back as two of the agents opened the door and six more streamed inside to secure it. While Jack couldn't see what was happening inside, he found it odd there was no sound – no shrieks of alarm or shouted orders from the raid team.

A few seconds later, Warner held his forefinger up to his earpiece, then turned to Jack. "This room is empty."

Jack's eyes narrowed. "He's scheduled to be in there, along with two hundred of his students."

Warner shrugged. "See for yourself."

Jack nodded and walked to the door. As soon as he looked inside, he knew Warner was right. The room was empty. "Where the fuck is he, then?"

"Office and caf teams came up empty." Warner barked an order and his men moved out. Then he turned back to Jack. "We're conducting secondary sweeps."

"What does that mean?"

"All target locations have come up with zilch, so we search room to room." Warner paused. "But it's a big campus, to be frank."

"We need to find him!" Jack felt all of his earlier hope go up in smoke. "Or else ten square blocks of this city won't be here in a week!"

Warner nodded and gestured for Jack to follow. They moved back outside in silence, as Warner did his best to keep abreast of the situation. This wasn't good. Eshkol was a very old man with very little mobility. He shouldn't have been able to elude so many heavily armed and well-trained agents. Either the information was wrong, or something else was. Jack froze.

"Agent Warner?"

"Yes?"

"What if someone else has him? Or he knew we were coming? This guy had one mole in the National Security Council, who's to say he doesn't have more?"

Warner seemed to chew on Jack's words for a minute. "Fuck."

"What now?"

He didn't hesitate. "I'll keep the secondary sweeps going and move the NYPD assets up to search surrounding streets. We can also get every beat cop in the city on the lookout and splash it across the media, if you like. But if he's slipped our containment then we're in all sorts of trouble. He could be anywhere."

"Yep – do it." Jack paused, trying to think of any other potential holes that Eshkol could slither out of. Then he considered one further thing. It would be universally loathed in New York City, but not as much as a nuke going off in Times Square. He dug into his pocket, pulled out his cell phone and dialed.

"Frank? This is Jack Emery. You're not going to like this."

"Hi, Jack." Frank Howard sounded tired. He'd been working hard since being promoted to National Security Advisor. "What's up?"

"I need every bridge and tunnel connected to Manhattan shut down." It sounded crazy as he said it, but it was necessary. "And I also need every security camera from here to New Jersey tasked with finding Zed Eshkol. He's slipped our net and we need to find him again."

There was a pause. "Jack, this will be a tall order. The blowback will be—"

"I don't care." Jack interrupted. "We're close to the leader of the Zionists."

"I'll take care of it."

He hung up and gestured for Warner to follow. Jack couldn't be sure that the professor was a senior member of the Zionist terrorists, but he was as close as possible to knowing without actually *knowing*. It was a particularly strong likelihood, given Eshkol had been so vocally against the peace agreement, was one of the fathers of the Samson Option and had very strong links to Tipping.

They made their way back to the vehicles and he climbed inside with Warner, ready to move at a second's notice. The rest of the SWAT team stayed behind, searching the university room by room. But Jack's attention was already diverted. Without being prompted, Warner made the vehicle's radio receiver loud enough so they could both hear as updates rolled in from across New York City.

They waited for hours. At some point, the rest of Warner's squad returned to the vehicles, their search of the campus completed. Jack's hopes fell with his energy, at least until an NYPD uniform fetched them coffee and a sandwich each. He started to wonder if he'd been right to suspect that Eshkol had been scooped up by someone else, or if the professor had simply left town.

He closed his eyes and let the radio reports roll over him, not really understanding the law enforcement shop talk but following enough of it to catch the gist: they had nothing. The search continued, with Federal assets working hard and the NYPD clocking some insane overtime, but it seemed like it was all for nothing.

"Turn it off." Jack opened his eyes and looked over at Warner. "He's gone. We've lost him."

"Shame, I thought we'd nailed that prick to the wall." Warner sighed and reached over to turn down the radio. "Now we'll have to—"

"*All units, all units, this is Prowler Two-One. Target located. Repeat, we have the target.*"

Instead of turning down the radio, Warner picked it up. "Prowler Two-One, this is Alpha Actual, report."

"Alpha Actual, target is cornered inside a diner with one unidentified female, armed, on 164th and Broadway."

"Don't let any harm come to him!" Jack hissed.

Warner nodded. "Prowler Two-One. Keep your distance unless the target is under threat. We need him alive. All SWAT converge to that location."

"Confirmed."

Warner put down the radio and nodded to the driver, who started the engine and hit the sirens. Jack held on as the Chevy did a quick one-eighty, tyres screeching and with the other two vehicles close behind. Jack and Warner sucked down the last of their coffee and scoffed some energy bars, rousing themselves after hours of inactivity, even as the vehicle shot past the speed limit.

Jack tried not to get his hopes up, but given how bad the situation had been a moment ago, having any trace of Eshkol at all was positive. Having him under threat by an unknown woman was a negative, sure, but it also meant that his hunch was probably correct: Eshkol was the lynchpin he was after. The man who could end this after he'd failed to catch Tipping.

"We're one block out." Warner turned his head to look at Jack. "I want you to wait in the car and—"

"No way." Jack shook his head. "I'm coming with you."

Warner looked like he might argue the point, but then relented and nodded. "Okay."

Jack's heart pounded as the vehicle pulled to a stop in the middle of Broadway. There were already four NYPD squad cars at the scene, with a dozen uniforms and a few plain clothes officers taking cover with weapons drawn. The scene was like something out of a movie, even before the Feds showed up. Jack just hoped they could end this with the professor still breathing.

He opened the door and followed Warner over to a waiting NYPD area commander. Given the body language of the two men, it was clear that once Warner arrived on scene, the show was his to run. Jack, invoking the President's authority, had made it clear that there would be no jurisdictional spats. This one had to be clean. Given the nuke in their city, the NYPD were happy to cooperate.

"I'm Agent Lance Warner." Warner crouched down behind the NYPD cruiser that the area commander was using as shelter. "This is Jack Emery."

Jack did the same, but felt a little stupid doing so. If the woman inside the diner wanted a shootout, she wouldn't have waited for the cavalry to arrive. "Hi."

"Lieutenant Henry Dillon." The NYPD man nodded. "Target is seated in a booth with unidentified female. She's armed. They're talking."

Jack glanced over the hood of the car at the diner. He could clearly see Zed Eshkol sitting opposite a woman. He smiled. "I'm just glad we found him."

"It's not that simple." Warner frowned, as SWAT teams kept arriving and flooding the scene with firepower. "What's her game?"

"Hell if I know." Dillon shrugged. "How do you gentleman want to handle this? She only has a pistol, from what we can see, and we can go in and get them."

"Too risky." Warner shook his head. "Sniper?"

"Impossible." Dillon laughed. "Would you believe it used to be a gun store? The windows are bullet proof."

"Almost like she planned it." Jack chanced another peek over the police cruiser. It was an unremarkable coffee and sandwich joint in a city full of them. The woman was seated with Eshkol in one of the front booths, talking with him as easy as you like. She didn't seemed concerned by the army of cops outside.

Warner looked over at Jack. "How do you want to play this, Jack? We can try to talk her out, or we can go in hot. There's not much else on offer if you want to get your boy out in one piece. And even those options don't come with a guarantee."

Jack didn't take his eyes off the woman. His eyes narrowed. Then they widened. "Motherfucker!"

"What?"

Jack stood, removed his pistol and handed it to Warner. "I'm going in. Don't shoot under any circumstances."

"I—"

Jack didn't give him a chance to respond, as he quickly rounded the cruiser and made for the diner. As he walked, he heard Warner curse after him, but Jack didn't look back. Once he reached the door, he opened it and stepped inside. Zed Eshkol looked in his direction, as did the woman who'd bailed Jack and Chen out of the German police van in Berlin, who he'd later discovered the identity of.

He approached the booth. "You better have a *fucking* good explanation for this, Anna."

"Looks like my cover wasn't as good as I thought it was." She smiled. "Hi again. I was just enjoying a sandwich and a cuppa with my good friend Zed here."

Eshkol had less humor. "I've been abducted by this woman and I want to go back to my university."

Jack pointed at Eshkol. "You. Shut up."

"I—"

He turned to Anna. "You. Talk."

She crossed her arms. "Hey, fuck you."

Jack flared. "Your dinner companion here might be the key to preventing a nuclear strike on this city. I need to take him in."

She reached for the pistol, which until now had been on the table. "Yeah, well, I've got my own problems."

"There's a lot of armed men outside."

She smiled and waved the pistol. "I've got the only gun that matters."

Jack exhaled through his teeth. He had to get Eshkol out of there, but couldn't quite see a way to do it without the professor ending up dead.

Eshkol started to laugh, long and deep and nasty. "This is too funny."

Jack glared at Eshkol. "What the fuck are you laughing at?"

The professor laughed so hard he coughed. "You're both fools. I've admitted that I'm the leader of the Zionists. Arrest me. But you're wasting time arguing. You can't stop the Samson Option. You'd be much better served applying your intellect on how to end the peace agreement."

Jack scoffed. "That's not going to happen, professor. I'm going to take you in and get the answers I need to end this."

"Is that so?" Anna pointed the pistol at Jack. "I need him for a little while longer, Mr. Emery, but I don't need you."

Jack suddenly regretted leaving his own pistol back with Agent Warner. He glanced outside, where SWAT were surrounding the building in ever increasing numbers. If he gave a nod, they'd storm the building in a second, but he'd be dead and Eshkol would fall in the crossfire. He was used to hairy situations, but this one seemed hopeless.

"So what do we do here?" He held his hands out. "We both need Eshkol, but we're stalemated."

"We both walk out of here. Equal access to Eshkol. That's the only thing I can agree to that my government will accept."

He considered it for a moment. He wasn't sure why Britain was so interested in the Zionists, but he didn't care. He needed Eshkol alive and needed to know where the nukes were. Nothing else would save the peace process and millions of lives. "Okay, we'll go with that. I suppose that's fair, since you found him."

"Stand down your goons."

"Pistol first."

Eshkol sighed. "You're both fools."

Anna glared at Eshkol then turned to Jack and lowered the pistol. "Okay. I—"

"*Freeze! Freeze!*"

Jack tensed. An FBI SWAT team was surging into the room through the kitchen with guns trained on each of them. Jack held his hands in place but cast a glance toward Anna. She looked down at her pistol, as if assessing her chances, then up to Jack. The look of fury on her face was terrifying. She held her hands up and let herself be subdued.

The scene froze for a few seconds, nobody moving or saying anything under the watchful guns of the SWAT team. Except Eshkol. The professor laughed and laughed and laughed until he started to cough and wheeze. Jack wanted to clobber the man, except it might earn him a bullet or two. Luckily his rage was interrupted by Warner entering the diner through the front door.

"You bastard." Jack scowled. "You could have ruined everything."

"I didn't." Warner shrugged. "Turns out the back door was open."

"What now?" Anna spoke softly.

"That's up to Mr. Emery." Warner looked to Jack. "I've disobeyed the President's man once today, I won't do it twice."

Jack exhaled slowly. It was time to take back the initiative. "Leave the pistol where it is, walk out of here and you'll be escorted to the airport. If you make a fuss, you'll be arrested and not even the special relationship between America and Britain will keep you out of prison for the next twenty years."

"Okay." Anna nodded and stood. Before she left, escorted by a pair of agents, she turned back. "Good luck. He's a tough old cookie."

Jack nodded and walked over to Eshkol. "Now, I think we got off on the wrong foot, professor. We've got a lot to talk about."

≈

ARON WOKE with a sigh and fumbled for the lamp. He squinted as the light pierced his solitude, nearly as irritating as the beeping that had woken him. He sat up in bed, rubbed his face and ran a hand through his hair. He looked down at his phone and read the message. There was only one thing that was permitted to override the do not disturb setting on his phone.

Zed Eshkol's emergency button.

He read the message again to confirm it, but he'd known as soon as he heard the phone beep. He didn't know what had happened to Zed Eshkol, nor did he have any care in finding out. The protocols were clear: the professor was compromised, so every single Zionist asset was to be activated. Now it was necessary to proceed with the contingency plan.

His work was not yet done.

ACT III

CHAPTER 15

The Federal Bureau of Investigation has so far resisted calls to reveal the identity of the Zionist leader, believed to have been detained after a massive manhunt through the streets of New York City. Sources have revealed that more than 300 police officers and Federal agents were involved in the arrest, which caused chaos across the city. The FBI has reiterated calls from the President for all Zionist members to hand themselves in and offered the largest reward in United States' history for information about the location of the three nuclear devices.

New York Standard

Jack closed his eyes and enjoyed the rest for just a moment. He took a few slow breaths, resisting the urge to sleep, though it tempted him like the final drink on a big night. It was never a good idea to be snoozing when the President walked into a National Security Council meeting, particularly with the world seven days away from nuclear catastrophe. Not even the fact he'd played a lead role in the scooping up of Zed Eshkol would get him off the hook for that one.

As if on cue, McGhinnist's voice boomed. "Thanks for coming in everyone. We ready to get started?"

Jack's eyes shot open and he caught sympathetic glances from a few of the other attendees. They'd all been burning the midnight oil, but some of the others had made a point of praising him for the work he'd put in and the progress he'd made. The recognition was nice, but felt a bit hollow at the moment. He'd only be satisfied when the good professor spilled the beans and they got their hands on the nuclear weapons.

He was still irritated that the SWAT unit had stormed the diner, putting everyone at risk. He thought he'd be able to talk Anna into handing Eshkol over, but instead they'd gone in hot. The professor had been bundled into an armored van and driven off, while Anna had been released and told in no uncertain terms to get on a plane. If she was from any other country, she'd have been locked up. The special relationship between the US and the UK still counted for something.

McGhinnist sat. "Lou, what do you have for us?"

Lou McColl – the FBI Director – removed his glasses, placed them on top of his papers and then smiled. "After the SWAT unit snapped up Eshkol, we moved him to a secure facility. He's currently being interrogated. He's holding out so far, but we could achieve more with enhanced techniques."

Jack snorted. "Torture, you mean?"

"Yes, Jack." McColl glared at him. "We don't have the luxury of a conscience when ten city blocks will soon be gone."

"Enough of that, gentlemen." McGhinnist sighed. "I won't authorize torture. Not while I'm still president. Has he told us where the bombs are yet?"

McColl placed both hands on the table, shook his head and let out a sigh. It was clear he thought Jack and the President were naive. "Not yet."

McGhinnist nodded. "We have seven days, but I want the weapons secured in one. If we wait any longer we're leaving it too close. Get it done."

"Yes, sir." McColl nodded then replaced his glasses, before scribbling a few notes on his pad. "We'll continue to rely on regular techniques."

"Okay." McGhinnist looked down at his papers. "Next item is the evacuation of Manhattan, twenty-four hours from now, should we fail to break Eshkol."

Jack winced. The thought of removing a few million people from the island was daunting. There would be panic, looting and chaos, at the end of which the greatest metropolis on Earth would resemble a ghost town. But there was a real chance they'd need to do it, given they didn't yet have the slightest clue where the weapon was. If they waited much longer there was no guarantee that the evacuation would be completed in time.

Admiral Bryson Tannenbaum – Chairman of the Joint Chiefs – nodded. "We've got several army and marine units readying to deploy to the city, if need be, along with every helicopter this side of the Atlantic. All assets will be at the disposal of the civilian authorities, sir, even if it's just to help direct people where to go."

"Can we pull it off?"

"Not a question for me, sir." Tannenbaum shrugged. "But the military can help get people out of the city and secure it when it's empty."

Jack leaned in. "Secure it how?"

"A small guard detail at each bridge along with helicopter and river patrols." Tannenbaum paused. "The minimum force required to keep people out."

The next question was obvious to Jack. "Men who could die if the bomb goes off in their vicinity?"

"Volunteers, Mr. Emery." Tannenbaum's look was hard. "These are extreme circumstances, but we've had plans in place to deal with them for seventy years."

Jack shook his head, but kept quiet. He understood the need to keep the city clamped down in the event of the bomb not being found. He spared a thought for the authorities going through the same preparations in Jerusalem and Mecca. It was far easier to button down a metropolis on an island, with all the resources of the United States government, than it was in those other locations. There would be lots of lives lost if the bombs couldn't be found.

"We have to break Eshkol." Jack was surprised by the pitch of his voice. "We can't let those devices go off. It'll be a catastrophe."

His words hung in the air until the phone in front of McGhinnist rang. Everyone at the meeting stared at it and Jack thought it unusual. Very few calls made it through to the President when the council was in session. McGhinnist frowned, lifted the handset and pressed the button to put the call onto speaker. It only took a moment for the President's secretary to announce that the Iranian President was on the line.

"Put him through, Steph." McGhinnist ran a hand through his hair. "President Gharazi, you're on the line with my National Security Council."

There was a slight pause, before a man spoke in heavily accented

English. "Mr. President, this is a warning. Iran will launch nuclear weapons at Israel if you can't guarantee the safety of Mecca. We will do it two hours before the peace agreement is due to come into force. I can't tolerate this threat to Mecca."

McGhinnist sighed, as if this was the last thing he needed. "President Gharazi, I can assure you we're doing everything we can to find the weapons. Such an act by Iran, against an ally, would be considered an act of war by the United States and we'd be forced to retaliate."

"I'm aware of all of this, Mr. President, but I can imagine the reaction if a Muslim had a nuke in Vatican City." The Iranian laughed. "We've made reforms and drawn closer to your country in some ways, but some things remain the same. This risk can't be tolerated."

"What good will nuking Israel do?"

"If there's no Israel, there's no peace agreement. Mecca will be spared."

Jack shook his head and shared a look with some other council members. It was a strange arithmetic the Iranian President was engaging in, but it made a mad sort of sense. Iran had been strong-armed by the United States to support the agreement – or at least turn a blind eye – and McGhinnist had hoped that untangling the Israeli–Palestinian mess would help to end the worst conflict in the region. Instead, it looked as if it might do the opposite.

"That's strange logic, Mr. President." McGhinnist seemed to read Jack's mind. "My understanding was that your country supported the peace process."

"We consider the agreement acceptable, if the weapons can be found." Gharazi's voice hardened. "If not, the whole region will go to hell, Mr. President. Palestine has no nuclear weapons, but it does have friends. It's Zionists who hold this dagger to our hearts, and it's Israel that will pay if it isn't dealt with."

The phone started to beep, indicating the call had been ended. Before anyone could speak, McGhinnist slammed a fist down on the table.

"Find those weapons!"

∾

ANNA LOOKED DOWN – a long way down – then stepped back and pulled the balaclava over her head. Once it was comfortably in place, she checked her weapons were on her hip, that her harness and combat vest were tight and secure, and that the small black remote with the single button that she carried was still showing a green light. Satisfied that she was as ready as she could be, she took a few long, deep breaths and then stepped to the ledge again.

Though she was usually okay with heights, the prospect of jumping off a perfectly good ledge and hanging from a zip line seventy-one stories above Broadway didn't really appeal to her. But, as she'd often found since joining MI6, the agent went where the work was to be found. In this case, the work was on the sixty-third level, in a small, off-the-books office that the FBI kept for interviewing important prisoners like Zed Eshkol.

As she connected the zip line to the metal ring on her harness, she cursed herself again for letting Eshkol slip out of her grasp. She'd taken a risk by questioning him in the open after she'd got him away from the campus. She'd wagered that there was no harm being seen with an academic in a diner and that, when he realized the jig was up, the professor would be forthcoming. Following that, he could be easily disposed of – an old man whose heart gave out.

But taking the risk had bitten her. She'd failed and he was now in American custody. What she hadn't counted on was Jack Emery linking Tipping to Eshkol and then Eshkol to the Zionists. Given the hit team had taken care of Tipping, she'd made a mistake in thinking her lead safe. Uncovering Eshkol's link with the Zionists had been a first-rate bit of research by Emery, which had unfortunately cost her dearly. Her overconfidence may have cost her country and the world.

Luckily, she had another chance. She'd easily escaped the security detail tasked with seeing her onto a plane, and Cunningham had made it clear any action she deemed necessary was on the board in order to get to Eshkol again and get the information out of him. Though he was in American hands, with the full menu of options at her disposal and the permission to use them, she was confident she could get to him.

That's how she found herself on top of a building, about to rappel down it. Eshkol was alive and she intended to make her claim on him. She gave the zip line a tug and eased herself over the side of the building. She winced at the strength of the wind that blew against her. Once she was suspended by nothing other than the line, she let her rubber shoes rest against the glass windows and started to lower herself slowly.

She knew the darkness was her friend and that there was little chance she'd be seen, but she still hurried as much as she dared. All it would take to expose her was one office worker staying back late. If that happened, she'd likely never make it out of the building and this part of the world would be radioactive in a week's time. As her confidence with the abseil grew, so did the speed of her descent.

Seventy-one.

Seventy.

She scanned each floor as she descended, reflecting on the huge disparity in office layout.

Sixty-nine.

Sixty-eight.

A third of the way there, and she hadn't seen a soul. With each floor lit by security lights and empty of people, her assessment of the situation improved.

Sixty-seven.

Sixty-six.

She started to slow her descent, but continued to bounce softly off of windows with her feet as she rappelled down.

Sixty-five.

Sixty-four.

Sixty-three.

Touching her feet to the window, she slowed to a stop. She pulled a lever on her rig to apply the brake, which freed her hands to get on with the job. After a quick dig in one of the many pockets on her combat vest, she found a small but powerful glass cutter. She fired it up, held it in one hand and reached for her remote with the other. The light on the remote was still green, meaning the security responsible for monitoring this window were still occupied.

After one final glance inside, she set to work creating a large enough circle to fit through. As the cutter bit into the glass, she winced at the noise it made, hoping that nobody was in a position to hear it. The work only took a few minutes, then she put the cutter back in her pocket and used a suction device to remove and secure the glass. Once she was done, she swung inside, careful not to make too much noise and alert security.

She unclipped the zip line and removed her harness, placing it near the window, then drew her pistol and scanned the room. Though MI6 had known about this location for years, nobody ever expected to use the information. Given they knew most of the possible locations that the

FBI would use to question Eshkol, simple signal interception had told MI6 which one Eshkol was being taken to. Now it was up to her.

She raised the pistol and advanced through the cubicle jungle, which looked like any other. If all went to plan, the floor should be deserted except for the agent on the security desk – who her little green light told her was under control – and however many agents were interrogating Eshkol. Her weapon swept from side to side, alert to any potential ambush from one of the vacant cubicles, but nothing pricked her senses amid darkness and silence.

She moved toward the target office, relaxed but alert for any movement or trouble. The first office had its door closed and no lights on, so she kept moving past. It was a process she repeated four more times, until she reached the sixth office. The curtains were drawn and the door was similarly shut, but this time light blazed at the edges of the window, where the curtains couldn't totally block it. She allowed herself a small smile and prepared for the violence to come.

There was no subtle way to do this, so she got on with it. She holstered her pistol and pulled out a taser, never taking her eyes off the door. Next she grabbed one of the metal cylinders attached to her combat vest, kicked the bottom of the door a few times, lifted the cylinder to her mouth and pulled out the pin. The door opened and she fired the taser. The contractor who'd opened the door dropped – courtesy of 50,000 volts – at the same time as she threw the cylinder inside and retreated from the doorway.

The flashbang exploded with noise and light, but she was shielded from the worst of it by the door frame. Once the fireworks concluded she rounded back into the doorway, her eyes scanning the small interview room. She made her way toward the second and final contractor, who was rubbing his eyes and in no position to threaten her, and aimed a kick at his knee. The man crumpled and she pulled some cuffs from her vest, restrained him and forced him outside. A few seconds later and the man she'd tasered was likewise restrained.

All was clear except for Eshkol.

She stood in front of the professor, savoring the look of fear and confusion on his face. He was seated with one hand cuffed to a steel ring on the table, but was too busy reacting to the flashbang to notice her enter. She sat opposite and stared at him, waiting for him to regain his composure and wishing he'd be quicker about it. The FBI didn't know she was here, but she was still in very hostile territory. That she'd been authorized to take this action showed how much Fraser and Cunningham wanted Eshkol's information. She drew her pistol.

"Hi again." She kept the weapon on him as she lifted the balaclava off her face. "I'm sorry our nice lunch was interrupted. We've got a lot to discuss."

The second his eyes adjusted to her, they narrowed. He glanced around for the Americans then back at Anna. "You."

"Me." She smiled, never taking the pistol off him. "I'm so glad to see you too, professor."

"You're going to kill me, then?" He continued to blink and spoke louder than normal, the flashbang having affected his hearing. "I gave you the location of the backpack weapons. There's nothing else I can tell you, no matter how fanciful your claims about a nuclear submarine."

"That you did." Anna stood and walked around the table. "And rest assured that I'll pass the location on to my American friends, but I need something else."

"What would that be?"

"Confirmation that HMS *Vigilant* has been compromised and an explanation on how you planned to activate the launch."

"This again?" He gave a sharp laugh. "You're wrong. The backpack nukes were the play. Get those, and you've silenced me."

She sighed. "You have an unknown number of minions, able to enact multiple plans at once. Redundancy."

"If you're so convinced then nothing I can say will change your mind." He closed his eyes and turned his head away. "Shoot me."

Anna had no intention of doing that, not until she had the information she needed. Despite his denials, she knew he had more to tell her. She placed the pistol down on the table, out of his reach but close enough to grab if they were interrupted. She unzipped one of the pockets on her vest and dug around inside, pulling out a small case not unlike one used to hold reading glasses. She opened the case, removing the syringe and a small flask with a rubber stopper. The stopper gave a small pop, then she filled the syringe with liquid.

"Last chance, professor." She pressed down on the plunger and squirted a small amount of the liquid in front of his face. "This won't be pleasant."

"I was in a Nazi camp for two years and came out the other side." He spat at her. "I'm not scared of you."

"You should be."

"My life is irrelevant. What matters is securing Israel." He paused. "Seven days from now a travesty will take place that I don't want to see occur. Kill me."

She shrugged, stabbed the needle into his arm and pressed down on the plunger. The liquid inside emptied out and she threw the empty vessel onto the floor. He had no reaction for the first few seconds, but then his eyes widened and he let out a small whimper. In the seconds that followed, he started to struggle against the handcuffs. Then he started to scream.

The poison was one of the most lethal on Earth and was completely fatal. What made it helpful, however, was the speed at which it acted. It caused immense, crippling pain within seconds of injection, but took a long while to bring the body to its eventual death. It was an eternity to be subjected to the pain of your nervous system dying, given the poison could take eight hours to kill.

She shook her head. Two hours, given his age. Still, a very long time.

"Professor, I know it hurts and it's going to get worse. You're going to die. But if you tell me what I need, a bullet will end you. If not, you'll slowly decay and your nervous system will tell your brain all about it for the next few hours. It really is your choice."

"Okay!" His shriek was piercing. "I'll tell you! Make it stop!"

"I can't stop it until I kill you, professor. Answer my questions." She leaned in to him. "Has the HMS *Vigilant* been compromised?"

"Yes!" he howled. "Joseph Cohen was my student and friend! He's the captain of the submarine!"

She ignored the upward inflection in his voice. He was getting desperate. "How is the launch activated?"

"By using the normal process!"

"That's impossible." She picked up the pistol. "No British Prime Minister would order the launch."

"No, not that way." His eyes were bulging now and saliva started to dribble from his mouth. "The Dead Man Letter!"

Her eyes widened. It was as if she'd found the missing piece to a jigsaw lying under the table. "You fucking bastard."

He laughed, a terrible sight given the pain he was in. "If only you knew. I've activated pieces all throughout your government. The world will burn with nuclear fire, and you'll watch as everything you thought secure is compromised before your eyes."

She raised the pistol and pulled the trigger. His head slumped forward. She gave a moment's thought to killing the men outside, but decided there was no point. They didn't know who she was and she didn't want to end the lives of men just doing their jobs. She stood and prepared to leave the lifeless corpse of one of the most brilliant minds the Western world had seen.

An intellect that may well end the world.

~

JACK CLINKED his champagne glass against Celeste's then took a sip. The vintage Dom Perignon fizzed in his mouth and he savored the taste. But, more than that, he was savoring the first real meal he'd had with Celeste in over a week. It had been the busiest week in a crazy month and he was feeling the fatigue in his muscles and his bones, in his mind and in his heart. The end of the twenty-eight–day countdown to the peace agreement couldn't come soon enough, if the nukes could be found, anyway.

"Thanks for coming up here for this, Celeste." He put his glass down and looked across the table at her. "I needed it."

"I don't mind bringing the party to you." She took a second sip of her own drink and then winked at him, a twinkle in her eye. "Are you okay?"

He opened his mouth to answer, then paused. It was a loaded question, akin to asking a rabbit staring into the headlights of an oncoming car if it was doing fine. He was tired, sure, and he was counting down the minutes until the peace, but until the nukes were found he'd have no rest. Now that Eshkol had been captured, that should only take a short while, but he couldn't relax until that moment. There was too much work to do, too much at stake and too many lives that could be lost.

"I'm fine." He smiled.

"Liar." She raised her eyebrows. "You need to look after yourself, Jack."

He shrugged. "There are a few million reasons for me to keep working. Once we find those bombs and we've got peace, I'll rest."

"Promise?"

"In fact, I'll do you one better." He paused, reached down into his pocket and pulled out a small box.

She gasped and her eyes flickered between his face and the box. "What're you doing?"

He never took his eyes off her as he stood and lowered himself to one knee. He opened the box, revealing the ring. "Marry me, Celeste?"

"Seriously?" She shook her head and gave a small laugh. "I had no idea this was coming."

"Seriously." He moved the box closer to her. "I know there's a bunch of trouble that comes with being with me, but I want you in my life forever. Marry me?"

He took a deep breath as she stared at the ring, then at him, then back again. It was if she was transfixed, and with each passing second the feeling in the pit of his stomach worsened. He hadn't planned this, not really, and had only purchased the ring in the afternoon after she'd told him she was coming to visit. There were so many reasons that marrying Celeste made sense to him, but he also knew that he was asking a lot. Trouble stalked him, and they'd had their own problems. It seemed unlikely that those two things would cease, but he knew he needed her.

"Sorry." She shook her head. "I was just thinking about how far we've come – both individually and together – since we first met."

He cracked a smile. "We definitely don't do boring. Stick with me, and there'll be more entertainment to come. That I can promise."

"It feels like I've packed in a million lifetimes worth of excitement with you already, Jack."

"Okay." He saw where this was going and started to lower the box. When he'd asked Erin to marry him, years ago, she'd said yes instantly. He felt like someone had punched him in the stomach. He swallowed hard and struggled to find some words, unable to believe he'd misread their relationship so badly. "I—"

"Give me that!" She reached out and plucked the box from his hand. "You didn't let me finish!"

He relinquished the package. "Okay."

"As I was saying, it's been exciting so far, and I wouldn't have it any other way." She pulled the ring from the box. "Of course I'll marry you."

He let out a small laugh and smiled so wide it hurt. He helped her with the ring. "Hope it fits."

She slid it on. "Perfect."

He leaned in to kiss her, but paused when Celeste's eyes flicked behind him and narrowed. "Jack, we've got company."

Jack followed her gaze and was surprised to see four Chevy Suburbans pulled up out the front, with DC Metro Police motorbikes along as outriders. Several black-suited Secret Service agents had taken up station outside the restaurant and one had the door to the restaurant open. Jack stood and waited for the agent to approach, even as Celeste tensed and reached for his hand.

"Evening." He smiled at the agent as he squeezed Celeste's hand. "This is quite a bit of a show to wish me congratulations on my engagement, isn't it?"

The agent acted like he didn't even hear the joke. He was all business. "Mr. Emery, you need to come with us, sir."

"Something wrong?"

"You need to come now, sir."

Jack nodded and turned back to Celeste. He leaned in to kiss her. "Sorry."

"I'll finish my meal and the bottle, but it's going on your card." She gave a small laugh as she pecked him on the lips. "Go save the world. I love you."

"I love you too."

He nodded at the agent and they walked outside the restaurant to the waiting convoy. He hoped whatever had interrupted his proposal was important, given that Celeste had flown from New York to be with him. He waited for the agent to indicate which vehicle he was to get inside, then climbed in. The agent closed the door behind him, and Jack wasn't surprised to see the President, given the size of the security detail. But he was surprised by the presence of a second man.

"Mr. President." Jack nodded at McGhinnist, then shifted his gaze to the other man. "Ambassador Hutchens."

David Hutchens had been UK Ambassador to the United States for the better part of a decade. In that time, he'd been a steady hand at the helm of the most important alliance both countries shared, during a time when the US had dealt with both Michelle Dominique and her Foundation for a New America and Richard Hall's authoritarian takeover. Since McGhinnist had won the Presidency, Hutchens had been a strong supporter. He'd also been at the forefront of the peace negotiations.

"Good to see you again, Jack." The ambassador held out his hand. "Wish it was under better circumstances."

Jack shook Hutchens' hand. "Likewise. Something's come up? I assume it's not good?"

"Sorry to interrupt your dinner, Jack." McGhinnist sounded like he meant it. "This one is on me."

"It'll be an expensive one to cover, Mr. President." Jack smiled. "There was a diamond on the menu."

"You proposed?" McGhinnist's eyes widened slightly and he gave a tired smile. "Good move."

Hutchens grinned at McGhinnist then at Jack. "Fantastic news, Jack. I wish I were congratulating you under better circumstances."

McGhinnist cleared his throat, cutting the celebrations short. "We know where some of the bombs are. A team in New York has already secured one and Jerusalem will be safe soon. Unfortunately, Mecca came up empty. Looks like the Zionists left that weapon with someone who has moved it somewhere else."

"Eshkol?" Jack's gaze moved between the other two men. He felt the temperature in the vehicle drop to freezing, but neither man spoke. "Well?"

Finally, the ambassador broke the silence. "He's dead. But he did give us the location of the bombs."

Jack started to speak. "How—"

"Leave it, Jack." McGhinnist's voice was laced with threat. Something bad had to have happened, leading to tension between the President and Hutchens.

Hutchens leaned forward. "Unfortunately, we're out of the frying pan and into the fire. We've received intelligence indicating that HMS *Vigilant* is under the command of an agent of the Zionists. Worse, it looks like the Zionists might have a plan to get off a launch. Needless to say this is thoroughly bad news."

Jack's eyes narrowed as he chewed on the ambassador's words. "Wait a minute, isn't that a—"

"A ballistic missile submarine capable of annihilating a fair percentage of humanity." The ambassador nodded. "Yes."

"Fuck."

Jack couldn't believe it. His heart had soared in the moment after McGhinnist had revealed the bombs had been found, but the taste of triumph after all his hard work had turned to ashes in his mouth. A British boomer was waiting silently beneath the ocean to unleash Zed

Eshkol's wrath from beyond the grave. After all the effort to find them, the backpack bombs had been a plot shouted to the world, when in reality the larger danger was lurking as quiet as a whisper beneath the ocean.

Hutchens sighed. "It can't be hunted down and it can't be ordered to the surface, so we've got seven days to figure out how to prevent a launch."

Jack scoffed. "Can it be done?"

"There's one way." Hutchens shrugged. "We're working on it, along with some of your people, but it won't be easy. It looks like Eshkol has agents all the way through Britain and the British Government. I imagine it's the same story in America – Tipping was just the start."

"Nor is it the only issue." McGhinnist's voice was nearly a whisper. "Iran hasn't changed its position."

Jack nearly laughed at the gall of the Iranian President. "Turns out they're playing realpolitik like everyone else."

"It'll take some concessions to get them to back down, I think. Until we can find the bomb in Mecca, they're playing hardball." McGhinnist placed a hand on his knee. "In the meantime, we're going to DEFCON 2. If we can't find a way to deal with that sub, and Iran, we need to be ready."

Jack nodded. The world was on the verge of catastrophe. "What can I do?"

McGhinnist smiled.

CHAPTER 16

The State Department has confirmed Israeli reports that the backpack nuclear device planted by the Zionist terrorists in Jerusalem has been secured, five days before the deadline. This follows a similar announcement by the Department of Homeland Security, confirming that the device in New York City has been found. State Department officials remain tight-lipped about the bomb in Mecca, suggesting that it has yet to be found, even as reports emerge of troop movements across the Middle East as enactment of the peace agreement draws near.

New York Standard

Joseph held his coffee in one hand and gripped the safety rail with the other, as the *Vigilant* ascended toward the surface. Though he didn't have to hold on and there was no danger of falling over, the practice was as instinctive as breathing, drilled into him over many years in the submarine service. As he looked around the bridge, he could see those who weren't seated doing the same thing. He gave a small smile as he felt the boat reach an even plane.

"We're at depth and level, captain." Jennings' voice broke the silence.

Joseph released the rail. "Unfurl the array and download communications."

Jennings nodded and started to fire off commands to the bridge crew, as Joseph sipped his tea and waited for the first batch of messages to come in. While at sea, British nuclear submarines never surfaced and communication with them was difficult, possible only in very short bursts – such as launch orders. They only climbed to periscope depth to receive longer messages a small handful of time during their tour. It was no coincidence that Joseph had chosen this date to do so.

Joseph hoped the first news they'd receive would be about the peace agreement being abandoned. Failing that, he hoped to read that Eshkol's main plan was proceeding well, with nuclear weapons ready for use in the event of the peace agreement being enacted. Though that would mean Israel was a step closer to being divided, it would be the next best result for Joseph. By far the worst would be news that the agreement was close and that Eshkol's plan had failed. In that case, Joseph would become the primary defender of Israel.

"Captain?"

Joseph shook his head, clearing the gloomy thoughts. "Report."

Jennings smiled and winked at his captain, like they shared a little secret. Since their chat in the wardroom, the other man had continued to confide in Joseph about his personal life, to the point where Joseph thought Jennings would walk over hot coals if asked to by his captain. He couldn't be totally sure, of course, but if the *Vigilant* and its warheads did have to become the final act in Eshkol's plan, with Jennings in hand Joseph considered it likely he'd be able to hold up his end. The rest of the crew would follow.

"Attention crew." Jennings spoke over the boat intercom. "News as follows: The separation of Israel and Palestine is five days away. The Zionist leader has been arrested and two of the nuclear weapons found, but Iran has threatened to attack Israel if the Mecca device isn't. In sport, Ipswich Town has been relegated."

Joseph cursed to himself. Even though there were no new orders from British command, the news contained all the orders he needed from his other master. He was now the last person standing in the way of Israel's destruction. Eshkol was incapacitated and two of the backpack bombs were off the board. The Iranian declaration was a surprise, but not relevant to his mission. All that was clear was that the start gun had fired for him and he now had some work to do in order to get ready.

He shook his head and focused on the deck. He turned to Jennings, who'd continued to read the less important news. "Tim?"

Jennings stopped mid-sentence and looked at Joseph, a confused look on his face. He took his finger off the intercom transmit button. "Captain?"

"I want to speak to the crew." Joseph stepped closer to the intercom and Jennings stepped back. Joseph pressed the button. "This is the captain. This news is unexpected, but not a surprise. The world was an unstable, dangerous place when we set out and it looks to have gotten worse. I'm not sure the world has ever faced such a strong possibility of nuclear war. It's important that we stay safe and that we look after each other, because we have a vital job to do. Amid this uncertainty, we're the only thing protecting Britain, however she may get caught up in this. Remain vigilant, do your jobs and we'll get through this."

Joseph took his finger off the intercom button and looked around the bridge. A few of the crew wore determined looks and Jennings nodded at him. Joseph considered the little speech as necessary in preparing Jennings for the eventuality of the launch. He trusted Eshkol to have things sorted, but nothing above the ocean would matter if Joseph failed to do his job below it. Enactment of the Samson Option and the prevention of the peace agreement now required two plans to proceed, one after the other, with no room for failure. It required choreography more difficult than stashing some nukes around the place.

He exhaled deeply at the burden. "Immediate drill: dive to launch depth and prepare a package with standard incoming orders. Two minutes."

Jennings' eyes narrowed. "I hadn't finished the news yet, sir. Maybe we should wait until—"

Joseph looked at his watch. "Fifteen seconds down, XO. I suggest you get moving."

~

ARON SMILED at the flight attendant, whose own smile was plastered on with practiced ease, then stepped past her and onto the skybridge. The cool, artificial air was replaced with the crisper air of a London morning and he strolled into the terminal humming a nameless tune. Since Eshkol's alert had sprung him into action he'd taken a slow and ponderous route to London to make sure he didn't appear on the radar of the authorities.

He regretted that two of the three backpack bombs he'd deployed had been located. So much effort had gone into their acquisition and placement that it seemed very anticlimactic to have them scooped up, but that had always been a risk. He hadn't counted on Eshkol being exposed and revealing their location, but there was no use worrying about it. There was still one bomb in place, which threatened to make Mecca glow.

The minute the New York bomb had been found it had been plastered all over the media and, hours later, the Jerusalem bomb had also been secured. Aron had expected to see coverage from Mecca not long after, but it hadn't happened. It meant the only bomb he'd left with a human being, rather than in a supposedly secure location, had been moved at the discretion of its caretaker. Aron hoped the man could keep from being found.

He couldn't count on it though, so he still had work to do. Aron was always restless on aircraft, but knowing the job that waited for him in London had made him all the more anxious to arrive and get started. He made his way through immigration and toward the luggage carousel. As he did, he thought about what needed doing over the next five days, whether or not the weapon in Mecca was located by the authorities.

He still hoped the agreement would be abandoned, but now considered it unlikely. The situation was ridiculous and the answer obvious, yet the signatories to the agreement had failed to blink as they were supposed to so more had to be done. A threat was only as good as the intent behind it and Eshkol wasn't bluffing. The professor's instructions had been clear and Aron intended to serve him faithfully.

By using the emergency button, Aron knew that Eshkol had activated every single asset he had. It was not a step taken lightly. Aron had his own assignment, for which he'd join up with others, but he knew that assets all around the world would have their jobs. Some may assist Aron, others may occur without him even knowing, but it would be the final flourish of a great mind who, in some way or another, had been compromised.

He reached the luggage carousel and his bag emerged quickly. With the large backpack over his shoulder, it didn't take him too long to clear customs and make his way to the exit. The sliding doors opened and he stepped outside and into the fresh air. He took a deep breath as he looked up at the overcast skies. If all went to plan, he might have emerged from an airport for the last time in his life. As odd as it felt to think it, he was at ease with his fate. Only the mission counted.

"It's good to see you again, my friend."

Aron smiled at the sound of the voice, which he hadn't heard in weeks. He turned and took in the sight of her for several moments. It felt like so much had changed since they'd parted in Russia. They'd studied together under Zed Eshkol, years ago, becoming fast friends and allies in the professor's network – two of the key pieces on his board. That they were both here now spoke to the gravity of the situation. All assets were in play.

"Miri." Aron placed his bag on the ground and held his arms wide. "I had no idea you'd be beside me for this final effort."

Miri Shaked laughed as she stepped into his hug. "You were the golden child, Aron, but you don't really think he'd trust you alone with this, do you?"

He pulled away and shrugged. "You know the plan?"

Her eyes twinkled. "I know my part in it."

Aron nearly laughed. Zed Eshkol's compartmentalization was legendary. "You're in contact with the local network?"

"Yes. That's what I've been doing while you were busy planting bombs. I don't know much about them." She paused. "Zed trusted them, though."

"Let's get going." Aron smiled and jerked his head toward the taxi line, keen to waste no time.

He'd flown in expecting to have to deal with a list of difficult targets with the help of strangers. Now he had Miri. Though he'd still be relying on Eshkol's local network for most of the heavy lifting, having one friend at his side made him all the more confident. She had skills that he lacked, but was also good at most of the things he was. He'd always found that quite frustrating, in truth, but now it would be an asset.

They climbed into the first available cab and rode in silence. Though they were both too experienced to speak in front of prying ears, they did share a few easy smiles. Aron closed his eyes, knowing he had some time before they reached their destination. He didn't sleep, but used the time to cycle through the list of targets in his head. He had five days to hit them all, with Miri and the local team available for support.

They arrived about an hour after they'd departed, which included being caught in some traffic. As the cab pulled up, Aron looked at the studios of BBC Radio 4 for the first time. Broadcasting House was a mix of the old and the new, a century-old building modernized with steel and glass. After he'd soaked it up, he looked at Miri, who was staring at him intently. It felt as if her eyes were asking hard questions, even if her mouth remained closed.

"What?" He unbuckled his belt.

"Just making sure you're focused."

Aron shrugged, paid the driver and climbed out of the cab. He collected his bag from the trunk, then hefted it over his shoulder and walked toward the building. Miri followed, and he felt her summing up him as much as the building. He couldn't blame her. The targets were ambitious, to say the least, and Aron actually considered the likelihood of success to be slim. He was dedicated to trying and dying, if need be. He wasn't sure she had the same commitment.

Knocking BBC Radio 4 off the air was not even the most difficult of the jobs, but it was one of the first. It was impossible for a pair of them to do it, and that's where Eshkol's local assets would come into play – warm bodies with lots of explosives and a few particular skills. Aron wasn't overly worried about the first target, he was concerned about the ones that followed. Even with all those men and guns and bombs, the size of the task seemed impossible.

"What're you thinking?" Miri placed a hand on his shoulder.

"How much I hate public broadcasting."

∾

JACK GAVE a deep sigh as he looked out the window of the car, then spoke into his cell phone. "Anything else, sir?"

McGhinnist laughed from the other end of the line. "You'll be fine, Jack. Stop worrying and remember: I sent you there. Any failure is mine."

Jack snorted. "I'm struggling to see things the same way, knowing that if I leave here empty-handed we'll either lose the peace or watch Israel get glassed."

McGhinnist said nothing for a moment. Jack knew the President well enough to know that he was looking for the right thing to say, the thing that would convince a man in hostile territory on the other side of the world that he could achieve the impossible. In this case, the impossible was convincing nuclear-armed Iranians not to take matters into their own hands, flattening Israel to ostensibly save Mecca, but probably starting a global nuclear war in the process.

"Sir?"

"I'd love to tell you that it doesn't matter if you succeed or not, Jack, but that'd be a lie." McGhinnist paused again. "You've been caught up in a whole bunch of crises in recent years, but now I need you to help solve another. With Karl gone and Zionists popping up all over the place, you're the one I trust for this."

"I'll do my best." He hoped his best would be good enough.

"Do whatever you need to do to get them to back down, Jack. Good luck."

The line went dead and Jack put the phone in his top pocket. He sat back in the soft leather seat and closed his eyes, feeling the weight of the expectation on him. The warning in the car outside the restaurant had been apt, and Eshkol's moles were turning everywhere. As they acted, they were exposed, but the damage had been done. It was terrifying how deep Eshkol's assets had burrowed into the American and British governments.

He sighed and tried to focus on the job. Before he'd called McGhinnist, the driver had told him he was ten minutes out from the Presidential palace. He'd hoped that McGhinnist would have good news – that the bomb in Mecca had been found – but Saudi authorities were still searching for it. He laughed at the ridiculousness of it all: the Iranians were prepared to nuke Israel over Mecca, and a small number of Israelis were prepared to nuke Mecca over Palestine.

The car stopped and Jack opened his eyes as the door was opened for him. Camera flashes greeted him as he climbed out of the vehicle. An honor guard greeted him – the Iranian Republican Guard, which he'd been forewarned about, and the Iranian President, which he hadn't been. Despite the location, he'd half expected to be meeting with a minor official, but the President's presence meant there was hope. He closed the distance between them, deliberately avoiding the temptation to look around too much. He couldn't let himself be overwhelmed.

"Mr. Emery." The President held out his hand. "Welcome to Iran."

Jack shook his hand. "President Gharazi, thanks for welcoming me."

"These are dire days, but there's still some time to eat. Join me."

Gharazi turned on his heel, gesturing for Jack to follow. As they walked, they made small talk while surrounded by the President's army of retainers and hangers on. They eventually reached a small dining room dominated by a six-seater table. Jack was pleased to see there were only two places set. He stood inside the door and waited for whatever was to come. Gharazi dismissed the support staff, leaving just the two of them.

"What now, Mr. President?" Jack felt a little prompting was necessary, given the situation. "I'm quite short on time."

"Aren't we all?" Gharazi smiled as he gestured toward the table. "Please, sit. It's just the two of us. We'll have to serve ourselves."

Jack nodded and sat in the seat the President had gestured him to. In a weaker moment, he might have made a wise crack about being alone with the President and his spy agencies, but he held his tongue. Gharazi had his secrets and Jack had his – such as the fact that a British nuclear submarine had been hijacked and posed a far greater threat to the world – and Mecca – than either backpack nukes or Iranian ones. Adding more fuel to this fire was not something he wanted to do.

"Now, Mr. Emery, you've come a long way." Gharazi rested his elbows on the table, his fingers steepled in front of his face. "I know why you're here, but you needn't have bothered. My terms were clear: the threat to Mecca must be removed or the peace abandoned."

Jack took a sip of water. He'd have preferred to have something stronger, but Gharazi was not a drinker. "Mr. President, I hope you appreciate the bind the United States is in. We've worked to broker a peace that makes everyone happy – including Iran – only to have it threatened by extremists."

Gharazi nodded. "I—"

Jack held up a hand. "Please, let me finish. As I said, this is a deal that's good for everybody, yet having your government make inflammatory threats places the peace and the whole world in danger. I'm simply here to ask that you take your threats, and your nuclear weapons, off the table."

Jack sat back. The other man's features were as hard as granite and his face showed no hint that Jack's words had influenced him at all. While in a sane world what he'd said to Gharazi would be enough, events had spiraled out of control. It was possible that Jack coming here could make things worse. Thankfully, McGhinnist had armed him with more than appeals to reason. The United States could throw a huge amount of resources at diplomatic problems when needed.

"If Iran agrees to take such action, President McGhinnist is willing to remove the last of the economic sanctions against Iran and to also normalize relations between the two countries." Jack smiled. "This is as tough a concession for a Republican president to offer as possible."

Gharazi's features cracked for the first time, as he gave the slightest hint of a smile. "I knew you'd come equipped with platitudes, threats and maybe baubles to dangle in front of me, Mr. Emery, but it appears your boss is more serious about this peace than I gave him credit for."

"He's taken us to the brink of nuclear catastrophe for it. We don't negotiate with terrorists as a matter of policy, but even if we did the President would stand behind the deal and ignore the Zionist demands. Their threat must be dealt with, because we won't relinquish the peace."

Gharazi nodded. "That answers my next question: Why not walk away? But I appreciate and respect a man of conviction."

Jack was pleased at not having to dwell on that point for too long. McGhinnist had repeatedly stated and shown that abandoning the peace was not an option, through dealing with the initial leaks to chasing Tipping to finding Eshkol and the first two bombs. Iranian brinkmanship was just another step along that road, at the end of which would either be a more peaceful Middle East, or a glowing one. Jack doubted he'd have the stones to be as resolute as McGhinnist had been.

They spoke for several hours, through three courses, dessert and coffee. While Jack appreciated the difficult position Gharazi was in, he was determined to do whatever he needed to in order to buy America, Israel and Palestine some extra time. They circled around the same terms, Jack sweetened them a little, Gharazi blustered and Jack bristled until, eventually, Jack felt he had gone as far as he could.

"Those are the best terms I can offer, Mr. President. The only thing I can add is that the US would consider a pre-emptive attack on Israel to be an act of war."

Gharazi laughed. "My people would consider an attack on Mecca to be the same."

"Then we're at a decision point." Jack held out his hands. "This is the chance to make the right decision, to try our best – together – to end the threat to Mecca and also lock in the two-state solution that has eluded us for generations. You don't like Israel, fine, but I suggest you can live with it if all else is put right."

"You ask much of me. If my people don't revolt at this deal, the spiritual leaders are likely to. You might see me on CNN hanging from my neck tomorrow." Gharazi lifted his water glass and took a long sip, but never took his eyes off Jack. "But we all must take risks to avert catastrophe."

Jack raised an eyebrow. "We have a deal?"

"We have a deal." Gharazi nodded. "But not exactly the one you wanted. Twenty-three hours is all I can give you. If I don't have a guarantee that Mecca is safe one hour prior to the expiry of the agreement, then I'll have no choice but to strike pre-emptively."

Jack stood and held out his hand, which Gharazi shook. Others would work out the detail of the deal, but it had been agreed in principle. It was good enough. It would have to be. Jack had bought McGhinnist, the peace process and the world an extra day. He'd given up nearly a day to do so, as well as mountains of US influence and treasure. But in the world of geopolitics, Jack thought it might just count as a win.

They'd had precious few of those recently.

CHAPTER 17

With less than 72 hours before the peace agreement between Israel and Palestine is enacted and a two-state solution realized, the nuclear device that Zionist extremists have placed near Mecca has still not been found. The bomb, which the Zionists claim will be detonated if the countdown expires, threatens to level the most holy Islamic site in the world. Saudi Arabia has already begun mass evacuations from the area, but the saving of lives is of little comfort to leaders in the Islamic world, who are facing the strongest possible demands from their people that something be done to prevent the peace and the explosion of the bomb.

New York Standard

Jack laughed. "It's hardly the Pentagon, is it?"

As the car he'd been riding in pulled to a stop, Jack's judgment of the UK Ministry of Defence headquarters was met with a few nods of agreement by his companions. Squat and grey, the building was about a dozen stories tall and offered little to distinguish itself from other government buildings the convoy had driven past. There was plenty to see in London, but the administration buildings of Whitehall weren't high on the list.

He waited while two of his escorts climbed out of the vehicle and secured the surrounds, an action mimicked by pairs from the other two vehicles. When prompted by the security detail, Jack opened the door and exited the vehicle, pulling his coat tight to guard against the chill.

Careful not to get in the way of his guards, Jack started toward the entrance as the six Navy SEALS fanned out, weapons gripped tightly as they scanned their surroundings.

Jack wasn't used to heavily armed SEALs escorting him wherever he went, but he didn't have a choice in the matter. As soon as he'd left the meeting with Gharazi, Jack had flown to the United Kingdom aboard a US Government jet. He'd never expected to be alone on a jet with a fighter escort, and upon landing there had been more surprises – Chen and a US Navy SEAL team waiting for him at Heathrow Airport.

"You're kidding me!" Jack put his hands on his hips when he saw who was waiting for them at the entrance of the building. His alarm caused several of the SEALs to raise their weapons at the woman – an entirely bad idea. "Cool it, guys, she's a friendly."

Anna Fowler glanced at the SEALs as they lowered their weapons, then smiled at him. "Hi, Jack. I should introduce myself. I'm Anna Fowler"

"The surprises keep on coming, don't they?" Jack sighed. "At least I know your surname now. Though I guess I shouldn't be surprised that you skulked back."

She winked at him. "Actually, I flew home first class. Not as nice as the jet you flew in on, but better than I usually get. Follow me. These guys stay outside."

Jack wanted to take issue with her ordering him around, given the mischief she'd caused, but he fell in behind her. Chen followed too, but the SEAL team remained outside. As they walked deeper into the bowels of the Ministry of Defence, the group caught some sideways glances from military and civilian staff. Jack barely noticed. His mind felt cloudy and he was struggling to process how Anna was back in his life after screwing him over so heartily.

She appeared to have landed on her feet, in her job, back home. While he had no proof, he was certain she was behind the death of Zed Eshkol. It was also very likely she was the one who'd found out about the location of the bombs and the Zionist plot to launch the missiles aboard HMS *Vigilant*. Swings and roundabouts. It made sense now, but he felt it would have been nice of McGhinnist or the NSC to tell him the whole story.

"We're here." Anna stopped outside an office, which had no sign or nameplate on the door she knocked on.

"What's the story?" Jack's eyes narrowed, searching her face for an indication of what she was up to. He didn't like being in the dark.

The door opened and two men stepped into the hallway. One of them, in a simple black suit, spoke to Anna. "This them?"

Anna took a small step back. "Jack Emery, sirs, along with Chen Shubian and a half-dozen Navy SEAL troops waiting outside."

"Mr. Emery, good to meet you. Your exploits have made for very interesting reading over the years." A British naval officer with a fruit salad worth of medals on his chest held out his hand. "Shame it's not under better circumstances, but we're glad you're here."

Jack shook the other man's hand. "Nice to meet you, Mr ..."

"Admiral Duncan Fraser, First Sea Lord and Chief of the Naval Staff." Fraser gestured toward his suited companion. "And this is Director Cunningham, MI6."

"Good to meet you, gentlemen." Jack shook Cunningham's hand. "This is Chen, my advisor."

"Advisor? Okay. Let's go with that." Cunningham raised an eyebrow and gave a slight smirk, showing he knew some of Chen's past. "We should get to work."

Jack nodded and followed them into a deceptively large office, where the five of them took seats on the large sofas inside. The UK Ambassador to the United States had ensured McGhinnist that Jack would have all necessary briefings and information once he arrived in London. Here, he'd find out exactly what was at stake over the next seventy-two hours. And how to stop it. Both governments were united in their effort to stop the Zionists, despite the moles in their ranks.

Cunningham spoke first. "As you know, Mr. Emery, we've got a missing ballistic missile submarine – HMS *Vigilant* – with a rogue commander aboard. Our fears were confirmed thanks to Ms. Fowler's efforts on US soil. This has potentially catastrophic ramifications."

Jack decided to leave the topic of Anna's actions to his superiors. Spy games between friendly powers wasn't the major issue here. "The ambassador wasn't clear about how the boat could launch in the absence of a clear, verified order. I was speaking to some of the SEALs, and US subs can't—"

"Britain isn't America." Fraser's voice was sharp. "Not all of our launch protocols are the same."

Jack shrugged. "Okay, explain it to me then. How can the submarine fire off a few nukes without an order to do so?"

Fraser let out a long breath and then leaned forward. "Your escorts were right about one aspect of a launch: under normal circumstances a British nuclear launch is as restricted as an American one. An order must be sent from the Prime Minister down through the chain of command to the sub, verified at each step along the way."

"It feels like there's a 'but' at the end of that."

Fraser nodded. "British ballistic missile submarines have a secondary safe, inside the safe holding the usual launch codes. Inside that safe is what's called a Dead Man Letter. These letters are written by the Prime Minister and personally addressed to the submarine's captain."

"This sounds ominous." Jack sighed.

"The letter contains orders for what action the captain should take in the event that Britain is attacked and command structures compromised."

"So it's like one giant dead man switch, then?" Jack scoffed. "No offence, but that sounds mad."

"Exactly." Cunningham ran a hand through his hair. "Revenge from beyond the grave. Not all that far removed from the Israeli Samson Option that's plaguing us."

"So how does this apply here? Unless the Zionists have turned the Prime Minister, or they have the capability to flatten Britain, there's no way to trigger either a launch order or the Dead Man Letter. If the captain tries to do it in the absence of an order, his crew will see right through him." Jack paused. "Right?"

"Not quite, and what I'm about to tell you has never been shared with a non-British citizen." Cunningham glanced at Chen and then back to Jack. "Despite my better judgment, I've been instructed to do so here. But this information is highly classified, as is your role in what's to come. Understood?"

Jack nodded and then looked left at Chen, who did the same. "Consider the riot act read."

Cunningham nodded. "Okay. Associated with the Dead Man Letters are a set of conditions that act as a test for our submarine captains, to tell them whether or not Britain is still intact. If all of those conditions are tested by the captain, and each fails, then he's to open the safe and the letter and proceed as ordered."

Jack's eyes widened. He couldn't quite believe that a king-sized salvo of nukes could be launched from a British sub by reading a letter. But, as Cunningham spoke, it became clear that the conditions for such a launch were quite specific. Cunningham detailed each, but Jack was unable to make notes or do anything but memorize them. The more Cunningham spoke, the more daunting a challenge was painted in Jack's head. Finally, the MI6 boss fell silent.

"It's clear that, in the absence of a launch order from the Prime Minister, the Zionists are going to create the preconditions for a launch using Cohen's Dead Man Letter." Jack looked from Fraser to Cunningham to Chen to Anna. "Do we know what the letter says?"

"Yes, we do." Fraser smiled sadly. "Turns out the lady we have isn't for turning, as it were. The Prime Minister has informed us that the letter orders a launch."

Jack sighed. "So we need to fight like hell to defend a few of those things and stop the letter from being opened."

Cunningham smiled. "Our thoughts exactly. Unfortunately, several targets have already been assaulted by Zionist attackers."

Jack frowned. "How did we not know about—"

"The British secret services still have much to be proud of." Cunningham waved a hand. "I suggest we focus on those targets that remain to be protected."

Cunningham spent thirty minutes detailing nearly a dozen targets that the Zionists would need to hit in order to make a Dead Man Letter launch viable. Some had already been hit, but only one needed to still be standing in seventy-two hours to deny Cohen the conditions he needed to open that safe, convince his crew and launch his missiles. The task was daunting, but Jack thought a country like Britain, with all its resources, should be able to pull it off.

"Why not just drop a battalion on top of each target? Put so many guns between the Zionists and their targets, it's impossible?"

Fraser shrugged. "Several targets have already been attacked by Zionist hit teams. Others have been hit by those who were supposed to be guarding them – friendly fire. We're doing our best to pick out any Zionist weeds from our security apparatus, but we're not sure who we can trust. We've found dozens already."

Jack whistled slowly as his mind processed the new information. He'd underestimated the extent of the Zionist penetration, particularly given they'd turned Tipping and a nuclear submarine captain, but the prospect of not being able to deploy armies or police forces because of that infiltration was terrifying. It was no surprise that the British had asked for America's help – there was no other way they could guarantee full coverage of the targets by friendly forces.

"So if we can't guarantee that the good guys are good guys, how can we defend the targets needed to activate the Dead Man Letters?"

"Pick two or three and focus on those." Chen spoke for the first time. "Against a capable infiltrator, if you try to protect all of them, you'll end up protecting none."

Cunningham and Fraser smiled at each other, then the admiral spoke. "Our thoughts exactly. We will deploy trusted assets at as many sites as we can, knowing that they could fall to direct Zionist assault or friendly infiltration. If we can keep a few standing, we'll win."

Cunningham smiled, then turned to the others. "On the most vital targets I intend to use you three, your SEAL team and the most reliable MI6 agents I have."

Jack turned and stared at Chen, who nodded, then turned back to the Britons. "Makes sense to me."

"All the other targets are expendable if we focus on three." Cunningham held up three fingers. "Our focus must be, firstly, protecting BBC Radio 4. Its longwave broadcasts are one of the preconditions required to open the letter. Second, we protect the Prime Minister, whose death or incapacitation is another."

"And third?" Jack raised an eyebrow.

Fraser smiled. "The Prime Minister's designated second."

"Who would that be?"

"Classified." Cunningham's voice was matter of fact.

Jack laughed. "Nice to know you'll use us, but won't fully trust us."

Fraser was completely deadpan. "We're British, Mr. Emery. We don't trust anyone. You wouldn't be in this room at all if the situation weren't so dire, but we need your help. Unfortunately, at this moment, for protecting these targets, I trust my own countrymen even less."

"Where to now, then?" Jack felt everything was getting a bit too heavy. "Any idea where they'll hit first?"

Fraser's eyes bored into him. "You'll head to the BBC shortly, once we finish your briefing. We hope the PM's security is enough, and her second isn't known."

"Like it or not, Jack." Anna placed a hand on his knee. "You and I may well be the last line of defense."

∽

Aron grunted at the strain of lifting the heavy toolbox out of the back of the utility, then turned to face the rest of his team. The ten of them were all dressed in coveralls and had a variety of tools, bags and toolboxes in their hands. They looked like a very large maintenance team. Miri Shaked was the only one he knew well, but Zed Eshkol had hand selected the others for this job, which was good enough for Aron.

"You look good in a uniform." Miri smiled. "I think you missed your calling in life, Aron."

Aron laughed. "I much prefer the line of work I'm in. There's more chance to see the world."

"For another few days, anyway." Miri turned to Broadcasting House. "Let's get going?"

Aron nodded and gestured for the others to follow. They fell in behind him, leaving their three utilities parked on All Souls' Place, and crossed the street to the entrance of Broadcasting House. As he walked, Aron noted the number of heavily armed police outside the building, hoping again that Zed had selected the right crew. Though the attack on the BBC required precision rather than brute force, he'd still prefer to have talented people along if things went poorly.

As he walked deeper inside the horseshoe-shaped grounds, Aron smiled at the old sandstone architecture that was mixed with modern steel and glass. As they drew closer to the entrance, one police officer stepped forward while several of his colleagues half-raised their submachine guns toward Aron and his team. Aron held up a hand. The entire team stopped and waited for the police to act.

"Hold it there." The lead officer stopped squarely in front of them. "I'll need to see identification and a work order."

Aron placed his toolbox on the ground. "Something wrong, officer? The administration booked us for this job a month ago."

"Precautions." The officer gestured at all of the contractors. "Must be a big job you guys are doing?"

"You could say that." Aron made a show of digging around in the pockets of his coveralls. He pulled out his wallet and some sheets of paper he'd folded up and handed them to the officer. As he did, the other members of the team dug out their identification.

"Okay, we'll just be a minute." The officer turned and walked back to his colleagues.

Aron waited, a little nervously, as several police officers checked the orders and the identification. The officer who'd taken their papers used his radio, no doubt checking the legitimacy of the work order and the identification of the contractors. While he was confident that it would all check out, Aron never liked jobs that were quite so public, because all it took was one mistake for the bullets to start flying.

Not today, though. The officer walked over to them and handed back the identification and the work orders. "Everything checks out."

Aron smiled as he found his fake identification and pocketed it, along with the work orders. "Lot of you guys here today. Security drill?"

"If only." The officer didn't share the humor. "I'll leave you all to it, you're free to enter. Have a good day and please keep to your designated areas."

Aron nodded, lifted the toolbox and resumed his walk. Once they were inside the lobby, it became clear that the majority of the extra security was outside – a very public show of force. While Eshkol's selection of the BBC as a target was somewhat confusing, Aron didn't question it. It was clear that British authorities were beefing up security at key sites in London. That changed nothing. He had intelligence from other moles and the team to get the job done.

They made their way through the lobby and into a relatively quiet hallway. Aron placed his toolbox on the ground for the last time. He opened it and pulled out the pair of machine pistols inside, then looked around to make sure the rest of his team were preparing themselves. Each of them had armed themselves with whatever small firearm they preferred. In addition, Aron spotted blades, grenades and explosives. They all pulled on balaclavas, then gathered tightly.

"Everyone ready?" Aron hefted the machine pistols and was answered by a set of nods. "We meet back at the utilities in ten minutes. Let's go."

The team split off into pairs. Two went to guard the front entrance. Another pair went to kill the alarms. The remaining groups prepared for the assault. Aron jogged toward his assigned target with Miri right behind him. They were there within moments, passing only a few shocked staff members along the way. Apart from squealing, the BBC employees hugged the walls and did nothing to stop them as they passed.

He paused near a door and looked at Miri, who lifted her pistol and gave a nod. Aron pushed the door open and entered the room, firing a couple of shots into the air from each of his machine pistols. The effect was instantaneous. Staff looked up from their desks and meeting tables, shock and fear painted on their faces, then either ran away or cowered in corners or under their desks. It didn't matter to Aron which they chose, the end result was inevitable.

He mowed down every member of the radio production staff he could find. The machine pistol in his left hand found a young blond woman. The one in his right found an older man. Left and right. Some ran, others cowered. He didn't worry about those who he'd missed, because Miri picked each off with a single shot before they could escape the room. It was over in less than a minute. The room fell silent and no alarms rang out.

"Take care of this equipment?" Aron turned to Miri as he reloaded both of his pistols in turn. "I'll take care of the studio."

Aron turned and walked to the end of the floor, where a closed door had an on air sign lit brightly above it. He pushed the door open and kept his machine pistol raised as he walked inside. The studio was dimly lit, but he could see one man cowering under the desk in the room. Aron fired a long burst toward him, then stepped inside and placed one of his pistols down on the desk as he dug the explosives out of the pockets of his coveralls.

As he placed the bombs on the equipment, he absentmindedly looked around the studio. It was hard to understand why Eshkol wanted this target flattened as part of his contingency plan, but it had proven easier than Aron had expected. The other members of his team who'd paired off were similarly gunning down key staff and destroying equipment. At the end of the raid, the intent was to take BBC Radio 4 off the air.

He placed two charges at opposite sides of the room, then left the studio. Back in the office spaces, Miri had finished her demolition job on other equipment and was waiting for him. He checked his watch – seven minutes down – then pointed at the door they'd entered through. She nodded and they walked together into the hall and back to the lobby. As they drew closer, Aron could hear gunfire – probably the police trying to force their way into the building.

He paused near the end of the hallway that led into the lobby. He tossed his machine pistols into the trash and then did the same with his balaclava. A quick check of his pockets showed that he had nothing incriminating left. When Miri had done the same, he held up a hand and they waited in silence. After a few moments, the gunfire ceased, only screams and piercing cries of fear and warning able to be heard.

He looked at his watch – ten minutes. "Time to go."

"Do it." Miri's voice was hard.

They ran out of the hallway and into the lobby, where a stream of civilians were rushing toward police, who shouted at them to freeze and put up their hands. Aron raised his hands high and stayed in the middle of the pack streaming toward the exit. The police had a choice – get out of the way or start shooting – and they chose the predictable path. They stepped aside and let the civilians move past them, out of the lobby and into the streets.

Aron spotted the police officer who'd let them in – his face was cut. He stopped next to the man. "What's going on?"

The officer glanced at Aron but didn't really look at him, his eyes scanning for threats as he gripped his submachine gun. "Terrorists. Get out of here."

Aron smiled slightly and nodded. He didn't look back as he made his way out of Broadcasting House and toward the utilities. Miri was alongside him and he could see another pair already at the vehicles. With some luck, there would only be a few lives lost among his team. But whatever the result, there wouldn't be much time to rest, because the assault on the next target was scheduled for tomorrow.

Mentally, he checked one more item off Zed Eshkol's list. He didn't envy the British authorities trying to figure it all out.

∼

JACK WALKED BEHIND ANNA, Chen and the Navy SEALs as they approached Broadcasting House, which was surrounded by armed police and vehicles with flashing lights and blaring sirens. The BBC headquarters had been attacked while he'd been in briefings. On the way over, the radio reports had been bleak – many were dead and critical equipment had been destroyed. The minute they'd seen the building, Jack had known it was too late.

"This is pointless." Jack gestured to the building, where police officers were doing their best to manage the throng of civilians that milled outside and the rush of emergency services in and out. "We need to move on to protecting the next target."

"Hold up." Anna placed an arm on his shoulder. "We don't know the situation yet, we can't rush in. The Prime Minister is okay, for now, and the terrorists don't know who her second is. We need to find out what happened here before we move on. The information about this attack might be the key to stopping the next."

Jack pushed her arm away. "The BBC is done for as far as the Dead Man Letters are concerned, but we can still stop the next attack!"

"Be patient, Jack. You're panicking." Her eyes narrowed. She handed him the pistol she was carrying. "Take this, I've got another. We work out what happened here and then move out to defend the next target. That's how we're going to play this, okay?"

He nodded, but didn't like it. If he was in charge, they'd rush straight on to defend either the PM or her designated second, but Anna was the boss. He took the weapon. A few years ago, he'd have been horrified by the idea of handling it, but now it was a no-brainer. It felt good having some steel in his hand, and he hefted the weapon as one of the SEALs handed Chen a pistol. They kept moving until they reached the outer checkpoint.

"*Stop and drop the weapons!*" Several police officers manning the checkpoint aimed their weapons and shouted at Jack and his group. "*This area is restricted!*"

"Take it easy!" Jack screamed as loudly as he could, to be heard over the shouts of the police officers. "We're friendlies!"

The police continued to target them, while the SEALs pointed carbines right back. Jack cursed. Though they'd probably win a firefight, they didn't have time for this – with each passing second there was more chance of the Zionists attacking their next target. He lifted his pistol with his thumb through the trigger guard, and kept his palms pointed out. It did no good – the SEALs didn't back down and the police didn't budge.

Anna mimicked his actions and slowly stepped forward. "We're here under authorization of the director of MI6. Can I show you?"

Several of the officers hesitated and a couple of them looked at each other, until one waved Anna forward. Jack stood, frozen in place, watching her cross no-man's-land to talk to the police. He couldn't hear what was being said, but after a moment she dug into her pocket and flashed some identification. As if by magic, the police attention melted away – the cops lowered their weapons and waved Jack and the others forward.

Jack led the group into the lobby of Broadcasting House. It was chaos. Police were everywhere, paramedics treated the wounded, several bodies lay uncovered and the few BBC staff who hadn't been allowed to leave appeared to be in shock. Jack looked at Anna. She nodded and led him toward the largest bunch of people in the room – a group of two police and a handful of BBC staff. The SEALs fanned out to cover the room while Chen looked around.

"Anna Fowler, MI6." Anna flashed the ID again – probably a rare occurrence for a secret agent – then jerked a thumb at Jack. "This is Jack Emery."

The most senior of the police officers nodded at Anna, though his eyes narrowed at the presence of a British secret service agent. "DCI Fiskin."

"What's the situation?" Jack slid his pistol down the back of his jeans. "We're in a bit of a hurry."

Fiskin nodded. "We're still trying to figure that out, Mr. Emery, but around ten attackers shot up the staff and studios. We've contained the scene and two of the attackers are dead, but it's all a bit chaotic. There's been significant damage to the facility and we've no idea where the other gunmen went."

Anna frowned. "You didn't capture or kill the attackers? How did that happen, exactly?"

"A mistake from one of my officers." Fiskin shrugged. "He tried to save civilians by letting those inside evacuate, but it looks like he let the terrorists escape as well."

Jack cursed. "Any chance of—"

An officer interrupted Jack, running up to the group with an iPad in his hand. "DCI Fiskin, we've got the footage from the camera feed."

"Show us." Fiskin gestured for them to gather round the officer, who played the video.

The video feed showed several gunmen with balaclavas mowing down civilians indiscriminately. Man, woman, old, young – everyone received the same treatment. If Jack hadn't known the Zionist endgame in attacking the BBC – the eradication of the entire network, but particularly longwave Radio 4 broadcasts – it would look like an indiscriminate office massacre. Instead, it just looked like they'd been thorough.

"They weren't messing around." Jack ran a hand through his hair. He'd worked in enough news rooms for all this to feel a bit too real. He thought of Celeste.

"Is the network compromised?" Anna looked up from the iPad. "Is the main broadcasting equipment intact?"

One of the BBC staff standing near Fiskin spoke up. "You're worried about the World Service? A hundred people just got killed!"

Jack glared at the man. "And a whole lot more will die if you don't get on with it. What's the status of BBC radio, particularly the longwave?"

The man snarled, but Fiskin put a hand on his arm and the BBC employee took a deep breath. Once he'd composed himself, he spoke. "It's all down. The equipment is as dead as most of the people who know how to use it, not that you care about them."

Jack ignored the crack. "We need to get it back online. I know it sounds callous, but you can't comprehend how important this is."

The man shook his head and turned away from Jack. It was hard not to feel sorry for him, given he'd just had his workplace shot up and his colleagues killed, but there was no time for sentiment. With each passing minute the chances of the Zionists bringing down the list of targets required to activate the Dead Man Letters increased. The minute that happened, there would be nothing that could be done to prevent a launch. They'd witness the end of the world.

Anna sighed, stepped forward and placed a hand on the man's shoulder. "What are the chances?"

"Of getting back online now?" The man shrugged off her touch and had tears streaking down his cheeks as he turned to face them. "None. We'll be lucky if we're up in a week. I don't think any of you understand the damage they've caused here."

She took half a step back. "Can we get the longwave signal up again?"

"No."

The longwave BBC Radio 4 signal was one of the checks British submarine captains went through to determine whether British society had been annihilated. If the signal was down, and Joseph Cohen did the check, he was one step closer to being able to crack open the safe and use the Dead Man Letter. Cunningham, Fraser, Anna, Chen and Jack had agreed to focus on preventing three of the preconditions from being met and, less than an hour later, one had already fallen.

"We're wasting our time here, Anna." Jack exhaled deeply. "We need to focus on the other two."

She nodded and then addressed DCI Fiskin and his colleagues. "Thanks for your time and good luck with the clean-up."

Jack stepped to the side and waited for her to join him. He spoke as firmly as he could. "I know the PM is the next target we're meant to be protecting, but I need to know the third. We can't act if we're not on the same page, and I'm out of the loop here."

She frowned. "Fraser and Cunningham swore me to secrecy, Jack. Nobody else in the entire United Kingdom besides the PM, the four captains, Cunningham, Fraser and I know who it is. I thought we'd deal with it if and when something happened to the PM."

"I need the name, Anna." Jack crossed his arms. He wasn't taking no for an answer. "The Prime Minister has a shit-ton of protection around her, I'm sure. If the attack against her succeeds, it will be in spite of anything we can do to help. But we can help to protect her second, if you let us."

Anna's eyes bored into him, then she nodded. She pulled a cell phone from her pocket, dialed and lifted it to her ear. In muted tones, she spoke about orders and about how much she could tell Jack. He assumed it was Cunningham on the other end, and the uptight director of MI6 was doing his best to stonewall her, until right at the end of the call she cursed loudly and hung up. She closed her eyes and took a deep breath.

"What's wrong?"

"Two more targets hit by traitors. We're running out of parachutes on this one, Jack." She shook her head. "Cunningham authorized me to tell you."

"Tell me what?"

"It's Patrick Ho. The PM's second is the Minister of State for Employment. We're to protect him at all costs."

CHAPTER 18

With potential nuclear catastrophe just a few days away, the attack on Broadcasting House has tipped the United Kingdom into outright panic. The Zionists have claimed responsibility for this and other attacks, though their motive is unclear. Added to this are reports of Zionist moles being uncovered throughout the government, causing havoc. In response to the attacks and nuclear threat, Britain has raised its threat level to Critical. Prime Minister Katherine Huxley has called for Britons and the world to remain resolute in the face of tyranny.

New York Standard

Jack handed the binoculars to Anna. "Seems quiet. Want to take a look?"

She nodded and used the binoculars to scan their surroundings – the front of the building, its visible windows, the surrounding rooftops and the street below – then lowered them, apparently satisfied that things were safe. Jack was glad he hadn't missed anything, but she was a professional with years of experience. As Anna placed the binoculars on the ground beside him and rubbed her eyes, he wondered how many times she'd been the one trying to crack security just like this during her time in MI6.

Jack didn't know how cops did this for a living, because every minute felt like torture. Cunningham and Fraser had been adamant: the

Minister for Employment couldn't be told about the threat unless it was absolutely necessary. Instead, Jack and Anna had been camped out since the previous evening, watching his office for any signs of danger. The SEAL team were similarly placed and a few trustworthy MI6 assets had also covered the minister's home. Minister Ho was wrapped tight in a security blanket he didn't know existed.

While they'd waited, cooling their heels and protecting the minister, other Zionist targets had fallen. Though the PM and Minister Ho were safe, a mix of armed assaults and infiltrations had steadily shrunk the safety net underneath the tightrope they were walking on. Each time Anna received a notification, her anger seemed to increase slightly, along with Jack's determination. He'd realized quickly that Fraser and Cunningham had been right to fear the extent of Zionist infiltration of Britain. He was feeling paranoid himself.

"You alright?" Jack studied Anna's face and saw deep bags under her eyes.

She took a sip of the coffee and winced. "Cold."

"It was cold an hour ago." He laughed. "You should rest."

"I'll rest when the world survives the greatest threat to its existence since the Cuban Missile Crisis." She took a second sip of the coffee, obviously deciding caffeine was more important than taste or temperature. "We fucked up, letting them hit the BBC."

Jack nodded. The result of the attack had been immediate. All BBC radio broadcasts had been affected and the likelihood of them returning before deadline were slim. Even though other assets were covering other likely Zionist targets, Cunningham had placed the only people he could fully trust in one place – protecting Minister Ho. It was a gutsy call, but Jack figured Cunningham was used to those. He wondered if he'd have made the same decisions as McGhinnist, Huxley, Schiller and others along the way, but parked the thought.

"He's pulling up." Anna edged closer to the window. "I can see the chase car, no sign of a threat, all looking good."

"Fingers crossed it stays that way." Jack glanced out the window to see the minister's sedan pulling to a stop in front of his office building.

The radio on the floor next to Anna and Jack crackled. *"This is Defender Four. The package is on site. Over."*

Anna picked up the radio. "Confirmed Defender Four, we'll take it from here. Over."

Jack watched as the black sedan that had been trailing the minister's

SUV kept driving, even as the minister started to climb out of his vehicle. It seemed a stupid risk not to squirrel him away somewhere to protect him from the Zionists, or at least tell the minister that his life was in danger, but the orders had been clear. Jack caressed the pistol Anna had given him back at the BBC studios and had made no effort to reclaim. If things got hairy here, there'd be nobody but him, Chen, Anna and a team of SEALs to protect the minister.

"Is it possible the Zionists don't know who the Prime Minister's designated second is?" Jack turned from watching the car and raised his eyebrows at Anna.

"Possible, sure." She shrugged her shoulders. "But they've shown a knack for kicking us in the teeth, so I'm not banking on it."

"Let's make a bet?" Jack smiled. "If we get out of this and the entire world isn't irradiated, I'll buy you a beer."

"Are you good for it?" She laughed. "I wouldn't want to—"

Jack instinctively turned his head and shielded his eyes as the world in front of him exploded in light and fire. The flash was followed by a terrible boom and sudden pain as the shattered window cut into his arms. He dropped to his hands and knees, his ears ringing and his lungs on fire. He coughed several times, but couldn't expel the dust and the other debris. He shook his head and tried to clear it, then glanced at Anna. She fumbled with the radio and Jack watched her speak into it but, strangely, couldn't hear what she was saying.

He crawled to the windowsill, which he gripped and used to pull himself up. As he did, the ringing in his ears slowly subsided. Once his eyes were level with the window he stared, mouth wide open, at the scene on the street below. Where the minister's car had been there was now just a blackened, flaming metal husk. The street was filled with smoke and victims splayed on the ground, while those who could still move ran from the scene. His eyes scanned the area for the minister, but Jack couldn't see him.

Anna gripped his shoulder and shouted close to his ear. "Grab your gun, Jack, we need to get down there."

He nodded and searched for the pistol, which he'd dropped as he'd gone down. He found it and then looked at her. "I'm ready."

"One more thing." She tore at her white blouse, which was stained and grimy from the explosion. She grabbed hold of his arm. "Hold still."

"Okay."

She wrapped a strip of cloth around the cuts on his arm, pulled it tight and then tied it. "It's only a temporary solution, but it'll do. Let's go."

He gripped the pistol as he followed her out of the stakeout and down the fire stairs. He pulled up short at the emergency exit, where Anna had paused to look at him. She raised an eyebrow, as if asking if he was ready, and Jack nodded. The door opened with a tortured squeal and Jack followed Anna out, down the lane and onto the main street. It was chaos. Flames licked the carcass of the minister's vehicle and debris was scattered throughout the street.

"Defender Actual is heading for the minister." Anna spoke into the radio in her hand as she ran, holding the pistol in the other.

"Defender One, no hostiles."

"Defender Two, we got nothing."

"Defender Three, nothing."

"Copy." She clipped the radio onto her belt, gripped her pistol with both hands and kept moving forward, a look of grim determination on her face.

Jack and Anna crossed the street and rounded the minister's vehicle, which continued to burn. Jack wanted to know how the Zionists had rigged the bomb in the minister's car, but it was moot now. Ho was face down on the pavement twenty feet from his vehicle, bloodied and unmoving. A couple of other casualties from the blast were scattered about, but there was no time to worry about anyone other than the minister – the world depended on it.

"I'll check him out." Jack pointed at the minister and then glanced at Anna. "You work on getting us some help."

"On it." She turned away from Jack, talking into her radio but never lowering her pistol.

Jack crouched beside Minister Ho, placing the pistol on the pavement beside the downed man. He gripped the other man's wrist and exhaled deeply when he felt a strong, steady pulse. Jack rolled the minister over, opened his suit jacket and felt around for any major wounds caused by shrapnel from the exploding vehicle. Thankfully, despite the blood, the wounds appeared minor. Ho had been knocked unconscious by the blast but was otherwise remarkably lucky.

"How is he?" Anna slid down alongside Jack. "Is he alive?"

"Fine, as far as I can tell." Jack looked sideways at her. "We need to move."

"Support is two minutes out and your SEALs are converging on our posit—"

"Who are you people?"

Jack's eyes darted back to the minister, who was blinking quickly and looking back and forth between him and Anna. "Minister, you're okay."

Anna leaned in closer. "Your vehicle exploded, sir. We've secured the scene and we're working to get you out of here."

"Oh, I understand."

Jack wasn't sure the minister could comprehend anything right now, judging from the look in his eyes. "Just relax, sir."

Jack could hear the hint of sirens off into the distance. He looked at Anna, who nodded. Help was on the way. They smiled at each other. Both knew that as long as either the PM or the Minister for Employment was alive and in contact, then all the terrorist attacks in the world couldn't get HMS *Vigilant* to launch its payload. As it was, he doubted they'd manage to get another bomb this close to Minister Ho, meaning that the Zionists had given the launch their best shot and failed. It had been a close call, but Jack felt like they'd caught a break.

And without that launch, the Zionist plot couldn't succeed, no matter how much chaos they caused in Britain.

～

Aron looked down at his watch and then up at his team. "Any moment now. Make sure you're ready. We'll only have a small window."

He was met with nods and grim faces as his six men and Miri went to work, checking their weapons and body armor. He looked down at his own weapon, a carbine far larger than the machine pistols he preferred. As he checked the weapon, he was glad for the distraction. It helped to keep his mind off the fact that this was most likely a one-way mission for all of them – a Hail Mary pass that had almost no chance of success but had to be thrown if they were going to win the game. Aron didn't know the reason, but the order was enough.

"Everyone is ready, Aron." Miri seemed to read his mind, but spoke softly enough that only the two of them could hear. "Trust in Eshkol, in us and yourself."

He looked at her and searched her eyes for doubt, but found none. He cursed himself for his weakness. Before he'd met Zed Eshkol, Aron would have found fanciful the idea that a small team on foot could assassinate the British Prime Minister, but he had to trust in the professor. Aron swallowed hard and warded off the negative thoughts. Eshkol knew what he was doing and Aron's team would succeed. They had to. To come this far and then fail was not a possibility he was prepared to entertain.

After the attack on Broadcasting House, they'd driven away in their utilities and then dumped them after less than five minutes on the road. They'd gone to ground in a nearby apartment building, where they'd cleaned up and rested in preparation for another attack. The apartment had been long readied for this purpose, less than a five-minute walk to Downing Street and packed full of guns and ammo. It was the perfect staging post for an attack on the Prime Minister of the United Kingdom.

It had one other thing of immense value. Aron gripped his gun and crossed the room to where a number of desktop PCs displayed feeds from webcams placed around the city. He leaned in to look and a smile broke out across his face as he watched a portion of the extra security forces around Downing Street rush away. It had all gone perfectly – a bomb timed to injure but not kill the Minister for Employment, stripping enough security away from the Prime Minister to let Aron and his team do what needed doing.

Aron smiled wider. "They're not sure who they can trust, so there's only a handful of men and women they can throw at problems."

"That's the problem when everything you know has been infiltrated and compromised." Miri laughed. "Zed has played it well."

"Time to go." He lifted his carbine again and turned to his team. "I don't know why Eshkol wants these two dead so badly, but it's not our job to ask why."

"We're ready, Aron." Miri touched his arm. "We'll take out Huxley and then deal with the Minister for Employment."

Aron nodded and led his team downstairs, where black sedans were idling with additional Zionists, fresh from other jobs, at the wheel. They drove in silence to Downing Street. Less than half a mile from the target, Aron gripped the overhead handle with one hand and his carbine with the other, shocked that they'd been able to get this close without being intercepted. He looked at his watch one last time, then lowered the gas mask resting on his head over his face.

As the sedans skidded to a halt next to a large yellow bulldozer, Aron nodded at Miri then opened the door and led his team out of their ride. Those in the other sedan did likewise, and shouts and gunfire started to boom out from the remaining defenders of Downing Street as the Zionists made for safety behind the construction vehicle. The minute he was joined behind the slab of steel by the rest of his team, Aron readied the underslung grenade launcher on his carbine.

"Launch tear gas." Aron spoke softly into his voice-activated headset. "And get the 'dozer moving."

Aron looked around. As the large bulldozer's engine turned over and started, Aron lifted his carbine and joined his team in lobbing gas canisters over the steel security fence blocking them from Downing Street. Each round launched with a *thunk*, exploded with a pop and hissed as they released the gas inside. The team had fired several dozen canisters inside of thirty seconds and when Aron peeked around the bulldozer he could see little but the gas.

The bulldozer's engine roared and the vehicle rolled forward. Already Aron could hear the rattle of gunfire and the hail-on-the-roof pinging of rounds against the bulldozer's scoop. Aron and the other Zionists advanced behind the giant slab of steel, unable to see anything past the bucket, but the crude cover worked to get them right to the gate. The bulldozer hit the fence with a crunch, which gave a sickening squeal as it strained against the force.

As the bulldozer shifted up a gear and pushed harder against the fence, Aron turned his attention to the defenders. It was a slaughter. Gunfire roared from his team as police and other security forces staggered in the street and were cut down. Aron wondered if the attack on the Minister for Employment had even been necessary. With such a brute display of force, it was possible that this would have worked without the ruse.

The gate groaned one final time, crashing against the road as the bulldozer came to a stop and the driver killed the engine. Aron peeked around it as silence fell in the street. Nothing moved except for the final wisps of dissipating tear gas. He grinned like a hyena as he reached up, removed his gas mask and tossed it to the ground. His team did likewise and started to advance, weapons raised, toward the famed tenth house on this very special street.

The team rushed the short distance between the gate and the Prime Minister's residence in a few seconds, then paired off and covered Miri as she moved to the door. Aron half expected another threat to emerge – snipers or reinforcements – but all was calm until he heard two dull thumps as the shaped charges did their work. He turned to face the door. It was wide open and Miri was standing next to it.

"Miri, Vadim, Abram – with me." Aron ejected the magazine from his weapon and reloaded. "The rest of you, cover our rear."

As those left outside took up defensive positions, Aron looked at his watch and led the smaller team inside with his carbine raised. They rushed through the house quicker than he'd like, but the clock was ticking. He fired a quick burst at one defender – dropping him – and Miri dropped two targets before they reached the back of the house. Aron breathed a sigh of relief when he saw British Prime Minister Katherine Huxley standing with her hands held out, showing no threat.

"Ms. Prime Minister." Aron halted a few steps away from her.

"Just who the hell are you?" Huxley hissed at them.

"It doesn't matter." Aron raised his carbine and pointed it at Huxley's chest.

"Britain doesn't negotiate with terrorists." Huxley nearly spat the words.

"Oh, I don't want to negotiate." Aron laughed. "I just want you dead."

"I—"

Aron squeezed the trigger of his carbine. The weapon chattered as it delivered a three-round burst into the Prime Minister's chest, a process repeated by his colleagues. Huxley's body toppled to the ground. A pool of blood was already forming and Aron could smell the stench of death – evacuated bowels – but he had to be sure. He took a step closer and fired a single round into her head.

"Time to go." Aron started toward the entrance as he looked down at his watch. "We're thirty seconds behind schedule."

He ran to the front of the house as quickly as he could while still being alert for any threat. Once outside, he was relieved to see the helicopters already grounded and half of his team already onboard. He rushed toward the second chopper and was the last inside after Miri. He slid the door shut and the pilot didn't waste one second in taking off. Less than a minute after they'd killed the PM, they were in the air.

Miri smiled at him and gave him a quizzical look. He knew instinctively what she was asking – whether it was safe to fly above London, having just killed the British PM. He nodded back to her, gave a thumbs-up and then turned away. Even if the Royal Air Force was zooming around in the sky, Aron was confident that Zed Eshkol had taken care of it. He had students – assets – everywhere and had proven to be in control.

Aron knew, whatever the final plan, it would succeed.

JACK'S EYES shot open and he sat up in a flash, looking for the source of the loud bang that had woken him from the deepest sleep he'd had in days. He slowly let out the breath he'd sucked in as he turned his head to stare at Anna Fowler. She had her head in her hands and was visibly shaking. He sighed and rubbed his eyes, then glanced down at the phone she'd tossed onto the floor of the vehicle. It was still lit up brightly as he leaned down and picked it up.

"Sorry." She opened her eyes and looked at him, then reached up and ran a hand over her face as she looked away. "Didn't realize you were asleep."

"What's wrong?" He held the phone out to her, but she wasn't watching him. "Anna? Is something wrong?"

"Cunningham just called." Anna turned and stared at the phone, then snatched it from him. "The Prime Minister is dead."

Jack's head spun with the news. They'd left the Minister for Employment's office building in a small convoy of vehicles and made their way straight out of London. Anna had coordinated it all, making sure the minister was well guarded for the drive and that nothing got in their way. Now they were speeding through the Welsh countryside, making their way to an abandoned manor kept off books by M16.

It was incomprehensible to Jack that the Prime Minister, with all of her protection, could have been killed. That changed the game and significantly increased the danger their little convoy was in, given Ho was now the only thing standing in the way of the Zionist threat to let the nukes fly. The decision by Cunningham, Fraser, Jack and Anna to focus on protecting only three targets had backfired.

"When?" He shook his head. "How did it happen?"

"Less than an hour ago. We pulled security from Downing Street to help protect the minister after the bomb." Anna sighed. "And the Zionists kicked us in the teeth."

"There wasn't enough to go around?" In the States, there would have been enough friendlies with guns to protect the President three times over.

She shrugged. "We can count on a very limited number of hands the amount of people we trust totally right now. Cohen's treachery has shocked the system."

Jack started to speak, then paused. It made so much sense. "If that's the case, why don't we just get more US boots on the ground to help protect the minister? We can surround the house with so much firepower that an army couldn't get through. All it will take is a phone call."

Anna shook her head. "I floated the idea, but Cunningham is as worried about US forces as he is about British ones. Our best chance, with the restrictions, is to keep everyone a mile away from Ho except those people already in this convoy. That means secrecy."

Jack turned and stared out the window, tapping his leg as he thought. Though the isolated location and the limited size of their convoy should have been enough to protect the minister, it all felt a bit tenuous. Eshkol had been one step ahead of them, and now Jack felt the caress of the professor from beyond the grave – a chill down his spine, a churn in his stomach. It felt impossible to believe that by hiding in the Welsh countryside it would all be over.

He made a decision. He dug into his pocket and dialed a number he knew by heart. It rang, over and over, until finally the line connected.

"Mr. President, it's Jack."

"Jack." There was a heavy dose of sleep in McGhinnist's voice. "How are you? What's the situation?"

"Prime Minister Huxley is dead."

"What?" McGhinnist suddenly sounded as if he had a drip line of black coffee hooked up to wake him. "How do you know this and we don't?"

Jack removed the phone from his ear and pressed the speaker button. "You're on speaker with Anna Fowler and I. There's another MI6 agent driving."

"Mr. President." Anna spoke close to the phone. "Wish we were speaking on better terms."

"Ms. Fowler." McGhinnist's voice was cold. "Tell me what's going on and why I don't know about it."

"The one and only, sir." Anna smiled darkly. "The Prime Minister was assassinated less than an hour ago by the Zionists. It'll hit the news any minute."

"Fucking hell." McGhinnist paused. "What's the situation?"

Jack leaned in to the phone. "We're one dead minister away from doom, sir."

"What support do you need, Jack? Name it."

Jack exhaled deeply. He wanted the next words he said to be a request for additional special forces troops, helicopters, warplanes and armored vehicles. He wanted a twenty-mile exclusion zone around the house they were nearing and satellites covering every inch of it. Finally, he wanted US missiles ready at a moment's notice to flatten anything that was spotted moving inside that exclusion zone. But he didn't ask for any of that.

One glance at Anna told him the only possible answer. The Zionists had so effectively infiltrated the British and US governments that nobody could guarantee any help would be worth the risk of exposure. Eshkol's network had everyone jumping at shadows, afraid of their own people and doubting plans designed to prevent attacks like the very ones they'd been facing. Jack couldn't risk asking the President for anything and revealing their location.

"Nothing, sir." Jack paused. "We're going off grid."

McGhinnist scoffed. "I've got armies on speed dial, you guys know?"

"We know." Jack and Anna spoke at the same time, but Jack kept speaking. "But the Zionists have played our security like a fiddle and we don't know who, or what assets, are compromised. We need secrecy and anonymity, not guns and heavy metal."

"Okay, Jack. I don't agree, but we'll go with your plan."

Jack smiled. "Thanks, Mr. President."

"Good luck. And let me know if you need support."

Jack turned to Anna as the line went dead. "There's not much I can do if you don't let me call in the cavalry."

She nodded. "We've done all we can, Jack. We just have to hope that they can't find us."

Jack crossed his arms and closed his eyes. He considered it highly unlikely that the attackers would be caught if they hadn't already been. The Zionist team had proven so immensely capable and a mile ahead of the British and American forces trying, desperately, to prevent nuclear disaster. That meant hiding was their only hope, but he wasn't sure that would work. As he drifted off to sleep, he wrapped his hand around the pistol resting on the seat beside him.

He hoped that in the next twenty-four hours, he wouldn't need it.

CHAPTER 19

With less than a day until the peace agreement between Israel and the soon-to-be-created state of Palestine is enacted, there is no sign that either signatory nor the United States intends to blink in the face of Zionist threats. US and Saudi authorities have stressed that they're close to locating the backpack nuclear device that threatens Mecca, though precautionary evacuations of the area are well underway. A strange silence has descended over Mecca as its doom approaches.

New York Standard

Jack cursed as his finger started to bleed, the fingernail bitten down so far it had started to seep at the edge. He sucked the blood as he glanced at his watch. The turn of the hour approached and, with it, the threat of an Iranian nuclear launch that would render all the blood and effort over the past few days pointless. An attack by Iran on Israel was likely to set off a chain reaction of launches across the world, though at least a manor house in the Welsh countryside might be safe.

"What's wrong?" Anna stared at him from across the table. "You've been on edge for twenty minutes."

Jack had to lie. "Nothing. Just feel like this is the first time we've stopped to catch our breath in weeks."

She smiled wearily, heavy bags under her eyes and a hollow look on her face. "You get used to it. We're okay here, Jack."

They'd arrived at the house late the previous evening. Anna had been right – it was deserted for miles around and still in relatively good upkeep. The SEALs and MI6 agents had made their position more defensible, the minister had gone to sleep, and Jack and Anna had set up in the dining hall with their phones at the ready. He hadn't told her about the Iranian launch threats, but the constant glances at his watch and his cell phone had obviously made her suspicious.

A lot of experiences had combined to make Jack the man he was – a lot of conflict, a lot of danger and a lot of alcohol – but he'd never felt more afraid than the moment his watch ticked over to 10.01pm GMT. He picked up his phone and unlocked it, then scanned the NSC feed for any launch activity originating in Iran. There were a few items, but nothing that looked like what Jack feared. After a few minutes, he tossed the phone on the table, leaned back and closed his eyes.

Then the phone rang. His eyes shot open and he stared at the caller ID for a moment, then answered. "Mr. President?"

"We've found it, Jack. We've found the bomb in Mecca." McGhinnist's voice had never sounded so good. "The Saudis called a few moments ago to tell us."

Jack laughed for several moments. "Did the Iranians indicate if they were going to launch or not? If I had any impact by going there?"

"Best we never know." McGhinnist laughed. "Let's focus on what matters. In two hours, we're through this. Stay safe and speak soon."

"Amen to that." Jack hung up the phone and tossed it on the table, where it rested next to the pistol he'd acquired from Anna.

"What was that about?"

"Oh, nothing." Jack smiled at her. "We just had a second potential nuclear disaster hanging over our heads. But don't worry, I sorted that one."

Anna's eyes narrowed and she looked like she might ask more, but she left it. "Well, I better make sure I take care of this one. I'd hate to owe you."

"I'll collect once this is all over." He smiled and closed his eyes. One disaster averted, one left to avoid, he felt himself starting to doze off.

His eyes shot open when he heard a popping sound. It was unmistakable – the chatter of automatic weapons fire. The chair he'd been sitting on fell back as he sprang to his feet, grabbed his phone and pistol and bolted toward the sound. He had no idea where Anna was, but he didn't care – there were six American special forces soldiers, a handful of MI6 agents and Chen standing between the attackers and the minister. He needed to help.

He ran down one of the four corridors, each of which had a pair of defenders posted at all times. They'd fortified the house as best they could, had eyes on all approaches and some excellent cover. On the downside, the defenders only had a mix of carbines and small arms, the Navy SEALs not having prepared for a full-blown defensive firefight. Their preparations were the best they could be with so few defenders. Secrecy had been their armor, which seemed to have failed them – another victim of Zionist infiltration of the British security services. Now, any sort of focused attack from any direction would stretch them. He reached the bedroom they were using as a defensive post and saw Chen and an MI6 agent on guard. They were crouched low, peering out windows with weapons ready.

"What's going on?" He slid down next to Chen and gripped the pistol tightly. "Are they here?"

"Yes." Chen glanced over his shoulder at Jack, then gestured at one of the windows. "Take that window."

Jack nodded and took up position. He glanced at his watch. 11.36pm GMT. "We hold for twenty-four minutes."

The others nodded and Jack turned his attention to the grounds outside the manor. A quick glance over the window frame showed Jack what he feared – complete darkness. But it was also met with a short burst of gunfire, which he heard slam into the stone on the outside of the house. Jack gripped the pistol and rested on his knees. After a deep breath, then another, Jack huffed and turned to peer over the window again, the pistol pointed out in front of him.

Automatic fire barked at him and in the dim light, Jack could see someone move in the distance. He squeezed the trigger, again and again, the pistol kicking slightly with each shot. No voices cried out in alarm or pain, so he'd probably hit dirt. He hesitated for just a second too long, and something ricocheted off the windowsill and cut into his cheek. Jack ducked down again and reached up to touch his face, where he could feel the slick of blood.

"Fuck." He pulled his hand away and considered the moisture on his palm. "Something hit me."

"It's nothing. You'll be alright." The MI6 agent squeezed off a few shots. "Get back on the job!"

Jack nodded. "Reloading!"

As he ejected the clip from the pistol and slid in another, Jack glanced at Chen. The ex-Taiwanese special forces soldier had rested a carbine on the windowsill and was as calm as ever as he waited for their enemy to emerge. Chen seemed to have infinite patience, firing off short bursts only when necessary and otherwise playing for time. Jack suddenly felt stupid for blazing away at the darkness, given the patience of the other defenders.

He felt useless, unable to see anything and unsure whether his adversaries could see him.

~

ARON WATCHED, safe in the darkness, as gunfire rattled back and forth between his comrades and the defenders. While it did, he held his fire and waited, with Miri and a pair of others by his side. They were all dressed in black and armed with their favorite weapons. Aron had reacquired his machine pistols but added a rather nasty combat knife. He had the feeling that this one was going to get up close and personal before the night was done.

They'd left Downing Street by helicopter, landed outside London and acquired vehicles. While on the road, he'd called the contact Eshkol had entrusted to him. With as much difficulty as ordering a pizza, the mole inside the bureaucracy had told Aron who'd taken the minister and where he was being taken. Though they were a few hours behind, the information had allowed Aron and his team to arrive at the house in the Welsh countryside with enough time to get the job done.

His team had halted their drive two miles from the house, then waited until darkness before embarking on their walk. They'd covered the distance quickly and then split up and moved to their assigned positions in silence. Planning had been completed on the road and there were no words to be said, only a job to be done. If anything, Aron felt like the hardest tasks were behind them and that this was the victory lap – the final target that Eshkol had asked him to take care of.

"We should move." Miri spoke softly from beside him. "The minister is there for the taking."

"Not yet." He could sense his team growing restless to join the fray and help their comrades.

A larger group of his men were attacking the house from the north, east and west. Ideally, one of the attacks would succeed and the feints wouldn't matter, but he doubted it. The British would have some of their best defending the minister, which meant something special was required to take him down. So Aron and his squad cooled their heels on the southern approach to the house, watching and waiting for the right moment to strike.

Though he had no more men than the defenders and they were dug in, he had tactical advantages they didn't enjoy. Timing was everything if his attack were to succeed. If he moved too early, his small squad would struggle to penetrate the defenses protecting their target. Too late, and he might have lost too many men for it to matter. He had his eyes locked on to one of the defenders, crouched low behind a window. The second they moved, so would Aron.

As if on cue with his thoughts, one of the figures in the window moved out of sight. They'd pulled assets from the south to reinforce elsewhere.

He smiled. "Go."

Next to him, Miri prepared her rifle for the most important shot of this engagement. Aron watched as she breathed, taking her time, then turned his head to the house as Miri took the shot. The suppressed rifle made barely a sound and the final defender, who'd only peeked over the windowsill, dropped suddenly. Miri threw the rifle on the ground and flashed him a grin. She was still every bit as good as advertised.

The small team stood and moved quickly to close the distance between their position and the house. As they drew closer, with Aron in the lead, there was no sign of a single defender – they'd left the back door open to stop the front door from blowing in. Aron and Miri crouched low, waiting as the other pair moved in first. They approached and climbed through the window, then peeked back and waved Aron and Miri forward.

Aron reached the window and leaped through, keeping low as he landed, eyes scanning the room for any threat. There was none and the room was quiet, except for the muted footsteps of his small squad as they started to move out of the corridor and deeper into the house. Aron and Miri cut north and the other pair moved for the eastern end of the house. In seconds they were behind the defenders and ready to end this.

Gripping his machine pistol in one hand and the combat knife in the other, Aron stalked toward the two defenders he could see. They were apparently so busy keeping his other forces outside that they had no clue what was inside. As he moved closer, he listened as the pair of them shouted at each other in between gunfire. One – an American – wanted to rush to help the others, while the man with the British accent wanted to hold firm.

Aron considered the quirk of circumstance that had brought US forces to defend a British minister in the Welsh countryside, and worried for a moment there might be more US forces close, but quickly disregarded the thought. If the US had more than a token force here, they'd have played their hand already. Aron raised the knife to strike just as the Briton glanced sideways, catching Miri in his peripheral vision.

"They're here!" The British man's shout ruined Aron and Miri's chance of doing this cleanly.

Aron lifted the knife and struck quickly as the American started to turn. The blade ran across the American's throat and Aron heard a gargling sound as blood gushed over the carpet in front of them. To be sure of it, he dug the knife into the base of the man's neck as he fell, going hilt deep and probably severing his spinal cord. As the American hit the floor, Aron glanced left and saw that Miri had already taken care of the British defender.

A gunshot boomed and Miri shrieked in agony. Aron raised the machine pistol and fired off a long burst at the woman who'd just put down his comrade, but she'd ducked back behind the doorframe. Aron cursed and dived behind a sofa, then looked beside him to see if Miri was alright. She was still moving, but was nursing a wound to her arm. Aron gritted his teeth, peered over the sofa and fired off another long burst at the woman who'd shot Miri down.

Any tactical advantage he'd gained through the feint would be lost if they got stuck in here, on the outskirts of the house and kept from his target.

~

ANNA GRUNTED as the wooden doorframe continued to splinter and shatter under the withering gunfire from the other side. Never more thankful for stone walls, she reloaded her pistol and gritted her teeth, safe for now but under no illusions that would last. She'd left Jack to cover one of the approaches to the house and moved to reinforce another herself, but little had she known that the Zionists were already inside the house and some of her people were dead.

She'd reached the position just as the attackers had engaged her comrades. Though she'd ruined their ambush and winged one of them, it might not make a difference. They'd turned on her and unleashed a withering barrage of fire, forcing her back behind cover. All she had to fire back with was her pistol, but if nothing else her interruption had made their path toward the minister a bit more difficult.

As she shied away from the gunfire, she lifted the radio clipped to her hip. "They're inside! They're inside the house! At least two attackers! North side!"

Following her report, the radio crackled with more from the other pairings: Emery and a SEAL were holding one direction; a pair of SEALs were holding another; and Chen had peeled off to protect the minister. There was silence from the other rooms, which probably explained how these Zionists had gained entry. Things were going to hell quickly, and she needed to think about more than the Zionist firing at her. She had to salvage the situation.

She spoke into the radio again. "All forces disengage. Everyone fall back to defend the minister."

She tossed the radio on to the ground. The tactical situation was dire. She breathed a sigh of relief that Chen had had the foresight to head straight to Ho, despite the pressure they were under elsewhere, but every other defender left breathing was fully engaged. There was nobody to help her hold off this group. All she could do was keep them here for a few crucial moments, to buy time for the others to reach Chen and the minister for the final stand.

They had to try to defend the inner corridors of the house and, if it came to it, the dining room. If the Zionists made it that far, there was an extremely high likelihood that the minister would eat a bullet, yet the defenders had no other choice. They'd gambled everything on keeping the Zionists outside. Failing that, they were now spread too thin against an unknown number of hostiles. They were probably fucked. She was definitely fucked.

She took a deep breath, peered round the doorframe and squeezed off two quick shots. She wasn't sure if she'd hit anything, because she was already back behind the wall. From the other side, a machine pistol chattered and a pistol barked in response. Anna wished she had a grenade handy. If she made it out of here, she'd be sure to tell MI6 to make them standard issue. As it was, all she had was her pistol and her wits.

"We're not here for you!" a voice shouted from inside the other room. "Bring the minister to me and you can go home."

She laughed. Talking was good – it bought time. "And let you nuke the whole planet? We didn't find your baby bombs only to let you fire ICBMs."

"There's no plan to nuke anyone. We're only after the minister."

"Come and get him then!"

There was silence, then the first attacker rushed through the door. The female Zionist went down quickly, two rounds through the chest, but in the time that took another was upon her. Anna squeezed the trigger one more time but missed. A long chain of machine pistol fire filled her ears and a burning pain seared her legs. She shrieked and fell to the ground, dropping the pistol on the way down before landing hard.

"Stupid bitch." The Zionist with the machine pistol kicked her pistol away then stomped on her chest, driving the wind from her.

"*Home plate secure.*" The long forgotten radio. It was Jack's voice. "*The minister is safe but we're under assault. Where are you, Anna?*"

Anna smiled and closed her eyes. "Hear that? You lose, you giant fucking wanker."

She heard a guttural growl then blackness overcame her.

CHAPTER 10

The New York Standard Online has reporters on the streets of Jerusalem, Gaza City and other population centers in Israel and Palestine less than ten minutes before the peace agreement enters into law. Crowds fill the streets, keen to witness history and send off one of the most divisive and heated conflicts of the past century. It appears as if the Zionist terrorists have failed in their efforts to divide the world with hatred and bigotry, in what looks to be a triumph for the future of a newly divided Israel and Palestine.

New York Standard

J ack kept his pistol trained on the doorway of the dining room. He glanced left, then right. Chen and one of the Navy SEALs were doing the same from behind the upturned oak dining table that they claimed might stop a bullet. It was the best cover they could manage in the circumstances. Behind them, deeper inside the room, Minister Ho lay underneath a few spare Kevlar vests. This was very much the final stand – for Jack, the peace agreement and civilization.

After Anna Fowler's radio warning, he'd withdrawn to help secure the dining room, where Chen and the minister were already busy. When he'd reached the room, he'd found it well prepared for a final stand. Unfortunately, only one SEAL had joined them since. He'd radioed Anna a moment ago, but there'd been no response. He didn't know how many Zionists were left, but he'd bet there were more attackers than defenders.

They might not have numbers, but they did have time on their side. If they could hold out for another eight minutes or so, the deed would be done, though it was unlikely Jack, Chen or the others would survive to be labeled heroes. They'd be anonymous to everyone except the uppermost leadership of the United States and Britain – anonymous men and women who'd spared the world nuclear armageddon and improved the lives of millions, but at the cost of their own.

Jack heard a series of pounding bangs on the wooden floor that grew louder as the attackers approached. "They're coming."

"Nice knowing you guys." The SEAL smiled, not taking his eyes off the door as he stared down his iron sights.

Jack looked at his watch as he continued to grip his pistol. "Seven minutes until midnight."

"That's only 420 seconds." The SEAL shouted as he squeezed the trigger of his carbine. "Contact!"

Gunfire erupted. The SEAL's carbine boomed in three-round bursts. Chen's more patient firing added to the cacophony in less frequent intervals. Jack, for his part, was careful only to fire when he had something to fire at. He squeezed off two shots at a Zionist who briefly appeared in his sights, but wasn't confident he'd hit anything. He didn't know how many attackers were left, but he'd be happy if he could take down one of them and help out those trained to do this.

Jack's breathing was fast, in, out, in, out, as he tried to stay calm. He focused on keeping as low a profile behind the upturned table as he could while maintaining his aim. He gasped when rounds fired from the attackers pounded into the hardwood table and he half expected to feel hot lead penetrate his body, but the cover held firm. He wasn't sure how many attackers there were, but he felt confident they might just be able to hold them for the next few minutes.

Until he watched a small, oval-shaped object fly overhead.

"Grenade!" the SEAL shouted.

Jack's eyes involuntarily tracked the grenade in flight, taking his focus off the hallway. A shout of alarm got stuck in his throat as he watched the SEAL drop his carbine and spring to his feet. As the grenade landed near the minister, the SEAL dived on top of it. There was an ear-splitting boom and the SEAL's body lifted slightly off the ground with the impact, but his sacrifice had saved the rest of them, the Minister and probably the world.

Jack turned back to the hallway, but the damage had been done. A pair of Zionists had forced their way inside the room and one was aiming at Chen. Jack swung his pistol and fired at the new threat just as Chen did the same thing. The Zionist dropped, bearing multiple bullet wounds, but Chen grunted and reached for his shoulder too. Jack ducked a little lower as he turned his gun toward what must have been the final attacker. Too slow.

The Zionist leaped over the table and kicked out at Jack's hand, striking hard and causing the pistol to drop to the ground. With a curse, Jack fell on his ass, but wasted no time in backing away from the new threat. As he did, the Zionist aimed a kick at Chen, who was in no position to block it. The blow connected with the head of Jack's last remaining ally and Chen slumped forward, unconscious from the blow to the head and bleeding from the gunshot wound to his shoulder.

Jack was on his own. With two or three minutes left before the deadline.

The Zionist advanced, his machine pistol pointed at Jack and with a nasty-looking knife in his other hand. "Come out, minister, and save this brave man."

"Stay where you are!" Jack shouted at Ho, who'd been told to stay behind cover no matter what happened. "I'll protect you!"

"You're joking." The Zionist let out a laugh as he tossed the machine pistol at Jack's feet.

Jack snarled as he picked up the machine pistol. The Zionist approached him with the knife as Jack lifted the weapon. "Confident, aren't you?"

The other man grinned as he flicked the knife into an underhand grip and stalked forward. "Why wouldn't I be? I've still got two minutes to kill my target."

Jack shouted at him to stop, but the Zionist kept coming. He gripped the machine pistol tight and then squeezed the trigger. He heard a click. "Fuck."

The Zionist slashed out at his face with the knife. Jack flinched and came away with a nasty cut, which was better than losing half of his face. He retreated, blood dripping from his cheek as he reached up to press his palm against the cut, but the Zionist didn't let up. He kicked out at Jack's knee, which buckled under the blow. Jack screamed in pain and fell to the floor, his mind protesting at the pain even as he tried to think about a way out of this.

"You lose." The Zionist raised the knife with the point facing downward, ready to pierce him.

"Do you know the consequences of killing him?" Jack sucked in breath. "Annihilation."

The Zionist laughed. "This is where I pause for twenty minutes to tell you my evil plan, is it? It's simple: kill the minister, because those are my orders."

Jack's eyes widened. "You don't know, do you? If you kill him, a British nuclear submarine launches enough nukes to end the world."

"It doesn't matter." The Zionist raised his arm then brought the blade down on Jack's thigh.

Jack screamed in agony as the blade went deep. He reached for the hilt and gripped it, but stopped short of pulling it out, remembering that doing so only increased your chance of bleeding out. His eyes locked on the Zionist, who'd picked up the machine pistol and reloaded it. At no point did the man show any hesitation or doubt about what Jack had told him. He pointed the weapon at the minister and fired a long burst.

All Jack could do was scream.

~

COHEN WAS GROWING FRUSTRATED with the communications officer, who was clearly stalling him. He gripped the man's chair and leaned his head next to the young seaman. "Anything? Is there any sign of broadcast on the longwave band? BBC Radio 4?"

To his credit, the young man didn't shy away. He turned in his chair, removed his headset and ran a hand over his face. "No signal on the longwave band, sir."

Cohen frowned and nodded. It was looking increasingly likely that he had a launch to conduct. "Check on the PM and the Minister for Employment."

With a slight nod, the officer replaced his headset and turned back to his console, fingers dancing across the keyboard at a speed Joseph could never hope to replicate. He left the man to his work, crossed the small bridge and stood alongside Jennings, who waited in silence for orders from his captain. His executive officer was as tense as the rest of the men and women on the bridge, a mood Joseph was sure would be replicated through the entire boat.

Launch prep.

A situation that all ballistic missile submariners prepare for but never really expect to do for real – end the world from safely beneath the ocean, knowing that minutes after pressing the button other states would do likewise. Once that happened friends, family and homes were as like as not to be reduced to ash. Simply contemplating it left a coppery taste in the mouth, but to actually go through with it would feel quite a lot worse. Or so Joseph imagined.

"No proper authentication from the Prime Minister on national command channels, captain." The comms officer turned and stared at his captain, then at the executive officer, then at a few of his crewmates. "The PM is dead or not able to authenticate."

To their credit, the crew kept their composure – the only reaction Joseph could hear was a few sharp intakes of breath – though it did feel like the temperature had dropped. The men and women aboard continued with their jobs. He was proud of them, though they were unwitting puppets in his own mission – acting on the orders Zed Eshkol had given him. He did sense an expectation that he should say or do something, though.

"Carry on with your jobs." Joseph did his best to project an air of calm. "Comms, try to make contact with the PM's second. XO, inform the crew."

As the crew went about their jobs, Joseph closed his eyes. In the few seconds he had to spare, he searched his soul and his heart for confirmation that he'd really go through with this – launch nuclear missiles as a final invocation of Zed Eshkol's Samson Option. That doctrine, developed decades ago by a fiery young Jew, was now the order of a man who was so old he wouldn't live to see the consequences.

Eshkol's age changed nothing, though. A younger Joseph had been taught by a younger professor, nearly two decades prior. He'd been a student of Eshkol's, then a friend, then a confidant and, finally, an agent. With a simple word from his lips, he had confirmed to the elderly Zionist that he'd do whatever was necessary should the existence of Israel ever be seriously threatened. He'd sworn a life of service and, in return, Eshkol's network had opened doors for Joseph.

"Captain?" The comms officer's voice was grave. "We have no proper authentication from the Prime Minister's second."

"Thank you. Stand by everyone." Joseph opened his eyes. He turned to Jennings. "Do you concur that command authority has been compromised?"

Jennings smiled sadly, as if the world had already gone to ash. "I concur, captain."

They went to the safe, wordlessly going through a process that was nearly automatic. Once it was open, Joseph ignored the contents of the safe and instead worked to open the second safe, inside the first. He turned the dial several times, using a code that only he knew to open the door. Inside was one crisp, white envelope. As he reached inside for the envelope, he still couldn't be sure if he'd go through with this.

He opened the envelope and extracted the letter, which was on good-quality paper and folded neatly into thirds. Once the letter was unfolded, his eyes scanned the words but his mind was already made up. The Prime Minister, Joseph wasn't surprised to read, had written to her submarine commanders and ordered them to launch. Not that it would have mattered if the letter said otherwise, given Joseph had no need to show anyone else.

The order was his.

He returned to the bridge and made his way to the ship's address system and picked up the radio. "Attention all crew. I regret to inform you all that the United Kingdom has been attacked and quite possibly rendered helpless. All tests we use to ascertain the viability of the UK government have failed.

"As a result, protocol dictates we open the Dead Man Letter, which dictates the action I'm to take in these circumstances. I've done so, and the Prime Minister's orders were to launch on those states deemed responsible for the destruction of Britain. We will now commence preparations for that launch."

Joseph replaced the radio and turned around. Jennings had his eyes locked on his captain, as did the rest of the crew. He nodded at them. "We have jobs to do."

"The targets, sir?" Jennings' voice had a slight break in it.

Joseph spoke as confidently as he could. "Jerusalem and Mecca."

The other man hesitated, then nodded. "Yes, sir."

The comms officer cut in. "Sir, I've run another check on the Minister for—"

Joseph glared at the junior officer. "Nobody told you—"

"He's alive!" The comms officer let out a cry of relief. "The minister is alive."

"We launch!" Joseph clenched his fists. "Nobody told you to run that check."

"But, sir, he's—"

Joseph held up a hand to cut the other man off, then turned to Jennings. "We proceed as planned."

"I don't think that's wise, sir. The government is still intact." Jennings reached a hand out, moving to place it on Joseph's shoulder.

Joseph reached for his pistol in its holster and raised it in one swift motion, until the muzzle was inches from Jennings' face. "We launch."

~

"WE'VE ONLY GOT A MINUTE, ANNA!" Jack's voice was unintentionally sharp, but he didn't bother apologizing. He leaned down to the minister and kept working.

"I'm on it."

As Anna struggled with the radio alongside the minister, Jack tried desperately to dress some of his more serious wounds. Despite her own wounds, Anna was doing her best to follow the minister's instructions even as his breathing became shallow. So far they'd established contact with the HMS *Vigilant*, but that was only the first part of the process to save the world.

Anna had limped into the room just after the Zionist had shot the minister. She had a gunshot wound to the leg, but had shot the Zionist with calm certainty. The minister was alive, but only barely, and Jack was working to keep him that way using his basic first aid training. Jack counted several wounds and shock was setting in as the minister's life blood seeped out of him.

The minister's life was one problem, the time this was taking was another. Jack looked at his watch and instantly regretted it. There was no way to hurry Anna and the minister but there was also no time to lose. The launch was scheduled to take place in less than a minute, and it was quite possible they were too late to avert it at any rate.

"They're communicating with us!" The relief in Anna's voice was edged with fear and the knowledge that they were probably too late. "Minister, it's time."

The minister nodded and sighed. He leaned his head ever so slightly toward the radio and spoke softly. "The United Kingdom ... is fine ..."

Jack waited for the minister to say more, as he pressed a fistful of gauze into the man's leg and wrapped a bandage hastily around it. But there was silence. He kept working, but the minister had more bullet holes than Jack had hands to press down. Anna helped out, shaking the minister several times and whispering something into his ear.

"The code is alpha, victor, tango, delta, seven, three, seven." The minister's eyes closed and his breathing slowed to nearly nothing. "One."

A glance at Anna was enough. She shook her head and Jack knew instantly that Minister Ho was dead. He let out a growl of frustration as he threw the gauze and bandages to the ground and then backed away from the body. He knew he should start CPR, but it was pointless. That the minister had lived long enough to get his broadcast out would have to do.

"It's okay, Jack. We got the message out. Four letters, four numbers – the minister was crystal clear on that."

Jack stared at her, too tired to feel anything. "In time?"

"We'll know in a few minutes."

Jack looked at his watch.

It still read 11.59.

EPILOGUE

J ack wasn't sure the explosives or the large, red plunger that would detonate them were necessary.

Using a crutch to support his weight, Jack watched as the Israeli Army engineers finished rigging up explosives to the security wall that had divided Israel and Palestine for years. It would have been far too simple to just pull down the wall. Instead, the powers that be had decided to blow it up in a grand display of peace, after which a fleet of construction vehicles would cart the debris away over the coming days.

He hadn't even wanted to come – content with his role in winning the peace, but not needing to see it enacted. Yet here he was, standing in a dark mood among dignitaries who had nothing to do with the peace or the sacrifices it had taken to achieve. President McGhinnist had insisted he attend, though, and Celeste had thought it might provide him with some closure. He scoffed at the thought.

For what felt like the hundredth time, he reached up and touched the deep cut on his face, which had been cleaned up and stitched but was still raw and painful. The doctor who'd patched him up had told him it would scar and that he might want to see a cosmetic surgeon, but Jack doubted he'd do that. To worry about vanity and appearance seemed the gravest possible insult to the men and women who'd clawed, scraped and ultimately died to prevent nuclear war.

Chen had lost a lot of blood by the time Jack could help him, minutes after the launch had been prevented and the minister had died. He was still in a medically induced coma and his long-term prognosis was unclear. For her part, Anna Fowler had been whisked away by MI6 and he hadn't seen her since. But her wounds had also been serious. Everyone had paid a price, though his own bill had been modest – a cut to the face and a combat knife buried in his leg.

It had all been worth it. The HMS *Vigilant* had surfaced not long after the deadline with the executive officer in charge and the captain under guard. Naval assets from a dozen countries had swarmed it, and bringing the boat back into the fold had nearly caused a war in its own right. Jack didn't know what had happened in those final, fateful minutes aboard the submarine, but the launch had been prevented.

With a sigh, he reached down and locked hands with Celeste, who was standing next to him. "Should be starting soon."

"You okay?" She turned her head, a look of concern painted across her face. "How's the leg?"

He shrugged. She'd flown in from the States along with a small battalion of other VIPs and dignitaries. They now stood, not in bleachers with bunting and brass bands, but in the dirt that – along with faith – had separated two states and two people, and had cost far too much blood and treasure. He still believed in the peace that had been won, but he resented the price that had been paid to get it over the line.

"Jack?" Her tone became more insistent.

"I'm fine." It was a lie. "Looking forward to the islands."

She smiled and gave his hand a squeeze as she turned back to the fence. The holiday had been his idea, but she'd been happy to go along with a month in the Greek islands. He couldn't think of a less explosive, more relaxing place on the planet to hide for a while. For the first time in years, Jack wanted to sit and do nothing for a very long time.

He glanced at the fence, an object of division and a catalyst of heartbreak. Not all wounds had been healed, but Jack hoped that everything the world had been through in the last month might show Israel and Palestine that peace was worth the effort. He hoped that his body and mind would heal as well, though he wasn't sure how likely that was at the moment.

A piercing squeal assaulted his ears and Jack tensed. Celeste squeezed his hand again. He was probably the only person in attendance with nerves so frayed that speaker feedback freaked him out, but he felt he had good reason to be paranoid. He shook his head and turned his attention back to the wall, where the Israeli Prime Minister stood next to the Palestinian President.

"Esteemed ladies and gentlemen, thank you for your patience. It took our engineers slightly longer than expected to prepare." The MC's voice boomed over loudspeakers positioned near the large throng of dignitaries. "Please welcome Prime Minister Schiller and President Fadi."

Jack joined in the light applause as the two leaders stepped forward. When they reached the lectern, they linked hands and pumped their fists high above their heads. This brought a smile to Jack's face and soft laughter from the crowd. As he listened to them mouth pleasantries to a long list of VIPs, he thought again of the people who should be here.

"Today, we will both act to bring down a symbol of division." Schiller pointed to the wall then gestured to Fadi.

The two leaders moved the short distance from the lectern to the small black box with a T-shaped plunger on top. Both pressed down on it and Jack heard the deep rumble of explosions long before he could see the detonations. After a few seconds, off into the distance, plumes of dust and smoke rose. Finally, the chain of explosions reached where they were standing.

The crowd cheered as the sections of fence nearest to them were destroyed by the orderly blasts and fell, cracking and crumbling, to the ground. Jack hadn't liked the idea of such theatrics, but it was an impressive scene. His gaze panned in time with the explosions and he followed them far off into the distance. Nobody spoke or moved until quiet and stillness settled.

President Fadi approached the lectern again. "This fence, long the bane of my people, is gone. The flags of two states – Israel and Palestine – now blow in the same wind, without anything to act as a break. It's my sincere hope this air remains fresh and light."

Applause broke out again when the simple speeches came to an end. As cameras flashed, Jack felt a momentary pang of loss. He'd have loved to cover this as a reporter, but instead he'd been pulled far deeper into the crisis. He turned away from the journalists and went with Celeste over to McGhinnist, who was surrounded by Secret Service agents and world leaders.

McGhinnist spotted Jack and disengaged from the conversation. Jack waited on his crutches for the President to approach, reflecting on the four years he'd worked for the man. McGhinnist's achievements had been enormous, and Jack had been at the heart of them, but with each win he felt like he had lost something of himself.

"Quite a display, wasn't it?" McGhinnist held out his hand. "How are you both?"

"We're fine, Bill." Jack shook the President's hand, then waited while Celeste did the same. "You flying back on Air Force One?"

"Tonight." McGhinnist sighed and gave a wry grin. "Malcolm wants to start on the election prep. He tells me there's no time to lose in capitalizing on this."

"Smart guy." Jack gave a thin smile.

"You're not coming." McGhinnist's tone was light. "Don't even think about it."

Celeste laughed. "He's got a date with a wonderful woman."

"A wonderful fiancée, you mean." McGhinnist smirked.

"Or that." She smiled.

"I'll leave you both to it. Don't hurry back to DC, Jack. Take all the time you need." McGhinnist patted them both on the shoulder and left them alone.

"Do you think it will last?" Celeste gripped his hand again as she gestured toward where the fence had stood.

Deep down, he knew it probably wouldn't – but he couldn't speak those words. It would be a betrayal of all that had been lost. "Yes."

"So what now?" She wrapped an arm around him.

"Sunshine and cocktails."

ACKNOWLEDGMENTS

Firstly, my wife, Vanessa Pratt. There's nobody and nothing more important to me or my writing. Her love and support is a constant foundation for the constant forays into imaginary lands. It'd be very hard to not get lost without her.

Putting roughly a quarter-million words into an anthology caused me to reflect on all the people who had a role in bringing each of the Jack Emery novels to market. So I've created about the most comprehensive list I can.

The team at Pan Macmillan / Momentum who published the novels were wonderful. Haylee Nash, Joel Naoum, Tara Goedjen, Shelley Cameron, Ashley Thomson, Patrick Lenton and Mark Harding have my thanks for all their hard work.

My editor, Kylie Mason, is the reason this anthology isn't closer to 300,000 words. Her cutting and her crafting and her ability to ask the hard question improved the novels immensely. Plus she's a pleasure to work with.

The individual novel covers were all designed by Xou Creative and they couldn't have a happier customer. Special thanks to Jon McDonald at Xou for being a master at his craft and a really nice guy, to boot.

The cover of the boxset was designed by Amanda Pillar, a busy lady who nevertheless found time to do me an amazing

An army of beta readers helped to beat the books into shape. Thanks to Gerard Burg, Andrew McLaughlin, Dave Sinclair, Kirstie Barry, Emily Swann, Ashley Pratt, Chris Nelson, Phillipa Martin, Raya Klinbail and Andrea Kenrick.

Finally, to the friends and family and fans who support my work, it's deeply appreciated.

ABOUT THE AUTHOR

Steve P. Vincent is the USA Today Bestselling Author of the Jack Emery and Mitch Herron conspiracy thriller series.

Steve has a degree in political science, a thesis on global terrorism, a decade as a policy advisor and training from the FBI and Australian Army in his conspiracy kit bag.

When he's not writing, Steve enjoys whisky, sports and travel.

You can contact Steve at all the usual places:
stevepvincent.com
steve@stevepvincent.com

Made in the USA
Columbia, SC
23 October 2020